PENGUIN TWEN

THREE EU

MADAME DE TREYME

Edith Wharton was born Edith Newbold Jones in New York in 1862. A member of a distinguished New York family, she was educated privately in the United States and abroad. In 1885 she married Edward Robbins Wharton, who was twelve years her senior and from whom she was divorced in 1913. She spent long periods in Europe, where she gained her intimacy with numerous continental languages and settings for her books. From 1910 until her death, she made her home in France. During the war she was an unflinching worker; in France she ran a workroom for unemployed skilled women workers in her quarter; she fed French and Belgian refugees in her restaurants below cost price; she took entire charge of 600 Belgian children who had to leave their orphanage at the time of the German advance. In 1915 the French government gave her the cross of the Legion of Honour. She died in 1937.

Edith Wharton was a unique American novelist, distinguished by her literary powers and at the same time by great popular appeal. She started writing in 1897, but it was not until 1905 that she had an outstanding success with *The House of Mirth*. During her life she published more than forty volumes: novels, stories, verse, essays, travel books and memoirs. While *Ethan Frome* (1911), the stark New England tragedy, is possibly her best-known work, it is the least typical of her art. This found full expression in her 'society' novels, such as *The Custom of the Country* and particularly *The Age of Innocence* (1920), for which she won the Pulitzer Prize and in which she brilliantly analysed the changing scene of fashionable American life, and contrasted the manners of the New World with those of Old Europe. Other works include *The Reef*, *The Buccaneers*, *Summer* and *The Muse's Tragedy and Other Stories*, all of which are available as Penguin Twentieth-Century Classics.

THREE EUROPEAN NOVELS

MADAME DE TREYMES
THE REEF
THE BUCCANEERS

EDITH WHARTON

PENGUIN BOOKS

PENGUIN BOOKS

Published by the Penguin Group
Penguin Books Ltd, 27 Wrights Lane, London w8 5TZ, England
Penguin Books USA Inc., 375 Hudson Street, New York, New York 10014, USA
Penguin Books Australia Ltd, Ringwood, Victoria, Australia
Penguin Books Canada Ltd, 10 Alcorn Avenue, Toronto, Ontario, Canada M4V 3B2
Penguin Books (NZ) Ltd, 182–190 Wairau Road, Auckland 10, New Zealand

Penguin Books Ltd, Registered Offices: Harmondsworth, Middlesex, England

Madame de Treymes first published 1907
Published in Penguin Books 1995

The Reef first published 1912
Published in Penguin Books 1994

The Buccaneers first published 1938
Published in Penguin Books 1994
Copyright 1938 by the Estate of Edith Wharton

This omnibus edition published in Penguin Books 1996
1 3 5 7 9 10 8 6 4 2

Set in 10/12pt Monotype Baskerville
Typeset by Datix International Limited, Bungay, Suffolk
Printed in England by Clays Ltd, St Ives plc

CONTENTS

MADAME DE TREYMES

I

John Durham, while he waited for Madame de Malrive to draw on her gloves, stood in the hotel doorway looking out across the rue de Rivoli at the afternoon brightness of the Tuileries gardens.

His European visits were infrequent enough to have kept unimpaired the freshness of his eye, and he was always struck anew by the vast and consummately ordered spectacle of Paris: by its look of having been boldly and deliberately planned as a background for the enjoyment of life, instead of being forced into grudging concessions to the festive instincts, or barricading itself against them in unenlightened ugliness, like his own lamentable New York.

But today, if the scene had never presented itself more alluringly, in that moist spring bloom between showers, when the horse-chestnuts dome themselves in unreal green against a gauzy sky, and the very dust of the pavement seems the fragrance of lilac made visible – today for the first time the sense of a personal stake in it all, of having to reckon individually with its effects and influences, kept Durham from an unrestrained yielding to the spell. Paris might still be – to the unimplicated it doubtless still was – the most beautiful city in the world; but whether it were the most lovable or the most detestable depended for him, in the last analysis, on the buttoning of the white glove over which Fanny de Malrive still lingered.

The mere fact of her having forgotten to draw on her gloves as they were descending in the hotel lift from his mother's drawing-room was, in this connection, charged with significance to Durham. She was the kind of woman who always presents herself to the mind's eye as completely equipped, as made up of exquisitely cared for and finely related details; and that the heat of her parting with his family should have left her unconscious that she was emerging gloveless into Paris, seemed, on the whole, to speak hopefully for Durham's future opinion of the city.

Even now, he could detect a certain confusion, a desire to draw breath and catch up with life, in the way she dawdled over the last buttons in the dimness of the porte-cochère, while her footman, outside, hung on her retarded signal.

When at length they emerged, it was to learn from that functionary that Madame la Marquise's carriage had been obliged to yield its place at the door, but was at the moment in the act of regaining it. Madame de Malrive cut the explanation short. 'I shall walk home. The carriage this evening at eight.'

As the footman turned away, she raised her eyes for the first time to Durham's.

'Will you walk with me? Let us cross the Tuileries. I should like to sit a moment on the terrace.'

She spoke quite easily and naturally, as if it were the most commonplace thing in the world for them to be straying afoot together over Paris; but even his vague knowledge of the world she lived in – a knowledge mainly acquired through the perusal of yellow-backed fiction – gave a thrilling significance to her naturalness. Durham, indeed, was beginning to find that one of the charms of a sophisticated society is that it lends point and perspective to the slightest contact between the sexes. If, in the old unrestricted New York days, Fanny Frisbee, from a brown-stone doorstep, had proposed that they should take a walk in the Park, the idea would have presented itself to her companion as agreeable but unimportant; whereas Fanny de Malrive's suggestion that they should stroll across the Tuileries was obviously fraught with unspecified possibilities.

He was so throbbing with the sense of these possibilities that he walked beside her without speaking down the length of the wide alley which follows the line of the rue de Rivoli, suffering her even, when they reached its farthest end, to direct him in silence up the steps to the terrace of the Feuillants. For, after all, the possibilities were double-faced, and her bold departure from custom might simply mean that what she had to say was so dreadful that it needed all the tenderest mitigation of circumstance.

There was apparently nothing embarrassing to her in his silence: it was a part of her long European discipline that she had learned to manage pauses with ease. In her Frisbee days she might have packed this one with a random fluency; now she was content to let it widen slowly before them like the spacious prospect opening at their feet.

The complicated beauty of this prospect, as they moved toward it between the symmetrically clipped limes of the lateral terrace, touched him anew through her nearness, as with the hint of some vast impersonal power, controlling and regulating her life in ways he could not guess, putting between himself and her the whole width of the civilization into which her marriage had absorbed her. And there was such fear in the thought – he read such derision of what he had to offer in the splendour of the great avenues tapering upward to the sunset glories of the Arch – that all he had meant to say when he finally spoke compressed itself at last into an abrupt unmitigated: 'Well?'

She answered at once – as though she had only awaited the call of the national interrogation – 'I don't know when I have been so happy.'

'So happy?' The suddenness of his joy flushed up through his fair skin.

'As I was just now – taking tea with your mother and sisters.'

Durham's 'Oh!' of surprise betrayed also a note of disillusionment, which she met only by the reconciling murmur: 'Shall we sit down?'

He found two of the springy yellow chairs indigenous to the spot, and placed them under the tree near which they had paused, saying reluctantly, as he did so: 'Of course it was an immense pleasure to *them* to see you again.'

'Oh, not in the same way. I mean –' she paused, sinking into the chair, and betraying, for the first time, a momentary inability to deal becomingly with the situation. 'I mean,' she resumed, smiling, 'that it was not an event for them, as it was for me.'

'An event?' He caught her up again, eagerly; for what, in the language of any civilization, could that word mean but just the one thing he most wished it to?

'To be with dear, good, sweet, simple, real Americans again!' she burst out, heaping up her epithets with reckless prodigality.

Durham's smile once more faded to impersonality, as he rejoined, just a shade on the defensive: 'If it's merely our Americanism you enjoyed – I've no doubt we can give you all you want in that line.'

'Yes, it's just that! But if you knew what the word means to me! It means – it means –' she paused as if to assure herself that they were

5

sufficiently isolated from the desultory groups beneath the other trees – 'it means that I'm *safe* with them; as safe as in a bank!'

Durham felt a sudden warmth behind his eyes and in his throat. 'I think I do know –'

'No, you don't, really; you can't know how dear and strange and familiar it all sounded: the old New York names that kept coming up in your mother's talk, and her charming quaint ideas about Europe – their all regarding it as a great big innocent pleasure-ground and shop for Americans; and your mother's missing the home-made bread and preferring the American asparagus – I'm so tired of Americans who despise even their own asparagus! And then your married sister's spending her summers at – where is it? – the Kittawittany House on Lake Pohunk –'

A vision of earnest women in Shetland shawls, with spectacles and thin knobs of hair, eating blueberry pie at unwholesome hours in a shingled dining-room on a bare New England hill-top, rose pallidly between Durham and the verdant brightness of the Champs Elysées, and he protested with a slight smile: 'Oh, but my married sister is the black sheep of the family – the rest of us never sank as low as that.'

'Low? I think it's beautiful – fresh and innocent and simple. I remember going to such a place once. They have early dinner – rather late – and go off in buckboards over terrible roads, and bring back golden rod and autumn leaves, and read nature books aloud on the piazza; and there is always one shy young man in flannels – only one – who has come to see the prettiest girl (though how he can choose among so many!) and who takes her off in a buggy for hours and hours –' She paused and summed up with a long sigh: 'It is fifteen years since I was in America.'

'And you're still so good an American.'

'Oh, a better and better one every day!'

He hesitated. 'Then why did you never come back?'

Her face altered instantly, exchanging its retrospective light for the look of slightly shadowed watchfulness which he had known as most habitual to it.

'It was impossible – it has always been so. My husband would not go; and since – since our separation – there have been family reasons.'

Durham sighed impatiently. 'Why do you talk of reasons? The

truth is, you have made your life here. You could never give all this up!' He made a discouraged gesture in the direction of the Place de la Concorde.

'Give it up! I would go tomorrow! But it could never, now, be for more than a visit. I must live in France on account of my boy.'

Durham's heart gave a quick beat. At last the talk had neared the point toward which his whole mind was straining, and he began to feel a personal application in her words. But that made him all the more cautious about choosing his own.

'It is an agreement – about the boy?' he ventured.

'I gave my word. They knew that was enough,' she said proudly; adding, as if to put him in full possession of her reasons: 'It would have been much more difficult for me to obtain complete control of my son if it had not been understood that I was to live in France.'

'That seems fair,' Durham assented after a moment's reflection: it was his instinct, even in the heat of personal endeavour, to pause a moment on the question of 'fairness'. The personal claim reasserted itself as he added tentatively: 'But when he *is* brought up – when he's grown up: then you would feel freer?'

She received this with a start, as a possibility too remote to have entered into her view of the future. 'He is only eight years old!' she objected.

'Ah, of course it would be a long way off?'

'A long way off; thank heaven! French mothers part late with their sons, and in that one respect I mean to be a French mother.'

'Of course – naturally – since he has only you,' Durham again assented.

He was eager to show how fully he took her point of view, if only to dispose her to the reciprocal fairness of taking his when the time came to present it. And he began to think that the time had now come; that their walk would not have thus resolved itself, without excuse or pretext, into a tranquil session beneath the trees, for any purpose less important than that of giving him his opportunity.

He took it, characteristically, without seeking a transition. 'When I spoke to you, the other day, about myself – about what I felt for you – I said nothing of the future, because, for the moment, my mind refused to travel beyond its immediate hope of happiness. But I felt, of course, even then, that the hope involved various difficulties – that we can't, as we might once have done, come together without any thought but for ourselves; and whatever your answer is to be, I want to tell you now that I am ready to accept my share of the difficulties.' He paused, and then added explicitly, 'If there's the least chance of your listening to me, I'm willing to live over here as long as you can keep your boy with you.'

2

Whatever Madame de Malrive's answer was to be, there could be no doubt as to her readiness to listen. She received Durham's words without sign of resistance, and took time to ponder them gently before she answered, in a voice touched by emotion, 'You are very generous – very unselfish; but when you fix a limit – no matter how remote – to my remaining here, I see how wrong it is to let myself consider for a moment such possibilities as we have been talking of.'

'Wrong? Why should it be wrong?'

'Because I shall want to keep my boy always! Not, of course, in the sense of living with him, or even forming an important part of his life; I am not deluded enough to think that possible. But I do believe it possible never to pass wholly out of his life; and while there is a hope of that, how can I leave him?' She paused, and turned on him a new face, a face on which the past of which he was still so ignorant showed itself like a shadow suddenly darkening a clear pane. 'How can I make you understand?' she went on urgently. 'It is not only because of my love for him – not only, I mean, because of my own happiness in being with him; that I can't, in imagination, surrender even the remotest hour of his future; it is because, the moment he passes out of my influence, he passes under that other – the influence I have been fighting against every hour since he was born! – I don't mean, you know,' she added, as Durham, with bent head, continued to offer her the silent fixity of his attention, 'I don't mean the special personal influence – except inasmuch as it represents something wider, more general, something that encloses and circulates through the whole world in which he belongs. That is what

I meant when I said you could never understand! There is nothing in your experience – in any American experience – to correspond with that far-reaching family organization, which is itself a part of the larger system, and which encloses a young man of my son's position in a network of accepted prejudices and opinions. Everything is prepared in advance – his political and religious convictions, his judgements of people, his sense of honour, his ideas of women, his whole view of life. He is taught to see vileness and corruption in every one not of his own way of thinking, and in every idea that does not directly serve the religious and political purposes of his class. The truth isn't a fixed thing: it's not used to test actions by, it's tested by them, and made to fit in with them. And this forming of the mind begins with the child's first consciousness; it's in his nursery stories, his baby prayers, his very games with his playmates! Already he is only half mine, because the Church has the other half, and will be reaching out for my share as soon as his education begins. But that other half is still mine, and I mean to make it the strongest and most living half of the two, so that, when the inevitable conflict begins, the energy and the truth and the endurance shall be on my side and not on theirs!'

She paused, flushing with the repressed fervour of her utterance, though her voice had not been raised beyond its usual discreet modulations; and Durham felt himself tingling with the transmitted force of her resolve. Whatever shock her words brought to his personal hope, he was grateful to her for speaking them so clearly, for having so sure a grasp of her purpose.

Her decision strengthened his own, and after a pause of deliberation he said quietly: 'There might be a good deal to urge on the other side – the ineffectualness of your sacrifice, the probability that when your son marries he will inevitably be absorbed back into the life of his class and his people; but I can't look at it in that way, because if I were in your place I believe I should feel just as you do about it. As long as there was a fighting chance I should want to keep hold of my half, no matter how much the struggle cost me. And one reason why I understand your feeling about your boy is that I have the same feeling about *you*: as long as there's a fighting chance of keeping my half of you – the half he is willing to spare me – I don't see how I can ever give it up.' He waited again, and then brought out firmly: 'If you'll marry me, I'll agree to live out here as long as you want, and we'll be two instead of one to keep hold of your half of him.'

He raised his eyes as he ended, and saw that hers met them through a quick clouding of tears.

'Ah, I am glad to have had this said to me! But I could never accept such an offer.'

He caught instantly at the distinction. 'That doesn't mean that you could never accept *me*?'

'Under such conditions –'

'But if I am satisfied with the conditions? Don't think that I am speaking rashly, under the influence of the moment. I have expected something of this sort, and I have thought out my side of the case. As far as material circumstances go, I have worked long enough and successfully enough to take my ease and take it where I choose. I mention that because the life I offer you is offered to your boy as well.' He let this sink into her mind before summing up gravely: 'The offer I make is made deliberately, and at least I have a right to a direct answer.'

She was silent again, and then lifted a cleared gaze to his. 'My direct answer then is: if I were still Fanny Frisbee I would marry you.'

He bent toward her persuasively. 'But you will be – when the divorce is pronounced.'

'Ah, the divorce –' She flushed deeply, with an instinctive shrinking back of her whole person which made him straighten himself in his chair.

'Do you so dislike the idea?'

'The idea of divorce? No – not in my case. I should like anything that would do away with the past – obliterate it all – make everything new in my life!'

'Then what –?' he began again, waiting with the patience of a wooer on the uneasy circling of her tormented mind.

'Oh, don't ask me; I don't know; I am frightened.'

Durham gave a deep sigh of discouragement. 'I thought your coming here with me today – and above all your going with me just now to see my mother – was a sign that you were *not* frightened!'

'Well, I was not when I was with your mother. She made everything seem easy and natural. She took me back into that clear American air where there are no obscurities, no mysteries –'

'What obscurities, what mysteries, are you afraid of?'

She looked about her with a faint shiver. 'I am afraid of everything!' she said.

'That's because you are alone; because you've no one to turn to. I'll clear the air for you fast enough if you'll let me.'

He looked forth defiantly, as if flinging his challenge at the great city which had come to typify the powers contending with him for her possession.

'You say that so easily! But you don't know; none of you know.'

'Know what?'

'The difficulties –'

'I told you I was ready to take my share of the difficulties – and my share naturally includes yours. You know Americans are great hands at getting over difficulties.' He drew himself up confidently. 'Just leave that to me – only tell me exactly what you're afraid of.'

She paused again, and then said: 'The divorce, to begin with – they will never consent to it.'

He noticed that she spoke as though the interests of the whole clan, rather than her husband's individual claim, were to be considered; and the use of the plural pronoun shocked his free individualism like a glimpse of some dark feudal survival.

'But you are absolutely certain of your divorce! I've consulted – of course without mentioning names –'

She interrupted him, with a melancholy smile: 'Ah, so have I. The divorce would be easy enough to get, if they ever let it come into the courts.'

'How on earth can they prevent that?'

'I don't know; my never knowing how they will do things is one of the secrets of their power.'

'Their power? What power?' he broke in with irrepressible contempt. 'Who are these bogeys whose machinations are going to arrest the course of justice in a – comparatively – civilized country? You've told me yourself that Monsieur de Malrive is the least likely to give you trouble; and the others are his uncle the Abbé, his mother and sister. That kind of a syndicate doesn't scare me much. A priest and two women *contra mundum*!'

She shook her head. 'Not *contra mundum*, but with it, their whole world is behind them. It's that mysterious solidarity that you can't understand. One doesn't know how far they may reach, or in how many directions. I have never known. They have always cropped up where I least expected them.'

Before this persistency of negation Durham's buoyancy began to flag, but his determination grew the more fixed.

'Well, then, supposing them to possess these supernatural powers; do you think it's to people of that kind that I'll ever consent to give you up?'

She raised a half-smiling glance of protest. 'Oh, they're not wantonly wicked. They'll leave me alone as long as –'

'As I do?' he interrupted. 'Do you want me to leave you alone? Was that what you brought me here to tell me?'

The directness of the challenge seemed to gather up the scattered strands of her hesitation, and lifting her head she turned on him a look in which, but for its underlying shadow, he might have recovered the full free beam of Fanny Frisbee's gaze.

'I don't know why I brought you here,' she said gently, 'except from the wish to prolong a little the illusion of being once more an American among Americans. Just now, sitting there with your mother and Katy and Nannie, the difficulties seemed to vanish; the problems grew as trivial to me as they are to you. And I wanted them to remain so a little longer; I wanted to put off going back to them. But it was of no use – they were waiting for me here. They are over there now in that house across the river. She indicated the grey sky-line of the Faubourg, shining in the splintered radiance of the sunset beyond the long sweep of the quays. 'They are a part of me – I belong to them. I must go back to them!' she sighed.

She rose slowly to her feet, as though her metaphor had expressed an actual fact and she felt herself bodily drawn from his side by the influences of which she spoke.

Durham had risen too. 'Then I go back with you!' he exclaimed energetically; and as she paused, wavering a little under the shock of his resolve: 'I don't mean into your house – but into your life!' he said.

She suffered him, at any rate, to accompany her to the door of the house, and allowed their debate to prolong itself through the almost monastic quiet of the quarter which led thither. On the way, he succeeded in wresting from her the confession that, if it were possible to ascertain in advance that her husband's family would not oppose her action, she might decide to apply for a divorce. Short of a positive assurance on this point, she made it clear that she would never move in the matter; there must be no scandal, no *retentissement*, nothing which her boy, necessarily brought up in the French tradition of scrupulously preserved appearances, could afterward regard as the faintest blur on his much-quartered escutcheon. But even this partial concession again raised fresh obstacles; for there seemed to be no one to whom she could entrust so delicate an investigation, and to apply directly to the Marquis de Malrive or his relatives appeared, in the light of her past experience, the last way of learning their intentions.

'But,' Durham objected, beginning to suspect a morbid fixity of idea in her perpetual attitude of distrust – 'but surely you have told me that your husband's sister – what is her name? Madame de Treymes? – was the most powerful member of the group, and that she has always been on your side.'

She hesitated. 'Yes, Christiane has been on my side. She dislikes her brother. But it would not do to ask her.'

'But could no one else ask her? Who are her friends?'

'She has a great many, and some, of course, are mine. But in a case like this they would be all hers; they wouldn't hesitate a moment between us.'

'Why should it be necessary to hesitate between you? Suppose Madame de Treymes sees the reasonableness of what you ask; suppose, at any rate, she sees the hopelessness of opposing you? Why should she make a mystery of your opinion?'

'It's not that; it is that, if I went to her friends, I should never get her real opinion from them. At least I should never know if it *was* her real opinion; and therefore I should be no farther advanced. Don't you see?'

Durham struggled between the sentimental impulse to soothe her, and the practical instinct that it was a moment for unmitigated frankness.

'I'm not sure that I do; but if you can't find out what Madame de Treymes thinks, I'll see what I can do myself.'

'Oh – *you!*' broke from her in mingled terror and admiration; and pausing on her doorstep to lay her hand in his before she touched the bell, she added with a half-whimsical flash of regret: 'Why didn't this happen to Fanny Frisbee?'

3

Why had it not happened to Fanny Frisbee?

Durham put the question to himself as he walked back along the quays, in a state of inner commotion which left him, for once, insensible to the ordered beauty of his surroundings. Propinquity had not been lacking: he had known Miss Frisbee since his college days. In unsophisticated circles, one family is apt to quote another; and the Durham ladies had always quoted the Frisbees. The Frisbees were bold, experienced, enterprising: they had what the novelists of the day called 'dash'. The beautiful Fanny was especially dashing; she had the showiest national attributes, tempered only by a native grace of softness, as the beam of her eyes was subdued by the length of their lashes. And yet young Durham, though not unsusceptible to such charms, had remained content to enjoy them from a safe distance of good fellowship. If he had been asked why, he could not have told; but the Durham of forty understood. It was because there were, with minor modifications, many other Fanny Frisbees; whereas never before, within his ken, had there been a Fanny de Malrive.

He had felt it in a flash, when, the autumn before, he had run across her one evening in the dining-room of the Beaurivage at Ouchy; when, after a furtive exchange of glances, they had simultaneously arrived at recognition, followed by an eager pressure of hands, and a long evening of reminiscence on the starlit terrace. She was the same, but so mysteriously changed! And it was the mystery, the sense of unprobed depths of initiation, which drew him to her as her freshness had never drawn him. He had not hitherto attempted to define the nature of the change: it remained for his sister Nannie to do that when, on his return to the rue de Rivoli, where the family were still sitting in conclave upon their recent visitor, Miss Durham summed up their groping comments in the phrase: 'I never saw anything so French!'

Durham, understanding what his sister's use of the epithet implied, recognized it instantly as the explanation of his own feelings. Yes, it was the finish, the modelling which Madame de Malrive's experience had given her that set her apart from the fresh uncomplicated personalities of which she had once been simply the most charming type. The influences that had lowered her voice, regulated her gestures, toned her down to harmony with the warm dim background of a long social past – these influences had lent to her natural fineness of perception a command of expression adapted to complex conditions. She had moved in surroundings through which one could hardly bounce and bang on the genial American plan without knocking the angles off a number of sacred institutions; and her acquired dexterity of movement seemed to Durham a crowning grace. It was a shock, now that he knew at what cost the dexterity had been acquired, to acknowledge this even to himself; he hated to think that she could owe anything to such conditions as she had been placed in. And it gave him a sense of the tremendous strength of the organization into which she had been absorbed, that in spite of her horror, her moral revolt, she had not reacted against its external forms. She might abhor her husband, her marriage, and the world to which it had introduced her, but she had become a product of that world in its outward expression, and no better proof of the fact was needed than her exotic enjoyment of Americanism.

The sense of the distance to which her American past had been removed was never more present to him than when, a day or two later, he went with his mother and sister to return her visit. The region beyond the river existed, for the Durham ladies, only as the unmapped environment of the Bon Marché; and Nannie Durham's exclamation on the pokiness of the streets and the dullness of the houses showed Durham, with a start, how far he had already travelled from the family point of view.

'Well, if this is all she got by marrying a Marquis!' the young lady summed up as they paused before the small sober hotel in its high-walled court; and Katy, following her mother through the stone-vaulted and stone-floored vestibule, murmured: 'It must be simply freezing in winter.'

In the softly-faded drawing-room, with its old pastels in old frames, its windows looking on the damp green twilight of a garden sunk deep in blackened walls, the American ladies might have been even more conscious of the insufficiency of their friend's compensations, had not the warmth of her welcome precluded all other reflections. It was not till she had gathered them about her in the corner beside the tea-table, that Durham identified the slender dark lady loitering negligently in the background, and introduced in a comprehensive murmur to the American group, as the redoubtable sister-in-law to whom he had declared himself ready to throw down his challenge.

There was nothing very redoubtable about Madame de Treymes, except perhaps the kindly yet critical observation which she bestowed on her sister-in-law's visitors: the unblinking attention of a civilized spectator observing an encampment of aborigines. He had heard of her as a beauty, and was surprised to find her, as Nannie afterward put it, a mere stick to hang clothes on (but they *did* hang!), with a small brown glancing face, like that of a charming little inquisitive animal. Yet before she had addressed ten words to him – nibbling at the hard English consonants like nuts – he owned the justice of the epithet. She was a beauty, if beauty, instead of being restricted to the cast of the face, is a pervasive attribute informing the hands, the voice, the gestures, the very fall of a flounce and tilt of a feather. In this impalpable *aura* of grace Madame de Treymes' dark meagre presence unmistakably moved, like a thin flame in a wide quiver of light. And as he realized that she looked much handsomer than she was, so, while they talked, he felt that she understood a great deal more than she betrayed. It was not through the groping speech which formed their apparent medium of communication that she imbibed her information: she found it in the air, she extracted it from Durham's look and manner, she caught it in the turn of her sister-in-law's defenceless eyes – for in her presence Madame de Malrive became Fanny Frisbee again! – she put it together, in short, out of just such unconsidered, indescribable trifles as differentiated the quiet felicity of her dress from Nannie and Katy's 'handsome' haphazard clothes.

Her actual converse with Durham moved, meanwhile, strictly in the conventional ruts: had he been long in Paris, which of the new plays did he like best, was it true that American *jeunes filles* were sometimes taken to the Boulevard theatres? And she threw an interrogative glance at the young ladies beside the tea-table. To Durham's reply that it depended how much French they knew, she shrugged and smiled, replying that his compatriots all spoke French like Parisians, inquiring, after a moment's thought, if they learned it, *là-bas, des nègres,* and laughing heartily when Durham's astonishment revealed her blunder.

When at length she had taken leave – enveloping the Durham ladies in a last puzzled, penetrating look – Madame de Malrive turned to Mrs Durham with a faintly embarrassed smile.

'My sister-in-law was much interested: I believe you are the first Americans she has ever known.'

'Good gracious!' ejaculated Nannie, as though such social darkness required immediate missionary action on someone's part.

'Well, she knows *us*,' said Durham, catching, in Madame de Malrive's rapid glance, a startled assent to his point.

'After all,' reflected the accurate Katy, as though seeking an excuse for Madame de Treymes' unenlightenment, '*we* don't know many French people, either.'

To which Nannie promptly if obscurely retorted: 'Ah, but we couldn't and *she* could!'

4

Madame de Treymes' friendly observation of her sister-in-law's visitors resulted in no expression on her part of a desire to renew her study of them. To all appearances, she passed out of their lives when Madame de Malrive's door closed on her; and Durham felt that the arduous task of making her acquaintance was still to be begun.

He felt also, more than ever, the necessity of attempting it; and in his determination to lose no time, and his perplexity how to set most speedily about the business, he bethought himself of applying to his cousin Mrs Boykin.

Mrs Elmer Boykin was a small plump woman, to whose vague

prettiness the lines of middle-age had given no meaning: as though whatever had happened to her had merely added to the sum total of her inexperience. After a Parisian residence of twenty-five years, spent in a state of feverish servitude to the great artists of the rue de la Paix, her dress and hair still retained a certain rigidity in keeping with the directness of her gaze and the unmodulated candour of her voice. Her very drawing-room had the hard bright atmosphere of her native skies, and one felt that she was still true at heart to the national ideals in electric lighting and plumbing.

She and her husband had left America owing to the impossibility of living there with the finish and decorum which the Boykin standard demanded; but in the isolation of their exile they had created about them a kind of phantom America, where the national prejudices continued to flourish unchecked by the national progressiveness: a little world sparsely peopled by compatriots in the same attitude of chronic opposition toward a society chronically unaware of them. In this uncontaminated air Mr and Mrs Boykin had preserved the purity of simpler conditions, and Elmer Boykin, returning rakishly from a Sunday's racing at Chantilly, betrayed, under his 'knowing' coat and the racing-glasses slung ostentatiously across his shoulder, the unmistakable cut of the American business man coming 'up town' after a long day in the office.

It was a part of the Boykins' uncomfortable but determined attitude – and perhaps a last expression of their latent patriotism – to live in active disapproval of the world about them, fixing in memory with little stabs of reprobation innumerable instances of what the abominable foreigner was doing; so that they reminded Durham of persons peacefully following the course of a horrible war by pricking red pins in a map. To Mrs Durham, with her gentle tourist's view of the European continent, as a vast Museum in which the human multitudes simply furnished the element of costume, the Boykins seemed abysmally instructed, and darkly expert in forbidden things; and her son, without sharing her simple faith in their omniscience, credited them with an ample supply of the kind of information of which he was in search.

Mrs Boykin, from the corner of an intensely modern Gobelin sofa, studied her cousin as he balanced himself insecurely on one of the small gilt chairs which always look surprised at being sat in.

'Fanny de Malrive? Oh, of course: I remember you were all very intimate with the Frisbees when they lived in West Thirty-third Street. But she has dropped all her American friends since her marriage. The excuse was that de Malrive didn't like them but as she's been separated for five or six years, I can't see – You say she's been very nice to your mother and the girls? Well, I daresay she is beginning to feel the need of friends she can really trust; for as for her French relations –! That Malrive set is the worst in the Faubourg. Of course you know what *he* is; even the family, for decency's sake, had to back her up, and urge her to get a separation. And Christiane de Treymes –'

Durham seized his opportunity. 'Is she so very reprehensible too?'

Mrs Boykin pursed up her small colourless mouth. 'I can't speak from personal experience. I know Madame de Treymes slightly – I have met her at Fanny's – but she never remembers the fact except when she wants me to go to one of her *ventes de charité*. They all remember us then; and some American women are silly enough to ruin themselves at the smart bazaars, and fancy they will get invitations in return. They say Mrs Addison G. Pack followed Madame d'Alglade around for a whole winter, and spent a hundred thousand francs at her stalls; and at the end of the season Madame d'Alglade asked her to tea, and when she got there she found *that* was for a charity too, and she had to pay a hundred francs to get in.'

Mrs Boykin paused with a smile of compassion. 'That is not *my* way,' she continued. 'Personally I have no desire to thrust myself into French society – I can't see how any American woman can do so without loss of self-respect. But any one can tell you about Madame de Treymes.'

'I wish you would, then,' Durham suggested.

'Well, I think Elmer had better,' said his wife mysteriously, as Mr Boykin, at this point, advanced across the wide expanse of Aubusson on which his wife and Durham were islanded in a state of propinquity without privacy.

'What's that, Bessy? Hah, Durham, how are you? Didn't see you at Auteuil this afternoon. You don't race? Busy sight-seeing, I suppose? What was that my wife was telling you? Oh, about Madame de Treymes.'

He stroked his pepper-and-salt moustache with a gesture intended rather to indicate than to conceal the smile of experience beneath it. 'Well, Madame de Treymes has not been like a happy country – she's had a history: several of 'em. Someone said she constituted the *feuilleton* of the Faubourg daily news. *La suite au prochain numéro* – you see the point? Not that I speak from personal knowledge. Bessy and I have never cared to force our way –' He paused, reflecting that his wife had probably anticipated him in the expression of this familiar sentiment, and added with a significant nod: 'Of course you know the Prince d'Armillac by sight? No? I'm surprised at that. Well, he's one of the choicest ornaments of the Jockey Club: very fascinating to the ladies I believe, but the deuce and all at baccarat. Ruined his mother and a couple of maiden aunts already – and now Madame de Treymes has put the family pearls up the spout, and is wearing imitation for love of him.'

'I had that straight from my maid's cousin, who is employed by Madame d'Armillac's jeweller,' said Mrs Boykin with conscious pride.

'Oh, it's straight enough – more than *she* is!' retorted her husband, who was slightly jealous of having his facts reinforced by any information not of his own gleaning.

'Be careful of what you say, Elmer,' Mrs Boykin interposed with archness. 'I suspect John of being seriously smitten by the lady.'

Durham let this pass unchallenged, submitting with a good grace to his host's low whistle of amusement, and the sardonic inquiry: 'Ever do anything with the foils? D'Armillac is what they call over here a *fine lame*.'

'Oh, I don't mean to resort to bloodshed unless it's absolutely necessary; but I mean to make the lady's acquaintance,' said Durham, falling into his key.

Mrs Boykin's lips tightened to the vanishing point. 'I am afraid you must apply for an introduction to more fashionable people than *we* are. Elmer and I so thoroughly disapprove of French society that we have always declined to take any part in it. But why should not Fanny de Malrive arrange a meeting for you?'

Durham hesitated. 'I don't think she is on very intimate terms with her husband's family –'

'You mean that she's not allowed to introduce *her* friends to them,' Mrs Boykin interjected sarcastically; while her husband added, with an air of portentous initiation: 'Ah, my dear fellow, the way they treat the Americans over here – that's another chapter, you know.'

'How some people can *stand* it!' Mrs Boykin chimed in; and as the footman, entering at that moment, tendered her a large coroneted envelope, she held it up as if in illustration of the indignities to which her countrymen were subjected.

'Look at that, my dear John,' she exclaimed – 'another card to one of their everlasting bazaars! Why, it's at Madame d'Armillac's, the Prince's mother. Madame de Treymes must have sent it, of course. The brazen way in which they combine religion and immorality! Fifty francs admission – *rien que cela!* – to see some of the most disreputable people in Europe. And if you're an American, you're expected to leave at least a thousand behind you. Their own people naturally get off cheaper.' She tossed over the card to her cousin. 'There's your opportunity to see Madame de Treymes.'

'Make it two thousand, and she'll ask you to tea,' Mr Boykin scathingly added.

<h1 style="text-align:center">5</h1>

In the monumental drawing-room of the Hôtel de Malrive – it had been a surprise to the American to read the name of the house emblazoned on black marble over its still more monumental gateway – Durham found himself surrounded by a buzz of feminine tea-sipping oddly out of keeping with the wigged and cuirassed portraits frowning high on the walls, the majestic attitude of the furniture, the rigidity of great gilt consoles drawn up like lords-in-waiting against the tarnished panels.

It was the old Marquise de Malrive's 'day', and Madame de Treymes, who lived with her mother, had admitted Durham to the heart of the enemy's country by inviting him, after his prodigal disbursements at the charity bazaar, to come in to tea on a Thursday. Whether, in thus fulfilling Mr Boykin's prediction, she had been aware of Durham's purpose, and had her own reasons for falling in with it; or whether she simply wished to reward his lavishness at the

fair, and permit herself another glimpse of an American so pictur-
esquely embodying the type familiar to French fiction – on these
points Durham was still in doubt.

Meanwhile, Madame de Treymes being engaged with a venerable
Duchess in a black shawl – all the older ladies present had the
sloping shoulders of a generation of shawl-wearers – her American
visitor, left in the isolation of his unimportance, was using it as a
shelter for a rapid survey of the scene.

He had begun his study of Fanny de Malrive's situation without
any real understanding of her fears. He knew the repugnance to
divorce existing in the French Catholic world, but since the French
laws sanctioned it, and in a case so flagrant as his injured friend's,
would inevitably accord it with the least possible delay and exposure,
he could not take seriously any risk of opposition on the part of the
husband's family. Madame de Malrive had not become a Catholic,
and since her religious scruples could not be played on, the only
weapon remaining to the enemy – the threat of fighting the divorce
– was one they could not wield without self-injury. Certainly, if the
chief object were to avoid scandal, common sense must counsel Monsieur de Malrive and his friends not to give the courts an opportunity
of exploring his past; and since the echo of such explorations, and
their ultimate transmission to her son, were what Madame de Malrive most dreaded, the opposing parties seemed to have a common
ground for agreement, and Durham could not but regard his friend's
fears as the result of over-taxed sensibilities. All this had seemed
evident enough to him as he entered the austere portals of the Hôtel
de Malrive and passed, between the faded liveries of old family
servants, to the presence of the dreaded dowager above. But he had
not been ten minutes in that presence before he had arrived at a
faint intuition of what poor Fanny meant. It was not in the exquisite
mildness of the old Marquise, a little grey-haired bunch of a woman
in dowdy mourning, or in the small, neat presence of the priestly
uncle, the Abbé, who had so obviously just stepped down from one
of the picture-frames overhead: it was not in the aspect of these
chief protagonists, so outwardly unformidable, that Durham read an
occult danger to his friend. It was rather in their setting, their surroundings, the little company of elderly and dowdy persons – so
uniformly clad in weeping blacks and purples that they might have

been assembled for some mortuary anniversary – it was in the remoteness and the solidarity of this little group that Durham had his first glimpse of the social force of which Fanny de Malrive had spoken. All these amiably chatting visitors, who mostly bore the stamp of personal insignificance on their mildly sloping or aristocratically beaked faces, hung together in a visible closeness of tradition, dress, attitude, and manner, as different as possible from the loose aggregation of a roomful of his own countrymen. Durham felt, as he observed them, that he had never before known what 'society' meant; nor understood that, in an organized and inherited system, it exists full-fledged where two or three of its members are assembled.

Upon this state of bewilderment, this sense of having entered a room in which the lights had suddenly been turned out, even Madame de Treymes' intensely modern presence threw no illumination. He was conscious, as she smilingly rejoined him, not of her points of difference from the others, but of the myriad invisible threads by which she held to them; he even recognized the audacious slant of her little brown profile in the portrait of a powdered ancestress beneath which she had paused a moment in advancing. She was simply one particular facet of the solid, glittering, impenetrable body which he had thought to turn in his hands and look through like a crystal; and when she said, in her clear staccato English, 'Perhaps you will like to see the other rooms,' he felt like crying out in his blindness: 'If I could only be sure of seeing *anything* here!' Was she conscious of his blindness, and was he as remote and unintelligible to her as she was to him? This possibility, as he followed her through the nobly-unfolding rooms of the great house, gave him his first hope of recoverable advantage. For, after all, he had some vague traditional lights on her world and its antecedents; whereas to her he was a wholly new phenomenon, as unexplained as a fragment of meteorite dropped at her feet on the smooth gravel of the garden-path they were pacing.

She had led him down into the garden, in response to his admiring exclamation, and perhaps also because she was sure that, in the chill spring afternoon, they would have its embowered privacies to themselves. The garden was small, but intensely rich and deep – one of those wells of verdure and fragrance which everywhere sweeten the air of Paris by wafts blown above old walls on quiet streets; and as Madame de Treymes paused against the ivy bank masking its farther boundary, Durham felt more than ever removed from the normal bearings of life.

His sense of strangeness was increased by the surprise of his companion's next speech.

'You wish to marry my sister-in-law?' she asked abruptly; and Durham's start of wonder was followed by an immediate feeling of relief. He had expected the preliminaries of their interview to be as complicated as the bargaining in an Eastern bazaar, and had feared to lose himself at the first turn in a labyrinth of 'foreign' intrigue.

'Yes, I do,' he said with equal directness; and they smiled together at the sharp report of question and answer.

The smile put Durham more completely at his ease, and after waiting for her to speak, he added with deliberation: 'So far, however, the wishing is entirely on my side.' His scrupulous conscience felt itself justified in this reserve by the conditional nature of Madame de Malrive's consent.

'I understand; but you have been given reason to hope –'

'Every man in my position gives himself his own reasons for hoping,' he interposed, with a smile.

'I understand that too,' Madame de Treymes assented. 'But still – you spent a great deal of money the other day at our bazaar.'

'Yes: I wanted to have a talk with you, and it was the readiest – if not the most distinguished – means of attracting your attention.'

'I understand,' she once more reiterated, with a gleam of amusement.

'It is because I suspect you of understanding everything that I have been so anxious for this opportunity.'

She bowed her acknowledgement, and said: 'Shall we sit a moment?' adding, as he drew their chairs under a tree, 'You permit me, then, to say that I believe I understand also a little of our good Fanny's mind?'

'On that point I have no authority to speak. I am here only to listen.'

'Listen, then: you have persuaded her that there would be no harm in divorcing my brother – since I believe your religion does not forbid divorce?'

'Madame de Malrive's religion sanctions divorce in such a case as –'

'As my brother has furnished? Yes, I have heard that your race is stricter in judging such *écarts*. But you must not think,' she added, 'that I defend my brother. Fanny must have told you that we have always given her our sympathy.'

'She has let me infer it from her way of speaking of you.'

Madame de Treymes arched her dramatic eyebrows. 'How cautious you are! I am so straightforward that I shall have no chance with you.'

'You will be quite safe, unless you are so straightforward that you put me on my guard.'

She met this with a low note of amusement.

'At this rate we shall never get any farther; and in two minutes I must go back to my mother's visitors. Why should we go on fencing? The situation is really quite simple. Tell me just what you wish to know. I have always been Fanny's friend, and that disposes me to be yours.'

Durham, during this appeal, had had time to steady his thoughts; and the result of his deliberation was that he said, with a return to his former directness: 'Well, then, what I wish to know is, what position your family would take if Madame de Malrive should sue for a divorce?' He added, without giving her time to reply: 'I naturally wish to be clear on this point before urging my cause with your sister-in-law.'

Madame de Treymes seemed in no haste to answer; but after a pause of reflection she said, not unkindly, 'My poor Fanny might have asked me that herself.'

'I beg you to believe that I am not acting as her spokesman,' Durham hastily interposed. 'I merely wish to clear up the situation before speaking to her in my own behalf.'

'You are the most delicate of suitors! But I understand your feeling. Fanny also is extremely delicate: it was a great surprise to us at first. Still, in this case –' Madame de Treymes paused – 'since she has no religious scruples, and she had no difficulty in obtaining a separation, why should she fear any in demanding a divorce?'

'I don't know that she does: but the mere fact of possible opposition might be enough to alarm the delicacy you have observed in her.'

'Ah – yes: on her boy's account.'

'Partly, doubtless, on her boy's account.'

'So that, if my brother objects to a divorce, all he has to do is to announce his objection? But, my dear sir, you are giving your case into my hands!' She flashed an amused smile on him.

'Since you say you are Madame de Malrive's friend, could there be a better place for it?'

As she turned her eyes on him he seemed to see, under the flitting lightness of her glance, the sudden concentrated expression of the ancestral will. 'I am Fanny's friend, certainly. But with us family considerations are paramount. And our religion forbids divorce.'

'So that, inevitably, your brother will oppose it?'

She rose from her seat, and stood fretting with her slender boot-tip the minute red pebbles of the path.

'I must really go in; my mother will never forgive me for deserting her.'

'But surely you owe me an answer?' Durham protested, rising also.

'In return for your purchases at my stall?'

'No: in return for the trust I have placed in you.'

She mused on this, moving slowly a step or two toward the house.

'Certainly I wish to see you again; you interest me,' she said smiling. 'But it is so difficult to arrange. If I were to ask you to come here again, my mother and uncle would be surprised. And at Fanny's –'

'Oh, not there!' he exclaimed.

'Where then? Is there any other house where we are likely to meet?'

Durham hesitated; but he was goaded by the flight of the precious minutes. 'Not unless you'll come and dine with me,' he said boldly.

'Dine with you? *Au cabaret?* Ah, that would be diverting – but impossible!'

'Well, dine with my cousin, then – I have a cousin, an American lady, who lives here,' said Durham, with suddenly soaring audacity.

She paused with puzzled brows. 'An American lady whom I know?'

'By name, at any rate. You send her cards for all your charity bazaars.'

She received the thrust with a laugh. 'We do exploit your compatriots.'

'Oh, I don't think she has ever gone to the bazaars.'

'But she might if I dined with her?'

'Still less, I imagine.'

She reflected on this, and then said with acuteness: 'I like that, and I accept – but what is the lady's name?'

6

On the way home, in the first drop of his exaltation, Durham had said to himself: 'But why on earth should Bessy invite her?'

He had, naturally, no very cogent reasons to give Mrs Boykin in support of his astonishing request, and could only, marvelling at his own growth in duplicity, suffer her to infer that he was really, shamelessly 'smitten' with the lady he thus proposed to thrust upon her hospitality. But, to his surprise, Mrs Boykin hardly gave herself time to pause upon his reasons. They were swallowed up in the fact that Madame de Treymes wished to dine with her, as the lesser luminaries vanish in the blaze of the sun.

'I am not surprised,' she declared, with a faint smile intended to check her husband's unruly wonder. 'I wonder *you* are, Elmer. Didn't you tell me that Armillac went out of his way to speak to you the other day at the races? And at Madame d'Alglade's sale – yes, I went there after all, just for a minute, because I found Katy and Nannie were so anxious to be taken – well, that day I noticed that Madame de Treymes was quite *empressée* when we went up to her stall. Oh, I didn't buy anything: I merely waited while the girls chose some lampshades. They thought it would be interesting to take home something painted by a real Marquise, and of course I didn't tell them that those women *never* make the things they sell at their stalls. But I repeat I'm not surprised: I suspected that Madame de Treymes had heard of our little dinners. You know they're really horribly bored in that poky old Faubourg. My poor John, I see now why she's been

27

making up to you! But on one point I am quite determined, Elmer; whatever you say, I shall *not* invite the Prince d'Armillac.'

Elmer, as far as Durham could observe, did not say much; but, like his wife, he continued in a state of pleasantly agitated activity till the momentous evening of the dinner.

The festivity in question was restricted in numbers, either owing to the difficulty of securing suitable guests, or from a desire not to have it appear that Madame de Treymes' hosts attached any special importance to her presence; but the smallness of the company was counterbalanced by the multiplicity of the courses.

The national determination not to be 'downed' by the despised foreigner, to show a wealth of material resource obscurely felt to compensate for the possible lack of other distinctions – this resolve had taken, in Mrs Boykin's case, the shape – or rather the multiple shapes – of a series of culinary feats, of gastronomic combinations, which would have commanded her deep respect had she seen them on any other table, and which she naturally relied on to produce the same effect on her guest. Whether or not the desired result was achieved, Madame de Treymes' manner did not specifically declare; but it showed a general complaisance, a charming willingness to be amused, which made Mr Boykin, for months afterward, allude to her among his compatriots as 'an old friend of my wife's – takes pot-luck with us, you know. Of course there's not a word of truth in any of those ridiculous stories.'

It was only when, to Durham's intense surprise, Mr Boykin hazarded to his neighbour the regret that they had not been so lucky as to 'secure the Prince' – it was then only that the lady showed, not indeed anything so simple and unprepared as embarrassment, but a faint play of wonder, an under-flicker of amusement, as though recognizing that, by some odd law of social compensation, the crudity of the talk might account for the complexity of the dishes.

But Mr Boykin was tremulously alive to hints, and the conversation at once slid to safer topics, easy generalizations which left Madame de Treymes ample time to explore the table, to use her narrowed gaze like a knife slitting open the unsuspicious personalities about her. Nannie and Katy Durham, who, after much discussion (to which their hostess candidly admitted them), had been included in the feast, were the special objects of Madame de

Treymes' observation. During dinner she ignored in their favour the other carefully selected guests – the fashionable art-critic, the old Legitimist general, the beauty from the English Embassy, the whole impressive marshalling of Mrs Boykin's social resources – and when the men returned to the drawing-room, Durham found her still fanning in his sisters the flame of an easily kindled enthusiasm. Since she could hardly have been held by the intrinsic interest of their converse, the sight gave him another swift intuition of the working of those hidden forces with which Fanny de Malrive felt herself encompassed. But when Madame de Treymes, at his approach, let him see that it was for him she had been reserving herself, he felt that so graceful an impulse needed no special explanation. She had the art of making it seem quite natural that they should move away together to the remotest of Mrs Boykin's far-drawn salons, and that there, in a glaring privacy of brocade and ormolu, she should turn to him with a smile which avowed her intentional quest of seclusion.

'Confess that I have done a great deal for you!' she exclaimed, making room for him on a sofa judiciously screened from the observation of the other rooms.

'In coming to dine with my cousin?' he inquired, answering her smile.

'Let us say, in giving you this half-hour.'

'For that I am duly grateful – and shall be still more so when I know what it contains for me.'

'Ah, I am not sure. You will not like what I am going to say.'

'Shall I not?' he rejoined, changing colour.

She raised her eyes from the thoughtful contemplation of her painted fan. 'You appear to have no idea of the difficulties.'

'Should I have asked your help if I had not had an idea of them?'

'But you are still confident that with my help you can surmount them?'

'I can't believe you have come here to take that confidence from me?'

She leaned back, smiling at him through her lashes. 'And all this I am to do for your *beaux yeux*?'

'No – for your own: that you may see with them what happiness you are conferring.'

'You are extremely clever, and I like you.' She paused, and then brought out with lingering emphasis: 'But my family will not hear of a divorce.'

She threw into her voice such an accent of finality that Durham, for the moment, felt himself brought up against an insurmountable barrier; but, almost at once, his fear was mitigated by the conviction that she would not have put herself out so much to say so little.

'When you speak of your family, do you include yourself?' he suggested.

She threw a surprised glance at him. 'I thought you understood that I am simply their mouthpiece.'

At this he rose quietly to his feet with a gesture of acceptance. 'I have only to thank you, then, for not keeping me longer in suspense.'

His air of wishing to put an immediate end to the conversation seemed to surprise her. 'Sit down a moment longer,' she commanded him kindly; and as he leaned against the back of his chair, without appearing to hear her request, she added in a low voice: 'I am very sorry for you and Fanny – but you are not the only persons to be pitied.'

'The only persons?'

'In our unhappy family.' She touched her breast with a sudden tragic gesture. 'I, for instance, whose help you ask – if you could guess how I need help myself!'

She had dropped her light manner as she might have tossed aside her fan, and he was startled at the intimacy of misery to which her look and movement abruptly admitted him. Perhaps no Anglo-Saxon fully understands the fluency in self-revelation which centuries of the confessional have given to the Latin races, and to Durham, at any rate, Madame de Treymes' sudden avowal gave the shock of a physical abandonment.

'I am so sorry,' he stammered – 'is there any way in which I can be of use to you?'

She sat before him with her hands clasped, her eyes fixed on his in a terrible intensity of appeal. 'If you would – if you would! Oh, there is nothing I would not do for you. I have still a great deal of influence with my mother, and what my mother commands we all do. I could help you – I am sure I could help you; but not if my own situation were known. And if nothing can be done it must be known in a few days.'

Durham had reseated himself at her side. 'Tell me what I can do,' he said in a low tone, forgetting his own preoccupations in his genuine concern for her distress.

She looked up at him through tears. 'How dare I? Your race is so cautious, so self-controlled – you have so little indulgence for the extravagances of the heart. And my folly has been incredible – and unrewarded.' She paused, and as Durham waited in a silence which she guessed to be compassionate, she brought out below her breath: 'I have lent money – my husband's, my brother's – money that was not mine, and now I have nothing to repay it with.'

Durham gazed at her in genuine astonishment. The turn the conversation had taken led quite beyond his uncomplicated experiences with the other sex. She saw his surprise, and extended her hands in deprecation and entreaty. 'Alas, what must you think of me? How can I explain my humiliating myself before a stranger? Only by telling you the whole truth – the fact that I am not alone in this disaster, that I could not confess my situation to my family without ruining myself, and involving in my ruin someone who, however undeservedly, has been as dear to me as – as you are to –'

Durham pushed his chair back with a sharp exclamation.

'Ah, even that does not move you!' she said.

The cry restored him to his senses by the long shaft of light it sent down the dark windings of the situation. He seemed suddenly to know Madame de Treymes as if he had been brought up with her in the inscrutable shades of the Hôtel de Malrive.

She, on her side, appeared to have a startled but uncomprehending sense of the fact that his silence was no longer completely sympathetic, that her touch called forth no answering vibration; and she made a desperate clutch at the one chord she could be certain of sounding.

'You have asked a great deal of me – much more than you can guess. Do you mean to give me nothing – not even your sympathy – in return? Is it because you have heard horrors of me? When are they not said of a woman who is married unhappily? Perhaps not in your fortunate country, where she may seek liberation without dishonour. But here –! You who have seen the consequences of our disastrous marriages – you who may yet be the victim of our cruel and abominable system; have you no pity for one who has suffered in the same way, and without the possibility of release?' She paused, laying her hand on his arm with a smile of deprecating irony. 'It is not because you are not rich. At such times the crudest way is the shortest, and I don't pretend to deny that I know I am asking you a trifle. You Americans, when you want a thing, always pay ten times what it is worth, and I am giving you the wonderful chance to get what you most want at a bargain.'

Durham sat silent, her little gloved hand burning his coat-sleeve as if it had been a hot iron. His brain was tingling with the shock of her confession. She wanted money, a great deal of money: that was clear, but it was not the point. She was ready to sell her influence, and he fancied she could be counted on to fulfil her side of the bargain. The fact that he could so trust her seemed only to make her more terrible to him – more supernaturally dauntless and baleful. For what was it that she exacted of him? She had said she must have money to pay her debts; but he knew that was only a pretext which she scarcely expected him to believe. She wanted the money for someone else; that was what her allusion to a fellow-victim meant. She wanted it to pay the Prince's gambling debts – it was at that price that Durham was to buy the right to marry Fanny de Malrive.

Once the situation had worked itself out in his mind, he found himself unexpectedly relieved of the necessity of weighing the arguments for and against it. All the traditional forces of his blood were in revolt, and he could only surrender himself to their pressure, without thought of compromise or parley.

He stood up in silence, and the abruptness of his movement caused Madame de Treymes' hand to slip from his arm.

'You refuse?' she exclaimed; and he answered with a bow: 'Only because of the return you propose to make me.'

She stood staring at him, in a perplexity so genuine and profound that he could almost have smiled at it through his disgust.

'Ah, you are all incredible,' she murmured at last, stooping to repossess herself of her fan; and as she moved past him to rejoin the group in the farther room, she added in an incisive undertone: 'You are quite at liberty to repeat our conversation to your friend!'

7

Durham did not take advantage of the permission thus strangely flung at him: of his talk with her sister-in-law he gave to Madame de Malrive only that part which concerned her.

Presenting himself for this purpose, the day after Mrs Boykin's dinner, he found his friend alone with her son; and the sight of the child had the effect of dispelling whatever illusive hopes had attended him to the threshold. Even after the governess's descent upon the scene had left Madame de Malrive and her visitor alone, the little boy's presence seemed to hover admonishingly between them, reducing to a bare statement of fact Durham's confession of the total failure of his errand.

Madame de Malrive heard the confession calmly; she had been too prepared for it not to have prepared a countenance to receive it. Her first comment was: 'I have never known them to declare themselves so plainly –' and Durham's baffled hopes fastened themselves eagerly on the words. Had she not always warned him that there was nothing so misleading as their plainness? And might it not be that, in spite of his advisedness, he had suffered too easy a rebuff? But second thoughts reminded him that the refusal had not been as unconditional as his necessary reservations made it seem in the repetition; and that, furthermore, it was his own act, and not that of his opponents, which had determined it. The impossibility of revealing this to Madame de Malrive only made the difficulty shut in more darkly around him, and in the completeness of his discouragement he scarcely needed her reminder of his promise to regard the subject as closed when once the other side had defined its position.

He was secretly confirmed in this acceptance of his fate by the knowledge that it was really he who had defined the position. Even now that he was alone with Madame de Malrive, and subtly aware of the struggle under her composure, he felt no temptation to abate his stand by a jot. He had not yet formulated a reason for his resistance: he simply went on feeling, more and more strongly with every precious sign of her participation in his unhappiness, that he could neither owe his escape from it to such a transaction, nor suffer her, innocently, to owe hers.

The only mitigating effect of his determination was in an increase of helpless tenderness toward her; so that, when she exclaimed, in answer to his announcement that he meant to leave Paris the next night, 'Oh, give me a day or two longer!' he at once resigned himself to saying, 'If I can be of the least use, I'll give you a hundred.'

She answered sadly that all he could do would be to let her feel that he was there – just for a day or two, till she had readjusted herself to the idea of going on in the old way; and on this note of renunciation they parted.

But Durham, however pledged to the passive part, could not long sustain it without rebellion. To 'hang round' the shut door of his hopes seemed, after two long days, more than even his passion required of him; and on the third he dispatched a note of goodbye to his friend. He was going off for a few weeks, he explained – his mother and sisters wished to be taken to the Italian lakes: but he would return to Paris, and say his real farewell to her, before sailing for America in July.

He had not intended his note to act as an ultimatum: he had no wish to surprise Madame de Malrive into unconsidered surrender. When, almost immediately, his own messenger returned with a reply from her, he even felt a pang of disappointment, a momentary fear lest she should have stooped a little from the high place where his passion had preferred to leave her; but her first words turned his fear into rejoicing.

'Let me see you before you go: something extraordinary has happened,' she wrote.

What had happened, as he heard from her a few hours later – finding her in a tremor of frightened gladness, with her door boldly closed to all the world but himself – was nothing less extraordinary than a visit from Madame de Treymes, who had come, officially delegated by the family, to announce that Monsieur de Malrive had decided not to oppose his wife's suit for divorce. Durham, at the news, was almost afraid to show himself too amazed; but his small signs of alarm and wonder were swallowed up in the flush of Madame de Malrive's incredulous joy.

'It's the long habit, you know, of not believing them – of looking for the truth always in what they *don't* say. It took me hours and hours to convince myself that there's no trick under it, that there can't be any,' she explained.

'Then you *are* convinced now?' escaped from Durham; but the shadow of his question lingered no more than the flit of a wing across her face.

'I am convinced because the facts are there to reassure me. Christiane tells me that Monsieur de Malrive has consulted his lawyers, and that they have advised him to free me. Maître Enguerrand has been instructed to see my lawyer whenever I wish it. They quite understand that I never should have taken the step in face of any opposition on their part – I am so thankful to you for making that perfectly clear to them! – and I suppose this is the return their pride makes to mine. For they *can* be proud collectively –' She broke off, and added, with happy hands outstretched: 'And I owe it all to you – Christiane said it was your talk with her that had convinced them.'

Durham, at this statement, had to repress a fresh sound of amazement; but with her hands in his, and, a moment after, her whole self drawn to him in the first yielding of her lips, doubt perforce gave way to the lover's happy conviction that such love was after all too strong for the powers of darkness.

It was only when they sat again in the blissful after-calm of their understanding, that he felt the pricking of an unappeased distrust.

'Did Madame de Treymes give you any reason for this change of front?' he risked asking, when he found the distrust was not otherwise to be quelled.

'Oh, yes: just what I've said. It was really her admiration of *you* – of your attitude – your delicacy. She said that at first she hadn't believed in it: they're always looking for a hidden motive. And when she found that yours was staring at her in the actual words you said: that you really respected my scruples, and would never, never try to coerce or entrap me – something in her – poor Christiane! – answered to it, she told me, and she wanted to prove to us that she was capable of understanding us too. If you knew her history you'd find it wonderful and pathetic that she can!'

Durham thought he knew enough of it to infer that Madame de Treymes had not been the object of many conscientious scruples on the part of the opposite sex; but this increased rather his sense of the strangeness than of the pathos of her action. Yet Madame de Malrive, whom he had once inwardly taxed with the morbid raising of obstacles, seemed to see none now; and he could only infer that her sister-in-law's actual words had carried more conviction than reached him in the repetition of them. The mere fact that he had so much to gain by leaving his friend's faith undisturbed was no doubt stirring his own suspicions to unnatural activity; and this sense gradually reasoned him back into acceptance of her view, as the most normal as well as the pleasantest he could take.

8

The uneasiness thus temporarily repressed slipped into the final disguise of hoping he should not again meet Madame de Treymes; and in this wish he was seconded by the decision, in which Madame de Malrive concurred, that it would be well for him to leave Paris while the preliminary negotiations were going on. He committed her interests to the best professional care, and his mother, resigning her dream of the lakes, remained to fortify Madame de Malrive by her mild, unimaginative view of the transaction, as an uncomfortable but commonplace necessity, like house-cleaning or dentistry. Mrs Durham would doubtless have preferred that her only son, even with his hair turning grey, should have chosen a Fanny Frisbee rather than a Fanny de Malrive; but it was a part of her acceptance of life on a general basis of innocence and kindliness, that she entered generously into his dream of rescue and renewal, and devoted herself without after-thought to keeping up Fanny's courage with so little to spare for herself.

The process, the lawyers declared, would not be a long one, since Monsieur de Malrive's acquiescence reduced it to a formality; and when, at the end of June, Durham returned from Italy with Katy and Nannie, there seemed no reason why he should not stop in Paris long enough to learn what progress had been made.

But before he could learn this he was to hear, on entering Madame de Malrive's presence, news more immediate if less personal. He found her, in spite of her gladness in his return, so evidently preoccupied and distressed that his first thought was one of fear for their own future. But she read and dispelled this by saying, before he could put his question: 'Poor Christiane is here. She is very unhappy. You have seen in the papers –'

'I have seen no papers since we left Turin. What has happened?'

'The Prince d'Armillac has come to grief. There has been some terrible scandal about money, and he has been obliged to leave France to escape arrest.'

'And Madame de Treymes has left her husband?'

'Ah, no, poor creature: they don't leave their husbands – they can't. But de Treymes has gone down to their place in Brittany, and as my mother-in-law is with another daughter in Auvergne, Christiane came here for a few days. With me, you see, she need not pretend – she can cry her eyes out.'

'And that is what she is doing?'

It was so unlike his conception of the way in which, under the most adverse circumstances, Madame de Treymes would be likely to occupy her time, that Durham was conscious of a note of scepticism in his query.

'Poor thing – if you saw her you would feel nothing but pity. She is suffering so horribly that I reproach myself for being happy under the same roof.'

Durham met this with a tender pressure of her hand; then he said, after a pause of reflection: 'I should like to see her.'

He hardly knew what prompted him to utter the wish, unless it were a sudden stir of compunction at the memory of his own dealings with Madame de Treymes. Had he not sacrificed the poor creature to a purely fantastic conception of conduct? She had said that she knew she was asking a trifle of him; and the fact that, materially, it would have been a trifle, had seemed at the moment only an added reason for steeling himself in his moral resistance to it. But now that he had gained his point – and through her own generosity, as it still appeared – the largeness of her attitude made his own seem cramped and petty. Since conduct, in the last resort, must be judged by its enlarging or diminishing effect on character, might it not be that the zealous weighing of the moral anise and cummin was less important than the unconsidered lavishing of the precious ointment? At any rate, he could enjoy no peace of mind under the burden of Madame de Treymes' magnanimity, and when he had assured himself that his own affairs were progressing favourably, he once more, at the risk of surprising his betrothed, brought up the possibility of seeing her relative.

Madame de Malrive evinced no surprise. 'It is natural, knowing what she has done for us, that you should want to show her your sympathy. The difficulty is that it is just the one thing you *can't* show her. You can thank her, of course, for ourselves, but even that at the moment –'

'Would seem brutal? Yes, I recognize that I should have to choose my words,' he admitted, guiltily conscious that his capability of dealing with Madame de Treymes extended far beyond her sister-in-law's conjecture.

Madame de Malrive still hesitated. 'I can tell her; and when you come back tomorrow –'

It had been decided that, in the interests of discretion – the interests, in other words, of the poor little future Marquis de Malrive – Durham was to remain but two days in Paris, withdrawing then with his family till the conclusion of the divorce proceedings permitted him to return in the acknowledged character of Madame de Malrive's future husband. Even on this occasion, he had not come to her alone; Nannie Durham, in the adjoining room, was chatting conspicuously with the little Marquis, whom she could with difficulty be restrained from teaching to call her 'Aunt Nannie'. Durham thought her voice had risen unduly once or twice during his visit, and when, on taking leave, he went to summon her from the inner room, he found the higher note of ecstasy had been evoked by the appearance of Madame de Treymes, and that the little boy, himself absorbed in a new toy of Durham's bringing, was being bent over by an actual as well as a potential aunt.

Madame de Treymes raised herself with a slight start at Durham's approach: she had her hat on, and had evidently paused a moment on her way out to speak with Nannie, without expecting to be surprised by her sister-in-law's other visitor. But her surprises never wore the awkward form of embarrassment, and she smiled beautifully on Durham as he took her extended hand.

The smile was made the more appealing by the way in which it lit up the ruin of her small dark face, which looked seared and hollowed as by a flame that might have spread over it from her fevered eyes. Durham, accustomed to the pale inward grief of the inexpressive races, was positively startled by the way in which she seemed to have been openly stretched on the pyre; he almost felt an indelicacy in the ravages so tragically confessed.

The sight caused an involuntary readjustment of his whole view of the situation, and made him, as far as his own share in it went, more than ever inclined to extremities of self-disgust. With him such sensations required, for his own relief, some immediate penitential escape, and as Madame de Treymes turned toward the door he addressed a glance of entreaty to his betrothed.

Madame de Malrive, whose intelligence could be counted on at such moments, responded by laying a detaining hand on her sister-in-law's arm.

'Dear Christiane, may I leave Mr Durham in your charge for two minutes? I have promised Nannie that she shall see the boy put to bed.'

Madame de Treymes made no audible response to this request, but when the door had closed on the other ladies she said, looking quietly at Durham: 'I don't think that, in this house, your time will hang so heavy that you need my help in supporting it.'

Durham met her glance frankly. 'It was not for that reason that Madame de Malrive asked you to remain with me.'

'Why, then? Surely not in the interest of preserving appearances, since she is safely upstairs with your sister?'

'No; but simply because I asked her to. I told her I wanted to speak to you.'

'How you arrange things! And what reason can you have for wanting to speak to me?'

He paused a moment. 'Can't you imagine? The desire to thank you for what you have done.'

She stirred restlessly, turning to adjust her hat before the glass above the mantelpiece.

'Oh, as for what I have done —'

'Don't speak as if you regretted it,' he interposed.

She turned back to him with a flash of laughter lighting up the haggardness of her face. 'Regret working for the happiness of two such excellent persons? Can't you fancy what a charming change it is for me to do something so innocent and beneficent?'

He moved across the room and went up to her, drawing down the hand which still flitted experimentally about her hat.

'Don't talk in that way, however much one of the persons of whom you speak may have deserved it.'

'One of the persons? Do you mean me?'

He released her hand, but continued to face her resolutely. 'I mean myself, as you know. You have been generous – extraordinarily generous.'

'Ah, but I was doing good in a good cause. You have made me see that there is a distinction.'

He flushed to the forehead. 'I am here to let you say whatever you choose to me.'

'Whatever I choose?' She made a slight gesture of deprecation. 'Has it never occurred to you that I may conceivably choose to say nothing?'

Durham paused, conscious of the increasing difficulty of the ad-vance. She met him, parried him, at every turn: he had to take his baffled purpose back to another point of attack.

'Quite conceivably,' he said: 'so much so that I am aware I must make the most of this opportunity, because I am not likely to get another.'

'But what remains of your opportunity, if it isn't one to me?'

'It still remains, for me, an occasion to abase myself –' He broke off, conscious of a grossness of allusion that seemed, on a closer approach, the real obstacle to full expression. But the moments were flying, and for his self-esteem's sake he must find some way of making her share the burden of his repentance.

'There is only one thinkable pretext for detaining you: it is that I may still show my sense of what you have done for me.'

Madame de Treymes, who had moved toward the door, paused at this and faced him, resting her thin brown hands on a slender sofa-back.

'How do you propose to show that sense?' she inquired.

Durham coloured still more deeply: he saw that she was deter-mined to save her pride by making what he had to say of the utmost difficulty. Well! he would let his expiation take that form, then – it was as if her slender hands held out to him the fool's cap he was condemned to press down on his own ears.

'By offering in return – in any form, and to the utmost – any service you are forgiving enough to ask of me.'

She received this with a low sound of laughter that scarcely rose to her lips. 'You are princely. But, my dear sir, does it not occur to you that I may, meanwhile, have taken my own way of repaying myself for any service I have been fortunate enough to render you?'

Durham, at the question, or still more, perhaps, at the tone in which it was put, felt, through his compunction, a vague faint chill of apprehension. Was she threatening him or only mocking him? Or was this barbed swiftness of retort only the wounded creature's way of defending the privacy of her own pain? He looked at her again, and read his answer in the last conjecture.

'I don't know how you can have repaid yourself for anything so disinterested – but I am sure, at least, that you have given me no chance of recognizing, ever so slightly, what you have done.'

She shook her head, with the flicker of a smile on her melancholy lips. 'Don't be too sure! You have given me a chance and I have taken it – taken it to the full. So fully,' she continued, keeping her eyes fixed on his, 'that if I were to accept any farther service you might choose to offer, I should simply be robbing you – robbing you shamelessly.' She paused, and added in an undefinable voice: 'I was entitled, wasn't I, to take something in return for the service I had the happiness of doing you?'

Durham could not tell whether the irony of her tone was self-directed or addressed to himself – perhaps it comprehended them both. At any rate, he chose to overlook his own share in it in replying earnestly: 'So much so, that I can't see how you can have left me nothing to add to what you say you have taken.'

'Ah, but you don't know what that is!' She continued to smile, elusively, ambiguously. 'And what's more, you wouldn't believe me if I told you.'

'How do you know?' he rejoined.

'You didn't believe me once before; and this is so much more incredible.'

He took the taunt full in the face. 'I shall go away unhappy unless you tell me – but then perhaps I have deserved to,' he confessed.

She shook her head again, advancing toward the door with the evident intention of bringing their conference to a close; but on the threshold she paused to launch her reply.

'I can't send you away unhappy, since it is in the contemplation of
your happiness that I have found my reward.'

9

The next day Durham left with his family for England, with the
intention of not returning till after the divorce should have been
pronounced in September.

To say that he left with a quiet heart would be to overstate the
case: the fact that he could not communicate to Madame de Malrive
the substance of his talk with her sister-in-law still hung upon him
uneasily. But of definite apprehensions the lapse of time gradually
freed him, and Madame de Malrive's letters, addressed more frequently to his mother and sisters than to himself, reflected, in their
reassuring serenity, the undisturbed course of events.

There was to Durham something peculiarly touching – as of an
involuntary confession of almost unbearable loneliness – in the way
she had regained, with her re-entry into the clear air of American
associations, her own fresh trustfulness of view. Once she had accustomed herself to the surprise of finding her divorce unopposed, she
had been, as it now seemed to Durham, in almost too great haste to
renounce the habit of weighing motives and calculating chances. It
was as though her coming liberation had already freed her from the
garb of a mental slavery, as though she could not too soon or too
conspicuously cast off the ugly badge of suspicion. The fact that
Durham's cleverness had achieved so easy a victory over forces apparently impregnable, merely raised her estimate of that cleverness to
the point of letting her feel that she could rest in it without farther
demur. He had even noticed in her, during his few hours in Paris, a
tendency to reproach herself for her lack of charity, and a desire,
almost as fervent as his own, to expiate it by exaggerated recognition
of the disinterestedness of her opponents – if opponents they could
still be called. This sudden change in her attitude was peculiarly
moving to Durham. He knew she would hazard herself lightly
enough wherever her heart called her; but that, with the precious
freight of her child's future weighing her down, she should commit

herself so blindly to his hand stirred in him the depths of tenderness. Indeed, had the actual course of events been less auspiciously regular, Madame de Malrive's confidence would have gone far toward unsettling his own; but with the process of law going on unimpeded, and the other side making no sign of open or covert resistance, the fresh air of good faith gradually swept through the inmost recesses of his distrust.

It was expected that the decision in the suit would be reached by mid-September; and it was arranged that Durham and his family should remain in England till a decent interval after the conclusion of the proceedings. Early in the month, however, it became necessary for Durham to go to France to confer with a business associate who was in Paris for a few days, and on the point of sailing from Cherbourg. The most zealous observance of appearances could hardly forbid Durham's return for such a purpose; but it had been agreed between himself and Madame de Malrive – who had once more been left alone by Madame de Treymes' return to her family – that, so close to the fruition of their wishes, they would propitiate fate by a scrupulous adherence to usage, and communicate only, during his hasty visit, by a daily interchange of notes.

The ingenuity of Madame de Malrive's tenderness found, however, the day after his arrival, a means of tempering their privation. 'Christiane,' she wrote, 'is passing through Paris on her way from Trouville, and has promised to see you for me if you will call on her today. She thinks there is no reason why you should not go to the Hôtel de Malrive, as you will find her there alone, the family having gone to Auvergne. She is really our friend and understands us.'

In obedience to this request – though perhaps inwardly regretting that it should have been made – Durham that afternoon presented himself at the proud old house beyond the Seine. More than ever, in the semi-abandonment of the *morte saison*, with reduced service, and shutters closed to the silence of the high-walled court, did it strike the American as the incorruptible custodian of old prejudices and strange social survivals. The thought of what he must represent to the almost human consciousness which such old houses seem to possess, made him feel like a barbarian desecrating the silence of a temple of the earlier faith. Not that there was anything venerable in the attestations of the Hôtel de Malrive, except in so far as, to a sensitive imagination, every concrete embodiment of a past order of things testifies to real convictions once suffered for. Durham, at any rate, always alive in practical issues to the view of the other side, had enough sympathy left over to spend it sometimes, whimsically, on such perceptions of difference. Today, especially, the assurance of success – the sense of entering like a victorious beleaguerer receiving the keys of the stronghold – disposed him to a sentimental perception of what the other side might have to say for itself, in the language of old portraits, old relics, old usages dumbly outraged by his mere presence.

On the appearance of Madame de Treymes, however, such considerations gave way to the immediate act of wondering how she meant to carry off her share of the adventure. Durham had not forgotten the note on which their last conversation had closed: the lapse of time serving only to give more precision and perspective to the impression he had then received.

Madame de Treymes' first words implied a recognition of what was in his thoughts.

'It is extraordinary, my receiving you here; but *que voulez-vous?* There was no other place, and I would do more than this for our dear Fanny.'

Durham bowed. 'It seems to me that you are also doing a great deal for me.'

'Perhaps you will see later that I have my reasons,' she returned, smiling. 'But before speaking for myself I must speak for Fanny.'

She signed to him to take a chair near the sofa-corner in which she had installed herself, and he listened in silence while she delivered Madame de Malrive's message, and her own report of the progress of affairs.

'You have put me still more deeply in your debt,' he said as she concluded; 'I wish you would make the expression of this feeling a large part of the message I send back to Madame de Malrive.'

She brushed this aside with one of her light gestures of deprecation. 'Oh, I told you I had my reasons. And since you are here – and the mere sight of you assures me that you are as well as Fanny charged me to find you – with all these preliminaries disposed of, I am going to relieve you, in a small measure, of the weight of your obligation.'

Durham raised his head quickly. 'By letting me do something in return?'

She made an assenting motion. 'By asking you to answer a question.'

'That seems very little to do.'

'Don't be so sure! It is never very little to your race.' She leaned back, studying him through half-dropped lids.

'Well, try me,' he protested.

She did not immediately respond; and when she spoke, her first words were explanatory rather than interrogative.

'I want to begin by saying that I believe I once did you an injustice, to the extent of misunderstanding your motive for a certain action.'

Durham's uneasy flush confessed his recognition of her meaning. 'Ah, if we must go back to *that* –'

'You withdraw your assent to my request?'

'By no means; but nothing consolatory you can find to say on that point can really make any difference.'

'Will not the difference in my view of you perhaps make a difference in your own?'

She looked at him earnestly, without a trace of irony in her eyes or on her lips. 'It is really I who have an *amende* to make, as I now understand the situation. I once turned to you for help in a painful extremity, and I have only now learned to understand your reasons for refusing to help me.'

'Oh, my reasons –' groaned Durham.

'I have learned to understand them,' she persisted, 'by being so much, lately, with Fanny.'

'But I never told her!' he broke in.

'Exactly. That was what told *me*. I understood you through her, and through your dealings with her. There she was – the woman you adored and longed to save and you would not lift a finger to make her yours by means which would have seemed – I see it now – a desecration of your feeling for each other.' She paused, as if to find the exact words for meanings she had never before had occasion to formulate. 'It came to me first – a light on your attitude – when I found you had never breathed to her a word of our talk together. She had confidently commissioned you to find a way for her, as the medieval lady sent a prayer to her knight to deliver her from captivity, and you came back, confessing you had failed, but never justifying yourself by so much as a hint of the reason why. And when I had lived a little in Fanny's intimacy – at a moment when circumstances helped to bring us extraordinarily close – I understood why you had done this; why you had let her take what view she pleased of your failure, your passive acceptance of defeat, rather than let her suspect the alternative offered you. You couldn't, even with my permission, betray to any one a hint of my miserable secret, and you couldn't, for your life's happiness, pay the particular price that I asked.' She leaned toward him in the intense, almost childlike, effort at full expression. 'Oh, we are of different races, with a different point of honour; but I understand, I see, that you are good people – just simply, courageously *good*!'

She paused, and then said slowly: 'Have I understood you? Have I put my hand on your motive?'

Durham sat speechless, subdued by the rush of emotion which her words set free.

'That, you understand, is my question,' she concluded with a faint smile; and he answered hesitatingly: 'What can it matter, when the upshot is something I infinitely regret?'

'Having refused me? Don't!' She spoke with deep seriousness, bending her eyes full on his: 'Ah, I have suffered – suffered! But I have learned also – my life has been enlarged. You see how I have understood you both. And that is something I should have been incapable of a few months ago.'

Durham returned her look. 'I can't think that you can ever have been incapable of any generous interpretation.'

She uttered a slight exclamation, which resolved itself into a laugh of self-directed irony.

'If you knew into what language I have always translated life! But that,' she broke off, ' is not what you are here to learn.'

'I think,' he returned gravely, 'that I am here to learn the measure of Christian charity.'

She threw him a new, odd look. 'Ah, no – but to show it!' she exclaimed.

'To show it? And to whom?'

She paused for a moment, and then rejoined, instead of answering: 'Do you remember that day I talked with you at Fanny's? The day after you came back from Italy?'

He made a motion of assent, and she went on: 'You asked me then what return I expected for my service to you, as you called it; and I answered, the contemplation of your happiness. Well, do you know what that meant in my old language – the language I was still speaking then? It meant that I knew there was horrible misery in store for you, and that I was waiting to feast my eyes on it: that's all!'

She had flung out the words with one of her quick bursts of self-abandonment, like a fevered sufferer stripping the bandage from a wound. Durham received them with a face blanching to the pallor of her own.

'What misery do you mean?' he exclaimed.

She leaned forward, laying her hand on his with just such a gesture as she had used to enforce her appeal in Mrs Boykin's boudoir. The remembrance made him shrink slightly from her touch, and she drew back with a smile.

'Have you never asked yourself,' she inquired, 'why our family consented so readily to a divorce?'

'Yes, often,' he replied, all his unformed fears gathering in a dark throng about him. 'But Fanny was so reassured, so convinced that we owed it to your good offices –'

She broke into a laugh. 'My good offices! Will you never, you Americans, learn that we do not act individually in such cases? That we are all obedient to a common principle of authority?'

'Then it was not you –'

She made an impatient shrugging motion. 'Oh, you are too confiding – it is the other side of your beautiful good faith!'

'The side you have taken advantage of, it appears?'

'I – we – all of us. I especially!' she confessed.

IO

There was another pause, during which Durham tried to steady himself against the shock of the impending revelation. It was an odd circumstance of the case that, though Madame de Treymes' avowal of duplicity was fresh in his ears, he did not for a moment believe that she would deceive him again. Whatever passed between them now would go to the root of the matter.

The first thing that passed was the long look they exchanged: searching on his part, tender, sad, undefinable on hers. As the result of it he said: 'Why, then, did you consent to the divorce?'

'To get the boy back,' she answered instantly; and while he sat stunned by the unexpectedness of the retort, she went on: 'Is it possible you never suspected? It has been our whole thought from the first. Everything was planned with that object.'

He drew a sharp breath of alarm. 'But the divorce – how could that give him back to you?'

'It was the only thing that could. We trembled lest the idea should occur to you. But we were reasonably safe, for there has only been one other case of the same kind before the courts.' She leaned back, the sight of his perplexity checking her quick rush of words. 'You didn't know,' she began again, 'that in that case, on the remarriage of the mother, the courts instantly restored the child to the father, though he had – well, given as much cause for divorce as my unfortunate brother?'

Durham gave an ironic laugh. 'Your French justice takes a grammar and dictionary to understand.'

She smiled. '*We* understand it – and it isn't necessary that you should.'

'So it would appear!' he exclaimed bitterly.

'Don't judge us too harshly – or not, at least, till you have taken the trouble to learn our point of view. You consider the individual – we think only of the family.'

'Why don't you take care to preserve it, then?'

'Ah, that's what we do; in spite of every aberration of the individual. And so, when we saw it was impossible that my brother and his wife should live together, we simply transferred our allegiance to the child – we constituted *him* the family.'

'A precious kindness you did him! If the result is to give him back to his father.'

'That, I admit, is to be deplored; but his father is only a fraction of the whole. What we really do is to give him back to his race, his religion, his true place in the order of things.'

'His mother never tried to deprive him of any of those inestimable advantages!'

Madame de Treymes unclasped her hands with a slight gesture of deprecation.

'Not consciously, perhaps; but silences and reserves can teach so much. His mother has another point of view –'

'Thank heaven!' Durham interjected.

'Thank heaven for *her* – yes – perhaps; but it would not have done for the boy.'

Durham squared his shoulders with the sudden resolve of a man breaking through a throng of ugly phantoms.

'You haven't yet convinced me that it won't have to do for him. At the time of Madame de Malrive's separation, the court made no difficulty about giving her the custody of her son; and you must pardon me for reminding you that the father's unfitness was the reason alleged.'

Madame de Treymes shrugged her shoulders. 'And my poor brother, you would add, has not changed; but the circumstances have, and that proves precisely what I have been trying to show you: that, in such cases, the general course of events is considered rather than the action of any one person.'

'Then why is Madame de Malrive's action to be considered?'

'Because it breaks up the unity of the family.'

'*Unity* –!' broke from Durham; and Madame de Treymes gently suffered his smile.

'Of the family tradition, I mean: it introduces new elements. You are a new element.'

'Thank heaven!' said Durham again.

She looked at him singularly. 'Yes – you may thank heaven. Why isn't it enough to satisfy Fanny?'

'Why isn't what enough?'

'Your being, as I say, a new element; taking her so completely into a better air. Why shouldn't she be content to begin a new life with you, without wanting to keep the boy too?'

Durham stared at her dumbly. 'I don't know what you mean,' he said at length.

'I mean that in her place –' she broke off, dropping her eyes. 'She may have another son – the son of the man she adores.'

Durham rose from his seat and took a quick turn through the room. She sat motionless, following his steps through her lowered lashes, which she raised again slowly as he stood before her.

'Your idea, then, is that I should tell her nothing?' he said.

'Tell her *now*? But, my poor friend, you would be ruined!'

'Exactly.' He paused. 'Then why have you told *me*?'

Under her dark skin he saw the faint colour stealing. 'We see things so differently – but can't you conceive that, after all that has passed, I felt it a kind of loyalty not to leave you in ignorance?'

'And you feel no such loyalty to her?'

'Ah, I leave her to you,' she murmured, looking down again.

Durham continued to stand before her, grappling slowly with his perplexity, which loomed larger and darker as it closed in on him.

'You don't leave her to me; you take her from me at a stroke! I suppose,' he added painfully, 'I ought to thank you for doing it before it's too late.'

She stared. 'I take her from you? I simply prevent your going to her unprepared. Knowing Fanny as I do, it seemed to me necessary that you should find a way in advance – a way of tiding over the first moment. That, of course, is what we had planned that you shouldn't have. We meant to let you marry, and then – Oh, there is no question about the result: we are certain of our case – our measures have been taken *de loin*.' She broke off, as if oppressed by his stricken silence. 'You will think me stupid, but my warning you of this is the only return I know how to make for your generosity. I could not bear to have you say afterward that I had deceived you twice.'

'Twice?' He looked at her perplexedly, and her colour rose.

'I deceived you once – that night at your cousin's, when I tried to get you to bribe me. Even then we meant to consent to the divorce – it was decided the first day that I saw you.' He was silent, and she added, with one of her mocking gestures, 'You see from what a *milieu* you are taking her!'

Durham groaned. 'She will never give up her son!'

'How can she help it? After you are married there will be no choice.'

'No – but there is one now.'

'*Now?*' She sprang to her feet, clasping her hands in dismay. 'Haven't I made it clear to you? Haven't I shown you your course?' She paused, and then brought out with emphasis: 'I love Fanny, and I am ready to trust her happiness to you.'

'I shall have nothing to do with her happiness,' he repeated doggedly.

She stood close to him, with a look intently fixed on his face. 'Are you afraid?' she asked with one of her mocking flashes.

'Afraid?'

'Of not being able to make it up to her –?'

Their eyes met, and he returned her look steadily.

'No; if I had the chance, I believe I could.'

'I know you could!' she exclaimed.

'That's the worst of it,' he said with a cheerless laugh.

'The worst –?'

'Don't you see that I can't deceive her? Can't trick her into marrying me now?'

Madame de Treymes continued to hold his eyes for a puzzled moment after he had spoken; then she broke out despairingly: 'Is happiness never more to you, then, than this abstract standard of truth?'

Durham reflected. 'I don't know – it's an instinct. There doesn't seem to be any choice.'

'Then I am a miserable wretch for not holding my tongue!'

He shook his head sadly. 'That would not have helped me; and it would have been a thousand times worse for her.'

'Nothing can be as bad for her as losing you! Aren't you moved by seeing her need?'

'Horribly – are not *you?*' he said, lifting his eyes to hers suddenly.

She started under his look. 'You mean, why don't I help you? Why don't I use my influence? Ah, if you knew how I have tried!'

'And you are sure that nothing can be done?'

'Nothing, nothing: what arguments can I use? We abhor divorce – we go against our religion in consenting to it – and nothing short of recovering the boy could possibly justify us.'

Durham turned slowly away. 'Then there is nothing to be done,' he said, speaking more to himself than to her.

He felt her light touch on his arm. 'Wait! There is one thing more –' She stood close to him, with entreaty written on her small passionate face. 'There is one thing more,' she repeated. 'And that is, to believe that I am deceiving you again.'

He stopped short with a bewildered stare. 'That you are deceiving me – about the boy?'

'Yes – yes; why shouldn't I? You're so credulous – the temptation is irresistible.'

'Ah, it would be too easy to find out –'

'Don't try, then! Go on as if nothing had happened. I have been lying to you,' she declared with vehemence.

'Do you give me your word of honour?' he rejoined.

'A liar's? I haven't any! Take the logic of the facts instead. What reason have you to believe any good of me? And what reason have I to do any to you? Why on earth should I betray my family for your benefit? Ah, don't let yourself be deceived to the end!' She sparkled up at him, her eyes suffused with mockery; but on the lashes he saw a tear.

He shook his head sadly. 'I should first have to find a reason for your deceiving me.'

'Why, I gave it to you long ago. I wanted to punish you – and now I've punished you enough.'

'Yes, you've punished me enough,' he conceded.

The tear gathered and fell down her thin cheek. 'It's you who are punishing me now. I tell you I'm false to the core. Look back and see what I've done to you!'

He stood silent, with his eyes fixed on the ground. Then he took one of her hands and raised it to his lips.

'You poor, good woman!' he said gravely.

Her hand trembled as she drew it away. 'You're going to her – straight from here?'

'Yes – straight from here.'

'To tell her everything – to renounce your hope?'

'That is what it amounts to, I suppose.'

She watched him cross the room and lay his hand on the door.

'Ah, you poor, good man!' she said with a sob.

THE REEF

BOOK ONE

I

'Unexpected obstacle. Please don't come till thirtieth. Anna.'

All the way from Charing Cross to Dover the train had hammered the words of the telegram into George Darrow's ears, ringing every change of irony on its commonplace syllables: rattling them out like a discharge of musketry, letting them, one by one, drip slowly and coldly into his brain, or shaking, tossing, transposing them like the dice in some game of the gods of malice; and now, as he emerged from his compartment at the pier, and stood facing the windswept platform and the angry sea beyond, they leapt out at him as if from the crest of the waves, stung and blinded him with a fresh fury of derision.

'Unexpected obstacle. Please don't come till thirtieth. Anna.'

She had put him off at the very last moment, and for the second time: put him off with all her sweet reasonableness, and for one of her usual 'good' reasons – he was certain that this reason, like the other (the visit of her husband's uncle's widow), would be 'good'! But it was that very certainty which chilled him. The fact of her dealing so reasonably with their case shed an ironic light on the idea that there had been any exceptional warmth in the greeting she had given him after their twelve years apart.

They had found each other again, in London, some three months previously, at a dinner at the American Embassy, and when she had caught sight of him her smile had been like a red rose pinned on her widow's mourning. He still felt the throb of surprise with which, among the stereotyped faces of the season's diners, he had come upon her unexpected face, with the dark hair banded above grave eyes; eyes in which he had recognized every little curve and shadow as he would have recognized, after half a life-time, the details of a room he had played in as a child. And as, in the plumed starred crowd, she had stood out for him, slender, secluded and different, so he had felt, the instant their glances met, that he as sharply

55

detached himself for her. All that and more her smile had said; had said not merely 'I remember,' but 'I remember just what you remember'; almost, indeed, as though her memory had aided his, her glance flung back on their recaptured moment its morning brightness. Certainly, when their distracted Ambassadress – with the cry: 'Oh, you know Mrs Leath? That's perfect, for General Farnham has failed me' – had waved them together for the march to the dining-room, Darrow had felt a slight pressure of the arm on his, a pressure faintly but unmistakably emphasizing the exclamation: 'Isn't it wonderful? – In London – in the season – in a mob?'

Little enough, on the part of most women; but it was a sign of Mrs Leath's quality that every movement, every syllable, told with her. Even in the old days, as an intent grave-eyed girl, she had seldom misplaced her light strokes; and Darrow, on meeting her again, had immediately felt how much finer and surer an instrument of expression she had become.

Their evening together had been a long confirmation of this feeling. She had talked to him, shyly yet frankly, of what had happened to her during the years when they had so strangely failed to meet. She had told him of her marriage to Fraser Leath, and of her subsequent life in France, where her husband's mother, left a widow in his youth, had been remarried to the Marquis de Chantelle, and where, partly in consequence of this second union, the son had permanently settled himself. She had spoken also, with an intense eagerness of affection, of her little girl Effie, who was now nine years old, and, in a strain hardly less tender, of Owen Leath, the charming clever young step-son whom her husband's death had left to her care . . .

A porter, stumbling against Darrow's bags, roused him to the fact that he still obstructed the platform, inert and encumbering as his luggage.

'Crossing, sir?'

Was he crossing? He really didn't know; but for lack of any more compelling impulse he followed the porter to the luggage van, singled out his property, and turned to march behind it down the gang-way. As the fierce wind shouldered him, building up a crystal wall against his efforts, he felt anew the derision of his case.

'Nasty weather to cross, sir,' the porter threw back at him as they beat their way down the narrow walk to the pier. Nasty weather, indeed; but luckily, as it had turned out, there was no earthly reason why Darrow should cross.

While he pushed on in the wake of his luggage his thoughts slipped back into the old groove. He had once or twice run across the man whom Anna Summers had preferred to him, and since he had met her again he had been exercising his imagination on the picture of what her married life must have been. Her husband had struck him as a characteristic specimen of the kind of American as to whom one is not quite clear whether he lives in Europe in order to cultivate an art, or cultivates an art as a pretext for living in Europe. Mr Leath's art was water-colour painting, but he practised it furtively, almost clandestinely, with the disdain of a man of the world for anything bordering on the professional, while he devoted himself more openly, and with religious seriousness, to the collection of enamelled snuffboxes. He was blond and well-dressed, with the physical distinction that comes from having a straight figure, a thin nose, and the habit of looking slightly disgusted – as who should not, in a world where authentic snuffboxes were growing daily harder to find, and the market was flooded with flagrant forgeries?

Darrow had often wondered what possibilities of communion there could have been between Mr Leath and his wife. Now he concluded that there had probably been none. Mrs Leath's words gave no hint of her husband's having failed to justify her choice; but her very reticence betrayed her. She spoke of him with a kind of impersonal seriousness, as if he had been a character in a novel or a figure in history; and what she said sounded as though it had been learned by heart and slightly dulled by repetition. This fact immensely increased Darrow's impression that his meeting with her had annihilated the intervening years. She, who was always so elusive and inaccessible, had grown suddenly communicative and kind: had opened the doors of her past, and tacitly left him to draw his own conclusions. As a result, he had taken leave of her with the sense that he was a being singled out and privileged, to whom she had entrusted something precious to keep. It was her happiness in their meeting that she had given him, had frankly left him to do with as he willed; and the frankness of the gesture doubled the beauty of the gift.

Their next meeting had prolonged and deepened the impression. They had found each other again, a few days later, in an old country house full of books and pictures, in the soft landscape of southern England. The presence of a large party, with all its aimless and agitated displacements, had served only to isolate the pair and give them (at least to the young man's fancy) a deeper feeling of communion, and their days there had been like some musical prelude, where the instruments, breathing low, seem to hold back the waves of sound that press against them.

Mrs Leath, on this occasion, was no less kind than before; but she contrived to make him understand that what was so inevitably coming was not to come too soon. It was not that she showed any hesitation as to the issue, but rather that she seemed to wish not to miss any stage in the gradual reflowering of their intimacy.

Darrow, for his part, was content to wait if she wished it. He remembered that once, in America, when she was a girl, and he had gone to stay with her family in the country, she had been out when he arrived, and her mother had told him to look for her in the garden. She was not in the garden, but beyond it he had seen her approaching down a long shady path. Without hastening her step she had smiled and signed to him to wait; and charmed by the lights and shadows that played upon her as she moved, and by the pleasure of watching her slow advance toward him, he had obeyed her and stood still. And so she seemed now to be walking to him down the years, the light and shade of old memories and new hopes playing variously on her, and each step giving him the vision of a different grace. She did not waver or turn aside; he knew she would come straight to where he stood; but something in her eyes said 'Wait', and again he obeyed and waited.

On the fourth day an unexpected event threw out his calculations. Summoned to town by the arrival in England of her husband's mother, she left without giving Darrow the chance he had counted on, and he cursed himself for a dilatory blunderer. Still, his disappointment was tempered by the certainty of being with her again before she left for France; and they did in fact see each other in London. There, however, the atmosphere had changed with the conditions. He could not say that she avoided him, or even that she was a shade less glad to see him; but she was beset by family duties and, as he thought, a little too readily resigned to them.

The Marquise de Chantelle, as Darrow soon perceived, had the same mild formidableness as the late Mr Leath: a sort of insistent self-effacement before which every one about her gave way. It was perhaps the shadow of this lady's presence – pervasive even during her actual brief eclipses – that subdued and silenced Mrs Leath. The latter was, moreover, preoccupied about her step-son, who, soon after receiving his degree at Harvard, had been rescued from a stormy love-affair, and finally, after some months of troubled drifting, had yielded to his step-mother's counsel and gone up to Oxford for a year of supplementary study. Thither Mrs Leath went once or twice to visit him, and her remaining days were packed with family obligations: getting, as she phrased it, 'frocks and governesses' for her little girl, who had been left in France, and having to devote the remaining hours to long shopping expeditions with her mother-in-law. Nevertheless, during her brief escapes from duty, Darrow had had time to feel her safe in the custody of his devotion, set apart for some inevitable hour; and the last evening, at the theatre, between the overshadowing Marquise and the unsuspicious Owen, they had had an almost decisive exchange of words.

Now, in the rattle of the wind about his ears, Darrow continued to hear the mocking echo of her message: 'Unexpected obstacle.' In such an existence as Mrs Leath's, at once so ordered and so exposed, he knew how small a complication might assume the magnitude of an 'obstacle'; yet, even allowing as impartially as his state of mind permitted for the fact that, with her mother-in-law always, and her stepson intermittently, under her roof, her lot involved a hundred small accommodations generally foreign to the freedom of widowhood – even so, he could not but think that the very ingenuity bred of such conditions might have helped her to find a way out of them. No, her 'reason', whatever it was, could, in this case, be nothing but a pretext; unless he leaned to the less flattering alternative that any reason seemed good enough for postponing him! Certainly, if her welcome had meant what he imagined, she could not, for the second time within a few weeks, have submitted so tamely to the disarrangement of their plans; a disarrangement which – his official duties considered – might, for all she knew, result in his not being able to go to her for months.

'Please don't come till thirtieth.' The thirtieth – and it was now the fifteenth! She flung back the fortnight on his hands as if he had been an idler indifferent to dates, instead of an active young diplomatist who, to respond to her call, had had to hew his way through a very jungle of engagements! 'Please don't come till thirtieth.' That was all. Not the shadow of an excuse or a regret; not even the perfunctory 'have written' with which it is usual to soften such blows. She didn't want him, and had taken the shortest way to tell him so. Even in his first moment of exasperation it struck him as characteristic that she should not have padded her postponement with a fib. Certainly her moral angles were not draped!

'If I asked her to marry me, she'd have refused in the same language. But thank heaven I haven't!' he reflected.

These considerations, which had been with him every yard of the way from London, reached a climax of irony as he was drawn into the crowd on the pier. It did not soften his feelings to remember that, but for her lack of forethought, he might, at this harsh end of the stormy May day, have been sitting before his club fire in London instead of shivering in the damp human herd on the pier. Admitting the sex's traditional right to change, she might at least have advised him of hers by telegraphing directly to his rooms. But in spite of their exchange of letters she had apparently failed to note his address, and a breathless emissary had rushed from the Embassy to pitch her telegram into his compartment as the train was moving from the station.

Yes, he had given her chance enough to learn where he lived; and this minor proof of her indifference became, as he jammed his way through the crowd, the main point of his grievance against her and of his derision of himself. Half way down the pier the prod of an umbrella increased his exasperation by rousing him to the fact that it was raining. Instantly the narrow ledge became a battle-ground of thrusting, slanting, parrying domes. The wind rose with the rain, and the harried wretches exposed to this double assault wreaked on their neighbours the vengeance they could not take on the elements.

Darrow, whose healthy enjoyment of life made him in general a good traveller, tolerant of agglutinated humanity, felt himself obscurely outraged by these promiscuous contacts. It was as though all the people about him had taken his measure and known his plight; as though they were contemptuously bumping and shoving him like the inconsiderable thing he had become. 'She doesn't want you, doesn't want you, doesn't want you,' their umbrellas and their elbows seemed to say.

He had rashly vowed, when the telegram was flung into his window: 'At any rate I won't turn back' – as though it might cause the sender a malicious joy to have him retrace his steps rather than keep on to Paris! Now he perceived the absurdity of the vow, and thanked his stars that he need not plunge, to no purpose, into the fury of waves outside the harbour.

With this thought in his mind he turned back to look for his porter; but the contiguity of dripping umbrellas made signalling impossible and, perceiving that he had lost sight of the man, he scrambled up again to the platform. As he reached it, a descending umbrella caught him in the collarbone; and the next moment, bent sideways by the wind, it turned inside out and soared up, kite-wise, at the end of a helpless female arm.

Darrow caught the umbrella, lowered its inverted ribs, and looked up at the face it exposed to him.

'Wait a minute,' he said; 'you can't stay here.'

As he spoke, a surge of the crowd drove the owner of the umbrella abruptly down on him. Darrow steadied her with extended arms, and regaining her footing she cried out: 'Oh, dear, oh, dear! It's in ribbons!'

Her lifted face, fresh and flushed in the driving rain, woke in him a memory of having seen it at a distant time and in a vaguely unsympathetic setting; but it was no moment to follow up such clues, and the face was obviously one to make its way on its own merits.

Its possessor had dropped her bag and bundles to clutch at the tattered umbrella. 'I bought it only yesterday at the Stores; and – yes – it's utterly done for!' she lamented.

Darrow smiled at the intensity of her distress. It was food for the moralist that, side by side with such catastrophes as his, human nature was still agitating itself over its microscopic woes!

'Here's mine if you want it!' he shouted back at her through the shouting of the gale.

The offer caused the young lady to look at him more intently. 'Why, it's Mr Darrow!' she exclaimed; and then, all radiant recognition: 'Oh, thank you! We'll share it, if you will.'

She knew him, then; and he knew her; but how and where had they met? He put aside the problem for subsequent solution, and drawing her into a more sheltered corner, bade her wait till he could find his porter.

When, a few minutes later, he came back with his recovered property, and the news that the boat would not leave till the tide had turned, she showed no concern.

'Not for two hours? How lucky – then I can find my trunk!'

Ordinarily Darrow would have felt little disposed to involve himself in the adventure of a young female who had lost her trunk; but at the moment he was glad of any pretext for activity. Even should he decide to take the next up train from Dover he still had a yawning hour to fill; and the obvious remedy was to devote it to the loveliness in distress under his umbrella.

'You've lost a trunk? Let me see if I can find it.'

It pleased him that she did not return the conventional 'Oh, *would* you?' Instead, she corrected him with a laugh – 'Not *a* trunk, but *my* trunk; I've no other –' and then added briskly: 'You'd better first see to getting your own things on the boat.'

This made him answer, as if to give substance to his plans by discussing them: 'I don't actually know that I'm going over.'

'Not going over?'

'Well . . . perhaps not by this boat.' Again he felt a stealing indecision. 'I may probably have to go back to London. I'm – I'm waiting . . . expecting a letter . . .' ('She'll think me a defaulter,' he reflected.) 'But meanwhile there's plenty of time to find your trunk.'

He picked up his companion's bundles, and offered her an arm which enabled her to press her slight person more closely under his umbrella; and as, thus linked, they beat their way back to the platform, pulled together and apart like marionettes on the wires of the wind, he continued to wonder where he could have seen her. He had immediately classed her as a compatriot; her small nose, her clear tints, a kind of sketchy delicacy in her face, as though she had been brightly but lightly washed in with water-colour, all confirmed the evidence of her high sweet voice and of her quick incessant gestures. She was clearly an American, but with the loose native quality strained through a closer woof of manners: the composite product of an enquiring and adaptable race. All this, however, did not help him to fit a name to her, for just such instances were perpetually pouring through the London Embassy, and the etched and angular American was becoming rarer than the fluid type.

More puzzling than the fact of his being unable to identify her was the persistent sense connecting her with something uncomfortable and distasteful. So pleasant a vision as that gleaming up at him between wet brown hair and wet brown boa should have evoked only associations as pleasing; but each effort to fit her image into his past resulted in the same memories of boredom and a vague discomfort . . .

2

'Don't you remember me now – at Mrs Murrett's?' She threw the question at Darrow across a table of the quiet coffee-room to which, after a vainly prolonged quest for her trunk, he had suggested taking her for a cup of tea.

In this musty retreat she had removed her dripping hat, hung it on the fender to dry, and stretched herself on tiptoe in front of the round eagle-crowned mirror, above the mantel vases of dyed immortelles, while she ran her fingers combwise through her hair. The gesture had acted on Darrow's numb feelings as the glow of the fire acted on his circulation; and when he had asked: 'Aren't your feet wet, too?' and, after frank inspection of a stout-shod sole, she had answered cheerfully: 'No – luckily I had on my new boots,' he began to feel that human intercourse would still be tolerable if it were always as free from formality.

The removal of his companion's hat, besides provoking this reflection, gave him his first full sight of her face; and this was so favourable that the name she now pronounced fell on him with a quite disproportionate shock of dismay.

'Oh, Mrs Murrett's – was it *there*?'

He remembered her now, of course: remembered her as one of the shadowy sidling presences in the background of that awful house in Chelsea, one of the dumb appendages of the shrieking unescapable

Mrs Murrett, into whose talons he had fallen in the course of his head-long pursuit of Lady Ulrica Crispin. Oh, the taste of stale follies! How insipid it was, yet how it clung!

'I used to pass you on the stairs,' she reminded him.

Yes: he had seen her slip by – he recalled it now – as he dashed up to the drawing-room in quest of Lady Ulrica. The thought made him steal a longer look. How could such a face have been merged in the Murrett mob? Its fugitive slanting lines, that lent themselves to all manner of tender tilts and foreshortenings, had the freakish grace of some young head of the Italian comedy. The hair stood up from her forehead in a boyish elf-lock, and its colour matched her auburn eyes flecked with black, and the little brown spot on her cheek, between the ear that was meant to have a rose behind it and the chin that should have rested on a ruff. When she smiled, the left corner of her mouth went up a little higher than the right; and her smile began in her eyes and ran down to her lips in two lines of light. He had dashed past that to reach Lady Ulrica Crispin!

'But of course you wouldn't remember me,' she was saying. 'My name is Viner – Sophy Viner.'

Not remember her? But of course he *did*! He was genuinely sure of it now. 'You're Mrs Murrett's niece,' he declared.

She shook her head. 'No; not even that. Only her reader.'

'Her reader? Do you mean to say she ever reads?'

Miss Viner enjoyed his wonder. 'Dear, no! But I wrote notes, and made up the visiting-book, and walked the dogs, and saw bores for her.'

Darrow groaned. 'That must have been rather bad!'

'Yes; but nothing like as bad as being her niece.'

'That I can well believe. I'm glad to hear,' he added, 'that you put it all in the past tense.'

She seemed to droop a little at the allusion; then she lifted her chin with a jerk of defiance. 'Yes. All is at an end between us. We've just parted in tears – but not in silence!'

'Just parted? Do you mean to say you've been there all this time?'

'Ever since you used to come there to see Lady Ulrica? Does it seem to you so awfully long ago?'

The unexpectedness of the thrust – as well as its doubtful taste – chilled his growing enjoyment of her chatter. He had really been getting to like her – had recovered, under the candid approval of her eye, his usual sense of being a personable young man, with all the privileges pertaining to the state, instead of the anonymous rag of humanity he had felt himself in the crowd on the pier. It annoyed him, at that particular moment, to be reminded that naturalness is not always consonant with taste.

She seemed to guess his thought. 'You don't like my saying that you came for Lady Ulrica?' she asked, leaning over the table to pour herself a second cup of tea.

He liked her quickness, at any rate. 'It's better,' he laughed, 'than your thinking I came for Mrs Murrett!'

'Oh, we never thought anybody came for Mrs Murrett! It was always for something else: the music, or the cook – when there was a good one – or the other people; generally *one* of the other people.'

'I see.'

She was amusing, and that, in his present mood, was more to his purpose than the exact shade of her taste. It was odd, too, to discover suddenly that the blurred tapestry of Mrs Murrett's background had all the while been alive and full of eyes. Now, with a pair of them looking into his, he was conscious of a queer reversal of perspective.

'Who were the "we"? Were you a cloud of witnesses?'

'There were a good many of us.' She smiled. 'Let me see – who was there in your time? Mrs Bolt – and Mademoiselle – and Professor Didymus and the Polish Countess. Don't you remember the Polish Countess? She crystal-gazed, and played accompaniments, and Mrs Murrett chucked her because Mrs Didymus accused her of hypnotizing the Professor. But of course you don't remember. We were all invisible to you; but we could see. And we all used to wonder about you –'

Again Darrow felt a redness in the temples. 'What about me?'

'Well – whether it was *you* or she who . . .'

He winced, but hid his disapproval. It made the time pass to listen to her.

'And what, if one may ask, was your conclusion?'

'Well, Mrs Bolt and Mademoiselle and the Countess naturally thought it was *she*; but Professor Didymus and Jimmy Brance – especially Jimmy –'

'Just a moment: who on earth is Jimmy Brance?'

She exclaimed in wonder: 'You *were* absorbed – not to remember Jimmy Brance! He must have been right about you, after all.' She let her amused scrutiny dwell on him. 'But how *could* you? She was false from head to foot!'

'False –?' In spite of time and satiety, the male instinct of ownership rose up and repudiated the charge.

Miss Viner caught his look and laughed. 'Oh, I only meant externally! You see, she often used to come to my room after tennis, or to touch up in the evenings, when they were going on; and I assure you she took apart like a puzzle. In fact I used to say to Jimmy – just to make him wild –: "I'll bet you anything you like there's nothing wrong, because I know she'd never dare un—"' She broke the word in two, and her quick blush made her face like a shallow-petalled rose shading to the deeper pink of the centre.

The situation was saved, for Darrow, by an abrupt rush of memories, and he gave way to a mirth which she as frankly echoed. 'Of course,' she gasped through her laughter, 'I only said it to tease Jimmy –'

Her amusement obscurely annoyed him. 'Oh, you're all alike!' he exclaimed, moved by an unaccountable sense of disappointment.

She caught him up in a flash – she didn't miss things! 'You say that because you think I'm spiteful and envious? Yes – I *was* envious of Lady Ulrica . . . Oh, not on account of you or Jimmy Brance! Simply because she had almost all the things I've always wanted: clothes and fun and motors, and admiration and yachting and Paris – why, Paris alone would be enough! – And how do you suppose a girl can see that sort of thing about her day after day, and never wonder why some women, who don't seem to have any more right to it, have it all tumbled into their laps, while others are writing dinner invitations, and straightening out accounts, and copying visiting lists, and finishing golf-stockings, and matching ribbons, and seeing that the dogs get their sulphur? One looks in one's glass, after all!'

She launched the closing words at him on a cry that lifted them above the petulance of vanity; but his sense of her words was lost in the surprise of her face. Under the flying clouds of her excitement it was no longer a shallow flowercup but a darkening gleaming mirror that might give back strange depths of feeling. The girl had stuff in her – he saw it; and she seemed to catch the perception in his eyes.

'That's the kind of education I got at Mrs Murrett's – and I never had any other,' she said with a shrug.

'Good Lord – were you there so long?'

'Five years. I stuck it out longer than any of the others.' She spoke as though it were something to be proud of.

'Well, thank God you're out of it now!'

Again a just perceptible shadow crossed her face. 'Yes – I'm out of it now fast enough.'

'And what – if I may ask – are you doing next?'

She brooded a moment behind drooped lids; then, with a touch of hauteur: 'I'm going to Paris: to study for the stage.'

'The stage?' Darrow stared at her, dismayed. All his confused contradictory impressions assumed a new aspect at this announcement; and to hide his surprise he added lightly: 'Ah – then you *will* have Paris, after all!'

'Hardly Lady Ulrica's Paris. It's not likely to be roses, roses all the way.'

'It's not, indeed.' Real compassion prompted him to continue: 'Have you any – any influence you can count on?'

She gave a somewhat flippant little laugh. 'None but my own. I've never had any other to count on.'

He passed over the obvious reply. 'But have you any idea how the profession is over-crowded? I know I'm trite –'

'I've a very clear idea. But I couldn't go on as I was.'

'Of course not. But since, as you say, you'd stuck it out longer than any of the others, couldn't you at least have held on till you were sure of some kind of an opening?'

She made no reply for a moment; then she turned a listless glance to the rain-beaten window. 'Oughtn't we be starting?' she asked, with a lofty assumption of indifference that might have been Lady Ulrica's.

Darrow, surprised by the change, but accepting her rebuff as a phase of what he guessed to be a confused and tormented mood, rose from his seat and lifted her jacket from the chairback on which she had hung it to dry. As he held it toward her she looked up at him quickly.

'The truth is, we quarrelled,' she broke out, 'and I left last night without my dinner – and without my salary.'

'Ah –' he groaned, with a sharp perception of all the sordid dangers that might attend such a break with Mrs Murrett.

'And without a character!' she added, as she slipped her arms into the jacket. 'And without a trunk, as it appears – but didn't you say that, before going, there'd be time for another look at the station?'

There was time for another look at the station; but the look again resulted in disappointment, since her trunk was nowhere to be found in the huge heap disgorged by the newly-arrived London express. The fact caused Miss Viner a moment's perturbation; but she promptly adjusted herself to the necessity of proceeding on her journey, and her decision confirmed Darrow's vague resolve to go to Paris instead of retracing his way to London.

Miss Viner seemed cheered at the prospect of his company, and sustained by his offer to telegraph to Charing Cross for the missing trunk; and he left her to wait in the fly while he hastened back to the telegraph office. The enquiry despatched, he was turning away from the desk when another thought struck him and he went back and indited a message to his servant in London: 'If any letters with French postmark received since departure forward immediately to Terminus Hotel Gare du Nord Paris.'

Then he rejoined Miss Viner, and they drove off through the rain to the pier.

3

Almost as soon as the train left Calais her head had dropped back into the corner, and she had fallen asleep.

Sitting opposite, in the compartment from which he had contrived to have other travellers excluded, Darrow looked at her curiously. He had never seen a face that changed so quickly. A moment since it had danced like a field of daisies in a summer breeze; now, under the pallid oscillating light of the lamp overhead, it wore the hard stamp of experience, as of a soft thing chilled into shape before its curves had rounded: and it moved him to see that care already stole upon her when she slept.

The story she had imparted to him in the wheezing shaking cabin, and at the Calais buffet – where he had insisted on offering her the dinner she had missed at Mrs Murrett's – had given a distincter outline to her figure. From the moment of entering the New York boarding-school to which a preoccupied guardian had hastily consigned her after the death of her parents, she had found herself alone in a busy and indifferent world. Her youthful history might, in fact, have been summed up in the statement that everybody had been too busy to look after her. Her guardian, a drudge in a big banking house, was absorbed by 'the office'; the guardian's wife, by her health and her religion; and an elder sister, Laura, married, unmarried, remarried, and pursuing, through all these alternating phases, some vaguely 'artistic' ideal on which the guardian and his wife looked askance, had (as Darrow conjectured) taken their disapproval as a pretext for not troubling herself about poor Sophy, to whom – perhaps for this reason – she had remained the incarnation of remote romantic possibilities.

In the course of time a sudden 'stroke' of the guardian's had thrown his personal affairs into a state of confusion from which – after his widely lamented death – it became evident that it would not be possible to extricate his ward's inheritance. No one deplored this more sincerely than his widow, who saw in it one more proof of her husband's life having been sacrificed to the innumerable duties imposed on him, and who could hardly – but for the counsels of religion – have brought herself to pardon the young girl for her indirect share in hastening his end. Sophy did not resent this point of view. She was really much sorrier for her guardian's death than for the loss of her insignificant fortune. The latter had represented only the means of holding her in bondage, and its disappearance was the occasion of her immediate plunge into the wide bright sea of life surrounding the island of her captivity. She had first landed – thanks to the intervention of the ladies who had directed her education – in a Fifth Avenue school-room where, for a few months, she acted as a buffer between three autocratic infants and their bodyguard of nurses and teachers. The too-pressing attentions of their father's valet had caused her to fly this sheltered spot, against the express advice of her educational superiors, who implied that, in their own case, refinement and self-respect had always sufficed to keep the most ungovernable passions at bay. The experience of the guardian's widow having been precisely similar, and the deplorable precedent of Laura's career being present to all their minds, none of these ladies felt any obligation to intervene farther in Sophy's affairs; and she was accordingly left to her own resources.

A schoolmate from the Rocky Mountains, who was taking her father and mother to Europe, had suggested Sophy's accompanying them, and 'going round' with her while her progenitors, in the care of the courier, nursed their ailments at a fashionable bath. Darrow gathered that the 'going round' with Mamie Hoke was a varied and diverting process; but this relatively brilliant phase of Sophy's career was cut short by the elopement of the inconsiderate Mamie with a 'matinée idol' who had followed her from New York, and by the precipitate return of her parents to negotiate for the repurchase of their child.

It was then – after an interval of repose with compassionate but impecunious American friends in Paris – that Miss Viner had been drawn into the turbid current of Mrs Murrett's career. The impecunious compatriots had found Mrs Murrett for her, and it was partly on their account (because they were such dears, and so unconscious, poor confiding things, of what they were letting her in for) that Sophy had stuck it out so long in the dreadful house in Chelsea. The Farlows, she explained to Darrow, were the best friends she had ever had (and the only ones who had ever 'been decent' about Laura, whom they had seen once, and intensely admired); but even after twenty years of Paris they were the most incorrigibly inexperienced angels, and quite persuaded that Mrs Murrett was a woman of great intellectual eminence, and the house at Chelsea 'the last of the *salons*' – Darrow knew what she meant? And she hadn't liked to undeceive them, knowing that to do so would be virtually to throw herself back on their hands, and feeling, moreover, after her previous experiences, the urgent need of gaining, at any cost, a name for stability; besides which – she threw it off with a slight laugh – no other chance, in all these years, had happened to come to her.

She had brushed in this outline of her career with light rapid strokes, and in a tone of fatalism oddly untinged by bitterness.

Darrow perceived that she classified people according to their greater or less 'luck' in life, but she appeared to harbour no resentment against the undefined power which dispensed the gift in such unequal measure. Things came one's way or they didn't; and meanwhile one could only look on, and make the most of small compensations, such as watching 'the show' at Mrs Murrett's, and talking over the Lady Ulricas and other footlight figures. And at any moment, of course, a turn of the kaleidoscope might suddenly toss a bright spangle into the grey pattern of one's days.

This light-hearted philosophy was not without charm to a young man accustomed to more traditional views. George Darrow had had a fairly varied experience of feminine types, but the women he had frequented had either been pronouncedly 'ladies' or they had not. Grateful to both for ministering to the more complex masculine nature, and disposed to assume that they had been evolved, if not designed, to that end, he had instinctively kept the two groups apart in his mind, avoiding that intermediate society which attempts to conciliate both theories of life. 'Bohemianism' seemed to him a cheaper convention than the other two, and he liked, above all, people who went as far as they could in their own line – liked his 'ladies' and their rivals to be equally unashamed of showing for exactly what they were. He had not indeed – the fact of Lady Ulrica was there to remind him – been without his experience of a third type; but that experience had left him with a contemptuous distaste for the woman who uses the privileges of one class to shelter the customs of another.

As to young girls, he had never thought much about them since his early love for the girl who had become Mrs Leath. That episode seemed, as he looked back on it, to bear no more relation to reality than a pale decorative design to the confused richness of a summer landscape. He no longer understood the violent impulses and dreamy pauses of his own young heart, or the inscrutable abandonments and reluctances of hers. He had known a moment of anguish at losing her – the mad plunge of youthful instincts against the barrier of fate; but the first wave of stronger sensation had swept away all but the outline of their story, and the memory of Anna Summers had made the image of the young girl sacred, but the class uninteresting.

Such generalizations belonged, however, to an earlier stage of his experience. The more he saw of life the more incalculable he found it; and he had learned to yield to his impressions without feeling the youthful need of relating them to others. It was the girl in the opposite seat who had roused in him the dormant habit of comparison. She was distinguished from the daughters of wealth by her avowed acquaintance with the real business of living, a familiarity as different as possible from their theoretical proficiency; yet it seemed to Darrow that her experience had made her free without hardness and self-assured without assertiveness.

The rush into Amiens, and the flash of the station lights into their compartment, broke Miss Viner's sleep, and without changing her position she lifted her lids and looked at Darrow. There was neither surprise nor bewilderment in the look. She seemed instantly conscious, not so much of where she was, as of the fact that she was with him; and that fact seemed enough to reassure her. She did not even turn her head to look out; her eyes continued to rest on him with a vague smile which appeared to light her face from within, while her lips kept their sleepy droop.

Shouts and the hurried tread of travellers came to them through the confusing cross-lights of the platform. A head appeared at the window, and Darrow threw himself forward to defend their solitude; but the intruder was only a train hand going his round of inspection. He passed on, and the lights and cries of the station dropped away, merged in a wider haze and a hollower resonance, as the train gathered itself up with a long shake and rolled out again into the darkness.

Miss Viner's head sank back against the cushion, pushing out a dusky wave of hair above her forehead. The swaying of the train loosened a lock over her ear, and she shook it back with a movement like a boy's, while her gaze still rested on her companion.

'You're not too tired?'

She shook her head with a smile.

'We shall be in before midnight. We're very nearly on time.' He verified the statement by holding up his watch to the lamp.

She nodded dreamily. 'It's all right. I telegraphed Mrs Farlow that they mustn't think of coming to the station; but they'll have told the *concierge* to look out for me.'

'You'll let me drive you there?'

She nodded again, and her eyes closed. It was very pleasant to Darrow that she made no effort to talk or to dissemble her sleepiness. He sat watching her till the upper lashes met and mingled with the lower, and their blent shadow lay on her cheek; then he stood up and drew the curtain over the lamp, drowning the compartment in a bluish twilight.

As he sank back into his seat he thought how differently Anna Summers – or even Anna Leath – would have behaved. She would not have talked too much; she would not have been either restless or embarrassed; but her adaptability, her appropriateness, would not have been nature but 'tact'. The oddness of the situation would have made sleep impossible, or, if weariness had overcome her for a moment, she would have waked with a start, wondering where she was, and how she had come there, and if her hair were tidy; and nothing short of hairpins and a glass would have restored her self-possession . . .

The reflection set him wondering whether the 'sheltered' girl's bringing-up might not unfit her for all subsequent contact with life. How much nearer to it had Mrs Leath been brought by marriage and motherhood, and the passage of fourteen years? What were all her reticences and evasions but the result of the deadening process of forming a 'lady'? The freshness he had marvelled at was like the unnatural whiteness of flowers forced in the dark.

As he looked back at their few days together he saw that their intercourse had been marked, on her part, by the same hesitations and reserves which had chilled their earlier intimacy. Once more they had had their hour together and she had wasted it. As in her girlhood, her eyes had made promises which her lips were afraid to keep. She was still afraid of life, of its ruthlessness, its danger and mystery. She was still the petted little girl who cannot be left alone in the dark . . . His memory flew back to their youthful story, and long-forgotten details took shape before him. How frail and faint the picture was! They seemed, he and she, like the ghostly lovers of the Grecian Urn, forever pursuing without ever clasping each other. To this day he did not quite know what had parted them: the break had been as fortuitous as the fluttering apart of two seed-vessels on a wave of summer air . . .

The very slightness, vagueness, of the memory gave it an added poignancy. He felt the mystic pang of the parent for a child which has just breathed and died. Why had it happened thus, when the least shifting of influences might have made it all so different? If she had been given to him then he would have put warmth in her veins and light in her eyes: would have made her a woman through and through. Musing thus, he had the sense of waste that is the bitterest harvest of experience. A love like his might have given her the divine gift of self-renewal; and now he saw her fated to wane into old age repeating the same gestures, echoing the words she had always heard, and perhaps never guessing that, just outside her glazed and curtained consciousness, life rolled away, a vast blackness starred with lights, like the night landscape beyond the windows of the train.

The engine lowered its speed for the passage through a sleeping station. In the light of the platform lamp Darrow looked across at his companion. Her head had dropped toward one shoulder, and her lips were just far enough apart for the reflection of the upper one to deepen the colour of the other. The jolting of the train had again shaken loose the lock above her ear. It danced on her cheek like the flit of a brown wing over flowers, and Darrow felt an intense desire to lean forward and put it back behind her ear.

4

As their motor-cab, on the way from the Gare du Nord, turned into the central glitter of the Boulevard, Darrow had bent over to point out an incandescent threshold.

'There!'

Above the doorway, an arch of flame flashed out the name of a great actress, whose closing performances in a play of unusual originality had been the theme of long articles in the Paris papers which Darrow had tossed into their compartment at Calais.

'That's what you must see before you're twenty-four hours older!'

The girl followed his gesture eagerly. She was all awake and alive now, as if the heady rumours of the streets, with their long effervescences of light, had passed into her veins like wine.

'Cerdine? Is that where she acts?' She put her head out of the window, straining back for a glimpse of the sacred threshold. As they flew past it she sank into her seat with a satisfied sigh.

'It's delicious enough just to *know* she's there! I've never seen her, you know. When I was here with Mamie Hoke we never went anywhere but to the music halls, because she couldn't understand any French; and when I came back afterward to the Farlows' I was dead broke, and couldn't afford the play, and neither could they; so the only chance we had was when friends of theirs invited us – and once it was to see a tragedy by a Roumanian lady, and the other time it was for "L'Ami Fritz" at the Français.'

Darrow laughed. 'You must do better than that now. "Le Vertige" is a fine thing, and Cerdine gets some wonderful effects out of it. You must come with me tomorrow evening to see it – with your friends, of course. – That is,' he added, 'if there's any sort of chance of getting seats.'

The flash of a street lamp lit up her radiant face. 'Oh, will you really take us? What fun to think that it's tomorrow already!'

It was wonderfully pleasant to be able to give such pleasure. Darrow was not rich, but it was almost impossible for him to picture the state of persons with tastes and perceptions like his own, to whom an evening at the theatre was an unattainable indulgence. There floated through his mind an answer of Mrs Leath's to his enquiry whether she had seen the play in question. 'No. I meant to, of course, but one is so overwhelmed with things in Paris. And then I'm rather sick of Cerdine – one is always being dragged to see her.'

That, among the people he frequented, was the usual attitude toward such opportunities. There were too many, they were a nuisance, one had to defend one's self! He even remembered wondering, at the moment, whether to a really fine taste the exceptional thing could ever become indifferent through habit; whether the appetite for beauty was so soon dulled that it could be kept alive only by privation. Here, at any rate, was a fine chance to experiment with such a hunger: he almost wished he might stay on in Paris long enough to take the measure of Miss Viner's receptivity.

She was still dwelling on his promise. 'It's too beautiful of you! Oh, don't you *think* you'll be able to get seats?' And then, after a pause of brimming appreciation: 'I wonder if you'll think me horrid? – but it may be my only chance; and if you can't get places for us all, wouldn't you perhaps just take *me*? After all, the Farlows may have seen it!'

He had not, of course, thought her horrid, but only the more engaging, for being so natural, and so unashamed of showing the frank greed of her famished youth. 'Oh, *you* shall go somehow!' he had gaily promised her; and she had dropped back with a sigh of pleasure as their cab passed into the dimly-lit streets of the Farlows' quarter beyond the Seine . . .

This little passage came back to him the next morning, as he opened his hotel window on the early roar of the Northern Terminus.

The girl was there, in the room next to him. That had been the first point in his waking consciousness. The second was a sense of relief at the obligation imposed on him by this unexpected turn of events. To wake to the necessity of action, to postpone perforce the fruitless contemplation of his private grievance, was cause enough for gratitude, even if the small adventure in which he found himself involved had not, on its own merits, roused an instinctive curiosity to see it through.

When he and his companion, the night before, had reached the Farlows' door in the rue de la Chaise, it was only to find, after repeated assaults on its panels, that the Farlows were no longer there. They had moved away the week before, not only from their apartment but from Paris; and Miss Viner's breach with Mrs Murrett had been too sudden to permit her letter and telegram to overtake them. Both communications, no doubt, still reposed in a pigeon-hole of the *loge*; but its custodian, when drawn from his lair, sulkily declined to let Miss Viner verify the fact, and only flung out, in return for Darrow's bribe, the statement that the Americans had gone to Joigny.

To pursue them there at that hour was manifestly impossible, and Miss Viner, disturbed but not disconcerted by this new obstacle, had quite simply acceded to Darrow's suggestion that she should return for what remained of the night to the hotel where he had sent his luggage.

The drive back through the dark hush before dawn, with the nocturnal blaze of the Boulevard fading around them like the false lights of a magician's palace, had so played on her impressionability that she seemed to give no farther thought to her own predicament. Darrow noticed that she did not feel the beauty and mystery of the spectacle as much as its pressure of human significance, all its hidden implications of emotion and adventure. As they passed the shadowy colonnade of the Français, remote and temple-like in the paling lights, he felt a clutch on his arm, and heard the cry: 'There are things *there* that I want so desperately to see!' and all the way back to the hotel she continued to question him, with shrewd precision and an artless thirst for detail, about the theatrical life of Paris. He was struck afresh, as he listened, by the way in which her naturalness eased the situation of constraint, leaving to it only a pleasant savour of good fellowship. It was the kind of episode that one might, in advance, have characterized as 'awkward', yet that was proving, in the event, as much outside such definitions as a sunrise stroll with a dryad in a dew-drenched forest; and Darrow reflected that mankind would never have needed to invent tact if it had not first invented social complications.

It had been understood, with his good-night to Miss Viner, that the next morning he was to look up the Joigny trains, and see her safely to the station; but, while he breakfasted and waited for a time-table, he recalled again her cry of joy at the prospect of seeing Cerdine. It was certainly a pity, since that most elusive and incalculable of artists was leaving the next week for South America, to miss what might be a last sight of her in her greatest part; and Darrow, having dressed and made the requisite excerpts from the time-table, decided to carry the result of his deliberations to his neighbour's door.

It instantly opened at his knock, and she came forth looking as if she had been plunged into some sparkling element which had curled up all her drooping tendrils and wrapped her in a shimmer of fresh leaves.

'Well, what do you think of me?' she cried; and with a hand at her waist she spun about as if to show off some miracle of Parisian dress-making.

'I think the missing trunk has come – and that it was worth waiting for!'

'You *do* like my dress?'

'I adore it! I always adore new dresses – why, you don't mean to say it's *not* a new one?'

She laughed out her triumph.

'No, no, no! My trunk hasn't come, and this is only my old rag of yesterday – but I never knew the trick to fail!' And, as he stared: 'You see,' she joyously explained, 'I've always had to dress in all kinds of dreary left-overs, and sometimes, when everybody else was smart and new, it used to make me awfully miserable. So one day, when Mrs Murrett dragged me down unexpectedly to fill a place at dinner, I suddenly thought I'd try spinning around like that, and say to every one: '*Well, what do you think of me?*' And, do you know, they were all taken in, including Mrs Murrett, who didn't recognize my old turned and dyed rags, and told me afterward it was awfully bad form to dress as if I were somebody that people would expect to know! And ever since, whenever I've particularly wanted to look nice, I've just asked people what they thought of my new frock; and they're always, always taken in!'

She dramatized her explanation so vividly that Darrow felt as if his point were gained.

'Ah, but this confirms your vocation – of course,' he cried, 'you must see Cerdine!' and, seeing her face fall at this reminder of the change in her prospects, he hastened to set forth his plan. As he did so, he saw how easy it was to explain things to her. She would either accept his suggestion, or she would not: but at least she would waste no time in protestations and objections, or any vain sacrifice to the idols of conformity. The conviction that one could, on any given point, almost predicate this of her, gave him the sense of having advanced far enough in her intimacy to urge his arguments against a hasty pursuit of her friends.

Yes, it would certainly be foolish – she at once agreed – in the case of such dear indefinite angels as the Farlows, to dash off after them without more positive proof that they were established at Joigny, and so established that they could take her in. She owned it was but too probable that they had gone there to 'cut down', and might be doing so in quarters too contracted to receive her; and it would be unfair, on that chance, to impose herself on them unannounced. The simplest way of getting farther light on the question would be to go back to the rue de la Chaise, where, at that more conversable hour, the *concierge* might be less chary of detail; and she could decide on her next step in the light of such facts as he imparted.

Point by point, she fell in with the suggestion, recognizing, in the light of their unexplained flight, that the Farlows might indeed be in a situation on which one could not too rashly intrude. Her concern for her friends seemed to have effaced all thought of herself, and this little indication of character gave Darrow a quite disproportionate pleasure. She agreed that it would be well to go at once to the rue de la Chaise, but met his proposal that they should drive by the declaration that it was a 'waste' not to walk in Paris; so they set off on foot through the cheerful tumult of the streets.

The walk was long enough for him to learn many things about her. The storm of the previous night had cleared the air, and Paris shone in morning beauty under a sky that was all broad wet washes of white and blue; but Darrow again noticed that her visual sensitiveness was less keen than her feeling for what he was sure the good Farlows – whom he already seemed to know – would have called 'the human interest'. She seemed hardly conscious of sensations of form and colour, or of any imaginative suggestion, and the spectacle before them – always, in its scenic splendour, so moving to her companion – broke up, under her scrutiny, into a thousand minor points: the things in the shops, the types of character and manner of occupation shown in the passing faces, the street signs, the names of the hotels they passed, the motley brightness of the flower-carts, the identity of the churches and public buildings that caught her eye. But what she liked best, he divined, was the mere fact of being free to walk abroad in the bright air, her tongue rattling on as it pleased, while her feet kept time to the mighty orchestration of the city's sounds. Her delight in the fresh air, in the freedom, light and sparkle of the morning, gave him a sudden insight into her stifled past; nor was it indifferent to him to perceive how much his presence evidently added to her enjoyment. If only as a sympathetic ear, he guessed what he must be worth to her. The girl had been dying for some one to talk to, some one before whom she could unfold and shake out to the light her poor little shut-away emotions. Years of repression were revealed in her sudden burst of confidence; and the pity she inspired made Darrow long to fill her few free hours to the brim.

She had the gift of rapid definition, and his questions as to the life she had led with the Farlows, during the interregnum between the Hoke and Murrett eras, called up before him a queer little corner of Parisian existence. The Farlows themselves – he a painter, she a 'magazine writer' – rose before him in all their incorruptible simplicity: an elderly New England couple, with vague yearnings for enfranchisement, who lived in Paris as if it were a Massachusetts suburb, and dwelt hopefully on the 'higher side' of the Gallic nature. With equal vividness she set before him the component figures of the circle from which Mrs Farlow drew the 'Inner Glimpses of French Life' appearing over her name in a leading New England journal: the Roumanian lady who had sent them tickets for her tragedy, an elderly French gentleman who, on the strength of a week's stay at Folkestone, translated English fiction for the provincial press, a lady from Wichita, Kansas, who advocated free love and the abolition of the corset, a clergyman's widow from Torquay who had written an 'English Ladies' Guide to Foreign Galleries' and a Russian sculptor who lived on nuts and was 'almost certainly' an anarchist. It was this nucleus, and its outer ring of musical, architectural and other American students, which posed successively to Mrs Farlow's versatile fancy as a centre of 'University Life', a 'Salon of the Faubourg St Germain', a group of Parisian 'Intellectuals' or a 'Cross-section of Montmartre'; but even her faculty for extracting from it the most varied literary effects had not sufficed to create a permanent demand for the 'Inner Glimpses', and there were days when – Mr Farlow's landscapes being equally unmarketable – a temporary withdrawal to the country (subsequently utilized as 'Peeps into Château Life') became necessary to the courageous couple.

Five years of Mrs Murrett's world, while increasing Sophy's tenderness for the Farlows, had left her with few illusions as to their power of advancing her fortunes; and she did not conceal from Darrow that her theatrical projects were of the vaguest. They hung mainly on the problematical goodwill of an ancient comédienne, with whom Mrs Farlow had a slight acquaintance (extensively utilized in 'Stars of the French Footlights' and 'Behind the Scenes at the Français'), and who had once, with signs of approval, heard Miss Viner recite the 'Nuit de Mai'.

'But of course I know how much that's worth,' the girl broke off, with one of her flashes of shrewdness. 'And besides, it isn't likely that a poor old fossil like Mme Dolle could get anybody to listen to her now, even if she really thought I had talent. But she might introduce me to people; or at least give me a few tips. If I could manage to earn enough to pay for lessons I'd go straight to some of the big people and work with them. I'm rather hoping the Farlows may find me a chance of that kind – an engagement with some American family in Paris who would want to be "gone round" with like the Hokes, and who'd leave me time enough to study.'

In the rue de la Chaise they learned little except the exact address of the Farlows, and the fact that they had sub-let their flat before leaving. This information obtained, Darrow proposed to Miss Viner that they should stroll along the quays to a little restaurant looking out on the Seine, and there, over the *plat du jour*, consider the next step to be taken. The long walk had given her cheeks a glow indicative of wholesome hunger, and she made no difficulty about satisfying it in Darrow's company. Regaining the river they walked on in the direction of Notre Dame, delayed now and again by the young man's irresistible tendency to linger over the bookstalls, and by his ever-fresh response to the shifting beauties of the scene. For two years his eyes had been subdued to the atmospheric effects of London, to the mysterious fusion of darkly-piled city and low-lying bituminous sky; and the transparency of the French air, which left the green gardens and silvery stones so classically clear yet so softly harmonized, struck him as having a kind of conscious intelligence. Every line of the architecture, every arch of the bridges, the very sweep of the strong bright river between them, while contributing to this effect, sent forth each a separate appeal to some sensitive memory; so that, for Darrow, a walk through the Paris streets was always like the unrolling of a vast tapestry from which countless stored fragrances were shaken out.

It was a proof of the richness and multiplicity of the spectacle that it served, without incongruity, for so different a purpose as the background of Miss Viner's enjoyment. As a mere drop-scene for her personal adventure it was just as much in its place as in the evocation of great perspectives of feeling. For her, as he again perceived when they were seated at their table in a low window above the Seine, Paris was 'Paris' by virtue of all its entertaining details, its endless ingenuities of pleasantness. Where else, for instance, could one find the dear little dishes of *hors d'oeuvre*, the symmetrically-laid anchovies and radishes, the thin golden shells of butter, or the wood strawberries and brown jars of cream that gave to their repast the last refinement of rusticity? Hadn't he noticed, she asked, that cooking always expressed the national character, and that French food was clever and amusing just because the people were? And in private houses, everywhere, how the dishes always resembled the talk – how the very same platitudes seemed to go into people's mouths and come out of them? Couldn't he see just what kind of menu it would make, if a fairy waved a wand and suddenly turned the conversation at a London dinner into joints and puddings? She always thought it a good sign when people liked Irish stew; it meant that they enjoyed changes and surprises, and taking life as it came; and such a beautiful Parisian version of the dish as the *navarin* that was just being set before them was like the very best kind of talk – the kind when one could never tell beforehand just what was going to be said!

Darrow, as he watched her enjoyment of their innocent feast, wondered if her vividness and vivacity were signs of her calling. She was the kind of girl in whom certain people would instantly have recognized the histrionic gift. But experience had led him to think that, except at the creative moment, the divine flame burns low in its possessors. The one or two really intelligent actresses he had known had struck him, in conversation, as either bovine or primitively 'jolly'. He had a notion that, save in the mind of genius, the creative process absorbs too much of the whole stuff of being to leave much surplus for personal expression; and the girl before him, with her changing face and flexible fancies, seemed destined to work in life itself rather than in any of its counterfeits.

The coffee and liqueurs were already on the table when her mind suddenly sprang back to the Farlows. She jumped up with one of her subversive movements and declared that she must telegraph at once. Darrow called for writing materials, and room was made at her elbow for the parched ink-bottle and saturated blotter of the Parisian restaurant; but the mere sight of these jaded implements seemed to paralyse Miss Viner's faculties. She hung over the telegraph-form with anxiously-drawn brow, the tip of the pen-handle pressed against her lip; and at length she raised her troubled eyes to Darrow's.

'I simply can't think how to say it.'

'What – that you're staying over to see Cerdine?'

'But *am* I – am I, really?' The joy of it flamed over her face.

Darrow looked at his watch. 'You could hardly get an answer to your telegram in time to take a train to Joigny this afternoon, even if you found your friends could have you.'

She mused for a moment, tapping her lip with the pen. 'But I must let them know I'm here. I must find out as soon as possible if they *can* have me.' She laid the pen down despairingly. 'I never *could* write a telegram!' she sighed.

'Try a letter, then, and tell them you'll arrive tomorrow.'

This suggestion produced immediate relief, and she gave an energetic dab at the ink-bottle; but after another interval of uncertain scratching she paused again.

'Oh, it's fearful! I don't know what on earth to say. I wouldn't for the world have them know how beastly Mrs Murrett's been.'

Darrow did not think it necessary to answer. It was no business of his, after all. He lit a cigar and leaned back in his seat, letting his eyes take their fill of indolent pleasure. In the throes of invention she had pushed back her hat, loosening the stray lock which had invited his touch the night before. After looking at it for a while he stood up and wandered to the window.

Behind him he heard her pen scrape on.

'I don't want to worry them – I'm so certain they've got bothers of their own.' The faltering scratches ceased again. 'I wish I weren't such an idiot about writing: all the words get frightened and scurry away when I try to catch them.'

He glanced back at her with a smile as she bent above her task like a school-girl struggling with a 'composition'. Her flushed cheek and frowning brow showed that her difficulty was genuine and not an artless device to draw him to her side. She was really powerless to put her thoughts in writing, and the inability seemed characteristic of her quick impressionable mind, and of the incessant come-and-go of her sensations. He thought of Anna Leath's letters, or rather of the few he had received, years ago, from the girl who had been Anna Summers. He saw the slender firm strokes of the pen, recalled the clear structure of the phrases, and, by an abrupt association of ideas, remembered that, at that very hour, just such a document might be awaiting him at the hotel.

What if it were there, indeed, and had brought him a complete explanation of her telegram? The revulsion of feeling produced by this thought made him look at the girl with sudden impatience. She struck him as positively stupid, and he wondered how he could have wasted half his day with her, when all the while Mrs Leath's letter might be lying on his table. At that moment, if he could have chosen, he would have left his companion on the spot; but he had her on his hands, and must accept the consequences.

Some odd intuition seemed to make her conscious of his change of mood, for she sprang from her seat, crumpling the letter in her hand.

'I'm too stupid; but I won't keep you any longer. I'll go back to the hotel and write there.'

Her colour deepened, and for the first time, as their eyes met, he noticed a faint embarrassment in hers. Could it be that his nearness was, after all, the cause of her confusion? The thought turned his vague impatience with her into a definite resentment toward himself. There was really no excuse for his having blundered into such an adventure. Why had he not shipped the girl off to Joigny by the evening train, instead of urging her to delay, and using Cerdine as a pretext? Paris was full of people he knew, and his annoyance was increased by the thought that some friend of Mrs Leath's might see him at the play, and report his presence there with a suspiciously good-looking companion. The idea was distinctly disagreeable: he did not want the woman he adored to think he could forget her for a moment. And by this time he had fully persuaded himself that a letter from her was awaiting him, and had even gone so far as to imagine that its contents might annul the writer's telegraphed injunction, and call him to her side at once . . .

5

At the porter's desk a brief '*Pas de lettres*' fell destructively on the fabric of these hopes.

Mrs Leath had not written – she had not taken the trouble to explain her telegram. Darrow turned away with a sharp pang of humiliation. Her frugal silence mocked his prodigality of hopes and fears. He had put his question to the porter once before, on returning to the hotel after luncheon; and now, coming back again in the late afternoon, he was met by the same denial. The second post was in, and had brought him nothing.

A glance at his watch showed that he had barely time to dress before taking Miss Viner out to dine; but as he turned to the lift a new thought struck him, and hurrying back into the hall he dashed off another telegram to his servant: 'Have you forwarded any letter with French postmark today? Telegraph answer Terminus.'

Some kind of reply would be certain to reach him on his return from the theatre, and he would then know definitely whether Mrs Leath meant to write or not. He hastened up to his room and dressed with a lighter heart.

Miss Viner's vagrant trunk had finally found its way to its owner; and, clad in such modest splendour as it furnished, she shone at Darrow across their restaurant table. In the reaction of his wounded vanity he found her prettier and more interesting than before. Her dress, sloping away from the throat, showed the graceful set of her head on its slender neck, and the wide brim of her hat arched above her hair like a dusky halo. Pleasure danced in her eyes and on her lips, and as she shone on him between the candle-shades Darrow felt that he should not be at all sorry to be seen with her in public. He even sent a careless glance about him in the vague hope that it might fall on an acquaintance.

At the theatre her vivacity sank into a breathless hush, and she sat intent in her corner of their *baignoire*, with the gaze of a neophyte about to be initiated into the sacred mysteries. Darrow placed himself behind her, that he might catch her profile between himself and the stage. He was touched by the youthful seriousness of her expression. In spite of the experiences she must have had, and of the twenty-four years to which she owned, she struck him as intrinsically young; and he wondered how so evanescent a quality could have been preserved in the desiccating Murrett air. As the play progressed he noticed that her immobility was traversed by swift flashes of perception. She was not missing anything, and her intensity of attention when Cerdine was on the stage drew an anxious line between her brows.

After the first act she remained for a few minutes rapt and motionless; then she turned to her companion with a quick patter of questions. He gathered from them that she had been less interested in following the general drift of the play than in observing the details of its interpretation. Every gesture and inflection of the great actress's had been marked and analysed; and Darrow felt a secret gratification in being appealed to as an authority on the histrionic art. His interest in it had hitherto been merely that of the cultivated young man curious of all forms of artistic expression; but in reply to her questions he found things to say about it which evidently struck his listener as impressive and original, and with which he himself was not, on the whole, dissatisfied. Miss Viner was much more concerned to hear his views than to express her own, and the deference with which she received his comments called from him more ideas about the theatre than he had ever supposed himself to possess.

With the second act she began to give more attention to the development of the play, though her interest was excited rather by what she called 'the story' than by the conflict of character producing it. Oddly combined with her sharp apprehension of things theatrical, her knowledge of technical 'dodges' and green-room precedents, her glibness about 'lines' and 'curtains', was the primitive simplicity of her attitude toward the tale itself, as toward something that was 'really happening' and at which one assisted as at a street-accident or a quarrel overheard in the next room. She wanted to know if Darrow thought the lovers 'really would' be involved in the catastrophe that threatened them, and when he reminded her that his predictions were disqualified by his having already seen the play, she exclaimed: 'Oh, then, please don't tell me what's going to happen!' and the next moment was questioning him about Cerdine's theatrical situation and her private history. On the latter point some of her enquiries were of a kind that it is not in the habit of young girls to make, or even to know how to make; but her apparent unconsciousness of the fact seemed rather to reflect on her past associates than on herself.

When the second act was over, Darrow suggested their taking a turn in the *foyer*; and seated on one of its cramped red velvet sofas they watched the crowd surge up and down in a glare of lights and gilding. Then, as she complained of the heat, he led her through the press to the congested *café* at the foot of the stairs, where orangeades were thrust at them between the shoulders of packed *consommateurs*, and Darrow, lighting a cigarette while she sucked her straw, knew the primitive complacency of the man at whose companion other men stare.

On a corner of their table lay a smeared copy of a theatrical journal. It caught Sophy's eye and after poring over the page she looked up with an excited exclamation.

'They're giving *Oedipe* tomorrow afternoon at the Français! I suppose you've seen it heaps and heaps of times?'

He smiled back at her. 'You must see it too. We'll go tomorrow.'

She sighed at his suggestion, but without discarding it. 'How can I? The last train for Joigny leaves at four.'

'But you don't know yet that your friends will want you.'

'I shall know tomorrow early. I asked Mrs Farlow to telegraph as soon as she got my letter.'

A twinge of compunction shot through Darrow. Her words recalled to him that on their return to the hotel after luncheon she had given him her letter to post, and that he had never thought of it again. No doubt it was still in the pocket of the coat he had taken off when he dressed for dinner. In his perturbation he pushed back his chair, and the movement made her look up at him.

'What's the matter?'

'Nothing. Only – you know I don't fancy that letter can have caught this afternoon's post.'

'Not caught it? Why not?'

'Why, I'm afraid it will have been too late.' He bent his head to light another cigarette.

She struck her hands together with a gesture which, to his amusement, he noticed she had caught from Cerdine.

'Oh, dear, I hadn't thought of that! But surely it will reach them in the morning?'

'Some time in the morning, I suppose. You know the French provincial post is never in a hurry. I don't believe your letter would have been delivered this evening in any case.' As this idea occurred to him he felt himself almost absolved.

'Perhaps, then, I ought to have telegraphed?'

'I'll telegraph for you in the morning if you say so.'

The bell announcing the close of the entr'acte shrilled through the *café*, and she sprang to her feet.

'Oh, come, come! We mustn't miss it!'

Instantly forgetful of the Farlows, she slipped her arm through his and turned to push her way back to the theatre.

As soon as the curtain went up she as promptly forgot her companion. Watching her from the corner to which he had returned, Darrow saw that great waves of sensation were beating deliciously against her brain. It was as though every starved sensibility were throwing out feelers to the mounting tide; as though everything she was seeing, hearing, imagining, rushed in to fill the void of all she had always been denied.

Darrow, as he observed her, again felt a detached enjoyment in her pleasure. She was an extraordinary conductor of sensation: she seemed to transmit it physically, in emanations that set the blood dancing in his veins. He had not often had the opportunity of studying the effects of a perfectly fresh impression on so responsive a temperament, and he felt a fleeting desire to make its chords vibrate for his own amusement.

At the end of the next act she discovered with dismay that in their transit to the *café* she had lost the beautiful pictured programme he had bought for her. She wanted to go back and hunt for it, but Darrow assured her that he would have no trouble in getting her another. When he went out in quest of it she followed him protestingly to the door of the box, and he saw that she was distressed at the thought of his having to spend an additional franc for her. This frugality smote Darrow by its contrast to her natural bright profusion; and again he felt the desire to right so clumsy an injustice.

When he returned to the box she was still standing in the doorway, and he noticed that his were not the only eyes attracted to her.

Then another impression sharply diverted his attention. Above the fagged faces of the Parisian crowd he had caught the fresh fair countenance of Owen Leath signalling a joyful recognition.

The young man, slim and eager, had detached himself from two companions of his own type, and was seeking to push through the press to his step-mother's friend. The encounter, to Darrow, could hardly have been more inopportune; it woke in him a confusion of feelings of which only the uppermost was allayed by seeing Sophy Viner, as if instinctively warned, melt back into the shadow of their box.

A minute later Owen Leath was at his side. 'I was sure it was you! Such luck to run across you! Won't you come off with us to supper after it's over? Montmartre, or wherever else you please. Those two chaps over there are friends of mine, at the Beaux Arts; both of them rather good fellows – and we'd be so glad –'

For half a second Darrow read in his hospitable eye the termination 'if you'd bring the lady too'; then it deflected into: 'We'd all be so glad if you'd come.'

Darrow, excusing himself with thanks, lingered on for a few minutes' chat, in which every word, and every tone of his companion's voice, was like a sharp light flashed into aching eyes. He was glad when the bell called the audience to their seats, and young Leath left him with the friendly question: 'We'll see you at Givré later on?'

When he rejoined Miss Viner, Darrow's first care was to find out, by a rapid inspection of the house, whether Owen Leath's seat had given him a view of their box. But the young man was not visible from it, and Darrow concluded that he had been recognized in the corridor and not at his companion's side. He scarcely knew why it seemed to him so important that this point should be settled; certainly his sense of reassurance was less due to regard for Miss Viner than to the persistent vision of grave offended eyes . . .

During the drive back to the hotel this vision was persistently kept before him by the thought that the evening post might have brought a letter from Mrs Leath. Even if no letter had yet come, his servant might have telegraphed to say that one was on its way; and at the thought his interest in the girl at his side again cooled to the fraternal, the almost fatherly. She was no more to him, after all, than an appealing young creature to whom it was mildly agreeable to have offered an evening's diversion; and when, as they rolled into the illuminated court of the hotel, she turned with a quick movement which brought her happy face close to his, he leaned away, affecting to be absorbed in opening the door of the cab.

At the desk the night porter, after a vain search through the pigeon-holes, was disposed to think that a letter or telegram had in fact been sent up for the gentleman; and Darrow, at the announcement, could hardly wait to ascend to his room. Upstairs, he and his companion had the long dimly-lit corridor to themselves, and Sophy paused on her threshold, gathering up in one hand the pale folds of her cloak, while she held the other out to Darrow.

'If the telegram comes early I shall be off by the first train; so I suppose this is good-bye,' she said, her eyes dimmed by a little shadow of regret.

Darrow, with a renewed start of contrition, perceived that he had again forgotten her letter; and as their hands met he vowed to himself that the moment she had left him he would dash downstairs to post it.

'Oh, I'll see you in the morning, of course!'

A tremor of pleasure crossed her face as he stood before her, smiling a little uncertainly.

'At any rate,' she said, 'I want to thank you now for my good day.'

He felt in her hand the same tremor he had seen in her face. 'But it's *you*, on the contrary –' he began, lifting the hand to his lips.

As he dropped it, and their eyes met, something passed through hers that was like a light carried rapidly behind a curtained window.

'Good night; you must be awfully tired,' he said with a friendly abruptness, turning away without even waiting to see her pass into her room. He unlocked his door, and stumbling over the threshold groped in the darkness for the electric button. The light showed him a telegram on the table, and he forgot everything else as he caught it up.

'No letter from France,' the message read.

It fell from Darrow's hand to the floor, and he dropped into a chair by the table and sat gazing at the dingy drab and olive pattern of the carpet. She had not written, then; she had not written, and it was manifest now that she did not mean to write. If she had had any intention of explaining her telegram she would certainly, within twenty-four hours, have followed it up by a letter. But she evidently did not intend to explain it, and her silence could mean only that she had no explanation to give, or else that she was too indifferent to be aware that one was needed.

Darrow, face to face with these alternatives, felt a recrudescence of boyish misery. It was no longer his hurt vanity that cried out. He told himself that he could have borne an equal amount of pain, if only it had left Mrs Leath's image untouched; but he could not bear to think of her as trivial or insincere. The thought was so intolerable that he felt a blind desire to punish some one else for the pain it caused him.

As he sat moodily staring at the carpet its silly intricacies melted into a blur from which the eyes of Mrs Leath again looked out at him. He saw the fine sweep of her brows, and the deep look beneath them as she had turned from him on their last evening in London. 'This will be good-bye, then,' she had said; and it occurred to him that her parting phrase had been the same as Sophy Viner's.

At the thought he jumped to his feet and took down from its hook the coat in which he had left Miss Viner's letter. The clock marked the third quarter after midnight, and he knew it would make no difference if he went down to the post-box now or early the next morning; but he wanted to clear his conscience, and having found the letter he went to the door.

A sound in the next room made him pause. He had become conscious again that, a few feet off, on the other side of a thin partition, a small keen flame of life was quivering and agitating the air. Sophy's face came back to him insistently. It was as vivid now as Mrs Leath's had been a moment earlier. He recalled with a faint smile of retrospective pleasure the girl's enjoyment of her evening, and the innumerable fine feelers of sensation she had thrown out to its impressions.

It gave him a curiously close sense of her presence to think that at that moment she was living over her enjoyment as intensely as he was living over his unhappiness. His own case was irremediable, but it was easy enough to give her a few more hours of pleasure. And did she not perhaps secretly expect it of him? After all, if she had been very anxious to join her friends she would have telegraphed them on reaching Paris, instead of writing. He wondered now that he had not been struck at the moment by so artless a device to gain more time. The fact of her having practised it did not make him think less well of her; it merely strengthened the impulse to use his opportunity. She was starving, poor child, for a little amusement, a little personal life – why not give her the chance of another day in Paris? If he did so, should he not be merely falling in with her own hopes?

At the thought his sympathy for her revived. She became of absorbing interest to him as an escape from himself and an object about which his thwarted activities could cluster. He felt less drearily alone because of her being there, on the other side of the door, and in his gratitude to her for giving him this relief he began, with indolent amusement, to plan new ways of detaining her. He dropped back into his chair, lit a cigar, and smiled a little at the image of her smiling face. He tried to imagine what incident of the day she was likely to be recalling at that particular moment, and what part he probably played in it. That it was not a small part he was certain, and the knowledge was undeniably pleasant.

Now and then a sound from her room brought before him more vividly the reality of the situation and the strangeness of the vast swarming solitude in which he and she were momentarily isolated, amid long lines of rooms each holding its separate secret. The nearness of all these other mysteries enclosing theirs gave Darrow a more intimate sense of the girl's presence, and through the fumes of his cigar his imagination continued to follow her to and fro, traced the curve of her slim young arms as she raised them to undo her hair, pictured the sliding down of her dress to the waist and then to the knees, and the whiteness of her feet as she slipped across the floor to bed . . .

He stood up and shook himself with a yawn, throwing away the end of his cigar. His glance, in following it, lit on the telegram which had dropped to the floor. The sounds in the next room had ceased, and once more he felt alone and unhappy.

Opening the window, he folded his arms on the sill and looked out on the vast light-spangled mass of the city, and then up at the dark sky, in which the morning planet stood.

6

At the Théâtre Français, the next afternoon, Darrow yawned and fidgeted in his seat.

The day was warm, the theatre crowded and airless, and the performance, it seemed to him, intolerably bad. He stole a glance at his companion, wondering if she shared his feelings. Her rapt profile betrayed no unrest, but politeness might have caused her to feign an interest that she did not feel. He leaned back impatiently, stifling another yawn, and trying to fix his attention on the stage. Great things were going forward there, and he was not insensible to the stern beauties of the ancient drama. But the interpretation of the play seemed to him as airless and lifeless as the atmosphere of the theatre. The players were the same whom he had often applauded in those very parts, and perhaps that fact added to the impression of staleness and conventionality produced by their performance. Surely it was time to infuse new blood into the veins of the moribund art. He had the impression that the ghosts of actors were giving a spectral performance on the shores of Styx.

Certainly it was not the most profitable way for a young man with a pretty companion to pass the golden hours of a spring afternoon. The freshness of the face at his side, reflecting the freshness of the season, suggested dapplings of sunlight through new leaves, the sound of a brook in the grass, the ripple of tree-shadows over breezy meadows . . .

When at length the fateful march of the cothurns was stayed by the single pause in the play, and Darrow had led Miss Viner out on the balcony overhanging the square before the theatre, he turned to see if she shared his feelings. But the rapturous look she gave him checked the depreciation on his lips.

'Oh, why did you bring me out here? One ought to creep away and sit in the dark till it begins again!'

'Is *that* the way they made you feel?'

'Didn't they *you*? . . . As if the gods were there all the while, just behind them, pulling the strings?' Her hands were pressed against the railing, her face shining and darkening under the wing-beats of successive impressions.

Darrow smiled in enjoyment of her pleasure. After all, he *had* felt all that, long ago; perhaps it was his own fault, rather than that of the actors, that the poetry of the play seemed to have evaporated . . . But no, he had been right in judging the performance to be dull and stale: it was simply his companion's inexperience, her lack of occasions to compare and estimate, that made her think it brilliant.

'I was afraid you were bored and wanted to come away.'

'*Bored?*' She made a little aggrieved grimace. 'You mean you thought me too ignorant and stupid to appreciate it?'

'No; not that.' The hand nearest him still lay on the railing of the balcony, and he covered it for a moment with his. As he did so he saw the colour rise and tremble in her cheek.

'Tell me just what you think,' he said, bending his head a little, and only half-aware of his words.

She did not turn her face to his, but began to talk rapidly, trying to convey something of what she felt. But she was evidently unused to analysing her aesthetic emotions, and the tumultuous rush of the drama seemed to have left her in a state of panting wonder, as though it had been a storm or some other natural cataclysm. She had no literary or historic associations to which to attach her impressions: her education had evidently not comprised a course in Greek literature. But she felt what would probably have been unperceived by many a young lady who had taken a first in classics: the ineluctable fatality of the tale, the dread sway in it of the same mysterious 'luck' which pulled the threads of her own small destiny. It was not literature to her, it was fact: as actual, as near by, as what was happening to her at the moment and what the next hour held in store. Seen in this light, the play regained for Darrow its supreme and poignant reality. He pierced to the heart of its significance through all the artificial accretions with which his theories of art and the conventions of the stage had clothed it, and saw it as he had never seen it: as life.

After this there could be no question of flight, and he took her back to the theatre, content to receive his own sensations through the medium of hers. But with the continuation of the play, and the oppression of the heavy air, his attention again began to wander, straying back over the incidents of the morning.

He had been with Sophy Viner all day, and he was surprised to find how quickly the time had gone. She had hardly attempted, as the hours passed, to conceal her satisfaction on finding that no telegram came from the Farlows. 'They'll have written,' she had simply said; and her mind had at once flown on to the golden prospect of an afternoon at the theatre. The intervening hours had been disposed of in a stroll through the lively streets, and a repast, luxuriously lingered over, under the chestnut-boughs of a restaurant in the Champs Elysées. Everything entertained and interested her, and Darrow remarked, with an amused detachment, that she was not insensible to the impression her charms produced. Yet there was no hard edge of vanity in her sense of her prettiness: she seemed simply to be aware of it as a note in the general harmony, and to enjoy sounding the note as a singer enjoys singing.

After luncheon, as they sat over their coffee, she had again asked an immense number of questions and delivered herself of a remarkable variety of opinions. Her questions testified to a wholesome and comprehensive human curiosity, and her comments showed, like her face and her whole attitude, an odd mingling of precocious wisdom and disarming ignorance. When she talked to him about 'life' – the word was often on her lips – she seemed to him like a child playing with a tiger's cub; and he said to himself that some day the child would grow up – and so would the tiger. Meanwhile, such expertness qualified by such candour made it impossible to guess the extent of her personal experience, or to estimate its effect on her character. She might be any one of a dozen definable types, or she might – more disconcertingly to her companion and more perilously to herself – be a shifting and uncrystallized mixture of them all.

Her talk, as usual, had promptly reverted to the stage. She was eager to learn about every form of dramatic expression which the metropolis of things theatrical had to offer, and her curiosity ranged from the official temples of the art to its less hallowed haunts. Her searching enquiries about a play whose production, on one of the latter scenes, had provoked a considerable amount of scandal, led Darrow to throw out laughingly: 'To see *that* you'll have to wait till you're married!' and his answer had sent her off at a tangent.

'Oh, I never mean to marry,' she had rejoined in a tone of youthful finality.

'I seem to have heard that before!'

'Yes; from girls who've only got to choose!' Her eyes had grown suddenly almost old. 'I'd like you to see the only men who've ever wanted to marry me! One was the doctor on the steamer, when I came abroad with the Hokes: he'd been cashiered from the navy for drunkenness. The other was a deaf widower with three grown-up daughters, who kept a clockshop in Bayswater! – besides,' she rambled on, 'I'm not so sure that I believe in marriage. You see I'm all for self-development and the chance to live one's life. I'm awfully modern, you know.'

It was just when she proclaimed herself most awfully modern that she struck him as most helplessly backward; yet the moment after, without any bravado, or apparent desire to assume an attitude, she would propound some social axiom which could have been gathered only in the bitter soil of experience.

All these things came back to him as he sat beside her in the theatre and watched her ingenuous absorption. It was on 'the story' that her mind was fixed, and in life also, he suspected, it would always be 'the story', rather than its remoter imaginative issues, that would hold her. He did not believe there were ever any echoes in her soul . . .

There was no question, however, that what she felt was felt with intensity: to the actual, the immediate, she spread vibrating strings. When the play was over, and they came out once more into the sunlight, Darrow looked down at her with a smile.

'Well?' he asked.

She made no answer. Her dark gaze seemed to rest on him without seeing him. Her cheeks and lips were pale, and the loose hair under her hat-brim clung to her forehead in damp rings. She looked like a young priestess still dazed by the fumes of the cavern.

'You poor child – it's been almost too much for you!'

She shook her head with a vague smile.

'Come,' he went on, putting his hand on her arm, 'let's jump into a taxi and get some air and sunshine. Look, there are hours of daylight left; and see what a night it's going to be!'

He pointed over their heads, to where a white moon hung in the misty blue above the roofs of the rue de Rivoli.

She made no answer, and he signed to a motor-cab, calling out to the driver: 'To the Bois!'

96

As the carriage turned toward the Tuileries she roused herself. 'I must go first to the hotel. There may be a message – at any rate I must decide on something.'

Darrow saw that the reality of the situation had suddenly forced itself upon her. 'I *must* decide on something,' she repeated.

He would have liked to postpone the return, to persuade her to drive directly to the Bois for dinner. It would have been easy enough to remind her that she could not start for Joigny that evening, and that therefore it was of no moment whether she received the Far-lows' answer then or a few hours later; but for some reason he hesitated to use this argument, which had come so naturally to him the day before. After all, he knew she would find nothing at the hotel – so what did it matter if they went there?

The porter, interrogated, was not sure. He himself had received nothing for the lady, but in his absence his subordinate might have sent a letter upstairs.

Darrow and Sophy mounted together in the lift, and the young man, while she went into her room, unlocked his own door and glanced at the empty table. For him at least no message had come; and on her threshold, a moment later, she met him with the ex-pected: 'No – there's nothing!'

He feigned an unregretful surprise. 'So much the better! And now, shall we drive out somewhere? Or would you rather take a boat to Bellevue? Have you ever dined there, on the terrace, by moonlight? It's not at all bad. And there's no earthly use in sitting here waiting.'

She stood before him in perplexity.

'But when I wrote yesterday I asked them to telegraph. I suppose they're horribly hard up, the poor dears, and they thought a letter would do as well as a telegram.' The colour had risen to her face. 'That's why *I* wrote instead of telegraphing; I haven't a penny to spare myself!'

Nothing she could have said could have filled her listener with a deeper contrition. He felt the red in his own face as he recalled the motive with which he had credited her in his midnight musings. But that motive, after all, had simply been trumped up to justify his own disloyalty: he had never really believed in it. The reflection deepened his confusion, and he would have liked to take her hand in his and confess the injustice he had done her.

She may have interpreted his change of colour as an involuntary protest at being initiated into such shabby details, for she went on with a laugh: 'I suppose you can hardly understand what it means to have to stop and think whether one can afford a telegram? But I've always had to consider such things. And I mustn't stay here any longer now – I must try to get a night train for Joigny. Even if the Farlows can't take me in, I can go to the hotel: it will cost less than staying here.' She paused again and then exclaimed: 'I ought to have thought of that sooner; I ought to have telegraphed yesterday! But I was sure I should hear from them today; and I wanted – oh, I *did* so awfully want to stay!' She threw a troubled look at Darrow. 'Do you happen to remember,' she asked, 'what time it was when you posted my letter?'

7

Darrow was still standing on her threshold. As she put the question he entered the room and closed the door behind him.

His heart was beating a little faster than usual and he had no clear idea of what he was about to do or say, beyond the definite conviction that, whatever passing impulse of expiation moved him, he would not be fool enough to tell her that he had not sent her letter. He knew that most wrongdoing works, on the whole, less mischief than its useless confession; and this was clearly a case where a passing folly might be turned, by avowal, into a serious offence.

'I'm so sorry – so sorry; but you must let me help you . . . You will let me help you?' he said.

He took her hands and pressed them together between his, counting on a friendly touch to help out the insufficiency of words. He felt her yield slightly to his clasp, and hurried on without giving her time to answer.

'Isn't it a pity to spoil our good time together by regretting anything you might have done to prevent our having it?'

She drew back, freeing her hands. Her face, losing its look of appealing confidence, was suddenly sharpened by distrust.

'You didn't forget to post my letter?'

Darrow stood before her, constrained and ashamed, and ever more keenly aware that the betrayal of his distress must be a greater offence than its concealment.

'What an insinuation!' he cried, throwing out his hands with a laugh.

Her face instantly melted to laughter. 'Well, then – I *won't* be sorry; I won't regret anything except that our good time is over!'

The words were so unexpected that they routed all his resolves. If she had gone on doubting him he could probably have gone on deceiving her; but her unhesitating acceptance of his word made him hate the part he was playing. At the same moment a doubt shot up its serpent head in his own bosom. Was it not he rather than she who was childishly trustful? Was she not almost too ready to take his word, and dismiss once for all the tiresome question of the letter? Considering what her experiences must have been, such trustfulness seemed open to suspicion. But the moment his eyes fell on her he was ashamed of the thought, and knew it for what it really was: another pretext to lessen his own delinquency.

'Why should our good time be over?' he asked. 'Why shouldn't it last a little longer?'

She looked up, her lips parted in surprise; but before she could speak he went on: 'I want you to stay with me – I want you, just for a few days, to have all the things you've never had. It's not always May and Paris – why not make the most of them now? You know me – we're not strangers – why shouldn't you treat me like a friend?'

While he spoke she had drawn away a little, but her hand still lay in his. She was pale, and her eyes were fixed on him in a gaze in which there was neither distrust or resentment, but only an ingenuous wonder. He was extraordinarily touched by her expression.

'Oh, do! You must. Listen: to prove that I'm sincere I'll tell you . . . I'll tell you I didn't post your letter . . . I didn't post it because I wanted so much to give you a few good hours . . . and because I couldn't bear to have you go.'

He had the feeling that the words were being uttered in spite of him by some malicious witness of the scene, and yet that he was not sorry to have them spoken.

The girl had listened to him in silence. She remained motionless for a moment after he had ceased to speak; then she snatched away her hand.

'You didn't post my letter? You kept it back on purpose? And you tell me so *now*, to prove to me that I'd better put myself under your protection?' She burst into a laugh that had in it all the piercing echoes of her Murrett past, and her face, at the same moment, underwent the same change, shrinking into a small malevolent white mask in which the eyes burned black. 'Thank you – thank you most awfully for telling me! And for all your other kind intentions! The plan's delightful – really quite delightful, and I'm extremely flattered and obliged.'

She dropped into a seat beside her dressing-table, resting her chin on her lifted hands, and laughing out at him under the elf-lock which had shaken itself down over her eyes.

Her outburst did not offend the young man; its immediate effect was that of allaying his agitation. The theatrical touch in her manner made his offence seem more venial than he had thought it a moment before.

He drew up a chair and sat down beside her. 'After all,' he said, in a tone of good-humoured protest, 'I needn't have told you I'd kept back your letter; and my telling you seems rather strong proof that I hadn't any very nefarious designs on you.'

She met this with a shrug, but he did not give her time to answer. 'My designs,' he continued with a smile, 'were not nefarious. I saw you'd been through a bad time with Mrs Murrett, and that there didn't seem to be much fun ahead for you; and I didn't see – and I don't yet see – the harm of trying to give you a few hours of amusement between a depressing past and a not particularly cheerful future.' He paused again, and then went on, in the same tone of friendly reasonableness: 'The mistake I made was not to tell you this at once – not to ask you straight out to give me a day or two, and let me try to make you forget all the things that are troubling you. I was a fool not to see that if I'd put it to you in that way you'd have accepted or refused, as you chose; but that at least you wouldn't have mistaken my intentions. – Intentions!' He stood up, walked the length of the room, and turned back to where she still sat motionless, her elbows propped on the dressing-table, her chin on her hands. 'What rubbish we talk about intentions! The truth is I hadn't any: I just liked being with you. Perhaps you don't know how extraordinarily one can like being with you ... I was depressed and adrift myself; and you made me forget my bothers; and when I found you were going – and going back to dreariness, as I was – I didn't see why we shouldn't have a few hours together first; so I left your letter in my pocket.'

He saw her face melt as she listened, and suddenly she unclasped her hands and leaned to him.

'But are *you* unhappy too? Oh, I never understood – I never dreamed it! I thought you'd always had everything in the world you wanted!'

Darrow broke into a laugh at this ingenuous picture of his state. He was ashamed of trying to better his case by an appeal to her pity, and annoyed with himself for alluding to a subject he would rather have kept out of his thoughts. But her look of sympathy had disarmed him; his heart was bitter and distracted; she was near him, her eyes were shining with compassion – he bent over her and kissed her hand.

'Forgive me – do forgive me,' he said.

She stood up with a smiling head-shake. 'Oh, it's not so often that people try to give me any pleasure – much less two whole days of it! I shan't forget how kind you've been. I shall have plenty of time to remember. But this *is* good-bye, you know. I must telegraph at once to say I'm coming.'

'To say you're coming? Then I'm not forgiven?'

'Oh, you're forgiven – if that's any comfort.'

'It's not, the very least, if your way of proving it is to go away!'

She hung her head in meditation. 'But, I can't stay. – How *can* I stay?' she broke out, as if arguing with some unseen monitor.

'Why can't you? No one knows you're here ... No one need ever know.'

She looked up, and their eyes exchanged meanings for a rapid minute. Her gaze was as clear as a boy's. 'Oh, it's not *that*,' she exclaimed, almost impatiently; 'it's not people I'm afraid of! They've never put themselves out for me – why on earth should I care about them?'

He liked her directness as he had never liked it before. 'Well, then, what is it? Not *me*, I hope?'

'No, not you: I like you. It's the money! With me that's always the root of the matter. I could never yet afford a treat in my life!'

'Is *that* all?' He laughed, relieved by her naturalness. 'Look here; since we're talking as man to man – can't you trust me about that too?'

'Trust you? How do you mean? You'd better not trust *me!*' she laughed back sharply. 'I might never be able to pay up!'

His gesture brushed aside the allusion. 'Money may be the root of the matter; it can't be the whole of it, between friends. Don't you think one friend may accept a small service from another without looking too far ahead or weighing too many chances? The question turns entirely on what you think of me. If you like me well enough to be willing to take a few days' holiday with me, just for the pleasure of the thing, and the pleasure you'll be giving me, let's shake hands on it. If you don't like me well enough we'll shake hands too; only I shall be sorry,' he ended.

'Oh, but I shall be sorry too!' Her face, as she lifted it to his, looked so small and young that Darrow felt a fugitive twinge of compunction, instantly effaced by the excitement of pursuit.

'Well, then?' He stood looking down on her, his eyes persuading her. He was now intensely aware that his nearness was having an effect which made it less and less necessary for him to choose his words, and he went on, more mindful of the inflections of his voice than of what he was actually saying: 'Why on earth should we say good-bye if we're both sorry to? Won't you tell me your reason? It's not a bit like you to let anything stand in the way of your saying just what you feel. You mustn't mind offending me, you know!'

She hung before him like a leaf on the meeting of cross-currents, that the next ripple may sweep forward or whirl back. Then she flung up her head with the odd boyish movement habitual to her in moments of excitement. 'What I feel? Do you want to know what I feel? That you're giving me the only chance I've ever had!'

She turned about on her heel and, dropping into the nearest chair, sank forward, her face hidden against the dressing-table.

Under the folds of her thin summer dress the modelling of her back and of her lifted arms, and the slight hollow between her shoulder-blades, recalled the faint curves of a terra-cotta statuette, some young image of grace hardly more than sketched in the clay. Darrow, as he stood looking at her, reflected that her character, for all its seeming firmness, its flashing edges of 'opinion', was probably no less immature. He had not expected her to yield so suddenly to his suggestion, or to confess her yielding in that way. At first he was slightly disconcerted; then he saw how her attitude simplified his own. Her behaviour had all the indecision and awkwardness of inexperience. It showed that she was a child after all; and all he could do – all he had ever meant to do – was to give her a child's holiday to look back to.

For a moment he fancied she was crying; but the next she was on her feet and had swept round on him a face she must have turned away only to hide the first rush of her pleasure.

For a while they shone on each other without speaking; then she sprang to him and held out both hands.

'Is it true? Is it really true? Is it really going to happen to *me*?'

He felt like answering: 'You're the very creature to whom it was bound to happen'; but the words had a double sense that made him wince, and instead he caught her proffered hands and stood looking at her across the length of her arms, without attempting to bend them or to draw her closer. He wanted her to know how her words had moved him; but his thoughts were blurred by the rush of the same emotion that possessed her, and his own words came with an effort.

He ended by giving her back a laugh as frank as her own, and declaring, as he dropped her hands: 'All that and more too – you'll see!'

8

All day, since the late reluctant dawn, the rain had come down in torrents. It streamed against Darrow's high-perched windows, reduced their vast prospect of roofs and chimneys to a black oily huddle, and filled the room with the drab twilight of an underground aquarium.

The streams descended with the regularity of a third day's rain, when trimming and shuffling are over, and the weather has settled down to do its worst. There were no variations of rhythm, no lyrical ups and downs: the grey lines streaking the panes were as dense and uniform as a page of unparagraphed narrative.

George Darrow had drawn his armchair to the fire. The time-table he had been studying lay on the floor, and he sat staring with dull acquiescence into the boundless blur of rain, which affected him like a vast projection of his own state of mind. Then his eyes travelled slowly about the room.

It was exactly ten days since his hurried unpacking had strewn it with the contents of his portmanteaux. His brushes and razors were spread out on the blotched marble of the chest of drawers. A stack of newspapers had accumulated on the centre table under the 'electrolier', and half a dozen paper novels lay on the mantelpiece among cigar-cases and toilet bottles; but these traces of his passage had made no mark on the featureless dullness of the room, its look of being the makeshift setting of innumerable transient collocations. There was something sardonic, almost sinister, in its appearance of having deliberately 'made up' for its anonymous part, all in noncommittal drabs and browns, with a carpet and paper that nobody would remember, and chairs and tables as impersonal as railway porters.

Darrow picked up the time-table and tossed it on to the table. Then he rose to his feet, lit a cigar and went to the window. Through the rain he could just discover the face of a clock in a tall building beyond the railway roofs. He pulled out his watch, compared the two time-pieces, and started the hands of his with such a rush that they flew past the hour and he had to make them repeat the circuit more deliberately. He felt a quite disproportionate irritation at the trifling blunder. When he had corrected it he went back to his chair and threw himself down, leaning back his head against his hands. Presently his cigar went out, and he got up, hunted for the matches, lit it again and returned to his seat.

The room was getting on his nerves. During the first few days, while the skies were clear, he had not noticed it, or had felt for it only the contemptuous indifference of the traveller toward a provisional shelter. But now that he was leaving it, was looking at it for the last time, it seemed to have taken complete possession of his mind, to be soaking itself into him like an ugly indelible blot. Every detail pressed itself on his notice with the familiarity of an accidental confidant: whichever way he turned, he felt the nudge of a transient intimacy . . .

The one fixed point in his immediate future was that his leave was over and that he must be back at his post in London the next morning. Within twenty-four hours he would again be in a daylight world of recognized activities, himself a busy, responsible, relatively necessary factor in the big whirring social and official machine. That fixed obligation was the fact he could think of with the least discomfort, yet for some unaccountable reason it was the one on which he found it most difficult to fix his thoughts. Whenever he did so, the room jerked him back into the circle of its insistent associations. It was extraordinary with what a microscopic minuteness of loathing he hated it all: the grimy carpet and wallpaper, the black marble mantelpiece, the clock with a gilt allegory under a dusty bell, the high-bolstered brown-counterpaned bed, the framed card of printed rules under the electric light switch, and the door of communication with the next room. He hated the door most of all . . .

At the outset, he had felt no special sense of responsibility. He was satisfied that he had struck the right note, and convinced of his power of sustaining it. The whole incident had somehow seemed, in spite of its vulgar setting and its inevitable prosaic propinquities, to be enacting itself in some unmapped region outside the pale of the usual. It was not like anything that had ever happened to him before, or in which he had ever pictured himself as likely to be involved; but that, at first, had seemed no argument against his fitness to deal with it.

Perhaps but for the three days' rain he might have got away without a doubt as to his adequacy. The rain had made all the difference. It had thrown the whole picture out of perspective, blotted out the mystery of the remoter planes and the enchantment of the middle distance, and thrust into prominence every commonplace fact of the foreground. It was the kind of situation that was not helped by being thought over; and by the perversity of circumstance he had been forced into the unwilling contemplation of its every aspect . . .

His cigar had gone out again, and he threw it into the fire and vaguely meditated getting up to find another. But the mere act of leaving his chair seemed to call for a greater exertion of the will than he was capable of, and he leaned his head back with closed eyes and listened to the drumming of the rain.

A different noise aroused him. It was the opening and closing of the door leading from the corridor into the adjoining room. He sat motionless, without opening his eyes; but now another sight forced itself under his lowered lids. It was the precise photographic picture of that other room. Everything in it rose before him and pressed itself upon his vision with the same acuity of distinctness as the objects surrounding him. A step sounded on the floor, and he knew which way the step was directed, what pieces of furniture it had to skirt, where it would probably pause, and what was likely to arrest it. He heard another sound, and recognized it as that of a wet umbrella placed in the black marble jamb of the chimneypiece, against the hearth. He caught the creak of a hinge, and instantly differentiated it as that of the wardrobe against the opposite wall. Then he heard the mouse-like squeal of a reluctant drawer, and knew it was the upper one in the chest of drawers beside the bed: the clatter which followed was caused by the mahogany toilet-glass jumping on its loosened pivots . . .

The step crossed the floor again. It was strange how much better he knew it than the person to whom it belonged! Now it was drawing near the door of communication between the two rooms. He opened his eyes and looked. The step had ceased and for a moment there was silence. Then he heard a low knock. He made no response, and after an interval he saw that the door-handle was being tentatively turned. He closed his eyes once more . . .

The door opened, and the step was in the room, coming cautiously toward him. He kept his eyes shut, relaxing his body to feign sleep. There was another pause, then a wavering soft advance, the rustle of a dress behind his chair, the warmth of two hands pressed for a moment on his lids. The palms of the hands had the lingering scent of some stuff that he had bought on the Boulevard . . . He looked up and saw a letter falling over his shoulder to his knee . . .

'Did I disturb you? I'm so sorry! They gave me this just now when I came in.'

The letter, before he could catch it, had slipped between his knees to the floor. It lay there, address upward, at his feet, and while he sat staring down at the strong slender characters on the blue-grey envelope an arm reached out from behind to pick it up.

'Oh, don't – *don't*!' broke from him, and he bent over and caught the arm. The face above it was close to his.

'Don't what?'

' – take the trouble,' he stammered.

He dropped the arm and stooped down. His grasp closed over the letter, he fingered its thickness and weight and calculated the number of sheets it must contain.

Suddenly he felt the pressure of the hand on his shoulder, and became aware that the face was still leaning over him, and that in a moment he would have to look up and kiss it . . .

He bent forward first and threw the unopened letter into the middle of the fire.

BOOK TWO

9

The light of the October afternoon lay on an old high-roofed house which enclosed in its long expanse of brick and yellowish stone the breadth of a grassy court filled with the shadow and sound of limes.

From the escutcheoned piers at the entrance of the court a level drive, also shaded by limes, extended to a white-barred gate beyond which an equally level avenue of grass, cut through a wood, dwindled to a blue-green blur against a sky banked with still white slopes of cloud.

In the court, half-way between house and drive, a lady stood. She held a parasol above her head, and looked now at the house-front, with its double flight of steps meeting before a glazed door under sculptured trophies, now down the drive toward the grassy cutting through the wood. Her air was less of expectancy than of contemplation: she seemed not so much to be watching for any one, or listening for an approaching sound, as letting the whole aspect of the place sink into her while she held herself open to its influence. Yet it was no less apparent that the scene was not new to her. There was no eagerness of investigation in her survey: she seemed rather to be looking about her with eyes to which, for some intimate inward reason, details long since familiar had suddenly acquired an unwonted freshness.

This was in fact the exact sensation of which Mrs Leath was conscious as she came forth from the house and descended into the sunlit court. She had come to meet her step-son, who was likely to be returning at that hour from an afternoon's shooting in one of the more distant plantations, and she carried in her hand the letter which had sent her in search of him; but with her first step out of the house all thought of him had been effaced by another series of impressions.

The scene about her was known to satiety. She had seen Givré at all seasons of the year, and for the greater part of every year, since the far-off day of her marriage; the day when, ostensibly driving through its gates at her husband's side, she had actually been carried there on a cloud of iris-winged visions.

The possibilities which the place had then represented were still vividly present to her. The mere phrase 'a French château' had called up to her youthful fancy a throng of romantic associations, poetic, pictorial and emotional; and the serene face of the old house seated in its park among the poplar-bordered meadows of middle France, had seemed, on her first sight of it, to hold out to her a fate as noble and dignified as its own mien.

Though she could still call up that phase of feeling it had long since passed, and the house had for a time become to her the very symbol of narrowness and monotony. Then, with the passing of years, it had gradually acquired a less inimical character, had become, not again a castle of dreams, evoker of fair images and romantic legend, but the shell of a life slowly adjusted to its dwelling: the place one came back to, the place where one had one's duties, one's habits and one's books, the place one would naturally live in till one died: a dull house, an inconvenient house, of which one knew all the defects, the shabbinesses, the discomforts, but to which one was so used that one could hardly, after so long a time, think one's self away from it without suffering a certain loss of identity.

Now, as it lay before her in the autumn mildness, its mistress was surprised at her own insensibility. She had been trying to see the house through the eyes of an old friend who, the next morning, would be driving up to it for the first time; and in so doing she seemed to be opening her own eyes upon it after a long interval of blindness.

The court was very still, yet full of a latent life: the wheeling and rustling of pigeons about the rectangular yews and across the sunny gravel; the sweep of rooks above the lustrous greyish-purple slates of the roof, and the stir of the tree-tops as they met the breeze which every day, at that hour, came punctually up from the river.

Just such a latent animation glowed in Anna Leath. In every nerve and vein she was conscious of that equipoise of bliss which the fearful human heart scarce dares acknowledge. She was not used to strong or full emotions; but she had always known that she should not be afraid of them. She was not afraid now; but she felt a deep inward stillness.

The immediate effect of the feeling had been to send her forth in quest of her step-son. She wanted to stroll back with him and have a quiet talk before they re-entered the house. It was always easy to talk to him, and at this moment he was the one person to whom she could have spoken without fear of disturbing her inner stillness. She was glad, for all sorts of reasons, that Madame de Chantelle and Effie were still at Ouchy with the governess, and that she and Owen had the house to themselves. And she was glad that even he was not yet in sight. She wanted to be alone a little longer; not to think, but to let the long slow waves of joy break over her one by one.

She walked out of the court and sat down on one of the benches that bordered the drive. From her seat she had a diagonal view of the long house-front and of the domed chapel terminating one of the wings. Beyond a gate in the court-yard wall the flower-garden drew its dark-green squares and raised its statues against the yellowing background of the park. In the borders only a few late pinks and crimsons smouldered, but a peacock strutting in the sun seemed to have gathered into his outspread fan all the summer glories of the place.

In Mrs Leath's hand was the letter which had opened her eyes to these things, and a smile rose to her lips at the mere feeling of the paper between her fingers. The thrill it sent through her gave a keener edge to every sense. She felt, saw, breathed the shining world as though a thin impenetrable veil had suddenly been removed from it.

Just such a veil, she now perceived, had always hung between herself and life. It had been like the stage gauze which gives an illusive air of reality to the painted scene behind it, yet proves it, after all, to be no more than a painted scene.

She had been hardly aware, in her girlhood, of differing from others in this respect. In the well-regulated well-fed Summers world the unusual was regarded as either immoral or ill-bred, and people with emotions were not visited. Sometimes, with a sense of groping in a topsy-turvy universe, Anna had wondered why everybody about her seemed to ignore all the passions and sensations which formed the stuff of great poetry and memorable action. In a community composed entirely of people like her parents and her parents' friends she did not see how the magnificent things one read about could ever have happened. She was sure that if anything of the kind had occurred in her immediate circle her mother would have consulted the family clergyman, and her father perhaps even have rung up the police; and her sense of humour compelled her to own that, in the given conditions, these precautions might not have been unjustified.

Little by little the conditions conquered her, and she learned to regard the substance of life as a mere canvas for the embroideries of poet and painter, and its little swept and fenced and tended surface as its actual substance. It was in the visioned region of action and emotion that her fullest hours were spent; but it hardly occurred to her that they might be translated into experience, or connected with anything likely to happen to a young lady living in West Fifty-fifth Street.

She perceived, indeed, that other girls, leading outwardly the same life as herself, and seemingly unaware of her world of hidden beauty, were yet possessed of some vital secret which escaped her. There seemed to be a kind of freemasonry between them; they were wider awake than she, more alert, and surer of their wants if not of their opinions. She supposed they were 'cleverer', and accepted her inferiority good-humouredly, half aware, within herself, of a reserve of unused power which the others gave no sign of possessing.

This partly consoled her for missing so much of what made their 'good time'; but the resulting sense of exclusion, of being somehow laughingly but firmly debarred from a share of their privileges, threw her back on herself and deepened the reserve which made envious mothers cite her as a model of ladylike repression.

Love, she told herself, would one day release her from this spell of unreality. She was persuaded that the sublime passion was the key to the enigma; but it was difficult to relate her conception of love to the forms it wore in her experience. Two or three of the girls she had envied for their superior acquaintance with the arts of life had contracted, in the course of time, what were variously described as 'romantic' or 'foolish' marriages; one even made a runaway match, and languished for a while under a cloud of social reprobation. Here, then, was passion in action, romance converted to reality; yet the heroines of these exploits returned from them untransfigured, and their husbands were as dull as ever when one had to sit next to them at dinner.

Her own case, of course, would be different. Some day she would find the magic bridge between West Fifty-fifth Street and life; once or twice she had even fancied that the clue was in her hand. The first time was when she had met young Darrow. She recalled even now the stir of the encounter. But his passion swept over her like a wind that shakes the roof of the forest without reaching its still glades or rippling its hidden pools. He was extra-ordinarily intelligent and agreeable, and her heart beat faster when he was with her. He had a tall fair easy presence and a mind in which the lights of irony played pleasantly through the shades of feeling. She liked to hear his voice almost as much as to listen to what he was saying, and to listen to what he was saying almost as much as to feel that he was looking at her; but he wanted to kiss her, and she wanted to talk to him about books and pictures, and have him insinuate the eternal theme of their love into every sub-ject they discussed.

Whenever they were apart a reaction set in. She wondered how she could have been so cold, called herself a prude and an idiot, questioned if any man could really care for her, and got up in the dead of night to try new ways of doing her hair. But as soon as he reappeared her head straightened itself on her slim neck and she sped her little shafts of irony, or flew her little kites of erudition, while hot and cold waves swept over her, and the things she really wanted to say choked in her throat and burned the palms of her hands.

Often she told herself that any silly girl who had waltzed through a season would know better than she how to attract a man and hold him; but when she said 'a man' she did not really mean George Darrow.

Then one day, at a dinner, she saw him sitting next to one of the silly girls in question: the heroine of the elopement which had shaken West Fifty-fifth Street to its base. The young lady had come back from her adventure no less silly than when she went; and across the table the partner of her flight, a fat young man with eye-glasses, sat stolidly eating terrapin and talking about polo and investments.

The young woman was undoubtedly as silly as ever; yet after

watching her for a few minutes Miss Summers perceived that she had somehow grown luminous, perilous, obscurely menacing to nice girls and the young men they intended eventually to accept. Suddenly, at the sight, a rage of possessorship awoke in her. She must save Darrow, assert her right to him at any price. Pride and reticence went down in a hurricane of jealousy. She heard him laugh, and there was something new in his laugh . . . She watched him talking, talking . . . He sat slightly sideways, a faint smile beneath his lids, lowering his voice as he lowered it when he talked to her. She caught the same inflections, but his eyes were different. It would have offended her once if he had looked at her like that. Now her one thought was that none but she had a right to be so looked at. And that girl of all others! What illusions could he have about a girl who, hardly a year ago, had made a fool of herself over the fat young man stolidly eating terrapin across the table? If that was where romance and passion ended, it was better to take to district visiting or algebra!

All night she lay awake and wondered: 'What was she saying to him? How shall I learn to say such things?' and she decided that her heart would tell her – that the next time they were alone together the irresistible word would spring to her lips. He came the next day, and they were alone, and all she found was: 'I didn't know that you and Kitty Mayne were such friends.'

He answered with indifference that he didn't know it either, and in the reaction of relief she declared: 'She's certainly ever so much prettier than she was . . . '

'She's rather good fun,' he admitted, as though he had not noticed her other advantages; and suddenly Anna saw in his eyes the look she had seen there the previous evening.

She felt as if he were leagues and leagues away from her. All her hopes dissolved, and she was conscious of sitting rigidly, with high head and straight lips, while the irresistible word fled with a last wing-beat into the golden mist of her illusions . . .

She was still quivering with the pain and bewilderment of this adventure when Fraser Leath appeared. She met him first in Italy, where she was travelling with her parents; and the following winter he came to New York. In Italy he had seemed interesting: in New York he became remarkable. He seldom spoke of his life in Europe, and let drop but the most incidental allusions to the friends, the tastes, the pursuits which filled his cosmopolitan days; but in the atmosphere of West Fifty-fifth Street he seemed the embodiment of a storied past. He presented Miss Summers with a prettily-bound anthology of the old French poets and, when she showed a discriminating pleasure in the gift, observed with his grave smile: 'I didn't suppose I should find any one here who would feel about these things as I do.' On another occasion he asked her acceptance of a half-effaced eighteenth-century pastel which he had surprisingly picked up in a New York auction-room. 'I know no one but you who would really appreciate it,' he explained.

He permitted himself no other comments, but these conveyed with sufficient directness that he thought her worthy of a different setting. That she should be so regarded by a man living in an atmosphere of art and beauty, and esteeming them the vital elements of life, made her feel for the first time that she was understood. Here was some one whose scale of values was the same as hers, and who thought her opinion worth hearing on the very matters which they both considered of supreme importance. The discovery restored her self-confidence, and she revealed herself to Mr Leath as she had never known how to reveal herself to Darrow.

As the courtship progressed, and they grew more confidential, her suitor surprised and delighted her by little explosions of revolutionary sentiment. He said: 'Shall you mind, I wonder, if I tell you that you live in a dreadfully conventional atmosphere?' and, seeing that she manifestly did not mind: 'Of course I shall say things now and then that will horrify your dear delightful parents – I shall shock them awfully, I warn you.'

In confirmation of this warning he permitted himself an occasional playful fling at the regular church-going of Mr and Mrs Summers, at the innocuous character of the literature in their library, and at their guileless appreciations in art. He even ventured to banter Mrs Summers on her refusal to receive the irrepressible Kitty Mayne, who, after a rapid passage with George Darrow, was now involved in another and more flagrant adventure.

'In Europe, you know, the husband is regarded as the only judge in such matters. As long as he accepts the situation –' Mr Leath explained to Anna, who took his view the more emphatically in order to convince herself that, personally, she had none but the most tolerant sentiments toward the lady.

The subversiveness of Mr Leath's opinions was enhanced by the distinction of his appearance and the reserve of his manners. He was like the anarchist with a gardenia in his buttonhole who figures in the higher melodrama. Every word, every allusion, every note of his agreeably-modulated voice, gave Anna a glimpse of a society at once freer and finer, which observed the traditional forms but had discarded the underlying prejudices; whereas the world she knew had discarded many of the forms and kept almost all the prejudices.

In such an atmosphere as his an eager young woman, curious as to all the manifestations of life, yet instinctively desiring that they should come to her in terms of beauty and fine feeling, must surely find the largest scope for self-expression. Study, travel, the contact of the world, the comradeship of a polished and enlightened mind, would combine to enrich her days and form her character; and it was only in the rare moments when Mr Leath's symmetrical blond mask bent over hers, and his kiss dropped on her like a cold smooth pebble, that she questioned the completeness of the joys he offered.

There had been a time when the walls on which her gaze now rested had shed a glare of irony on these early dreams. In the first years of her marriage the sober symmetry of Givré had suggested only her husband's neatly-balanced mind. It was a mind, she soon learned, contentedly absorbed in formulating the conventions of the unconventional. West Fifty-fifth Street was no more conscientiously concerned than Givré with the momentous question of 'what people did'; it was only the type of deed investigated that was different. Mr Leath collected his social instances with the same seriousness and patience as his snuff-boxes. He exacted a rigid conformity to his rules of non-conformity and his scepticism had the absolute accent of a dogma. He even cherished certain exceptions to his rules as the book-collector prizes a 'defective' first edition. The Protestant church-going of Anna's parents had provoked his gentle sarcasm; but he prided himself on his mother's devoutness, because Madame de Chantelle, in embracing her second husband's creed, had become part of a society which still observes the outward rites of piety.

Anna, in fact, had discovered in her amiable and elegant mother-in-law an unexpected embodiment of the West Fifty-fifth Street ideal. Mrs Summers and Madame de Chantelle, however strongly they would have disagreed as to the authorized source of Christian dogma, would have found themselves completely in accord on all the momentous minutiae of drawing-room conduct; yet Mr Leath treated his mother's foibles with a respect which Anna's experience of him forbade her to attribute wholly to filial affection.

In the early days, when she was still questioning the Sphinx instead of trying to find an answer to it, she ventured to tax her husband with his inconsistency.

'You say your mother won't like it if I call on that amusing little woman who came here the other day, and was let in by mistake; but Madame de Chantelle tells me she lives with her husband, and when mother refused to visit Kitty Mayne you said –'

Mr Leath's smile arrested her. 'My dear child, I don't pretend to apply the principles of logic to my poor mother's prejudices.'

'But if you admit that they *are* prejudices –?'

'There are prejudices and prejudices. My mother, of course, got hers from Monsieur de Chantelle, and they seem to me as much in their place in this house as the pot-pourri in your hawthorn jar. They preserve a social tradition of which I should be sorry to lose the least perfume. Of course I don't expect you, just at first, to feel the difference, to see the *nuance*. In the case of little Madame de Vireville, for instance: you point out that she's still under her husband's roof. Very true; and if she were merely a Paris acquaintance – especially if you had met her, as one still might, in the *right kind* of house in Paris – I should be the last to object to your visiting her. But in the country it's different. Even the best provincial society is what you would call narrow: I don't deny it; and if some of our friends met Madame de Vireville at Givré – well, it would produce a bad impression. You're inclined to ridicule such considerations, but gradually you'll come to see their importance; and meanwhile, do trust me when I ask you to be guided by my mother. It is always well for a stranger in an old society to err a little on the side of what you call its prejudices but I should rather describe as its traditions.'

After that she no longer tried to laugh or argue her husband out of his convictions. They *were* convictions, and therefore unassailable. Nor was any insincerity implied in the fact that they sometimes seemed to coincide with hers. There were occasions when he really did look at things as she did; but for reasons so different as to make the distance between them all the greater. Life, to Mr Leath, was like a walk through a carefully classified museum, where, in moments of doubt, one had only to look at the number and refer to one's catalogue; to his wife it was like groping about in a huge dark lumber-room where the exploring ray of curiosity lit up now some shape of breathing beauty and now a mummy's grin.

In the first bewilderment of her new state these discoveries had had the effect of dropping another layer of gauze between herself and reality. She seemed farther than ever removed from the strong joys and pangs for which she felt herself made. She did not adopt her husband's views, but insensibly she began to live his life. She tried to throw a compensating ardour into the secret excursions of her spirit, and thus the old vicious distinction between romance and reality was re-established for her, and she resigned herself again to the belief that 'real life' was neither real nor alive.

The birth of her little girl swept away this delusion. At last she felt herself in contact with the actual business of living: but even this impression was not enduring. Everything but the irreducible crude fact of child-bearing assumed, in the Leath household, the same ghostly tinge of unreality. Her husband, at the time, was all that his own ideal of a husband required. He was attentive, and even suitably moved; but as he sat by her bedside, and thoughtfully proffered to her the list of people who had 'called to enquire', she looked first at him, and then at the child between them, and wondered at the blundering alchemy of Nature . . .

With the exception of the little girl herself, everything connected with that time had grown curiously remote and unimportant. The days that had moved so slowly as they passed seemed now to have plunged down headlong steeps of time; and as she sat in the autumn sun, with Darrow's letter in her hand, the history of Anna Leath appeared to its heroine like some grey shadowy tale that she might have read in an old book, one night as she was falling asleep . . .

10

Two brown blurs emerging from the farther end of the wood-vista gradually defined themselves as her step-son and an attendant game-keeper. They grew slowly upon the bluish background, with occa-sional delays and re-effacements, and she sat still, waiting till they should reach the gate at the end of the drive, where the keeper would turn off to his cottage and Owen continue on to the house.

She watched his approach with a smile. From the first days of her marriage she had been drawn to the boy, but it was not until after Effie's birth that she had really begun to know him. The eager obser-vation of her own child had shown her how much she had still to learn about the slight fair boy whom the holidays periodically re-stored to Givré. Owen, even then, both physically and morally, fur-nished her with the oddest of commentaries on his father's mien and mind. He would never, the family sighingly recognized, be nearly as handsome as Mr Leath; but his rather charmingly unbalanced face, with its brooding forehead and petulant boyish smile, suggested to Anna what his father's countenance might have been could one have pictured its neat features disordered by a rattling breeze. She even pushed the analogy farther, and descried in her step-son's mind a quaintly-twisted reflection of her husband's. With his bursts of door-slamming activity, his fits of bookish indolence, his crude revolution-ary dogmatizing and his flashes of precocious irony, the boy was not unlike a boisterous embodiment of his father's theories. It was as though Fraser Leath's ideas, accustomed to hang like marionettes on their pegs, should suddenly come down and walk. There were mo-ments, indeed, when Owen's humours must have suggested to his progenitor the gambols of an infant Frankenstein; but to Anna they were the voice of her secret rebellions, and her tenderness to her step-son was partly based on her severity toward herself. As he had the courage she had lacked, so she meant him to have the chances she had missed; and every effort she made for him helped to keep her own hopes alive.

Her interest in Owen led her to think more often of his mother, and sometimes she would slip away and stand alone before her pre-decessor's portrait. Since her arrival at Givré the picture – a 'full-length' by a once fashionable artist – had undergone the successive displacements of an exiled consort removed farther and farther from the throne; and Anna could not help noting that these stages co-incided with the gradual decline of the artist's fame. She had a fancy that if his credit had been in the ascendant the first Mrs Leath might have continued to throne over the drawing-room mantelpiece, even to the exclusion of her successor's effigy. Instead of this, her peregrina-tions had finally landed her in the shrouded solitude of the billiard-room, an apartment which no one ever entered, but where it was understood that 'the light was better', or might have been if the shutters had not been always closed.

Here the poor lady, elegantly dressed, and seated in the middle of a large lonely canvas, in the blank contemplation of a gilt console, had always seemed to Anna to be waiting for visitors who never came.

'Of course they never came, you poor thing! I wonder how long it took you to find out that they never would?' Anna had more than once apostrophized her, with a derision addressed rather to herself than to the dead; but it was only after Effie's birth that it occurred to her to study more closely the face in the picture, and speculate on the kind of visitors that Owen's mother might have hoped for.

'She certainly doesn't look as if they would have been the same kind as mine: but there's no telling, from a portrait that was so obviously done "to please the family", and that leaves Owen so unaccounted for. Well, they never came, the visitors; they never came; and she died of it. She died of it long before they buried her: I'm certain of that. Those are stone-dead eyes in the picture . . . The loneliness must have been awful, if even Owen couldn't keep her from dying of it. And to feel it so she must have *had* feelings – real live ones, the kind that twitch and tug. And all she had to look at all her life was a gilt console – yes, that's it, a gilt console screwed to the wall! That's exactly and absolutely what he is!'

She did not mean, if she could help it, that either Effie or Owen should know that loneliness, or let her know it again. They were three, now, to keep each other warm, and she embraced both chil-dren in the same passion of motherhood, as though one were not enough to shield her from her predecessor's fate.

Sometimes she fancied that Owen Leath's response was warmer

than that of her own child. But then Effie was still hardly more than a baby, and Owen, from the first, had been almost 'old enough to understand': certainly *did* understand now, in a tacit way that yet perpetually spoke to her. This sense of his understanding was the deepest element in their feeling for each other. There were so many things between them that were never spoken of, or even indirectly alluded to, yet that, even in their occasional discussions and differences, formed the unadduced arguments making for final agreement . . .

Musing on this, she continued to watch his approach; and her heart began to beat a little faster at the thought of what she had to say to him. But when he reached the gate she saw him pause, and after a moment he turned aside as if to gain a cross-road through the park.

She started up and waved her sunshade, but he did not see her. No doubt he meant to go back with the game-keeper, perhaps to the kennels, to see a retriever who had hurt his leg. Suddenly she was seized by the whim to overtake him. She threw down the parasol, thrust her letter into her bodice, and catching up her skirts began to run.

She was slight and light, with a natural ease and quickness of gait, but she could not recall having run a yard since she had romped with Owen in his school-days; nor did she know what impulse moved her now. She only knew that run she must, that no other motion, short of flight, would have been buoyant enough for her humour. She seemed to be keeping pace with some inward rhythm, seeking to give bodily expression to the lyric rush of her thoughts. The earth always felt elastic under her, and she had a conscious joy in treading it; but never had it been as soft and springy as today. It seemed actually to rise and meet her as she went, so that she had the feeling, which sometimes came to her in dreams, of skimming miraculously over short bright waves. The air, too, seemed to break in waves against her, sweeping by on its current all the slanted lights and moist sharp perfumes of the failing day. She panted to herself: 'This is nonsense!' Her blood hummed back: 'But it's glorious!' and she sped on till she saw that Owen had caught sight of her and was striding back in her direction. Then she stopped and waited, flushed and laughing, her hands clasped against the letter in her breast.

'No, I'm not mad,' she called out; 'but there's something in the air today – don't you feel it? – And I wanted to have a little talk with you,' she added as he came up to her, smiling at him and linking her arm in his.

He smiled back, but above the smile she saw the shade of anxiety which, for the last two months, had kept its fixed line between his handsome eyes.

'Owen, don't look like that! I don't want you to!' she said imperiously.

He laughed. 'You said that exactly like Effie. What do you want me to do? To race with you as I do Effie? But I shouldn't have a show!' he protested, still with the little frown between his eyes.

'Where are you going?' she asked.

'To the kennels. But there's not the least need. The vet has seen Garry and he's all right. If there's anything you wanted to tell me –'

'Did I say there was? I just came out to meet you – I wanted to know if you'd had good sport.'

The shadow dropped on him again. 'None at all. The fact is I didn't try. Jean and I have just been knocking about in the woods. I wasn't in a sanguinary mood.'

They walked on with the same light gait, so nearly of a height that keeping step came as naturally to them as breathing. Anna stole another look at the young face on a level with her own.

'You *did* say there was something you wanted to tell me,' her step-son began after a pause.

'Well, there is.' She slackened her pace involuntarily, and they came to a pause and stood facing each other under the limes.

'Is Darrow coming?' he asked.

She seldom blushed, but at the question a sudden heat suffused her. She held her head high.

'Yes: he's coming. I've just heard. He arrives tomorrow. But that's not –' She saw her blunder and tried to rectify it. 'Or rather, yes, in a way it *is* my reason for wanting to speak to you –'

'Because he's coming?'

'Because he's not yet here.'

'It's about him, then?'

He looked at her kindly, half-humorously, an almost fraternal wisdom in his smile.

'About –? No, no: I meant that I wanted to speak today because it's our last day alone together.'

'Oh, I see.' He had slipped his hands into the pockets of his tweed shooting jacket and lounged along at her side, his eyes bent on the moist ruts of the drive, as though the matter had lost all interest for him.

'Owen –'

He stopped again and faced her. 'Look here, my dear, it's no sort of use.'

'What's no use?'

'Anything on earth you can any of you say.'

She challenged him: 'Am *I* one of "any of you"?'

He did not yield. 'Well, then – anything on earth that even *you* can say.'

'You don't in the least know what I can say – or what I mean to.'

'Don't I, generally?'

She gave him this point, but only to make another. 'Yes; but this is particularly. I want to say . . . Owen, you've been admirable all through.'

He broke into a laugh in which the odd elder-brotherly note was once more perceptible.

'Admirable,' she emphasized. 'And so has *she*.'

'Oh, and so have you to *her*!' His voice broke down to boyishness. 'I've never lost sight of that for a minute. It's been altogether easier for her, though,' he threw off presently.

'On the whole, I suppose it has. Well –' she summed up with a laugh, 'aren't you all the better pleased to be told you've behaved as well as she?'

'Oh, you know, I've not done it for *you*,' he tossed back at her, without the least note of hostility in the affected lightness of his tone.

'Haven't you, though, perhaps – the least bit? Because, after all, you knew I understood?'

'You've been awfully kind about pretending to.'

She laughed. 'You don't believe me? You must remember I had your grandmother to consider.'

'Yes: and my father – and Effie, I suppose – and the outraged shades of Givré!' He paused, as if to lay more stress on the boyish sneer: 'Do you likewise include the late Monsieur de Chantelle?'

His step-mother did not appear to resent the thrust. She went on, in the same tone of affectionate persuasion: 'Yes: I must have seemed to you too subject to Givré. Perhaps I have been. But you know that was not my real object in asking you to wait, to say nothing to your grandmother before her return.'

He considered. 'Your real object, of course, was to gain time.'

'Yes – but for whom? Why not for *you*?'

'For me?' He flushed up quickly. 'You don't mean –?'

She laid her hand on his arm and looked gravely into his handsome eyes.

'I mean that when your grandmother gets back from Ouchy I shall speak to her –'

'You'll speak to her . . .?'

'Yes; if only you'll promise to give me time –'

'Time for her to send for Adelaide Painter?'

'Oh, she'll undoubtedly send for Adelaide Painter!'

The allusion touched a spring of mirth in both their minds, and they exchanged a laughing look.

'Only you must promise not to rush things. You must give me time to prepare Adelaide too,' Mrs Leath went on.

'Prepare her too?' He drew away for a better look at her. 'Prepare her for what?'

'Why, to prepare your grandmother! For your marriage. Yes, that's what I mean. I'm going to see you through, you know –'

His feint of indifference broke down and he caught her hand. 'Oh, you dear divine thing! I didn't dream –'

'I know you didn't.' She dropped her gaze and began to walk on slowly. 'I can't say you've convinced me of the wisdom of the step. Only I seem to see that other things matter more – and that not missing things matters most. Perhaps I've changed – or *your* not changing has convinced me. I'm certain now that you won't budge. And that was really all I ever cared about.'

'Oh, as to not budging – I told you so months ago: you might have been sure of that! And how can you be any surer today than yesterday?'

'I don't know. I suppose one learns something every day –'

'Not at Givré!' he laughed, and shot a half-ironic look at her. 'But you haven't really *been* at Givré lately – not for months! Don't you suppose I've noticed that, my dear?'

She echoed his laugh to merge it in an undenying sigh. 'Poor Givré . . .'

'Poor empty Givré! With so many rooms full and yet not a soul in it – except of course my grandmother, who *is* its soul!'

They had reached the gateway of the court and stood looking with a common accord at the long soft-hued façade on which the autumn light was dying. 'It looks so made to be happy in –' she murmured.

'Yes – today, today!' He pressed her arm a little. 'Oh, you darling – to have given it that look for me!' He paused, and then went on in a lower voice: 'Don't you feel we owe it to the poor old place to do what we can to give it that look? You, too, I mean? Come, let's make it grin from wing to wing! I've such a mad desire to say outrageous things to it – haven't you? After all, in old times there must have been living people here!'

Loosening her arm from his she continued to gaze up at the house-front, which seemed, in the plaintive decline of light, to send her back the mute appeal of something doomed.

'It *is* beautiful,' she said.

'A beautiful memory! Quite perfect to take out and turn over when I'm grinding at the law in New York, and you're –' He broke off and looked at her with a questioning smile. 'Come! Tell me. You and I don't have to say things to talk to each other. When you turn suddenly absent-minded and mysterious I always feel like saying: "Come back. All is discovered".'

She returned his smile. 'You know as much as I know. I promise you that.'

He wavered, as if for the first time uncertain how far he might go. 'I don't know Darrow as much as you know him,' he presently risked.

She frowned a little. 'You said just now we didn't need to say things –'

'Was *I* speaking? I thought it was your eyes –' He caught her by both elbows and spun her half-way round, so that the late sun shed a betraying gleam on her face. 'They're such awfully conversational eyes! Don't you suppose they told me long ago why it's just today you've made up your mind that people have got to live their own lives – even at Givré?'

II

'This is the south terrace,' Anna said. 'Should you like to walk down to the river?'

She seemed to listen to herself speaking from a far-off airy height, and yet to be wholly gathered into the circle of consciousness which drew its glowing ring about herself and Darrow. To the aerial listener her words sounded flat and colourless, but to the self within the ring each one beat with a separate heart.

It was the day after Darrow's arrival, and he had come down early, drawn by the sweetness of the light on the lawns and gardens below his window. Anna had heard the echo of his step on the stairs, his pause in the stone-flagged hall, his voice as he asked a servant where to find her. She was at the end of the house, in the brown-panelled sitting-room which she frequented at that season because it caught the sunlight first and kept it longest. She stood near the window, in the pale band of brightness, arranging some salmon-pink geraniums in a shallow porcelain bowl. Every sensation of touch and sight was thrice-alive in her. The grey-green fur of the geranium leaves caressed her fingers and the sunlight wavering across the irregular surface of the old parquet floor made it seem as bright and shifting as the brown bed of a stream.

Darrow stood framed in the door-way of the farthest drawing-room, a light-grey figure against the black and white flagging of the hall; then he began to move toward her down the empty pale-panelled vista, crossing one after another the long reflections which a projecting cabinet or screen cast here and there upon the shining floors.

As he drew nearer, his figure was suddenly displaced by that of her husband, whom, from the same point, she had so often seen advancing down the same perspective. Straight, spare, erect, looking to right and left with quick precise turns of the head, and stopping now and then to straighten a chair or alter the position of a vase, Fraser Leath used to march toward her through the double file of furniture like a general reviewing a regiment drawn up for his inspection. At a certain point, midway across the second room, he always stopped before the mantelpiece of pinkish-yellow marble and looked at himself in the tall garlanded glass that surmounted it. She could not remember that he had ever found anything to straighten or alter in his own studied attire, but she had never known him to omit the inspection when he passed that particular mirror.

When it was over he continued more briskly on his way, and the resulting expression of satisfaction was still on his face when he entered the oak sitting-room to greet his wife . . .

The spectral projection of this little daily scene hung but for a moment before Anna, but in that moment she had time to fling a wondering glance across the distance between her past and present. Then the footsteps of the present came close, and she had to drop the geraniums to give her hand to Darrow . . .

'Yes, let us walk down to the river.'

They had neither of them, as yet, found much to say to each other. Darrow had arrived late on the previous afternoon, and during the evening they had had between them Owen Leath and their own thoughts. Now they were alone for the first time and the fact was enough in itself. Yet Anna was intensely aware that as soon as they began to talk more intimately they would feel that they knew each other less well.

They passed out on to the terrace and down the steps to the gravel walk below. The delicate frosting of dew gave the grass a bluish shimmer, and the sunlight, sliding in emerald streaks along the tree-boles, gathered itself into great luminous blurs at the end of the wood-walks, and hung above the fields a watery glory like the ring about an autumn moon.

'It's good to be here,' Darrow said.

They took a turn to the left and stopped for a moment to look back at the long pink house-front, plainer, friendlier, less adorned than on the side toward the court. So prolonged yet delicate had been the friction of time upon its bricks that certain expanses had the bloom and texture of old red velvet, and the patches of gold lichen spreading over them looked like the last traces of a dim embroidery. The dome of the chapel, with its gilded cross, rose above one wing, and the other ended in a conical pigeon-house, above which the birds were flying, lustrous and slaty, their breasts merged in the blue of the roof when they dropped down on it.

'And this is where you've been all these years.'

They turned away and began to walk down a long tunnel of yellowing trees. Benches with mossy feet stood against the mossy edges of the path, and at its farther end it widened into a circle about a basin rimmed with stone, in which the opaque water strewn with leaves looked like a slab of gold-flecked agate. The path, growing narrower, wound on circuitously through the woods, between slender serried trunks twined with ivy. Patches of blue appeared above them through the dwindling leaves, and presently the trees drew back and showed the open fields along the river.

They walked on across the fields to the tow-path. In a curve of the wall some steps led up to a crumbling pavilion with openings choked with ivy. Anna and Darrow seated themselves on the bench projecting from the inner wall of the pavilion and looked across the river at the slopes divided into blocks of green and fawn-colour, and at the chalk-tinted village lifting its squat church-tower and grey roofs against the precisely drawn lines of the landscape. Anna sat silent, so intensely aware of Darrow's nearness that there was no surprise in the touch he laid on her hand. They looked at each other, and he smiled and said: 'There are to be no more obstacles now.'

'Obstacles?' The word startled her. 'What obstacles?'

'Don't you remember the wording of the telegram that turned me back last May? "Unforeseen obstacle": that was it. What *was* the earth-shaking problem, by the way? Finding a governess for Effie, wasn't it?'

'But I gave you my reason: the reason why it *was* an obstacle. I wrote you fully about it.'

'Yes, I know you did.' He lifted her hand and kissed it. 'How far off it all seems, and how little it all matters today!'

She looked at him quickly. 'Do you feel that? I suppose I'm different. I want to draw all those wasted months into today – to make them a part of it.'

'But they *are*, to me. You reach back and take everything – back to the first days of all.'

She frowned a little, as if struggling with an inarticulate perplexity. 'It's curious how, in those first days, too, something that I didn't understand came between us.'

'Oh, in those days we neither of us understood, did we? It's part of what's called the bliss of being young.'

'Yes, I thought that, too: thought it, I mean, in looking back. But it couldn't, even then, have been as true of you as of me; and now –'

'Now,' he said, 'the only thing that matters is that we're sitting here together.'

He dismissed the rest with a lightness that might have seemed conclusive evidence of her power over him. But she took no pride in such triumphs. It seemed to her that she wanted his allegiance and his adoration not so much for herself as for their mutual love, and that in treating lightly any past phase of their relation he took something from its present beauty. The colour rose to her face.

'Between you and me everything matters.'

'Of course!' She felt the unperceiving sweetness of his smile. 'That's why,' he went on, ' "everything", for me, is here and now: on this bench, between you and me.'

She caught at the phrase. 'That's what I meant: it's here and now; we can't get away from it.'

'Get away from it? Do you want to? *Again?*'

Her heart was beating unsteadily. Something in her, fitfully and with reluctance, struggled to free itself, but the warmth of his nearness penetrated every sense as the sunlight steeped the landscape. Then, suddenly, she felt that she wanted no less than the whole of her happiness.

' "Again?" But wasn't it *you*, the last time –?'

She paused, the tremor in her of Psyche holding up the lamp. But in the interrogative light of her pause her companion's features underwent no change.

'The last time? Last spring? But it was you who – for the best of reasons, as you've told me – turned me back from your very door last spring!'

She saw that he was good-humouredly ready to 'thresh out', for her sentimental satisfaction, a question which, for his own, Time had so conclusively dealt with; and the sense of his readiness reassured her.

'I wrote as soon as I could,' she rejoined. 'I explained the delay and asked you to come. And you never even answered my letter.'

'It was impossible to come then. I had to go back to my post.'

'And impossible to write and tell me so?'

'Your letter was a long time coming. I had waited a week – ten days. I had some excuse for thinking, when it came, that you were in no great hurry for an answer.'

'You thought that – really – after reading it?'

'I thought it.'

Her heart leaped up to her throat. 'Then why are you here today?'

He turned on her with a quick look of wonder. 'God knows – if you can ask me that!'

'You see I was right to say I didn't understand.'

He stood up abruptly and stood facing her, blocking the view over the river and the checkered slopes. 'Perhaps I might say so too.'

'No, no: we must neither of us have any reason for saying it again.' She looked at him gravely. 'Surely you and I needn't arrange the lights before we show ourselves to each other. I want you to see me just as I am, with all my irrational doubts and scruples; the old ones and the new ones too.'

He came back to his seat beside her. 'Never mind the old ones. They were justified – I'm willing to admit it. With the governess having suddenly to be packed off, and Effie on your hands, and your mother-in-law ill, I see the impossibility of your letting me come. I even see that, at the moment, it was difficult to write and explain. But what does all that matter now? The new scruples are the ones I want to tackle.'

Again her heart trembled. She felt her happiness so near, so sure, that to strain it closer might be like a child's crushing a pet bird in its caress. But her very security urged her on. For so long her doubts had been knife-edged: now they had turned into bright harmless toys that she could toss and catch without peril!

'You didn't come, and you didn't answer my letter; and after waiting four months I wrote another.'

'And I answered that one; and I'm here.'

'Yes.' She held his eyes. 'But in my last letter I repeated exactly what I'd said in the first – the one I wrote you last June. I told you then that I was ready to give you the answer to what you'd asked me in London; and in telling you that, I told you what the answer was.'

'My dearest! My dearest!' Darrow murmured.

'You ignored that letter. All summer you made no sign. And all I ask now is that you should frankly tell me why.'

'I can only repeat what I've just said. I was hurt and unhappy and I doubted you. I suppose if I'd cared less I should have been more confident. I cared so much that I couldn't risk another failure. For you'd made me feel that I'd miserably failed. So I shut my eyes and set my teeth and turned my back. There's the whole pusillanimous truth of it!'

'Oh, if it's the *whole* truth –!' She let him clasp her. 'There's my torment, you see. I thought that was what your silence meant till I made you break it. Now I want to be sure that I was right.'

'What can I tell you to make you sure?'

'You can let me tell *you* everything first.' She drew away, but without taking her hands from him. 'Owen saw you in Paris,' she began.

She looked at him and he faced her steadily. The light was full on his pleasantly-browned face, his grey eyes, his frank white forehead. She noticed for the first time a seal-ring in a setting of twisted silver on the hand he had kept on hers.

'In Paris? Oh, yes . . . So he did.'

'He came back and told me. I think you talked to him a moment in a theatre. I asked if you'd spoken of my having put you off – or if you'd sent me any message. He didn't remember that you had.'

'In a crush – in a Paris *foyer*? My dear!'

'It was absurd of me! But Owen and I have always been on odd kind of brother-and-sister terms. I think he guessed about us when he saw you with me in London. So he teased me a little and tried to make me curious about you; and when he saw he'd succeeded he told me he hadn't had time to say much to you because you were in such a hurry to get back to the lady you were with.'

He still held her hands, but she felt no tremor in his, and the blood did not stir in his brown cheek. He seemed to be honestly turning over his memories.

'Yes: and what else did he tell you?'

'Oh, not much, except that she was awfully pretty. When I asked him to describe her he said you had her tucked away in a *baignoire* and he hadn't actually seen her; but he saw the tail of her cloak, and somehow knew from that that she was pretty. One *does*, you know . . . I think he said the cloak was pink.'

Darrow broke into a laugh. 'Of course it was – they always are! So that was at the bottom of your doubts?'

'Not at first. I only laughed. But afterward, when I wrote you and you didn't answer – Oh, you *do* see?' she appealed to him.

He was looking at her gently. 'Yes: I see.'

'It's not as if this were a light thing between us. I want you to know me as I am. If I thought that at that moment . . . when you were on your way here, almost –'

He dropped her hand and stood up. 'Yes, yes – I understand.'

'But do you?' Her look followed him. 'I'm not a goose of a girl. I know . . . of course I *know* . . . but there are things a woman feels . . . when what she knows doesn't make any difference. It's not that I want you to explain – I mean about that particular evening. It's only that I want you to have the whole of my feeling. I didn't know what it was till I saw you again. I never dreamed I should say such things to you!'

'I never dreamed I should be here to hear you say them!' He turned back and lifting a floating end of her scarf put his lips to it. 'But now that you have, *I* know – *I* know,' he smiled down at her.

'You know –?'

'That this is no light thing between us. Now you may ask me anything you please! That was all I wanted to ask *you*.'

For a long moment they looked at each other without speaking. She saw the dancing spirit in his eyes turn grave and darken to a passionate sternness. He stooped and kissed her, and she sat as if folded in wings.

12

It was in the natural order of things that, on the way back to the house, their talk should have turned to the future.

Anna was not eager to define it. She had an extraordinary sensitiveness to the impalpable elements of happiness, and as she walked at Darrow's side her imagination flew back and forth, spinning luminous webs of feeling between herself and the scene about her. Every heightening of emotion produced for her a new effusion of beauty in visible things, and with it the sense that such moments should be lingered over and absorbed like some unrenewable miracle. She understood Darrow's impatience to see their plans take shape. She knew it must be so, she would not have had it otherwise; but to reach a point where she could fix her mind on his appeal for dates and decisions was like trying to break her way through the silver tangle of an April wood.

Darrow wished to use his diplomatic opportunities as a means of studying certain economic and social problems with which he presently hoped to deal in print; and with this in view he had asked for, and obtained, a South American appointment. Anna was ready to follow where he led, and not reluctant to put new sights as well as new thoughts between herself and her past. She had, in a direct way, only Effie and Effie's education to consider; and there seemed, after due reflection, no reason why the most anxious regard for these should not be conciliated with the demands of Darrow's career. Effie, it was evident, could be left to Madame de Chantelle's care till the couple should have organized their life; and she might even, as long as her future step-father's work retained him in distant posts, continue to divide her year between Givré and the antipodes.

As for Owen, who had reached his legal majority two years before, and was soon to attain the age fixed for the taking over of his paternal inheritance, the arrival of this date would reduce his step-mother's responsibility to a friendly concern for his welfare. This made for the prompt realization of Darrow's wishes, and there seemed no reason why the marriage should not take place within the six weeks that remained of his leave.

They passed out of the wood-walk into the open brightness of the garden. The noon sunlight sheeted with gold the bronze flanks of the polygonal yews. Chrysanthemums, russet, saffron and orange, glowed like the efflorescence of an enchanted forest; belts of red begonia purpling to wine-colour ran like smouldering flame among the borders; and above this outspread tapestry the house extended its harmonious length, the soberness of its lines softened to grace in the luminous misty air.

Darrow stood still, and Anna felt that his glance was travelling from her to the scene about them and then back to her face.

'You're sure you're prepared to give up Givré? You look so made for each other!'

'Oh, Givré –' She broke off suddenly, feeling as if her too careless tone had delivered all her past into his hands; and with one of her instinctive movements of recoil she added: 'When Owen marries I shall have to give it up.'

'When Owen marries? That's looking some distance ahead! I want to be told that meanwhile you'll have no regrets.'

She hesitated. Why did he press her to uncover to him her poor starved past? A vague feeling of loyalty, a desire to spare what could no longer harm her, made her answer evasively: 'There will probably be no "meanwhile". Owen may marry before long.'

She had not meant to touch on the subject, for her step-son had sworn her to provisional secrecy; but since the shortness of Darrow's leave necessitated a prompt adjustment of their own plans, it was, after all, inevitable that she should give him at least a hint of Owen's.

'Owen marry? Why, he always seems like a faun in flannels! I hope he's found a dryad. There might easily be one left in these blue-and-gold woods.'

'I can't tell you yet where he found his dryad, but she *is* one, I believe: at any rate she'll become the Givré woods better than I do. Only there may be difficulties –'

'Well! At that age they're not always to be wished away.'

She hesitated. 'Owen, at any rate, has made up his mind to overcome them; and I've promised to see him through.'

She went on, after a moment's consideration, to explain that her step-son's choice was, for various reasons, not likely to commend itself to his grandmother. 'She must be prepared for it, and I've promised to do the preparing. You know I always *have* seen him through things, and he rather counts on me now.'

She fancied that Darrow's exclamation had in it a faint note of annoyance, and wondered if he again suspected her of seeking a pretext for postponement.

'But once Owen's future is settled, you won't, surely, for the sake of what you call seeing him through, ask that I should go away again without you?' He drew her closer as they walked. 'Owen will understand, if you don't. Since he's in the same case himself I'll throw myself on his mercy. He'll see that I have the first claim on you; he won't even want you not to see it.'

'Owen sees everything: I'm not afraid of that. But his future isn't settled. He's very young to marry – too young, his grandmother is sure to think – and the marriage he wants to make is not likely to convince her to the contrary.'

'You don't mean that it's like his first choice?'

'Oh, no! But it's not what Madame de Chantelle would call a good match; it's not even what I call a wise one.'

'Yet you're backing him up?'

'Yet I'm backing him up.' She paused. 'I wonder if you'll understand? What I've most wanted for him, and shall want for Effie, is that they shall always feel free to make their own mistakes, and never, if possible, be persuaded to make other people's. Even if Owen's marriage is a mistake, and has to be paid for, I believe he'll learn and grow in the paying. Of course I can't make Madame de Chantelle see this; but I can remind her that, with his character – his big rushes of impulse, his odd intervals of ebb and apathy – she may drive him into some worse blunder if she thwarts him now.'

'And you mean to break the news to her as soon as she comes back from Ouchy?'

'As soon as I see my way to it. She knows the girl and likes her: that's our hope. And yet it may, in the end, prove our danger, make it harder for us all, when she learns the truth, than if Owen had chosen a stranger. I can't tell you more till I've told her: I've promised Owen not to tell any one. All I ask you is to give me time, to give me a few days at any rate. She's been wonderfully "nice", as she would call it, about you, and about the fact of my having soon to leave Givré; but that, again, may make it harder for Owen. At any rate, you can see, can't you, how it makes me want to stand by him? You see, I couldn't bear it if the least fraction of my happiness seemed to be stolen from his – as if it were a little scrap of happiness that had to be pieced out with other people's!' She clasped her hands on Darrow's arm. 'I want our life to be like a house with all the windows lit: I'd like to string lanterns from the roof and chimneys!'

She ended with an inward tremor. All through her exposition and her appeal she had told herself that the moment could hardly have been less well chosen. In Darrow's place she would have felt, as he doubtless did, that her carefully developed argument was only the disguise of an habitual indecision. It was the hour of all others when she would have liked to affirm herself by brushing aside every obstacle to his wishes; yet it was only by opposing them that she could show the strength of character she wanted him to feel in her.

But as she talked she began to see that Darrow's face gave back no reflection of her words, that he continued to wear the abstracted look of a man who is not listening to what is said to him. It caused her a slight pang to discover that his thoughts could wander at such a moment; then, with a flush of joy she perceived the reason.

In some undefinable way she had become aware, without turning her head, that he was steeped in the sense of her nearness, absorbed in contemplating the details of her face and dress; and the discovery made the words throng to her lips. She felt herself speak with ease, authority, conviction. She said to herself: 'He doesn't care what I say – it's enough that I say it – even if it's stupid he'll like me better for it . . .' She knew that every inflexion of her voice, every gesture, every characteristic of her person – its very defects, the fact that her fore-head was too high, that her eyes were not large enough, that her hands, though slender, were not small, and that the fingers did not taper – she knew that these deficiencies were so many channels through which her influence streamed to him; that she pleased him in spite of them, perhaps because of them; that he wanted her as she was, and not as she would have liked to be; and for the first time she felt in her veins the security and lightness of happy love.

They reached the court and walked under the limes toward the house. The hall door stood wide, and through the windows opening on the terrace the sun slanted across the black and white floor, the faded tapestry chairs, and Darrow's travelling coat and cap, which lay among the cloaks and rugs piled on a bench against the wall.

The sight of these garments, lying among her own wraps, gave her a sense of homely intimacy. It was as if her happiness came down from the skies and took on the plain dress of daily things. At last she seemed to hold it in her hand.

As they entered the hall her eye lit on an unstamped note conspicu-ously placed on the table.

'From Owen! He must have rushed off somewhere in the motor.'

She felt a secret stir of pleasure at the immediate inference that she and Darrow would probably lunch alone. Then she opened the note and stared at it in wonder.

'Dear,' Owen wrote, 'after what you said yesterday I can't wait another hour, and I'm off to Francheuil, to catch the Dijon express and travel back with them. Don't be frightened; I won't speak unless it's safe to. Trust me for that – but I had to go.'

She looked up slowly.

'He's gone to Dijon to meet his grandmother. Oh, I hope I haven't made a mistake!'

'You? Why, what have you to do with his going to Dijon?'

She hesitated. 'The day before yesterday I told him, for the first time, that I meant to see him through, no matter what happened. And I'm afraid he's lost his head, and will be imprudent and spoil things. You see, I hadn't meant to say a word to him till I'd had time to prepare Madame de Chantelle.'

She felt that Darrow was looking at her and reading her thoughts, and the colour flew to her face. 'Yes: it was when I heard you were coming that I told him. I wanted him to feel as I felt . . . it seemed too unkind to make him wait!'

Her hand was in his, and his arm rested for a moment on her shoulder.

'It *would* have been too unkind to make him wait.'

They moved side by side toward the stairs. Through the haze of bliss enveloping her, Owen's affairs seemed curiously unimportant and remote. Nothing really mattered but this torrent of light in her veins. She put her foot on the lowest step, saying: 'It's nearly luncheon time – I must take off my hat . . .' and as she started up the stairs Darrow stood below in the hall and watched her. But the distance between them did not make him seem less near: it was as if his thoughts moved with her and touched her like endearing hands.

In her bedroom she shut the door and stood still, looking about her in a fit of dreamy wonder. Her feelings were unlike any she had ever known: richer, deeper, more complete. For the first time everything in her, from head to foot, seemed to be feeding the same full current of sensation.

She took off her hat and went to the dressing-table to smooth her hair. The pressure of the hat had flattened the dark strands on her forehead; her face was paler than usual, with shadows about the eyes. She felt a pang of regret for the wasted years. 'If I look like this today,' she said to herself, 'what will he think of me when I'm ill or worried?' She began to run her fingers through her hair, rejoicing in its thickness; then she desisted and sat still, resting her chin on her hands.

'I want him to see me as I am,' she thought.

Deeper than the deepest fibre of her vanity was the triumphant sense that *as she was*, with her flattened hair, her tired pallor, her thin sleeves a little tumbled by the weight of her jacket, he would like her even better, feel her nearer, dearer, more desirable, than in all the splendours she might put on for him. In the light of this discovery she studied her face with a new intentness, seeing its defects as she had never seen them, yet seeing them through a kind of radiance, as though love were a luminous medium into which she had been bodily plunged.

She was glad now that she had confessed her doubts and her jealousy. She divined that a man in love may be flattered by such involuntary betrayals, that there are moments when respect for his liberty appeals to him less than the inability to respect it: moments so propitious that a woman's very mistakes and indiscretions may help to establish her dominion. The sense of power she had been aware of in talking to Darrow came back with ten-fold force. She felt like testing him by the most fantastic exactions, and at the same moment she longed to humble herself before him, to make herself the shadow and echo of his mood. She wanted to linger with him in a world of fancy and yet to walk at his side in the world of fact. She wanted him to feel her power and yet to love her for her ignorance and humility. She felt like a slave, and a goddess, and a girl in her teens . . .

13

Darrow, late that evening, threw himself into an armchair before his fire and mused.

The room was propitious to meditation. The red-veiled lamp, the corners of shadow, the splashes of firelight on the curves of old full-bodied wardrobes and cabinets, gave it an air of intimacy increased by its faded hangings, its slightly frayed and threadbare rugs. Everything in it was harmoniously shabby, with a subtle sought-for shabbiness in which Darrow fancied he discerned the touch of Fraser Leath. But Fraser Leath had grown so unimportant a factor in the scheme of things that these marks of his presence caused the young man no emotion beyond that of a faint retrospective amusement.

The afternoon and evening had been perfect.

After a moment of concern over her step-son's departure, Anna had surrendered herself to her happiness with an impetuosity that Darrow had never suspected in her. Early in the afternoon they had gone out in the motor, traversing miles of sober-tinted landscape in which, here and there, a scarlet vineyard flamed, clattering through the streets of stony villages, coming out on low slopes above the river, or winding through the pale gold of narrow wood-roads with the blue of clear-cut hills at their end. Over everything lay a faint sun-shine that seemed dissolved in the still air, and the smell of wet roots and decaying leaves was merged in the pungent scent of burning underbrush. Once, at the turn of a wall, they stopped the motor before a ruined gateway and, stumbling along a road full of ruts, stood before a little old deserted house, fantastically carved and chim-neyed, which lay in a moat under the shade of ancient trees. They paced the paths between the trees, found a mouldy Temple of Love on an islet among reeds and plantains, and, sitting on a bench in the stable-yard, watched the pigeons circling against the sunset over their cot of patterned brick. Then the motor flew on into the dusk . . .

When they came in they sat beside the fire in the oak drawing-room, and Darrow noticed how delicately her head stood out against the sombre panelling, and mused on the enjoyment there would always be in the mere fact of watching her hands as they moved about among the tea-things . . .

They dined late, and facing her across the table, with its low lights and flowers, he felt an extraordinary pleasure in seeing her again in evening dress, and in letting his eyes dwell on the proud shy set of her head, the way her dark hair clasped it, and the girlish thinness of her neck above the slight swell of the breast. His imagination was struck by the quality of reticence in her beauty. She suggested a fine portrait kept down to a few tones, or a Greek vase on which the play of light is the only pattern.

After dinner they went out on the terrace for a look at the moon-misted park. Through the crepuscular whiteness the trees hung in blotted masses. Below the terrace, the garden drew its dark diagrams between statues that stood like muffled conspirators on the edge of the shadow. Farther off, the meadows unrolled a silver-shot tissue to the mantling of mist above the river; and the autumn stars trembled overhead like their own reflections seen in dim water.

He lit his cigar, and they walked slowly up and down the flags in the languid air, till he put an arm about her, saying: 'You mustn't stay till you're chilled'; then they went back into the room and drew up their chairs to the fire.

It seemed only a moment later that she said: 'It must be after eleven,' and stood up and looked down on him, smiling faintly. He sat still, absorbing the look, and thinking: 'There'll be evenings and evenings' – till she came nearer, bent over him, and with a hand on his shoulder said: 'Good night.'

He got to his feet and put his arms about her.

'Good night,' he answered, and held her fast; and they gave each other a long kiss of promise and communion.

The memory of it glowed in him still as he sat over his crumbling fire; but beneath his physical exultation he felt a certain gravity of mood. His happiness was in some sort the rallying-point of many scattered purposes. He summed it up vaguely by saying to himself that to be loved by a woman like that made 'all the difference' . . . He was a little tired of experimenting on life; he wanted to 'take a line', to follow things up, to centralize and concentrate, and produce results. Two or three more years of diplomacy – with her beside him! – and then their real life would begin: study, travel and book-making for him, and for her – well, the joy, at any rate, of getting out of an atmosphere of bric-à-brac and card-leaving into the open air of competing activities.

The desire for change had for some time been latent in him, and his meeting with Mrs Leath the previous spring had given it a definite direction. With such a comrade to focus and stimulate his energies he felt modestly but agreeably sure of 'doing something'. And under this assurance was the lurking sense that he was somehow worthy of his opportunity. His life, on the whole, had been a creditable affair. Out of modest chances and middling talents he had built himself a fairly marked personality, known some exceptional people, done a number of interesting and a few rather difficult things, and found himself, at thirty-seven, possessed of an intellectual ambition sufficient to occupy the passage to a robust and energetic old age. As for the private and personal side of his life, it had come up to the current standards, and if it had dropped, now and then, below a more ideal measure, even these declines had been brief, parenthetic, incidental. In the recognized essentials he had always remained strictly within the limit of his scruples.

From this reassuring survey of his case he came back to the contemplation of its crowning felicity. His mind turned again to his first meeting with Anna Summers and took up one by one the threads of their faintly sketched romance. He dwelt with pardonable pride on the fact that fate had so early marked him for the high privilege of possessing her: it seemed to mean that they had really, in the truest sense of the ill-used phrase, been made for each other.

Deeper still than all these satisfactions was the mere elemental sense of well-being in her presence. That, after all, was what proved her to be the woman for him: the pleasure he took in the set of her head, the way her hair grew on her forehead and at the nape, her steady gaze when he spoke, the grave freedom of her gait and gestures. He recalled every detail of her face, the fine veinings of the temples, the bluish-brown shadows in her upper lids, and the way the reflections of two stars seemed to form and break up in her eyes when he held her close to him . . .

If he had had any doubt as to the nature of her feeling for him those dissolving stars would have allayed it. She was reserved, she was shy even, was what the shallow and effusive would call 'cold'. She was like a picture so hung that it can be seen only at a certain angle: an angle known to no one but its possessor. The thought flattered his sense of possessorship . . . He felt that the smile on his lips would have been fatuous had it had a witness. He was thinking of her look when she had questioned him about his meeting with Owen at the theatre: less of her words than of her look, and of the effort the question cost her: the reddening of her cheek, the deepening of the strained line between her brows, the way her eyes sought shelter and then turned and drew on him. Pride and passion were in the conflict – magnificent qualities in a wife! The sight almost made up for his momentary embarrassment at the rousing of a memory which had no place in his present picture of himself. Yes! It was worth a good deal to watch that fight between her instinct and her intelligence, and know one's self the object of the struggle . . .

Mingled with these sensations were considerations of another order. He reflected with satisfaction that she was the kind of woman with whom one would like to be seen in public. It would be distinctly agreeable to follow her into drawing-rooms, to walk after her down the aisle of a theatre, to get in and out of trains with her, to say 'my wife' of her to all sorts of people. He draped these details in the handsome phrase 'She's a woman to be proud of', and felt that this fact somehow justified and ennobled his instinctive boyish satisfaction in loving her.

He stood up, rambled across the room and leaned out for a while into the starry night. Then he dropped again into his armchair with a sigh of deep content.

'Oh, hang it,' he suddenly exclaimed, 'it's the best thing that's ever happened to me, anyhow!'

The next day was even better. He felt, and knew she felt, that they had reached a clearer understanding of each other. It was as if, after a swim through bright opposing waves, with a dazzle of sun in their eyes, they had gained an inlet in the shades of a cliff, where they could float on the still surface and gaze far down into the depths.

Now and then, as they walked and talked, he felt a thrill of youthful wonder at the coincidence of their views and their experiences, at the way their minds leapt to the same point in the same instant.

'The old delusion, I suppose,' he smiled to himself. 'Will Nature never tire of the trick?'

But he knew it was more than that. There were moments in their talk when he felt, distinctly and unmistakably, the solid ground of friendship underneath the whirling dance of his sensations. 'How I should like her if I didn't love her!' he summed it up, wondering at the miracle of such a union.

In the course of the morning a telegram had come from Owen Leath, announcing that he, his grandmother and Effie would arrive from Dijon that afternoon at four. The station of the main line was eight or ten miles from Givré, and Anna, soon after three, left in the motor to meet the travellers.

When she had gone Darrow started for a walk, planning to get back late, in order that the reunited family might have the end of the afternoon to themselves. He roamed the countryside till long after dark, and the stable-clock of Givré was striking seven as he walked up the avenue to the court.

In the hall, coming down the stairs, he encountered Anna. Her face was serene, and his first glance showed him that Owen had kept his word and that none of her forebodings had been fulfilled.

She had just come down from the school-room, where Effie and the governess were having supper; the little girl, she told him, looked immensely better for her Swiss holiday, but was dropping with sleep after the journey, and too tired to make her habitual appearance in the drawing-room before being put to bed. Madame de Chantelle was resting, but would be down for dinner; and as for Owen, Anna supposed he was off somewhere in the park – he had a passion for prowling about the park at nightfall . . .

Darrow followed her into the brown room, where the tea-table had been left for him. He declined her offer of tea, but she lingered a moment to tell him that Owen had in fact kept his word, and that Madame de Chantelle had come back in the best of humours, unsuspicious of the blow about to fall.

'She has enjoyed her month at Ouchy, and it has given her a lot to talk about – her symptoms, and the rival doctors, and the people at the hotel. It seems she met your Ambassadress there, and Lady Wantley, and some other London friends of yours, and she's heard what she calls "delighted things" about you: she told me to tell you so. She attaches great importance to the fact that your grandmother was an Everard of Albany. She's prepared to open her arms to you. I don't know whether it won't make it harder for poor Owen . . . the contrast, I mean . . . There are no Ambassadresses or Everards to vouch for *his* choice! But you'll help me, won't you? You'll help me to help him? To-morrow I'll tell you the rest. Now I must rush up and tuck in Effie . . .'

'Oh, you'll see, we'll pull it off for him!' he assured her; 'together, we can't fail to pull it off.'

He stood and watched her with a smile as she fled down the half-lit vista to the hall.

14

If Darrow, on entering the drawing-room before dinner, examined its new occupant with unusual interest, it was more on Owen Leath's account than his own.

Anna's hints had roused his interest in the lad's love affair, and he wondered what manner of girl the heroine of the coming conflict might be. He had guessed that Owen's rebellion symbolized for his step-mother her own long struggle against the Leath conventions, and he understood that if Anna so passionately abetted him it was partly because, as she owned, she wanted his liberation to coincide with hers.

The lady who was to represent, in the impending struggle, the forces of order and tradition was seated by the fire when Darrow entered. Among the flowers and old furniture of the large pale-panelled room, Madame de Chantelle had the inanimate elegance of a figure introduced into a 'still-life' to give the scale. And this, Darrow reflected, was exactly what she doubtless regarded as her chief obligation: he was sure she thought a great deal of 'measure', and approved of most things only up to a certain point.

She was a woman of sixty, with a figure at once young and old-fashioned. Her fair faded tints, her quaint corseting, the *passementerie* on her tight-waisted dress, the velvet band on her tapering arm, made her resemble a 'carte de visite' photograph of the middle sixties. One saw her, younger but no less invincibly lady-like, leaning on a chair with a fringed back, a curl in her neck, a locket on her tuckered bosom, toward the end of an embossed morocco album beginning with 'The Beauties of the Second Empire'.

She received her daughter-in-law's suitor with an affability which implied her knowledge and approval of his suit. Darrow had already guessed her to be a person who would instinctively oppose any suggested changes, and then, after one had exhausted one's main arguments, unexpectedly yield to some small incidental reason, and adhere doggedly to her new position. She boasted of her old-fashioned prejudices, talked a good deal of being a grandmother, and made a show of reaching up to tap Owen's shoulder, though his height was little more than hers.

She was full of a small pale prattle about the people she had seen at Ouchy, as to whom she had the minute statistical information of a gazetteer, without any apparent sense of personal differences. She said to Darrow: 'They tell me things are very much changed in America . . . Of course in my youth there *was* a Society' . . . She had no desire to return there: she was sure the standards must be so different. 'There are charming people everywhere . . . and one must always look on the best side . . . but when one has lived among Traditions it's difficult to adapt one's self to the new ideas . . . These dreadful views of marriage . . . it's so hard to explain them to my French relations . . . I'm thankful to say I don't pretend to understand them myself! But *you're* an Everard – I told Anna last spring in London that one sees that instantly . . .'

She wandered off to the cooking and the service of the hotel at Ouchy. She attached great importance to gastronomic details and to the manners of hotel servants. There, too, there was a falling off, she said. 'I don't know, of course; but people say it's owing to the Americans. Certainly my waiter had a way of slapping down the dishes . . . they tell me that many of them are Anarchists . . . belong to Unions, you know.' She appealed to Darrow's reported knowledge of economic conditions to confirm this ominous rumour.

After dinner Owen Leath wandered into the next room, where the piano stood, and began to play among the shadows. His step-mother presently joined him, and Darrow sat alone with Madame de Chantelle.

She took up the thread of her mild chat and carried it on at the same pace as her knitting. Her conversation resembled the large loose-stranded web between her fingers: now and then she dropped a stitch, and went on regardless of the gap in the pattern.

Darrow listened with a lazy sense of well-being. In the mental lull of the after-dinner hour, with harmonious memories murmuring through his mind, and the soft tints and shadowy spaces of the fine old room charming his eyes to indolence, Madame de Chantelle's discourse seemed not out of place. He could understand that, in the long run, the atmosphere of Givré might be suffocating; but in his present mood its very limitations had a grace.

Presently he found the chance to say a word in his own behalf; and thereupon measured the advantage, never before particularly apparent to him, of being related to the Everards of Albany. Madame de Chantelle's conception of her native country – to which she had not returned since her twentieth year – reminded him of an ancient geographer's map of the Hyperborean regions. It was all a foggy blank, from which only one or two fixed outlines emerged; and one of these belonged to the Everards of Albany.

The fact that they offered such firm footing – formed, so to speak, a friendly territory on which the opposing powers could meet and treat – helped him through the task of explaining and justifying himself as the successor of Fraser Leath. Madame de Chantelle could not resist such incontestable claims. She seemed to feel her son's hovering and discriminating presence, and she gave Darrow the sense that he was being tested and approved as a last addition to the Leath Collection.

She also made him aware of the immense advantage he possessed in belonging to the diplomatic profession. She spoke of this humdrum calling as a Career, and gave Darrow to understand that she supposed him to have been seducing Duchesses when he was not negotiating Treaties. He heard again quaint phrases which romantic old ladies had used in his youth: 'Brilliant diplomatic society ... social advantages ... the *entrée everywhere* ... *nothing else forms* a young man in the same way ...' and she sighingly added that she could have wished her grandson had chosen the same path to glory.

Darrow prudently suppressed his own view of the profession, as well as the fact that he had adopted it provisionally, and for reasons less social than sociological; and the talk presently passed on to the subject of his future plans.

Here again, Madame de Chantelle's awe of the Career made her admit the necessity of Anna's consenting to an early marriage. The fact that Darrow was 'ordered' to South America seemed to put him in the romantic light of a young soldier charged to lead a forlorn hope: she sighed and said: 'At such moments a wife's duty is at her husband's side.'

The problem of Effie's future might have disturbed her, she added; but since Anna, for a time, consented to leave the little girl with her, that problem was at any rate deferred. She spoke plaintively of the responsibility of looking after her granddaughter, but

145

Darrow divined that she enjoyed the flavour of the word more than she felt the weight of the fact.

'Effie's a perfect child. She's more like my son, perhaps, than dear Owen. She'll never intentionally give me the least trouble. But of course the responsibility will be great . . . I'm not sure I should dare to undertake it if it were not for her having such a treasure of a governess. Has Anna told you about our little governess? After all the worry we had last year, with one impossible creature after another, it seems providential, just now, to have found her. At first we were afraid she was too young; but now we've the greatest confidence in her. So clever and amusing – and *such* a lady! I don't say her education's all it might be . . . no drawing or singing . . . but one can't have everything; and she speaks Italian . . .'

Madame de Chantelle's fond insistence on the likeness between Effie Leath and her father, if not particularly gratifying to Darrow, had at least increased his desire to see the little girl. It gave him an odd feeling of discomfort to think that she should have any of the characteristics of the late Fraser Leath: he had, somehow, fantastically pictured her as the mystical offspring of the early tenderness between himself and Anna Summers.

His encounter with Effie took place the next morning, on the lawn below the terrace, where he found her, in the early sunshine, knocking about golf balls with her brother. Almost at once, and with infinite relief, he saw that the resemblance of which Madame de Chantelle boasted was mainly external. Even that discovery was slightly distasteful, though Darrow was forced to own that Fraser Leath's straight-featured fairness had lent itself to the production of a peculiarly finished image of childish purity. But it was evident that other elements had also gone to the making of Effie, and that another spirit sat in her eyes. Her serious handshake, her 'pretty' greeting, were worthy of the Leath tradition, and he guessed her to be more malleable than Owen, more subject to the influences of Givré; but the shout with which she returned to her romp had in it the note of her mother's emancipation.

He had begged a holiday for her, and when Mrs Leath appeared he and she and the little girl went off for a ramble. Anna wished her daughter to have time to make friends with Darrow before learning in what relation he was to stand to her; and the three roamed the woods and fields till the distant chime of the stable-clock made them turn back for luncheon.

Effie, who was attended by a shaggy terrier, had picked up two or three subordinate dogs at the stable; and as she trotted on ahead with her yapping escort, Anna hung back to throw a look at Darrow.

'Yes,' he answered it, 'she's exquisite . . . Oh, I see what I'm asking of you! But she'll be quite happy here, won't she? And you must remember it won't be for long . . .'

Anna sighed her acquiescence. 'Oh, she'll be happy here. It's her nature to be happy. She'll apply herself to it, conscientiously, as she does to her lessons, and to what she calls "being good" . . . In a way, you see, that's just what worries me. Her idea of "being good" is to please the person she's with – she puts her whole dear little mind on it! And so, if ever she's with the wrong person –'

'But surely there's no danger of that just now? Madame de Chantelle tells me that you've at last put your hand on a perfect governess –'

Anna, without answering, glanced away from him toward her daughter.

'It's lucky, at any rate,' Darrow continued, 'that Madame de Chantelle thinks her so.'

'Oh, I think very highly of her too.'

'Highly enough to feel quite satisfied to leave her with Effie?'

'Yes. She's just the person for Effie. Only, of course, one never knows . . . She's young, and she might take it into her head to leave us . . .' After a pause she added: 'I'm naturally anxious to know what you think of her.'

When they entered the house the hands of the hall clock stood within a few minutes of the luncheon hour. Anna led Effie off to have her hair smoothed and Darrow wandered into the oak sitting-room, which he found untenanted. The sun lay pleasantly on its brown walls, on the scattered books and the flowers in old porcelain vases. In his eyes lingered the vision of the dark-haired mother mounting the stairs with her little fair daughter. The contrast between them seemed a last touch of grace in the complex harmony of things. He stood in the window, looking out at the park, and brooding inwardly upon his happiness . . .

He was roused by Effie's voice and the scamper of her feet down the long floors behind him.

'Here he is! Here he is!' she cried, flying over the threshold.

He turned and stooped to her with a smile, and as she caught his hand he perceived that she was trying to draw him toward some one who had paused behind her in the doorway, and whom he supposed to be her mother.

'*Here* he is!' Effie repeated, with her sweet impatience.

The figure in the doorway came forward and Darrow, looking up, found himself face to face with Sophy Viner. They stood still, a yard or two apart, and looked at each other without speaking.

As they paused there, a shadow fell across one of the terrace windows, and Owen Leath stepped whistling into the room. In his rough shooting clothes, with the glow of exercise under his fair skin, he looked extraordinarily light-hearted and happy. Darrow, with a quick side-glance, noticed this, and perceived also that the glow on the youth's cheek had deepened suddenly to red. He too stopped short, and the three stood there motionless for a barely perceptible beat of time. During its lapse, Darrow's eyes had turned back from Owen's face to that of the girl between them. He had the sense that, whatever was done, it was he who must do it, and that it must be done immediately. He went forward and held out his hand.

'How do you do, Miss Viner?'

She answered: 'How do you do?' in a voice that sounded clear and natural; and the next moment he again became aware of steps behind him, and knew that Mrs Leath was in the room.

To his strained senses there seemed to be another just measurable pause before Anna said, looking gaily about the little group: 'Has Owen introduced you? This is Effie's friend, Miss Viner.'

Effie, still hanging on her governess's arm, pressed herself closer with a little gesture of appropriation; and Miss Viner laid her hand on her pupil's hair.

Darrow felt that Anna's eyes had turned to him.

'I think Miss Viner and I have met already – several years ago in London.'

'I remember,' said Sophy Viner, in the same clear voice.

'How charming! Then we're all friends. But luncheon must be ready,' said Mrs Leath.

She turned back to the door, and the little procession moved down the two long drawing-rooms, with Effie waltzing on ahead.

15

Madame de Chantelle and Anna had planned, for the afternoon, a visit to a remotely situated acquaintance whom the introduction of the motor had transformed into a neighbour. Effie was to pay for her morning's holiday by an hour or two in the school-room, and Owen suggested that he and Darrow should betake themselves to a distant covert in the desultory quest for pheasants.

Darrow was not an ardent sportsman, but any pretext for physical activity would have been acceptable at the moment; and he was glad both to get away from the house and not to be left to himself.

When he came downstairs the motor was at the door, and Anna stood before the hall mirror, swathing her hat in veils. She turned at the sound of his step and smiled at him for a long full moment.

'I'd no idea you knew Miss Viner,' she said, as he helped her into her long coat.

'It came back to me, luckily, that I'd seen her two or three times in London, several years ago. She was secretary, or something of the sort, in the background of a house where I used to dine.'

He loathed the slighting indifference of the phrase, but he had uttered it deliberately, had been secretly practising it all through the interminable hour at the luncheon-table. Now that it was spoken, he shivered at its note of condescension. In such cases one was almost sure to overdo . . . But Anna seemed to notice nothing unusual.

'Was she really? You must tell me all about it – tell me exactly how she struck you. I'm so glad it turns out that you know her.'

' "Know" is rather exaggerated: we used to pass each other on the stairs.'

Madame de Chantelle and Owen appeared together as he spoke, and Anna, gathering up her wraps, said: 'You'll tell me about that, then. Try and remember everything you can.'

As he tramped through the woods at his young host's side, Darrow felt the partial relief from thought produced by exercise and the obligation to talk. Little as he cared for shooting, he had the habit of concentration which makes it natural for a man to throw himself wholly into whatever business he has in hand, and there were moments of the afternoon when a sudden whirr in the undergrowth, a vivider gleam against the hazy browns and greys of the woods, was enough to fill the foreground of his attention. But all the while, behind these voluntarily emphasized sensations, his secret consciousness continued to revolve on a loud wheel of thought. For a time it seemed to be sweeping him through deep gulfs of darkness. His sensations were too swift and swarming to be disentangled. He had an almost physical sense of struggling for air, of battling helplessly with material obstructions, as though the russet covert through which he trudged were the heart of a maleficent jungle . . .

Snatches of his companion's talk drifted to him intermittently through the confusion of his thoughts. He caught eager self-revealing phrases, and understood that Owen was saying things about himself, perhaps hinting indirectly at the hopes for which Darrow had been prepared by Anna's confidences. He had already become aware that the lad liked him, and had meant to take the first opportunity of showing that he reciprocated the feeling. But the effort of fixing his attention on Owen's words was so great that it left no power for more than the briefest and most inexpressive replies.

Young Leath, it appeared, felt that he had reached a turning-point in his career, a height from which he could impartially survey his past progress and projected endeavour. At one time he had had musical and literary yearnings, visions of desultory artistic indulgence; but these had of late been superseded by the resolute determination to plunge into practical life.

'I don't want, you see,' Darrow heard him explaining, 'to drift into what my grandmother, poor dear, is trying to make of me: an adjunct of Givré. I don't want – hang it all! – to slip into collecting sensations as my father collected snuff-boxes. I want Effie to have Givré – it's my grandmother's, you know, to do as she likes with; and I've understood lately that if it belonged to me it would gradually gobble me up. I want to get out of it, into a life that's big and ugly and struggling. If I can extract beauty out of *that*, so much the better: that'll prove my vocation. But I want to *make* beauty, not be drowned in the ready-made, like a bee in a pot of honey.'

Darrow knew that he was being appealed to for corroboration of these views and for encouragement in the course to which they pointed. To his own ears his answers sounded now curt, now irrelevant: at one moment he seemed chillingly indifferent, at another he heard himself launching out on a flood of hazy discursiveness. He dared not look at Owen, for fear of detecting the lad's surprise at these senseless transitions. And through the confusion of his inward struggles and outward loquacity he heard the ceaseless trip-hammer beat of the question: 'What in God's name shall I do?' . . .

To get back to the house before Anna's return seemed his most pressing necessity. He did not clearly know why: he simply felt that he ought to be there. At one moment it occurred to him that Miss Viner might want to speak to him alone – and again, in the same flash, that it would probably be the last thing she would want . . . At any rate, he felt he ought to try to speak to *her*, or at least be prepared to do so, if the chance should occur . . .

Finally, toward four, he told his companion that he had some letters on his mind and must get back to the house and despatch them before the ladies returned. He left Owen with the beater and walked on to the edge of the covert. At the park gates he struck obliquely through the trees, following a grass avenue at the end of which he had caught a glimpse of the roof of the chapel. A grey haze had blotted out the sun and the still air clung about him tepidly. At length the house-front raised before him its expanse of damp-silvered brick, and he was struck afresh by the high decorum of its calm lines and soberly massed surfaces. It made him feel, in the turbid coil of his fears and passions, like a muddy tramp forcing his way into some pure sequestered shrine . . .

By and by, he knew, he should have to think the complex horror out, slowly, systematically, bit by bit; but for the moment it was whirling him about so fast that he could just clutch at its sharp spikes and be tossed off again. Only one definite immediate fact stuck in his quivering grasp. He must give the girl every chance – must hold himself passive till she had taken them . . .

In the court Effie ran up to him with her leaping terrier.

'I was coming out to meet you – you and Owen. Miss Viner was coming, too, and then she couldn't because she's got such a headache. I'm afraid I gave it to her because I did my division so disgracefully. It's too bad, isn't it? But won't you walk back with me? Nurse won't mind the least bit; she'd so much rather go in to tea.'

Darrow excused himself laughingly, on the plea that he had letters to write, which was much worse than having a headache, and not infrequently resulted in one.

'Oh, then you can go and write them in Owen's study. That's where gentlemen always write their letters.'

She flew on with her dog and Darrow pursued his way to the house. Effie's suggestion struck him as useful. He had pictured himself as vaguely drifting about the drawing-rooms, and had perceived the difficulty of Miss Viner's having to seek him there; but the study, a small room on the right of the hall, was in easy sight from the staircase, and so situated that there would be nothing marked in his being found there in talk with her.

He went in, leaving the door open, and sat down at the writing-table. The room was a friendly heterogeneous place, the one repository, in the well-ordered and amply-servanted house, of all its unclassified odds and ends: Effie's croquet-box and fishing rods, Owen's guns and golf-sticks and racquets, his step-mother's flower-baskets and gardening implements, even Madame de Chantelle's embroidery frame, and the back numbers of the *Catholic Weekly*. The early twilight had begun to fall, and presently a slanting ray across the desk showed Darrow that a servant was coming across the hall with a lamp. He pulled out a sheet of note-paper and began to write at random, while the man, entering, put the lamp at his elbow and vaguely 'straightened' the heap of newspapers tossed on the divan. Then his steps died away and Darrow sat leaning his head on his locked hands.

Presently another step sounded on the stairs, wavered a moment and then moved past the threshold of the study. Darrow got up and walked into the hall, which was still unlighted. In the dimness he saw Sophy Viner standing by the hall door in her hat and jacket. She stopped at sight of him, her hand on the door-bolt, and they stood for a second without speaking.

'Have you seen Effie?' she suddenly asked. 'She went out to meet you.'

'She *did* meet me, just now, in the court. She's gone on to join her brother.'

Darrow spoke as naturally as he could, but his voice sounded to his own ears like an amateur actor's in a 'light' part.

Miss Viner, without answering, drew back the bolt. He watched her in silence as the door swung open; then he said: 'She has her nurse with her. She won't be long.'

She stood irresolute, and he added: 'I was writing in there – won't you come and have a little talk? Every one's out.'

The last words struck him as not well-chosen, but there was no time to choose. She paused a second longer and then crossed the threshold of the study. At luncheon she had sat with her back to the window, and beyond noting that she had grown a little thinner, and had less colour and vivacity, he had seen no change in her; but now, as the lamplight fell on her face, its whiteness startled him.

'Poor thing . . . poor thing . . . what in heaven's name can she suppose?' he wondered.

'Do sit down – I want to talk to you,' he said and pushed a chair toward her.

She did not seem to see it, or, if she did, she deliberately chose another seat. He came back to his own chair and leaned his elbows on the blotter. She faced him from the farther side of the table.

'You promised to let me hear from you now and then,' he began awkwardly, and with a sharp sense of his awkwardness.

A faint smile made her face more tragic. 'Did I? There was nothing to tell. I've had no history – like the happy countries . . .'

He waited a moment before asking: 'You *are* happy here?'

'– I *was*,' she said with a faint emphasis.

'Why do you say "was"? You're surely not thinking of going? There can't be kinder people anywhere.' Darrow hardly knew what he was saying; but her answer came to him with deadly definiteness.

'I suppose it depends on you whether I go or stay.'

'On me?' He stared at her across Owen's scattered papers. 'Good God! What can you think of me, to say that?'

The mockery of the question flashed back at him from her wretched face. She stood up, wandered away, and leaned an instant in the darkening window-frame. From there she turned to fling back at him: 'Don't imagine I'm the least bit sorry for anything!'

He steadied his elbows on the table and hid his face in his hands. It was harder, oh, damnably harder, than he had expected! Arguments, expedients, palliations, evasions, all seemed to be slipping away from him: he was left face to face with the mere graceless fact of his inferiority. He lifted his head to ask at random: 'You've been here, then, ever since –?'

'Since June; yes. It turned out that the Farlows were hunting for me – all the while – for *this*.'

She stood facing him, her back to the window, evidently impatient to be gone, yet with something still to say, or that she expected to hear him say. The sense of her expectancy benumbed him. What in heaven's name could he say to her that was not an offence or a mockery?

'Your idea of the theatre – you gave that up at once, then?'

'Oh, the theatre!' She gave a little laugh. 'I couldn't wait for the theatre. I had to take the first thing that offered; I took this.'

He pushed on haltingly: 'I'm glad – extremely glad – you're happy here . . . I'd counted on your letting me know if there was anything I could do . . . The theatre, now – if you still regret it – if you're not contented here . . . I know people in that line in London – I'm certain I can manage it for you when I get back –'

She moved up to the table and leaned over it to ask, in a voice that was hardly above a whisper: 'Then you *do* want me to leave? Is that it?'

He dropped his arms with a groan. 'Good heavens! How can you think such things? At the time, you know, I begged you to let me do what I could, but you wouldn't hear of it . . . and ever since I've been wanting to be of use – to do something, anything, to help you . . .'

She heard him through, motionless, without a quiver of the clasped hands she rested on the edge of the table.

'If you want to help me, then – you can help me to stay here,' she brought out with low-toned intensity.

Through the stillness of the pause which followed, the bray of a motor-horn sounded far down the drive. Instantly she turned, with a last white look at him, and fled from the room and up the stairs. He stood motionless, benumbed by the shock of her last words. She was *afraid*, then – afraid of him – sick with fear of him! The discovery beat him down to a lower depth . . .

The motor-horn sounded again, close at hand, and he turned and went up to his room. His letter-writing was a sufficient pretext for not immediately joining the party about the tea-table, and he wanted to be alone and try to put a little order into his tumultuous thinking.

Upstairs, the room held out the intimate welcome of its lamp and fire. Everything in it exhaled the same sense of peace and stability which, two evenings before, had lulled him to complacent meditation. His armchair again invited him from the hearth, but he was too agitated to sit still, and with sunk head and hands clasped behind his back he began to wander up and down the room.

His five minutes with Sophy Viner had flashed strange lights into the shadowy corners of his consciousness. The girl's absolute candour, her hard ardent honesty, was for the moment the vividest point in his thoughts. He wondered anew, as he had wondered before, at the way in which the harsh discipline of life had stripped her of false sentiment without laying the least touch on her pride. When they had parted, five months before, she had quietly but decidedly rejected all his offers of help, even to the suggestion of his trying to further her theatrical aims: she had made it clear that she wished their brief alliance to leave no trace on their lives save that of its own smiling memory. But now that they were unexpectedly confronted in a situation which seemed, to her terrified fancy, to put her at his mercy, her first impulse was to defend her right to the place she had won, and to learn as quickly as possible if he meant to dispute it. While he had pictured her as shrinking away from him in a tremor of self-effacement she had watched his movements, made sure of her opportunity, and come straight down to 'have it out' with him. He was so struck by the frankness and energy of the proceeding that for a moment he lost sight of the view of his own character implied in it.

'Poor thing . . . poor thing!' he could only go on saying; and with the repetition of the words the picture of himself as she must see him pitiably took shape again.

He understood then, for the first time, how vague, in comparison with hers, had been his own vision of the part he had played in the brief episode of their relation. The incident had left in him a sense of exasperation and self-contempt, but that, as he now perceived, was chiefly, if not altogether, as it bore on his preconceived ideal of his attitude toward another woman. He had fallen below his own standard of sentimental loyalty, and if he thought of Sophy Viner it was mainly as the chance instrument of his lapse. These considerations were not agreeable to his pride, but they were forced on him by the example of her valiant common-sense. If he had cut a sorry figure in the business, he owed it to her not to close his eyes to the fact any longer . . .

But when he opened them, what did he see? The situation, detestable at best, would yet have been relatively simple if protecting Sophy Viner had been the only duty involved in it. The fact that that duty was paramount did not do away with the contingent obligations. It was Darrow's instinct, in difficult moments, to go straight to the bottom of the difficulty; but he had never before had to take so dark a dive as this, and for the minute he shivered on the brink . . . Well, his first duty, at any rate, was to the girl: he must let her see that he meant to fulfil it to the last jot, and then try to find out how to square the fulfilment with the other problems already in his path . . .

16

In the oak room he found Mrs Leath, her mother-in-law and Effie. The group, as he came toward it down the long drawing-rooms, composed itself prettily about the tea-table. The lamps and the fire crossed their gleams on silver and porcelain, on the bright haze of Effie's hair and on the whiteness of Anna's forehead, as she leaned back in her chair behind the tea-urn.

She did not move at Darrow's approach, but lifted to him a deep gaze of peace and confidence. The look seemed to throw about him the spell of a divine security: he felt the joy of a convalescent suddenly waking to find the sunlight on his face.

Madame de Chantelle, across her knitting, discoursed of their afternoon's excursion, with occasional pauses induced by the hypnotic effect of the fresh air; and Effie, kneeling on the hearth, softly but insistently sought to implant in her terrier's mind some notion of the relation between a vertical attitude and sugar.

Darrow took a chair behind the little girl, so that he might look across at her mother. It was almost a necessity for him, at the moment, to let his eyes rest on Anna's face, and to meet, now and then, the proud shyness of her gaze.

Madame de Chantelle presently enquired what had become of Owen, and a moment later the window behind her opened, and her grandson, gun in hand, came in from the terrace. As he stood there in the lamp-light, with dead leaves and bits of bramble clinging to his mud-spattered clothes, the scent of the night about him and its chill on his pale bright face, he really had the look of a young faun strayed in from the forest.

Effie abandoned the terrier to fly to him. 'Oh, Owen, where in the world have you been? I walked miles and miles with Nurse and couldn't find you, and we met Jean and he said he didn't know where you'd gone.'

'Nobody knows where I go, or what I see when I get there – that's the beauty of it!' he laughed back at her. 'But if you're good,' he added, 'I'll tell you about it one of these days.'

'Oh, now, Owen, now! I don't really believe I'll ever be much better than I am now.'

'Let Owen have his tea first,' her mother suggested; but the young man, declining the offer, propped his gun against the wall, and, lighting a cigarette, began to pace up and down the room in a way that reminded Darrow of his own caged wanderings. Effie pursued him with her blandishments, and for a while he poured out to her a low-voiced stream of nonsense; then he sat down beside his step-mother and leaned over to help himself to tea.

'Where's Miss Viner?' he asked, as Effie climbed up on him. 'Why isn't she here to chain up this ungovernable infant?'

'Poor Miss Viner has a headache. Effie says she went to her room as soon as lessons were over, and sent word that she wouldn't be down for tea.'

'Ah,' said Owen, abruptly setting down his cup. He stood up, lit another cigarette, and wandered away to the piano in the room beyond.

From the twilight where he sat a lonely music, borne on fantastic chords, floated to the group about the tea-table. Under its influence Madame de Chantelle's meditative pauses increased in length and frequency, and Effie stretched herself on the hearth, her drowsy head against the dog. Presently her nurse appeared, and Anna rose at the same time. 'Stop a minute in my sitting-room on your way up,' she paused to say to Darrow as she went.

A few hours earlier, her request would have brought him instantly to his feet. She had given him, on the day of his arrival, an inviting glimpse of the spacious booklined room above stairs in which she had gathered together all the tokens of her personal tastes: the retreat in which, as one might fancy, Anna Leath had hidden the restless ghost of Anna Summers; and the thought of a talk with her there had been in his mind ever since. But now he sat motionless, as if spellbound by the play of Madame de Chantelle's needles and the pulsations of Owen's fitful music.

'She will want to ask me about the girl,' he repeated to himself, with a fresh sense of the insidious taint that embittered all his thoughts; the hand of the slender-columned clock on the mantel-piece had spanned a half-hour before shame at his own indecision finally drew him to his feet.

From her writing-table, where she sat over a pile of letters, Anna lifted her happy smile. The impulse to press his lips to it made him come close and draw her upward. She threw her head back, as if surprised at the abruptness of the gesture; then her face leaned to his with the slow droop of a flower. He felt again the sweep of the secret tides, and all his fears went down in them.

She sat down in the sofa-corner by the fire and he drew an arm-chair close to her. His gaze roamed peacefully about the quiet room.

'It's just like you – it *is* you,' he said, as his eyes came back to her.

'It's a good place to be alone in – I don't think I've ever before cared to talk with any one here.'

'Let's be quiet, then: it's the best way of talking.'

'Yes; but we must save it up till later. There are things I want to say to you now.'

He leaned back in his chair. 'Say them, then, and I'll listen.'

'Oh, no. I want you to tell me about Miss Viner.'

'About Miss Viner?' He summoned up a look of faint interrogation.

He thought she seemed surprised at his surprise. 'It's important, naturally,' she explained, 'that I should find out all I can about her before I leave.'

'Important on Effie's account?'

'On Effie's account – of course.'

'Of course . . . But you've every reason to be satisfied, haven't you?'

'Every apparent reason. We all like her. Effie's very fond of her, and she seems to have a delightful influence on the child. But we know so little, after all – about her antecedents, I mean, and her past history. That's why I want you to try and recall everything you heard about her when you used to see her in London.'

'Oh, on that score I'm afraid I sha'n't be of much use. As I told you, she was a mere shadow in the background of the house I saw her in – and that was four or five years ago . . .'

'When she was with a Mrs Murrett?'

'Yes; an appalling woman who runs a roaring dinner-factory that used now and then to catch me in its wheels. I escaped from them long ago; but in my time there used to be half a dozen fagged "hands" to tend the machine, and Miss Viner was one of them. I'm glad she's out of it, poor girl!'

'Then you never really saw anything of her there?'

'I never had the chance. Mrs Murrett discouraged any competition on the part of her subordinates.'

'Especially such pretty ones, I suppose?' Darrow made no comment, and she continued: 'And Mrs Murrett's own opinion – if she'd offered you one – probably wouldn't have been of much value?'

'Only in so far as her disapproval would, on general principles, have been a good mark for Miss Viner. But surely,' he went on after a pause, 'you could have found out about her from the people through whom you first heard of her?'

Anna smiled. 'Oh, we heard of her through Adelaide Painter –'; and in reply to his glance of interrogation she explained that the lady in question was a spinster of South Braintree, Massachusetts, who, having come to Paris some thirty years earlier, to nurse a brother through an illness, had ever since protestingly and provisionally camped there in a state of contemptuous protestation oddly manifested by her never taking the slip-covers off her drawing-room chairs. Her long residence on Gallic soil had not mitigated her hostility toward the creed and customs of the race, but though she always referred to the Catholic Church as the Scarlet Woman and took the darkest views of French private life, Madame de Chantelle placed great reliance on her judgment and experience, and in every domestic crisis the irreducible Adelaide was immediatcly summoned to Givré.

'It's all the odder because my mother-in-law, since her second marriage, has lived so much in the country that she's practically lost sight of all her other American friends. Besides which, you can see how completely she has identified herself with Monsieur de Chantelle's nationality and adopted French habits and prejudices. Yet when anything goes wrong she always sends for Adelaide Painter, who's more American than the Stars and Stripes, and might have left South Braintree yesterday, if she hadn't, rather, brought it over with her in her trunk.'

Darrow laughed. 'Well, then, if South Braintree vouches for Miss Viner –'

'Oh, but only indirectly. When we had that odious adventure with Mademoiselle Grumeau, who'd been so highly recommended by Monsieur de Chantelle's aunt, the Chanoinesse, Adelaide was of course sent for, and she said at once: "I'm not the least bit surprised. I've always told you that what you wanted for Effie was a sweet American girl, and not one of these nasty foreigners." Unluckily she couldn't, at the moment, put her hand on a sweet American; but she presently heard of Miss Viner through the Farlows, an excellent couple who live in the Quartier Latin and write about French life for the American papers. I was only too thankful to find anyone who was vouched for by decent people; and so far I've had no cause to regret my choice. But I know, after all, very little about Miss Viner; and there are all kinds of reasons why I want, as soon as possible, to find out more – to find out all I can.'

'Since you've got to leave Effie I understand your feeling in that way. But is there, in such a case, any recommendation worth half as much as your own direct experience?'

'No; and it's been so favourable that I was ready to accept it as conclusive. Only, naturally, when I found you'd known her in London I was in hopes you'd give me some more specific reasons for liking her as much as I do.'

'I'm afraid I can give you nothing more specific than my general vague impression that she seems very plucky and extremely nice.'

'You don't, at any rate, know anything specific to the contrary?'

'To the contrary? How should I? I'm not conscious of ever having heard any one say two words about her. I only infer that she must have pluck and character to have stuck it out so long at Mrs Murrett's.'

'Yes, poor thing! She has pluck, certainly; and pride, too; which must have made it all the harder.' Anna rose to her feet. 'You don't know how glad I am that your impression's on the whole so good. I particularly wanted you to like her.'

He drew her to him with a smile. 'On that condition I'm prepared to love even Adelaide Painter.'

'I almost hope you won't have the chance to – poor Adelaide! Her appearance here always coincides with a catastrophe.'

'Oh, then I must manage to meet her elsewhere.' He held Anna closer, saying to himself, as he smoothed back the hair from her forehead: 'What does anything matter but just *this*? – Must I go now?' he added aloud.

She answered absently: 'It must be time to dress'; then she drew back a little and laid her hands on his shoulders. 'My love – oh, my dear love!' she said.

It came to him that they were the first words of endearment he had heard her speak, and their rareness gave them a magic quality of reassurance, as though no danger could strike through such a shield.

A knock on the door made them draw apart. Anna lifted her hand to her hair and Darrow stooped to examine a photograph of Effie on the writing-table.

'Come in!' Anna said.

The door opened and Sophy Viner entered. Seeing Darrow, she drew back.

'Do come in, Miss Viner,' Anna repeated, looking at her kindly.

The girl, a quick red in her cheeks, still hesitated on the threshold.

'I'm so sorry; but Effie has mislaid her Latin grammar, and I thought she might have left it here. I need it to prepare for tomor-row's lesson.'

'Is this it?' Darrow asked, picking up a book from the table.

'Oh, thank you!'

He held it out to her and she took it and moved to the door.

'Wait a minute, please, Miss Viner,' Anna said; and as the girl turned back, she went on with her quiet smile: 'Effie told us you'd gone to your room with a headache. You mustn't sit up over tomorrow's lessons if you don't feel well.'

Sophy's blush deepened. 'But you see I have to. Latin's one of my weak points, and there's generally only one page of this book between me and Effie.' She threw the words off with a half-ironic smile. 'Do excuse my disturbing you,' she added.

'You didn't disturb me,' Anna answered. Darrow perceived that she was looking intently at the girl, as though struck by something tense and tremulous in her face, her voice, her whole mien and attitude. 'You *do* look tired. You'd much better go straight to bed. Effie won't be sorry to skip her Latin.'

'Thank you – but I'm really all right,' murmured Sophy Viner. Her glance, making a swift circuit of the room, dwelt for an appreciable instant on the intimate propinquity of armchair and sofa-corner; then she turned back to the door.

BOOK THREE

17

At dinner that evening Madame de Chantelle's slender monologue was thrown out over gulfs of silence. Owen was still in the same state of moody abstraction as when Darrow had left him at the piano; and even Anna's face, to her friend's vigilant eye, revealed not, perhaps, a personal preoccupation, but a vague sense of impending disturbance.

She smiled, she bore a part in the talk, her eyes dwelt on Darrow's with their usual deep reliance; but beneath the surface of her serenity his tense perceptions detected a hidden stir.

He was sufficiently self-possessed to tell himself that it was doubtless due to causes with which he was not directly concerned. He knew the question of Owen's marriage was soon to be raised, and the abrupt alteration in the young man's mood made it seem probable that he was himself the centre of the atmospheric disturbance. For a moment it occurred to Darrow that Anna might have employed her afternoon in preparing Madame de Chantelle for her grandson's impending announcement; but a glance at the elder lady's unclouded brow showed that he must seek elsewhere the clue to Owen's taciturnity and his step-mother's concern. Possibly Anna had found reason to change her own attitude in the matter, and had made the change known to Owen. But this, again, was negatived by the fact that, during the afternoon's shooting, young Leath had been in a mood of almost extravagant expansiveness, and that, from the moment of his late return to the house till just before dinner, there had been, to Darrow's certain knowledge, no possibility of a private talk between himself and his step-mother.

This obscured, if it narrowed, the field of conjecture; and Darrow's gropings threw him back on the conclusion that he was probably reading too much significance into the moods of a lad he hardly knew, and who had been described to him as subject to sudden changes of humour. As to Anna's fancied perturbation, it might simply be due to the fact that she had decided to plead Owen's cause the next day, and had perhaps already had a glimpse of the difficulties awaiting her. But Darrow knew that he was too deep in his own perplexities to judge the mental state of those about him. It might be, after all, that the variations he felt in the currents of communication were caused by his own inward tremor.

Such, at any rate, was the conclusion he had reached when, shortly after the two ladies left the drawing-room, he bade Owen good-night and went up to his room. Ever since the rapid self-colloquy which had followed on his first sight of Sophy Viner, he had known there were other questions to be faced behind the one immediately confronting him. On the score of that one, at least, his mind, if not easy, was relieved. He had done what was possible to reassure the girl, and she had apparently recognized the sincerity of his intention. He had patched up as decent a conclusion as he could to an incident that should obviously have had no sequel; but he had known all along that with the securing of Miss Viner's peace of mind only a part of his obligation was discharged, and that with that part his remaining duty was in conflict. It had been his first business to convince the girl that their secret was safe with him; but it was far from easy to square this with the equally urgent obligation of safe-guarding Anna's responsibility toward her child. Darrow was not much afraid of accidental disclosures. Both he and Sophy Viner had too much at stake not to be on their guard. The fear that beset him was of another kind, and had a profounder source. He wanted to do all he could for the girl, but the fact of having had to urge Anna to confide Effie to her was peculiarly repugnant to him. His own ideas about Sophy Viner were too mixed and indeterminate for him not to feel the risk of such an experiment; yet he found himself in the intolerable position of appearing to press it on the woman he desired above all others to protect . . .

Till late in the night his thoughts revolved in a turmoil of indecision. His pride was humbled by the discrepancy between what Sophy Viner had been to him and what he had thought of her. This discrepancy, which at the time had seemed to simplify the incident, now turned out to be its most galling complication. The bare truth, indeed, was that he had hardly thought of her at all, either at the time or since, and that he was ashamed to base his judgment of her on his meagre memory of their adventure.

The essential cheapness of the whole affair – as far as his share in it was concerned – came home to him with humiliating distinctness. He would have liked to be able to feel that, at the time at least, he had staked something more on it, and had somehow, in the sequel, had a more palpable loss to show. But the plain fact was that he hadn't spent a penny on it; which was no doubt the reason of the prodigious score it had since been rolling up. At any rate, beat about the case as he would, it was clear that he owed it to Anna – and incidentally to his own peace of mind – to find some way of securing Sophy Viner's future without leaving her installed at Givré when he and his wife should depart for their new post.

The night brought no aid to the solving of this problem; but it gave him, at any rate, the clear conviction that no time was to be lost. His first step must be to obtain from Miss Viner the chance of another and calmer talk; and he resolved to seek it at the earliest hour.

He had gathered that Effie's lessons were preceded by an early scamper in the park, and conjecturing that her governess might be with her he betook himself the next morning to the terrace, whence he wandered on to the gardens and the walks beyond.

The atmosphere was still and pale. The muffled sunlight gleamed like gold tissue through grey gauze, and the beech alleys tapered away to a blue haze blent of sky and forest. It was one of those elusive days when the familiar forms of things seem about to dissolve in a prismatic shimmer.

The stillness was presently broken by joyful barks, and Darrow, tracking the sound, overtook Effie flying down one of the long alleys at the head of her pack. Beyond her he saw Miss Viner seated near the stone-rimmed basin beside which he and Anna had paused on their first walk to the river.

The girl, coming forward at his approach, returned his greeting almost gaily. His first glance showed him that she had regained her composure, and the change in her appearance gave him the measure of her fears. For the first time he saw in her again the sidelong grace that had charmed his eyes in Paris; but he saw it now as in a painted picture.

THE REEF

'Shall we sit down a minute?' he asked, as Effie trotted off.

The girl looked away from him. 'I'm afraid there's not much time; we must be back at lessons at half-past nine.'

'But it's barely ten minutes past. Let's at least walk a little way toward the river.'

She glanced down the long walk ahead of them and then back in the direction of the house. 'If you like,' she said in a low voice, with one of her quick fluctuations of colour; but instead of taking the way he proposed she turned toward a narrow path which branched off obliquely through the trees.

Darrow was struck, and vaguely troubled, by the change in her look and tone. There was in them an undefinable appeal, whether for help or forbearance he could not tell. Then it occurred to him that there might have been something misleading in his so pointedly seeking her, and he felt a momentary constraint. To ease it he made an abrupt dash at the truth.

'I came out to look for you because our talk of yesterday was so unsatisfactory. I want to hear more about you – about your plans and prospects. I've been wondering ever since why you've so completely given up the theatre.'

Her face instantly sharpened to distrust. 'I had to live,' she said in an off-hand tone.

'I understand perfectly that you should like it here – for a time.' His glance strayed down the gold-roofed windings ahead of them. 'It's delightful: you couldn't be better placed. Only I wonder a little at your having so completely given up any idea of a different future.'

She waited for a moment before answering: 'I suppose I'm less restless than I used to be.'

'It's certainly natural that you should be less restless here than at Mrs Murrett's; yet somehow I don't seem to see you permanently given up to forming the young.'

'What – exactly – *do* you seem to see me permanently given up to? You know you warned me rather emphatically against the theatre.' She threw off the statement without impatience, as though they were discussing together the fate of a third person in whom both were benevolently interested.

Darrow considered his reply. 'If I did, it was because you so emphatically refused to let me help you to a start.'

166

She stopped short and faced him. 'And you think I may let you now?'

Darrow felt the blood in his cheek. He could not understand her attitude – if indeed she had consciously taken one, and her changes of tone did not merely reflect the involuntary alternations of her mood. It humbled him to perceive once more how little he had to guide him in his judgement of her. He said to himself: 'If I'd ever cared a straw for her I should know how to avoid hurting her now' – and his insensibility struck him as no better than a vulgar obtuseness. But he had a fixed purpose ahead and could only push on to it.

'I hope, at any rate, you'll listen to my reasons. There's been time, on both sides, to think them over since –' He caught himself back and hung helpless on the 'since': whatever words he chose, he seemed to stumble among reminders of their past.

She walked on beside him, her eyes on the ground. 'Then I'm to understand – definitely – that you *do* renew your offer?' she asked.

'With all my heart! If you'll only let me –'

She raised a hand, as though to check him. 'It's extremely friendly of you – I *do* believe you mean it as a friend – but I don't quite understand why, finding me, as you say, so well placed here, you should show more anxiety about my future than at a time when I was actually, and rather desperately, adrift.'

'Oh, no, not more!'

'If you show any at all, it must, at any rate, be for different reasons. – In fact, it can only be,' she went on, with one of her disconcerting flashes of astuteness, 'for one of two reasons; either because you feel you ought to help me, or because, for some reason, you think you owe it to Mrs Leath to let her know what you know of me.'

Darrow stood still in the path. Behind him he heard Effie's call, and at the child's voice he saw Sophy turn her head with the alertness of one who is obscurely on the watch. The look was so fugitive that he could not have said wherein it differed from her normal professional air of having her pupil on her mind.

Effie sprang past them, and Darrow took up the girl's challenge.

'What you suggest about Mrs Leath is hardly worth answering. As to my reasons for wanting to help you, a good deal depends on the words one uses to define rather indefinite things. It's true enough that I want to help you; but the wish isn't due to ... to any past kindness on your part, but simply to my own interest in you. Why not put it that our friendship gives me the right to intervene for what I believe to be your benefit?'

She took a few hesitating steps and then paused again. Darrow noticed that she had grown pale and that there were rings of shade about her eyes.

'You've known Mrs Leath a long time?' she asked him suddenly.

He paused with a sense of approaching peril. 'A long time – yes.'

'She told me you were friends – great friends.'

'Yes,' he admitted, 'we're great friends.'

'Then you might naturally feel yourself justified in telling her that you don't think I'm the right person for Effie.' He uttered a sound of protest, but she disregarded it. 'I don't say you'd *like* to do it. You wouldn't: you'd hate it. And the natural alternative would be to try to persuade me that I'd be better off somewhere else than here. But supposing that failed, and you saw I was determined to stay? *Then* you might think it your duty to tell Mrs Leath.'

She laid the case before him with a cold lucidity. 'I should, in your place, I believe,' she ended with a little laugh.

'I shouldn't feel justified in telling her, behind your back, if I thought you unsuited for the place; but I should certainly feel justified,' he rejoined after a pause, 'in telling *you* if I thought the place unsuited to you.'

'And that's what you're trying to tell me now?'

'Yes; but not for the reasons you imagine.'

'What, then, are your reasons, if you please?'

'I've already implied them in advising you not to give up all idea of the theatre. You're too various, too gifted, too personal, to tie yourself down, at your age, to the dismal drudgery of teaching.'

'And is *that* what you've told Mrs Leath?'

She rushed the question out at him as if she expected to trip him up over it. He was moved by the simplicity of the stratagem.

'I've told her exactly nothing,' he replied.

'And what – exactly – do you mean by "nothing"? You and she were talking about me when I came into her sitting-room yesterday.'

Darrow felt his blood rise at the thrust.

'I've told her, simply, that I'd seen you once or twice at Mrs Murrett's.'

'And not that you've ever seen me since?'

'And not that I've ever seen you since . . .'

'And she believes you – she completely believes you?'

He uttered a protesting exclamation, and his flush reflected itself in the girl's cheek.

'Oh, I beg your pardon! I didn't mean to ask you that.' She halted, and again cast a rapid glance behind and ahead of her. Then she held out her hand. 'Well, then, thank you – and let me relieve your fears. I shan't be Effie's governess much longer.'

At the announcement, Darrow tried to merge his look of relief into the expression of friendly interest with which he grasped her hand. 'You really do agree with me, then? And you'll give me a chance to talk things over with you?'

She shook her head with a faint smile. 'I'm not thinking of the stage. I've had another offer: that's all.'

The relief was hardly less great. After all, his personal responsibility ceased with her departure from Givré.

'You'll tell me about that, then – won't you?'

Her smile flickered up. 'Oh, you'll hear about it soon . . . I must catch Effie now and drag her back to the blackboard.'

She walked on for a few yards, and then paused again and confronted him. 'I've been odious to you – and not quite honest,' she broke out suddenly.

'Not quite honest?' he repeated, caught in a fresh wave of wonder.

'I mean, in seeming not to trust you. It's come over me again as we talked that, at heart, I've always *known* I could . . .'

Her colour rose in a bright wave, and her eyes clung to his for a swift instant of reminder and appeal. For the same space of time the past surged up in him confusedly; then a veil dropped between them.

'Here's Effie now!' she exclaimed.

He turned and saw the little girl trotting back to them, her hand in Owen Leath's.

Even through the stir of his subsiding excitement Darrow was at once aware of the change effected by the young man's approach. For a moment Sophy Viner's cheeks burned redder; then they faded to the paleness of white petals. She lost, however, nothing of the bright bravery which it was her way to turn on the unexpected. Perhaps no one less familiar with her face than Darrow would have discerned the tension of the smile she transferred from himself to Owen Leath, or have remarked that her eyes had hardened from misty grey to a shining darkness. But her observer was less struck by this than by the corresponding change in Owen Leath. The latter, when he came in sight, had been laughing and talking unconcernedly with Effie; but as his eye fell on Miss Viner his expression altered as suddenly as hers.

The change, for Darrow, was less definable; but, perhaps for that reason, it struck him as more sharply significant. Only – just what did it signify? Owen, like Sophy Viner, had the kind of face which seems less the stage on which emotions move than the very stuff they work in. In moments of excitement his odd irregular features seemed to grow fluid, to unmake and remake themselves like the shadows of clouds on a stream. Darrow, through the rapid flight of the shadows, could not seize on any specific indication of feeling: he merely perceived that the young man was unaccountably surprised at finding him with Miss Viner, and that the extent of his surprise might cover all manner of implications.

Darrow's first idea was that Owen, if he suspected that the conversation was not the result of an accidental encounter, might wonder at his step-mother's suitor being engaged, at such an hour, in private talk with her little girl's governess. The thought was so disturbing that, as the three turned back to the house, he was on the point of saying to Owen: 'I came out to look for your mother.' But, in the contingency he feared, even so simple a phrase might seem like an awkward attempt at explanation; and he walked on in silence at Miss Viner's side. Presently he was struck by the fact that Owen Leath and the girl were silent also; and this gave a new turn to his thoughts. Silence may be as variously shaded as speech; and that which enfolded Darrow and his two companions seemed to his watchful perceptions to be quivering with cross-threads of communication. At first he was aware only of those that centred in his own troubled consciousness; then it occurred to him that an equal activity of intercourse was going on outside of it. Something was in fact passing mutely and rapidly between young Leath and Sophy Viner; but what it was, and whither it tended, Darrow, when they reached the house, was but just beginning to divine . . .

18

Anna Leath, from the terrace, watched the return of the little group.

She looked down on them, as they advanced across the garden, from the serene height of her unassailable happiness. There they were, coming toward her in the mild morning light, her child, her step-son, her promised husband: the three beings who filled her life. She smiled a little at the happy picture they presented, Effie's gambols encircling it in a moving frame within which the two men came slowly forward in the silence of friendly understanding. It seemed part of the deep intimacy of the scene that they should not be talking to each other, and it did not till afterward strike her as odd that neither of them apparently felt it necessary to address a word to Sophy Viner.

Anna herself, at the moment, was floating in the mid-current of felicity, on a tide so bright and buoyant that she seemed to be one with its warm waves. The first rush of bliss had stunned and dazzled her; but now that, each morning, she woke to the calm certainty of its recurrence, she was growing used to the sense of security it gave.

'I feel as if I could trust my happiness to carry me; as if it had grown out of me like wings.' So she phrased it to Darrow, as, later in the morning, they paced the garden-paths together. His answering look gave her the same assurance of safety. The evening before he had seemed preoccupied, and the shadow of his mood had faintly encroached on the great golden orb of their blessedness; but now it was uneclipsed again, and hung above them high and bright as the sun at noon.

Upstairs in her sitting-room, that afternoon, she was thinking of these things. The morning mists had turned to rain, compelling the postponement of an excursion in which the whole party were to have joined. Effie, with her governess, had been despatched in the motor to do some shopping at Francheuil; and Anna had promised Darrow to join him, later in the afternoon, for a quick walk in the rain.

He had gone to his room after luncheon to get some belated letters off his conscience; and when he had left her she had continued to sit in the same place, her hands crossed on her knees, her head slightly bent, in an attitude of brooding retrospection. As she looked back at her past life, it seemed to her to have consisted of one ceaseless effort to pack into each hour enough to fill out its slack folds; but now each moment was like a miser's bag stretched to bursting with pure gold.

She was roused by the sound of Owen's step in the gallery outside her room. It paused at her door and in answer to his knock she called out 'Come in!'

As the door closed behind him she was struck by his look of pale excitement, and an impulse of compunction made her say: 'You've come to ask me why I haven't spoken to your grandmother!'

He sent about him a glance vaguely reminding her of the strange look with which Sophy Viner had swept the room the night before; then his brilliant eyes came back to her.

'I've spoken to her myself,' he said.

Anna started up, incredulous.

'You've spoken to her? When?'

'Just now. I left her to come here.'

Anna's first feeling was one of annoyance. There was really something comically incongruous in this boyish surrender to impulse on the part of a young man so eager to assume the responsibilities of life. She looked at him with a faintly veiled amusement.

'You asked me to help you and I promised you I would. It was hardly worth while to work out such an elaborate plan of action if you intended to take the matter out of my hands without telling me.'

'Oh, don't take that tone with me!' he broke out, almost angrily.

'That tone? What tone?' She stared at his quivering face. 'I might,' she pursued, still half-laughing, 'more properly make that request of *you*!'

Owen reddened and his vehemence suddenly subsided.

'I meant that I *had* to speak – that's all. You don't give me a chance to explain . . .'

She looked at him gently, wondering a little at her own impatience.

'Owen! Don't I always want to give you every chance? It's because I *do* that I wanted to talk to your grandmother first – that I was waiting and watching for the right moment . . .'

'The right moment? So was I. That's why I've spoken.' His voice rose again and took the sharp edge it had in moments of high pressure.

His step-mother turned away and seated herself in her sofa-corner. 'Oh, my dear, it's not a privilege to quarrel over! You've taken a load off my shoulders. Sit down and tell me all about it.'

He stood before her, irresolute. 'I can't sit down,' he said.

'Walk about, then. Only tell me: I'm impatient.'

His immediate response was to throw himself into the armchair at her side, where he lounged for a moment without speaking, his legs stretched out, his arms locked behind his thrown-back head. Anna, her eyes on his face, waited quietly for him to speak.

'Well – of course it was just what one expected.'

'She takes it so badly, you mean?'

'All the heavy batteries were brought up: my father, Givré, Monsieur de Chantelle, the throne and the altar. Even my poor mother was dragged out of oblivion and armed with imaginary protests.'

Anna sighed out her sympathy. 'Well – you were prepared for all that?'

'I thought I was, till I began to hear her say it. Then it sounded so incredibly silly that I told her so.'

'Oh, Owen – Owen!'

'Yes: I know. I was a fool; but I couldn't help it.'

'And you've mortally offended her, I suppose? That's exactly what I wanted to prevent.' She laid a hand on his shoulder. 'You tiresome boy, not to wait and let me speak for you!'

He moved slightly away, so that her hand slipped from its place. 'You don't understand,' he said, frowning.

'I don't see how I can, till you explain. If you thought the time had come to tell your grandmother, why not have asked me to do it? I had my reasons for waiting; but if you'd told me to speak I should have done so, naturally.'

He evaded her appeal by a sudden turn. 'What *were* your reasons for waiting?'

Anna did not immediately answer. Her step-son's eyes were on her face, and under his gaze she felt a faint disquietude.

'I was feeling my way . . . I wanted to be absolutely sure . . .'

'Absolutely sure of what?'

She delayed again for a just perceptible instant. 'Why, simply of *our* side of the case.'

'But you told me you were, the other day, when we talked it over before they came back from Ouchy.'

'Oh, my dear – if you think that, in such a complicated matter, every day, every hour, doesn't more or less modify one's surest sureness!'

'That's just what I'm driving at. I want to know what has modified yours.'

She made a slight gesture of impatience. 'What does it matter, now the thing's done? I don't know that I could give any clear reason . . .'

He got to his feet and stood looking down on her with a tormented brow. 'But it's absolutely necessary that you should.'

At his tone her impatience flared up. 'It's not necessary that I should give you any explanation whatever, since you've taken the matter out of my hands. All I can say is that I was trying to help you: that no other thought ever entered my mind.' She paused a moment and then added: 'If you doubted it, you were right to do what you've done.'

'Oh, I never doubted *you*!' he retorted, with a fugitive stress on the pronoun. His face had cleared to its old look of trust. 'Don't be offended if I've seemed to,' he went on. 'I can't quite explain myself, either . . . it's all a kind of tangle, isn't it? That's why I thought I'd better speak at once; or rather why I didn't think at all, but just suddenly blurted the thing out –'

Anna gave him back his look of conciliation. 'Well, the how and why don't much matter now. The point is how to deal with your grandmother. You've not told me what she means to do.'

'Oh, she means to send for Adelaide Painter.'

The name drew a faint note of mirth from him and relaxed both their faces to a smile.

'Perhaps,' Anna added, 'it's really the best thing for us all.'

Owen shrugged his shoulders. 'It's too preposterous and humiliating. Dragging that woman into our secrets –!'

'This could hardly be a secret much longer.'

He had moved to the hearth, where he stood pushing about the small ornaments on the mantelshelf; but at her answer he turned back to her.

'You haven't, of course, spoken of it to any one?'

'No; but I intend to now.'

She paused for his reply, and as it did not come she continued: 'If Adelaide Painter's to be told there's no possible reason why I shouldn't tell Mr Darrow.'

Owen abruptly set down the little statuette between his fingers. 'None whatever: I want every one to know.'

She smiled a little at his over-emphasis, and was about to meet it with a word of banter when he continued, facing her: 'You haven't, as yet, said a word to him?'

'I've told him nothing, except what the discussion of our own plans – his and mine – obliged me to: that you were thinking of marrying, and that I wasn't willing to leave France till I'd done what I could to see you through.'

At her first words the colour had rushed to his forehead; but as she continued she saw his face compose itself and his blood subside.

'You're a brick, my dear!' he exclaimed.

'You had my word, you know.'

'Yes; yes – I know.' His face had clouded again. 'And that's all – positively all – you've ever said to him?'

'Positively all. But why do you ask?'

He had a moment's embarrassed hesitation. 'It was understood, wasn't it, that my grandmother was to be the first to know?'

'Well – and so she has been, hasn't she, since you've told her?'

He turned back to his restless shifting of the knick-knacks.

'And you're sure that nothing you've said to Darrow could possibly have given him a hint –?'

'Nothing I've said to him – certainly.'

He swung about on her. 'Why do you put it in that way?'

'In what way?'

'Why – as if you thought some one else might have spoken . . .'

'Some one else? Who else?' She rose to her feet. 'What on earth, my dear boy, can you be driving at?'

'I'm trying to find out whether you think he knows anything definite.'

'Why should I think so? Do *you*?'

'I don't know. I want to find out.'

She laughed at his obstinate insistence. 'To test my veracity, I suppose?' At the sound of a step in the gallery she added: 'Here he is – you can ask him yourself.'

She met Darrow's knock with an invitation to enter, and he came into the room and paused between herself and Owen. She was struck, as he stood there, by the contrast between his happy careless good-looks and her step-son's frowning agitation.

Darrow met her eyes with a smile. 'Am I too soon? Or is our walk given up?'

'No; I was just going to get ready.' She continued to linger between the two, looking slowly from one to the other. 'But there's something we want to tell you first: Owen is engaged to Miss Viner.'

The sense of an indefinable interrogation in Owen's mind made her, as she spoke, fix her eyes steadily on Darrow.

He had paused just opposite the window, so that, even in the rainy afternoon light, his face was clearly open to her scrutiny. For a second, immense surprise was alone visible on it: so visible that she half turned to her step-son, with a faint smile for his refuted suspicions. Why, she wondered, should Owen have thought that Darrow had already guessed his secret, and what, after all, could be so disturbing to him in this not improbable contingency? At any rate, his doubt must have been dispelled: there was nothing feigned about Darrow's astonishment. When her eyes turned back to him he was already crossing to Owen with outstretched hand, and she had, through an unaccountable faint flutter of misgiving, a mere confused sense of their exchanging the customary phrases. Her next perception was of Owen's tranquillized look, and of his smiling return of Darrow's congratulatory grasp. She had the eerie feeling of having been overswept by a shadow which there had been no cloud to cast . . .

A moment later Owen had left the room and she and Darrow were alone. He had turned away to the window and stood staring out into the down-pour.

'You're surprised at Owen's news?' she asked.

'Yes: I am surprised,' he answered.

'You hadn't thought of its being Miss Viner?'

'Why should I have thought of Miss Viner?'

'You see now why I wanted so much to find out what you knew about her.' He made no comment, and she pursued: 'Now that you *do* know it's she, if there's anything –'

He moved back into the room and went up to her. His face was serious, with a slight shade of annoyance. 'What on earth should there be? As I told you, I've never in my life heard any one say two words about Miss Viner.'

Anna made no answer and they continued to face each other without moving. For the moment she had ceased to think about Sophy Viner and Owen: the only thought in her mind was that Darrow was alone with her, close to her, and that, for the first time, their hands and lips had not met.

He glanced back doubtfully at the window. 'It's pouring. Perhaps you'd rather not go out?'

She hesitated, as if waiting for him to urge her. 'I suppose I'd better not. I ought to go at once to my mother-in-law – Owen's just been telling her,' she said.

'Ah.' Darrow hazarded a smile. 'That accounts for my having, on my way up, heard some one telephoning for Miss Painter!'

At the allusion they laughed together, vaguely, and Anna moved toward the door. He held it open for her and followed her out.

19

He left her at the door of Madame de Chantelle's sitting-room, and plunged out alone into the rain.

The wind flung about the stripped tree-tops of the avenue and dashed the stinging streams into his face. He walked to the gate and then turned into the high-road and strode along in the open, buffeted by slanting gusts. The evenly ridged fields were a blurred waste of mud, and the russet coverts which he and Owen had shot through the day before shivered desolately against a driving sky.

Darrow walked on and on, indifferent to the direction he was taking. His thoughts were tossing like the tree-tops. Anna's announcement had not come to him as a complete surprise: that morning, as he strolled back to the house with Owen Leath and Miss Viner, he had had a momentary intuition of the truth. But it had been no more than an intuition, the merest faint cloud-puff of surmise; and now it was an attested fact, darkening over the whole sky.

In respect of his own attitude, he saw at once that the discovery made no appreciable change. If he had been bound to silence before, he was no less bound to it now; the only difference lay in the fact that what he had just learned had rendered his bondage more intolerable. Hitherto he had felt for Sophy Viner's defenceless state a sympathy profoundly tinged with compunction. But now he was half-conscious of an obscure indignation against her. Superior as he had fancied himself to ready-made judgments, he was aware of cherishing the common doubt as to the disinterestedness of the woman who tries to rise above her past. No wonder she had been sick with fear on meeting him! It was in his power to do her more harm than he had dreamed . . .

Assuredly he did not want to harm her; but he did desperately want to prevent her marrying Owen Leath. He tried to get away from the feeling, to isolate and exteriorize it sufficiently to see what motives it was made of; but it remained a mere blind motion of his blood, the instinctive recoil from the thing that no amount of arguing can make 'straight'. His tramp, prolonged as it was, carried him no nearer to enlightenment; and after trudging through two or three sallow mudstained villages he turned about and wearily made his way back to Givré. As he walked up the black avenue, making for the lights that twinkled through its pitching branches, he had a sudden realization of his utter helplessness. He might think and combine as he would; but there was nothing, absolutely nothing, that he could do . . .

He dropped his wet coat in the vestibule and began to mount the stairs to his room. But on the landing he was overtaken by a sober-faced maid who, in tones discreetly lowered, begged him to be so kind as to step, for a moment, into the Marquise's sitting-room. Somewhat disconcerted by the summons, he followed its bearer to the door at which, a couple of hours earlier, he had taken leave of Mrs Leath. It opened to admit him to a large lamp-lit room which he immediately perceived to be empty; and the fact gave him time to note, even through his disturbance of mind, the interesting degree to which Madame de Chantelle's apartment 'dated' and completed her. Its looped and corded curtains, its purple satin upholstery, the Sèvres jardinières, the rose-wood fire-screen, the little velvet tables edged with lace and crowded with silver knick-knacks and simpering minia-tures, reconstituted an almost perfect setting for the blonde beauty of the 'sixties. Darrow wondered that Fraser Leath's filial respect should have prevailed over his aesthetic scruples to the extent of permitting such an anachronism among the eighteenth-century graces of Givré; but a moment's reflection made it clear that, to its late owner, the attitude would have seemed exactly in the traditions of the place.

Madame de Chantelle's emergence from an inner room snatched Darrow from these irrelevant musings. She was already beaded and bugled for the evening, and, save for a slight pinkness of the eye-lids, her elaborate appearance revealed no mark of agitation; but Darrow noticed that, in recognition of the solemnity of the occasion, she pinched a lace handkerchief between her thumb and forefinger.

She plunged at once into the centre of the difficulty, appealing to him, in the name of all the Everards, to descend there with her to the rescue of her darling. She wasn't, she was sure, addressing her- self in vain to one whose person, whose 'tone', whose traditions so brilliantly declared his indebtedness to the principles she besought him to defend. Her own reception of Darrow, the confidence she had at once accorded him, must have shown him that she had instinc- tively felt their unanimity of sentiment on these fundamental ques- tions. She had in fact recognized in him the one person whom, without pain to her maternal piety, she could welcome as her son's successor; and it was almost as to Owen's father that she now appealed to Darrow to aid in rescuing the wretched boy.

'Don't think, please, that I'm casting the least reflection on Anna, or showing any want of sympathy for her, when I say that I consider her partly responsible for what's happened. Anna is "modern" – I believe that's what it's called when you read unsettling books and admire hideous pictures. Indeed,' Madame de Chantelle continued, leaning confidentially forward, 'I myself have always more or less lived in that atmosphere: my son, you know, was very revolutionary. Only he didn't, of course, apply his ideas: they were purely intellec- tual. That's what dear Anna has always failed to understand. And I'm afraid she's created the same kind of confusion in Owen's mind – led him to mix up things you read about with things you do . . . You know, of course, that she sides with him in this wretched business?'

Developing at length upon this theme, she finally narrowed down to the point of Darrow's intervention. 'My grandson, Mr Darrow, calls me illogical and uncharitable because my feelings toward Miss

Viner have changed since I've heard this news. Well! You've known her, it appears, for some years: Anna tells me you used to see her when she was a companion, or secretary or something, to a dreadfully vulgar Mrs Murrett. And I ask you as a friend, I ask you as one of *us*, to tell me if you think a girl who has had to knock about the world in that kind of position, and at the orders of all kinds of people, is fitted to be Owen's wife . . . I'm not implying anything against her! I *liked* the girl, Mr Darrow . . . But what's that got to do with it? I don't want her to marry my grand-son. If I'd been looking for a wife for Owen, I shouldn't have applied to the Farlows to find me one. That's what Anna won't understand; and what you must help me to make her see.'

Darrow, to this appeal, could oppose only the repeated assurance of his inability to interfere. He tried to make Madame de Chantelle see that the very position he hoped to take in the household made his intervention the more hazardous. He brought up the usual arguments, and sounded the expected note of sympathy; but Madame de Chantelle's alarm had dispelled her habitual imprecision, and, though she had not many reasons to advance, her argument clung to its point like a frightened sharp-clawed animal.

'Well, then,' she summed up, in response to his repeated assertions that he saw no way of helping her, 'you can, at least, even if you won't say a word to the others, tell me frankly and fairly – and quite between ourselves – your personal opinion of Miss Viner, since you've known her so much longer than we have.'

He protested that, if he had known her longer, he had known her much less well, and that he had already, on this point, convinced Anna of his inability to pronounce an opinion.

Madame de Chantelle drew a deep sigh of intelligence. 'Your opinion of Mrs Murrett is enough! I don't suppose you pretend to conceal *that*? And heaven knows what other unspeakable people she's been mixed up with. The only friends she can produce are called *Hoke* . . . Don't try to reason with me, Mr Darrow. There are feelings that go deeper than facts . . . And I *know* she thought of studying for the stage . . .' Madame de Chantelle raised the corner of her lace handkerchief to her eyes. 'I'm old-fashioned – like my furniture,' she murmured. 'And I thought I could count on you, Mr Darrow . . .'

*

When Darrow, that night, regained his room, he reflected with a flash of irony that each time he entered it he brought a fresh troop of perplexities to trouble its serene seclusion. Since the day after his arrival, only forty-eight hours before, when he had set his window open to the night, and his hopes had seemed as many as its stars, each evening had brought its new problem and its renewed distress. But nothing, as yet, had approached the blank misery of mind with which he now set himself to face the fresh questions confronting him.

Sophy Viner had not shown herself at dinner, so that he had had no glimpse of her in her new character, and no means of divining the real nature of the tie between herself and Owen Leath. One thing, however, was clear: whatever her real feelings were, and however much or little she had at stake, if she had made up her mind to marry Owen she had more than enough skill and tenacity to defeat any arts that poor Madame de Chantelle could oppose to her.

Darrow himself was in fact the only person who might possibly turn her from her purpose: Madame de Chantelle, at haphazard, had hit on the surest means of saving Owen – if to prevent his marriage were to save him! Darrow, on this point, did not pretend to any fixed opinion; one feeling alone was clear and insistent in him: he did not mean, if he could help it, to let the marriage take place.

How he was to prevent it he did not know: to his tormented imagination every issue seemed closed. For a fantastic instant he was moved to follow Madame de Chantelle's suggestion and urge Anna to withdraw her approval. If his reticence, his efforts to avoid the subject, had not escaped her, she had doubtless set them down to the fact of his knowing more, and thinking less, of Sophy Viner than he had been willing to admit; and he might take advantage of this to turn her mind gradually from the project. Yet how to do so without betraying his insincerity? If he had had nothing to hide he could easily have said: 'It's one thing to know nothing against the girl, it's another to pretend that I think her a good match for Owen.' But could he say even so much without betraying more? It was not Anna's questions, or his answers to them, that he feared, but what might cry aloud in the intervals between them. He understood now that ever since Sophy Viner's arrival at Givré he had felt in Anna the lurking sense of something unexpressed, and perhaps inexpressible,

between the girl and himself . . . Whcn at last he fell asleep he had
fatalistically committed his next step to the chances of the morrow.

The first that offered itself was an encounter with Mrs Leath as
he descended the stairs the next morning. She had come down
already hatted and shod for a dash to the park lodge, where one
of the gatekeeper's children had had an accident. In her compact
dark dress she looked more than usually straight and slim, and her
face wore the pale glow it took on at any call on her energy: a
kind of warrior brightness that made her small head, with its
strong chin and closebound hair, like that of an amazon in a
frieze.

It was their first moment alone since she had left him, the afternoon before, at her mother-in-law's door; and after a few words
about the injured child their talk inevitably reverted to Owen.

Anna spoke with a smile of her 'scene' with Madame de Chantelle, who belonged, poor dear, to a generation when 'scenes' (in the
ladylike and lachrymal sense of the term) were the tribute which
sensibility was expected to pay to the unusual. Their conversation
had been, in every detail, so exactly what Anna had foreseen that it
had clearly not made much impression on her; but she was eager to
know the result of Darrow's encounter with her mother-in-law.

'She told me she'd sent for you: she always "sends for" people in
emergencies. That again, I suppose, is *de l'époque*. And failing Adelaide Painter, who can't get here till this afternoon, there was no one
but poor you to turn to.'

She put it all lightly, with a lightness that seemed to his tight-
strung nerves slightly, undefinably over-done. But he was so aware of
his own tension that he wondered, the next moment, whether anything would ever again seem to him quite usual and insignificant and
in the common order of things.

As they hastened on through the drizzle in which the storm of the
night was weeping itself out, Anna drew close under his umbrella,
and at the pressure of her arm against his he recalled his walk up the
Dover pier with Sophy Viner. The mcmory gave him a startled
vision of the inevitable occasions of contact, confidence, familiarity,
which his future relationship to the girl would entail, and the countless chances of betrayal that every one of them involved.

'Do tell me just what you said,' he heard Anna pleading; and with sudden resolution he affirmed: 'I quite understand your mother-in-law's feeling as she does.'

The words, when uttered, seemed a good deal less significant than they had sounded to his inner ear; and Anna replied without surprise: 'Of course. It's inevitable that she should. But we shall bring her round in time.' Under the dripping dome she raised her face to his. 'Don't you remember what you said the day before yesterday? "Together we can't fail to pull it off for him!" I've told Owen that, so you're pledged and there's no going back.'

The day before yesterday! Was it possible that, no longer ago, life had seemed a sufficiently simple business for a sane man to hazard such assurances?

'Anna,' he questioned her abruptly, 'why are you so anxious for this marriage?'

She stopped short to face him. 'Why? But surely I've explained to you – or rather I've hardly had to, you seemed so in sympathy with my reasons!'

'I didn't know, then, who it was that Owen wanted to marry.'

The words were out with a spring and he felt a clearer air in his brain. But her logic hemmed him in.

'You knew yesterday; and you assured me then that you hadn't a word to say –'

'Against Miss Viner?' The name, once uttered, sounded on and on in his ears. 'Of course not. But that doesn't necessarily imply that I think her a good match for Owen.'

Anna made no immediate answer. When she spoke it was to question: 'Why don't you think her a good match for Owen?'

'Well – Madame de Chantelle's reasons seem to me not quite as negligible as you think.'

'You mean the fact that she's been Mrs Murrett's secretary, and that the people who employed her before were called Hoke? For, as far as Owen and I can make out, these are the gravest charges against her.'

'Still, one can understand that the match is not what Madame de Chantelle had dreamed of.'

'Oh, perfectly – if that's all you mean.'

The lodge was in sight, and she hastened her step. He strode on beside her in silence, but at the gate she checked him with the question: 'Is it really all you mean?'

'Of course,' he heard himself declare.

'Oh, then I think I shall convince you – even if I can't, like Madame de Chantelle, summon all the Everards to my aid!' She lifted to him the look of happy laughter that sometimes brushed her with a gleam of spring.

Darrow watched her hasten along the path between the dripping chrysanthemums and enter the lodge. After she had gone in he paced up and down outside in the drizzle, waiting to learn if she had any message to send back to the house; and after the lapse of a few minutes she came out again.

The child, she said, was badly, though not dangerously, hurt, and the village doctor, who was already on hand, had asked that the surgeon, already summoned from Francheuil, should be told to bring with him certain needful appliances. Owen had started by motor to fetch the surgeon, but there was still time to communicate with the latter by telephone. The doctor furthermore begged for an immediate provision of such bandages and disinfectants as Givré itself could furnish, and Anna bade Darrow address himself to Miss Viner, who would know where to find the necessary things, and would direct one of the servants to bicycle with them to the lodge.

Darrow, as he hurried off on this errand, had at once perceived the opportunity it offered of a word with Sophy Viner. What that word was to be he did not know; but now, if ever, was the moment to make it urgent and conclusive. It was unlikely that he would again have such a chance of unobserved talk with her.

He had supposed he should find her with her pupil in the schoolroom; but he learned from a servant that Effie had gone to Francheuil with her step-brother, and that Miss Viner was still in her room. Darrow sent her word that he was the bearer of a message from the lodge, and a moment later he heard her coming down the stairs.

20

For a second, as she approached him, the quick tremor of her glance showed her all intent on the same thought as himself. He transmitted his instructions with mechanical precision, and she answered in the same tone, repeating his words with the intensity of attention of a child not quite sure of understanding. Then she disappeared up the stairs.

Darrow lingered on in the hall, not knowing if she meant to return, yet inwardly sure she would. At length he saw her coming down in her hat and jacket. The rain still streaked the window panes, and, in order to say something, he said: 'You're not going to the lodge yourself?'

'I've sent one of the men ahead with the things; but I thought Mrs Leath might need me.'

'She didn't ask for you,' he returned, wondering how he could detain her; but she answered decidedly: 'I'd better go.'

He held open the door, picked up his umbrella and followed her out. As they went down the steps she glanced back at him. 'You've forgotten your mackintosh.'

'I sha'n't need it.'

She had no umbrella, and he opened his and held it out to her. She rejected it with a murmur of thanks and walked on through the thin drizzle, and he kept the umbrella over his own head, without offering to shelter her.

Rapidly and in silence they crossed the court and began to walk down the avenue. They had traversed a third of its length before Darrow said abruptly: 'Wouldn't it have been fairer, when we talked together yesterday, to tell me what I've just heard from Mrs Leath?'

'Fairer –?' She stopped short with a startled look.

'If I'd known that your future was already settled I should have spared you my gratuitous suggestions.'

She walked on, more slowly, for a yard or two. 'I couldn't speak yesterday. I meant to have told you today.'

'Oh, I'm not reproaching you for your lack of confidence. Only, if you *had* told me, I should have been more sure of your really meaning what you said to me yesterday.'

She did not ask him to what he referred, and he saw that her parting words to him lived as vividly in her memory as in his.

'Is it so important that you should be sure?' she finally questioned.

'Not to you, naturally,' he returned with involuntary asperity. It was incredible, yet it was a fact, that for the moment his immediate purpose in seeking to speak to her was lost under a rush of resentment at counting for so little in her fate. Of what stuff, then, was his feeling for her made? A few hours earlier she had touched his thoughts as little as his senses; but now he felt old sleeping instincts stir in him . . .

A rush of rain dashed against his face, and, catching Sophy's hat, strained it back from her loosened hair. She put her hands to her head with a familiar gesture . . . He came closer and held his umbrella over her . . .

At the lodge he waited while she went in. The rain continued to stream down on him and he shivered in the dampness and stamped his feet on the flags. It seemed to him that a long time elapsed before the door opened and she reappeared. He glanced into the house for a glimpse of Anna, but obtained none; yet the mere sense of her nearness had completely altered his mood.

The child, Sophy told him, was doing well; but Mrs Leath had decided to wait till the surgeon came. Darrow, as they turned away, looked through the gates, and saw the doctor's old-fashioned carriage by the road-side.

'Let me tell the doctor's boy to drive you back,' he suggested; but Sophy answered: 'No; I'll walk,' and he moved on toward the house at her side. She expressed no surprise at his not remaining at the lodge, and again they walked on in silence through the rain. She had accepted the shelter of his umbrella, but she kept herself at such a carefully measured distance that even the slight swaying movements produced by their quick pace did not once bring her arm in touch with his; and, noticing this, he perceived that every drop of her blood must be alive to his nearness.

'What I meant just now,' he began, 'was that you ought to have been sure of my good wishes.'

She seemed to weigh the words. 'Sure enough for what?'

'To trust me a little farther than you did.'

'I've told you that yesterday I wasn't free to speak.'

'Well, since you are now, may I say a word to you?'

She paused perceptibly, and when she spoke it was in so low a tone that he had to bend his head to catch her answer. 'I can't think what you can have to say.'

'It's not easy to say here, at any rate. And indoors I sha'n't know where to say it.' He glanced about him in the rain. 'Let's walk over to the spring-house for a minute.'

To the right of the drive, under a clump of trees, a little stucco pavilion crowned by a balustrade rose on arches of mouldering brick over a flight of steps that led down to a spring. Other steps curved up to a door above. Darrow mounted these, and opening the door entered a small circular room hung with loosened strips of painted paper whereon spectrally faded Mandarins executed elongated gestures. Some black and gold chairs with straw seats and an unsteady table of cracked lacquer stood on the floor of red-glazed tile.

Sophy had followed him without comment. He closed the door after her, and she stood motionless, as though waiting for him to speak.

'Now we can talk quietly,' he said, looking at her with a smile into which he tried to put an intention of the frankest friendliness.

She merely repeated: 'I can't think what you can have to say.'

Her voice had lost the note of half-wistful confidence on which their talk of the previous day had closed, and she looked at him with a kind of pale hostility. Her tone made it evident that his task would be difficult, but it did not shake his resolve to go on. He sat down, and mechanically she followed his example. The table was between them and she rested her arms on its cracked edge and her chin on her interlocked hands. He looked at her and she gave him back his look.

'Have you nothing to say to *me*?' he asked at length.

A faint smile lifted, in the remembered way, the left corner of her narrowed lips.

'About my marriage?'

'About your marriage.'

She continued to consider him between half-drawn lids. 'What can I say that Mrs Leath has not already told you?'

'Mrs Leath has told me nothing whatever but the fact – and her pleasure in it.'

'Well; aren't those the two essential points?'

'The essential points to *you*? I should have thought –'

'Oh, to *you*, I meant,' she put in keenly.

He flushed at the retort, but steadied himself and rejoined: 'The essential point to me is, of course, that you should be doing what's really best for you.'

She sat silent, with lowered lashes. At length she stretched out her arm and took up from the table a little threadbare Chinese hand-screen. She turned its ebony stem once or twice between her fingers, and as she did so Darrow was whimsically struck by the way in which their evanescent slight romance was symbolized by the fading lines on the frail silk.

'Do you think my engagement to Mr Leath not really best for me?' she asked at length.

Darrow, before answering, waited long enough to get his words into the tersest shape – not without a sense, as he did so, of his likeness to the surgeon deliberately poising his lancet for a clean incision. 'I'm not sure,' he replied, 'of its being the best thing for either of you.'

She took the stroke steadily, but a faint red swept her face like the reflection of a blush. She continued to keep her lowered eyes on the screen.

'From whose point of view do you speak?'

'Naturally, that of the persons most concerned.'

'From Owen's, then, of course? You don't think me a good match for him?'

'From yours, first of all. I don't think him a good match for you.'

He brought the answer out abruptly, his eyes on her face. It had grown extremely pale, but as the meaning of his words shaped itself in her mind he saw a curious inner light dawn through her set look. She lifted her lids just far enough for a veiled glance at him, and a smile slipped through them to her trembling lips. For a moment the change merely bewildered him; then it pulled him up with a sharp jerk of apprehension.

'I don't think him a good match for you,' he stammered, groping for the lost thread of his words.

She threw a vague look about the chilly rain-dimmed room. 'And you've brought me here to tell me why?'

The question roused him to the sense that their minutes were numbered, and that if he did not immediately get to his point there might be no other chance of making it.

'My chief reason is that I believe he's too young and inexperienced to give you the kind of support you need.'

At his words her face changed again, freezing to a tragic coldness. She stared straight ahead of her, perceptibly struggling with the tremor of her muscles; and when she had controlled it she flung out a pale-lipped pleasantry. 'But you see I've always had to support myself!'

'He's a boy,' Darrow pushed on, 'a charming, wonderful boy; but with no more notion than a boy how to deal with the inevitable daily problems . . . the trivial stupid unimportant things that life is chiefly made up of.'

'I'll deal with them for him,' she rejoined.

'They'll be more than ordinarily difficult.'

She shot a challenging glance at him. 'You must have some special reason for saying so.'

'Only my clear perception of the facts.'

'What facts do you mean?'

Darrow hesitated. 'You must know better than I,' he returned at length, 'that the way won't be made easy to you.'

'Mrs Leath, at any rate, has made it so.'

'Madame de Chantelle will not.'

'How do *you* know that?' she flung back.

He paused again, not sure how far it was prudent to reveal himself in the confidence of the household. Then, to avoid involving Anna, he answered: 'Madame de Chantelle sent for me yesterday.'

'Sent for you – to talk to you about me?' The colour rose to her forehead and her eyes burned black under lowered brows. 'By what right, I should like to know? What have you to do with me, or with anything in the world that concerns me?'

Darrow instantly perceived what dread suspicion again possessed her, and the sense that it was not wholly unjustified caused him a passing pang of shame. But it did not turn him from his purpose.

'I'm an old friend of Mrs Leath's. It's not unnatural that Madame de Chantelle should talk to me.'

She dropped the screen on the table and stood up, turning on him the same small mask of wrath and scorn which had glared at him, in

Paris, when he had confessed to his suppression of her letter. She walked away a step or two and then came back.

'May I ask what Madame de Chantelle said to you?'

'She made it clear that she should not encourage the marriage.'

'And what was her object in making that clear to *you*?'

Darrow hesitated. 'I suppose she thought –'

'That she could persuade you to turn Mrs Leath against me?'

He was silent, and she pressed him: 'Was that it?'

'That was it.'

'But if you don't – if you keep your promise –'

'My promise?'

'To say nothing . . . nothing whatever . . .' Her strained look threw a haggard light along the pause.

As she spoke, the whole odiousness of the scene rushed over him. 'Of course I shall say nothing . . . you know that . . .' He leaned to her and laid his hand on hers. 'You know I wouldn't for the world . . .'

She drew back and hid her face with a sob. Then she sank again into her seat, stretched her arms across the table and laid her face upon them. He sat still, overwhelmed with compunction. After a long interval, in which he had painfully measured the seconds by her hard-drawn breathing, she looked up at him with a face washed clear of bitterness.

'Don't suppose I don't know what you must have thought of me!'

The cry struck him down to a lower depth of self-abasement. 'My poor child,' he felt like answering, 'the shame of it is that I've never thought of you at all!' But he could only uselessly repeat: 'I'll do anything I can to help you.'

She sat silent, drumming the table with her hand. He saw that her doubt of him was allayed, and the perception made him more ashamed, as if her trust had first revealed to him how near he had come to not deserving it. Suddenly she began to speak.

'You think, then, I've no right to marry him?'

'No right? God forbid! I only meant –'

'That you'd rather I didn't marry any friend of yours.' She brought it out deliberately, not as a question, but as a mere dispassion-ate statement of fact.

Darrow in turn stood up and wandered away helplessly to the

window. He stood staring out through its small discoloured panes at the dim brown distances; then he moved back to the table.

'I'll tell you exactly what I meant. You'll be wretched if you marry a man you're not in love with.'

He knew the risk of misapprehension that he ran, but he estimated his chances of success as precisely in proportion to his peril. If certain signs meant what he thought they did, he might yet – at what cost he would not stop to think – make his past pay for his future.

The girl, at his words, had lifted her head with a movement of surprise. Her eyes slowly reached his face and rested there in a gaze of deep interrogation. He held the look for a moment; then his own eyes dropped and he waited.

At length she began to speak. 'You're mistaken – you're quite mistaken.'

He waited a moment longer. 'Mistaken –?'

'In thinking what you think. I'm as happy as if I deserved it!' she suddenly proclaimed with a laugh.

She stood up and moved toward the door. '*Now* are you satisfied?' she asked, turning her vividest face to him from the threshold.

21

Down the avenue there came to them, with the opening of the door, the voice of Owen's motor. It was the signal which had interrupted their first talk, and again, instinctively, they drew apart at the sound. Without a word Darrow turned back into the room, while Sophy Viner went down the steps and walked back alone toward the court.

At luncheon the presence of the surgeon, and the non-appearance of Madame de Chantelle – who had excused herself on the plea of a headache – combined to shift the conversational centre of gravity; and Darrow, under shelter of the necessarily impersonal talk, had time to adjust his disguise and to perceive that the others were engaged in the same re-arrangement. It was the first time that he had seen young Leath and Sophy Viner together since he had learned of their engagement; but neither revealed more emotion than befitted the occasion. It was evident that Owen was deeply under the girl's charm, and that at the least sign from her his bliss would have broken bounds; but her reticence was justified by the tacitly recognized fact of Madame de Chantelle's disapproval. This also visibly weighed on Anna's mind, making her manner to Sophy, if no less kind, yet a trifle more constrained than if the moment of final understanding had been reached. So Darrow interpreted the tension perceptible under the fluent exchange of commonplaces in which he was diligently sharing. But he was more and more aware of his inability to test the moral atmosphere about him: he was like a man in fever testing another's temperature by the touch.

After luncheon Anna, who was to motor the surgeon home, suggested to Darrow that he should accompany them. Effie was also of the party; and Darrow inferred that Anna wished to give her stepson a chance to be alone with his betrothed. On the way back, after the surgeon had been left at his door, the little girl sat between her mother and Darrow, and her presence kept their talk from taking a personal turn. Darrow knew that Mrs Leath had not yet told Effie of the relation in which he was to stand to her. The premature divulging of Owen's plans had thrown their own into the background, and by common consent they continued, in the little girl's presence, on terms of an informal friendliness.

The sky had cleared after luncheon, and to prolong their excursion they returned by way of the ivy-mantled ruin which was to have been the scene of the projected picnic. This circuit brought them back to the park gates not long before sunset, and as Anna wished to stop at the lodge for news of the injured child Darrow left her there with Effie and walked on alone to the house. He had the impression that she was slightly surprised at his not waiting for her; but his inner restlessness vented itself in an intense desire for bodily movement. He would have liked to walk himself into a state of torpor; to tramp on for hours through the moist winds and the healing darkness and come back staggering with fatigue and sleep. But he had no pretext for such a flight, and he feared that, at such a moment, his prolonged absence might seem singular to Anna.

As he approached the house, the thought of her nearness produced a swift reaction of mood. It was as if an intenser vision of her had scattered his perplexities like morning mists. At this moment, wherever she was, he knew he was safely shut away in her thoughts, and the knowledge made every other fact dwindle away to a shadow. He and she loved each other, and their love arched over them open and ample as the day: in all its sunlit spaces there was no cranny for a fear to lurk. In a few minutes he would be in her presence and would read his reassurance in her eyes. And presently, before dinner, she would contrive that they should have an hour by themselves in her sitting-room, and he would sit by the hearth and watch her quiet movements, and the way the bluish lustre on her hair purpled a little as she bent above the fire.

A carriage drove out of the court as he entered it, and in the hall his vision was dispelled by the exceedingly substantial presence of a lady in a waterproof and a tweed hat, who stood firmly planted in the centre of a pile of luggage, as to which she was giving involved but lucid directions to the footman who had just admitted her. She went on with these directions regardless of Darrow's entrance, merely fixing her small pale eyes on him while she proceeded, in a deep contralto voice, and a fluent French pronounced with the purest Boston accent, to specify the destination of her bags; and this enabled Darrow to give her back a gaze protracted enough to take in all the details of her plain thick-set person, from the square sallow face beneath bands of grey hair to the blunt boot-toes protruding under her wide walking skirt.

She submitted to this scrutiny with no more evidence of surprise than a monument examined by a tourist; but when the fate of her luggage had been settled she turned suddenly to Darrow and, dropping her eyes from his face to his feet, asked in trenchant accents: 'What sort of boots have you got on?'

Before he could summon his wits to the consideration of this question she continued in a tone of suppressed indignation: 'Until Americans get used to the fact that France is under water for half the year they're perpetually risking their lives by not being properly protected. I suppose you've been tramping through all this nasty clammy mud as if you'd been taking a stroll on Boston Common.'

Darrow, with a laugh, affirmed his previous experience of French dampness, and the degree to which he was on his guard against it; but the lady, with a contemptuous snort, rejoined: 'You young men are all alike—'; to which she appended, after another hard look at him: 'I suppose you're George Darrow? I used to know one of your mother's cousins, who married a Tunstall of Mount Vernon Street. My name is Adelaide Painter. Have you been in Boston lately? No? I'm sorry for that. I hear there have been several new houses built at the lower end of Commonwealth Avenue and I hoped you could tell me about them. I haven't been there for thirty years myself.'

Miss Painter's arrival at Givré produced the same effect as the wind's hauling around to the north after days of languid weather. When Darrow joined the group about the tea-table she had already given a tingle to the air. Madame de Chantelle still remained invisible above stairs; but Darrow had the impression that even through her drawn curtains and bolted doors a stimulating whiff must have entered.

Anna was in her usual seat behind the tea-tray, and Sophy Viner presently led in her pupil. Owen was also there, seated, as usual, a little apart from the others, and following Miss Painter's massive movements and equally substantial utterances with a smile of secret intelligence which gave Darrow the idea of his having been in clandestine parley with the enemy. Darrow further took note that the girl and her suitor perceptibly avoided each other; but this might be a natural result of the tension Miss Painter had been summoned to relieve.

Sophy Viner would evidently permit no recognition of the situation save that which it lay with Madame de Chantelle to accord; but meanwhile Miss Painter had proclaimed her tacit sense of it by summoning the girl to a seat at her side.

Darrow, as he continued to observe the newcomer, who was perched on her armchair like a granite image on the edge of a cliff, was aware that, in a more detached frame of mind, he would have found an extreme interest in studying and classifying Miss Painter. It was not that she said anything remarkable, or betrayed any of those unspoken perceptions which give significance to the most commonplace utterances. She talked of the lateness of her train, of an impending crisis in international politics, of the difficulty of buying English tea in Paris and of the enormities of which French servants were capable; and her views on these subjects were enunciated with a uniformity of emphasis implying complete unconsciousness of any difference in their interest and importance. She always applied to the

French race the distant epithet of 'those people', but she betrayed an intimate acquaintance with many of its members, and an encyclopaedic knowledge of the domestic habits, financial difficulties and private complications of various persons of social importance. Yet, as she evidently felt no incongruity in her attitude, so she revealed no desire to parade her familiarity with the fashionable, or indeed any sense of it as a fact to be paraded. It was evident that the titled ladies whom she spoke of as Mimi or Simone or Odette were as much 'those people' to her as the *bonne* who tampered with her tea and steamed the stamps off her letters ('when, by a miracle, I don't put them in the box myself'). Her whole attitude was of a vast grim tolerance of things-as-they-came, as though she had been some wonderful automatic machine which recorded facts but had not yet been perfected to the point of sorting or labelling them.

All this, as Darrow was aware, still fell short of accounting for the influence she obviously exerted on the persons in contact with her. It brought a slight relief to his state of tension to go on wondering, while he watched and listened, just where the mystery lurked. Perhaps, after all, it was in the fact of her blank insensibility, an insensibility so devoid of egotism that it had no hardness and no grimaces, but rather the freshness of a simpler mental state. After living, as he had, as they all had, for the last few days, in an atmosphere perpetually tremulous with echoes and implications, it was restful and fortifying merely to walk into the big blank area of Miss Painter's mind, so vacuous for all its accumulated items, so echoless for all its vacuity.

His hope of a word with Anna before dinner was dispelled by her rising to take Miss Painter up to Madame de Chantelle; and he wandered away to his own room, leaving Owen and Miss Viner engaged in working out a picture-puzzle for Effie.

Madame de Chantelle – possibly as the result of her friend's ministrations – was able to appear at the dinner-table, rather pale and pink-nosed, and casting tenderly reproachful glances at her grandson, who faced them with impervious serenity; and the situation was relieved by the fact that Miss Viner, as usual, had remained in the school-room with her pupil.

Darrow conjectured that the real clash of arms would not take place till the morrow; and wishing to leave the field open to the contestants he set out early on a solitary walk. It was nearly luncheon-time when he returned from it and came upon Anna just emerging from the house. She had on her hat and jacket and was apparently coming forth to seek him, for she said at once: 'Madame de Chantelle wants you to go up to her.'

'To go up to her? Now?'

'That's the message she sent. She appears to rely on you to do something.' She added with a smile: 'Whatever it is, let's have it over!'

Darrow, through his rising sense of apprehension, wondered why, instead of merely going for a walk, he had not jumped into the first train and got out of the way till Owen's affairs were finally settled.

'But what in the name of goodness can I do?' he protested, following Anna back into the hall.

'I don't know. But Owen seems so to rely on you, too –'

'Owen! Is *he* to be there?'

'No. But you know I told him he could count on you.'

'But I've said to your mother-in-law all I could.'

'Well, then you can only repeat it.'

This did not seem to Darrow to simplify his case as much as she appeared to think; and once more he had a movement of recoil. 'There's no possible reason for my being mixed up in this affair!'

Anna gave him a reproachful glance. 'Not the fact that *I* am?' she reminded him; but even this only stiffened his resistance.

'Why should you be, either – to this extent?'

The question made her pause. She glanced about the hall, as if to be sure they had it to themselves; and then, in a lowered voice: 'I don't know,' she suddenly confessed; 'but, somehow, if *they're* not happy I feel as if we shouldn't be.'

'Oh, well –' Darrow acquiesced, in the tone of the man who perforce yields to so lovely an unreasonableness. Escape was, after all, impossible, and he could only resign himself to being led to Madame de Chantelle's door.

Within, among the bric-à-brac and furbelows, he found Miss Painter seated in a redundant purple armchair with the incongruous air of a horseman bestriding a heavy mount. Madame de Chantelle sat opposite, still a little wan and disordered under her elaborate hair, and clasping the handkerchief whose visibility symbolized her distress. On the young man's entrance she sighed out a plaintive welcome, to which she immediately appended: 'Mr Darrow, I can't help feeling that at heart you're with me!'

The directness of the challenge made it easier for Darrow to protest, and he reiterated his inability to give an opinion on either side.

'But Anna declares you have – on hers!'

He could not restrain a smile at this faint flaw in an impartiality so scrupulous. Every evidence of feminine inconsequence in Anna seemed to attest her deeper subjection to the most inconsequent of passions. He had certainly promised her his help – but before he knew what he was promising.

He met Madame de Chantelle's appeal by replying: 'If there were anything I could possibly say I should want it to be in Miss Viner's favour.'

'You'd want it to be – yes! But could you make it so?'

'As far as facts go, I don't see how I can make it either for or against her. I've already said that I know nothing of her except that she's charming.'

'As if that weren't enough – weren't all there *ought* to be!' Miss Painter put in impatiently. She seemed to address herself to Darrow, though her small eyes were fixed on her friend.

'Madame de Chantelle seems to imagine,' she pursued, 'that a young American girl ought to have a *dossier* – a police-record, or whatever you call it: what those awful women in the streets have here. In our country it's enough to know that a young girl's pure and lovely: people don't immediately ask her to show her bank-account and her visiting-list.'

Madame de Chantelle looked plaintively at her sturdy monitress. 'You don't expect me not to ask if she's got a family?'

'No; nor to think the worse of her if she hasn't. The fact that she's an orphan ought, with your ideas, to be a merit. You won't have to invite her father and mother to Givré!'

'Adelaide – Adelaide!' the mistress of Givré lamented.

'Lucretia Mary,' the other returned – and Darrow spared an instant's amusement to the quaint incongruity of the name – 'you know you sent for Mr Darrow to refute me; and how can he, till he knows what I think?'

'You think it's perfectly simple to let Owen marry a girl we know nothing about?'

'No; but I don't think it's perfectly simple to prevent him.'

The shrewdness of the answer increased Darrow's interest in Miss Painter. She had not hitherto struck him as being a person of much penetration, but he now felt sure that her gimlet gaze might bore to the heart of any practical problem.

Madame de Chantelle sighed out her recognition of the difficulty.

'I haven't a word to say against Miss Viner; but she's knocked about so, as it's called, that she must have been mixed up with some rather dreadful people. If only Owen could be made to see that – if one could get at a few facts, I mean. She says, for instance, that she has a sister; but it seems she doesn't even know her address!'

'If she does, she may not want to give it to you. I daresay the sister's one of the dreadful people. I've no doubt that with a little time you could rake up dozens of them: have her "traced", as they call it in detective stories. I don't think you'd frighten Owen, but you might: it's natural enough he should have been corrupted by those foreign ideas. You might even manage to part him from the girl; but you couldn't keep him from being in love with her. I saw that when I looked them over last evening. I said to myself: "It's a real old-fashioned American case, as sweet and sound as home-made bread." Well, if you take his loaf away from him, what are you going to feed him with instead? Which of your nasty Paris poisons do you think he'll turn to? Supposing you succeed in keeping him out of a really bad mess – and, knowing the young man as I do, I rather think that, at this crisis, the only way to do it would be to marry him slap off to somebody else – well, then, who, may I ask, would you pick out? One of your sweet French *ingénues*, I suppose? With as much mind as a minnow and as much snap as a soft-boiled egg. You might hustle him into that kind of marriage; I daresay you could – but if I know Owen, the natural thing would happen before the first baby was weaned.'

'I don't know why you insinuate such odious things against Owen!'

'Do you think it would be odious of him to return to his real love when he'd been forcibly parted from her? At any rate, it's what your French friends do, every one of them! Only they don't generally have the grace to go back to an old love; and I believe, upon my word, Owen would!'

Madame de Chantelle looked at her with a mixture of awe and exultation. 'Of course you realize, Adelaide, that in suggesting this you're insinuating the most shocking things against Miss Viner?'

'When I say that if you part two young things who are dying to be happy in the lawful way it's ten to one they'll come together in an unlawful one? I'm insinuating shocking things against *you*, Lucretia Mary, in suggesting for a moment that you'll care to assume such a responsibility before your Maker. And you wouldn't, if you talked things straight out with him, instead of merely sending him messages through a miserable sinner like yourself!'

Darrow expected this assault on her adopted creed to provoke in Madame de Chantelle an explosion of pious indignation; but to his surprise she merely murmured: 'I don't know what Mr Darrow'll think of you!'

'Mr Darrow probably knows his Bible as well as I do,' Miss Painter calmly rejoined; adding a moment later, without the least perceptible change of voice or expression: 'I suppose you've heard that Gisèle de Folembray's husband accuses her of being mixed up with the Duc d'Arcachon in that business of trying to sell a lot of imitation pearls to Mrs Homer Pond, the Chicago woman the Duke's engaged to? It seems the jeweller says Gisèle brought Mrs Pond there, and got twenty-five per cent – which of course she passed on to d'Arcachon. The poor old Duchess is in a fearful state – so afraid her son'll lose Mrs Pond! When I think that Gisèle is old Bradford Wagstaff's grand-daughter, I'm thankful he's safe in Mount Auburn!'

22

It was not until late that afternoon that Darrow could claim his postponed hour with Anna. When at last he found her alone in her sitting-room it was with a sense of liberation so great that he sought no logical justification of it. He simply felt that all their destinies were in Miss Painter's grasp, and that, resistance being useless, he could only enjoy the sweets of surrender.

Anna herself seemed as happy, and for more explicable reasons. She had assisted, after luncheon, at another debate between Madame de Chantelle and her confidante, and had surmised, when she withdrew from it, that victory was permanently perched on Miss Painter's banners.

'I don't know how she does it, unless it's by the dead weight of her convictions. She detests the French so that she'd back up Owen even if she knew nothing – or knew too much – of Miss Viner. She somehow regards the match as a protest against the corruption of European morals. I told Owen that was his great chance, and he's made the most of it.'

'What a tactician you are! You make me feel that I hardly know the rudiments of diplomacy.' Darrow smiled at her, abandoning himself to a perilous sense of well-being.

She gave him back his smile. 'I'm afraid I think nothing short of my own happiness is worth wasting any diplomacy on!'

'That's why I mean to resign from the service of my country,' he rejoined with a laugh of deep content.

The feeling that both resistance and apprehension were vain was working like wine in his veins. He had done what he could to deflect the course of events: now he could only stand aside and take his chance of safety. Underneath this fatalistic feeling was the deep sense of relief that he had, after all, said and done nothing that could in the least degree affect the welfare of Sophy Viner. That fact took a millstone off his neck.

Meanwhile he gave himself up once more to the joy of Anna's presence. They had not been alone together for two long days, and he had the lover's sense that he had forgotten, or at least underestimated, the strength of the spell she cast. Once more her eyes and her smile seemed to bound his world. He felt that their light would always move with him as the sunset moves before a ship at sea.

The next day his sense of security was increased by a decisive incident. It became known to the expectant houschold that Madame de Chantelle had yielded to the tremendous impact of Miss Painter's determination and that Sophy Viner had been 'sent for' to the purple satin sitting-room.

At luncheon, Owen's radiant countenance proclaimed the happy sequel, and Darrow, when the party had moved back to the oak-room for coffee, deemed it discreet to wander out alone to the terrace with his cigar. The conclusion of Owen's romance brought his own plans once more to the front. Anna had promised that she would consider dates and settle details as soon as Madame de Chantelle and her grandson had been reconciled, and Darrow was eager to go into the question at once, since it was necessary that the preparations for his marriage should go forward as rapidly as possible. Anna, he knew, would not seek any farther pretext for delay; and he strolled up and down contentedly in the sunshine, certain that she would come out and reassure him as soon as the reunited family had claimed its due share of her attention.

But when she finally joined him her first word was for the younger lovers.

'I want to thank you for what you've done for Owen,' she began, with her happiest smile.

'Who – I?' he laughed. 'Are you confusing me with Miss Painter?'

'Perhaps I ought to say for *me*,' she corrected herself. 'You've been even more of a help to us than Adelaide.'

'My dear child! What on earth have I done?'

'You've managed to hide from Madame de Chantelle that you don't really like poor Sophy.'

Darrow felt the pallor in his cheek. 'Not like her? What put such an idea into your head?'

'Oh, it's more than an idea – it's a feeling. But what difference does it make, after all? You saw her in such a different setting that it's natural you should be a little doubtful. But when you know her better I'm sure you'll feel about her as I do.'

'It's going to be hard for me not to feel about everything as you do.'

'Well, then – please begin with my daughter-in-law!'

He gave her back in the same tone of banter: 'Agreed: if you'll agree to feel as I do about the pressing necessity of our getting married.'

'I want to talk to you about that too. You don't know what a weight is off my mind! With Sophy here for good, I shall feel so differently about leaving Effie. I've seen much more accomplished governesses – to my cost! – but I've never seen a young thing more gay and kind and human. You must have noticed, though you've seen them so little together, how Effie expands when she's with her. And that, you know, is what I want. Madame de Chantelle will provide the necessary restraint.' She clasped her hands on his arm. 'Yes, I'm ready to go with you now. But first of all – this very moment! – you must come with me to Effie. She knows, of course, nothing of what's been happening; and I want her to be told first about *you*.'

Effie, sought throughout the house, was presently traced to the school-room, and thither Darrow mounted with Anna. He had never seen her so alight with happiness, and he had caught her buoyancy of mood. He kept repeating to himself: 'It's over – it's over,' as if some monstrous midnight hallucination had been routed by the return of day.

As they approached the school-room door the terrier's barks came to them through laughing remonstrances.

'She's giving him his dinner,' Anna whispered, her hand in Darrow's.

'Don't forget the gold-fish!' they heard another voice call out.

Darrow halted on the threshold. 'Oh – not now!'

'Not now?'

'I mean – she'd rather have you tell her first. I'll wait for you both downstairs.'

He was aware that she glanced at him intently. 'As you please. I'll bring her down at once.'

She opened the door, and as she went in he heard her say: 'No, Sophy, don't go! I want you both.'

The rest of Darrow's day was a succession of empty and agitating scenes. On his way down to Givré, before he had seen Effie Leath, he had pictured somewhat sentimentally the joy of the moment when he should take her in his arms and receive her first filial kiss. Everything in him that egotistically craved for rest, stability, a comfortably organized middle-age, all the home-building instincts of the man who has sufficiently wooed and wandered, combined to throw a charm about the figure of the child who might – who should – have been his. Effie came to him trailing the cloud of glory of his first romance, giving him back the magic hour he had missed and mourned. And how different the realization of his dream had been!

The child's radiant welcome, her unquestioning acceptance of this new figure in the family group, had been all that he had hoped and fancied. If Mother was so awfully happy about it, and Owen and Granny, too, how nice and cosy and comfortable it was going to be for all of them, her beaming look seemed to say; and then, suddenly, the small pink fingers he had been kissing were laid on the one flaw in the circle, on the one point which must be settled before Effie could, with complete unqualified assurance, admit the newcomer to full equality with the other gods of her Olympus.

'And is Sophy awfully happy about it too?' she had asked, loosening her hold on Darrow's neck to tilt back her head and include her mother in her questioning look.

'Why, dearest, didn't you see she was?' Anna had exclaimed, leaning to the group with radiant eyes.

'I think I should like to ask her,' the child rejoined, after a minute's shy consideration; and as Darrow set her down her mother laughed: 'Do, darling, do! Run off at once, and tell her we expect her to be awfully happy too.'

The scene had been succeeded by others less poignant but almost as trying. Darrow cursed his luck in having, at such a moment, to run the gauntlet of a houseful of interested observers. The state of being 'engaged', in itself an absurd enough predicament, even to a man only intermittently exposed, became intolerable under the continuous scrutiny of a small circle quivering with participation. Darrow was furthermore aware that, though the case of the other couple ought to have made his own less conspicuous, it was rather they who found a refuge in the shadow of his prominence. Madame de Chantelle, though she had consented to Owen's engagement and formally welcomed his betrothed, was nevertheless not sorry to show, by her reception of Darrow, of what finely-shaded degrees of cordiality she was capable. Miss Painter, having won the day for Owen, was also free to turn her attention to the newer candidate for her sympathy; and Darrow and Anna found themselves immersed in a warm bath of sentimental curiosity.

It was a relief to Darrow that he was under a positive obligation to end his visit within the next forty-eight hours. When he left London, his Ambassador had accorded him a ten days' leave. His fate being definitely settled and openly published he had no reason for asking to have the time prolonged, and when it was over he was to return to his post till the time fixed for taking up his new duties. Anna and he had therefore decided to be married, in Paris, a day or two before the departure of the steamer which was to take them to South America; and Anna, shortly after his return to England, was to go up to Paris and begin her own preparations.

In honour of the double betrothal Effie and Miss Viner were to appear that evening at dinner; and Darrow, on leaving his room, met the little girl springing down the stairs, her white ruffles and coral-coloured bows making her look like a daisy with her yellow hair for its centre. Sophy Viner was behind her pupil, and as she came into the light Darrow noticed a change in her appearance and wondered vaguely why she looked suddenly younger, more vivid, more like the little luminous ghost of his Paris memories. Then it occurred to him that it was the first time she had appeared at dinner since his arrival at Givré, and the first time, consequently, that he had seen her in evening dress. She was still at the age when the least adornment embellishes; and no doubt the mere uncovering of her young throat and neck had given her back her former brightness. But a second glance showed a more precise reason for his impression. Vaguely though he retained such details, he felt sure she was wearing the dress he had seen her in every evening in Paris. It was a simple enough dress, black, and transparent on the arms and shoulders, and he would probably not have recognized it if she had not called his attention to it in Paris by confessing that she hadn't any other. 'The same dress? That proves that she's forgotten!' was his first half-ironic thought; but the next moment, with a pang of compunction, he said to himself that she had probably put it on for the same reason as before: simply because she hadn't any other.

He looked at her in silence, and for an instant, above Effie's bobbing head, she gave him back his look in a full bright gaze.

'Oh, there's Owen!' Effie cried, and whirled away down the gallery to the door from which her step-brother was emerging. As Owen bent to catch her, Sophy Viner turned abruptly back to Darrow.

'You, too?' she said with a quick laugh. 'I didn't know –' And as Owen came up to them she added, in a tone that might have been meant to reach his ear: 'I wish you all the luck that we can spare!'

About the dinner-table, which Effie, with Miss Viner's aid, had lavishly garlanded, the little party had an air of somewhat self-conscious festivity. In spite of flowers, champagne and a unanimous attempt at ease, there were frequent lapses in the talk, and moments of nervous groping for new subjects. Miss Painter alone seemed not only unaffected by the general perturbation but as tightly sealed up in her unconsciousness of it as a diver in his bell. To Darrow's strained attention even Owen's gusts of gaiety seemed to betray an inward sense of insecurity. After dinner, however, at the piano, he broke into a mood of extravagant hilarity and flooded the room with the splash and ripple of his music.

Darrow, sunk in a sofa corner in the lee of Miss Painter's granite bulk, smoked and listened in silence, his eyes moving from one figure to another. Madame de Chantelle, in her armchair near the fire, clasped her little granddaughter to her with the gesture of a drawing-room Niobe, and Anna, seated near them, had fallen into one of the attitudes of vivid calm which seemed to Darrow to express her inmost quality. Sophy Viner, after moving uncertainly about the room, had placed herself beyond Mrs Leath, in a chair near the piano, where she sat with head thrown back and eyes attached to the musician, in the same rapt fixity of attention with which she had followed the players at the Français. The accident of her having fallen into the same attitude, and of her wearing the same dress, gave Darrow, as he watched her, a strange sense of double consciousness. To escape from it, his glance turned back to Anna; but from the point at which he was placed his eyes could not take in the one face without the other, and that renewed the disturbing duality of the impression. Suddenly Owen broke off with a crash of chords and jumped to his feet.

'What's the use of this, with such a moon to say it for us?'

Behind the uncurtained window a low golden orb hung like a ripe fruit against the glass.

'Yes – let's go out and listen,' Anna answered. Owen threw open the window, and with his gesture a fold of the heavy star-sprinkled sky seemed to droop into the room like a drawn-in curtain. The air that entered with it had a frosty edge, and Anna bade Effie run to the hall for wraps.

Darrow said: 'You must have one too,' and started toward the door; but Sophy, following her pupil, cried back: 'We'll bring things for everybody.'

Owen had followed her, and in a moment the three reappeared, and the party went out on the terrace. The deep blue purity of the night was unveiled by mist, and the moonlight rimmed the edges of the trees with a silver blur and blanched to unnatural whiteness the statues against their walls of shade.

Darrow and Anna, with Effie between them, strolled to the farther corner of the terrace. Below them, between the fringes of the park, the lawn sloped dimly to the fields above the river. For a few minutes they stood silently side by side, touched to peace beneath the trembling beauty of the sky. When they turned back, Darrow saw that Owen and Sophy Viner, who had gone down the steps to the garden, were also walking in the direction of the house. As they advanced, Sophy paused in a patch of moonlight, between the sharp shadows of the yews, and Darrow noticed that she had thrown over her shoulders a long cloak of some light colour, which suddenly evoked her image as she had entered the restaurant at his side on the night of their first dinner in Paris. A moment later they were all together again on the terrace, and when they re-entered the drawing-room the older ladies were on their way to bed.

Effie, emboldened by the privileges of the evening, was for coaxing Owen to round it off with a game of forfeits or some such reckless climax; but Sophy, resuming her professional rôle, sounded the summons to bed. In her pupil's wake she made her round of good-nights; but when she proffered her hand to Anna, the latter ignoring the gesture held out both arms.

'Good-night, dear child,' she said impulsively, and drew the girl to her kiss.

BOOK FOUR

23

The next day was Darrow's last at Givré and foreseeing that the afternoon and evening would have to be given to the family, he had asked Anna to devote an early hour to the final consideration of their plans. He was to meet her in the brown sitting-room at ten, and they were to walk down to the river and talk over their future in the little pavilion abutting on the wall of the park.

It was just a week since his arrival at Givré, and Anna wished, before he left, to return to the place where they had sat on their first afternoon together. Her sensitiveness to the appeal of inanimate things, to the colour and texture of whatever wove itself into the substance of her emotion, made her want to hear Darrow's voice, and to feel his eyes on her, in the spot where bliss had first flowed into her heart.

That bliss, in the interval, had wound itself into every fold of her being. Passing, in the first days, from a high shy tenderness to the rush of a secret surrender, it had gradually widened and deepened, to flow on in redoubled beauty. She thought she now knew exactly how and why she loved Darrow, and she could see her whole sky reflected in the deep and tranquil current of her love.

Early the next day, in her sitting-room, she was glancing through the letters which it was Effie's morning privilege to carry up to her. Effie meanwhile circled inquisitively about the room, where there was always something new to engage her infant fancy; and Anna, looking up, saw her suddenly arrested before a photograph of Darrow which, the day before, had taken its place on the writing-table.

Anna held out her arms with a faint blush. 'You do like him, don't you, dear?'

'Oh, most awfully, dearest,' Effie, against her breast, leaned back to assure her with a limpid look. 'And so do Granny and Owen – and I *do* think Sophy does too,' she added, after a moment's earnest pondering.

'I hope so,' Anna laughed. She checked the impulse to continue: 'Has she talked to you about him, that you're so sure?' She did not know what had made the question spring to her lips, but she was glad she had closed them before pronouncing it. Nothing could have been more distasteful to her than to clear up such obscurities by turning on them the tiny flame of her daughter's observation. And what, after all, now that Owen's happiness was secured, did it matter if there were certain reserves in Darrow's approval of his marriage?

A knock on the door made Anna glance at the clock. 'There's Nurse to carry you off.'

'It's Sophy's knock,' the little girl answered, jumping down to open the door; and Miss Viner in fact stood on the threshold.

'Come in,' Anna said with a smile, instantly remarking how pale she looked.

'May Effie go out for a turn with Nurse?' the girl asked. 'I should like to speak to you a moment.'

'Of course. This ought to be *your* holiday, as yesterday was Effie's. Run off, dear,' she added, stooping to kiss the little girl.

When the door had closed she turned back to Sophy Viner with a look that sought her confidence. 'I'm so glad you came, my dear. We've got so many things to talk about, just you and I together.'

The confused intercourse of the last days had, in fact, left little time for any speech with Sophy but such as related to her marriage and the means of overcoming Madame de Chantelle's opposition to it. Anna had exacted of Owen that no one, not even Sophy Viner, should be given a hint of her own projects till all contingent questions had been disposed of. She had felt, from the outset, a secret reluctance to intrude her securer happiness on the doubts and fears of the young pair.

From the sofa-corner to which she had dropped back she pointed to Darrow's chair. 'Come and sit by me, dear. I wanted to see you alone. There's so much to say that I hardly know where to begin.'

She leaned forward, her hands clasped on the arms of the sofa, her eyes bent smilingly on Sophy's. As she did so, she noticed that the girl's unusual pallor was partly due to the slight veil of powder on her face. The discovery was distinctly disagreeable. Anna had never before noticed, on Sophy's part, any recourse to cosmetics, and, much as she wished to think herself exempt from old-fashioned prejudices, she suddenly became aware that she did not like her daughter's governess to have a powdered face. Then she reflected that the girl who sat opposite her was no longer Effie's governess, but her own future daughter-in-law; and she wondered whether Miss Viner had chosen this odd way of celebrating her independence, and whether, as Mrs Owen Leath, she would present to the world a bedizened countenance. This idea was scarcely less distasteful than the other, and for a moment Anna continued to consider her without speaking. Then, in a flash, the truth came to her: Miss Viner had powdered her face because Miss Viner had been crying.

Anna leaned forward impulsively. 'My dear child, what's the matter?' She saw the girl's blood rush up under the white mask, and hastened on: 'Please don't be afraid to tell me. I do so want you to feel that you can trust me as Owen does. And you know you mustn't mind if, just at first, Madame de Chantelle occasionally relapses.'

She spoke eagerly, persuasively, almost on a note of pleading. She had, in truth, so many reasons for wanting Sophy to like her: her love for Owen, her solicitude for Effie, and her own sense of the girl's fine mettle. She had always felt a romantic and almost humble admiration for those members of her sex who, from force of will, or the constraint of circumstances, had plunged into the conflict from which fate had so persistently excluded her. There were even moments when she fancied herself vaguely to blame for her immunity, and felt that she ought somehow to have affronted the perils and hardships which refused to come to her. And now, as she sat looking at Sophy Viner, so small, so slight, so visibly defenceless and undone, she still felt, through all the superiority of her worldly advantages and her seeming maturity, the same odd sense of ignorance and inexperience. She could not have said what there was in the girl's manner and expression to give her this feeling, but she was reminded, as she looked at Sophy Viner, of the other girls she had known in her youth, the girls who seemed possessed of a secret she had missed. Yes, Sophy Viner had their look – almost the obscurely menacing look of Kitty Mayne . . . Anna, with an inward smile, brushed aside the image of this forgotten rival. But she had felt, deep down, a twinge of the old pain, and she was sorry that, even for the flash of a thought, Owen's betrothed should have reminded her of so different a woman . . .

She laid her hand on the girl's. 'When his grand-mother sees how happy Owen is she'll be quite happy herself. If it's only that, don't be distressed. Just trust to Owen – and the future.'

Sophy Viner, with an almost imperceptible recoil of her whole slight person, had drawn her hand from under the palm enclosing it.

'That's what I wanted to talk to you about – the future.'

'Of course! We've all so many plans to make – and to fit into each other's. Please let's begin with yours.'

The girl paused a moment, her hands clasped on the arms of her chair, her lids dropped under Anna's gaze; then she said: 'I should like to make no plans at all . . . just yet . . .'

'No plans?'

'No – I should like to go away . . . my friends the Farlows would let me go to them . . .' Her voice grew firmer and she lifted her eyes to add: 'I should like to leave today, if you don't mind.'

Anna listened with a rising wonder.

'You want to leave Givré at once?' She gave the idea a moment's swift consideration. 'You prefer to be with your friends till your marriage? I understand that – but surely you needn't rush off today? There are so many details to discuss; and before long, you know, I shall be going away too.'

'Yes, I know.' The girl was evidently trying to steady her voice. 'But I should like to wait a few days – to have a little more time to myself.'

Anna continued to consider her kindly. It was evident that she did not care to say why she wished to leave Givré so suddenly, but her disturbed face and shaken voice betrayed a more pressing motive than the natural desire to spend the weeks before her marriage under her old friends' roof. Since she had made no response to the allusion to Madame de Chantelle, Anna could but conjecture that she had had a passing disagreement with Owen; and if this were so, random interference might do more harm than good.

'My dear child, if you really want to go at once I shan't, of course, urge you to stay. I suppose you have spoken to Owen?'

'No. Not yet . . .'

Anna threw an astonished glance at her. 'You mean to say you haven't told him?'

'I wanted to tell you first. I thought I ought to, on account of Effie.' Her look cleared as she put forth this reason.

'Oh, Effie! –' Anna's smile brushed away the scruple: 'Owen has a right to ask that you should consider him before you think of his sister . . . Of course you shall do just as you wish,' she went on, after another thoughtful interval.

'Oh, thank you,' Sophy Viner murmured and rose to her feet.

Anna rose also, vaguely seeking for some word that should break down the girl's resistance. 'You'll tell Owen at once?' she finally asked.

Miss Viner, instead of replying, stood before her in manifest uncertainty, and as she did so there was a light tap on the door, and Owen Leath walked into the room.

Anna's first glance told her that his face was unclouded. He met her greeting with his happiest smile and turned to lift Sophy's hand to his lips. The perception that he was utterly unconscious of any cause for Miss Viner's agitation came to his step-mother with a sharp thrill of surprise.

'Darrow's looking for you,' he said to her. 'He asked me to remind you that you'd promised to go for a walk with him.'

Anna glanced at the clock. 'I'll go down presently.' She waited and looked again at Sophy Viner, whose troubled eyes seemed to commit their message to her. 'You'd better tell Owen, my dear.'

Owen's look also turned on the girl. 'Tell me what? Why, what's happened?'

Anna summoned a laugh to ease the vague tension of the moment. 'Don't look so startled! Nothing, except that Sophy proposes to desert us for a while for the Farlows.'

Owen's brow cleared. 'I was afraid she'd run off before long.' He glanced at Anna. 'Do please keep her here as long as you can!'

Sophy intervened: 'Mrs Leath's already given me leave to go.'

'Already? To go when?'

'Today,' said Sophy in a low tone, her eyes on Anna's.

'Today? Why on earth should you go today?' Owen dropped back a step or two, flushing and paling under his bewildered frown. His eyes seemed to search the girl more closely. 'Something's happened.'

He too looked at his step-mother. 'I suppose she must have told you what it is?'

Anna was struck by the suddenness and vehemence of his appeal. It was as though some smouldering apprehension had lain close under the surface of his security.

'She's told me nothing except that she wishes to be with her friends. It's quite natural that she should want to go to them.'

Owen visibly controlled himself. 'Of course – quite natural.' He spoke to Sophy. 'But why didn't you tell me so? Why did you come first to my step-mother?'

Anna intervened with her calm smile. 'That seems to me quite natural, too. Sophy was considerate enough to tell me first because of Effie.'

He weighed it. 'Very well, then: that's quite natural, as you say. And of course she must do exactly as she pleases.' He still kept his eyes on the girl. 'Tomorrow,' he abruptly announced, 'I shall go up to Paris to see you.'

'Oh, no – no!' she protested.

Owen turned back to Anna. '*Now* do you say that nothing's happened?'

Under the influence of his agitation Anna felt a vague tightening of the heart. She seemed to herself like someone in a dark room about whom unseen presences are groping.

'If it's anything that Sophy wishes to tell you, no doubt she'll do so. I'm going down now, and I'll leave you here to talk it over by yourselves.'

As she moved to the door the girl caught up with her. 'But there's nothing to tell: why should there be? I've explained that I simply want to be quiet.' Her look seemed to detain Mrs Leath.

Owen broke in: 'Is that why I mayn't go up tomorrow?'

'Not tomorrow!'

'Then when may I?'

'Later . . . in a little while . . . a few days . . .'

'In how many days?'

'Owen!' his step-mother interposed; but he seemed no longer aware of her. 'If you go away today, the day that our engagement's made known, it's only fair,' he persisted, 'that you should tell me when I am to see you.'

Sophy's eyes wavered between the two and dropped down wearily. 'It's you who are not fair – when I've said I wanted to be quiet.'

'But why should my coming disturb you? I'm not asking now to come tomorrow. I only ask you not to leave without telling me when I'm to see you.'

'Owen, I don't understand you!' his step-mother exclaimed.

'You don't understand my asking for some explanation, some assurance, when I'm left in this way, without a word, without a sign? All I ask her to tell me is when she'll see me.'

Anna turned back to Sophy Viner, who stood straight and tremulous between the two.

'After all, my dear, he's not unreasonable!'

'I'll write – I'll write,' the girl repeated.

'*What* will you write?' he pressed her vehemently.

'Owen,' Anna exclaimed, 'you *are* unreasonable!'

He turned from Sophy to his step-mother. 'I only want her to say what she means: that she's going to write to break off our engagement. Isn't that what you're going away for?'

Anna felt the contagion of his excitement. She looked at Sophy, who stood motionless, her lips set, her whole face drawn to a silent fixity of resistance.

'You ought to speak, my dear – you ought to answer him.'

'I only ask him to wait –'

'Yes,' Owen broke in, 'and you won't say how long!'

Both instinctively addressed themselves to Anna, who stood, nearly as shaken as themselves, between the double shock of their struggle. She looked again from Sophy's inscrutable eyes to Owen's stormy features; then she said: 'What can I do, when there's clearly something between you that I don't know about?'

'Oh, if it *were* between us! Can't you see it's outside of us – outside of her, dragging at her, dragging her away from me?' Owen wheeled round again upon his step-mother.

Anna turned from him to the girl. 'Is it true that you want to break your engagement? If you do, you ought to tell him now.'

Owen burst into a laugh. 'She doesn't dare to – she's afraid I'll guess the reason!'

A faint sound escaped from Sophy's lips, but she kept them close on whatever answer she had ready.

'If she doesn't wish to marry you, why should she be afraid to have you know the reason?'

'She's afraid to have *you* know it – not me!'

'To have *me* know it?'

He laughed again, and Anna, at his laugh, felt a sudden rush of indignation.

'Owen, you must explain what you mean!'

He looked at her hard before answering; then: 'Ask Darrow!' he said.

'Owen – Owen!' Sophy Viner murmured.

24

Anna stood looking from one to the other. It had become apparent to her in a flash that Owen's retort, though it startled Sophy, did not take her by surprise; and the discovery shot its light along dark distances of fear.

The immediate inference was that Owen had guessed the reason of Darrow's disapproval of his marriage, or that, at least, he suspected Sophy Viner of knowing and dreading it. This confirmation of her own obscure doubt sent a tremor of alarm through Anna. For a moment she felt like exclaiming: 'All this is really no business of mine, and I refuse to have you mix me up in it –' but her secret fear held her fast.

Sophy Viner was the first to speak.

'I should like to go now,' she said in a low voice, taking a few steps toward the door.

Her tone woke Anna to the sense of her own share in the situation. 'I quite agree with you, my dear, that it's useless to carry on this discussion. But since Mr Darrow's name has been brought into it, for reasons which I fail to guess, I want to tell you that you're both mistaken if you think he's not in sympathy with your marriage. If that's what Owen means to imply, the idea's a complete delusion.'

She spoke the words deliberately and incisively, as if hoping that the sound of their utterance would stifle the whisper in her bosom.

Sophy's only answer was a vague murmur, and a movement that

brought her nearer to the door; but before she could reach it Owen had placed himself in her way.

'I don't mean to imply what you think,' he said, addressing his step-mother but keeping his eyes on the girl. 'I don't say Darrow doesn't like our marriage; I say it's Sophy who's hated it since Darrow's been here!'

He brought out the charge in a tone of forced composure, but his lips were white and he grasped the door-knob to hide the tremor of his hand.

Anna's anger surged up with her fears. 'You're absurd, Owen! I don't know why I listen to you. Why should Sophy dislike Mr Darrow, and if she does, why should that have anything to do with her wishing to break her engagement?'

'I don't say she dislikes him! I don't say she likes him; I don't know what it is they say to each other when they're shut up together alone.'

'Shut up together alone?' Anna stared. Owen seemed like a man in delirium; such an exhibition was degrading to them all. But he pushed on without seeing her look.

'Yes – the first evening she came, in the study; the next morning, early, in the park; yesterday, again, in the springhouse, when you were at the lodge with the doctor . . . I don't know what they say to each other, but they've taken every chance they could to say it . . . and to say it when they thought that no one saw them.'

Anna longed to silence him, but no words came to her. It was as though all her confused apprehensions had suddenly taken definite shape. There was 'something' – yes, there was 'something' . . . Darrow's reticences and evasions had been more than a figment of her doubts.

The next instant brought a recoil of pride. She turned indignantly on her step-son.

'I don't half understand what you've been saying; but what you seem to hint is so preposterous, and so insulting both to Sophy and to me, that I see no reason why we should listen to you any longer.'

Though her tone steadied Owen, she perceived at once that it would not deflect him from his purpose. He spoke less vehemently, but with all the more precision.

'How can it be preposterous, since it's true? Or insulting, since I don't know, any more than *you*, the meaning of what I've been seeing? If you'll be patient with me I'll try to put it quietly. What I mean is that Sophy has completely changed since she met Darrow here, and that, having noticed the change, I'm hardly to blame for having tried to find out its cause.'

Anna made an effort to answer him with the same composure. 'You're to blame, at any rate, for so recklessly assuming that you *have* found it out. You seem to forget that, till they met here, Sophy and Mr Darrow hardly knew each other.'

'If so, it's all the stranger that they've been so often closeted together!'

'Owen, Owen –' the girl sighed out.

He turned his haggard face to her. 'Can I help it, if I've seen and known what I wasn't meant to? For God's sake give me a reason – any reason I can decently make out with! Is it my fault if, the day after you arrived, when I came back late through the garden, the curtains of the study hadn't been drawn, and I saw you there alone with Darrow?'

Anna laughed impatiently. 'Really, Owen, if you make it a grievance that two people who are staying in the same house should be seen talking together –!'

'They were not talking. That's the point –'

'Not talking? How do you know? You could hardly hear them from the garden!'

'No; but I could see. *He* was sitting at my desk, with his face in his hands. *She* was standing in the window, looking away from him . . .'

He waited, as if for Sophy Viner's answer; but still she neither stirred nor spoke.

'That was the first time,' he went on; 'and the second was the next morning in the park. It was natural enough, their meeting there. Sophy had gone out with Effie, and Effie ran back to look for me. She told me she'd left Sophy and Darrow in the path that leads to the river, and presently we saw them ahead of us. They didn't see us at first, because they were standing looking at each other; and this time they were not speaking either. We came up close before they heard us, and all that time they never spoke, or stopped looking at each other. After that I began to wonder; and so I watched them.'

'Oh, Owen!'

'Oh, I only had to wait. Yesterday, when I motored you and the doctor back from the lodge, I saw Sophy coming out of the spring-house. I supposed she'd taken shelter from the rain, and when you got out of the motor I strolled back down the avenue to meet her. But she'd disappeared – she must have taken a short cut and come into the house by the side door. I don't know why I went on to the spring-house; I suppose it was what you'd call spying. I went up the steps and found the room empty; but two chairs had been moved out from the wall and were standing near the table; and one of the Chinese screens that lie on it had dropped to the floor.'

Anna sounded a faint note of irony. 'Really? Sophy'd gone there for shelter, and she dropped a screen and moved a chair?'

'I said two chairs –'

'Two? What damning evidence – of I don't know what!'

'Simply of the fact that Darrow'd been there with her. As I looked out of the window I saw him close by, walking away. He must have turned the corner of the spring-house just as I got to the door.'

There was another silence, during which Anna paused, not only to collect her own words but to wait for Sophy Viner's; then, as the girl made no sign, she turned to her.

'I've absolutely nothing to say to all this; but perhaps you'd like me to wait and hear your answer?'

Sophy raised her head with a quick flash of colour. 'I've no answer either – except that Owen must be mad.'

In the interval since she had last spoken she seemed to have re-gained her self-control, and her voice rang clear, with a cold edge of anger.

Anna looked at her step-son. He had grown extremely pale, and his hand fell from the door with a discouraged gesture. 'That's all then? You won't give me any reason?'

'I didn't suppose it was necessary to give you or any one else a reason for talking with a friend of Mrs Leath's under Mrs Leath's own roof.'

Owen hardly seemed to feel the retort: he kept his dogged stare on her face.

'I won't ask for one, then. I'll only ask you to give me your assur-ance that your talks with Darrow have had nothing to do with your suddenly deciding to leave Givré.'

She hesitated, not so much with the air of weighing her answer as of questioning his right to exact any. 'I give you my assurance; and now I should like to go,' she said.

As she turned away, Anna intervened. 'My dear, I think you ought to speak.'

The girl drew herself up with a faint laugh. 'To him – or to *you*?'

'To him.'

She stiffened. 'I've said all there is to say.'

Anna drew back, her eyes on her step-son. He had left the threshold and was advancing toward Sophy Viner with a motion of desperate appeal; but as he did so there was a knock on the door. A moment's silence fell on the three; then Anna said: 'Come in!'

Darrow came into the room. Seeing the three together, he looked rapidly from one to the other; then he turned to Anna with a smile.

'I came up to see if you were ready; but please send me off if I'm not wanted.'

His look, his voice, the simple sense of his presence, restored Anna's shaken balance. By Owen's side he looked so strong, so urbane, so experienced, that the lad's passionate charges dwindled to mere boyish vapourings. A moment ago she had dreaded Darrow's coming; now she was glad that he was there.

She turned to him with sudden decision. 'Come in, please; I want you to hear what Owen has been saying.'

She caught a murmur from Sophy Viner, but disregarded it. An illuminating impulse urged her on. She, habitually so aware of her own lack of penetration, her small skill in reading hidden motives and detecting secret signals, now felt herself mysteriously inspired. She addressed herself to Sophy Viner. 'It's much better for you both that this absurd question should be cleared up now.' Then, turning to Darrow, she continued: 'For some reason that I don't pretend to guess, Owen has taken it into his head that you've influenced Miss Viner to break her engagement.'

She spoke slowly and deliberately, because she wished to give time and to gain it; time for Darrow and Sophy to receive the full impact of what she was saying, and time to observe its full effect on them. She had said to herself: 'If there's nothing between them, they'll look at each other; if there *is* something, they won't;' and as she ceased to speak she felt as if all her life were in her eyes.

Sophy, after a start of protest, remained motionless, her gaze on the ground. Darrow, his face grown grave, glanced slowly from Owen Leath to Anna. With his eyes on the latter he asked: 'Has Miss Viner broken her engagement?'

A moment's silence followed his question; then the girl looked up and said: 'Yes!'

Owen, as she spoke, uttered a smothered exclamation and walked out of the room. She continued to stand in the same place, without appearing to notice his departure, and without vouchsafing an additional word of explanation; then, before Anna could find a cry to detain her, she too turned and went out.

'For God's sake, what's happened?' Darrow asked; but Anna, with a drop of the heart, was saying to herself that he and Sophy Viner had not looked at each other.

25

Anna stood in the middle of the room, her eyes on the door. Darrow's questioning gaze was still on her, and she said to herself with a quick-drawn breath: 'If only he doesn't come near me!'

It seemed to her that she had been suddenly endowed with the fatal gift of reading the secret sense of every seemingly spontaneous look and movement, and that in his least gesture of affection she would detect a cold design.

For a moment longer he continued to look at her enquiringly; then he turned away and took up his habitual stand by the mantelpiece. She drew a deep breath of relief.

'Won't you please explain?' he said.

'I can't explain: I don't know. I didn't even know – till she told you – that she really meant to break her engagement. All I know is that she came to me just now and said she wished to leave Givré today; and that Owen, when he heard of it – for she hadn't told him – at once accused her of going away with the secret intention of throwing him over.'

'And you think it's a definite break?' She perceived, as she spoke, that his brow had cleared.

'How should I know? Perhaps you can tell me.'

'I?' She fancied his face clouded again, but he did not move from his tranquil attitude.

'As *I* told you,' she went on, 'Owen has worked himself up to imagining that for some mysterious reason you've influenced Sophy against him.'

Darrow still visibly wondered. 'It must indeed be a mysterious reason! He knows how slightly I know Miss Viner. Why should he imagine anything so wildly improbable?'

'I don't know that either.'

'But he must have hinted at some reason.'

'No: he admits he doesn't know your reason. He simply says that Sophy's manner to him has changed since she came back to Givré and that he's seen you together several times – in the park, the spring-house, I don't know where – talking alone in a way that seemed confidential – almost secret; and he draws the preposterous conclusion that you've used your influence to turn her against him.'

'My influence? What kind of influence?'

'He doesn't say.'

Darrow again seemed to turn over the facts she gave him. His face remained grave, but without the least trace of discomposure. 'And what does Miss Viner say?'

'She says it's perfectly natural that she should occasionally talk to my friends when she's under my roof – and refuses to give him any other explanation.'

'That at least is perfectly natural!'

Anna felt her cheeks flush as she answered: 'Yes – but there *is* something –'

'Something –?'

'Some reason for her sudden decision to break her engagement. I can understand Owen's feeling, sorry as I am for his way of showing it. The girl owes him some sort of explanation, and as long as she refuses to give it his imagination is sure to run wild.'

'She would have given it, no doubt, if he'd asked it in a different tone.'

'I don't defend Owen's tone – but she knew what it was before she accepted him. She knows he's excitable and undisciplined.'

'Well, she's been disciplining him a little – probably the best thing that could happen. Why not let the matter rest there?'

'Leave Owen with the idea that you *have* been the cause of the break?'

He met the question with his easy smile. 'Oh, as to that – leave him with any idea of me he chooses! But leave him, at any rate, free.'

'Free?' she echoed in surprise.

'Simply let things be. You've surely done all you could for him and Miss Viner. If they don't hit it off it's their own affair. What possible motive can you have for trying to interfere now?'

Her gaze widened to a deeper wonder. 'Why – naturally, what he says of you!'

'I don't care a straw what he says of me! In such a situation a boy in love will snatch at the most far-fetched reason rather than face the mortifying fact that the lady may simply be tired of him.'

'You don't quite understand Owen. Things go deep with him, and last long. It took him a long time to recover from his other unlucky love affair. He's romantic and extravagant: he can't live on the interest of his feelings. He worships Sophy and she seemed to be fond of him. If she's changed it's been very sudden. And if they part like this, angrily and inarticulately, it will hurt him horribly – hurt his very soul. But that, as you say, is between the two. What concerns me is his associating you with their quarrel. Owen's like my own son – if you'd seen him when I first came here you'd know why. We were like two prisoners who talk to each other by tapping on the wall. He's never forgotten it, nor I. Whether he breaks with Sophy, or whether they make it up, I can't let him think you had anything to do with it.'

She raised her eyes entreatingly to Darrow's, and read in them the forbearance of the man resigned to the discussion of non-existent problems.

'I'll do whatever you want me to,' he said; 'but I don't yet know what it is.'

His smile seemed to charge her with inconsequence, and the prick to her pride made her continue: 'After all, it's not so unnatural that Owen, knowing you and Sophy to be almost strangers, should wonder what you were saying to each other when he saw you talking together.'

She felt a warning tremor as she spoke, as though some instinct deeper than reason surged up in defence of its treasure. But Darrow's face was unstirred save by the flit of his half-amused smile.

'Well, my dear – and couldn't you have told him?'

'I?' she faltered out through her blush.

'You seem to forget, one and all of you, the position you put me in when I came down here: your appeal to me to see Owen through, your assurance to him that I would, Madame de Chantelle's attempt to win me over; and most of all, my own sense of the fact you've just recalled to me: the importance, for both of us, that Owen should like me. It seemed to me that the first thing to do was to get as much light as I could on the whole situation; and the obvious way of doing it was to try to know Miss Viner better. Of course I've talked with her alone – I've talked with her as often as I could. I've tried my best to find out if you were right in encouraging Owen to marry her.'

She listened with a growing sense of reassurance, struggling to separate the abstract sense of his words from the persuasion in which his eyes and voice enveloped them.

'I see – I do see,' she murmured.

'You must see, also, that I could hardly say this to Owen without offending him still more, and perhaps increasing the breach between Miss Viner and himself. What sort of figure should I cut if I told him I'd been trying to find out if he'd made a proper choice? In any case, it's none of my business to offer an explanation of what she justly says doesn't need one. If she declines to speak, it's obviously on the ground that Owen's insinuations are absurd; and that surely pledges me to silence.'

'Yes, yes! I see,' Anna repeated. 'But I don't want you to explain anything to Owen.'

'You haven't yet told me what you do want.'

She hesitated, conscious of the difficulty of justifying her request; then: 'I want you to speak to Sophy,' she said.

Darrow broke into an incredulous laugh. 'Considering what my previous attempts have resulted in –!'

She raised her eyes quickly. 'They haven't, at least, resulted in your liking her less, in your thinking less well of her than you've told me?'

She fancied he frowned a little. 'I wonder why you go back to that?'

'I want to be sure – I owe it to Owen. Won't you tell me the exact impression she's produced on you?'

'I have told you – I like Miss Viner.'

'Do you still believe she's in love with Owen?'

'There was nothing in our short talks to throw any particular light on that.'

'You still believe, though, that there's no reason why he shouldn't marry her?'

Again he betrayed a restrained impatience. 'How can I answer that without knowing her reasons for breaking with him?'

'That's just what I want you to find out from her.'

'And why in the world should she tell me?'

'Because, whatever grievance she has against Owen, she can certainly have none against me. She can't want to have Owen connect me in his mind with this wretched quarrel; and she must see that he will until he's convinced you've had no share in it.'

Darrow's elbow dropped from the mantelpiece and he took a restless step or two across the room. Then he halted before her.

'Why can't you tell her this yourself?'

'Don't you see?'

He eyed her intently, and she pressed on: 'You must have guessed that Owen's jealous of you.'

'Jealous of me?' The blood flew up under his brown skin.

'Blind with it – what else would drive him to this folly? And I can't have her think me jealous too! I've said all I could, short of making her think so; and she's refused a word more to either of us. Our only chance now is that she should listen to you – that you should make her see the harm her silence may do.'

Darrow uttered a protesting exclamation. 'It's all too preposterous – what you suggest! I can't, at any rate, appeal to her on such a ground as that!'

Anna laid her hand on his arm. 'Appeal to her on the ground that I'm almost Owen's mother, and that any estrangement between you and him would kill me. She knows what he is – she'll understand. Tell her to say anything, do anything, she wishes; but not to go away without speaking, not to leave *that* between us when she goes!'

She drew back a step and lifted her face to his, trying to look into his eyes more deeply than she had ever looked; but before she could discern what they expressed he had taken hold of her hands and bent his head to kiss them.

'You'll see her? You'll see her?' she entreated; and he answered: 'I'll do anything in the world you want me to.'

26

Darrow waited alone in the sitting-room.

No place could have been more distasteful as the scene of the talk that lay before him; but he had acceded to Anna's suggestion that it would seem more natural for her to summon Sophy Viner than for him to go in search of her. As his troubled pacings carried him back and forth a relentless hand seemed to be tearing away all the tender fibres of association that bound him to the peaceful room. Here, in this very place, he had drunk his deepest draughts of happiness, had had his lips at the fountain-head of its overflowing rivers; but now that source was poisoned and he would taste no more of an untainted cup.

For a moment he felt an actual physical anguish; then his nerves hardened for the coming struggle. He had no notion of what awaited him; but after the first instinctive recoil he had seen in a flash the urgent need of another word with Sophy Viner. He had been insincere in letting Anna think that he had consented to speak because she asked it. In reality he had been feverishly casting about for the pretext she had given him; and for some reason this trivial hypocrisy weighed on him more than all his heavy burden of deceit.

At length he heard a step behind him and Sophy Viner entered. When she saw him she paused on the threshold and half drew back.

'I was told that Mrs Leath had sent for me.'

'Mrs Leath *did* send for you. She'll be here presently; but I asked her to let me see you first.'

He spoke very gently, and there was no insincerity in his gentleness. He was profoundly moved by the change in the girl's appearance.

At sight of him she had forced a smile; but it lit up her wretchedness like a candle-flame held to a dead face.

She made no reply, and Darrow went on: 'You must understand my wanting to speak to you, after what I was told just now.'

She interposed, with a gesture of protest: 'I'm not responsible for Owen's ravings!'

'Of course –'. He broke off and they stood facing each other. She lifted a hand and pushed back her loose lock with the gesture that was burnt into his memory; then she looked about her and dropped into the nearest chair.

'Well, you've got what you wanted,' she said.

'What do you mean by what I wanted?'

'My engagement's broken – you heard me say so.'

'Why do you say that's what I wanted? All I wished, from the beginning, was to advise you, to help you as best I could –'

'That's what you've done,' she rejoined. 'You've convinced me that it's best I shouldn't marry him.'

Darrow broke into a despairing laugh. 'At the very moment when you'd convinced me to the contrary!'

'Had I?' Her smile flickered up. 'Well, I really believed it till you showed me . . . warned me . . .'

'Warned you?'

'That I'd be miserable if I married a man I didn't love.'

'Don't you love him?'

She made no answer, and Darrow started up and walked away to the other end of the room. He stopped before the writing-table, where his photograph, well-dressed, handsome, self-sufficient – the portrait of a man of the world, confident of his ability to deal adequately with the most delicate situations – offered its huge fatuity to his gaze. He turned back to her. 'It's rather hard on Owen, isn't it, that you should have waited until now to tell him?'

She reflected a moment before answering. 'I told him as soon as I knew.'

'Knew that you couldn't marry him?'

'Knew that I could never live here with him.' She looked about the room, as though the very walls must speak for her.

For a moment Darrow continued to search her face perplexedly; then their eyes met in a long disastrous gaze.

'Yes –' she said, and stood up.

Below the window they heard Effie whistling for her dogs, and then, from the terrace, her mother calling her.

'There – *that* for instance,' Sophy Viner said.

Darrow broke out: 'It's I who ought to go!'

She kept her small pale smile. 'What good would that do any of us – now?'

He covered his face with his hands. 'Good God!' he groaned. 'How could I tell?'

'You couldn't tell. We neither of us could.' She seemed to turn the problem over critically. 'After all, it might have been *you* instead of me!'

He took another distracted turn about the room and coming back to her sat down in a chair at her side. A mocking hand seemed to dash the words from his lips. There was nothing on earth that he could say to her that wasn't foolish or cruel or contemptible . . .

'My dear,' he began at last, 'oughtn't you, at any rate, to try?'

Her gaze grew grave. 'Try to forget you?'

He flushed to the forehead. 'I meant, try to give Owen more time; to give him a chance. He's madly in love with you; all the good that's in him is in your hands. His step-mother felt that from the first. And she thought – she believed –'

'She thought I could make him happy. Would she think so now?'

'Now . . .? I don't say now. But later? Time modifies . . . rubs out . . . more quickly than you think . . . Go away, but let him hope . . . I'm going too – *we're* going –' he stumbled on the plural – 'in a very few weeks: going for a long time, probably. What you're thinking of now may never happen. We may not all be here together again for years.'

She heard him out in silence, her hands clasped on her knee, her eyes bent on them. 'For me,' she said, 'you'll always be here.'

'Don't say that – oh, don't! Things change . . . people change . . . You'll see!'

'You don't understand. I don't want anything to change. I don't want to forget – to rub out. At first I imagined I did; but that was a foolish mistake. As soon as I saw you again I knew it . . . It's not being here with you that I'm afraid of – in the sense you think. It's being here, or anywhere, with Owen.' She stood up and bent her tragic smile on him. 'I want to keep you all to myself.'

The only words that came to him were futile denunciations of his folly; but the sense of their futility checked them on his lips. 'Poor child – you poor child!' he heard himself vainly repeating.

Suddenly he felt the strong reaction of reality and its impetus brought him to his feet. 'Whatever happens, I intend to go – to go for good,' he exclaimed. 'I want you to understand that. Oh, don't be afraid – I'll find a reason. But it's perfectly clear that I must go.'

She uttered a protesting cry. 'Go away? You? Don't you see that that would tell everything – drag everybody into the horror?'

He found no answer, and her voice dropped back to its calmer note. 'What good would your going do? Do you suppose it would change anything for me?' She looked at him with a musing wistfulness. 'I wonder what your feeling for me was? It seems queer that I've never really known – I suppose we *don't* know much about that kind of feeling. Is it like taking a drink when you're thirsty? . . . I used to feel as if all of me was in the palm of your hand . . .'

He bowed his humbled head, but she went on almost exultantly. 'Don't for a minute think I'm sorry! It was worth every penny it cost. My mistake was in being ashamed, just at first, of its having cost such a lot. I tried to carry it off as a joke – to talk of it to myself as an "adventure". I'd always wanted adventures, and you'd given me one, and I tried to take your attitude about it, to "play the game" and convince myself that I hadn't risked any more on it than you. Then, when I met you again, I suddenly saw that I *had* risked more, but that I'd won more, too – such worlds! I'd been trying all the while to put everything I could between us; now I want to sweep everything away. I'd been trying to forget how you looked; now I want to remember you always. I'd been trying not to hear your voice; now I never want to hear any other. I've made my choice – that's all: I've had you and I mean to keep you.' Her face was shining like her eyes. 'To keep you hidden away here,' she ended, and put her hand upon her breast.

After she had left him, Darrow continued to sit motionless, staring back into their past. Hitherto it had lingered on the edge of his mind in a vague pink blur, like one of the little rose-leaf clouds that a setting sun drops from its disk. Now it was a huge looming darkness, through which his eyes vainly strained. The whole episode was still obscure to him, save where here and there, as they talked, some phrase or gesture or intonation of the girl's had lit up a little spot in the night.

She had said: 'I wonder what your feeling for me was?' and he found himself wondering too . . . He remembered distinctly enough that he had not meant the perilous passion – even in its most transient form – to play a part in their relation. In that respect his attitude had been above reproach. She was an unusually original and attractive creature, to whom he had wanted to give a few days of harmless pleasuring, and who was alert and expert enough to understand his intention and spare him the boredom of hesitations and misinterpretations. That had been his first impression, and her subsequent demeanour had justified it. She had been, from the outset, just the frank and easy comrade he had expected to find her. Was it he, then, who, in the sequel, had grown impatient of the bounds he had set himself? Was it his wounded vanity that, seeking balm for its hurt, yearned to dip deeper into the healing pool of her compassion? In his confused memory of the situation he seemed not to have been guiltless of such yearnings . . . Yet for the first few days the experiment had been perfectly successful. Her enjoyment had been unclouded and his pleasure in it undisturbed. It was very gradually – he seemed to see – that a shade of lassitude had crept over their intercourse. Perhaps it was because, when her light chatter about people failed, he found she had no other fund to draw on, or perhaps simply because of the sweetness of her laugh, or of the charm of the gesture with which, one day in the woods of Marly, she had tossed off her hat and tilted back her head at the call of a cuckoo; or because, whenever he looked at her unexpectedly, he found that she was looking at him and did not want him to know it; or perhaps, in varying degrees, because of all these things, that there had come a moment when no word seemed to fly high enough or dive deep enough to utter the sense of well-being each gave to the other, and the natural substitute for speech had been a kiss.

The kiss, at all events, had come at the precise moment to save their venture from disaster. They had reached the point when her amazing reminiscences had begun to flag, when her future had been exhaustively discussed, her theatrical prospects minutely studied, her quarrel with Mrs Murrett retold with the last amplification of detail, and when, perhaps conscious of her exhausted resources and his dwindling interest, she had committed the fatal error of saying that she could see he was unhappy, and entreating him to tell her why . . .

From the brink of estranging confidences, and from the risk of unfavourable comparisons, his gesture had snatched her back to safety; and as soon as he had kissed her he felt that she would never bore him again. She was one of the elemental creatures whose emotion is all in their pulses, and who become inexpressive or senti-mental when they try to turn sensation into speech. His caress had restored her to her natural place in the scheme of things, and Darrow felt as if he had clasped a tree and a nymph had bloomed from it . . .

The mere fact of not having to listen to her any longer added immensely to her charm. She continued, of course, to talk to him, but it didn't matter, because he no longer made any effort to follow her words, but let her voice run on as a musical undercurrent to his thoughts. She hadn't a drop of poetry in her, but she had some of the qualities that create it in others; and in moments of heat the imagination does not always feel the difference . . .

Lying beside her in the shade, Darrow felt her presence as a part of the charmed stillness of the summer woods, as the element of vague well-being that suffused his senses and lulled to sleep the ache of wounded pride. All he asked of her, as yet, was a touch on the hand or on the lips – and that she should let him go on lying there through the long warm hours, while a blackbird's song throbbed like a fountain, and the summer wind stirred in the trees, and close by, between the nearest branches and the brim of his tilted hat, a slight white figure gathered up all the floating threads of joy . . .

He recalled, too, having noticed, as he lay staring at a break in the tree-tops, a stream of mares'-tails coming up the sky. He had said to himself: 'It will rain tomorrow,' and the thought had made the air seem warmer and the sun more vivid on her hair . . . Perhaps if the mares'-tails had not come up the sky their adventure might have had no sequel. But the cloud brought rain, and next morning he looked out of his window into a cold grey blur. They had planned an all-day excursion down the Seine, to the two Andelys and Rouen, and now, with the long hours on their hands, they were both a little at a loss . . . There was the Louvre, of course, and the Luxembourg; but he had tried looking at pictures with her, she had first so persistently admired the worst things, and then so frankly lapsed into indifference, that he had no wish to repeat the experiment. So they went out, aimlessly, and took a cold wet walk, turning at length into the deserted arcades of the Palais Royal, and finally drifting into one of its equally deserted restaurants, where they lunched alone and somewhat dolefully, served by a wan old waiter with the look of a castaway who has given up watching for a sail . . . It was odd how the waiter's face came back to him . . .

Perhaps but for the rain it might never have happened; but what was the use of thinking of that now? He tried to turn his thoughts to more urgent issues; but, by a strange perversity of association, every detail of the day was forcing itself on his mind with an insistence from which there was no escape. Reluctantly he relived the long wet walk back to the hotel, after a tedious hour at a cinematograph show on the Boulevard. It was still raining when they withdrew from this stale spectacle, but she had obstinately refused to take a cab, had even, on the way, insisted on loitering under the dripping awnings of shop-windows and poking into draughty passages, and finally, when they had nearly reached their destination, had gone so far as to suggest that they should turn back to hunt up some show she had heard of in a theatre at the Batignolles. But at that he had somewhat irritably protested: he remembered that, for the first time, they were both rather irritable, and vaguely disposed to resist one another's suggestions. His feet were wet, and he was tired of walking, and sick of the smell of stuffy unaired theatres, and he had said he must really get back to write some letters – and so they had kept on to the hotel . . .

27

Darrow had no idea how long he had sat there when he heard Anna's hand on the door. The effort of rising, and of composing his face to meet her, gave him a factitious sense of self-control. He said to himself: 'I must decide on something –' and that lifted him a hair's breadth above the whirling waters.

She came in with a lighter step, and he instantly perceived that something unforeseen and reassuring had happened.

'She's been with me. She came and found me on the terrace. We've had a long talk and she's explained everything. I feel as if I'd never known her before!'

Her voice was so moved and tender that it checked his start of apprehension.

'She's explained –?'

'It's natural, isn't it, that she should have felt a little sore at the kind of inspection she's been subjected to? Oh, not from *you* – I don't mean that! But Madame de Chantelle's opposition – and her sending for Adelaide Painter! She told me frankly she didn't care to owe her husband to Adelaide Painter . . . She thinks now that her annoyance at feeling herself so talked over and scrutinized may have shown itself in her manner to Owen, and set him imagining the insane things he did . . . I understand all she must have felt, and I agree with her that it's best she should go away for a while. She's made me,' Anna summed up, 'feel as if I'd been dreadfully thick-skinned and obtuse!'

'*You?*'

'Yes. As if I'd treated her like the bric-à-brac that used to be sent down here "on approval", to see if it would look well with the other pieces.' She added, with a sudden flush of enthusiasm: 'I'm glad she's got it in her to make one feel like that!'

She seemed to wait for Darrow to agree with her, or to put some other question, and he finally found voice to ask: 'Then you think it's not a final break?'

'I hope not – I've never hoped it more! I had a word with Owen, too, after I left her, and I think he understands that he must let her go without insisting on any positive promise. She's excited . . . he must let her calm down . . .'

Again she waited, and Darrow said: 'Surely you can make him see that.'

'She'll help me to – she's to see him, of course, before she goes. She starts immediately, by the way, with Adelaide Painter, who is motoring over to Francheuil to catch the one o'clock express – and who, of course, knows nothing of all this, and is simply to be told that Sophy has been sent for by the Farlows.'

Darrow mutely signed his comprehension, and she went on: 'Owen is particularly anxious that neither Adelaide nor his grandmother should have the least inkling of what's happened. The need of shielding Sophy will help him to control himself. He's coming to his senses, poor boy; he's ashamed of his wild talk already. He asked me to tell you so; no doubt he'll tell you so himself.'

Darrow made a movement of protest. 'Oh, as to that – the thing's not worth another word.'

'Or another thought, either?' She brightened. 'Promise me you won't even think of it – promise me you won't be hard on him!'

He was finding it easier to smile back at her. 'Why should you think it necessary to ask my indulgence for Owen?'

She hesitated a moment, her eyes wandering from him. Then they came back with a smile. 'Perhaps because I need it for myself.'

'For yourself?'

'I mean, because I understand better how one can torture one's self over unrealities.'

As Darrow listened, the tension of his nerves began to relax. Her gaze, so grave and yet so sweet, was like a deep pool into which he could plunge and hide himself from the hard glare of his misery. As this ecstatic sense enveloped him he found it more and more difficult to follow her words and to frame an answer; but what did anything matter, except that her voice should go on, and the syllables fall like soft touches on his tortured brain?

'Don't you know,' she continued, 'the bliss of waking from a bad dream in one's own quiet room, and going slowly over all the horror without being afraid of it any more? That's what I'm doing now. And that's why I understand Owen . . .' She broke off, and he felt her touch on his arm. '*Because I'd dreamed the horror too!*'

He understood her then, and stammered: 'You?'

'Forgive me! And let me tell you! . . . It will help you to understand Owen . . . There *were* little things . . . little signs . . . once I had begun to watch for them: your reluctance to speak about her . . . her reserve with you . . . a sort of constraint we'd never seen in her before . . .'

She laughed up at him, and with her hands in his he contrived to say: '*Now* you understand why –?'

'Oh, I understand; of course I understand; and I want you to laugh at me – with me! Because there were other things too . . . crazier things still . . . There was even – last night on the terrace – her pink cloak . . .'

'Her pink cloak?' Now he honestly wondered, and as she saw it she blushed.

'You've forgotten about the cloak? The pink cloak that Owen saw you with at the play in Paris? Yes . . . yes . . . I was mad enough for that! . . . It does me good to laugh about it now! But you ought to know that I'm going to be a jealous woman . . . a ridiculously jealous woman . . . you ought to be warned of it in time . . .'

He had dropped her hands, and she leaned close and lifted her arms to his neck with one of her rare gestures of surrender.

'I don't know why it is; but it makes me happier now to have been so foolish!'

Her lips were parted in a noiseless laugh and the tremor of her lashes made their shadow move on her cheek. He looked at her through a mist of pain and saw all her offered beauty held up like a cup to his lips; but as he stooped to it a darkness seemed to fall between them, her arms slipped from his shoulders and she drew away from him abruptly.

'But she *was* with you, then?' she exclaimed; and then, as he stared at her: 'Oh, don't say no! Only go and look at your eyes!'

He stood speechless, and she pressed on: 'Don't deny it – oh, don't deny it! What will be left for me to imagine if you do? Don't you see how every single thing cries it out? Owen sees it – he saw it again just now! When I told him she'd relented, and would see him, he said: "Is that Darrow's doing too?"'

Darrow took the onslaught in silence. He might have spoken, have summoned up the usual phrases of banter and denial; he was not even certain that they might not, for the moment, have served their purpose if he could have uttered them without being seen. But he was as conscious of what had happened to his face as if he had obeyed Anna's bidding and looked at himself in the glass. He knew he could no more hide from her what was written there than he could efface from his soul the fiery record of what he had just lived through. There before him, staring him in the eyes, and reflecting itself in all his lineaments, was the overwhelming fact of Sophy Viner's passion and of the act by which she had attested it.

Anna was talking again, hurriedly, feverishly, and his soul was wrung by the anguish in her voice. 'Do speak at last – you must speak! I don't want to ask you to harm the girl; but you must see that your silence is doing her more harm than your answering my questions could. You're leaving me only the worst things to think of her . . . she'd see that herself if she were here. What worse injury can you do her than to make me hate her – to make me feel she's plotted with you to deceive us?'

'Oh, not that!' Darrow heard his own voice before he was aware that he meant to speak. 'Yes; I did see her in Paris,' he went on after a pause; 'but I was bound to respect her reason for not wanting it known.'

Anna paled. 'It *was* she at the theatre that night?'

'I was with her at the theatre one night.'

'Why should she have asked you not to say so?'

'She didn't wish it known that I'd met her.'

'Why shouldn't she have wished it known?'

'She had quarrelled with Mrs Murrett and come over suddenly to Paris, and she didn't want the Farlows to hear of it. I came across her by accident, and she asked me not to speak of having seen her.'

'Because of her quarrel? Because she was ashamed of her part in it?'

'Oh, no. There was nothing for her to be ashamed of. But the Farlows had found the place for her, and she didn't want them to know how suddenly she'd had to leave, and how badly Mrs Murrett had behaved. She was in a terrible plight – the woman had even kept back her month's salary. She knew the Farlows would be awfully upset, and she wanted more time to prepare them.'

Darrow heard himself speak as though the words had proceeded from other lips. His explanation sounded plausible enough, and he half-fancied Anna's look grew lighter. She waited a moment, as though to be sure he had no more to add; then she said: 'But the Farlows *did* know; they told me all about it when they sent her to me.'

He flushed as if she had laid a deliberate trap for him. 'They may know *now*; they didn't then –'

'That's no reason for her continuing now to make a mystery of having met you.'

'It's the only reason I can give you.'

'Then I'll go and ask her for one myself.' She turned and took a few steps toward the door.

'Anna!' He started to follow her, and then checked himself. 'Don't do that!'

'Why not?'

'It's not like you . . . not generous . . .'

She stood before him straight and pale, but under her rigid face he saw the tumult of her doubt and misery.

'I don't want to be ungenerous; I don't want to pry into her secrets. But things can't be left like this. Wouldn't it be better for me to go to her? Surely she'll understand – she'll explain . . . It may be some mere trifle she's concealing: something that would horrify the Farlows, but that I shouldn't see any harm in . . .' She paused, her eyes searching his face. 'A love affair, I suppose . . . that's it? You met her with some man at the theatre – and she was frightened and begged you to fib about it? Those poor young things that have to go about among us like machines – oh, if you knew how I pity them!'

'If you pity her, why not let her go?'

She stared. 'Let her go – go for good, you mean? Is that the best you can say for her?'

'Let things take their course. After all, it's between herself and Owen.'

'And you and me – and Effie, if Owen marries her, and I leave my child with them! Don't you see the impossibility of what you're asking? We're all bound together in this coil.'

Darrow turned away with a groan. 'Oh, let her go – let her go.'

'Then there *is* something – something really bad? She *was* with some one when you met her? Some one with whom she was –' She broke off, and he saw her struggling with new thoughts. 'If it's *that*, of course . . . Oh, don't you see,' she desperately appealed to him, 'that I must find out, and that it's too late now for you not to speak? Don't be afraid that I'll betray you . . . I'll never, never let a soul suspect. But I must know the truth, and surely it's best for her that I should find it out from you.'

Darrow waited a moment; then he said slowly: 'What you imagine's mere madness. She was at the theatre with me.'

'With you?' He saw a tremor pass through her, but she controlled it instantly and faced him straight and motionless as a wounded creature in the moment before it feels its wound. 'Why should you both have made a mystery of that?'

'I've told you the idea was not mine.' He cast about. 'She may have been afraid that Owen –'

'But that was not a reason for her asking you to tell me that you hardly knew her – that you hadn't even seen her for years.' She broke off and the blood rose to her face and forehead. 'Even if *she* had other reasons, there could be only one reason for your obeying her –'

Silence fell between them, a silence in which the room seemed to become suddenly resonant with voices. Darrow's gaze wandered to the window and he noticed that the gale of two days before had nearly stripped the tops of the lime-trees in the court. Anna had moved away and was resting her elbows against the mantelpiece, her head in her hands. As she stood there he took in with a new intensity of vision little details of her appearance that his eyes had often cherished: the branching blue veins in the backs of her hands, the warm shadow that her hair cast on her ear, and the colour of the hair itself, dull black with a tawny under-surface, like the wings of certain birds. He felt it to be useless to speak.

After a while she lifted her head and said: 'I shall not see her again before she goes.'

He made no answer, and turning to him she added: 'That *is* why she's going, I suppose? Because she loves you and won't give you up?'

Darrow waited. The paltriness of conventional denial was so apparent to him that even if it could have delayed discovery he could no longer have resorted to it. Under all his other fears was the dread of dishonouring the hour.

'She *has* given me up,' he said at last.

28

When he had gone out of the room Anna stood where he had left her. 'I must believe him! I must believe him!' she said.

A moment before, at the moment when she had lifted her arms to his neck, she had been wrapped in a sense of complete security. All the spirits of doubt had been exorcized, and her love was once more the clear habitation in which every thought and feeling could move in blissful freedom. And then, as she raised her face to Darrow's and met his eyes, she had seemed to look into the very ruins of his soul. That was the only way she could express it. It was as though he and she had been looking at two sides of the same thing, and the side she had seen had been all light and life, and his a place of graves . . .

She didn't now recall who had spoken first, or even, very clearly, what had been said. It seemed to her only a moment later that she had found herself standing at the other end of the room – the room which had suddenly grown so small that, even with its length between them, she felt as if he touched her – crying out to him 'It *is* because of you she's going!' and reading the avowal in his face.

That was his secret, then, *their* secret: he had met the girl in Paris and helped her in her straits – lent her money, Anna vaguely conjectured – and she had fallen in love with him, and on meeting him again had been suddenly overmastered by her passion. Anna, dropping back into her sofa-corner, sat staring these facts in the face.

The girl had been in a desperate plight – frightened, penniless, outraged by what had happened, and not knowing (with a woman like Mrs Murrett) what fresh injury might impend; and Darrow, meeting her in this distracted hour, had pitied, counselled, been kind to her, with the fatal, the inevitable result. There were the facts as Anna made them out: that, at least, was their external aspect, was as much of them as she had been suffered to see; and into the secret intricacies they might cover she dared not yet project her thoughts.

'I must believe him . . . I must believe him . . .' She kept on repeating the words like a talisman. It was natural, after all, that he should have behaved as he had: defended the girl's piteous secret to the last. She too began to feel the contagion of his pity – the stir, in her breast, of feelings deeper and more native to her than the pains of jealousy. From the security of her blessedness she longed to lean over with compassionate hands . . . But Owen? What was Owen's part to be? She owed herself first to him – she was bound to protect him not only from all knowledge of the secret she had surmised, but also – and chiefly! – from its consequences. Yes: the girl must go – there could be no doubt of it – Darrow himself had seen it from the first; and at the thought she had a wild revulsion of relief, as though she had been trying to create in her heart the delusion of a generosity she could not feel . . .

The one fact on which she could stay her mind was that Sophy was leaving immediately; would be out of the house within an hour. Once she was gone, it would be easier to bring Owen to the point of understanding that the break was final; if necessary, to work upon the girl to make him see it. But that, Anna was sure, would not be necessary. It was clear that Sophy Viner was leaving Givré with no thought of ever seeing it again . . .

Suddenly, as she tried to put some order in her thoughts, she heard Owen's call at the door: 'Mother! –' a name he seldom gave her. There was a new note in his voice: the note of a joyous impatience. It made her turn hastily to the glass to see what face she was about to show him; but before she had had time to compose it he was in the room and she was caught in a school-boy hug.

'It's all right! It's all right! And it's all your doing! I want to do the worst kind of penance – bell and candle and the rest. I've been through it with *her*, and now she hands me on to you, and you're to call me any names you please.' He freed her with his happy laugh. 'I'm to be stood in the corner till next week, and then I'm to go up to see her. And she says I owe it all to you!'

'To me?' It was the first phrase she found to clutch at as she tried to steady herself in the eddies of his joy.

'Yes: you were so patient, and so dear to her; and you saw at once what a damned ass I'd been!' She tried a smile, and it seemed to pass muster with him, for he sent it back in a broad beam. 'That's not so difficult to see? No, I admit it doesn't take a microscope. But you were so wise and wonderful – you always are. I've been mad these last days, simply mad – you and she might well have washed your hands of me! And instead, it's all right – all right!'

She drew back a little, trying to keep the smile on her lips and not let him get the least glimpse of what it hid. Now if ever, indeed, it behoved her to be wise and wonderful!

'I'm so glad, dear; so glad. If only you'll always feel like that about me . . .' She stopped, hardly knowing what she said, and aghast at the idea that her own hands should have retied the knot she imagined to be broken. But she saw he had something more to say; something hard to get out, but absolutely necessary to express. He caught her hands, pulled her close, and, with his forehead drawn into its whimsical smiling wrinkles, 'Look here,' he cried, 'if Darrow wants to call me a damned ass too you're not to stop him!'

It brought her back to a sharper sense of her central peril: of the secret to be kept from him at whatever cost to her racked nerves.

'Oh, you know, he doesn't always wait for orders!' On the whole it sounded better than she'd feared.

'You mean he's called me one already?' He accepted the fact with his gayest laugh. 'Well, that saves a lot of trouble; now we can pass to the order of the day –' he broke off and glanced at the clock – 'which is, you know, dear, that she's starting in about an hour; she and Adelaide must already be snatching a hasty sandwich. You'll come down to bid them goodbye?'

'Yes – of course.'

There had, in fact, grown upon her while he spoke the urgency of seeing Sophy Viner again before she left. The thought was deeply distasteful: Anna shrank from encountering the girl till she had cleared a way through her own perplexities. But it was obvious that since they had separated, barely an hour earlier, the situation had taken a new shape. Sophy Viner had apparently reconsidered her decision to break amicably but definitely with Owen, and stood again in their path, a menace and a mystery; and confused impulses of resistance stirred in Anna's mind.

She felt Owen's touch on her arm. 'Are you coming?'

'Yes . . . yes . . . presently.'

'What's the matter? You look so strange.'

'What do you mean by strange?'

'I don't know: startled – surprised –' She read what her look must be by its sudden reflection in his face.

'Do I? No wonder! You've given us all an exciting morning.'

He held to his point. 'You're more excited now that there's no cause for it. What on earth has happened since I saw you?'

He looked about the room, as if seeking the clue to her agitation, and in her dread of what he might guess she answered: 'What has happened is simply that I'm rather tired. Will you ask Sophy to come up and see me here?'

*

239

While she waited she tried to think what she should say when the girl appeared; but she had never been more conscious of her inability to deal with the oblique and the tortuous. She had lacked the hard teachings of experience, and an instinctive disdain for whatever was less clear and open than her own conscience had kept her from learning anything of the intricacies and contradictions of other hearts. She said to herself: 'I must find out –' yet everything in her recoiled from the means by which she felt it must be done . . .

Sophy Viner appeared almost immediately, dressed for departure, her little bag on her arm. She was still pale to the point of haggardness, but with a light upon her that struck Anna with surprise. Or was it, perhaps, that she was looking at the girl with new eyes: seeing her, for the first time, not as Effie's governess, not as Owen's bride, but as the embodiment of that unknown peril lurking in the background of every woman's thoughts about her lover? Anna, at any rate, with a sudden sense of estrangement, noted in her graces and snares never before perceived. It was only the flash of a primitive instinct, but it lasted long enough to make her ashamed of the darknesses it lit up in her heart . . .

She signed to Sophy to sit down on the sofa beside her. 'I asked you to come up to me because I wanted to say goodbye quietly,' she explained, feeling her lips tremble, but trying to speak in a tone of friendly naturalness.

The girl's only answer was a faint smile of acquiescence, and Anna, disconcerted by her silence, went on: 'You've decided, then, not to break your engagement?'

Sophy Viner raised her head with a look of surprise. Evidently the question, thus abruptly put, must have sounded strangely on the lips of so ardent a partisan as Mrs Leath! 'I thought that was what you wished,' she said.

'What I wished?' Anna's heart shook against her side. 'I wish, of course, whatever seems best for Owen . . . It's natural, you must understand, that that consideration should come first with me . . .'

Sophy was looking at her steadily. 'I supposed it was the only one that counted with you.'

The curtness of retort roused Anna's latent antagonism. 'It is,' she said, in a hard voice that startled her as she heard it. Had she ever spoken so to any one before? She felt frightened, as though her very nature had changed without her knowing it . . . Feeling the girl's astonished gaze still on her, she continued: 'The suddenness of the change has naturally surprised me. When I left you it was understood that you were to reserve your decision –'

'Yes.'

'And now –?' Anna waited for a reply that did not come. She did not understand the girl's attitude, the edge of irony in her short syllables, the plainly premeditated determination to lay the burden of proof on her interlocutor. Anna felt the sudden need to lift their intercourse above this mean level of defiance and distrust. She looked appealingly at Sophy.

'Isn't it best that we should speak quite frankly? It's this change on your part that perplexes me. You can hardly be surprised at that. It's true, I asked you not to break with Owen too abruptly – and I asked it, believe me, as much for your sake as for his: I wanted you to take time to think over the difficulty that seems to have arisen between you. The fact that you felt it required thinking over seemed to show you wouldn't take the final step lightly – wouldn't, I mean, accept of Owen more than you could give him. But your change of mind obliges me to ask the question I thought you would have asked yourself. Is there any reason why you shouldn't marry Owen?'

She stopped a little breathlessly, her eyes on Sophy Viner's burning face. 'Any reason –? What do you mean by a reason?'

Anna continued to look at her gravely. 'Do you love some one else?' she asked.

Sophy's first look was one of wonder and a faint relief; then she gave back the other's scrutiny in a glance of indescribable reproach. 'Ah, you might have waited!' she exclaimed.

'Waited –?'

'Till I'd gone: till I was out of the house. You might have known . . . you might have guessed . . .' She turned her eyes again on Anna. 'I only meant to let him hope a little longer, so that he shouldn't suspect anything; of course I can't marry him,' she said.

Anna stood motionless, silenced by the shock of the avowal. She too was trembling, less with anger than with a confused compassion. But the feeling was so blent with others, less generous and more obscure, that she found no words to express it, and the two women faced each other without speaking.

'I'd better go,' Sophy murmured at length with lowered head.

The words roused in Anna a latent impulse of compunction. The girl looked so young, so exposed and desolate! And what thoughts must she be hiding in her heart! It was impossible that they should part in such a spirit.

'I want you to know that no one said anything . . . It was I who . . .'

Sophy looked at her. 'You mean that Mr Darrow didn't tell you? Of course not: do you suppose I thought he did? You found it out, that's all – I knew you would. In your place I should have guessed it sooner.'

The words were spoken simply, without irony or emphasis; but they went through Anna like a sword. Yes, the girl would have had divinations, promptings that she had not had! She felt half envious of such a sad precocity of wisdom.

'I'm so sorry . . . so sorry . . .' she murmured.

'Things happen that way. Now I'd better go. I'd like to say goodbye to Effie.'

'Oh –' it broke in a cry from Effie's mother. 'Not like this – you mustn't! I feel – you make me feel too horribly: as if I were driving you away . . .' The words had rushed up from the depths of her bewildered pity.

'No one is driving me away: I had to go,' she heard the girl reply.

There was another silence, during which passionate impulses of magnanimity warred in Anna with her doubts and dreads. At length, her eyes on Sophy's face: 'Yes, you must go now,' she began; 'but later on . . . after a while, when all this is over . . . if there's no reason why you shouldn't marry Owen –' she paused a moment on the words – 'I shouldn't want you to think I stood between you . . .'

'You?' Sophy flushed again, and then grew pale. She seemed to try to speak, but no words came.

'Yes! It was not true when I said just now that I was thinking only of Owen. I'm sorry – oh, so sorry! – for you too. Your life – I know how hard it's been; and mine . . . mine's so full . . . Happy women understand best!' Anna drew near and touched the girl's hand; then she began again, pouring all her soul into the broken phrases: 'It's terrible now . . . you see no future; but if, by and by . . . you know best . . . but you're so young . . . and at your age things *do* pass. If there's no reason, no real reason, why you shouldn't marry Owen, I *want* him to hope, I'll help him to hope . . . if you say so . . .'

With the urgency of her pleading her clasp tightened on Sophy's hand, but it warmed to no responsive tremor: the girl seemed numb, and Anna was frightened by the stony silence of her look. 'I suppose I'm not more than half a woman,' she mused, 'for I don't want my happiness to hurt her'; and aloud she repeated: 'If only you'll tell me there's no reason –'

The girl did not speak; but suddenly, like a snapped branch, she bent, stooped down to the hand that clasped her, and laid her lips upon it in a stream of weeping. She cried silently, continuously, abundantly, as though Anna's touch had released the waters of some deep spring of pain; then, as Anna, moved and half afraid, leaned over her with a sound of pity, she stood up and turned away.

'You're going, then – for good – like this?' Anna moved toward her and stopped. Sophy stopped too, with eyes that shrank from her.

'Oh –' Anna cried, and hid her face.

The girl walked across the room and paused again in the doorway. From there she flung back: 'I wanted it – I chose it. He was good to me – no one ever was so good!'

The door-handle turned, and Anna heard her go.

29

Her first thought was: 'He's going too in a few hours – I needn't see him again before he leaves . . .' At that moment the possibility of having to look in Darrow's face and hear him speak seemed to her more unendurable than anything else she could imagine. Then, on the next wave of feeling, came the desire to confront him at once and wring from him she knew not what: avowal, denial, justification, anything that should open some channel of escape to the flood of her pent-up anguish.

She had told Owen she was tired, and this seemed a sufficient reason for remaining upstairs when the motor came to the door and Miss Painter and Sophy Viner were borne off in it; sufficient also for sending word to Madame de Chantelle that she would not come down till after luncheon. Having despatched her maid with this message, she lay down on her sofa and stared before her into darkness . . .

She had been unhappy before, and the vision of old miseries flocked like hungry ghosts about her fresh pain: she recalled her youthful disappointment, the failure of her marriage, the wasted years that followed; but those were negative sorrows, denials and postponements of life. She seemed in no way related to their shadowy victim, she who was stretched on this fiery rack of the irreparable. She had suffered before – yes, but lucidly, reflectively, elegiacally: now she was suffering as a hurt animal must, blindly, furiously, with the single fierce animal longing that the awful pain should stop . . .

She heard her maid knock, and she hid her face and made no answer. The knocking continued, and the discipline of habit at length made her lift her head, compose her face and hold out her hand to the note the woman brought her. It was a word from Darrow – 'May I see you?' – and she said at once, in a voice that sounded thin and empty: 'Ask Mr Darrow to come up.'

The maid enquired if she wished to have her hair smoothed first, and she answered that it didn't matter; but when the door had closed, the instinct of pride drew her to her feet and she looked at herself in the glass above the mantelpiece and passed her hands over her hair. Her eyes were burning and her face looked tired and thinner; otherwise she could see no change in her appearance, and she wondered that at such a moment her body should seem as unrelated to the self that writhed within her as if it had been a statue or a picture.

The maid reopened the door to show in Darrow, and he paused a moment on the threshold, as if waiting for Anna to speak. He was extremely pale, but he looked neither ashamed nor uncertain, and she said to herself, with a perverse thrill of appreciation: 'He's as proud as I am.'

Aloud she asked: 'You wanted to see me?'

'Naturally,' he replied in a grave voice.

'Don't! It's useless. I know everything. Nothing you can say will help.'

At the direct affirmation he turned even paler, and his eyes, which he kept resolutely fixed on her, confessed his misery.

'You allow me no voice in deciding that?'

'Deciding what?'

'That there's nothing more to be said?' He waited for her to answer, and then went on: 'I don't even know what you mean by "everything".'

'Oh, I don't know what more there is! I know enough. I implored her to deny it, and she couldn't . . . What can you and I have to say to each other?' Her voice broke into a sob. The animal anguish was upon her again – just a blind cry against her pain!

Darrow kept his head high and his eyes steady. 'It must be as you wish; and yet it's not like you to be afraid.'

'Afraid?'

'To talk things out – to face them.'

'It's for *you* to face this – not me!'

'All I ask is to face it – but with you.' Once more he paused. 'Won't you tell me what Miss Viner told you?'

'Oh, she's generous – to the utmost!' The pain caught her like a physical throe. It suddenly came to her how the girl must have loved him to be so generous – what memories there must be between them!

'Oh, go, please go. It's too horrible! Why should I have to see you?' she stammered, lifting her hands to her eyes.

With her face hidden she waited to hear him move away, to hear the door open and close again, as, a few hours earlier, it had opened and closed on Sophy Viner. But Darrow made no sound or movement: he too was waiting. Anna felt a thrill of resentment: his presence was an outrage on her sorrow, a humiliation to her pride. It was strange that he should wait for her to tell him so!

'You want me to leave Givré?' he asked at length. She made no answer, and he went on: 'Of course I'll do as you wish; but if I go now am I not to see you again?'

His voice was firm: his pride was answering her pride!

She faltered: 'You must see it's useless –'

'I might remind you that you're dismissing me without a hearing –'

'Without a hearing? I've heard you both!'

'– but I won't,' he continued, 'remind you of that, or of any-thing or any one but Owen.'

'Owen –'

'Yes; if we could somehow spare him –'

She had dropped her hands and turned her startled eyes on him. It seemed to her an age since she had thought of Owen!

'You see, don't you,' Darrow continued, 'that if you send me away now –'

She interrupted: 'Yes, I see –' and there was a long silence be-tween them. At length she said, very low: 'I don't want any one else to suffer as I'm suffering . . .'

'Owen knows I meant to leave tomorrow,' Darrow went on. 'Any sudden change of plan may make him think . . .'

Oh, she saw his inevitable logic: the horror of it was on every side of her! It had seemed possible to control her grief and face Darrow calmly while she was upheld by the belief that this was their last hour together, that after he had passed out of the room there would be no fear of seeing him again, no fear that his nearness, his look, his voice, and all the unseen influences that flowed from him, would dissolve her soul to weakness. But her courage failed at the idea of having to conspire with him to shield Owen, of keeping up with him, for Owen's sake, a feint of union and felicity. To live at Darrow's side in seeming intimacy and harmony for another twenty-four hours seemed harder than to live without him for all the rest of her days. Her strength failed her, and she threw herself down and buried her sobs in the cushions where she had so often hidden a face aglow with happiness.

'Anna –' His voice was close to her. 'Let me talk to you quietly. It's not worthy of either of us to be afraid.'

Words of endearment would have offended her; but her heart rose at the call to her courage.

'I've no defence to make,' he went on. 'The facts are miserable enough; but at least I want you to see them as they are. Above all, I want you to know the truth about Miss Viner –'

The name sent the blood to Anna's forehead. She raised her head and faced him. 'Why should I know more of her than what she's told me? I never wish to hear her name again!'

'It's because you feel about her in that way that I ask you – in the name of common charity – to let me give you the facts as they are, and not as you've probably imagined them.'

'I've told you I don't think uncharitably of her. I don't want to think of her at all!'

'That's why I tell you you're afraid.'

'Afraid?'

'Yes. You've always said you wanted, above all, to look at life, at the human problem, as it is, without fear and without hypocrisy; and it's not always a pleasant thing to look at.' He broke off, and then began again: 'Don't think this a plea for myself! I don't want to say a word to lessen my offence. I don't want to talk of myself at all. Even if I did, I probably couldn't make you understand – I don't, myself, as I look back. Be just to me – it's your right; all I ask you is to be generous to Miss Viner . . .'

She stood up trembling. 'You're free to be as generous to her as you please!'

'Yes: you've made it clear to me that I'm free. But there's nothing I can do for her that will help her half as much as your understanding her would.'

'Nothing you can do for her? You can marry her!'

His face hardened. 'You certainly couldn't wish her a worse fate!'

'It must have been what she expected . . . relied on . . .' He was silent, and she broke out: 'Or what *is* she? What are you? It's too horrible! On your way here . . . to *me* . . .' She felt the tears in her throat and stopped.

'That was it,' he said bluntly. She stared at him.

'I was on my way to you – after repeated delays and postponements of your own making. At the very last you turned me back with a mere word – and without explanation. I waited for a letter; and none came. I'm not saying this to justify myself. I'm simply trying to make you understand. I felt hurt and bitter and bewildered. I thought you meant to give me up. And suddenly, in my way, I found some one to be sorry for, to be of use to. That, I swear to you, was the way it began. The rest was a moment's folly . . . a flash of madness . . . as such things are. We've never seen each other since . . .'

Anna was looking at him coldly. 'You sufficiently describe her in saying that!'

'Yes, if you measure her by conventional standards – which is what you always declare you never do.'

'Conventional standards? A girl who –' She was checked by a sudden rush of almost physical repugnance. Suddenly she broke out: 'I always thought her an adventuress!'

'Always?'

'I don't mean always . . . but after you came . . .'

'She's not an adventuress.'

'You mean that she professes to act on the new theories? The stuff that awful women rave about on platforms?'

'Oh, I don't think she pretended to have a theory –'

'She hadn't even *that* excuse?'

'She had the excuse of her loneliness, her unhappiness – of miseries and humiliations that a woman like you can't even guess. She had nothing to look back to but indifference or unkindness – nothing to look forward to but anxiety. She saw I was sorry for her and it touched her. She made too much of it – she exaggerated it. I ought to have seen the danger, but I didn't. There's no possible excuse for what I did.'

Anna listened to him in speechless misery. Every word he spoke threw back a disintegrating light on their own past. He had come to her with an open face and a clear conscience – come to her from this! If his security was the security of falsehood it was horrible; if it meant that he had forgotten, it was worse. She would have liked to stop her ears, to close her eyes, to shut out every sight and sound and suggestion of a world in which such things could be; and at the same time she was tormented by the desire to know more, to understand better, to feel herself less ignorant and inexpert in matters which made so much of the stuff of human experience. What did he mean by 'a moment's folly, a flash of madness'? How did people enter on such adventures, how pass out of them without more visible traces of their havoc? Her imagination recoiled from the vision of a sudden debasing familiarity: it seemed to her that her thoughts would never again be pure . . .

'I swear to you,' she heard Darrow saying, 'it was simply that, and nothing more.'

She wondered at his composure, his competence, at his knowing so exactly what to say. No doubt men often had to make such explanations: they had the formulas by heart . . . A leaden lassitude descended on her. She passed from flame and torment into a colourless cold world where everything surrounding her seemed equally indifferent and remote. For a moment she simply ceased to feel.

She became aware that Darrow was waiting for her to speak, and she made an effort to represent to herself the meaning of what he had just said; but her mind was as blank as a blurred mirror. Finally she brought out: 'I don't think I understand what you've told me.'

'No; you don't understand,' he returned with sudden bitterness; and on his lips the charge of incomprehension seemed an offence to her.

'I don't want to – about such things!'

He answered almost harshly: 'Don't be afraid . . . you never will . . .' and for an instant they faced each other like enemies. Then the tears swelled in her throat at his reproach.

'You mean I don't feel things – I'm too hard?'

'No: you're too high . . . too fine . . . such things are too far from you.'

He paused, as if conscious of the futility of going on with whatever he had meant to say, and again, for a short space, they confronted each other, no longer as enemies – so it seemed to her – but as beings of different language who had forgotten the few words they had learned of each other's speech.

Darrow broke the silence. 'It's best, on all accounts, that I should stay till tomorrow; but I needn't intrude on you; we needn't meet again alone. I only want to be sure I know your wishes.' He spoke the short sentences in a level voice, as though he were summing up the results of a business conference.

Anna looked at him vaguely. 'My wishes?'

'As to Owen –'

At that she started. 'They must never meet again!'

'It's not likely they will. What I meant was, that it depends on you to spare him . . .'

She answered steadily: 'He shall never know,' and after another interval Darrow said: 'This is good-bye, then.'

At the word she seemed to understand for the first time whither the flying moments had been leading them. Resentment and indignation died down, and all her consciousness resolved itself into the mere visual sense that he was there before her, near enough for her to lift her hand and touch him, and that in another instant the place where he stood would be empty.

She felt a mortal weakness, a craven impulse to cry out to him to stay, a longing to throw herself into his arms, and take refuge there from the unendurable anguish he had caused her. Then the vision called up another thought: 'I shall never know what that girl has known . . .' and the recoil of pride flung her back on the sharp edges of her anguish.

'Good-bye,' she said, in dread lest he should read her face; and she stood motionless, her head high, while he walked to the door and went out.

BOOK FIVE

30

Anna Leath, three days later, sat in Miss Painter's drawing-room in the rue de Matignon.

Coming up precipitately that morning from the country, she had reached Paris at one o'clock and Miss Painter's landing some ten minutes later. Miss Painter's mouldy little manservant, dissembling a napkin under his arm, had mildly attempted to oppose her entrance; but Anna, insisting, had gone straight to the dining-room and surprised her friend – who ate as furtively as certain animals – over a strange meal of cold mutton and lemonade. Ignoring the embarrassment she caused, she had set forth the object of her journey, and Miss Painter, always hatted and booted for action, had immediately hastened out, leaving her to the solitude of the bare fireless drawing-room with its eternal slip-covers and 'bowed' shutters.

In this inhospitable obscurity Anna had sat alone for close upon two hours. Both obscurity and solitude were acceptable to her, and impatient as she was to hear the result of the errand on which she had despatched her hostess, she desired still more to be alone. During her long meditation in a white-swathed chair before the muffled hearth she had been able for the first time to clear a way through the darkness and confusion of her thoughts. The way did not go far, and her attempt to trace it was as weak and spasmodic as a convalescent's first efforts to pick up the thread of living. She seemed to herself like some one struggling to rise from a long sickness of which it would have been so much easier to die. At Givré she had fallen into a kind of torpor, a deadness of soul traversed by wild flashes of pain; but whether she suffered or whether she was numb, she seemed equally remote from her real living and doing self.

It was only the discovery – that very morning – of Owen's unannounced departure for Paris that had caught her out of her dream and forced her back to action. The dread of what this flight might imply, and of the consequences that might result from it, had roused her to the sense of her responsibility, and from the moment when she had resolved to follow her step-son, and had made her rapid preparations for pursuit, her mind had begun to work again, feverishly, fitfully, but still with something of its normal order. In the train she had been too agitated, too preoccupied with what might next await her, to give her thoughts to anything but the turning over of dread alternatives; but Miss Painter's imperviousness had steadied her, and while she waited for the sound of the latch-key she resolutely returned upon herself.

With respect to her outward course she could at least tell herself that she had held to her purpose. She had, as people said, 'kept up' during the twenty-four hours preceding George Darrow's departure; had gone with a calm face about her usual business, and even contrived not too obviously to avoid him. Then, the next day before dawn, from behind the closed shutters where she had kept for half the night her dry-eyed vigil, she had heard him drive off to the train which brought its passengers to Paris in time for the Calais express.

The fact of his taking that train, of his travelling so straight and far away from her, gave to what had happened the implacable outline of reality. He was gone; he would not come back; and her life had ended just as she had dreamed it was beginning. She had no doubt, at first, as to the absolute inevitability of this conclusion. The man who had driven away from her house in the autumn dawn was not the man she had loved; he was a stranger with whom she had not a single thought in common. It was terrible, indeed, that he wore the face and spoke in the voice of her friend, and that, as long as he was under one roof with her, the mere way in which he moved and looked could bridge at a stroke the gulf between them. That, no doubt, was the fault of her exaggerated sensibility to outward things: she was frightened to see how it enslaved her. A day or two before she had supposed the sense of honour was her deepest sentiment: if she had smiled at the conventions of others it was because they were too trivial, not because they were too grave. There were certain dishonours with which she had never dreamed that any pact could be made: she had had an incorruptible passion for good faith and fairness.

She had supposed that, once Darrow was gone, once she was safe from the danger of seeing and hearing him, this high devotion would sustain her. She had believed it would be possible to separate the image of the man she had thought him from that of the man he was. She had even foreseen the hour when she might raise a mournful shrine to the memory of the Darrow she had loved, without fear that his double's shadow would desecrate it. But now she had begun to understand that the two men were really one. The Darrow she worshipped was inseparable from the Darrow she abhorred; and the inevitable conclusion was that both must go, and she be left in the desert of a sorrow without memories . . .

But if the future was thus void, the present was all too full. Never had blow more complex repercussions; and to remember Owen was to cease to think of herself. What impulse, what apprehension, had sent him suddenly to Paris? And why had he thought it needful to conceal his going from her? When Sophy Viner had left, it had been with the understanding that he was to await her summons; and it seemed improbable that he would break his pledge, and seek her without leave, unless his lover's intuition had warned him of some fresh danger. Anna recalled how quickly he had read the alarm in her face when he had rushed back to her sitting-room with the news that Miss Viner had promised to see him again in Paris. To be so promptly roused, his suspicions must have been but half-asleep; and since then, no doubt, if she and Darrow had dissembled, so had he. To her proud directness it was degrading to think that they had been living together like enemies who spy upon each other's movements: she felt a desperate longing for the days which had seemed so dull and narrow, but in which she had walked with her head high and her eyes unguarded.

She had come up to Paris hardly knowing what peril she feared, and still less how she could avert it. If Owen meant to see Miss Viner – and what other object could he have? – they must already be together, and it was too late to interfere. It had indeed occurred to Anna that Paris might not be his objective point: that his real purpose in leaving Givré without her knowledge had been to follow Darrow to London and exact the truth of him. But even to her alarmed imagination this seemed improbable. She and Darrow, to the last, had kept up so complete a feint of harmony that, whatever Owen had surmised, he could scarcely have risked acting on his suspicions. If he still felt the need of an explanation, it was almost certainly of Sophy Viner that he would ask it; and it was in quest of Sophy Viner that Anna had despatched Miss Painter.

She had found a blessed refuge from her perplexities in the stolid Adelaide's unawareness. One could so absolutely count on Miss Painter's guessing no more than one chose, and yet acting astutely on such hints as one vouchsafed her! She was like a well-trained retriever whose interest in his prey ceases when he lays it at his master's feet. Anna, on arriving, had explained that Owen's unannounced flight had made her fear some fresh misunderstanding between himself and Miss Viner. In the interests of peace she had thought it best to follow him; but she hastily added that she did not wish to see Sophy, but only, if possible, to learn from her where Owen was. With these brief instructions Miss Painter had started out; but she was a woman of many occupations, and had given her visitor to understand that before returning she should have to call on a friend who had just arrived from Boston, and afterward despatch to another exiled compatriot a supply of cranberries and brandied peaches from the American grocery in the Champs Elysées.

Gradually, as the moments passed, Anna began to feel the reaction which, in moments of extreme nervous tension, follows on any effort of the will. She seemed to have gone as far as her courage would carry her, and she shrank more and more from the thought of Miss Painter's return, since whatever information the latter brought would necessitate some fresh decision. What should she say to Owen if she found him? What could she say that should not betray the one thing she would give her life to hide from him? 'Give her life' – how the phrase derided her! It was a gift she would not have bestowed on her worst enemy. She would not have had Sophy Viner live the hours she was living now . . .

She tried again to look steadily and calmly at the picture that the image of the girl evoked. She had an idea that she ought to accustom herself to its contemplation. If life was like that, why the sooner one got used to it the better . . . But no! Life was not like that. Her adventure was a hideous accident. She dreaded above all the temptation to generalize from her own case, to doubt the high things she had lived by and seek a cheap solace in belittling what fate had refused her. There *was* such love as she had dreamed, and she meant to go on believing in it, and cherishing the thought that she was worthy of it. What had happened to her was grotesque and mean and miserable; but she herself was none of these things, and never, never would she make of herself the mock that fate had made of her . . .

She could not, as yet, bear to think deliberately of Darrow; but she kept on repeating to herself 'By and by that will come too.' Even now she was determined not to let his image be distorted by her suffering. As soon as she could, she would try to single out for remembrance the individual things she had liked in him before she had loved him altogether. No 'spiritual exercise' devised by the discipline of piety could have been more torturing; but its very cruelty attracted her. She wanted to wear herself out with new pains . . .

31

The sound of Miss Painter's latch-key made her start. She was still a bundle of quivering fears to whom each coming moment seemed a menace.

There was a slight interval, and a sound of voices in the hall; then Miss Painter's vigorous hand was on the door.

Anna stood up as she came in. 'You've found him?'

'I've found Sophy.'

'And Owen? – has she seen him? Is he here?'

'*She's* here: in the hall. She wants to speak to you.'

'Here – *now*?' Anna found no voice for more.

'She drove back with me,' Miss Painter continued in the tone of impartial narrative. 'The cabman was impertinent. I've got his number.' She fumbled in a stout black reticule.

'Oh, I can't –' broke from Anna; but she collected herself, remembering that to betray her unwillingness to see the girl was to risk revealing much more.

'She thought you might be too tired to see her: she wouldn't come in till I'd found out.'

Anna drew a quick breath. An instant's thought had told her that Sophy Viner would hardly have taken such a step unless something more important had happened. 'Ask her to come, please,' she said.

Miss Painter, from the threshold, turned back to announce her intention of going immediately to the police station to report the cabman's delinquency; then she passed out, and Sophy Viner entered.

The look in the girl's face showed that she had indeed come unwillingly; yet she seemed animated by an eager resoluteness that made Anna ashamed of her tremors. For a moment they looked at each other in silence, as if the thoughts between them were packed too thick for speech; then Anna said, in a voice from which she strove to take the edge of hardness: 'You know where Owen is, Miss Painter tells me.'

'Yes; that was my reason for asking you to see me.' Sophy spoke simply, without constraint or hesitation.

'I thought he'd promised you –' Anna interposed.

'He did; but he broke his promise. That's what I thought I ought to tell you.'

'Thank you.' Anna went on tentatively: 'He left Givré this morning without a word. I followed him because I was afraid . . .'

She broke off again and the girl took up her phrase. 'You were afraid he'd guessed? He *has* . . .'

'What do you mean – guessed what?'

'That you know something he doesn't . . . something that made you glad to have me go.'

'Oh –' Anna moaned. If she had wanted more pain she had it now. 'He's told you this?' she faltered.

'He hasn't told me, because I haven't seen him. I kept him off – I made Mrs Farlow get rid of him. But he's written me what he came to say; and that was it.'

'Oh, poor Owen!' broke from Anna. Through all the intricacies of her suffering she felt the separate pang of his.

'And I want to ask you,' the girl continued, 'to let me see him; for of course,' she added in the same strange voice of energy, 'I wouldn't unless you consented.'

'To see him?' Anna tried to gather together her startled thoughts. 'What use would it be? What could you tell him?'

'I want to tell him the truth,' said Sophy Viner.

The two women looked at each other, and a burning blush rose to Anna's forehead. 'I don't understand,' she faltered.

Sophy waited a moment; then she lowered her voice to say: 'I don't want him to think worse of me than he need . . .'

'Worse?'

'Yes – to think such things as you're thinking now . . . I want him to know exactly what happened . . . then I want to bid him good-bye.'

Anna tried to clear a way through her own wonder and confusion. She felt herself obscurely moved.

'Wouldn't it be worse for him –?'

'To hear the truth? It would be better, at any rate, for you and Mr Darrow.'

At the sound of the name Anna lifted her head quickly. 'I've only my step-son to consider!'

The girl threw a startled look at her. 'You don't mean – you're not going to give him up?'

Anna felt her lips harden. 'I don't think it's of any use to talk of that.'

'Oh, I know! It's my fault for not knowing how to say what I want you to hear. Your words are different; you know how to choose them. Mine offend you . . . and the dread of it makes me blunder. That's why, the other day, I couldn't say anything . . . couldn't make things clear to you. But now I *must*, even if you hate it!' She drew a step nearer, her slender figure swayed forward in a passion of entreaty. 'Do listen to me! What you've said is dreadful. How can you speak of him in that voice? Don't you see that I went away so that he shouldn't have to lose you?'

Anna looked at her coldly. 'Are you speaking of Mr Darrow? I don't know why you think your going or staying can in any way affect our relations.'

'You mean that you *have* given him up – because of me? Oh, how could you? You can't really love him! – And yet,' the girl suddenly added, 'you must, or you'd be more sorry for me!'

'I'm very sorry for you,' Anna said, feeling as if the iron band about her heart pressed on it a little less inexorably.

'Then why won't you hear me? Why won't you try to understand? It's all so different from what you imagine!'

'I've never judged you.'

'I'm not thinking of myself. He loves you!'

'I thought you'd come to speak of Owen.'

Sophy Viner seemed not to hear her. 'He's never loved any one else. Even those few days . . . I knew it all the while . . . he never cared for me.'

'Please don't say any more!' Anna said.

'I know it must seem strange to you that I should say so much. I shock you, I offend you: you think me a creature without shame. So I am – but not in the sense you think! I'm not ashamed of having loved him; no; and I'm not ashamed of telling you so. It's that that justifies me – and him too . . . Oh, let me tell you how it happened! He was sorry for me: he saw I cared. I *knew* that was all he ever felt. I could see he was thinking of some one else. I knew it was only for a week . . . He never said a word to mislead me . . . I wanted to be happy just once – and I didn't dream of the harm I might be doing him?'

Anna could not speak. She hardly knew, as yet, what the girl's words conveyed to her, save the sense of their tragic fervour; but she was conscious of being in the presence of an intenser passion than she had ever felt.

'I am sorry for you.' She paused. 'But why do you say this to me?' After another interval she exclaimed: 'You'd no right to let Owen love you.'

'No; that was wrong. At least what's happened since has made it so. If things had been different I think I could have made Owen happy. You were all so good to me – I wanted so to stay with you! I suppose you'll say that makes it worse: my daring to dream I had the right . . . But all that doesn't matter now. I won't see Owen unless you're willing. I should have liked to tell him what I've tried to tell you; but you must know better; you feel things in a finer way. Only you'll have to help him if I can't. He cares a great deal . . . it's going to hurt him . . .'

Anna trembled. 'Oh, I know! What can I do?'

'You can go straight back to Givré – now, at once! So that Owen shall never know you've followed him.' Sophy's clasped hands reached out urgently. 'And you can send for Mr Darrow – bring him back. Owen must be convinced that he's mistaken, and nothing else will convince him. Afterward I'll find a pretext – oh, I promise you! But first he must see for himself that nothing's changed for you.'

Anna stood motionless, subdued and dominated. The girl's ardour swept her like a wind.

'Oh, can't I move you? Some day you'll know!' Sophy pleaded, her eyes full of tears.

Anna saw them, and felt a fullness in her throat. Again the band about her heart seemed loosened. She wanted to find a word, but could not: all within her was too dark and violent. She gave the girl a speechless look.

'I do believe you,' she said suddenly; then she turned and walked out of the room.

32

She drove from Miss Painter's to her own apartment. The maid-servant who had it in charge had been apprised of her coming, and had opened one or two of the rooms, and prepared a fire in her bedroom. Anna shut herself in, refusing the woman's ministrations. She felt cold and faint, and after she had taken off her hat and cloak she knelt down by the fire and stretched her hands to it.

In one respect, at least, it was clear to her that she would do well to follow Sophy Viner's counsel. It had been an act of folly to follow Owen, and her first business was to get back to Givré before him. But the only train leaving that evening was a slow one, which did not reach Francheuil till midnight, and she knew that her taking it would excite Madame de Chantelle's wonder and lead to interminable talk. She had come up to Paris on the pretext of finding a new governess for Effie, and the natural thing was to defer her return till the next morning. She knew Owen well enough to be sure that he would make another attempt to see Miss Viner, and failing that, would write again and await her answer; so that there was no likelihood of his reaching Givré till the following evening.

Her sense of relief at not having to start out at once showed her for the first time how tired she was. The *bonne* had suggested a cup of tea, but the dread of having any one about her had made Anna refuse, and she had eaten nothing since morning but a sandwich bought at a buffet. She was too tired to get up, but stretching out her arm she drew toward her the armchair which stood beside the hearth and rested her head against its cushions. Gradually the warmth of the fire stole into her veins and her heaviness of soul was replaced by a dreamy buoyancy. She seemed to be seated on the hearth in her sitting-room at Givré, and Darrow was beside her, in the chair against which she leaned. He put his arms about her shoulders and drawing her head back looked into her eyes. 'Of all the ways you do your hair, that's the way I like best,' he said . . .

A log dropped, and she sat up with a start. There was a warmth in her heart, and she was smiling. Then she looked about her, and saw where she was, and the glory fell. She hid her face and sobbed.

Presently she perceived that it was growing dark, and getting up stiffly she began to undo the things in her bag and spread them on the dressing-table. She shrank from lighting the lights, and groped her way about, trying to find what she needed. She seemed immeasurably far off from every one, and most of all from herself. It was as if her consciousness had been transmitted to some stranger whose thoughts and gestures were indifferent to her . . .

Suddenly she heard a shrill tinkle, and with a beating heart she stood still in the middle of the room. It was the telephone in her dressing-room – a call, no doubt, from Adelaide Painter. Or could Owen have learned she was in town? The thought alarmed her and she opened the door and stumbled across the unlit room to the instrument. She held it to her ear, and heard Darrow's voice pronounce her name.

'Will you let me see you? I've come back – I had to come. Miss Painter told me you were here.'

She began to tremble, and feared that he would guess it from her voice. She did not know what she answered: she heard him say: 'I can't hear.' She called 'Yes!' and laid the telephone down, and caught it up again – but he was gone. She wondered if her 'Yes' had reached him.

She sat in her chair and listened. Why had she said that she would see him? What did she mean to say to him when he came? Now and then, as she sat there, the sense of his presence enveloped her as in her dream, and she shut her eyes and felt his arms about her. Then she woke to reality and shivered. A long time elapsed, and at length she said to herself: 'He isn't coming.'

The door-bell rang as she said it, and she stood up, cold and trembling. She thought: 'Can he imagine there's any use in coming?' and moved forward to bid the servant say she could not see him.

The door opened and she saw him standing in the drawing-room. The room was cold and fireless, and a hard glare fell from the wall-lights on the shrouded furniture and the white slips covering the curtains. He looked pale and stern, with a frown of fatigue between his eyes; and she remembered that in three days he had travelled from Givré to London and back. It seemed incredible that all that had befallen her should have been compressed within the space of three days!

'Thank you,' he said as she came in.

She answered: 'It's better, I suppose –'

He came toward her and took her in his arms. She struggled a little, afraid of yielding, but he pressed her to him, not bending to her but holding her fast, as though he had found her after a long search: she heard his hurried breathing. It seemed to come from her own breast, so close he held her; and it was she who, at last, lifted up her face and drew down his.

She freed herself and went and sat on a sofa at the other end of the room. A mirror between the shrouded window-curtains showed her crumpled travelling dress and the white face under her disordered hair.

She found her voice, and asked him how he had been able to leave London. He answered that he had managed – he'd arranged it; and she saw he hardly heard what she was saying.

'I had to see you,' he went on, and moved nearer, sitting down at her side.

'Yes; we must think of Owen –'

'Oh, Owen –!'

Her mind had flown back to Sophy Viner's plea that she should let Darrow return to Givré in order that Owen might be persuaded of the folly of his suspicions. The suggestion was absurd, of course. She could not ask Darrow to lend himself to such a fraud, even had she had the inhuman courage to play her part in it. She was suddenly overwhelmed by the futility of every attempt to reconstruct her ruined world. No, it was useless; and since it was useless, every moment with Darrow was pure pain . . .

'I've come to talk of myself, not of Owen,' she heard him saying.

'When you sent me away the other day I understood that it couldn't be otherwise – then. But it's not possible that you and I should part like that. If I'm to lose you, it must be for a better reason.'

'A better reason?'

'Yes: a deeper one. One that means a fundamental disaccord between us. This one doesn't – in spite of everything it doesn't. That's what I want you to see, and have the courage to acknowledge.'

'If I saw it I should have the courage!'

'Yes: courage was the wrong word. You have that. That's why I'm here.'

'But I don't see it,' she continued sadly. 'So it's useless, isn't it? – and so cruel . . .' He was about to speak, but she went on: 'I shall never understand it – never!'

He looked at her. 'You will some day: you were made to feel everything –'

'I should have thought this was a case of not feeling –'

'On my part, you mean?' He faced her resolutely. 'Yes, it was: to my shame . . . What I meant was that when you've lived a little longer you'll see what complex blunderers we all are: how we're struck blind sometimes, and mad sometimes – and then, when our sight and our senses come back, how we have to set to work, and build up, little by little, bit by bit, the precious things we'd smashed to atoms without knowing it. Life's just a perpetual piecing together of broken bits.'

She looked up quickly. 'That's what I feel: that you ought to –'

He stood up, interrupting her with a gesture. 'Oh, don't – don't say what you're going to! Men don't give their lives away like that. If you won't have mine, it's at least my own, to do the best I can with.'

'The best you can – that's what I mean! How can there be a "best" for you that's made of some one else's worst?'

He sat down again with a groan. 'I don't know! It seemed such a slight thing – all on the surface – and I've gone aground on it because it *was* on the surface. I see the horror of it just as you do. But I see, a little more clearly, the extent, and the limits, of my wrong. It's not as black as you imagine.'

She lowered her voice to say: 'I suppose I shall never understand; but she seems to love you . . .'

'There's my shame! That I didn't guess it, didn't fly from it. You say you'll never understand: but why shouldn't you? Is it anything to be proud of, to know so little of the strings that pull us? If you knew a little more, I could tell you how such things happen without offending you; and perhaps you'd listen without condemning me.'

'I don't condemn you.' She was dizzy with struggling impulses. She longed to cry out: 'I *do* understand! I've understood ever since you've been here!' For she was aware, in her own bosom, of sensations so separate from her romantic thoughts of him that she saw her body and soul divided against themselves. She recalled having read somewhere that in ancient Rome the slaves were not allowed to wear a distinctive dress lest they should recognize each other and learn their numbers and their power. So, in herself, she discerned for the first time instincts and desires, which, mute and unmarked, had gone to and fro in the dim passages of her mind, and now hailed each other with a cry of mutiny.

'Oh, I don't know what to think!' she broke out. 'You say you didn't know she loved you. But you know it now. Doesn't that show you how you can put the broken bits together?'

'Can you seriously think it would be doing so to marry one woman while I care for another?'

'Oh, I don't know . . . I don't know . . .' The sense of her weakness made her try to harden herself against his arguments.

'You do know! We've often talked of such things: of the monstrousness of useless sacrifices. If I'm to expiate, it's not in that way.' He added abruptly: 'It's in having to say this to you now . . .'

She found no answer.

Through the silent apartment they heard the sudden peal of the door-bell, and she rose to her feet. 'Owen!' she instantly exclaimed.

'Is Owen in Paris?'

She explained in a rapid undertone what she had learned from Sophy Viner.

'Shall I leave you?' Darrow asked.

'Yes . . . no . . .' She moved to the dining-room door, with the half-formed purpose of making him pass out, and then turned back. 'It may be Adelaide.'

They heard the outer door open, and a moment later Owen walked into the room. He was pale, with excited eyes: as they fell on

Darrow, Anna saw his start of wonder. He made a slight sign of recognition, and then went up to his step-mother with an air of exaggerated gaiety.

'You furtive person! I ran across the omniscient Adelaide and heard from her that you'd rushed up suddenly and secretly –' He stood between Anna and Darrow, strained, questioning, dangerously on edge.

'I came up to meet Mr Darrow,' Anna answered. 'His leave's been prolonged – he's going back with me.'

The words seemed to have uttered themselves without her will, yet she felt a great sense of freedom as she spoke them.

The hard tension of Owen's face changed to incredulous surprise. He looked at Darrow.

'The merest luck ... a colleague whose wife was ill ... I came straight back,' she heard the latter tranquilly explaining. His self-command helped to steady her, and she smiled at Owen.

'We'll all go back together tomorrow morning,' she said as she slipped her arm through his.

33

Owen Leath did not go back with his step-mother to Givré. In reply to her suggestion he announced his intention of staying on a day or two longer in Paris.

Anna left alone by the first train the next morning. Darrow was to follow in the afternoon. When Owen had left them the evening before, Darrow waited a moment for her to speak; then, as she said nothing, he asked her if she really wished him to return to Givré. She made a mute sign of assent, and he added: 'For you know that, much as I'm ready to do for Owen, I can't do that for him – I can't go back to be sent away again.'

'No – no!'

He came nearer, and looked at her, and she went to him. All her fears seemed to fall from her as he held her. It was a different feeling from any she had known before: confused and turbid, as if secret shames and rancours stirred in it, yet richer, deeper, more enslaving.

She leaned her head back and shut her eyes beneath his kisses. She knew now that she could never give him up.

Nevertheless she asked him, the next morning, to let her go back alone to Givré. She wanted time to think. She was convinced that what had happened was inevitable, that she and Darrow belonged to each other, and that he was right in saying no past folly could ever put them asunder. If there was a shade of difference in her feeling for him it was that of an added intensity. She felt restless, insecure out of his sight: she had a sense of incompleteness, of passionate dependence, that was somehow at variance with her own conception of her character.

It was partly the consciousness of this change in herself that made her want to be alone. The solitude of her inner life had given her the habit of these hours of self-examination, and she needed them as she needed her morning plunge into cold water.

During the journey she tried to review what had happened in the light of her new decision and of her sudden relief from pain. She seemed to herself to have passed through some fiery initiation from which she had emerged seared and quivering, but clutching to her breast a magic talisman. Sophy Viner had cried out to her: 'Some day you'll know!' and Darrow had used the same words. They meant, she supposed, that when she had explored the intricacies and darknesses of her own heart her judgment of others would be less absolute. Well, she knew now – knew weaknesses and strengths she had not dreamed of, and the deep discord and still deeper complicities between what thought in her and what blindly wanted . . .

Her mind turned anxiously to Owen. At least the blow that was to fall on him would not seem to have been inflicted by her hand. He would be left with the impression that his breach with Sophy Viner was due to one of the ordinary causes of such disruptions: though he must lose her, his memory of her would not be poisoned. Anna never for a moment permitted herself the delusion that she had renewed her promise to Darrow in order to spare her step-son this last refinement of misery. She knew she had been prompted by the irresistible impulse to hold fast to what was most precious to her, and that Owen's arrival on the scene had been the pretext for her decision, and not its cause; yet she felt herself fortified by the thought of what she had spared him. It was as though a star she had been used to follow had shed its familiar ray on ways unknown to her.

All through these meditations ran the undercurrent of an absolute trust in Sophy Viner. She thought of the girl with a mingling of antipathy and confidence. It was humiliating to her pride to recognize kindred impulses in a character which she would have liked to feel completely alien to her. But what indeed was the girl really like? She seemed to have no scruples and a thousand delicacies. She had given herself to Darrow, and concealed the episode from Owen Leath, with no more apparent sense of debasement than the vulgarest of adventuresses; yet she had instantly obeyed the voice of her heart when it bade her part from the one and serve the other.

Anna tried to picture what the girl's life must have been: what experiences, what initiations, had formed her. But her own training had been too different: there were veils she could not lift. She looked back at her married life, and its colourless uniformity took on an air of high restraint and order. Was it because she had been so incurious that it had worn that look to her? It struck her with amazement that she had never given a thought to her husband's past, or wondered what he did and where he went when he was away from her. If she had been asked what she supposed he thought about when they were apart, she would instantly have answered: his snuff-boxes. It had never occurred to her that he might have passions, interests, preoccupations of which she was absolutely ignorant. Yet he went up to Paris rather regularly: ostensibly to attend sales and exhibitions, or to confer with dealers and collectors. She tried to picture him, straight, trim, beautifully brushed and varnished, walking furtively down a quiet street, and looking about him before he slipped into a doorway. She understood now that she had been cold to him: what more likely than that he had sought compensations? All men were like that, she supposed – no doubt her simplicity had amused him.

In the act of transposing Fraser Leath into a Don Juan she was pulled up by the ironic perception that she was simply trying to justify Darrow. She wanted to think that all men were 'like that' because Darrow was 'like that': she wanted to justify her acceptance of the fact by persuading herself that only through such concessions could women like herself hope to keep what they could not give up. And suddenly she was filled with anger at her blindness, and then at her disastrous attempt to see. Why had she forced the truth out of Darrow? If only she had held her tongue nothing need ever have been known. Sophy Viner would have broken her engagement, Owen would have been sent around the world, and her own dream would have been unshattered. But she had probed, insisted, cross-examined, not rested till she had dragged the secret to the light. She was one of the luckless women who always have the wrong audacities, and who always know it . . .

Was it she, Anna Leath, who was picturing herself to herself in that way? She recoiled from her thoughts as if with a sense of demoniac possession, and there flashed through her the longing to return to her old state of fearless ignorance. If at that moment she could have kept Darrow from following her to Givré she would have done so . . .

But he came; and with the sight of him the turmoil fell and she felt herself reassured, rehabilitated. He arrived toward dusk, and she motored to Francheuil to meet him. She wanted to see him as soon as possible, for she had divined, through the new insight that was in her, that only his presence could restore her to a normal view of things. In the motor, as they left the town and turned into the high-road, he lifted her hand and kissed it, and she leaned against him, and felt the currents flow between them. She was grateful to him for not saying anything, and for not expecting her to speak. She said to herself: 'He never makes a mistake – he always knows what to do'; and then she thought with a start that it was doubtless because he had so often been in such situations. The idea that his tact was a kind of professional expertness filled her with repugnance, and insensibly she drew away from him. He made no motion to bring her nearer, and she instantly thought that that was calculated too. She sat beside him in frozen misery, wondering whether, henceforth, she would measure in this way his every look and gesture. Neither of them spoke again till the motor turned under the dark arch of the avenue, and they saw the lights of Givré twinkling at its end. Then Darrow laid his hand on hers and said: 'I know, dear –' and the hardness in her melted. 'He's suffering as I am,' she thought; and for a moment the baleful fact between them seemed to draw them closer instead of walling them up in their separate wretchedness.

It was wonderful to be once more re-entering the doors of Givré with him, and as the old house received them into its mellow silence she had again the sense of passing out of a dreadful dream into the reassurance of kindly and familiar things. It did not seem possible that these quiet rooms, so full of the slowly-distilled accumulations of a fastidious taste, should have been the scene of tragic dissensions. The memory of them seemed to be shut out into the night with the closing and barring of its doors.

At the tea-table in the oak-room they found Madame de Chantelle and Effie. The little girl, catching sight of Darrow, raced down the drawing-rooms to meet him, and returned in triumph on his shoulder. Anna looked at them with a smile. Effie, for all her graces, was chary of such favours, and her mother knew that in according them to Darrow she had admitted him to the circle where Owen had hitherto ruled.

Over the tea-table Darrow gave Madame de Chantelle the explanation of his sudden return from England. On reaching London, he told her, he had found that the secretary he was to have replaced was detained there by the illness of his wife. The Ambassador, knowing Darrow's urgent reasons for wishing to be in France, had immediately proposed his going back, and awaiting at Givré the summons to relieve his colleague; and he had jumped into the first train, without even waiting to telegraph the news of his release. He spoke naturally, easily, in his usual quiet voice, taking his tea from Effie, helping himself to the toast she handed, and stooping now and then to stroke the dozing terrier. And suddenly, as Anna listened to his explanation, she asked herself if it were true.

The question, of course, was absurd. There was no possible reason why he should invent a false account of his return, and every probability that the version he gave was the real one. But he had looked and spoken in the same way when he had answered her probing questions about Sophy Viner, and she reflected with a chill of fear that she would never again know if he were speaking the truth or not. She was sure he loved her, and she did not fear his insincerity as much as her own distrust of him. For a moment it seemed to her that this must corrupt the very source of love; then she said to herself: 'By and by, when I am altogether his, we shall be so near each other that there will be no room for any doubts between us.' But the doubts were there now, one moment lulled to quiescence, the next more torturingly alert. When the nurse appeared to summon Effie, the little girl, after kissing her grandmother, entrenched herself on Darrow's knee with the imperious demand to be carried up to bed; and Anna, while she laughingly protested, said to herself with a pang: 'Can I give her a father about whom I think such things?'

The thought of Effie, and of what she owed to Effie, had been the fundamental reason for her delays and hesitations when she and Darrow had come together again in England. Her own feeling was so clear that but for that scruple she would have put her hand in his at once. But till she had seen him again she had never considered the possibility of remarriage, and when it suddenly confronted her it seemed, for the moment, to disorganize the life she had planned for herself and her child. She had not spoken of this to Darrow because it appeared to her a subject to be debated within her own conscience. The question, then, was not as to his fitness to become the guide and guardian of her child; nor did she fear that her love for him would deprive Effie of the least fraction of her tenderness, since she did not think of love as something measured and exhaustible but as a treasure perpetually renewed. What she questioned was her right to introduce into her life any interests and duties which might rob Effie of a part of her time, or lessen the closeness of their daily intercourse.

She had decided this question as it was inevitable that she should; but now another was before her. Assuredly, at her age, there was no possible reason why she should cloister herself to bring up her daughter; but there was every reason for not marrying a man in whom her own faith was not complete . . .

34

When she woke the next morning she felt a great lightness of heart. She recalled her last awakening at Givré, three days before, when it had seemed as though all her life had gone down in darkness. Now Darrow was once more under the same roof with her, and once more his nearness sufficed to make the looming horror drop away. She could almost have smiled at her scruples of the night before: as she looked back on them they seemed to belong to the old ignorant timorous time when she had feared to look life in the face, and had been blind to the mysteries and contradictions of the human heart because her own had not been revealed to her. Darrow had said: 'You were made to feel everything'; and to feel was surely better than to judge.

When she came downstairs he was already in the oak-room with Effie and Madame de Chantelle, and the sense of reassurance which his presence gave her was merged in the relief of not being able to speak of what was between them. But there it was, inevitably, and whenever they looked at each other they saw it. In her dread of giving it a more tangible shape she tried to devise means of keeping the little girl with her, and, when the latter had been called away by the nurse, found an excuse for following Madame de Chantelle up-stairs to the purple sitting-room. But a confidential talk with Madame de Chantelle implied the detailed discussion of plans of which Anna could hardly yet bear to consider the vaguest outline: the date of her marriage, the relative advantages of sailing from London or Lisbon, the possibility of hiring a habitable house at their new post; and, when these problems were exhausted, the application of the same method to the subject of Owen's future.

His grandmother, having no suspicion of the real reason of Sophy Viner's departure, had thought it 'extremely suitable' of the young girl to withdraw to the shelter of her old friends' roof in the hour of bridal preparation. This maidenly retreat had in fact impressed Madame de Chantelle so favourably that she was disposed for the first time to talk over Owen's projects; and as every human event translated itself for her into terms of social and domestic detail, Anna had perforce to travel the same round again. She felt a momen-tary relief when Darrow presently joined them; but his coming served only to draw the conversation back to the question of their own future, and Anna felt a new pang as she heard him calmly and lucidly discussing it. Did such self-possession imply indifference or insincerity? In that problem her mind perpetually revolved; and she dreaded the one answer as much as the other.

She was resolved to keep on her course as though nothing had happened: to marry Darrow and never let the consciousness of the past intrude itself between them; but she was beginning to feel that the only way of attaining to this state of detachment from the irreparable was once for all to turn back with him to its contemplation. As soon as this desire had germinated it became so strong in her that she regretted having promised Effie to take her out for the afternoon. But she could think of no pretext for disappointing the little girl, and soon after luncheon the three set forth in the motor to show Darrow a château famous in the annals of the region. During their excursion Anna found it impossible to guess from his demeanour if Effie's presence between them was as much of a strain to his composure as to hers. He remained imperturbably good-humoured and appreciative while they went the round of the monument, and she remarked only that when he thought himself unnoticed his face grew grave and his answers came less promptly.

On the way back, two or three miles from Givré, she suddenly proposed that they should walk home through the forest which skirted that side of the park. Darrow acquiesced, and they got out and sent Effie on in the motor. Their way led through a bit of sober French woodland, flat as a faded tapestry, but with gleams of live emerald lingering here and there among its browns and ochres. The luminous grey air gave vividness to its dying colours, and veiled the distant glimpses of the landscape in soft uncertainty. In such a solitude Anna had fancied it would be easier to speak; but as she walked beside Darrow over the deep soundless flooring of brown moss the words on her lips took flight again. It seemed impossible to break the spell of quiet joy which his presence laid on her, and when he began to talk of the place they had just visited she answered his questions and then waited for what he should say next . . . No, decidedly she could not speak; she no longer even knew what she had meant to say . . .

The same experience repeated itself several times that day and the next. When she and Darrow were apart she exhausted herself in appeal and interrogation, she formulated with a fervent lucidity every point in her imaginary argument. But as soon as she was alone with him something deeper than reason and subtler than shyness laid its benumbing touch upon her, and the desire to speak became merely a dim disquietude, through which his looks, his words, his touch, reached her as through a mist of bodily pain. Yet this inertia was torn by wild flashes of resistance, and when they were apart she began to prepare again what she meant to say to him.

She knew he could not be with her without being aware of this inner turmoil, and she hoped he would break the spell by some releasing word. But she presently understood that he recognized the futility of words, and was resolutely bent on holding her to her own purpose of behaving as if nothing had happened. Once more she inwardly accused him of insensibility, and her imagination was beset by tormenting visions of his past . . . Had such things happened to him before? If the episode had been an isolated accident – 'a moment of folly and madness', as he had called it – she could understand, or at least begin to understand (for at a certain point her imagination always turned back); but if it were a mere link in a chain of similar experiments, the thought of it dishonoured her whole past . . .

Effie, in the interregnum between governesses, had been given leave to dine downstairs; and Anna, on the evening of Darrow's return, kept the little girl with her till long after the nurse had signalled from the drawing-room door. When at length she had been carried off, Anna proposed a game of cards, and after this diversion had drawn to its languid close she said good-night to Darrow and followed Madame de Chantelle upstairs. But Madame de Chantelle never sat up late, and the second evening, with the amiably implied intention of leaving Anna and Darrow to themselves, she took an earlier leave of them than usual.

Anna sat silent, listening to her small stiff steps as they minced down the hall and died out in the distance. Madame de Chantelle had broken her wooden embroidery frame, and Darrow, having offered to repair it, had drawn his chair up to a table that held a lamp. Anna watched him as he sat with bent head and knitted brows, trying to fit together the disjoined pieces. The sight of him, so tranquilly absorbed in this trifling business, seemed to give to the quiet room a perfume of intimacy, to fill it with a sense of sweet familiar habit; and it came over her again that she knew nothing of the inner thoughts of this man who was sitting by her as a husband might. The lamplight fell on his white forehead, on the healthy brown of his cheek, the backs of his thin sun-burnt hands. As she watched the hands her sense of them became as vivid as a touch, and she said to herself: 'That other woman has sat and watched him as I am doing. She has known him as I have never known him . . . Perhaps he is thinking of that now. Or perhaps he has forgotten it all as completely as I have forgotten everything that happened to me before he came . . .'

He looked young, active, stored with strength and energy; not the man for vain repinings or long memories. She wondered what she had to hold or satisfy him. He loved her now; she had no doubt of that; but how could she hope to keep him? They were so nearly of an age that already she felt herself his senior. As yet the difference was not visible; outwardly at least they were matched; but ill-health or unhappiness would soon do away with this equality. She thought with a pang of bitterness: 'He won't grow any older because he doesn't feel things; and because he doesn't, I *shall* . . .'

And when she ceased to please him, what then? Had he the tradition of faith to the spoken vow, or the deeper piety of the unspoken dedication? What was his theory, what his inner conviction in such matters? But what did she care for his convictions or his theories? No doubt he loved her now, and believed he would always go on loving her, and was persuaded that, if he ceased to, his loyalty would be proof against the change. What she wanted to know was not what he thought about it in advance, but what would impel or restrain him at the crucial hour. She put no faith in her own arts: she was too sure of having none! And if some beneficent enchanter had bestowed them on her, she knew now that she would have rejected the gift. She could hardly conceive of wanting the kind of love that was a state one could be cozened into . . .

Darrow, putting away the frame, walked across the room and sat down beside her; and she felt he had something special to say.

'They're sure to send for me in a day or two now,' he began.

She made no answer, and he continued: 'You'll tell me before I go what day I'm to come back and get you?'

It was the first time since his return to Givré that he had made any direct allusion to the date of their marriage; and instead of answering him she broke out: 'There's something I've been wanting you to know. The other day in Paris I saw Miss Viner.'

She saw him flush with the intensity of his surprise.

'You sent for her?'

'No; she heard from Adelaide that I was in Paris and she came. She came because she wanted to urge me to marry you. I thought you ought to know what she had done.'

Darrow stood up. 'I'm glad you've told me.' He spoke with a visible effort at composure. Her eyes followed him as he moved away.

'Is that all?' he asked after an interval.

'It seems to me a great deal.'

'It's what she'd already asked me.' His voice showed her how deeply he was moved, and a throb of jealousy shot through her.

'Oh, it was for your sake, I know!' He made no answer, and she added: 'She's been exceedingly generous . . . Why shouldn't we speak of it?'

She had lowered her head, but through her dropped lids she seemed to be watching the crowded scene of his face.

'I've not shrunk from speaking of it.'

'Speaking of *her*, then, I mean. It seems to me that if I could talk to you about her I should know better –'

She broke off, confused, and he questioned: 'What is it you want to know better?'

The colour rose to her forehead. How could she tell him what she scarcely dared own to herself? There was nothing she did not want to know, no fold or cranny of his secret that her awakened imagination did not strain to penetrate; but she could not expose Sophy Viner to the base fingerings of a retrospective jealousy, nor Darrow to the temptation of belittling her in the effort to better his own case. The girl had been magnificent, and the only worthy return that Anna could make was to take Darrow from her without a question if she took him at all . . .

She lifted her eyes to his face. 'I think I only wanted to speak her name. It's not right that we should seem so afraid of it. If I were really afraid of it I should have to give you up,' she said.

He bent over her and caught her to him. 'Ah, you can't give me up now!' he exclaimed.

She suffered him to hold her fast without speaking; but the old dread was between them again, and it was on her lips to cry out: 'How can I help it, when I *am* so afraid?'

35

The next morning the dread was still there, and she understood that she must snatch herself out of the torpor of the will into which she had been gradually sinking, and tell Darrow that she could not be his wife.

The knowledge came to her in the watches of a sleepless night, when, through the tears of disenchanted passion, she stared back upon her past. There it lay before her, her sole romance, in all its paltry poverty, the cheapest of cheap adventures, the most pitiful of sentimental blunders. She looked about her room, the room where, for so many years, if her heart had been quiescent her thoughts had been alive, and pictured herself henceforth cowering before a throng of mean suspicions, of unavowed compromises and concessions. In that moment of self-searching she saw that Sophy Viner had chosen the better part, and that certain renunciations might enrich where possession would have left a desert.

Passionate reactions of instinct fought against these efforts of her will. Why should past or future coerce her, when the present was so securely hers? Why insanely surrender what the other would after all never have? Her sense of irony whispered that if she sent away Darrow it would not be to Sophy Viner, but to the first woman who crossed his path – as, in a similar hour, Sophy Viner herself had crossed it . . . But the mere fact that she could think such things of him sent her shuddering back to the opposite pole. She pictured herself gradually subdued to such a conception of life and love, she pictured Effie growing up under the influence of the woman she saw herself becoming – and she hid her eyes from the humiliation of the picture . . .

They were at luncheon when the summons that Darrow expected was brought to him. He handed the telegram to Anna, and she learned that his Ambassador, on the way to a German cure, was to be in Paris the next evening and wished to confer with him there before he went back to London. The idea that the decisive moment was at hand was so agitating to her that when luncheon was over she slipped away to the terrace and thence went down alone to the garden. The day was grey but mild, with the heaviness of decay in the air. She rambled on aimlessly, following under the denuded boughs the path she and Darrow had taken on their first walk to the river. She was sure he would not try to overtake her: sure he would guess why she wished to be alone. There were moments when it seemed to double her loneliness to be so certain of his reading her heart while she was so desperately ignorant of his . . .

She wandered on for more than an hour, and when she returned to the house she saw, as she entered the hall, that Darrow was seated at the desk in Owen's study. He heard her step, and looking up turned in his chair without rising. Their eyes met, and she saw that his were clear and smiling. He had a heap of papers at his elbow and was evidently engaged in some official correspondence. She wondered that he could address himself so composedly to his task, and then ironically reflected that such detachment was a sign of his superiority. She crossed the threshold and went toward him; but as she advanced she had a sudden vision of Owen, standing outside in the cold autumn dusk and watching Darrow and Sophy Viner as they faced each other across the lamplit desk . . . The evocation was so vivid that it caught her breath like a blow, and she sank down helplessly on the divan among the piled-up books. Distinctly, at the moment, she understood that the end had come. 'When he speaks to me I will tell him!' she thought . . .

Darrow, laying aside his pen, looked at her for a moment in silence; then he stood up and shut the door.

'I must go tomorrow early,' he said, sitting down beside her. His voice was grave, with a slight tinge of sadness. She said to herself: 'He knows what I am feeling . . .' and now the thought made her feel less alone. The expression of his face was stern and yet tender: for the first time she understood what he had suffered.

She had no doubt as to the necessity of giving him up, but it was impossible to tell him so then. She stood up and said: 'I'll leave you to your letters.' He made no protest, but merely answered: 'You'll come down presently for a walk?' and it occurred to her at once that she would walk down to the river with him, and give herself for the last time the tragic luxury of sitting at his side in the little pavilion. 'Perhaps,' she thought, 'it will be easier to tell him there.'

It did not, on the way home from their walk, become any easier to tell him; but her secret decision to do so before he left gave her a kind of factitious calm and laid a melancholy ecstasy upon the hour. Still skirting the subject that fanned their very faces with its flame, they clung persistently to other topics, and it seemed to Anna that their minds had never been nearer together than in this hour when their hearts were so separate. In the glow of interchanged love she had grown less conscious of that other glow of interchanged thought which had once illumined her mind. She had forgotten how Darrow had widened her world and lengthened out all her perspectives, and with a pang of double destitution she saw herself alone among her shrunken thoughts.

For the first time, then, she had a clear vision of what her life would be without him. She imagined herself trying to take up the daily round, and all that had lightened and animated it seemed equally lifeless and vain. She tried to think of herself as wholly absorbed in her daughter's development, like other mothers she had seen; but she supposed those mothers must have had stored memories of happiness to nourish them. She had had nothing, and all her starved youth still claimed its due.

When she went up to dress for dinner she said to herself: 'I'll have my last evening with him, and then, before we say good night, I'll tell him.'

This postponement did not seem unjustified. Darrow had shown her how he dreaded vain words, how resolved he was to avoid all fruitless discussion. He must have been intensely aware of what had been going on in her mind since his return, yet when she had attempted to reveal it to him he had turned from the revelation. She was therefore merely following the line he had traced in behaving, till the final moment came, as though there were nothing more to say . . .

That moment seemed at last to be at hand when, at her usual hour after dinner, Madame de Chantelle rose to go upstairs. She lingered a little to bid good-bye to Darrow, whom she was not likely to see in the morning; and her affable allusions to his prompt return sounded in Anna's ear like the note of destiny.

A cold rain had fallen all day, and for greater warmth and intimacy they had gone after dinner to the oakroom, shutting out the chilly vista of the farther drawing-rooms. The autumn wind, coming up from the river, cried about the house with a voice of loss and separation; and Anna and Darrow sat silent, as if they feared to break the hush that shut them in. The solitude, the fire-light, the harmony of soft hangings and old dim pictures, wove about them a spell of security through which Anna felt, far down in her heart, the muffled beat of an inextinguishable bliss. How could she have thought that this last moment would be the moment to speak to him, when it seemed to have gathered up into its flight all the scattered splendours of her dream?

36

Darrow continued to stand by the door after it had closed. Anna felt that he was looking at her, and sat still, disdaining to seek refuge in any evasive word or movement. For the last time she wanted to let him take from her the fullness of what the sight of her could give.

He crossed over and sat down on the sofa. For a moment neither of them spoke; then he said: 'Tonight, dearest, I must have my answer.'

She straightened herself under the shock of his seeming to take the very words from her lips.

'Tonight?' was all that she could falter.

'I must be off by the early train. There won't be more than a moment in the morning.'

He had taken her hand, and she said to herself that she must free it before she could go on with what she had to say. Then she rejected this concession to a weakness she was resolved to defy. To the end she would leave her hand in his hand, her eyes in his eyes: she would not, in their final hour together, be afraid of any part of her love for him.

'You'll tell me tonight, dear,' he insisted gently; and his insistence gave her the strength to speak.

'There's something I must ask you,' she broke out, perceiving, as she heard her words, that they were not in the least what she had meant to say.

He sat still, waiting, and she pressed on: 'Do such things happen to men often?'

The quiet room seemed to resound with the long reverberations of her question. She looked away from him, and he released her and stood up.

'I don't know what happens to other men. Such a thing never happened to me . . .'

She turned her eyes back to his face. She felt like a traveller on a giddy path between a cliff and a precipice: there was nothing for it now but to go on.

'Had it . . . had it begun . . . before you met her in Paris?'

'No; a thousand times no! I've told you the facts as they were.'

'All the facts?'

He turned abruptly. 'What do you mean?'

Her throat was dry and the loud pulses drummed in her temples.

'I mean – about her . . . Perhaps you knew . . . knew things about her . . . beforehand.'

She stopped. The room had grown profoundly still. A log dropped to the hearth and broke there in a hissing shower.

Darrow spoke in a clear voice. 'I knew nothing, absolutely nothing,' he said.

She had the answer to her inmost doubt – to her last shameful unavowed hope. She sat powerless under her woe.

He walked to the fireplace and pushed back the broken log with his foot. A flame shot out of it, and in the upward glare she saw his pale face, stern with misery.

'Is that all?' he asked.

She made a slight sign with her head and he came slowly back to her. 'Then is this to be good-bye?'

Again she signed a faint assent, and he made no effort to touch her or draw nearer. 'You understand that I sha'n't come back?'

He was looking at her, and she tried to return his look, but her eyes were blind with tears, and in dread of his seeing them she got up and walked away. He did not follow her, and she stood with her back to him, staring at a bowl of carnations on a little table strewn with books. Her tears magnified everything she looked at, and the streaked petals of the carnations, their fringed edges and frail curled stamens, pressed upon her, huge and vivid. She noticed among the books a volume of verse he had sent her from England, and tried to remember whether it was before or after . . .

She felt that he was waiting for her to speak, and at last she turned to him. 'I shall see you tomorrow before you go . . .'

He made no answer.

She moved toward the door and he held it open for her. She saw his hand on the door, and his seal ring in its setting of twisted silver; and the sense of the end of all things came to her.

They walked down the drawing-rooms, between the shadowy reflections of screens and cabinets, and mounted the stairs side by side. At the end of the gallery, a lamp brought out turbid gleams in the smoky battle-piece above it.

On the landing Darrow stopped; his room was the nearest to the stairs. 'Good night,' he said, holding out his hand.

As Anna gave him hers the springs of grief broke loose in her. She struggled with her sobs, and subdued them; but her breath came unevenly, and to hide her agitation she leaned on him and pressed her face against his arm.

'Don't – don't,' he whispered, soothing her.

Her troubled breathing sounded loudly in the silence of the sleeping house. She pressed her lips tight, but could not stop the nervous pulsations in her throat, and he put an arm about her and, opening his door, drew her across the threshold of his room. The door shut behind her and she sat down on the lounge at the foot of the bed. The pulsations in her throat had ceased, but she knew they would begin again if she tried to speak.

Darrow walked away and leaned against the mantelpiece. The red-veiled lamp shone on his books and papers, on the armchair by the fire, and the scattered objects on his dressing-table. A log glimmered on the hearth, and the room was warm and faintly smoke-scented. It was the first time she had ever been in a room he lived in, among his personal possessions and the traces of his daily usage. Every object about her seemed to contain a particle of himself: the whole air breathed of him, steeping her in the sense of his intimate presence.

Suddenly she thought: 'This is what Sophy Viner knew' . . . and with a torturing precision she pictured them alone in such a scene . . . Had he taken the girl to an hotel . . . where did people go in such cases? Wherever they were, the silence of night had been around them, and the things he used had been strewn about the room . . . Anna, ashamed of dwelling on the detested vision, stood up with a confused impulse of flight; then a wave of contrary feeling arrested her and she paused with lowered head.

Darrow had come forward as she rose, and she perceived that he was waiting for her to bid him good night. It was clear that no other possibility had even brushed his mind; and the fact, for some dim reason, humiliated her. 'Why not . . . why not?' something whispered in her, as though his forbearance, his tacit recognition of her pride, were a slight on other qualities she wanted him to feel in her.

'In the morning, then?' she heard him say.

'Yes, in the morning,' she repeated.

She continued to stand in the same place, looking vaguely about the room. For once before they parted – since part they must – she longed to be to him all that Sophy Viner had been; but she remained rooted to the floor, unable to find a word or imagine a gesture that should express her meaning. Exasperated by her helplessness, she thought: 'Don't I feel things as other women do?'

Her eye fell on a note-case she had given him. It was worn at the corners with the friction of his pocket and distended with thickly packed papers. She wondered if he carried her letters in it, and she put her hand out and touched it.

All that he and she had ever felt or seen, their close encounters of word and look, and the closer contact of their silences, trembled through her at the touch. She remembered things he had said that had been like new skies above her head: ways he had that seemed a part of the air she breathed. The faint warmth of her girlish love came back to her, gathering heat as it passed through her thoughts; and her heart rocked like a boat on the surge of its long long memories. 'It's because I love him in too many ways,' she thought; and slowly she turned to the door.

She was aware that Darrow was still silently watching her, but he neither stirred nor spoke till she had reached the threshold. Then he met her there and caught her in his arms.

'Not tonight – don't tell me tonight!' he whispered; and she leaned away from him, closing her eyes for an instant, and then slowly opening them to the flood of light in his.

37

Anna and Darrow, the next day, sat alone in a compartment of the Paris train.

Anna, when they entered it, had put herself in the farthest corner and placed her bag on the adjoining seat. She had decided suddenly to accompany Darrow to Paris, had even persuaded him to wait for a later train in order that they might travel together. She had an intense longing to be with him, an almost morbid terror of losing sight of him for a moment: when he jumped out of the train and ran back along the platform to buy a newspaper for her she felt as though she should never see him again, and shivered with the cold misery of her last journey to Paris, when she had thought herself parted from him forever. Yet she wanted to keep him at a distance, on the other side of the compartment, and as the train moved out of the station she drew from her bag the letters she had thrust in it as she left the house, and began to glance over them so that her lowered lids should hide her eyes from him.

She was his now, his for life: there could never again be any question of sacrificing herself to Effie's welfare, or to any other abstract conception of duty. Effie of course would not suffer; Anna would pay for her bliss as a wife by redoubled devotion as a mother. Her scruples were not overcome; but for the time their voices were drowned in the tumultuous rumour of her happiness.

As she opened her letters she was conscious that Darrow's gaze was fixed on her, and gradually it drew her eyes upward, and she drank deep of the passionate tenderness in his. Then the blood rose to her face and she felt again the desire to shield herself. She turned back to her letters and her glance lit on an envelope inscribed in Owen's hand.

Her heart began to beat oppressively: she was in a mood when the simplest things seemed ominous. What could Owen have to say to her? Only the first page was covered, and it contained simply the announcement that, in the company of a young compatriot who was studying at the Beaux Arts, he had planned to leave for Spain the following evening.

'He hasn't seen her, then!' was Anna's instant thought; and her feeling was a strange compound of humiliation and relief. The girl had kept her word, lived up to the line of conduct she had set herself; and Anna had failed in the same attempt. She did not reproach herself with her failure; but she would have been happier if there had been less discrepancy between her words to Sophy Viner and the act which had followed them. It irritated her obscurely that the girl should have been so much surer of her power to carry out her purpose . . .

Anna looked up and saw that Darrow's eyes were on the newspaper. He seemed calm and secure, almost indifferent to her presence. 'Will it become a matter of course to him so soon?' she wondered with a twinge of jealousy. She sat motionless, her eyes fixed on him, trying to make him feel the attraction of her gaze as she felt his. It surprised and shamed her to detect a new element in her love for him: a sort of suspicious tyrannical tenderness that seemed to deprive it of all serenity. Finally he looked up, his smile enveloped her, and she felt herself his in every fibre, his so completely and inseparably that she saw the vanity of imagining any other fate for herself.

To give herself a countenance she held out Owen's letter. He took it and glanced down the page, his face grown grave. She waited nervously till he looked up.

'That's a good plan; the best thing that could happen,' he said, a just perceptible shade of constraint in his tone.

'Oh, yes,' she hastily assented. She was aware of a faint current of relief silently circulating between them. They were both glad that Owen was going, that for a while he would be out of their way; and it seemed to her horrible that so much of the stuff of their happiness should be made of such unavowed feelings . . .

'I shall see him this evening,' she said, wishing Darrow to feel that she was not afraid of meeting her step-son.

'Yes, of course; perhaps he might dine with you.'

The words struck her as strangely obtuse. Darrow was to meet his Ambassador at the station on the latter's arrival, and would in all probability have to spend the evening with him, and Anna knew he had been concerned at the thought of having to leave her alone. But how could he speak in that careless tone of her dining with Owen? She lowered her voice to say: 'I'm afraid he's desperately unhappy.'

He answered, with a tinge of impatience: 'It's much the best thing that he should travel.'

'Yes – but don't you feel . . .' She broke off. She knew how he disliked these idle returns on the irrevocable, and her fear of doing or saying what he disliked was tinged by a new instinct of subserviency against which her pride revolted. She thought to herself: 'He will see the change, and grow indifferent to me as he did to *her* . . .' and for a moment it seemed to her that she was reliving the experience of Sophy Viner.

Darrow made no attempt to learn the end of her unfinished sentence. He handed back Owen's letter and returned to his newspaper; and when he looked up from it a few minutes later it was with a clear brow and a smile that irresistibly drew her back to happier thoughts.

The train was just entering a station, and a moment later their compartment was invaded by a commonplace couple preoccupied with the bestowal of bulging packages. Anna, at their approach, felt the possessive pride of the woman in love when strangers are between herself and the man she loves. She asked Darrow to open the window, to place her bag in the net, to roll her rug into a cushion for her feet; and while he was thus busied with her she was conscious of a new devotion in his tone, in his way of bending over her and meeting her eyes. He went back to his seat, and they looked at each other like lovers smiling at a happy secret.

Anna, before going back to Givré, had suggested Owen's moving into her apartment, but he had preferred to remain at the hotel to which he had sent his luggage, and on arriving in Paris she decided to drive there at once. She was impatient to have the meeting over, and glad that Darrow was obliged to leave her at the station in order to look up a colleague at the Embassy. She dreaded his seeing Owen again, and yet dared not tell him so; and to ensure his remaining away she mentioned an urgent engagement with her dress-maker and a long list of commissions to be executed for Madame de Chantelle.

'I shall see you tomorrow morning,' she said; but he replied with a smile that he would certainly find time to come to her for a moment on his way back from meeting the Ambassador; and when he had put her in a cab he leaned through the window to press his lips to hers.

She blushed like a girl, thinking, half vexed, half happy: 'Yesterday he would not have done it . . .' and a dozen scarcely definable differences in his look and manner seemed all at once to be summed up in the boyish act. 'After all, I'm engaged to him,' she reflected, and then smiled at the absurdity of the word. The next instant, with a pang of self-reproach, she remembered Sophy Viner's cry: 'I knew all the while he didn't care . . .' 'Poor thing, oh poor thing!' Anna murmured . . .

At Owen's hotel she waited in a tremor while the porter went in search of him. Word was presently brought back that he was in his room and begged her to come up, and as she crossed the hall she caught sight of his portmanteaux lying on the floor, already labelled for departure.

Owen sat at a table writing, his back to the door; and when he stood up the window was behind him, so that, in the rainy afternoon light, his features were barely discernible.

'Dearest – so you're really off?' she said, hesitating a moment on the threshold.

He pushed a chair forward, and they sat down, each waiting for the other to speak. Finally she put some random question about his travelling-companion, a slow shy meditative youth whom he had once or twice brought down to Givré. She reflected that it was natural he should have given this uncommunicative comrade the preference over his livelier acquaintances, and aloud she said: 'I'm so glad Fred Rempson can go with you.'

Owen answered in the same tone, and for a few minutes their talk dragged itself on over a dry waste of commonplaces. Anna noticed that, though ready enough to impart his own plans, Owen studiously abstained from putting any questions about hers. It was evident from his allusions that he meant to be away for some time, and he presently asked her if she would give instructions about packing and sending after him some winter clothes he had left at Givré. This gave her the opportunity to say that she expected to go back within a day or two and would attend to the matter as soon as she returned. She added: 'I came up this morning with George, who is going on to London tomorrow,' intending, by the use of Darrow's Christian name, to give Owen the chance to speak of her marriage. But he made no comment, and she continued to hear the name sounding on unfamiliarly between them.

The room was almost dark, and she finally stood up and glanced about for the light-switch, saying: 'I can't see you, dear.'

'Oh, don't – I hate the light!' Owen exclaimed, catching her by the wrist and pushing her back into her seat. He gave a nervous laugh and added: 'I'm half-blind with neuralgia. I suppose it's this beastly rain.'

'Yes; it will do you good to get down to Spain.'

She asked if he had the remedies the doctor had given him for a previous attack, and on his replying that he didn't know what he'd done with the stuff, she sprang up, offering to go to the chemist's. It was a relief to have something to do for him, and she knew from his 'Oh, thanks – would you?' that it was a relief to him to have a pretext for not detaining her. His natural impulse would have been to declare that he didn't want any drugs, and would be all right in no time; and his acquiescence showed her how profoundly he felt the uselessness of their trying to prolong their talk. His face was now no more than a white blur in the dusk, but she felt its indistinctness as a veil drawn over aching intensities of expression. 'He knows . . . he knows . . .' she said to herself, and wondered whether the truth had been revealed to him by some corroborative fact or by the sheer force of divination.

He had risen also, and was clearly waiting for her to go, and she turned to the door, saying: 'I'll be back in a moment.'

'Oh, don't come up again, please!' He paused, embarrassed. 'I mean – I may not be here. I've got to go and pick up Rempson, and see about some final things with him.'

She stopped on the threshold with a sinking heart. He meant this to be their leave-taking, then – and he had not even asked her when she was to be married, or spoken of seeing her again before she set out for the other side of the world.

'Owen!' she cried, and turned back.

He stood mutely before her in the dimness.

'You haven't told me how long you're to be gone.'

'How long? Oh, you see . . . that's rather vague . . . I hate definite dates, you know . . .'

He paused and she saw he did not mean to help her out. She tried to say: 'You'll be here for my wedding?' but could not bring the words to her lips. Instead she murmured: 'In six weeks I shall be going too . . .' and he rejoined, as if he had expected the announce- ment and prepared his answer: 'Oh, by that time, very likely . . .'

'At any rate, I won't say good-bye,' she stammered, feeling the tears beneath her veil.

'No, no; rather not!' he declared; but he made no movement, and she went up and threw her arms about him. 'You'll write me, won't you?'

'Of course, of course —'

Her hands slipped down into his, and for a minute they held each other dumbly in the darkness; then he gave a vague laugh and said: 'It's really time to light up.' He pressed the electric button with one hand while with the other he opened the door; and she passed out without daring to turn back, lest the light on his face should show her what she feared to see.

38

Anna drove to the chemist's for Owen's remedy. On the way she stopped her cab at a book-shop, and emerged from it laden with literature. She knew what would interest Owen, and what he was likely to have read, and she had made her choice among the newest publications with the promptness of a discriminating reader. But on the way back to the hotel she was overcome by the irony of adding this mental panacea to the other. There was something grotesque and almost mocking in the idea of offering a judicious selection of literature to a man setting out on such a journey. 'He knows . . . he knows . . .' she kept on repeating; and giving the porter the parcel from the chemist's she drove away without leaving the books.

She went to her apartment, whither her maid had preceded her. There was a fire in the drawing-room and the tea-table stood ready by the hearth. The stormy rain beat against the uncurtained win- dows, and she thought of Owen, who would soon be driving through it to the station, alone with his bitter thoughts. She had been proud of the fact that he had always sought her help in difficult hours; and now, in the most difficult of all, she was the one being to whom he could not turn. Between them, henceforth, there would always be the wall of an insurmountable silence . . . She strained her aching thoughts to guess how the truth had come to him. Had he seen the girl, and had she told him? Instinctively, Anna rejected this conjecture. But what need was there of assuming an explicit statement, when every breath they had drawn for the last weeks had been charged with the immanent secret? As she looked back over the days since Darrow's first arrival at Givré she perceived that at no time had any one deliberately spoken, or anything been accidentally disclosed. The truth had come to light by the force of its irresistible pressure; and the perception gave her a startled sense of hidden powers, of a chaos of attractions and repulsions far beneath the ordered surfaces of intercourse. She looked back with melancholy derision on her old conception of life, as a kind of well-lit and well-policed suburb to dark places one need never know about. Here they were, these dark places, in her own bosom, and henceforth she would always have to traverse them to reach the beings she loved best!

She was still sitting beside the untouched tea-table when she heard Darrow's voice in the hall. She started up, saying to herself: 'I must tell him that Owen knows . . .' but when the door opened and she saw his face, still lit by the same smile of boyish triumph, she felt anew the uselessness of speaking . . . Had he ever supposed that Owen would not know? Probably, from the height of his greater experience, he had seen long since that all that happened was inevitable; and the thought of it, at any rate, was clearly not weighing on him now.

He was already dressed for the evening, and as he came toward her he said: 'The Ambassador's booked for an official dinner and I'm free after all. Where shall we dine?'

Anna had pictured herself sitting alone all the evening with her wretched thoughts, and the fact of having to put them out of her mind for the next few hours gave her an immediate sensation of relief. Already her pulses were dancing to the tune of Darrow's, and as they smiled at each other she thought: 'Nothing can ever change the fact that I belong to him.'

'Where shall we dine?' he repeated gaily, and she named a well-known restaurant for which she had once heard him express a preference. But as she did so she fancied she saw a shadow on his face, and instantly she said to herself: 'It was there he went with her!'

'Oh, no, not there, after all!' she interrupted herself; and now she was sure his colour deepened.

'Where shall it be, then?'

She noticed that he did not ask the reason of her change, and this convinced her that she had guessed the truth, and that he knew she had guessed it. 'He will always know what I am thinking, and he will never dare to ask me,' she thought; and she saw between them the same insurmountable wall of silence as between herself and Owen, a wall of glass through which they could watch each other's faintest motions but which no sound could ever traverse . . .

They drove to a restaurant on the Boulevard, and there, in their intimate corner of the serried scene, the sense of what was unspoken between them gradually ceased to oppress her. He looked so light-hearted and handsome, so ingenuously proud of her, so openly happy at being with her, that no other fact could seem real in his presence. He had learned that the Ambassador was to spend two days in Paris, and he had reason to hope that in consequence his own departure for London would be deferred. He was exhilarated by the prospect of being with Anna for a few hours longer, and she did not ask herself if his exhilaration were a sign of insensibility, for she was too conscious of his power of swaying her moods not to be secretly proud of affecting his.

They lingered for some time over the fruit and coffee, and when they rose to go Darrow suggested that, if she felt disposed for the play, they were not too late for the second part of the programme at one of the smaller theatres.

His mention of the hour recalled Owen to her thoughts. She saw his train rushing southward through the storm, and, in a corner of the swaying compartment, his face, white and indistinct as it had loomed on her in the rainy twilight. It was horrible to be thus perpetu-ally paying for her happiness!

Darrow had called for a theatrical journal, and he presently looked up from it to say: 'I hear the second play at the Athéné is amusing.'

It was on Anna's lips to acquiesce; but as she was about to speak she wondered if it were not at the Athéné that Owen had seen

Darrow with Sophy Viner. She was not sure he had even mentioned the theatre, but the mere possibility was enough to darken her sky. It was hateful to her to think of accompanying Darrow to places where the girl had been with him. She tried to reason away this scruple, she even reminded herself with a bitter irony that whenever she was in Darrow's arms she was where the girl had been before her – but she could not shake off her superstitious dread of being with him in any of the scenes of the Parisian episode.

She replied that she was too tired for the play, and they drove back to her apartment. At the foot of the stairs she half-turned to wish him good night, but he appeared not to notice her gesture and followed her up to her door.

'This is ever so much better than the theatre,' he said as they entered the drawing-room.

She had crossed the room and was bending over the hearth to light the fire. She knew he was approaching her, and that in a moment he would have drawn the cloak from her shoulders and laid his lips on her neck, just below the gathered-up hair. These privileges were his and, however deferently and tenderly he claimed them, the joyous ease of his manner marked a difference and proclaimed a right.

'After the theatre they came home like this,' she thought; and at the same instant she felt his hands on her shoulders and shrank back.

'Don't – oh, don't!' she cried, drawing her cloak about her. She saw from his astonished stare that her face must be quivering with pain.

'Anna! What on earth is the matter?'

'Owen knows!' she broke out, with a confused desire to justify herself.

Darrow's countenance changed. 'Did he tell you so? What did he say?'

'Nothing! I knew it from the things he didn't say.'

'You had a talk with him this afternoon?'

'Yes: for a few minutes. I could see he didn't want me to stay.'

She had dropped into a chair, and sat there huddled, still holding her cloak about her shoulders.

Darrow did not dispute her assumption, and she noticed that he expressed no surprise. He sat down at a little distance from her, turning about in his fingers the cigar-case he had drawn out as they came in. At length he said: 'Had he seen Miss Viner?'

She shrank from the sound of the name. 'No . . . I don't think so . . . I'm sure he hadn't . . .'

They remained silent, looking away from one another. Finally Darrow stood up and took a few steps across the room. He came back and paused before her, his eyes on her face.

'I think you ought to tell me what you mean to do.'

She raised her head and gave him back his look. 'Nothing I do can help Owen!'

'No; but things can't go on like this.' He paused, as if to measure his words. 'I fill you with aversion,' he exclaimed.

She started up, half-sobbing. 'No – oh, no!'

'Poor child – you can't see your face!'

She lifted her hands as if to hide it, and turning away from him bowed her head upon the mantel-shelf. She felt that he was standing a little way behind her, but he made no attempt to touch her or come nearer.

'I know you've felt as I've felt,' he said in a low voice – 'that we belong to each other and that nothing can alter that. But other thoughts come, and you can't banish them. Whenever you see me you remember . . . you associate me with things you abhor . . . You've been generous – immeasurably. You've given me all the chances a woman could; but if it's only made you suffer, what's the use?'

She turned to him with a tear-stained face. 'It hasn't only done that.'

'Oh, no! I know . . . There've been moments . . .' He took her hand and raised it to his lips. 'They'll be with me as long as I live. But I can't see you paying such a price for them. I'm not worth what I'm costing you.'

She continued to gaze at him through tear-dilated eyes; and suddenly she flung out the question: 'Wasn't it the Athéné you took her to that evening?'

'Anna – Anna!'

'Yes; I want to know now: to know everything. Perhaps that will make me forget. I ought to have made you tell me before. Wherever we go, I imagine you've been there with her . . . I see you together. I want to know how it began, where you went, why you left her . . . I can't go on in this darkness any longer!'

She did not know what had prompted her passionate outburst, but already she felt lighter, freer, as if at last the evil spell were broken. 'I want to know everything,' she repeated. 'It's the only way to make me forget.'

After she had ceased speaking Darrow remained where he was, his arms folded, his eyes lowered, immovable. She waited, her gaze on his face.

'Aren't you going to tell me?'

'No.'

The blood rushed to her temples. 'You won't? Why not?'

'If I did, do you suppose you'd forget that?'

'Oh –' she moaned, and turned away from him.

'You see it's impossible,' he went on. 'I've done a thing I loathe, and to atone for it you ask me to do another. What sort of satisfaction would that give you? It would put something irremediable between us.'

She leaned her elbow against the mantel-shelf and hid her face in her hands. She had the sense that she was vainly throwing away her last hope of happiness, yet she could do nothing, think of nothing, to save it. The conjecture flashed through her: 'Should I be at peace if I gave him up?' and she remembered the desolation of the days after she had sent him away, and understood that that hope was vain. The tears welled through her lids and ran slowly down between her fingers.

'Good-bye,' she heard him say, and his footsteps turned to the door.

She tried to raise her head, but the weight of her despair bowed it down. She said to herself: 'This is the end . . . he won't try to appeal to me again . . .' and she remained in a sort of tranced rigidity, perceiving without feeling the fateful lapse of the seconds. Then the cords that bound her seemed to snap, and she lifted her head and saw him going.

'Why, he's mine – he's mine! He's no one else's!' His face was turned to her and the look in his eyes swept away all her terrors. She no longer understood what had prompted her senseless outcry; and the mortal sweetness of loving him became again the one real fact in the world.

39

Anna, the next day, woke to a humiliated memory of the previous evening.

Darrow had been right in saying that their sacrifice would benefit no one; yet she seemed dimly to discern that there were obligations not to be tested by that standard. She owed it, at any rate, as much to his pride as to hers to abstain from the repetition of such scenes; and she had learned that it was beyond her power to do so while they were together. Yet when he had given her the chance to free herself, everything had vanished from her mind but the blind fear of losing him; and she saw that he and she were as profoundly and inextricably bound together as two trees with interwoven roots.

For a long time she brooded on her plight, vaguely conscious that the only escape from it must come from some external chance. And slowly the occasion shaped itself in her mind. It was Sophy Viner only who could save her – Sophy Viner only who could give her back her lost serenity. She would seek the girl out and tell her that she had given Darrow up; and that step once taken there would be no retracing it, and she would perforce have to go forward alone.

Any pretext for action was a kind of anodyne, and she despatched her maid to the Farlows' with a note asking if Miss Viner would receive her. There was a long delay before the maid returned, and when at last she appeared it was with a slip of paper on which an address was written, and a verbal message to the effect that Miss Viner had left some days previously, and was staying with her sister in a hotel near the Place de l'Etoile. The maid added that Mrs Farlow, on the plea that Miss Viner's plans were uncertain, had at first made some difficulty about giving this information; and Anna guessed that the girl had left her friends' roof, and instructed them to withhold her address, with the object of avoiding Owen. 'She's kept faith with herself and I haven't,' Anna mused; and the thought was a fresh incentive to action.

Darrow had announced his intention of coming soon after luncheon, and the morning was already so far advanced that Anna, still mistrustful of her strength, decided to drive immediately to the address Mrs Farlow had given. On the way there she tried to recall

what she had heard of Sophy Viner's sister, but beyond the girl's
enthusiastic report of the absent Laura's loveliness she could remember only certain vague allusions of Mrs Farlow's to her artistic endow-
ments and matrimonial vicissitudes. Darrow had mentioned her but
once, and in the briefest terms, as having apparently very little concern for Sophy's welfare, and being, at any rate, too geographically
remote to give her any practical support; and Anna wondered what
chance had brought her to her sister's side at this conjunction. Mrs
Farlow had spoken of her as a celebrity (in what line Anna failed to
recall); but Mrs Farlow's celebrities were legion, and the name on the
slip of paper – Mrs McTarvie-Birch – did not seem to have any
definite association with fame.

While Anna waited in the dingy vestibule of the Hôtel Chicago she
had so distinct a vision of what she meant to say to Sophy Viner that
the girl seemed already to be before her; and her heart dropped from
all the height of its courage when the porter, after a long delay,
returned with the announcement that Miss Viner was no longer in
the hotel. Anna, doubtful if she understood, asked if he merely
meant that the young lady was out at the moment; but he replied
that she had gone away the day before. Beyond this he had no
information to impart, and after a moment's hesitation Anna sent
him back to enquire if Mrs McTarvie-Birch would receive her. She
reflected that Sophy had probably pledged her sister to the same
secrecy as Mrs Farlow, and that a personal appeal to Mrs Birch
might lead to less negative results.

There was another long interval of suspense before the porter
reappeared with an affirmative answer; and a third while an exigu-
ous and hesitating lift bore her up past a succession of shabby
landings.

When the last was reached, and her guide had directed her down
a winding passage that smelt of sea-going luggage, she found herself
before a door through which a strong odour of tobacco reached her
simultaneously with the sounds of a suppressed altercation. Her
knock was followed by a silence, and after a minute or two the door
was opened by a handsome young man whose ruffled hair and general air of creased disorder led her to conclude that he had just risen
from a long-limbed sprawl on a sofa strewn with tumbled cushions.
This sofa, and a grand piano bearing a basket of faded roses, a

biscuit-tin and a devastated breakfast tray, almost filled the narrow sitting-room, in the remaining corner of which another man, short, swarthy and humble, sat examining the lining of his hat.

Anna paused in doubt; but on her naming Mrs Birch the young man politely invited her to enter, at the same time casting an impatient glance at the mute spectator in the background.

The latter, raising his eyes, which were round and bulging, fixed them, not on the young man but on Anna, whom, for a moment, he scrutinized as searchingly as the interior of his hat. Under his gaze she had the sense of being minutely catalogued and valued; and the impression, when he finally rose and moved toward the door, of having been accepted as a better guarantee than he had had any reason to hope for. On the threshold his glance crossed that of the young man in an exchange of intelligence as full as it was rapid; and this brief scene left Anna so oddly enlightened that she felt no surprise when her companion, pushing an armchair forward, sociably asked her if she wouldn't have a cigarette. Her polite refusal provoked the remark that he would, if she'd no objection; and while he groped for matches in his loose pockets, and behind the photographs and letters crowding the narrow mantel-shelf, she ventured another enquiry for Mrs Birch.

'Just a minute,' he smiled; 'I think the *masseur*'s with her.' He spoke in a smooth denationalized English, which, like the look in his long-lashed eyes and the promptness of his charming smile, suggested a long training in all the arts of expediency. Having finally discovered a match-box on the floor beside the sofa, he lit his cigarette and dropped back among the cushions; and on Anna's remarking that she was sorry to disturb Mrs Birch he replied that that was all right, and that she always kept everybody waiting.

After this, through the haze of his perpetually renewed cigarettes, they continued to chat for some time of indifferent topics; but when at last Anna again suggested the possibility of her seeing Mrs Birch he rose from his corner with a slight shrug, and murmuring: 'She's perfectly hopeless,' lounged off through an inner door.

Anna was still wondering when and in what conjunction of circumstances the much-married Laura had acquired a partner so conspicuous for his personal charms, when the young man returned to announce: 'She says it's all right, if you don't mind seeing her in bed.'

He drew aside to let Anna pass, and she found herself in a dim untidy scented room, with a pink curtain pinned across its single window, and a lady with a great deal of fair hair and uncovered neck smiling at her from a pink bed on which an immense powder-puff trailed.

'You don't mind, do you? He costs such a frightful lot that I can't afford to send him off,' Mrs Birch explained, extending a thickly-ringed hand to Anna, and leaving her in doubt as to whether the person alluded to were her *masseur* or her husband. Before a reply was possible there was a convulsive stir beneath the pink expanse, and something that resembled another powder-puff hurled itself at Anna with a volley of sounds like the popping of Lilliputian champagne corks. Mrs Birch, flinging herself forward, gasped out: 'If you'd just give him a caramel . . . there, in that box on the dressing-table . . . it's the only earthly thing to stop him . . .' and when Anna had proffered this sop to her assailant, and he had withdrawn with it beneath the bedspread, his mistress sank back with a laugh.

'Isn't he a beauty? The Prince gave him to me down at Nice the other day – but he's perfectly awful,' she confessed, beaming intimately on her visitor. In the roseate penumbra of the bed-curtains she presented to Anna's startled gaze an odd chromo-like resemblance to Sophy Viner, or a suggestion, rather, of what Sophy Viner might, with the years and in spite of the powder-puff, become. Larger, blonder, heavier-featured, she yet had glances and movements that disturbingly suggested what was freshest and most engaging in the girl; and as she stretched her bare plump arm across the bed she seemed to be pulling back the veil from dingy distances of family history.

'Do sit down, if there's a place to sit on,' she cordially advised; adding, as Anna took the edge of a chair hung with miscellaneous raiment: 'My singing takes so much time that I don't get a chance to walk the fat off – that's the worst of being an artist.'

Anna murmured an assent. 'I hope it hasn't inconvenienced you to see me; I told Mr Birch –'

'Mr *who*?' the recumbent beauty asked; and then: 'Oh, *Jimmy*!' She faintly laughed, as if more for her own enlightenment than Anna's.

The latter continued eagerly: 'I understand from Mrs Farlow that your sister was with you, and I ventured to come up because I wanted to ask you when I should have a chance of finding her.'

Mrs McTarvie-Birch threw back her head with a long stare. 'Do you mean to say the idiot at the door didn't tell you? Sophy went away last night.'

'Last night?' Anna echoed. A sudden terror had possessed her. Could it be that the girl had tricked them all and gone with Owen? The idea was incredible, yet it took such hold of her that she could hardly steady her lips to say: 'The porter did tell me, but I thought perhaps he was mistaken. Mrs Farlow seemed to think that I should find her here.'

'It was all so sudden that I don't suppose she had time to let the Farlows know. She didn't get Mrs Murrett's wire till yesterday, and she just pitched her things into a trunk and rushed –'

'Mrs Murrett?'

'Why, yes. Sophy's gone to India with Mrs Murrett; they're to meet at Brindisi,' Sophy's sister said with a calm smile.

Anna sat motionless, gazing at the disordered room, the pink bed, the trivial face among the pillows.

Mrs McTarvie-Birch pursued: 'They had a fearful kick-up last spring – I daresay you knew about it – but I told Sophy she'd better lump it, as long as the old woman was willing to . . . As an artist, of course, it's perfectly impossible for me to have her with me . . .'

'Of course,' Anna mechanically assented.

Through the confused pain of her thoughts she was hardly aware that Mrs Birch's explanations were still continuing. 'Naturally I didn't altogether approve of her going back to that beast of a woman. I said all I could . . . I told her she was a fool to chuck up such a place as yours. But Sophy's restless – always was – and she's taken it into her head she'd rather travel . . .'

Anna rose from her seat, groping for some formula of leave-taking. The pushing back of her chair roused the white dog's smouldering animosity, and he drowned his mistress's further confidences in another outburst of hysterics. Through the tumult Anna signed an inaudible farewell, and Mrs Birch, having momentarily succeeded in suppressing her pet under a pillow, called out: 'Do come again! I'd love to sing to you.'

Anna murmured a word of thanks and turned to the door. As she opened it she heard her hostess crying after her: 'Jimmy! Do you hear me? Jimmy *Brance*!' and then, there being no response from the person summoned: '*Do* tell him he must go and call the lift for you!'

THE END

THE BUCCANEERS

BOOK ONE

I

It was the height of the racing-season at Saratoga.

The thermometer stood over ninety, and a haze of sun-powdered dust hung in the elms along the street facing the Grand Union Hotel, and over the scant triangular lawns planted with young firs, and protected by a low white rail from the depredations of dogs and children.

Mrs St George, whose husband was one of the gentlemen most interested in the racing, sat on the wide hotel verandah, a jug of iced lemonade at her elbow and a palmetto fan in one small hand, and looked out between the immensely tall white columns of the portico, which so often reminded cultured travellers of the Parthenon at Athens (Greece). On Sunday afternoons this verandah was crowded with gentlemen in tall hats and frock-coats, enjoying cool drinks and Havana cigars, and surveying the long country street planted with spindling elms; but today the gentlemen were racing, and the rows of chairs were occupied by ladies and young girls listlessly awaiting their return, in a drowsy atmosphere of swayed fans and iced refreshments.

Mrs St George eyed most of these ladies with a melancholy dis-favour, and sighed to think how times had changed since she had first – some ten years earlier – trailed her crinolined skirts up and down that same verandah.

Mrs St George's vacant hours, which were many, were filled by such wistful reflexions. Life had never been easy, but it had certainly been easier when Colonel St George devoted less time to poker, and to Wall Street; when the children were little, crinolines were still worn, and Newport had not yet eclipsed all rival watering-places. What, for instance, could be prettier, or more suitable for a lady, than a black alpaca skirt looped up like a window-drapery above a scarlet serge underskirt, the whole surmounted by a wide-sleeved black poplin jacket with ruffled muslin undersleeves, and a flat 'pork-pie'

301

hat like the one the Empress Eugénie was represented as wearing on the beach at Biarritz? But now there seemed to be no definite fashions. Everybody wore what they pleased, and it was as difficult to look like a lady in those tight perpendicular polonaises bunched up at the back that the Paris dress-makers were sending over as in the outrageously low square-cut evening gowns which Mrs St George had viewed with disapproval at the Opera in New York. The fact was, you could hardly tell a lady now from an actress, or – er – the other kind of woman; and society at Saratoga, now that all the best people were going to Newport, had grown as mixed and confusing as the fashions.

Everything was changed since crinolines had gone out and bustles come in. Who, for instance, was that new woman, a Mrs Closson, or some such name, who had such a dusky skin for her auburn hair, such a fat body for her small uncertain feet, and who, when she wasn't strumming on the hotel piano, was credibly reported by the domestics to lie for hours on her bedroom sofa smoking – yes, *smoking* big Havana cigars? The gentlemen, Mrs St George believed, treated the story as a good joke; to a woman of refinement it could be only a subject for painful meditation.

Mrs St George had always been rather distant in her manner to the big and exuberant Mrs Elmsworth who was seated at this moment near by on the verandah. (Mrs Elmsworth was always 'edging up'.) Mrs St George was instinctively distrustful of the advances of ladies who had daughters of the age of her own, and Lizzy Elmsworth, the eldest of her neighbour's family, was just about the age of Virginia St George, and might by some (those who preferred the brunette to the very blond type) be thought as handsome. And besides, where did the Elmsworths come from, as Mrs St George had often asked her husband, an irreverent jovial man who invariably replied: 'If you were to begin by telling me where *we* do!' . . . so absurd on the part of a gentleman as well-known as Colonel St George in some unspecified district of what Mrs St George called the Sa-outh.

But at the thought of that new dusky Closson woman with the queer-looking girl who was so ugly now, but might suddenly turn into a beauty (Mrs St George had seen such cases), the instinct of organized defence awoke in her vague bosom, and she felt herself drawn to Mrs Elmsworth, and to the two Elmsworth girls, as to whom one already knew just how good-looking they were going to be.

A good many hours of Mrs St George's days were spent in mentally cataloguing and appraising the physical attributes of the young ladies in whose company her daughters trailed up and down the verandahs, and waltzed and polka-ed for hours every night in the long bare hotel parlours, so conveniently divided by sliding doors which slipped into the wall and made the two rooms into one. Mrs St George remembered the day when she had been agreeably awe-struck by this vista, with its expectant lines of bent-wood chairs against the walls, and its row of windows draped in crimson broca-telle heavily festooned from overhanging gilt cornices. In those days the hotel ball-room had been her idea of a throne-room in a palace; but since her husband had taken her to a ball at the Seventh Regiment Armoury in New York her standards had changed, and she regarded the splendours of the Grand Union almost as contemptu-ously as the arrogant Mrs Eglinton of New York, who had arrived there the previous summer on her way to Lake George, and after being shown into the yellow damask 'bridal suite' by the obsequious landlord, had said she supposed it would do well enough for one night.

Mrs St George, in those earlier years, had even been flattered by an introduction to Mrs Elmsworth, who was an older habituée of Saratoga than herself, and had a big showy affable husband with lustrous black whiskers, who was reported to have made a handsome fortune on the New York Stock Exchange. But that was in the days when Mrs Elmsworth drove daily to the races in a high barouche sent from New York, which attracted perhaps too much attention. Since then Mr Elmsworth's losses in Wall Street had obliged his wife to put down her barouche, and stay at home on the hotel verandah with the other ladies, and she now no longer inspired Mrs St George with awe or envy. Indeed, had it not been for this new Closson danger Mrs Elmsworth in her present situation would have been negligible; but now that Virginia St George and Lizzy Elmsworth were 'out' (as Mrs St George persisted in calling it, though the girls could not see much difference in their lives) – now that Lizzy Elmsworth's looks seemed to Mrs St George at once more to be admired and less to be feared, and Mabel, the second Elmsworth girl, who was a year older than her own youngest, to be too bony and lantern-jawed for future danger, Mrs St George began to wonder whether she and her neighbour might not organize some sort of joint defence against new women with daughters. Later it would not so much matter, for Mrs St George's youngest, Nan, though certainly not a beauty like Virginia, was going to be what was called fascinating, and by the time her hair was put up the St George girls need fear no rivalry.

Week after week, day after day, the anxious mother had gone over Miss Elmsworth's points, comparing them one by one with Virginia's. As regards hair and complexion, there could be no doubt; Virginia, all rose and pearl, with sheaves of full fair hair heaped above her low forehead, was as pure and luminous as an apple-blossom. But Lizzy's waist was certainly at least an inch smaller (some said two), Lizzy's dark eyebrows had a bolder curve, and Lizzy's foot – ah, where in the world did an upstart Elmsworth get that arrogant instep? Yes, but it was some comfort to note that Lizzy's complexion was opaque and lifeless compared to Virginia's, and that her fine eyes showed temper, and would be likely to frighten the young men away. Still, she had to an alarming degree what was called 'style', and Mrs St George suspected that in the circles to which she longed to introduce her daughters style was valued even more highly than beauty.

These were the problems among which her thoughts moved during the endless sweltering afternoon hours, like torpid fish turning about between the weary walls of a too-small aquarium. But now a new presence had invaded that sluggish element. Mrs St George no longer compared her eldest daughter and Lizzy Elmsworth with each other; she began to compare them both with the newcomer, the daughter of the unknown Mrs Closson. It was small comfort to Mrs St George (though she repeated it to herself so often) that the Clossons were utterly unknown, that though Colonel St George played poker with Mr Closson, and had what the family called 'business connections' with him, they were nowhere near the stage when it becomes a pleasing duty for a man to introduce a colleague to his family. Neither did it matter that Mrs Closson's own past was if anything obscurer than her husband's, and that those who said she was a poor Brazilian widow when Closson had picked her up on a business trip to Rio were smiled at and corrected by others, presumably better informed, who suggested that *divorcée* was the word, and not widow. Even the fact that the Closson girl (so called) was known not to be Closson's daughter, but to bear some queer exotic name like Santos-Dios ('the Colonel says that's not swearing, it's the language,' Mrs St George explained to Mrs Elmsworth when they talked the newcomers over) – even this was not enough to calm Mrs St George. The girl, whatever her real name, was known as Conchita Closson; she addressed as 'Father' the non-committal pepper-and-salt-looking man who joined his family over Sundays at the Grand Union; and it was of no use for Mrs St George to say to herself that Conchita was plain and therefore negligible, for she had the precise kind of plainness which, as mothers of rival daughters know, may suddenly blaze into irresistible beauty. At present Miss Closson's head was too small, her neck was too long, she was too tall and thin, and her hair – well, her hair (oh, horror!) was nearly red. And her skin was dark, under the powder which (yes, my dear – at eighteen!) Mrs St George was sure she applied to it; and the combination of red hair and sallow complexion would have put off anybody who had heard a description of them, instead of seeing them triumphantly embodied in Conchita Closson. Mrs St George shivered under her dotted muslin ruffled with Valenciennes, and drew a tippet edged with swansdown over her shoulders. At that moment her own daughters, Virginia and Nan, wandered by, one after the other; and the sight somehow increased Mrs St George's irritation.

'Virginia!' she called. Virginia halted, seemed to hesitate as to whether the summons were worth heeding, and then sauntered across the verandah toward her mother.

'Virginia, I don't want you should go round any more with that strange girl,' Mrs St George began.

Virginia's sapphire eyes rested with a remote indifferent gaze on the speaker's tightly buttoned bronze kid boots; and Mrs St George suddenly wondered if she had burst a buttonhole.

'What girl?' Virginia drawled.

'How do I know? Goodness knows who they are. Your pa says she was a widow from one of those South American countries when she married Mr Closson – the mother was, I mean.'

'Well, if he says so, I suppose she was.'

'But some people say she was just divorced. And I don't want my daughters associating with that kind of people.'

Virginia removed her blue gaze from her mother's boots to the little mantle trimmed with swansdown. 'I should think you'd roast with that thing on,' she remarked.

'Jinny! Now you listen to what I say,' her mother ineffectually called after her.

Nan St George had taken no part in the conversation; at first she had hardly heeded what was said. Such wrangles between mother and daughter were of daily, almost hourly, occurrence; Mrs St George's only way of guiding her children was to be always crying out to them not to do this or that. Nan St George, at sixteen, was at the culminating phase of a passionate admiration for her elder sister. Virginia was all that her junior longed to be: perfectly beautiful, completely self-possessed, calm and sure of herself. Nan, whose whole life was a series of waves of the blood, hot rushes of enthusiasm, icy chills of embarrassment and self-depreciation, looked with envy and admiration at her goddess-like elder. The only thing she did not quite like about Virginia was the latter's tone of superiority with her mother; to get the better of Mrs St George was too easy, too much like what Colonel St George called 'shooting a bird sitting'. Yet so strong was Virginia's influence that in her presence Nan always took the same tone with their mother, in the secret hope of attracting her sister's favourable notice. She had even gone so far as to mime for Virginia (who was no mimic) Mrs St George looking shocked at an untidy stocking ('mother wondering where we were brought up'), Mrs St George smiling in her sleep in church ('mother listening to the angels'), or Mrs St George doubtfully mustering new arrivals ('mother smelling a drain'). But Virginia took such demonstrations for granted, and when poor Nan afterward, in an agony of remorse, stole back alone to her mother, and whispered through penitent kisses: 'I didn't mean to be naughty to you, Mamma,' Mrs St George, raising a nervous hand to her crimped *bandeaux*, would usually reply apprehensively: 'I'm sure you didn't, darling; only don't get my hair all in a muss again.'

Expiation unresponded to embitters the blood, and something within Nan shrank and hardened with each of these rebuffs. But she now seldom exposed herself to them, finding it easier to follow Virginia's lead and ignore their parent's admonitions. At the moment, however, she was actually wavering in her allegiance to Virginia. Since she had seen Conchita Closson she was no longer sure that features and complexion were woman's crowning glory. Long before Mrs St George and Mrs Elmsworth had agreed on a valuation of the newcomer Nan had fallen under her spell. From the day when she had first seen her come whistling around the corner of the verandah, her restless little head crowned by a flapping Leghorn hat with a rose under the brim, and dragging after her a reluctant poodle with a large red bow, Nan had felt the girl's careless power. What would Mrs St George have said if one of her daughters had strolled along the verandah whistling, and dragging a grotesque-looking toy-shop animal at her heels? Miss Closson seemed troubled by no such considerations. She sat down on the upper step of the verandah, pulled a lump of molasses candy from her pocket, and invited the poodle to 'get up and waltz for it'; which the uncanny animal did by rising on his hind legs and performing a series of unsteady circles before his mistress while she licked the molasses from her fingers. Every rocking-chair on the verandah stopped creaking as its occupant sat upright to view the show. 'Circus performance!' Mrs St George commented to Mrs Elmsworth; and the latter retorted with her vulgar laugh: 'Looks as if the two of 'em were used to showing off, don't it?'

Nan overheard the comments, and felt sure the two mothers were mistaken. The Closson girl was obviously unaware that any one was looking at her and her absurd dog; it was that absence of self-consciousness which fascinated Nan. Virginia was intensely self-conscious; she really thought just as much as her mother of 'what people would say'; and even Lizzy Elmsworth, though she was so much cleverer at concealing her thoughts, was not really simple and natural; she merely affected unaffectedness. It frightened Nan a little to find herself thinking these things; but they forced themselves upon her, and when Mrs St George issued the order that her daughters were not to associate with 'the strange girl' (as if they didn't all know her name!) Nan felt a rush of anger. Virginia sauntered on, probably content to have shaken her mother's confidence in the details of her dress (a matter of much anxious thought to Mrs St George); but Nan stopped short.

'Why can't I go with Conchita if she wants me to?'

Mrs St George's faintly withered pink turned pale. 'If she *wants you to*? Annabel St George, what do you mean by talking to me that way? What on earth do you care for what a girl like that *wants*?'

Nan ground her heels into the crack between the verandah boards. 'I think she's lovely.'

Mrs St George's small nose was wrinkled with disdain. The small mouth under it drooped disgustedly. She was 'mother smelling a drain'.

'Well, when that new governess comes next week I guess you'll find she feels just the way I do about those people. And you'll have to do what *she* tells you, anyhow,' Mrs St George helplessly concluded.

A chill of dismay rushed over Nan. The new governess! She had never really believed in that remote bogey. She had an idea that Mrs St George and Virginia had cooked up the legend between them, in order to be able to say 'Annabel's governess', as they had once heard that tall proud Mrs Eglinton from New York, who had stayed only one night at the hotel, say to the landlord: 'You must be sure to put my daughter's governess in the room next to her.' Nan had never believed that the affair of the governess would go beyond talking; but now she seemed to hear the snap of the hand-cuffs on her wrists.

'A governess – me?'

Mrs St George moistened her lips nervously. 'All stylish girls have governesses the year before they come out.'

'I'm not coming out next year – I'm only sixteen,' Nan protested.

'Well, they have them for two years before. That Eglinton girl had.'

'Oh, that Eglinton girl! She looked at us all as if we weren't there.'

'Well, that's the way for a lady to look at strangers,' said Mrs St George heroically.

Nan's heart grew black within her. 'I'll kill her if she tries to interfere with me.'

'You'll drive down to the station on Monday to meet her,' Mrs St George shrilled back, defiant. Nan turned on her heel and walked away.

2

The Closson girl had already disappeared with her dog, and Nan suspected that she had taken him for a game of ball in the rough field adjoining the meagre grounds of the hotel. Nan went down the steps of the porch, and crossing the drive espied the slim Conchita whirling a ball high overhead while the dog spun about frantically at her feet. Nan had so far exchanged only a few shy words with her, and in ordinary circumstances would hardly have dared to join her now. But she had reached an acute crisis in her life, and her need for sympathy and help overcame her shyness. She vaulted over the fence into the field and went up to Miss Closson.

'That's a lovely dog,' she said.

Miss Closson flung the ball for her poodle, and turned with a smile to Nan. 'Isn't he a real darling?'

Nan stood twisting one foot about the other. 'Have you ever had a governess?' she asked abruptly.

Miss Closson opened with a stare of wonder the darkly fringed eyes which shone like pale aquamarines on her small dusky face. 'Me? A governess? Mercy, no – what for?'

'That's what I say! My mother and Virginia have cooked it up between them. I'm going to have one next week.'

'Land's sake! You're not? She's coming here?' Nan nodded sulkily.

'*Well* –' Conchita murmured.

'What'll I do about it – what would you?' Nan burst out, on the brink of tears.

Miss Closson drew her lids together meditatively; then she stooped with deliberation to the poodle, and threw the ball for him again.

'I said I'd kill her,' broke from Nan in a hoarse whisper.

The other laughed. 'I wouldn't do that; not right off, anyhow. I'd get round her first.'

'Get round her? How can I? I've got to do whatever she wants.'

'No, you haven't. Make her want whatever *you* want.'

'How can I? Oh, can I call you Conchita? It's such a lovely name. Mine's Annabel, really, but everybody calls me Nan . . . Well, but how can I get round that governess? She'll try to make me learn lists of dates . . . that's what she's paid for.'

Conchita's expressive face became one grimace of disapproval. 'Well, I should hate that like castor-oil. But perhaps she won't. I knew a girl at Rio who had a governess, and she was hardly any older than the girl, and she used to . . . well, carry messages and letters for her, the governess did . . . and in the evening she used to slip out to . . . to see a friend . . . and she and the girl knew all each other's secrets; so you see they couldn't tell on each other, neither one of them couldn't . . .'

'Oh, I see,' said Nan, with a feigned air of knowingness. But she was suddenly conscious of a queer sensation in her throat, almost of physical sickness. Conchita's laughing eyes seemed whispering to her through half-drawn lids. She admired Conchita as much as ever – but she was not sure she liked her at that moment.

Conchita was obviously not aware of having produced an unfavour-able impression. 'Out in Rio I knew a girl who got married that way. The governess carried her notes for her . . . Do you want to get married?' she asked abruptly.

Nan flushed and stared. Getting married was an inexhaustible theme of confidential talk between her sister and the Elmsworth girls; but she felt herself too young and inexperienced to take part in their discussions. Once, at one of the hotel dances, a young fellow called Roy Gilling had picked up her handkerchief, and refused to give it back. She had seen him raise it meaningly to his young mous-tache before he slipped it into his pocket; but the incident had left her annoyed and bewildered rather than excited, and she had not been sorry when soon afterward he rather pointedly transferred his attentions to Mabel Elmsworth. She knew Mabel Elmsworth had already been kissed behind a door; and Nan's own sister Virginia had too, Nan suspected. She herself had no definite prejudices in the matter; she simply felt unprepared as yet to consider matrimonial plans. She stooped to stroke the poodle, and answered, without look-ing up: 'Not to anybody I've seen yet.'

The other considered her curiously. 'I suppose you like love-making better, eh?' She spoke in a soft drawl, with a languid rippling of the Rs.

Nan felt her blood mounting again; one of her quick blushes steeped her in distress. Did she – didn't she – like 'love-making', as this girl crudely called it (the others always spoke of it as flirting)? Nan had not been subjected to any warmer advances than Mr Gilling's, and the obvious answer was that she didn't know, having had no experience of such matters; but she had the reluctance of youth to confess to its youthfulness, and she also felt that her likes and dislikes were no business of this strange girl's. She gave a vague laugh and said loftily: 'I think it's silly.'

Conchita laughed too; a low deliberate laugh, full of repressed and tantalizing mystery. Once more she flung the ball for her intently watching poodle; then she thrust a hand into a fold of her dress, and pulled out a crumpled packet of cigarettes. 'Here – have one! Nobody'll see us out here,' she suggested amicably.

Nan's heart gave an excited leap. Her own sister and the Elmsworth girl already smoked in secret, removing the traces of their indiscretion by consuming little highly perfumed pink lozenges furtively acquired from the hotel barber; but they had never offered to induct Nan into these forbidden rites, which, by awful oaths, they bound her not to reveal to their parents. It was Nan's first cigarette, and while her fingers twitched for it she asked herself in terror: 'Suppose it should make me sick right before her?'

But Nan, in spite of her tremors, was not the girl to refuse what looked like a dare, nor even to ask if in this open field they were really safe from unwanted eyes. There was a clump of low shrubby trees at the farther end, and Conchita strolled there and mounted the fence-rail, from which her slender uncovered ankles dangled gracefully. Nan swung up beside her, took a cigarette, and bent toward the match which her companion proffered. There was an awful silence while she put the forbidden object to her lips and drew a frightened breath: the acrid taste of the tobacco struck her palate sharply, but in another moment a pleasant fragrance filled her nose and throat. She puffed again, and knew she was going to like it. Instantly her mood passed from timidity to triumph, and she wrinkled her nose critically and threw back her head, as her father did when he was tasting a new brand of cigar. 'These are all right – where do you get them?' she enquired with a careless air; and then, suddenly forgetful of the experience her tone implied, she rushed on in a breathless little-girl voice: 'Oh, Conchita, won't you show me how you make those lovely rings? Jinny doesn't really do them right, nor the Elmsworth girls either.'

Miss Closson in turn threw back her head with a smile. She drew a deep breath, and removing the cigarette from her lips, curved them to a rosy circle through which she sent a wreath of misty smoke-rings. 'That's how,' she laughed, and pushed the packet into Nan's hands. 'You can practise at night,' she said good-humouredly, as she jumped from the rail.

Nan wandered back to the hotel, so much elated by her success as a smoker that her dread of the governess grew fainter. On the hotel steps she was further reassured by the glimpse, through the lobby doors, of a tall broad-shouldered man in a Panama hat and light grey suit who, his linen duster over his arm, his portmanteaux at his feet, had paused to light a big cigar and shake hands with the clerk. Nan gave a start of joy. She had not known that her father was arriving that afternoon, and the mere sight of him banished all her cares. Nan had a blind faith in her father's faculty for helping people out of difficulties – a faith based not on actual experience (for Colonel St George usually dealt with difficulties by a wave of dismissal which swept them into somebody else's lap), but on his easy contempt for feminine fusses, and his way of saying to his youngest daughter: 'You just call on me, child, when things want straightening out.' Perhaps he would straighten out even this nonsense about the governess; and meanwhile the mere thought of his large powerful presence, his big cologne-scented hands, his splendid yellow moustache and easy rolling gait, cleared the air of the cobwebs in which Mrs St George was always enveloped.

'Hullo, daughter! What's the news?' The Colonel greeted Nan with a resounding kiss, and stood with one arm about her, scrutiniz-ing her lifted face.

'I'm glad you've come, father,' she said, and then shrank back a little, fearful lest a whiff of cigarette smoke should betray her.

'Your mother taking her afternoon nap, I suppose?' the Colonel continued jovially. 'Well, come along with me. See here, Charlie' (to the clerk), 'send those things right along to my room, will you? There's something in them of interest to this young lady.'

The clerk signalled to a black porter, and preceded by his bags the Colonel mounted the stairs with Nan.

'Oh, father! It's lovely to have you! What I want to ask you is –'

But the Colonel was digging into the depths of one of the port-manteaux and scattering over the bed various parts of a showy but somewhat crumpled wardrobe. 'Here now; you wait,' he puffed, pausing to mop his broad white forehead with a fine cambric handkerchief. He pulled out two parcels, and beckoned to Nan. 'Here's some fancy notions for you and Jinny; the girl in the store said it was what the Newport belles are wearing this summer. And this is for your mother, when she wakes up.' He took the tissue-paper wrappings from a small red-morocco case and pressed the spring of the lid. Before Nan's dazzled eyes lay a diamond brooch formed of a spray of briar-roses. She gave an admiring gasp. 'Well, how's that for style?' laughed her father.

'Oh, father –' She paused, and looked at him with a faint touch of apprehension.

'Well?' the Colonel repeated. His laugh had an emptiness under it, like the hollow under a loud wave; Nan knew the sound. 'Is it a present for mother?' she asked doubtfully.

'Why, who'd you think it was for – not you?' he joked, his voice slightly less assured.

Nan twisted one foot about the other. 'It's terribly expensive, isn't it?'

'Why, you critical imp, you – what's the matter if it is?'

'Well, the last time you brought mother a piece of jewellery there was an all-night row after it, about cards or something,' said Nan judicially.

The Colonel burst out laughing, and pinched her chin. 'Well, well! You fear the Greeks, eh, do you? How does it go? *Timeo Danaos* . . .'

'What Greeks?'

Her father raised his handsome ironic eyebrows. Nan knew he was proud of his far-off smattering of college culture, and wished she could have understood the allusion. 'Haven't they even taught you that much Latin at your school? Well, I guess your mother's right; you *do* need a governess.'

Nan paled, and forgot the Greeks. 'Oh, father; that's what I wanted to speak to you about –'

'What about?'

'That governess. I'm going to hate her, you know. She's going to make me learn lists of dates, the way the Eglinton girl had to. And mother'll fill her up with silly stories about us, and tell her we mustn't do this, and we mustn't say that. I don't believe she'll even let me go with Conchita Closson, because mother says Mrs Closson's divorced.'

The Colonel looked up sharply. 'Oh, your mother says that, does she? She's down on the Clossons? I supposed she would be.' He picked up the morocco case and examined the brooch critically. 'Yes; that's a good piece; Black, Starr and Frost. And I don't mind telling you that you're right; it cost me a pretty penny. But I've got to persuade your mother to be polite to Mrs Closson – see?' He wrinkled up his face in the funny way he had, and took his daughter by the shoulders. 'Business matter, you understand – strictly between ourselves. I need Closson; got to have him. And he's fretted to death about the way all the women cold-shoulder his wife . . . I'll tell you what, Nan; suppose you and I form a league, defensive and offensive? You help me to talk round your mother, and get her to be decent to Mrs Closson, and persuade the others to be, and to let the girl go round with all of you; and I'll fix it up with the governess so you don't have to learn too many dates.'

Nan uttered a cry of joy. Already the clouds were lifting. 'Oh, father, you're perfectly grand! I knew everything would be all right as soon as you got here! I'll do all I can about mother – and you'll tell the governess I'm to go round all I like with Conchita?' She flung herself into the Colonel's comforting embrace.

3

Mrs St George, had she looked back far enough, could have recalled a time when she had all of Nan's faith in the Colonel's restorative powers; when to carry her difficulties to him seemed the natural thing, and his way of laughing at them gave her the illusion that they were solved. Those days were past; she had long been aware that most of her difficulties came from the Colonel instead of being solved by him. But she admired him as much as ever – thought him in fact even handsomer than when, before the Civil War, he had dawned on her dazzled sight at a White Sulphur Springs ball, in the uniform of a captain of militia; and now that he had become prominent in Wall Street, where life seemed to grow more feverish every day, it was only natural that he should require a little relaxation, though she deplored its always meaning poker and whisky, and sometimes, she feared, the third element celebrated in the song. Though Mrs St George was now a worried middle-aged woman with grown-up daughters, it cost her as much to resign herself to this as when she had first found in her husband's pocket a letter she was not meant to read. But there was nothing to be done about it, or about the whisky and poker, and the visits to establishments where game and champagne were served at all hours, and gentlemen who had won at roulette or the races supped in meretricious company. All this had long since been part of Mrs St George's consciousness, yet she was half consoled, when the Colonel joined his family at Long Branch or Saratoga, by the knowledge that all the other worried and middle-aged wives in the long hotel dining-room envied her her splendid husband.

And small wonder, thought Mrs St George, contemptuously picturing the gentlemen those ladies had to put up with: that loud red-faced Elmsworth, who hadn't yet found out that big lumps of black whisker were no longer worn except by undertakers, or the poor dyspeptic Closson, who spent such resigned and yawning hours beside the South American woman to whom he was perhaps not married at all. Closson was particularly obnoxious to Mrs St George; much as she despised Mrs Closson, she could almost have pitied her for having nothing better to show as a husband – even if he was that, as Mrs St George would add in her confidential exchanges with Mrs Elmsworth.

Even now, though of late the Colonel had been so evasive and unsatisfactory, and though she wasn't yet sure if he would turn up for the morrow's races, Mrs St George reflected thankfully that if he *did* she wouldn't have to appear in the hotel dining-room with a man about whom a lady need feel apologetic. But when, after her siesta, as she was re-arranging her hair before going back to the verandah, she heard his laugh outside of her door, her slumbering apprehensions started up. 'He's too cheerful,' she thought, nervously folding away her dressing-gown and slippers; for when the Colonel was worried he was always in the highest spirits.

'Well, my dear! Thought I'd surprise the family, and see what you were all up to. Nan's given me a fairly good report, but I haven't run down Jinny yet.' He laid a hand on his wife's greying blond hair, and brushed her care-worn forehead with the tip of his moustache; a ritual gesture which convinced him that he had kissed her, and Mrs St George that she had been kissed. She looked up at him with admiring eyes.

'That governess is coming on Monday,' she began. At the moment of his last successful 'turn-over', a few months earlier, his wife had wrung from him the permission to engage a governess; but now she feared a renewal of the discussion about the governess's salary, and yet she knew the girls, and Nan especially, must have some kind of social discipline. 'We've got to have her,' Mrs St George added.

The Colonel was obviously not listening. 'Of course, of course,' he agreed, measuring the room with his large strides (his inability to remain seated was another trial to his sedentary wife). Suddenly he paused before her and fumbled in his pocket, but produced nothing from it. Mrs St George noted the gesture, and thought: 'It's the coal bill! But he *knew* I couldn't get it down any lower . . .'

'Well, well, my dear,' the Colonel continued, 'I don't know what you've all been up to, but I've had a big stroke of luck, and it's only fair you three girls should share in it.' He jerked the morocco case out of another pocket. 'Oh, Colonel,' his wife gasped as he pressed the spring. 'Well, take it – it's for you!' he joked.

Mrs St George gazed blankly at the glittering spray; then her eyes filled, and her lip began to tremble. 'Tracy . . .' she stammered. It was years since she had called him by his name. 'But you oughtn't to,' she protested, 'with all our expenses . . . It's too grand – it's like a wedding present . . .'

'Well, we're married, ain't we?' The Colonel laughed resonantly. 'There's the first result of my turn-over, madam. And I brought the girls some gimcracks too. I gave Nan the parcel; but I haven't seen Jinny. I suppose she's off with some of the other girls.'

Mrs St George detached herself from ecstatic contemplation of the jewel. 'You mustn't spoil the girls, Colonel. I've got my hands full with them. I want you to talk to them seriously about not going with that Closson girl . . .'

Colonel St George blew a faint whistle through his moustache, and threw himself into the rocking-chair facing his wife's. 'Going with the Closson girl? Why, what's the matter with the Closson girl? She's as pretty as a peach, anyhow.'

'I guess your own daughters are pretty enough without having to demean themselves running after that girl. I can't keep Nan away from her.' Mrs St George knew that Nan was the Colonel's favourite, and she spoke with an inward tremor. But it would never do to have this fashionable new governess (who had been with the Russell Parmores of Tarrytown, and with the Duchess of Tintagel in England) imagine that her new charges were hand in glove with the Clossons.

Colonel St George tilted himself back in his chair, felt for a cigar and lit it thoughtfully. (He had long since taught Mrs St George that smoking in her bedroom was included among his marital rights.) 'Well,' he said, 'what's wrong with the Clossons, my dear?'

Mrs St George felt weak and empty inside. When he looked at her in that way, half laughing, half condescending, all her reasons turned to a puff of mist. And there lay the jewel on the dressing-table – and timorously she began to understand. But the girls must be rescued, and a flicker of maternal ardour stirred in her. Perhaps in his large careless way her husband had simply brushed by the Clossons without heeding them.

'I don't know any of the particulars, naturally. People *do* say . . . but Mrs Closson (if that's her name) is not a woman I could ever associate with, so I haven't any means of knowing . . .'

The Colonel gave his all-effacing laugh. 'Oh, well – if you haven't any means of knowing, we'll fix that up all right. But I've got business reasons for wanting you to make friends with Mrs Closson first; we'll investigate her history afterward.'

Make friends with Mrs Closson! Mrs St George looked at her husband with dismay. He wanted her to do the thing that would most humiliate her; and it was so important to him that he had probably spent his last dollar on this diamond bribe. Mrs St George was not unused to such situations; she knew that a gentleman's financial situation might at any moment necessitate compromises and concessions. All the ladies of her acquaintance were inured to them; up one day, down the next, as the secret gods of Wall Street decreed. She measured her husband's present need by the cost of the probably unpaid-for jewel, and her heart grew like water.

'But, Colonel –'

'Well, what's wrong with the Clossons, anyhow? I've done business with Closson off and on for some years now, and I don't know a squarer fellow. He's just put me on to a big thing, and if you're going to wreck the whole business by turning up your nose at his wife . . .'

Mrs St George gathered strength to reply: 'But, Colonel, the talk is that they're not even married . . .'

Her husband jumped up and stood before her with flushed face and irritated eyes. 'If you think I'm going to let my making a big rake-off depend on whether the Clossons had a parson to tie the knot, or only the town-clerk . . .'

'I've got the girls to think of,' his wife faltered.

'It's the girls I'm thinking of, too. D'you suppose I'd sweat and slave down town the way I do if it wasn't for the girls?'

'But I've got to think of the girls they go with, if they're to marry nice young men.'

'The nice young men'll show up in larger numbers if I can put this deal through. And what's the matter with the Closson girl? She's as pretty as a picture.'

Mrs St George marvelled once more at the obtuseness of the most brilliant men. Wasn't that one of the very reasons for not encouraging the Closson girl?

'She powders her face, and smokes cigarettes . . .'

'Well, don't our girls and the two Elmsworths do as much? I'll swear I caught a whiff of smoke when Nan kissed me just now.'

Mrs St George grew pale with horror. 'If you'll say that of your daughters you'll say anything!' she protested.

There was a knock at the door, and without waiting for it to be answered Virginia flew into her father's arms. 'Oh, father, how sweet of you! Nan gave me the locket. It's too lovely; with my monogram on it – and in diamonds!'

She lifted her radiant lips, and he bent to them with a smile. 'What's that new scent you're using, Miss St George? Or have you been stealing one of your papa's lozenges?' He sniffed and then held her at arm's-length, watching her quick flush of alarm, and the way in which her deeply fringed eyes pleaded with his.

'See here, Jinny. Your mother says she don't want you to go with the Closson girl because she smokes. But I tell her I'll answer for it that you and Nan would never follow such a bad example – eh?'

Their eyes and their laugh met. Mrs St George turned from the sight with a sense of helplessness. 'If he's going to let them smoke now . . .'

'I don't think your mother's fair to the Closson girl, and I've told her so. I want she should be friends with Mrs Closson. I want her to begin right off. Oh, here's Nan,' he added, as the door opened again. 'Come along, Nan; I want you to stick up for your friend Conchita. You like her, don't you?'

But Mrs St George's resentment was stiffening. She could fight for her daughters, helpless as she was for herself. 'If you're going to rely on the girls to choose who they associate with! They say the girl's name isn't Closson at all. Nobody knows what it is, or who any of them are. And the brother travels round with a guitar tied with ribbons. No nice girls will go with your daughters if you want them seen everywhere with those people.'

The Colonel stood frowning before his wife. When he frowned she suddenly forgot all her reasons for opposing him, but the blind instinct of opposition remained. 'You wouldn't invite the Clossons to join us at supper tonight?' he suggested.

Mrs St George moistened her dry lips with her tongue. 'Colonel –'

'You won't?'

'Girls, your father's joking,' she stammered, turning with a tremulous gesture to her daughters. She saw Nan's eyes darken, but Virginia laughed – a laugh of complicity with her father. He joined in it.

'Girls, I see your mother's not satisfied with the present I've brought her. She's not as easily pleased as you young simpletons.' He waved his hand to the dressing-table, and Virginia caught up the morocco box. 'Oh, mother – is this for *you*? Oh, I never saw anything so beautiful! You must invite Mrs Closson, just to see how envious it makes her. I guess that's what father wants you to do – isn't it?'

The Colonel looked at her sympathetically. 'I've told your mother the plain truth. Closson's put me on to a good thing, and the only return he wants is for you ladies to be a little humane to his womenfolk. Is that too unreasonable? He's coming today, by the afternoon train, bringing two young fellows with him, by the way – his step-son and a young Englishman who's been working out in Brazil on Mrs Closson's estancia. The son of an Earl, or something. How about that, girls? Two new dancing-partners! And you ain't any too well off in that line, are you?' This was a burning question, for it was common knowledge that, if their dancing-partners were obscure and few, it was because all the smart and eligible young men of whom Virginia and the Elmsworths read in the 'society columns' of the newspapers had deserted Saratoga for Newport.

'Mother knows we generally have to dance with each other,' Virginia murmured sulkily.

'Yes – or with the beaux from Buffalo!' Nan laughed.

· 'Well, I call that mortifying; but of course, if your mother disapproves of Mrs Closson, I guess the young fellows that Closson's bringing'll have to dance with the Elmsworth girls instead of you.'

Mrs St George stood trembling beside the dressing-table. Virginia had put down the box, and the diamonds sparkled in a sunset ray that came through the slats of the shutters.

Mrs St George did not own many jewels, but it suddenly occurred to her that each one marked the date of a similar episode. Either a woman, or a business deal – something she had to be indulgent about. She liked trinkets as well as any woman, but at that moment she wished that all of hers were at the bottom of the sea. For each time she had yielded – as she knew she was going to yield now. And her husband would always think that it was because he had bribed her . . .

The readjustment of seats necessary to bring together the St George and Closson parties at the long hotel supper-table caused a flutter in the room. Mrs St George was too conscious of it not to avoid Mrs Elmsworth's glance of surprise; but she could not deafen herself to Mrs Elmsworth's laugh. She had always thought the woman had an underbred laugh. And to think that, so few seasons ago, she had held her chin high in passing Mrs Elmsworth on the verandah, just as she had done till this very afternoon – and how much higher! – in passing Mrs Closson. Now Mrs Elmsworth, who did not possess the art of the lifted chin, but whispered and nudged and giggled where a 'lady' would have sailed by – now it would be in her power to practise on Mrs St George these vulgar means of reprisal. The diamond spray burned like hot lead on Mrs St George's breast; yet through all her misery there pierced the old thrill of pride as the Colonel entered the dining-room in her wake, and she saw him reflected in the other women's eyes. Ah, poor Mrs

Elmsworth, with her black-whiskered undertaker, and Mrs Closson with her cipher of a husband – and all the other ladies, young or elderly, of whom not one could boast a man of Colonel St George's quality! Evidently, like Mrs St George's diamonds, he was a costly possession, but (unlike the diamonds, she suspected) he had been paid for – oh, how dearly! – and she had a right to wear him with her head high.

But in the eyes of the other guests it was not only the Colonel's entrance that was reflected. Mrs St George saw there also the excitement and curiosity occasioned by the re-grouping of seats, and the appearance, behind Mrs Closson – who came in with her usual somnambulist's walk, and thick-lashed stare – of two young men, two authentic new dancers for the hotel beauties. Mrs St George knew all about them. The little olive-faced velvet-eyed fellow, with the impudently curly black hair, was Teddy de Santos-Dios, Mr Closson's Brazilian step-son, over on his annual visit to the States; the other, the short heavy-looking young man with a low forehead pressed down by a shock of drab hair, an uncertain mouth under a thick drab moustache, and small eyes, slow, puzzled, not unkindly yet not reliable, was Lord Richard Marable, the impecunious younger son of an English Marquess, who had picked up a job on the Closson estancia, and had come over for his holiday with Santos-Dios. Two 'foreigners', and certainly ineligible ones, especially the little black popinjay who travelled with his guitar – but, after all, dancers for the girls, and therefore not wholly unwelcome even to Mrs St George, whose heart often ached at the thought of the Newport ball-rooms, where black coat-tails were said to jam every doorway; while at Saratoga the poor girls—

Ah, but there they were, the girls! – the privileged few whom she grouped under that designation. The fancy had taken them to come in late, and to arrive all together; and now, arm-in-arm, a blushing bevy, they swayed across the threshold of the dining-room like a branch hung with blossoms, drawing the dull middle-aged eyes of the other guests from lobster salad and fried chicken, and eclipsing even the refulgent Colonel – happy girls, with two new dancers for the week-end, they had celebrated the unwonted wind-fall by extra touches of adornment: a red rose in the fold of a fichu, a loose curl on a white shoulder, a pair of new satin slippers, a fresh *moiré* ribbon.

Seeing them through the eyes of the new young men Mrs St George felt their collective grace with a vividness almost exempt from envy. To her, as to those two foreigners, they embodied 'the American girl', the world's highest achievement; and she was as ready to enjoy Lizzy Elmsworth's brilliant darkness, and that dry sparkle of Mab's, as much as her own Virginia's roses, and Nan's alternating frowns and dimples. She was even able to recognize that the Closson girl's incongruous hair gilded the whole group like a sunburst. Could Newport show anything lovelier, she wondered half-bitterly, as she seated herself between Mr Closson and young Santos-Dios.

Mrs Closson, from the Colonel's right, leaned across the table with her soft ambiguous smile. 'What lovely diamonds, Mrs St George! I wish I hadn't left all mine in the safe at New York!'

Mrs St George thought: 'She means the place isn't worth bringing jewels to. As if she ever went out anywhere in New York!' But her eyes wandered beyond Mrs Closson to Lord Richard Marable; it was the first time she had ever sat at table with any one even remotely related to a British nobleman, and she fancied the young man was ironically observing the way in which she held her fork. But she saw that his eyes, which were sand-coloured like his face, and sandy-lashed, had found another occupation. They were fixed on Conchita Closson, who sat opposite to him; they rested on her unblinkingly, immovably, as if she had been a natural object, a landscape or a cathedral, that one had travelled far to see, and had the right to look at as long as one chose. 'He's drinking her up like blotting-paper. I thought they were better brought up over in England!' Mrs St George said to herself, austerely thankful that he was not taking such liberties with *her* daughters ('but men always know the difference,' she reflected), and suddenly not worrying any longer about how she held her fork.

THE BUCCANEERS

4

Miss Laura Testvalley stood on the wooden platform of the railway
station at Saratoga Springs, N.Y., and looked about her. It was not
an inspiriting scene; but she had not expected that it would be, and
would not have greatly cared if it had. She had been in America for
eighteen months, and it was not for its architectural or civic beauties
that she had risked herself so far. Miss Testvalley had small means,
and a derelict family to assist; and her successful career as a governess in the households of the English aristocracy had been curtailed
by the need to earn more money. English governesses were at a
premium in the United States, and one of Miss Testvalley's former
pupils, whose husband was attached to the British Legation in Wash-
ington, had recommended her to Mrs Russell Parmore, a cousin of
the Eglintons and the van der Luydens – the best, in short, that New
York had to offer. The salary was not as high as Miss Testvalley had
hoped for; but her ex-pupil at the Legation had assured her that
among the 'new' coal and steel people, who could pay more, she
would certainly be too wretched. Miss Testvalley was not sure of
this. She had not come to America in search of distinguished manners any more than of well-kept railway stations; but she decided on
reflection that the Parmore household might be a useful spring-
board, and so it proved. Mrs Russell Parmore was certainly very
distinguished, and so were her pallid daughter and her utterly
rubbed-out husband; and how could they know that to Miss Testvalley they represented at best a *milieu* of retired Colonials at Chelten-
ham, or the household of a minor canon in a cathedral town? Miss
Testvalley had been used to a more vivid setting, and accustomed to
social dramas and emotions which Mrs Russell Parmore had only
seen hinted at in fiction; and as the pay was low, and the domestic
economies were painful (Mrs Russell Parmore would have thought it
ostentatious and vulgar to live largely), Miss Testvalley, after conscientiously 'finishing' Miss Parmore (a young lady whom Nature
seemed scarcely to have begun), decided to seek, in a different field,
ampler opportunities of action. She consulted a New York governesses' agency, and learned that the 'new people' would give 'almost
anything' for such social training as an accomplished European

323

governess could impart. Miss Testvalley fixed a maximum wage, and in a few days was notified by the agency that Mrs Tracy St George was ready to engage her. 'It was Mrs Russell Parmore's reference that did it,' said the black-wigged lady at the desk as they exchanged fees and congratulations. 'In New York that counts more than all your Duchesses'; and Miss Testvalley again had reason to rate her own good sense at its just value. Life at the Parmores', on poor pay and a scanty diet, had been a weary business; but it had been worth while. Now she had in her pocket the promise of eighty dollars a month, and the possibility of a more exciting task; for she understood that the St Georges were very 'new', and the prospect of comparing the manners and customs of the new and the not-new might be amusing. 'I wonder,' she thought ironically, 'if the Duchess would see the slightest difference . . .' the Duchess meaning always *hers*, the puissant lady of Tintagel, where Miss Testvalley had spent so many months shivering with cold, and bandaging the chilblains of the younger girls, while the other daughters, with their particular 'finishing' duenna, accompanied their parents from one ducal residence to another. The Duchess of Tintagel, who had beaten Miss Testvalley's salary well-nigh down to the level of an upper housemaid's, who had so often paid it after an embarrassingly long delay, who had been surprised that a governess should want a fire in her room, or a hot soup for her school-room dinner – the Duchess was now (all unknown to herself) making up for her arrears toward Miss Testvalley. By giving Mrs Parmore the chance to say, when she had friends to dine: 'I happen to know, for instance, that at Tintagel Castle there are only open fires, and the halls and corridors are not heated at all', Miss Testvalley had gained several small favours from her parsimonious employer: and by telling her, in the strictest confidence, that their Graces had at one time felt a good deal of anxiety about their only son – oh, a simple sweet-natured young man if ever there was one; but then, the temptations which beset a Marquess! – Miss Testvalley had obtained from Mrs Parmore a letter of recommendation which placed her at the head of the educational sisterhood in the United States.

Miss Testvalley needed this, and every other form of assistance she could obtain. It would have been difficult for either Mrs Parmore or the Duchess of Tintagel to imagine how poor she was, or how many people had (or so she thought) a lien on her pitiful savings. It was the penalty of the family glory. Miss Testvalley's grand-father was the illustrious patriot, Gennaro Testavaglia of Modena, fomenter of insurrections, hero of the Risorgimento, author of those once famous historical novels, *Arnaldo da Brescia* and *La Donna della Fortezza*, but whose fame lingered in England chiefly because he was the cousin of the old Gabriele Rossetti, father of the decried and illustrious Dante Gabriel. The Testavaglias, fleeing from the Austrian inquisition, had come to England at the same time as the Rossettis, and contracting their impossible name to the scope of English lips, had intermarried with other exiled revolutionaries and anti-papists, producing sons who were artists and agnostics, and daughters who were evangelicals of the strictest pattern, and governesses in the highest families. Laura Test valley had obediently followed the family tradition; but she had come after the heroic days of evangelical great ladies who required governesses to match; competition was more active, there was less demand for drawing-room Italian and prayerful considerations on the Collects, and more for German and the natural sciences, in neither of which Miss Testvalley excelled. And in the intervening years the mothers and aunts of the family had grown rheumatic and impotent, the heroic old men lingered on in their robust senility, and the drain on the younger generation grew heavier with every year. At thirty-nine Laura had found it impossible, on her English earnings, to keep the grand-mother (wife of the Risorgimento hero), and to aid her own infirm mother in supporting an invalid brother and a married sister with six children, whose husband had disappeared in the wilds of Australia. Laura was sure that it was not her vocation to minister to others, but she had been forced into the task early, and continued in it from family pride – and because, after all, she belonged to the group, and the Risorgimento and the Pre-Raphaelites were her chief credentials. And so she had come to America.

At the Parmores' she had learned a good deal about one phase of American life, and she had written home some droll letters on the subject; but she had suspected from the first that the real America was elsewhere, and had been tempted and amused by the idea that among the Wall Street *parvenus* she might discover it. She had an unspoiled taste for oddities and contrasts, and nothing could have been more alien to her private sentiments than the family combination of revolutionary radicalism, Exeter Hall piety, and awestruck reverence for the aristocratic households in which the Testvalley governesses earned the keep of their ex-carbonari. 'If I'd been a man,' she sometimes thought, 'Dante Gabriel might not have been the only cross in the family.' And the idea obscurely comforted her when she was correcting her pupils' compositions, or picking up the dropped stitches in their knitting.

She was used to waiting in strange railway stations, her old black beaded 'dolman' over her arm, her modest horse-hair box at her feet. Servants often forget to order the fly which is to fetch the governess, and the lady herself, though she may have meant to come to the station, is not infrequently detained by shopping or calling. So Miss Testvalley, without impatience, watched the other travellers drive off in the spidery high-wheeled vehicles in which people bounced across the humps and ruts of the American country roads. It was the eve of the great race-week, and she was amused by the showy garb of the gentlemen and the much-flounced elegance of their ladies, though she felt sure Mrs Parmore would have disdained them.

One by one the travellers scattered, their huge 'Saratogas' (she knew that expression also) hoisted into broken-down express-carts that crawled off in the wake of the owners; and at last a new dust-cloud formed down the road and floated slowly nearer, till there emerged from it a lumbering vehicle of the kind which Miss Testvalley knew to be classed as hotel hacks. As it drew up she was struck by the fact that the driver, a small dusky fellow in a white linen jacket and a hat-brim of exotic width, had an orange bow tied to his whip, and a beruffled white poodle with a bigger orange bow perched between himself and the shabby young man in overalls who shared his seat; while from within she felt herself laughingly surveyed by two tiers of bright young eyes. The driver pulled up with a queer guttural cry to his horses, the poodle leapt down and began to dance on his hind legs, and out of the hack poured a spring torrent of muslins, sash-ends, and bright cheeks under swaying hat-brims. Miss Testvalley found herself in a circle of nymphs shaken by hysterical laughter, and as she stood there, small, brown, interrogative, there swept through her mind a shred of verse which Dante Gabriel used to be fond of reciting:

> *Whence came ye, merry damsels, whence came ye,*
> *So many and so many, and such glee?*

and she smiled at the idea that Endymion should greet her at the Saratoga railway station. For it was clearly in search of her that the rabble rout had come. The dancing nymphs hailed her with joyful giggles, the poodle sprang on her with dusty paws, and then turned a somersault in her honour, and from the driver's box came the twang of a guitar and the familiar wail of: *Nita, Juanita, ask thy soul if we must part?*

'No, certainly not!' cried Miss Testvalley, tossing up her head toward the driver, who responded with doffed sombrero and hand on heart. 'That is to say,' she added, 'if my future pupil is one of the young ladies who have joined in this very flattering welcome.'

The enchanted circle broke, and the nymphs, still hand in hand, stretched a straight line of loveliness before her. 'Guess which!' chimed simultaneously from five pairs of lips, while five deep curtsies swept the platform; and Miss Testvalley drew back a step and scanned them thoughtfully.

Her first thought was that she had never seen five prettier girls in a row; her second (tinged with joy) that Mrs Russell Parmore would have been scandalized by such an exhibition, on the Saratoga railway platform, in full view of departing travellers, gazing employees, and delighted station loafers; her third that, whichever of the beauties was to fall to her lot, life in such company would be infinitely more amusing than with the Parmores. And still smiling she continued to examine the mirthful mocking faces.

No dominant beauty, was her first impression; no proud angelic heads, ready for coronets or haloes, such as she was used to in England; unless indeed the tall fair girl with such heaps of wheat-coloured hair and such gentian-blue eyes – or the very dark one, who was too pale for her black hair, but had the small imperious nose of a Roman empress . . . yes, those two were undoubtedly beautiful, yet they were not beauties. They seemed rather to have reached the last height of prettiness, and to be perched on that sunny lower slope, below the cold divinities. And with the other three, taken one by one, fault might have been found on various counts; for the one in the striped pink and white organdy, though she looked cleverer than the others, had a sharp nose, and her laugh showed too many teeth; and the one in white, with a big orange-coloured sash the colour of the poodle's bow (no doubt she was his mistress) was sallow and red-haired, and you had to look into her pale starry eyes to forget that she was too tall, and stooped a little. And as for the fifth, who seemed so much younger – hardly more than a child – her small face was such a flurry of frowns and dimples that Miss Testvalley did not know how to define her.

'Well, young ladies, my first idea is that I wish you were all to be my pupils; and the second –' she paused, weighed the possibilities and met the eyes – 'the second is that this is Miss Annabel St George, who is, I believe, to be my special charge.' She put her hand on Nan's arm.

'How did you know?' burst from Nan, on the shrill note of a netted bird; and the others broke into laughter.

'Why, you silly, we told you so! Anybody can see you're nothing but a baby!'

Nan faced about, blazing and quivering. 'Well, if I'm a baby, what I want is a nurse, and not a beastly English governess!'

Her companions laughed again and nudged each other; then, abashed, they glanced at the newcomer, as if trying to read in her face what would come next.

Miss Testvalley laughed also. 'Oh, I'm used to both jobs,' she rejoined briskly. 'But meanwhile hadn't we better be getting off to the hotel? Get into the carriage, please, Annabel,' she said with sudden authority.

She turned to look for her trunk; but it had already been shouldered by the nondescript young man in overalls, who hoisted it to the roof of the carriage, and then, jumping down, brushed the soot and dust off his hands. As he did so Miss Testvalley confronted him, and her hand dropped from Nan's arm.

'Why – Lord Richard!' she exclaimed; and the young man in overalls gave a sheepish laugh. 'I suppose at home they all think I'm in Brazil,' he said in an uncertain voice.

'I know nothing of what they think,' retorted Miss Testvalley drily, following the girls into the carriage. As they drove off, Nan, who was crowded in between Mab Elmsworth and Conchita, burst into sudden tears. 'I didn't mean to call you "beastly",' she whispered, stealing a hand toward the new governess; and the new governess, clasping the hand, answered with her undaunted smile: 'I didn't hear you call me so, my dear.'

5

Mrs St George had gone to the races with her husband – an ordeal she always dreaded and yet prayed for. Colonel St George, on these occasions, was so handsome, and so splendid in his light racing suit and grey top hat, that she enjoyed a larger repetition of her triumph in the hotel dining-room; but when this had been tasted to the full there remained her dread of the mysterious men with whom he was hail-fellow-well-met in the paddock, and the dreadful painted women in open carriages, who leered and beckoned (didn't she see them?) under the fringes of their sunshades.

She soon wearied of the show, and would have been glad to be back rocking and sipping lemonade on the hotel verandah; yet when the Colonel helped her into the carriage, suggesting that if she wanted to meet the new governess it was time to be off, she instantly concluded that the rich widow at the Congress Springs Hotel, about whom there was so much gossip, had made him a secret sign, and was going to carry him off to the gambling rooms for supper – if not worse. But when the Colonel chose his arts were irresistible, and in another moment Mrs St George was driving away alone, her heart heavy with this new anxiety superposed on so many others.

When she reached the hotel all the frequenters of the verandah, gathered between the columns of the porch, were greeting with hysterical laughter a motley group who were pouring out of the familiar vehicle from which Mrs St George had expected to see Nan descend with the dreaded and longed-for governess. The party was headed by Teddy de Santos-Dios, grotesquely accoutred in a hotel waiter's white jacket, and twanging his guitar to the antics of Conchita's poodle, while Conchita herself, the Elmsworth sisters and Mrs St George's own two girls, danced up the steps surrounding a small soberly garbed figure, whom Mrs St George instantly identified as the governess. Mrs Elmsworth and Mrs Closson stood on the upper step, smothering their laughter in lace handkerchiefs; but Mrs St George sailed past them with set lips, pushing aside a shabby-looking young man in overalls who seemed to form part of the company.

'Virginia – Annabel,' she gasped, 'what is the meaning . . . Oh, Miss Testvalley – what *must* you think?' she faltered with trembling lips.

'I think it very kind of Annabel's young friends to have come with her to meet me,' said Miss Testvalley; and Mrs St George noted with bewilderment and relief that she was actually smiling, and that she had slipped her arm through Nan's.

For a moment Mrs St George thought it might be easier to deal with a governess who was already on such easy terms with her pupil; but by the time Miss Testvalley, having removed the dust of travel, had knocked at her employer's door, the latter had been assailed by new apprehensions. It would have been comparatively simple to receive, with what Mrs St George imagined to be the dignity of a Duchess, a governess used to such ceremonial; but the disconcerting circumstances of Miss Testvalley's arrival, and the composure with which she met them, had left Mrs St George with her dignity on her hands. Could it be –? But no; Mrs Russell Parmore, as well as the Duchess, answered for Miss Testvalley's unquestionable respectability. Mrs St George fanned herself nervously.

'Oh, come in. Do sit down, Miss Testvalley.' (Mrs St George had expected some one taller, more majestic. She would have thought Miss Testvalley insignificant, could the term be applied to any one coming from Mrs Parmore.) 'I don't know how my daughters can have been induced to do anything so – so undignified. Unfortunately the Closson girl –.' She broke off, embarrassed by the recollection of the Colonel's injunctions.

'The tall young girl with auburn hair? I understand that one of the masqueraders was her brother.'

'Yes; her half-brother. Mrs Closson is a Brazilian' – but again Mrs St George checked the note of disparagement. 'Brazilian' was bad enough, without adding anything pejorative. 'The Colonel – Colonel St George – has business relations with Mr Closson. I never met them before . . .'

'Ah,' said Miss Testvalley.

'And I'm sure my girls and the Elmsworths would never . . .'

'Oh, quite so; I understood. I've no doubt the idea was Lord Richard's.'

She uttered the name as though it were familiar to her, and Mrs St George caught at Lord Richard. 'You knew him already? He appears to be a friend of the Clossons.'

'I knew him in England; yes. I was with Lady Brightlingsea for two years – as his sisters' governess.'

Mrs St George gazed awestruck down this new and resonant perspective. 'Lady Brittlesey?' (It was thus that Miss Testvalley had pronounced the name.)

'The Marchioness of Brightlingsea; his mother. It's a very large family. I was with two of the younger daughters. Lady Honoria and Lady Ulrica Marable. I think Lord Richard is the third son. But one saw him at home so very seldom . . .'

Mrs St George drew a deep breath. She had not bargained for this glimpse into the labyrinth of the peerage, and she felt a little dizzy, as though all the Brightlingseas and the Marables were in the room, and she ought to make the proper gestures, and didn't even know what to call them without her husband's being there to tell her. She wondered whether the experiment of an English governess might not after all make life too complicated. And this one's eyebrows were so black and ironical.

'Lord Richard,' continued Miss Testvalley, 'always has to have his little joke.' Her tone seemed to dismiss him, and all his titled relations with him. Mrs St George was relieved. 'But your daughter Annabel – perhaps,' Miss Testvalley continued, 'you would like to give me some general idea of the stage she has reached in her different studies?' Her manner was now distinctly professional, and Mrs St George's spirits drooped again. If only the Colonel had been there – as he would have been, but for that woman! Or even Nan herself . . . Mrs St George looked helplessly at the governess. But suddenly an inspiration came to her. 'I have always left these things to the girls' teachers,' she said with majesty.

'Oh, quite –' Miss Testvalley assented.

'And their father; their father takes a great interest in their studies – when time permits . . .' Mrs St George continued. 'But of course his business interests . . . which are enormous . . .'

'I think I understand,' Miss Testvalley softly agreed.

Mrs St George again sighed her relief. A governess who understood without the need of tiresome explanations – was it not more than she had hoped for? Certainly Miss Testvalley looked insignificant; but the eyes under her expressive eyebrows were splendid, and she had an air of firmness. And the miracle was that Nan should already have taken a fancy to her. If only the other girls didn't laugh her out of it! 'Of course,' Mrs St George began again, 'what I attach most importance to is that my girls should be taught to – to behave like ladies.'

Miss Testvalley murmured: 'Oh, yes. Drawing-room accomplishments.'

'I may as well tell you that I don't care very much for the girls they associate with here. Saratoga is not what it used to be. In New York of course it will be different. I hope you can persuade Annabel to study.'

She could not think of anything else to say, and the governess, who seemed singularly discerning, rose with a slight bow, and murmured: 'If you will allow me . . .'

Miss Testvalley's room was narrow and bare; but she had already discovered that the rooms of summer hotels in the States were all like that; the luxury and gilding were reserved for the public parlours. She did not much mind; she had never been used to comfort, and her Italian nature did not crave it. To her mind the chief difference between the governess's room at Tintagel, or at Allfriars, the Brightlingsea seat, and those she had occupied since her arrival in America, was that the former were larger (and therefore harder to heat) and were furnished with threadbare relics of former splendour, and carpets in which you caught your heel; whereas at Mrs Parmore's, and in this big hotel, though the governess's quarters were cramped, they were neat and the furniture was in good repair. But this afternoon Miss Testvalley was perhaps tired, or oppressed by the heat, or perhaps only by an unwonted sense of loneliness. Certainly it was odd to find one's self at the orders of people who wished their daughters to be taught to 'behave like ladies'. (The alternative being – what, she wondered? Perhaps a disturbing apparition like Conchita Closson.)

At any rate, Miss Testvalley was suddenly aware of a sense of loneliness, of far-away-ness, of a quite unreasonable yearning for the dining-room at the back of a certain shabby house at Denmark Hill, where her mother, in a widow's cap of white crêpe, sat on one side of the scantily filled grate, turning with rheumatic fingers the pages of the Reverend Frederick Maurice's sermons, while, facing her across the hearth, old Gennaro Testavaglia, still heavy and powerful in his extreme age, brooded with fixed eyes in a big parchment-coloured face, and repeated over and over some forgotten verse of his own revolutionary poems. In that room, with its chronic smell of cold coffee and smouldering coals, of Elliman's liniment and human old age, Miss Testvalley had spent some of the most disheartening hours of her life. '*Le mie prigioni,*' she had once called it; yet was it not for that detested room that she was homesick!

Only fifteen minutes in which to prepare for supper! (She had been warned that late dinners were still unknown in American hotels.) Miss Testvalley, setting her teeth against the vision of the Denmark Hill dining-room, went up to the chest of drawers on which she had already laid out her modest toilet appointments; and there she saw, between her yellowish-backed brush and faded pin-cushion, a bunch of freshly gathered geraniums and mignonette. The flowers had certainly not been there when she had smoothed her hair before waiting on Mrs St George; nor had they, she was sure, been sent by that lady. They were not bought flowers, but flowers lovingly gathered; and some one else must have entered in Miss Testvalley's absence, and hastily deposited the humble posy.

The governess sat down on the hard chair beside the bed, and her eyes filled with tears. Flowers, she had noticed, did not abound in the States; at least not in summer. In winter, in New York, you could see them banked up in tiers in the damp heat of the florists' windows; plumy ferns, forced lilac, and those giant roses, red and pink, which rich people offered to each other so lavishly in long white card-board boxes. It was very odd; the same ladies who exchanged these costly tributes in mid-winter lived through the summer without a flower, or with nothing but a stiff bed of dwarf foliage plants before the door, or a tub or two of the inevitable hydrangeas. Yet some one had apparently managed to snatch these flowers from the meagre border before the hotel porch, and had put them there to fill Miss Testvalley's bedroom with scent and colour. And who could have done it but her new pupil?

*

Quarter of an hour later Miss Testvalley, her thick hair re-braided and glossed with brilliantine, her black merino exchanged for a plum-coloured silk with a crochet lace collar, and lace mittens on her small worn hands, knocked at the door of the Misses St George. It opened, and the governess gave a little 'oh!' of surprise. Virginia stood there, a shimmer of ruffled white drooping away from her young throat and shoulders. On her heaped-up wheat-coloured hair lay a wreath of cornflowers; and a black velvet ribbon with a locket hanging from it intensified her fairness like the black stripe on a ring-dove's throat.

'What elegance for a public dining-room!' thought Miss Testvalley; and then reflected: 'But no doubt it's her only chance of showing it.'

Virginia opened wondering blue eyes, and the governess explained: 'The supper-bell has rung, and I thought you and your sister might like me to go down with you.'

'Oh–' Virginia murmured; and added: 'Nan's lost her slipper. She's hunting for it.'

'Very well; shall I help her? And you'll go down and excuse us to your mamma?'

Virginia's eyes grew wider. 'Well, I guess mother's used to waiting,' she said, as she sauntered along the corridor to the staircase.

Nan St George lay face downward on the floor, poking with a silk parasol under the wardrobe. At the sound of Miss Testvalley's voice she raised herself sulkily. Her small face was flushed and frowning. ('None of her sister's beauty,' Miss Testvalley thought.) 'It's there, but I can't get at it,' Nan proclaimed.

'My dear, you'll tumble your lovely frock –'

'Oh, it's not lovely. It's one of Jinny's last year's organdies.'

'Well, it won't improve it to crawl about on the floor. Is your shoe under the wardrobe? Let me try to get it. My silk won't be damaged.'

Miss Testvalley put out her hand for the sunshade, and Nan scrambled to her feet. 'You can't reach it,' she said, still sulkily. But Miss Testvalley, prostrate on the floor, had managed to push a thin arm under the wardrobe, and the parasol presently re-appeared with a little bronze slipper on its tip. Nan gave a laugh.

'Well, you *are* handy!' she said.

Miss Testvalley echoed the laugh. 'Put it on quickly, and let me help you to tidy your dress. And, oh dear, your sash is untied –.' She spun the girl about, re-tied the sash and smoothed the skirt with airy touches; for all of which, she noticed, Nan uttered no word of thanks.

'And your handkerchief, Annabel?' In Miss Testvalley's opinion no lady should appear in the evening without a scrap of lace-edged cambric, folded into a triangle and held between gloved or mittened fingertips. Nan shrugged. 'I never know where my handkerchiefs are – I guess they get lost in the wash, wandering round in hotels the way we do.'

Miss Testvalley sighed at this nomadic wastefulness. Perhaps because she had always been a wanderer herself she loved orderly drawers and shelves, and bunches of lavender between delicately fluted under-garments.

'Do you always live in hotels, my dear?'

'We did when I was little. But father's bought a house in New York now. Mother made him do it because the Elmsworths did. She thought maybe, if we had one, Jinny'd be invited out more; but I don't see much difference.'

'Well, I shall have to help you to go over your linen,' the governess continued; but Nan showed no interest in the offer. Miss Testvalley saw before her a cold impatient little face – and yet . . .

'Annabel,' she said, slipping her hand through the girl's thin arm, 'how did you guess I was fond of flowers?'

The blood rose from Nan's shoulders to her cheeks, and a half-guilty smile set the dimples racing across her face. 'Mother said we'd acted like a lot of savages, getting up that circus at the station – and what on earth would you think of us?'

'I think that I shall like you all very much; and you especially, because of those flowers.'

Nan gave a shy laugh. 'Lord Richard said you'd like them.'

'Lord Richard?'

'Yes. He says in England everybody has a garden, with lots of flowers that smell sweet. And so I stole them from the hotel border . . . He's crazy about Conchita, you know. Do you think she'll catch him?'

Miss Testvalley stiffened. She felt her upper lip lengthen, though she tried to smile. 'I don't think it's a question that need concern us, do you?'

Nan stared. 'Well, she's my greatest friend – after Jinny, I mean.'

'Then we must wish her something better than Lord Richard. Come, my dear, or those wonderful American griddle-cakes will all be gone.'

Early in her career Miss Testvalley had had to learn the difficult art of finding her way about – not only as concerned the tastes and temper of the people she lived with, but the topography of their houses. In those old winding English dwellings, half fortress, half palace, where suites and galleries of stately proportions abruptly tapered off into narrow twists and turns, leading to unexpected rooms tucked away in unaccountable corners, and where school-room and nurseries were usually at the far end of the labyrinth, it behoved the governess to blaze her trail by a series of private aids to memory. It was important, in such houses, not only to know the way you were meant to take, but the many you were expected to avoid, and a young governess turning too often down the passage leading to the young gentlemen's wing, or getting into the way of the master of the house in his dignified descent to the breakfast-room, might sud-denly have her services dispensed with. To any one thus trained the simple plan of an American summer hotel offered no mysteries; and when supper was over and, after a sultry hour or two in the red and gold ball-room, the St George ladies ascended to their apartments, Miss Testvalley had no difficulty in finding her way up another flight to her own room. She was already aware that it was in the wing of the hotel, and had noted that from its window she could look across into that from which, before supper, she had seen Miss Closson signal to her brother and Lord Richard, who were smoking on the gravel below.

It was no business of Miss Testvalley's to keep watch on what went on in the Closson rooms – or would not have been, she corrected herself, had Nan St George not spoken of Conchita as her dearest friend. Such a tie did seem to the governess to require vigilance. Miss Closson was herself an unknown quantity, and Lord Richard was one only too well known to Miss Testvalley. It was therefore not unnatural that, after silence had fallen on the long corridors of the hotel, the governess, finding sleep impossible in her small suffocating room, should put out her candle, and gaze across from her window at that from which she had seen Conchita lean.

Light still streamed from it, though midnight was past, and presently came laughter, and the twang of Santos-Dios's guitar, and a burst of youthful voices joining in song. Was her pupil's among them? Miss Testvalley could not be sure; but soon, detaching itself from Teddy de Santos-Dios's reedy tenor, she caught the hoarse barytone of another voice.

Imprudent children! It was bad enough to be gathered at that hour in a room with a young man and a guitar; but at least the young man was Miss Closson's brother, and Miss Testvalley had noticed, at the supper-table, much exchange of civilities between the St Georges and the Clossons. But Richard Marable – that was inexcusable, that was scandalous! The hotel would be ringing with it tomorrow . . .

Ought not Miss Testvalley to find some pretext for knocking at Conchita's door, gathering her charges back to safety, and putting it in their power to say that their governess had assisted at the little party? Her first impulse was to go; but governesses who act on first impulses seldom keep their places. 'As long as there's so much noise,' she thought, 'there can't be any mischief . . .' and at that moment, in a pause of the singing, she caught Nan's trill of little-girl laughter. Miss Testvalley started up, and went to her door; but once more she drew back. Better wait and see – interfering might do more harm than good. If only some exasperated neighbour did not ring to have the rejoicings stopped!

At length music and laughter subsided. Silence followed. Miss Testvalley, drawing an austere purple flannel garment over her night-dress, unbolted her door and stole out into the passage. Where it joined the main corridor she paused and waited. A door had opened half way down the corridor – Conchita's door – and the governess saw a flutter of light dresses, and heard subdued laughter and good nights. Both the St George and Elmsworth families were lodged below, and in the weak glimmer of gas she made sure of four girls hurrying toward her wing. She drew back hastily. Glued to her door she listened, and heard a heavy but cautious step passing by, and a throaty voice humming 'Champagne Charlie'. She drew a breath of relief, and sat down before her glass to finish her toilet for the night.

Her hair carefully waved on its pins, her evening prayer recited, she slipped into bed and blew out the light. But still sleep did not come, and she lay in the sultry darkness and listened, she hardly knew for what. At last she heard the same heavy step returning cautiously, passing her door, gaining once more the main corridor – the step she would have known in a thousand, the step she used to listen for at Allfriars after midnight, groping down the long passage to the governess's room.

She started up. Forgetful of crimping-pins and bare feet, she opened her door again. The last flicker of gas had gone out, and secure in the blackness she crept after the heavy step to the corner. It sounded ahead of her half way down the long row of doors; then it stopped, a door opened . . . and Miss Testvalley turned back on leaden feet . . .

Nothing of that fugitive adventure at Allfriars had ever been known. Of that she was certain. An ill-conditioned youth, the boon companion of his father's grooms, and a small brown governess, ten years his elder, and known to be somewhat curt and distant with every one except her pupils and their parents – who would ever have thought of associating the one with the other? The episode had been brief; the peril was soon over; and when, the very same year, Lord Richard was solemnly banished from his father's house, it was not because of his having once or twice stolen down the school-room passage at undue hours; but for reasons so far more deplorable that poor Lady Brightlingsea, her reserve utterly broken down, had sobbed out on Miss Testvalley's breast: 'Anything, anything else I know his father would have forgiven.' (Miss Testvalley wondered . . .)

6

When Colonel St George bought his house in Madison Avenue it seemed to him fit to satisfy the ambitions of any budding millionaire. That it had been built and decorated by one of the Tweed ring, who had come to grief earlier than his more famous fellow-criminals, was to Colonel St George convincing proof that it was a suitable setting for wealth and elegance. But social education is acquired rapidly in New York, even by those who have to absorb it through the cracks of the sacred edifice; and Mrs St George had already found out that no one lived in Madison Avenue, that the front hall should have been painted Pompeian red with a stencilled frieze, and not with naked Cupids and humming birds on a sky-blue ground, and that base-ment dining-rooms were unknown to the fashionable. So much she had picked up almost at once from Jinny and Jinny's school-friends; and when she called on Mrs Parmore to enquire about the English governess, the sight of the Parmore house, small and simple as it was, completed her disillusionment.

But it was too late to change. The Colonel, who was insensitive to details, continued to be proud of his house; even when the Elmsworths, suddenly migrating from Brooklyn, had settled them-selves in Fifth Avenue he would not admit his mistake, or feel the humiliation of the contrast. And yet what a difference it made to a lady to be able to say 'Fifth Avenue' in giving her address to Black, Starr and Frost, or to Mrs Connelly, the fashionable dress-maker! In establishments like that they classed their customers at once, and 'Madison Avenue' stood at best for a decent mediocrity.

Mrs St George at first ascribed to this unfortunate locality her failure to make a social situation for her girls; yet after the Elmsworths had come to Fifth Avenue she noted with satisfaction that Lizzy and Mabel were not asked out much more than Virginia. Of course Mr Elmsworth was an obstacle; and so was Mrs Elms-worth's laugh. It was difficult – it was even painful – to picture the Elmsworths dining at the Parmores' or the Eglintons'. But the St Georges did not dine there either. And the question of ball-going was almost as discouraging. One of the young men whom the girls had met at Saratoga had suggested to Virginia that he might get her a card for the first Assembly; but Mrs St George, when sounded, declined indignantly, for she knew that in the best society girls did not go to balls without their parents.

These subscription balls were a peculiar source of bitterness to Mrs St George. She could not understand how her daughters could be excluded from entertainment for which one could buy a ticket. She knew all about the balls from her hair-dresser, the celebrated Katie Wood. Katie did everybody's hair, and innocently planted dagger after dagger in Mrs St George's anxious breast by saying: 'If you and Jinny want me next Wednesday week for the first Assembly you'd better say so right off, because I've got every minute be-spoke already from three o'clock on,' or: 'If you're invited to the opening night of the Opera, I might try the new chignon with the bunch of curls on the left shoulder,' or worse still: 'I suppose Jinny belongs to the Thursday Evening Dances, don't she? The débutantes are going to wear wreaths of apple-blossom or rose-buds a good deal this winter – or forget-me-not would look lovely, with her eyes.'

Lovely, indeed. But if Virginia had not been asked to belong, and if Mrs St George had vainly tried to have her own name added to the list of the Assembly balls, or to get a box for the opening night of the Opera, what was there to do but to say indifferently: 'Oh, I don't know if we shall be here – the Colonel's thinking a little of carrying us off to Florida if he can get away . . .' knowing all the while how much the hair-dresser believed of that excuse, and also aware that, in speaking of Miss Eglinton and Miss Parmore, Katie did not call them by their Christian names . . .

Mrs St George could not understand why she was subjected to this cruel ostracism. The Colonel knew everybody – that is, all the gentlemen he met down town, or at his clubs, and he belonged to many clubs. Their dues were always having to be paid, even when the butcher and the grocer were clamouring. He often brought gentle-men home to dine, and gave them the best champagne and Madeira in the cellar; and they invited him back, but never included Mrs St George and Virginia in their invitations.

It was small comfort to learn one day that Jinny and Nan had been invited to act as Conchita Closson's bridesmaids. She thought it unnatural that the Clossons, who were strangers in New York, and still camping at the Fifth Avenue Hotel, should be marrying their daughter before Virginia was led to the altar. And then the bride-groom! – well, everybody knew that he was only a younger son, and that in England, even in the great aristocratic families, younger sons were of small account unless they were clever enough to make their own way – an ambition which seemed never to have troubled Dick Marable. Moreover, there were dark rumours about him, reports of warning discreetly transmitted through the British Legation in Wash-ington, and cruder tales among the clubs. Still, nothing could alter the fact that Lord Richard Marable was the son of the Marquess of Brightlingsea, and that his mother had been a Duke's daughter – and who knows whether the Eglintons and Parmores, though they thanked heaven their dear girls would never be exposed to such risks, were not half envious of the Clossons? But then there was the indecent haste of it. The young people had met for the first time in August; and they were to be married in November! In good society it was usual for a betrothal to last at least a year; and among the Eglintons and Parmores even that time-allowance was thought to betray an undue haste. 'The young people should be given time to get to know each other,' the mothers of Fifth Avenue decreed; and Mrs Parmore told Miss Testvalley, when the latter called to pay her respects to her former employer, that she for her part hoped her daughter would never consent to an engagement of less than two years. 'But I suppose, dear Miss Testvalley, that among the people you're with now there are no social traditions.'

'None except those they are making for themselves,' Miss Testvalley was tempted to rejoin; but that would not have been what she called a 'governess's answer', and she knew a governess should never be more on her guard than when conversing with a former employer. Especially, Miss Testvalley thought, when the employer had a long nose with a slight droop, and pale lips like Mrs Parmore's. She murmured that there were business reasons, she understood; Mr Closson was leaving shortly for Brazil.

'Ah, so they *say*. But of course, the rumours one hears about this young man . . . a son of Lord Brightlingsea's, I understand? But, Miss Testvalley, you were with the Brightlingseas; you must have known him?'

'It's a very big family, and when I went there the sons were already scattered. I usually remained at Allfriars with the younger girls.'

Mrs Parmore nodded softly. 'Quite so. And by that time this unfortunate young man had already begun his career of dissipation in London. He *has* been dissipated, I believe?'

'Lately I think he's been trying to earn his living on Mr Closson's plantation in Brazil.'

'Poor young man! Do his family realize what a deplorable choice he has made? Whatever his past may have been, it's a pity he should marry in New York, and leave it again, without having any idea of it beyond what can be had in the Closson set. If he'd come in different circumstances, we should all have been so happy . . . Mr Parmore would have put him down at his clubs . . . he would have been invited everywhere . . . Yes, it does seem unfortunate . . . But of course no one knows the Clossons.'

'I suppose the young couple will go back to Brazil after the marriage,' said Miss Testvalley evasively.

Mrs Parmore gave an ironic smile. 'I don't imagine Miss Closson is marrying the son of a Marquess to go and live on a plantation in Brazil. When I took Alida to Mrs Connelly's to order her dress for the Assembly, Mrs Connelly told me she'd heard from Mrs Closson's maid that Mr Closson meant to give the young couple a house in London. Do you suppose this is likely? They can't keep up any sort of establishment in London without a fairly large income; and I hear Mr Closson's position in Wall Street is rather shaky.'

Miss Testvalley took refuge in one of her Italian gestures of conjecture. 'Governesses, you know, Mrs Parmore, hear so much less gossip than dress-makers and ladies'-maids; and I'm not Miss Closson's governess.'

'No; fortunately for you! For I believe there were rather unpleasant rumours at Saratoga. People were bound to find a reason for such a hurried marriage . . . But your pupils have been asked to be bridesmaids, I understand?'

'The girls got to know each other last summer. And you know how exciting it is, especially for a child of Annabel St George's age, to figure for the first time in a wedding procession.'

'Yes. I suppose they haven't many chances . . . But shouldn't you like to come upstairs and see Alida's Assembly dress? Mrs Connelly has just sent it home, and your pupils might like to hear about it. White tulle, of course – nothing will ever replace white tulle for a débutante, will it?'

Miss Testvalley, after that visit, felt that she had cast in her lot once for all with the usurpers and the adventurers. Perhaps because she herself had been born in exile, her sympathies were with the social as well as the political outcasts – with the weepers by the waters of

Babylon rather than those who barred the doors of the Assembly against them. Describe Miss Parmore's white tulle to her pupils, indeed! What she meant – but how accomplish it? – was to get cards for the Assembly for Mrs St George and Virginia, and to see to it that the latter's dress outdid Miss Parmore's as much as her beauty over-shadowed that young woman's.

But how? Through Lord Richard Marable? Well, that was per-haps not impossible . . . Miss Testvalley had detected, in Mrs Parmore, a faint but definite desire to make the young man's acquaintance, even to have him on the list of her next dinner. She would like to show him, poor young fellow, her manner implied, that there are houses in New York where a scion of the English aristocracy may feel himself at home, and discover (though, alas, too late!) that there are American girls comparable to his own sisters in education and breeding.

Since the announcement of Conchita's engagement, and the return of the two families to New York, there had been a good deal of coming and going between the St George and Closson house-holds – rather too much to suit Miss Testvalley. But she had early learned to adapt herself to her pupils' whims while maintaining her authority over them, and she preferred to accompany Nan to the Fifth Avenue Hotel rather than let her go there without her. Virginia, being 'out', could come and go as she pleased; but among the Par-mores and Eglintons, in whose code Mrs St George was profoundly versed, girls in the school-room did not walk about New York alone, much less call at hotels, and Nan, fuming yet resigned – for she had already grown unaccountably attached to her governess – had to submit to Miss Testvalley's conducting her to the Closson apartment, and waiting below when she was to be fetched. Sometimes, at Mrs Closson's request, the governess went in with her charge. Mrs Clos-son was almost always in her sitting-room, since leaving it necessi-tated encasing her soft frame in stays and a heavily whale-boned dress; and she preferred sitting at her piano, or lying on the sofa with a novel and a cigarette, in an atmosphere of steam-heat and heavily scented flowers, and amid a litter of wedding presents and bridal finery. She was a good-natured woman, friendly and even confiden-tial with everybody who came her way, and when she caught sight of Miss Testvalley behind her charge, often called to her to come in and take a look at the lovely dress Mrs Connelly had just sent home, or the embossed soup-tureen of Baltimore silver offered by Mr Closson's business friends. Miss Testvalley did not always accept; but sometimes she divined that Mrs Closson wished to consult her, or to confide in her, and, while her pupil joined the other girls, she would clear the finery from a chair and prepare to receive Mrs Closson's confidences – which were usually connected with points of social etiquette, indifferent to the lady herself, but preoccupying to Mr Closson.

'He thinks it's funny that Dick's family haven't cabled, or even written. Do they generally do so in England? I tell Mr Closson there hasn't been time yet – I'm so bad about answering letters myself that I can't blame anybody else for not writing! But Mr Closson seems to think it's meant for a slight. Why should it be? If Dick's family are not satisfied with Conchita, they will be when they see her, don't you think so?' Yes, certainly, Miss Testvalley thought so. 'Well, then – what's the use of worrying? But Mr Closson is a business man, and he expects everybody to have business habits. I don't suppose the Marquess is in business, is he?'

Miss Testvalley said no, she thought not; and for a moment there flickered up in Mrs Closson a languid curiosity to know more of her daughter's future relatives. 'It's a big family, isn't it? Dick says he can never remember how many brothers and sisters he has; but I suppose that's one of his jokes . . . He's a great joker, isn't he; like my Ted! Those two are always playing tricks on everybody. But how many brothers and sisters are there, really?'

Miss Testvalley, after a moment's calculation, gave the number as eight; Lord Seadown, the heir, Lord John, Lord Richard – and five girls; yes, there were five girls. Only one married as yet; the Lady Camilla. Her own charges, the Ladies Honoria and Ulrica, were now out; the other two were still in the school-room. Yes; it was a large family – but not so very large, as English families went. Large enough, however, to preoccupy Lady Brightlingsea a good deal – especially as concerned the future of her daughters.

Mrs Closson listened with her dreamy smile. Her attention had none of the painful precision with which Mrs St George tried to master the details of social life in the higher spheres, nor of the eager curiosity gleaming under Mrs Parmore's pale eyelashes. Mrs

Closson really could not see that there was much difference between one human being and another, except that some had been favoured with more leisure than others – and leisure was her idea of heaven.

'I should think Lady Brightlingsea would be worn out, with all those girls to look after. I don't suppose she's had much time to think about the boys.'

'Well, of course she's devoted to her sons too.'

'Oh, I suppose so. And you say the other two sons are not married?' No, not as yet, Miss Testvalley repeated.

A flicker of interest was again perceptible between Mrs Closson's drowsy lids. 'If they don't either of them marry, Dick will be the Marquess some day, won't he?'

Miss Testvalley could not restrain a faint amusement. 'But Lord Seadown is certain to marry. In those great houses it's a family obligation for the heir to marry.'

Mrs Closson's head sank back contentedly. 'Mercy! How many obligations they all seem to have. I guess Conchita'll be happier just making a love-match with Lord Richard. He's passionately in love with her, isn't he?' Mrs Closson pursued with her confidential smile.

'It would appear so, certainly,' Miss Testvalley rejoined.

'All I want is that she should be happy; and he *will* make her happy, won't he?' the indulgent mother concluded, as though Miss Testvalley's words had completely reassured her.

At that moment the door was flung open, and the bride herself whirled into the room. 'Oh, mother!' Conchita paused to greet Miss Testvalley; her manner, like her mother's, was always considerate and friendly. 'You're not coming to take Nan away already, are you?' Reassured by Miss Testvalley, she put her hands on her hips and spun lightly around in front of the two ladies.

'Mother! Isn't it a marvel? – It's my Assembly dress,' she explained, laughing, to the governess.

It was indeed a marvel; the money these American mothers spent on their daughters' clothes never ceased to astonish Miss Testvalley; but while her appreciative eye registered every costly detail her mind was busy with the incredible fact that Conchita Closson – 'the Closson girl' in Mrs Parmore's vocabulary – had contrived to get an invitation to the Assembly, while her own charges, who were so much lovelier and more lovable . . . But here they were, Virginia, Nan, and Lizzy Elmsworth, all circling gaily about the future bride, applauding, criticizing, twitching as critically at her ruffles and ribbons as though these were to form a part of their own adornment. Miss Testvalley, looking closely, saw no trace of envy in their radiant faces, though Virginia's was perhaps a trifle sad. 'So they've not been invited to the ball, and Conchita *has*,' she reflected, and felt a sudden irritation against Miss Closson.

But the irritation did not last. This was Mrs Parmore's doing, the governess was sure; to secure Lord Richard she had no doubt persuaded the patronesses of the Assembly – that stern tribunal – to include his fiancée among their guests. Only – how had she, or the others, managed to accept the idea of introducing the fiancée's mother into their hallowed circle? The riddle was answered by Mrs Closson herself. 'First I was afraid I'd have to take Conchita – just imagine it! Get up out of my warm bed in the middle of the night, and rig myself up in satin and whale-bones, and feathers on my head – they say I'd have had to wear feathers!' Mrs Closson laughed luxuriously over this plumed and armoured vision, 'But luckily they didn't even invite me. They invited my son instead – it seems in New York a girl can go to a ball with her brother, even to an Assembly ball . . . and Conchita was so crazy to accept that Mr Closson said we'd better let her . . .'

Conchita spun around again, her flexible arms floating like a dancer's on her outspread flounces. 'Oh, girls, it's a perfect shame you're not coming too! They ought to have invited all my bridesmaids, oughtn't they, Miss Testvalley?' She spoke with evident good will, and the governess reflected how different Miss Parmore's view would have been, had she been invited to an exclusive entertainment from which her best friends were omitted. But then no New York entertainment excluded Miss Parmore's friends.

Miss Testvalley, as she descended the stairs, turned the problem over in her mind. She had never liked her girls (as she already called them) as much as she did at that moment. Nan, of course, was a child, and could comfort herself with the thought that her time for ball-going had not yet come; but Virginia – well, Virginia, whom Miss Testvalley had not altogether learned to like, was behaving as generously as her sister. Her quick hands had displaced the rosegarland on Conchita's shoulder, re-arranging it in a more becoming way. Conchita was careless about her toilet, and had there been any malice in Virginia she might have spoilt her friend's dress instead of improving it. No act of generosity appealed in vain to Miss Testvalley, and as she went down the stairs to the hotel entrance she muttered to herself: 'If I only could – if I only knew how!'

7

She was so busy with her thoughts that she was startled by the appearance, at the foot of the stairs, of a young man who stood there visibly waiting.

'Lord Richard!' she exclaimed, almost as surprised as when she had first recognized him, disguised in grimy overalls, at the Saratoga station.

Since then she had, of necessity, run across him now and then, at the St Georges' as well as at Mrs Closson's; but if he had not perceptibly avoided her, neither had he sought her out, and for that she was thankful. The Lord Richard chapter was a closed one, and she had no wish to re-open it. She had paid its cost in some brief fears and joys, and one night of agonizing tears; but perhaps her Italian blood had saved her from ever, then or after, regarding it as a moral issue. In her busy life there was no room for dead love-affairs; and besides, did the word 'love' apply to such passing follies? Fatalistically, she had registered the episode and pigeon-holed it. If ever she were to know an abiding grief it must be caused by one that engaged the soul.

Lord Richard stood before her awkwardly. He was always either sullen or too hearty, and she hoped he was not going to be hearty. But perhaps since those days life had formed him . . .

'I saw you go upstairs just now – and I waited.'

'You waited? For me?'

'Yes,' he muttered, still more awkwardly. 'Could I speak to you?'

Miss Testvalley reflected. She could not imagine what he wanted, but experience told her that it would almost certainly be something disagreeable. However, it was not her way to avoid issues – and perhaps he only wanted to borrow money. She could not give him much, of course . . . but if it were only that, so much the better. 'We can go in there, I suppose,' she said, pointing to the door of the public sitting-room. She lifted the *portière*, and finding the room empty, led the way to a ponderous rose-wood sofa. Lord Richard shambled after her, and seated himself on the other side of the table before the sofa.

'You'd better be quick – there are always people here receiving visitors.'

The young man, thus admonished, was still silent. He sat sideways on his chair, as though to avoid facing Miss Testvalley. A frown drew the shock of drab hair still lower over his low forehead, and he pulled nervously at his drab moustache.

'Well?' said Miss Testvalley.

'I – look here. I'm no hand at explaining . . . never was . . . But you were always a friend of mine . . .'

'I've no wish to be otherwise.'

His frown relaxed slightly. 'I never know how to say things . . .'

'What is it you wish to say?'

'I – well, Mr Closson asked me yesterday if there was any reason why I shouldn't marry Conchita.'

His eyes still avoided her, but she kept hers resolutely on his face. 'Do you know what made him ask?'

'Well, you see – there's been no word from home. I rather fancy he expected the governor to write, or even to cable. They seem to do such a lot of cabling in this country, don't they?'

Miss Testvalley reflected. 'How long ago did you write? Has there been time enough for an answer to come? It's not likely that your family would cable.'

Lord Richard looked embarrassed; which meant, she suspected, that his letter had not been sent as promptly as he had let the Clossons believe. Sheer dilatoriness might even have kept him from sending it at all. 'You have written, I suppose?' she enquired sternly.

'Oh, yes, I've written.'

'And told them everything – I mean about Miss Closson's family?'

'Of course,' he repeated, rather sulkily. 'I haven't got much of a head for that kind of thing; but I got Santos-Dios to write it all out for me.'

'Then you'll certainly have an answer. No doubt it's on the way now.'

'It ought to be. But Mr Closson's always in such a devil of a hurry. Everybody's in a hurry in America. He asked me if there was any reason why my people shouldn't write.'

'Well – is there?'

Lord Richard turned in his chair, and glanced at her with an uncomfortable laugh. 'You must see now what I'm driving at.'

'No, I don't. Unless you count on me to reassure the Clossons?'

'No –. Only, if they should take it into their heads to question you . . .'

She felt a faint shiver of apprehension. To question her – about what? Did he imagine that any one, at this hour, and at this far end of the world, would disinter that old unhappy episode? If this was what he feared, it meant her career to begin all over again, those poor old ancestors of Denmark Hill without support or comfort, and no one on earth to help her to her feet . . . She lifted her head sternly. 'Nonsense, Lord Richard – speak out.'

'Well, the fact is, I know my mother blurted out all that stupid business to you before I left Allfriars – I mean about the cheque,' he muttered half-audibly.

Miss Testvalley suddenly became aware that her heart had stopped beating by the violent plunge of relief it now gave. Her whole future, for a moment, had hung there in the balance. And after all, it was only the cheque he was thinking of. Now she didn't care what happened! She even saw, in a flash, that she had him at a disadvantage, and her past fear nerved her to use her opportunity.

'Yes, your mother did, as you say, blurt out something . . .'

The young man, his elbows on the table, had crossed his hands and rested his chin on them. She knew what he was waiting for – but she let him wait.

'I was a poor young fool – I didn't half know what I was doing . . . My father was damned hard on me, you know.'

'I think he was,' said Miss Testvalley.

Lord Richard lifted his head and looked at her. He hardly ever smiled, but when he did his face cleared, and became almost boyish again, as though a mask had been removed from it. 'You're a brick, Laura – you always were.'

'We're not here to discuss my merits, Lord Richard. Indeed you seem to have doubted them a moment ago.' He stared, and she remembered that subtlety was always lost on him. 'You imagined, knowing that I was in your mother's confidence, that I might betray it. Was that it?'

His look of embarrassment returned. 'I – you're so hard on a fellow . . .'

'I don't want to be hard on you. But, since you suspected I might tell your secrets, you must excuse my suspecting *you* –'

'Me? Of what?'

Miss Testvalley was silent. A hundred thoughts rushed through her brain – preoccupations both grave and trivial. It had always been thus with her, and she could never see that it was otherwise with life itself, where unimportant trifles and grave anxieties so often darkened the way with their joint shadows. At Nan St George's age, Miss Testvalley, though already burdened with the care and responsi- bilities of middle life, had longed with all Nan's longing to wear white tulle and be invited to a ball. She had never been invited to a ball, had never worn white tulle; and now, at nearly forty, and scarred by hardships and disappointments, she still felt that early pang, still wondered what, in life, ought to be classed as trifling, and what as grave. She looked again at Lord Richard. 'No,' she said, 'I've only one stipulation to make.'

He cleared his throat. 'Er – yes?'

'Lord Richard – are you truly and sincerely in love with Conchita?'

The young man's sallow face crimsoned to the roots of his hair, and even his freckled hands, with their short square fingers, grew red. 'In love with her?' he stammered. 'I . . . I never saw a girl that could touch her . . .'

There was something curiously familiar about the phrase; and she reflected that the young man had not renewed his vocabulary. Miss Testvalley smiled faintly. 'Conchita's very charming,' she continued. 'I wouldn't for the world have anything   anything that I could prevent – endanger her happiness.'

Lord Richard's flush turned to a sudden pallor. 'I – I swear to you I'd shoot myself sooner than let anything harm a hair of her head.'

Miss Testvalley was silent again. Lord Richard stirred uneasily in his chair, and she saw that he was trying to interpret her meaning. She stood up and gathered her old beaded dolman about her shoulders. 'I mean to believe you, Lord Richard,' she announced abruptly. 'I hope I'm not wrong.'

'Wrong? God bless you, Laura.' He held out his blunt hand. 'I'll never forget – never.'

'Never forget your promise about Conchita. That's all I ask.' She began to move toward the door, and slowly, awkwardly, he moved at her side. On the threshold she turned back to him. 'No, it's not all – there's something else.' His face clouded again, and his look of alarm moved her. Poor blundering boy that he still was! Perhaps his father *had* been too hard on him.

'What I'm going to ask is a trifle . . . yet at that age nothing is a trifle . . . Lord Richard, I'll back you up through thick and thin if you'll manage to get Miss Closson's bridesmaids invited to the Assembly ball next week.'

He looked at her in bewilderment. 'The Assembly ball?'

'Yes. They've invited you, I know; and your fiancée. In New York it's considerd a great honour – almost' (she smiled) 'like being invited to Court in England . . .'

'Oh, come,' he interjected. 'There's nothing like a Court here.'

'No; but this is the nearest approach. And my two girls, the St Georges, and their friends the Elmsworths, are not very well-known in the fashionable set which manages the Assemblies. Of course they can't all be invited; and indeed Nan is too young for balls. But Virginia St George and Lizzy Elmsworth ought not to be left out. Such things hurt young people cruelly. They've just been helping Conchita to arrange her dress, knowing all the while they were not going themselves. I thought it charming of them . . .'

Lord Richard stood before her in perplexity. 'I'm dreadfully sorry. It is hard on them, certainly. I'd forgotten all about that ball. But can't their parents –?'

'Their parents, I'm afraid, are the obstacle.'

He bent his puzzled eyes on the ground, but at length light seemed to break on him. 'Oh, I see. They're not in the right set? They seem to think a lot about sets in the States, don't they?'

'Enormously. But as you've been invited – through Mrs Parmore, I understand – and Mr de Santos-Dios also, you two, between you, can certainly get invitations for Virginia and Lizzy. You can count on me, Lord Richard, and I shall count on you. I've never asked you a favour before, have I?'

'Oh, but I say – I'd do anything, of course. But how the devil can I, when I'm a stranger here?'

'Because you're a stranger – because you're Lord Richard Marable. I should think you need only ask one of the patronesses. Or that clever monkey Santos-Dios will help you, as he has with your correspondence.' Lord Richard reddened. 'In any case,' Miss Testvalley continued, 'I don't wish to know how you do it; and of course you must not say that it's my suggestion. Any mention of that would ruin everything. But you must get those invitations, Lord Richard.'

She held him for a second with her quick decisive smile, just touched his hand, and walked out of the hotel.

New York society in the 'seventies was a nursery of young beauties, and Mrs Parmore and Mrs Eglinton would have told any newcomer from the old world that he would see at an Assembly ball faces to outrival all the court-beauties of Europe. There were rumours, now and then, that others even surpassing the Assembly standard had been seen at the Opera (on off-nights, when the fashionable let, or gave away, their boxes, or at such promiscuous annual entertainments as the Charity ball, the Seventh Regiment ball, and so on. And of late, more particularly, people had been talking of a Miss Closson, daughter or step-daughter of a Mr Closson, who was a stock-broker or railway-director – or was he a coffee planter in South America? The facts about Mr Closson were few and vague, but he had a certain notoriety in Wall Street and on the fashionable race-courses, and had now come into newspaper prominence through the engagement of his daughter (or step-daughter) to Lord Richard Marable, a younger son of the Marquess of Brightlingsea . . . (No, my dear, you must pronounce it Brittlesey.) Some of the fashionable young men had met Miss Closson, and spoken favourably, even enthusiastically, of her charms; but then young men are always attracted by novelty, and by a slight flavour of, shall we say fastness, or anything just a trifle off-colour?

The Assembly ladies felt it would be surprising if any Miss Closson could compete in loveliness with Miss Alida Parmore, Miss Julia

Vandercamp, or, among the married, with the radiant Mrs Casimir Dulac, or Mrs Fred Alston, who had been a van der Luyden. They were not afraid, as they gathered on the shining floor of Delmonico's ball-room, of any challenge to the supremacy of these beauties.

Miss Closson's arrival was, nevertheless, awaited with a certain curiosity. Mrs Parmore had been very clever about her invitation. It was impossible to invite Lord Richard without his fiancée, since their wedding was to take place the following week; and the ladies were eager to let a scion of the British nobility see what a New York Assembly had to show. But to invite the Closson parents was obviously impossible. No one knew who they were, or where they came from (beyond the vague tropical background), and Mrs Closson was said to be a *divorcée*, and to lie in bed all day smoking enormous cigars. But Mrs Parmore, whose daughter's former governess was now with a family who knew the Clossons, had learned that there was a Closson step-son, a clever little fellow with a Spanish name, who was a great friend of Lord Richard's, and was to be his best man; and of course it was perfectly proper to invite Miss Closson with her own brother. One or two of the more conservative patronesses had indeed wavered, and asked what further concessions this might lead to; but Mrs Parmore's party gained the day, and rich was their reward, for at the eleventh hour Mrs Parmore was able to announce that Lord Richard's sisters, the Ladies Ulrica and Honoria, had unexpectedly arrived for their brother's wedding, and were anxious, they too – could anything be more gratifying? – to accompany him to the ball.

Their appearance, for a moment, over-shadowed Miss Closson's; yet perhaps (or so some of the young men said afterward) each of the three girls was set off by the charms of the others. They were so complementary in their graces, each seemed to have been so especially created by Providence, and adorned by coiffeur and dressmaker, to make part of that matchless trio, that their entrance was a sight long remembered, not only by the young men thronging about them to be introduced but by the elderly gentlemen who surveyed them from a distance with critical and reminiscent eyes. The patronesses, whose own daughters risked a momentary eclipse, were torn between fears and admiration; but after all these lovely English girls, one so dazzlingly fair, the other so darkly vivid, who

framed Miss Closson in their contrasting beauty were only transient visitors; and Miss Closson was herself soon to rejoin them in
England, and might some day, as the daughter-in-law of a Marquess, remember gratefully that New York had set its social seal on
her.

No such calculations troubled the dancing men. They had found
three new beauties to waltz with – and how they waltzed! The
rumour that London dancing was far below the New York standard
was not likely to find credit with any one who had danced with the
Ladies Marable. The tall fair one – was she the Lady Honoria? –
was perhaps the more harmonious in her movements; but the Lady
Ulrica, as befitted her flashing good looks, was as nimble as a gipsy;
and if Conchita Closson polka-ed and waltzed as well as the English
girls, these surpassed her in the gliding elegance of the square
dances.

At supper they were as bewitching as on the floor. Nowhere in the
big supper-room, about the flower-decked tables, was the talk mer-
rier, the laughter louder (a shade too loud, perhaps? – but that may
have been the fault of the young men), than in the corner where the
three girls, enclosed in a dense body-guard of admirers, feasted on
champagne and terrapin. As Mrs Eglinton, with some bitterness,
afterward remarked to Mrs Parmore, it was absurd to say that English girls had no conversation, when these charming creatures had
chattered all night like magpies. She hoped it would teach their own
girls that there were moments when a little innocent *abandon* was not
unsuitable.

In the small hours of the same night a knock at her door waked Miss
Testvalley out of an uneasy sleep. She sat up with a start, and lighting her candle beheld a doleful little figure in a beribboned pink
wrapper.

'Why, Annabel – aren't you well?' she exclaimed, setting down her
candle beside the Book of Common Prayer and the small volume of
poems which always lay together on her night-table.

'Oh, don't call me Annabel, please! I can't sleep, and I feel so
lonely . . .'

'My poor Nan! Come and sit on the bed. What's the matter, child?
You're half frozen!' Miss Testvalley, thankful that before going to bed

she had wound her white net scarf over her crimping-pins, sat up
and drew the quilt around her pupil.

'I'm not frozen; I'm just lonely. I *did* want to go to that ball,' Nan
confessed, throwing her arms about her governess.

'Well, my dear, there'll be plenty of other balls for you when the
time comes.'

'Oh, but will there? I'm not a bit sure; and Jinny's not either. She
only got asked to this one because Lord Richard fixed it up. I don't
know how he did it; but I suppose those old Assembly scare-crows
are such snobs –'

'Annabel!'

'Oh, bother! When you know they are. If they hadn't been,
wouldn't they have invited Jinny and Lizzy long ago to all their
parties?'

'I don't think that question need trouble us. Now that your sister
and Lizzy Elmsworth have been seen they're sure to be invited again;
and when your turn comes . . .'

Suddenly she felt herself pushed back against her pillows by her
pupil's firm young hands. 'Miss Testvalley! How can you talk like
that, when you know the only way they got invited –'

Miss Testvalley, rearing herself up severely, shook off Nan's clutch.
'Annabel! I've no idea how they were invited; I can't imagine what
you mean. And I must ask you not to be impertinent.'

Nan gazed at her for a moment, and then buried her face among
the pillows in a wild rush of laughter.

'Annabel!' the governess repeated, still more severely; but Nan's
shoulders continued to shake with mirth.

'My dear, you told me you'd waked me up because you felt lonely.
If all you wanted was some one to giggle with, you'd better go back
to bed, and wait for your sister to come home.'

Nan lifted a penitent countenance to her governess. 'Oh, she
won't be home for hours. And I promise I won't laugh any more.
Only it *is* so funny! But do let me stay a little longer; please! Read
aloud to me, there's a darling; read me some poetry, won't you?'

She wriggled down under the bed-quilt, and crossing her arms
behind her, laid her head back against them, so that her brown curls
overflowed on the pillow. Her face had grown wistful again, and her
eyes were full of entreaty.

Miss Testvalley reached out for *Hymns Ancient and Modern*. But after a moment's hesitation she put it back beside the prayer-book, and took up instead the volume of poetry which always accompanied her on her travels.

'Now listen; listen very quietly, or I won't go on.' Almost solemnly she began to read.

> 'The blessèd damozel leaned out
>   From the gold bar of Heaven:
> Her eyes were deeper than the depth
>   Of waters stilled at even;
> She had three lilies in her hand,
>   And the stars in her hair were seven.'

Miss Testvalley read slowly, chantingly, with a rich murmur of vowels, and a lingering stress on the last word of the last line, as though it symbolized something grave and mysterious. *Seven . . .*

'That's lovely,' Nan sighed. She lay motionless, her eyes wide, her lips a little parted.

> 'Her robe, ungirt from clasp to hem,
>   No wrought flowers did adorn,
> But a white rose of Mary's gift . . .'

'I shouldn't have cared much for that kind of dress, should you? I suppose it had angel sleeves, if she was in heaven. When I go to my first ball I want to have a dress that *fits*; and I'd like it to be pale blue velvet, embroidered all over with seed-pearls, like I saw . . .'

'My dear, if you want to talk about ball-dresses, I should advise you to go to the sewing-room and get the maid's copy of *Butterick's Magazine*,' said Miss Testvalley icily.

'No, no! I want to hear the poem – I do! Please read it to me, Miss Testvalley. See how good I am.'

Miss Testvalley resumed her reading. The harmonious syllables flowed on, weaving their passes about the impatient young head on the pillow. Presently Miss Testvalley laid the book aside, and folding her hands continued her murmur of recital.

> 'And still she bowed herself and stooped
>   Out of the circling charm;

> *Until her bosom must have made*
> *The bar she leaned on warm . . .'*

She paused, hesitating for the next line, and Nan's drowsy eyes drifted to her face. 'How heavenly! But you know it all by heart.'

'Oh, yes; I know it by heart.'

'I never heard anything so lovely. Who wrote it?'

'My cousin, Dante Gabriel.'

'Your own cousin?' Nan's eyes woke up.

'Yes, dear. Listen:

> *'And the lilies lay as if asleep*
> *Along her bended arm . . .*
>
> *The sun was gone now; the curled moon*
> *Was like a little feather . . .'*

'Do you mean to say he's your very own cousin? Aren't you madly in love with him, Miss Testvalley?'

'Poor Dante Gabriel! My dear, he's a widower, and very stout – and has caused all the family a good deal of trouble.'

Nan's face fell. 'Oh – a widower? What a pity . . . If I had a cousin who was a poet I should be madly in love with him. And I should desert my marble palace to flee with him to the isles of Greece.'

'Ah – and when are you going to live in a marble palace?'

'When I'm an ambassadress, of course. Lord Richard says that ambassadresses . . . Oh, darling, don't stop! I do long to hear the rest . . . I do, really . . .'

Miss Testvalley resumed her recital, sinking her voice as she saw Nan's lids gradually sink over her questioning eyes till at last the long lashes touched her cheeks. Miss Testvalley murmured on, ever more softly, to the end; then, blowing out the candle, she slid down to Nan's side so gently that the sleeper did not move. 'She might have been my own daughter,' the governess thought, composing her narrow frame to rest, and listening in the darkness to Nan's peaceful breathing.

Miss Testvalley did not fall asleep herself. She lay speculating rather nervously over the meaning of her pupil's hysterical burst of giggling. She was delighted that Lord Richard had succeeded in getting invitations to the ball for Virginia and Lizzy Elmsworth; but she could not understand why Nan regarded his having done so as particularly droll. Probably, she reflected, it was because the invitations had been asked for and obtained without Mrs St George's knowledge. Everything was food for giggles when that light-hearted company were together, and nothing amused them more than to play a successful trick on Mrs St George. In any case, the girls had had their evening – and a long evening it must have been, since the late winter dawn was chilling the windows when Miss Testvalley at length heard Virginia on the stairs.

Lord Richard Marable, as it turned out, had underrated his family's interest in his projected marriage. No doubt, as Miss Testvalley had surmised, his announcement of the event had been late in reaching them; but the day before the wedding a cable came. It was not, however, addressed to Lord Richard, or to his bride, but to Miss Testvalley, who, having opened it with surprise (for she had never before received a cable) read it in speechless perplexity.

'Is she black his anguished mother Selina Brightlingsea.'

For some time the governess pored in vain over this cryptic communication; but at last light came to her, and she leaned her head back against her chair and laughed. She understood just what must have happened. Though there were two splendid globes, terrestrial and celestial, at opposite ends of the Allfriars library, no one in the house had ever been known to consult them; and Lady Brightlingsea's geographical notions, even measured by the family standard, were notoriously hazy. She could not imagine why any one should ever want to leave England, and her idea of the continent was one enormous fog from which two places called Paris and Rome indistinctly emerged; while the whole western hemisphere was little more clear to her than to the fore-runners of Columbus. But Miss Testvalley remembered that on one wall of the Vandyke saloon, where the family sometimes sat after dinner, there hung a great tapestry, brilliant in colour, rich and elaborate in design, in the foreground of which a shapely young Negress flanked by ruddy savages and attended by parakeets and monkeys was seen offering a tribute of tropical fruits to a lolling divinity. The housekeeper, Miss Testvalley also remembered, in showing this tapestry to visitors, on the day when Allfriars was open to the public, always designated it as 'The Spanish Main and the Americas – ' and what could be more natural than that poor bewildered Lady Brightlingsea should connect her son's halting explanations with this instructive scene?

Miss Testvalley pondered for a long time over her reply; then, for once forgetting to make a 'governess's answer', she cabled back to Lady Brightlingsea: 'No, but comely.'

BOOK TWO

8

On a June afternoon of the year 1875 one of the biggest carriages in London drew up before one of the smallest houses in Mayfair – the very smallest in that exclusive quarter, its occupant, Miss Jacqueline March, always modestly averred.

The tiny dwelling, a mere two-windowed wedge, with a bulging balcony under a striped awning, had been newly painted a pale buff, and freshly festooned with hanging pink geraniums and intensely blue lobelias. The carriage, on the contrary, a vast old-fashioned barouche of faded yellow, with impressive armorial bearings, and coachman and footman to scale, showed no signs of recent renovation; and the lady who descended from it was, like her conveyance, large and rather shabby though undeniably impressive.

A freshly starched parlour-maid let her in with a curtsey of recognition. 'Miss March is in the drawing-room my lady.' She led the visitor up the narrow stairs and announced from the threshold: 'Please, Miss, Lady Brightlingsea.'

Two ladies sat in the drawing-room in earnest talk. One of the two was vaguely perceived by Lady Brightlingsea to be small and brown, with burning black eyes which did not seem to go with her stiff purple poplin and old-fashioned beaded dolman.

The other lady was also very small, but extremely fair and elegant, with natural blond curls touched with grey, and a delicate complexion. She hurried hospitably forward.

'Dearest Lady Brightlingsea! What a delightful surprise! – You're not going to leave us, Laura?'

It was clear that the dark lady addressed as Laura was meant to do exactly what her hostess suggested she should not. She pressed the latter's hand in a resolute brown kid glove, bestowed a bow and a slanting curtsey on the Marchioness of Brightlingsea, and was out of the room with the ease and promptness of a person long practised in self-effacement.

Lady Brightlingsea sent a vague glance after the retreating figure. 'Now who was that, my dear? I seem to know . . .'

Miss March, who had a touch of firmness under her deprecating exterior, replied without hesitation: 'An old friend, dear Lady Bright-lingsea, Miss Testvalley, who used to be governess to the Duchess's younger girls at Tintagel.'

Lady Brightlingsea's long pale face grew still vaguer. 'At Tintagel? Oh, but of course. It was I who recommended her to Blanche Tintagel . . . Testvalley? The name is so odd. She was with us, you know; she was with Honoria and Ulrica before Madame Champion-net finished them.'

'Yes. I remember you used to think well of her. I believe it was at Allfriars I first met her.'

Lady Brightlingsea looked plaintively at Miss March. Her face always grew plaintive when she was asked to squeeze one more fact – even one already familiar – into her weary and over-crowded memory. 'Oh, yes . . . oh, yes!'

Miss March, glancing brightly at her guest, as though to re-animate the latter's failing energy, added: 'I wish she could have stayed. You might have been interested in her experiences in America.'

'In America?' Lady Brightlingsea's vagueness was streaked by a gleam of interest. 'She's been in America?'

'In the States. In fact, I think she was governess to that new beauty who's being talked about a good deal just now. A Miss St George – Virginia St George. You may have heard of her?'

Lady Brightlingsea sighed at this new call upon her powers of concentration. 'I hear of nothing but Americans. My son's house is always full of them.'

'Oh, yes; and I believe Miss St George is a particular friend of Lady Richard's.'

'Very likely. Is she from the same part of the States – from Brazil?'

Miss March, who was herself a native of the States, had in her youth been astonished at enquiries of this kind, and slightly resentful of them; but long residence in England, and a desire to appear at home in her adopted country, had accustomed her to such geogra-phy as Lady Brightlingsea's. 'Slightly farther north, I think,' she said.

'Ah? But they make nothing of distances in those countries, do they? Is this new young woman rich?' asked Lady Brightlingsea abruptly.

Miss March reflected, and then decided to say: 'According to Miss Testvalley the St Georges appear to live in great luxury.'

Lady Brightlingsea sank back wearily. 'That means nothing. My daughter-in-law's people do that too. But the man has never paid her settlements. Her step-father, I mean – I never can remember any of their names. I don't see how they can tell each other apart, all herded together, without any titles or distinctions. It's unfortunate that Richard did nothing about settlements; and now, barely two years after their marriage, the man says he can't go on paying his step-daughter's allowance. And I'm afraid the young people owe a great deal of money.'

Miss March heaved a deep sigh of sympathy. 'A bad coffee-year, I suppose.'

'That's what he says. But how can one tell? Do you suppose those other people would lend them the money?'

Miss March counted it as one of the many privileges of living in London that two or three times a year her friend Lady Brightlingsea came to see her. In Miss March's youth a great tragedy had befallen her – a sorrow which had darkened all her days. It had befallen her in London, and all her American friends – and they were many – had urged her to return at once to her home in New York. A proper sense of dignity, they insisted, should make it impossible for her to remain in a society where she had been so cruelly, so publicly offended. Miss March listened, hesitated – and finally remained in London. 'They simply don't know,' she explained to an American friend who also lived there, 'what they're asking me to give up.' And the friend sighed her assent.

'The first years will be difficult,' Miss March had continued courageously, 'but I think in the end I shan't be sorry.' And she was right. At first she had been only a poor little pretty American who had been jilted by an eminent nobleman; yes, and after the wedding-dress was ordered – the countermanding of that wedding-dress had long been one of her most agonizing memories. But since the unhappy date over thirty years had slipped by; and gradually, as they passed, and as people found out how friendly and obliging she was, and what a sweet little house she lived in, she had become the centre of a circle of warm friends, and the oracle of transatlantic pilgrims in quest of a social opening. These pilgrims had learned that Jacky March's narrow front door led straight into the London world, and a number had already slipped in through it. Miss March had a kind heart, and could never resist doing a friend a good turn; and if her services were sometimes rewarded by a cheque, or a new drawing-room carpet, or a chinchilla tippet and muff, she saw no harm in this way of keeping herself and her house in good shape. 'After all, if my friends are kind enough to come here, I want my house and myself, tiny as we both are, to be presentable.'

All this passed through Miss March's active mind while she sat listening to Lady Brightlingsea. Even should friendship so incline them, she doubted if the St George family would be able to come to the aid of the young Dick Marables, but there might be combinations, arrangements – who could tell? Laura Testvalley might enlighten her. It was never Miss March's policy to oppose a direct refusal to a friend.

'Dear Lady Brightlingsea, I'm so dreadfully distressed at what you tell me.'

'Yes. It's certainly very unlucky. And most trying for my husband. And I'm afraid poor Dick's not behaving as well as he might. After all, as he says, he's been deceived.'

Miss March knew that this applied to Lady Richard's money and not to her morals, and she sighed again. 'Mr St George was a business associate of Mr Closson's at one time, I believe. Those people generally back each other up. But of course they all have their ups and downs. At any rate I'll see, I'll make enquiries . . .'

'Their ways are so odd, you know,' Lady Brightlingsea pursued. It never seemed to occur to her that Miss March was one of 'them', and Miss March emitted a murmur of sympathy, for these new people seemed as alien to her as to her visitor. 'So very odd. And they speak so fast – I can't understand them. But I suppose one would get used to that. What I *cannot* see is their beauty – the young girls, I mean. They toss about so – they're never still. And they don't know how to carry themselves.' She paused to add in a lower tone: 'I believe my daughter-in-law dances to some odd instrument – quite like a ballet dancer. I hope her skirts are not as short. And sings in Spanish. Is Spanish their native language still?'

Miss March, despairing of making it clear to Lady Brightlingsea that Brazil was not one of the original Thirteen States, evaded this by saying: 'You must remember they've not had the social training which only a Court can give. But some of them seem to learn very quickly.'

'Oh, I hope so,' Lady Brightlingsea exclaimed, as if clutching at a floating spar. Slowly she drew herself up from the sofa-corner. She was so tall that the ostrich plumes on her bonnet might have brushed Miss March's ceiling had they not drooped instead of towering. Miss March had often wondered how her friend managed to have such an air of majesty when everything about her flopped and dangled. 'Ah – it's their secret,' she thought, and rejoiced that at least she could recognize and admire the attribute in her noble English friends. So many of her travelling compatriots seemed not to understand, or even to perceive, the difference. They were the ones who could not see what she 'got out' of her little London house, and her little London life.

Lady Brightlingsea stood in the middle of the room, looking uncertainly about her. At last she said: 'We're going out of town in a fortnight. You must come down to Allfriars later, you know.'

Miss March's heart leapt up under her trim black satin bodice. (She wore black often, to set off her still fair complexion.) She could never quite master the excitement of an invitation to Allfriars. In London she did not expect even to be offered a meal; the Brightlingseas always made a short season, and there were so many important people whom they had to invite. Besides, being asked down to stay in the country, *en famille*, was really much more flattering – more intimate. Miss March felt herself blushing to the roots of her fair curls. 'It's so kind of you, dear Lady Brightlingsea. Of course you know there's nothing I should like better. I'm never as happy anywhere as at Allfriars.'

Lady Brightlingsea gave a mirthless laugh. 'You're not like my daughter-in-law. She says she'd as soon spend a month in the family vault. In fact she'd never be with us at all if they hadn't had to let their house for the season.'

Miss March's murmur of horror was inarticulate. Words failed her. These dreadful new Americans – would London ever be able to educate them? In her confusion she followed Lady Brightlingsea to the landing without speaking. There her visitor suddenly turned toward her. 'I wish we could marry Seadown,' she said.

This allusion to the heir of the Brightlingseas was a fresh surprise to Miss March. 'But surely – in Lord Seadown's case it will be only too easy,' she suggested with a playful smile.

Lady Brightlingsea produced no answering smile. 'You must have heard, I suppose, of his wretched entanglement with Lady Churt. It's much worse, you know, than if she were a disreputable woman. She costs him a great deal more, I mean. And we've tried everything . . . But he won't look at a nice girl . . .' She paused, her wistful eyes bent entreatingly on Miss March's responsive face. 'And so, in sheer despair, I thought perhaps, if this friend of my daughter-in-law's is rich, really rich, it might be better to try . . . There's something about these foreigners that seems to attract the young men.'

Yes – there was, as Jacky March had reason to know. Her own charm had been subtler and more discreet, and in the end it had failed her; but the knowledge that she had possessed it gave her a feeling of affinity with this new band of marauders, social aliens though they were: the wild gipsy who had captured Dick Marable, and her young friends who, two years later, had come out to look over the ground, and do their own capturing.

Miss March, who was always on her watch-tower, had already sighted and classified them; the serenely lovely Virginia St George, whom Lady Brightlingsea had singled out for Lord Seadown, and her younger sister Nan, negligible as yet compared with Virginia, but odd and interesting too, as her sharp little observer perceived. It was a novel kind of invasion, and Miss March was a-flutter with curiosity, and with an irrepressible sympathy. In Lady Brightlingsea's company she had quite honestly blushed for the crude intruders; but freed from the shadow of the peerage she felt herself mysteriously akin to them, eager to know more of their plans, and even to play a secret part in the adventure.

Miss Testvalley was an old friend, and her arrival in London with a family of obscure but wealthy Americans had stirred the depths of Miss March's social curiosity. She knew from experience that Miss Testvalley would never make imprudent revelations concerning her employers, much less betray their confidence; but her shrewd eye and keen ear must have harvested, in the transatlantic field, much that would be of burning interest to Miss March, and the latter was impatient to resume their talk. So far, she knew only that the St George girls were beautiful, and their parents rich, yet that fashionable New York had rejected them. There was much more to learn, and there was also this strange outbreak of Lady Brightlingsea's to hint at, if not reveal, to Miss Testvalley.

It was certainly a pity that their talk had been interrupted by Lady Brightlingsea; yet Miss March would not for the world have missed the latter's visit, and above all, her unexpected allusion to her eldest son. For years Miss March had carried in her bosom the heavy weight of the Marable affairs, and this reference to Seadown had thrown her into such agitation that she sat down on the sofa and clasped her small wrinkled hands over her anxious heart. Seadown to marry an American – what news to communicate to Laura Testvalley!

Miss March rose and went quickly to her miniature writing-desk. She wrote a hurried note in her pretty flowing script, sealed it with silver-grey wax, and rang for the beruffled parlour-maid. Then she turned back into the room. It was crowded with velvet-covered tables and quaint corner-shelves, all laden with photographs in heavy silver or morocco frames, surmounted by coronets, from the baronial to the ducal – one, even, royal (in a place of honour by itself, on the mantel). Most of these photographs were of young or middle-aged women, with long necks and calm imperious faces, crowned with diadems or nodded over by court feathers. 'Selina Brightlingsea', 'Blanche Tintagel', 'Elfrida Marable', they were signed in tall slanting hands. The hand-writing was as uniform as the features, and nothing but the signatures seemed to differentiate these carven images. But in a corner by itself (pushed behind a lamp at Lady Brightlingsea's arrival) was one, 'To Jacky from her friend Idina Churt', which Miss March now drew forth and studied with a furtive interest. What chance had an untaught transatlantic beauty against this reprehensible creature, with her tilted nose and impertinent dark fringe? Yet, after studying the portrait for a while, Miss March, as she set it down, simply murmured: 'Poor Idina.'

9

In the long summer twilight a father and son were pacing the terrace of an old house called Honourslove, on the edge of the Cotswolds. The irregular silver-grey building, when approached from the village by a drive winding under ancient beech-trees, seemed, like so many old dwellings in England, to lie almost in a hollow, screened to the north by hanging woods, and surveying from its many windows only its own lawns and trees; but the terrace on the other front overlooked an immensity of hill and vale, with huddled village roofs and floating spires. Now, in the twilight, though the sky curved above so clear and luminous, everything below was blurred, and the spires were hardly distinguishable from the tree-trunks; but to the two men strolling up and down before the house long familiarity made every fold of the landscape visible.

The Cotswolds were in the blood of the Thwartes, and their rule at Honourslove reached back so far that the present baronet, Sir Helmsley Thwarte, had persuaded himself that only by accident (or treachery – he was given to suspecting treachery) had their title to the estate dropped out of Domesday.

His only son, Guy, was not so sure; but, as Sir Helmsley said, the young respect nothing and believe in nothing, least of all in the validity of tradition. Guy did, however, believe in Honourslove, the beautiful old place which had come to be the first and last article of the family creed. Tradition, as embodied in the ancient walls and the ancient trees of Honourslove, seemed to him as priceless a quality as it did to Sir Helmsley; and indeed he sometimes said to himself that if ever he succeeded to the baronetcy he would be a safer and more vigilant guardian than his father, who loved the place and yet had so often betrayed it.

'I'd have shot myself rather than sell the Titian,' Guy used to think in moments of bitterness. 'But then my father's sure to outlive me – so what's the odds?'

As they moved side by side that summer evening it would have been hard for a looker-on to decide which had the greater chance of longevity; the heavy vigorous man approaching the sixties, a little flushed after his dinner and his bottle of Burgundy, but obliged to curb his quick stride to match his son's more leisurely gait; or the son, tall and lean, and full of the balanced energy of the hard rider and quick thinker.

'You don't adapt yourself to the scene, sir. It's an insult to Honourslove to treat the terrace as if it were the platform at Euston, and you were racing for your train.'

Sir Helmsley was secretly proud of his own activity, and nothing pleased him better than his son's disrespectful banter on his over-youthfulness. He slackened his pace with a gruff laugh.

'I suppose you young fellows expect the grey-beards to drag their gouty feet and lean on staves, as they do in *Oedipe-roi* at the *Français*.'

'Well, sir, as your beard's bright auburn, that strikes me as irrele-vant.' Guy knew this would not be unwelcome either; but a moment later he wondered if he had not overshot the mark. His father stopped short and faced him. 'Bright auburn, indeed? Look here, my dear fellow, what is there behind this indecent flattery?' His voice hardened. 'Not another bill to be met – eh?'

Guy gave a short laugh. He *had* wanted something, and had per-haps resorted to flattery in the hope of getting it; but his admiration for his brilliant and impetuous parent, even when not disinterested, was sincere.

'A bill –?' He laughed again. That would have been easier – though it was never easy to confess a lapse to Sir Helmsley. Guy had never learned to take his father's tropical fits of rage without win-cing. But to make him angry about money would have been less dangerous; and, at any rate, the young man was familiar with the result. It always left him seared, but still upright; whereas . . .

'Well?'

'Nothing, sir.'

The father gave one of his angry 'foreign' shrugs (reminiscent of far-off Bohemian days in the Quartier Latin), and the two men walked on in silence.

There were moments during their talks – and this was one – when the young man felt that, if each could have read the other's secret mind, they would have found little to unite them except a joint love of their house and the land it stood on. But that love was so strong, and went so deep, that it sometimes seemed to embrace all the divergences. Would it now, Guy wondered? 'How the devil shall I tell him?' he thought.

The two had paused, and stood looking out over the lower terraces to the indistinct blue reaches beyond. Lights were beginning to prick the dusk, and every roof which they revealed had a name and a meaning to Guy Thwarte. Red Farm, where the famous hazel copse was, Ausprey with its decaying Norman church, Little Ausprey with the old heronry at the Hall, Odcote, Sudcote, Lowdon, the ancient borough with its market-cross and its rich minster – all were thick with webs of memory for the youth whose people had so long been rooted in their soil. And those frail innumerable webs tightened about him like chains at the thought that in a few weeks he was to say goodbye to it all, probably for many months.

After preparing for a diplomatic career, and going through a first stage at the Foreign Office, and a secretaryship in Brazil, Guy Thwarte had suddenly decided that he was not made for diplomacy, and braving his father's wrath at this unaccountable defection had settled down to a period of hard drudgery with an eminent firm of civil engineers who specialized in railway building. Though he had a natural bent for the work he would probably never have chosen it had he not hoped it would be a quick way to wealth. The firm employing him had big contracts out for building railways in Far Eastern and South American lands, and Guy's experience in Brazil had shown him that in those regions there were fortunes to be made by energetic men with a practical knowledge of the conditions. He preferred making a fortune to marrying one, and it was clear that sooner or later a great deal of money would be needed to save Honourslove and keep it going. Sir Helmsley's financial ventures had been even costlier than his other follies, and the great Titian which was the glory of the house had been sold to cover the loss of part of the fortune which Guy had inherited from his mother, and which, during his minority, had been in Sir Helmsley's imprudent hands. The subject was one never touched upon between father and son, but it had imperceptibly altered their relations, though not the tie of affection between them.

The truth was that the son's case was hardly less perplexing than the father's. Contradictory impulses strove in both. Each had the same love for the ancient habitation of their race, which enchanted but could not satisfy them, each was anxious to play the part fate had allotted to him, and each was dimly conscious of an inability to remain confined in it, and painfully aware that their secret problems would have been unintelligible to most men of their own class and kind. Sir Helmsley had been a grievous disappointment to the county, and it was expected that Guy should make up for his father's short-comings by conforming to the accepted standards, should be a hard rider, a good shot, a conscientious landlord and magistrate, and should in due time (and as soon as possible) marry a wife whose settlements would save Honourslove from the consequences of Sir Helmsley's follies.

The county was not conscious of anything incomprehensible about Guy. Sir Helmsley had dabbled dangerously in forbidden things; but Guy had a decent reputation about women, and it was incredible that a man so tall and well set-up, and such a brilliant point-to-point rider, should mess about with poetry or painting. Guy knew what was expected of him, and secretly agreed with his observers that the path they would have him follow was the right one for a man in his situation. But since Honourslove had to be saved, he would rather try to save it by his own labour than with a rich woman's money.

Guy's stage of drudgery as an engineer was now over, and he had been chosen to accompany one of the members of the firm on a big railway-building expedition in South America. His knowledge of the country, and the fact that his diplomatic training had included the mastering of two or three foreign languages, qualified him for the job, which promised to be lucrative as well as adventurous, and might, he hoped, lead to big things. Sir Helmsley accused him of undergoing the work only for the sake of adventure; but, aggrieved though he was by his son's decision, he respected him for sticking to it. 'I've been only a brilliant failure myself,' he had grumbled at the end of their discussion; and Guy had laughed back: 'Then I'll try to be a dingy success.'

The memory of this talk passed through the young man's mind, and with it the new impulse which, for the last week, had never been long out of his thoughts, and now threatened to absorb them. Struggle as he would, there it was, fighting in him for control. 'As if my father would ever listen to reason!' But was this reason? He leaned on the balustrade, and let his mind wander over the rich darkness of the country-side.

Though he was not yet thirty, his life had been full of dramatic disturbances; indeed, to be the only son of Sir Helmsley Thwarte was in itself a potential drama. Sir Helmsley had been born with the passionate desire to be an accomplished example of his class: the ideal English squire, the model landowner, crack shot, leader and champion in all traditionally British pursuits and pleasures; but a contrary streak in his nature was perpetually driving him toward art and poetry and travel, odd intimacies with a group of painters and decorators of socialistic tendencies, reckless dalliance with ladies, and a loud contempt for the mental inferiority of his county neighbours. Against these tendencies he waged a spasmodic and unavailing war, accusing and excusing himself in the same breath, and expecting his son to justify his vagaries, and to rescue him from their results. During Lady Thwarte's life the task had been less difficult; she had always, as Guy now understood, kept a sort of cold power over her husband. To Guy himself she remained an enigma; the boy had never found a crack through which to penetrate beyond the porcelain-like surface of her face and mind. But while she lived things had gone more smoothly at Honourslove. Her husband's oddest experiments had been tried away from home, and had never lasted long; her presence, her power, her clear conception of what the master of Honourslove ought to be, always drew him back to her and to conformity.

Guy summed it up by saying to himself: 'If she'd lived the Titian never would have gone.' But she had died, and left the two men and their conflicting tendencies alone in the old house . . . Yes; she had been the right mistress for such a house. Guy was thinking of that now, and knew that the same thought was in his father's mind, and that his own words had roused it to the pitch of apprehension. Who was to come after her? father and son were both thinking.

'Well, out with it!' Sir Helmsley broke forth abruptly.

Guy straightened himself with a laugh. 'You seem to expect a confession of bankruptcy or murder. I'm afraid I shall disappoint you. All I want is to have you ask some people to tea.'

'Ah –? Some "people"?' Sir Helmsley puffed dubiously at his cigar. 'I suppose they've got names and a local habitation?'

'The former, certainly. I can't say as to the rest. I ran across them the other day in London, and as I know they're going to spend next Sunday at Allfriars I thought –'

Sir Helmsley Thwarte drew the cigar from his lips, and looked along it as if it were a telescope at the end of which he saw an enemy approaching.

'Americans?' he queried, in a shrill voice so unlike his usual impressive baritone that it had been known to startle servants and trespassers almost out of their senses, and even in his family to cause a painful perturbation.

'Well – yes.'

'Ah –' said Sir Helmsley again. Guy proffered no remark, and his father broke out irritably: 'I suppose it's because you know how I hate the whole spitting tobacco-chewing crew, the dressed-up pushing women dragging their reluctant backswoodsmen after them, that you suggest polluting my house, and desecrating our last few days together, by this barbarian invasion – eh?'

There had been a time when his father's outbursts, even when purely rhetorical, were so irritating to Guy that he could meet them only with silence. But the victory of choosing his career had given him a lasting advantage. He smiled, and said: 'I don't seem to recognize my friends from your description.'

'Your friends – your friends? How many of them are there?'

'Only two sisters – the Miss St Georges. Lady Richard would drive them over, I imagine.'

'Lady Richard? What's she? Some sort of West Indian octoroon, I believe?'

'She's very handsome, and has auburn hair.'

Sir Helmsley gave an angry laugh. 'I suppose you think the similarity in our colouring will be a tie between us.'

'Well, sir, I think she'll amuse you.'

'I hate women who try to amuse me.'

'Oh, she won't try – she's too lazy.'

'But what about the sisters?'

Guy hesitated. 'Well, the rumour is that the eldest is going to marry Seadown.'

'Seadown – marry Seadown? Good God, are the Brightlingseas out of their minds? It was well enough to get rid of Dick Marable at

THE BUCCANEERS

any price. There wasn't a girl in the village safe from him, and his
father was forever buying people off. But Seadown – Seadown marry
an American! There won't be a family left in England without that
poison in their veins.'

Sir Helmsley walked away a few paces and then returned to
where his son was standing. 'Why do you want these people asked
here?'

'I – I like them,' Guy stammered, suddenly feeling as shamefaced
as a guilty school-boy.

'Like them!' In the darkness, the young man felt his father's nervous clutch on his arm. 'Look here, my boy – you know all the plans I
had for you. Plans – dreams, they turned out to be! I wanted you to
be all I'd meant to be myself. The enlightened landlord, the successful ambassador, the model MP, the ideal MFH. The range was
wide enough – or ought to have been. Above all, I wanted you to
have a steady career on an even keel. Just the reverse of the crazy
example I've set you.'

'You've set me the example of having too many talents to keep
any man on an even keel. There's not much danger of my following
you in that.'

'Let's drop compliments, Guy. You're a gifted fellow; too much so,
probably, for your job. But you've more persistency than I ever had,
and I haven't dared to fight your ideas because I could see they were
more definite than mine. And now –'

'Well, sir?' his son queried, forcing a laugh.

'And now – are you going to wreck everything, as I've done so
often?' He paused, as if waiting for an answer; but none came. 'Guy,
why do you want those women here? Is it because you've lost your
head over one of them? I've a right to an answer, I think.'

Guy Thwarte appeared to have none ready. Too many thoughts
were crowding through his mind. The first was: 'How like my father
to corner me when anybody with a lighter hand would have let the
thing pass unnoticed! But he's always thrown himself against life
head foremost . . .' The second: 'Well, and isn't that what I'm doing
now? It's the family folly, I suppose . . . Only, if he'd said nothing . . .
When I spoke I really hadn't got beyond . . . well, just wanting to see
her again . . . and now . . .'

Through the summer dark he could almost feel the stir of his

373

father's impatience. 'Am I to take your silence as an answer?' Sir Helmsley challenged him.

Guy relieved the tension with a laugh. 'What nonsense! I ask you to let me invite some friends and neighbours to tea . . .'

'To begin with, I hate these new-fangled intermediate meals. Why can't people eat enough at luncheon to last till dinner?'

'Well, sir, to dine and sleep, if you prefer.'

'Dine and sleep? A pack of strange women under my roof?' Sir Helmsley gave a grim laugh. 'I should like to see Mrs Bolt's face if she were suddenly told to get their rooms ready! Everything's a foot deep in dust and moths, I imagine.'

'Well, it might be a good excuse for a clean-up,' rejoined his son good-humouredly. But Sir Helmsley ignored this.

'For God's sake, Guy – you're not going to bring an American wife to Honourslove? I shan't shut an eye tonight unless you tell me.'

'And you won't shut an eye if I tell you "yes"?'

'Damn it, man – don't fence.'

'I'm not fencing, sir; I'm laughing at your way of jumping at conclusions. I shan't take any wife till I get back from South America; and there's not much chance that this one would wait for me till then – even if I happened to want her to.'

'Ah, well. I suppose, this last week, if you were to ask me to invite the devil I should have to do it.'

From her post of observation in the window of the housekeeper's room, Mrs Bolt saw the two red cigar-tips pass along the front of the house and disappear. The gentlemen were going in, and she could ring to have the front door locked, and the lights put out everywhere but in the baronet's study and on the stairs.

Guy followed his father across the hall, and into the study. The lamp on the littered writing-table cast a circle of light on crowded book-shelves, on Sienese predellas, and bold unsteady water-colours and charcoal-sketches by Sir Helmsley himself. Over the desk hung a small jewel-like picture in a heavy frame, with D. G. Rossetti inscribed beneath. Sir Helmsley glanced about him, selected a pipe from the rack, and filled and lit it. Then he lifted up the lamp.

'Well, Guy, I'm going to assume that you mean to have a good night's sleep.'

'The soundest, sir.'

Lamp in hand, Sir Helmsley moved toward the door. He paused – was it voluntarily? – half way across the room, and the lamplight touched the old yellow marble of the carved mantel, and struck upward to a picture above it, set in elaborate stucco scrolls. It was the portrait of a tall thin woman in white, her fair hair looped under a narrow diadem. As she looked forth from the dim background, expressionless, motionless, white, so her son remembered her in their brief years together. She had died, still young, during his last year at Eton – long ago, in another age, as it now seemed. Sir Helmsley, still holding the lifted lamp, looked up too. 'She was the most beautiful woman I ever saw,' he said abruptly – and added as if in spite of himself: 'But utterly unpaintable; even Millais found her so.'

Guy offered no comment, but went up the stairs in silence after his father.

10

The St George girls had never seen anything as big as the house at Allfriars except a public building, and as they drove toward it down the long avenue, and had their first glimpse of Inigo Jones's most triumphant expression of the Palladian dream, Virginia said with a little shiver: 'Mercy – it's just like a gaol.'

'Oh, no – a palace,' Nan corrected.

Virginia gave an impatient laugh. 'I'd like to know where you've ever seen a palace.'

'Why, hundreds of times, I have, in my dreams.'

'You mustn't tell your dreams. Miss Testvalley says nothing bores people so much as being told other people's dreams.'

Nan said nothing, but an iron gate seemed to clang shut in her; the gate that was so often slammed by careless hands. As if any one could be bored by such dreams as hers!

'Oh,' said Virginia, 'I never saw anything so colossal. Do you suppose they live all over it? I guess our clothes aren't half dressy enough. I told mother we ought to have something better for the afternoon than those mauve organdies.'

Nan shot a side-glance at the perfect curve of her sister's cheek.

'Mauve's the one colour that simply murders me. But nobody who sees *you* will bother to notice what you've got on.'

'You little silly, you, shut up . . . Look, there's Conchita and the poodle!' cried Virginia in a burst of reassurance. For there, on the edge of the drive, stood their friend, in a crumpled but picturesque yellow muslin and flapping garden hat, and a first glance at her smiling waving figure assured the two girls of her welcome. They sprang out, leaving the brougham to be driven on with maid and luggage, and instantly the trio were in each other's arms.

'Oh, girls, girls – I've been simply pining for you! I can't believe you're really here!' Lady Richard cried, with a tremor of emotion in her rich Creole voice.

'Conchita! Are you really glad?' Virginia drew back and scanned her anxiously. 'You're lovelier than ever; but you look terribly tired. Don't she look tired, Nan?'

'Don't talk about me. I've looked like a fright ever since the baby was born. But he's a grand baby, and they say I'll be all right soon. Jinny, darling, you can't think how I've missed you both! Little Nan, let me have a good look at you. How big your eyes have grown . . . Jinny, you and I must be careful, or this child will crowd us out of the running . . .'

Linked arm in arm, the three loitered along the drive, the poodle caracoling ahead. As they approached the great gateway, Conchita checked their advance. 'Look, girls! It *is* a grand house, isn't it?'

'Yes; but I'm not a bit afraid any more,' Nan laughed, pressing her arm.

'Afraid? What were you afraid of?'

'Virginia said you'd be as grand as the house. She didn't believe you'd be really glad to see us. We were scared blue of coming.'

'Nan – you little idiot!'

'Well, you did say so, Jinny. You said we must expect her to be completely taken up with her lords and ladies.'

Conchita gave a dry little laugh. 'Well, you wait,' she said.

Nan stood still, gazing up at the noble façade of the great house. 'It *is* grand. I'm so glad I'm not afraid of it,' she murmured, following the other two up the steps between the mighty urns and columns of the doorway.

*

It was a relief to the girls – though somewhat of a surprise – that there was no one to welcome them when they entered the big domed hall hung with tall family portraits and moth-eaten trophies of the chase. Conchita, seeing that they hesitated, said: 'Come along to your room – you won't see any of the in-laws till dinner'; and they went with her up the stairs, and down a succession of long corridors, glad that the dread encounter was postponed. Miss Jacky March, to whom they had been introduced by Miss Testvalley, had assured them that Lady Brightlingsea was the sweetest and kindest of women; but this did not appear to be Conchita's view, and they felt eager to hear more of her august relatives before facing them at dinner.

In the room with dark heavy bed-curtains and worn chintz arm-chairs which had been assigned to the sisters, the lady's-maid was already shaking out their evening toilets. Nan had wanted to take Miss Testvalley to Allfriars, and had given way to a burst of childish weeping when it was explained to her that girls who were 'out' did not go visiting with their governesses. Maids were a new feature in the St George household, and when, with Miss Jacky March's aid, Laura Testvalley had run down a paragon, and introduced her into the family, Mrs St George was even more terrified than the girls. But Miss Testvalley laughed. 'You were afraid of me once,' she said to Virginia. 'You and Nan must get used to being waited on, and having your clothes kept in order. And don't let the woman see that you're not used to it. Behave as if you'd never combed your own hair or rummaged for your stockings. Try and feel that you're as good as any of these people you're going about with,' the dauntless governess ordained.

'I guess we're as good as anybody,' Virginia replied haughtily. 'But they act differently from us, and we're not used to them yet.'

'Well, act in your own way, as you call it – that will amuse them much more than if you try to copy them.'

After deliberating with the maid and Conchita over the choice of dinner-dresses, they followed their friend along the corridor to her own bedroom. It was too late to disturb the baby, who was in the night-nursery in the other wing; but in Conchita's big shabby room, after inspecting everything it contained, the sisters settled themselves down happily on a wide sofa with broken springs. Dinner at Allfriars was not till eight, and they had an hour ahead of them before the dressing-gong. 'Tell us about everything, Conchita darling,' Virginia commanded.

'Well, you'll find only a family party, you know. They don't have many visitors here, because they have to bleed themselves white to keep the place going and there's not much left for entertaining. They're terribly proud of it – they couldn't imagine living in any other way. At least my father-in-law couldn't. He thinks God made Allfriars for him to live in, and Frenshaw – the other place, in Essex; but he doesn't understand why God gave him so little money to do it on. He's so busy thinking about that, that he doesn't take much notice of anybody. You mustn't mind. My mother-in-law's good-natured enough; only she never can think of anything to say to people she isn't used to. Dick talks a little when he's here; but he so seldom is, what with racing and fishing and shooting. I believe he's at Newmarket now; but he seldom keeps me informed of his movements.' Her aquamarine eyes darkened as she spoke her husband's name.

'But aren't your sisters-in-law here?' Virginia asked.

Conchita smiled. 'Oh, yes, poor dears; there's nowhere else for them to go. But they're too shy to speak when my mother-in-law doesn't; sometimes they open their mouths to begin, but they never get as far as the first sentence. You must get used to an ocean of silence, and just swim about in it as well as you can. I haven't drowned yet, and you won't. Oh – and Seadown's here this week. I think you'll like him; only he doesn't say much either.'

'Who does talk, then?' Nan broke in, her spirits sinking at this picture of an Allfriars evening.

'Well, I do; too much so, my mother-in-law says. But this evening you two will have to help me out. Oh, and the Rector thinks of something to say every now and then; and so does Jacky March. She's just arrived, by the way. You know her, don't you?'

'That little Miss March with the funny curls, that Miss Testvalley took us to see?'

'Yes. She's an American, you know – but she's lived in England for years and years. I'll tell you something funny – only you must swear not to let on. She was madly in love with Lord Brightlingsea – with my father-in-law. Isn't that a good one?' said Conchita with her easy laugh.

'Mercy! In love? But she must be sixty,' cried Virginia, scandalized.

'Well,' said Nan gravely, 'I can imagine being in love at sixty.'

'There's nothing crazy you can't imagine,' her sister retorted. 'But can you imagine being in love with Miss March?'

'Oh, she wasn't sixty when it happened,' Conchita continued. 'It was ages and ages ago. She *says* they were actually engaged, and that he jilted her after the wedding-dress was ordered; and I believe he doesn't deny it. But of course he forgot all about her years ago; and after a time she became a great friend of Lady Brightlingsea's, and comes here often, and gives all the children the loveliest presents. Don't you call that funny?'

Virginia drew herself up. 'I call it demeaning herself; it shows she hasn't any proper pride. I'm sorry she's an American.'

Nan sat brooding in her corner. 'I think it just shows she loves him better than she does her pride.'

The two elder girls laughed, and she hung her head with a sudden blush. 'Well,' said Virginia, 'if mother heard that she'd lock you up.'

The dressing-gong boomed through the passages, and the sisters sprang up and raced back to their room.

The Marquess of Brightlingsea stood with his coat-tails to the monumental mantelpiece of the red drawing-room, and looked severely at his watch. He was still, at sixty, a splendid figure of a man, firm-muscled, well set-up, with the sloping profile and coldly benevolent air associated, in ancestral portraits, with a tie-wig, and ruffles crossed by an Order. Lord Brightlingsea was a just man, and having assured himself that it still lacked five minutes to eight he pocketed his watch with a milder look, and began to turn about busily in the empty shell of his own mind. His universe was a brilliantly illuminated circle extending from himself at its centre to the exact limit of his occupations and interests. These comprised his dealings with his tenantry and his man of business, his local duties as Lord Lieutenant of the County and MFH, and participation in the manly sports suitable to his rank and age. The persons ministering to these pursuits were necessarily in the foreground, and the local clergy and magistracy in the middle distance, while his family clung in a precarious half-light on the periphery, and all beyond was blackness. Lady

Brightlingsea considered it her duty to fish out of this outer darkness, and drag for a moment into the light, any person or obligation entitled to fix her husband's attention; but they always faded back into night as soon as they had served their purpose.

Lord Brightlingsea had learned from his valet that several guests had arrived that afternoon, his own eldest son among them. Lord Seadown was seldom at Allfriars except in the hunting season, and his father's first thought was that if he had come at so unlikely a time it was probably to ask for money. The thought was excessively unpleasant, and Lord Brightlingsea was eager to be rid of it, or at least to share it with his wife, who was more used to such burdens. He looked about him impatiently; but Lady Brightlingsea was not in the drawing-room, nor in the Vandyke saloon beyond. Lord Brightlingsea, as he glanced down the length of the saloon, said to himself: 'Those tapestries ought to be taken down and mended' – but that too was an unpleasant thought, associated with much trouble and expense, and therefore belonging distinctly to his wife's province. Lord Brightlingsea was well aware of the immense value of the tapestries, and knew that if he put them up for sale all the big London dealers would compete for them; but he would have kicked out of the house any one who approached him with an offer. 'I'm not sunk as low as Thwarte,' he muttered to himself, shuddering at the sacrilege of the Titian carried off from Honourslove to the auction-room.

'Where the devil's your mother?' he asked, as a big-boned girl in a faded dinner-dress entered the drawing-room.

'Mamma's talking with Seadown, I think; I saw him go into her dressing-room,' Lady Honoria Marable replied.

Lord Brightlingsea cast an unfavourable glance on his daughter. ('If her upper teeth had been straightened when she was a child we might have had her married by this time,' he thought. But that again was Lady Brightlingsea's affair.)

'It's an odd time for your mother to be talking in her dressing-room. Dinner'll be on the table in a minute.'

'Oh, I'm sure Mamma will be down before the others. And Conchita's always late, you know.'

'Conchita knows that I won't eat my soup cold on her account. Who are the others?'

'No one in particular. Two American girls who are friends of Conchita's.'

'H'm. And why were they invited, may I ask?'

Honoria Marable hesitated. All the girls feared their father less than they did their mother, because she remembered and he did not. Honoria feared him least of all, and when Lady Brightlingsea was not present was almost at her ease with him. 'Mamma told Conchita to ask them down, I think. She says they're very rich. I believe their father's in the American army. They call him "Colonel".'

'The American army? There isn't any. And they call dentists "Colonel" in the States.' But Lord Brightlingsea's countenance had softened. 'Seadown . . .' he thought. If that were the reason for his son's visit, it altered the situation, of course. And, much as he disliked to admit such considerations to his mind, he repeated carelessly: 'You say these Americans are very rich?'

'Mamma has heard so. I think Miss March knows them, and she'll be able to tell her more about them. Miss March is here too, you know.'

'Miss March?' Lord Brightlingsea's sloping brow was wrinkled in an effort of memory. He repeated: 'March – March. Now that's a name I know . . .'

Lady Honoria smiled. 'I should think so, Papa!'

'Now why? Do you mean that I know her too?'

'Yes. Mamma told me to be sure to remind you.'

'Remind me of what?'

'Why, that you jilted her, and broke her heart. Don't you remember? You're to be particularly nice to her, Papa; and be sure not to ask her if she's ever seen Allfriars before.'

'I – what? Ah, yes, of course . . . That old nonsense! I hope I'm "nice", as you call it, to every one who comes to my house,' Lord Brightlingsea rejoined, pulling down the lapels of his dress-coat, and throwing back his head majestically.

At the same moment the drawing-room door opened again, and two girls came into the room. Lord Brightlingsea, gazing at them from the hearth, gave a faint exclamation, and came forward with extended hand. The elder and taller of the two advanced to meet it.

'You're Lord Brightlingsea, aren't you? I'm Miss St George, and this is my sister Annabel,' the young lady said, in a tone that was fearless without being familiar.

Lord Brightlingsea fixed on her a gaze of undisguised bene-volence. It was a long time since his eyes had rested on anything so fresh and fair, and he found the sensation very agreeable. It was a pity, he reflected, that his eldest son lacked his height, and had freckles and white eye-lashes. 'Gad,' he thought, 'if I were Seadown's age . . .'

But before he could give further expression to his approval an-other guest had appeared. This time it was some one vaguely known to him; a small elderly lady, dressed with a slightly antiquated ele-gance, who came toward him reddening under her faint touch of rouge. 'Oh, Lord Brightlingsea—' and, as he took her trembling little hand he repeated to himself: 'My wife's old friend, of course; Miss March. The name's perfectly familiar to me – what the deuce else did Honoria say I was to remember about her?'

II

When the St George girls, following candle in hand the bedward procession headed by Lady Brightlingsea, had reached the door of their room, they could hardly believe that the tall clock ticking so loudly in the corner had not gone back an hour or two.

'Why, is it only half past ten?' Virginia exclaimed.

Conchita, who had followed them in, threw herself on the sofa with a laugh. 'That's what I always think when I come down from town. But it's not the clocks at Allfriars that are slow; my father-in-law sees to that. It's the place itself.' She sighed. 'In London the night's just beginning. And the worst of it is that when I'm here I feel as dead with sleep by ten o'clock as if I'd been up till daylight.'

'I suppose it's the struggling to talk,' said Nan irrepressibly.

'That, and the awful certainty that when anybody does speak nothing will be said that one hasn't heard a million times before. Poor little Miss March! What a fight she put up; but it's no use. My father-in-law can never think of anything to say to her. – Well, Jinny, what did you think of Seadown?'

Virginia coloured; the challenge was a trifle too direct. 'Why, I thought he looked pretty sad, too; like all the others.'

'Well, he *is* sad, poor old Seedy. The fact is – it's no mystery – he's tangled up with a rapacious lady who can't afford to let him go; and I suspect he's so sick of it that if any nice girl came along and held out her hand . . .'

Virginia, loosening her bright tresses before the mirror, gave them a contemptuous toss. 'In America girls don't have to hold out their hands –'

'Oh, I mean, just be kind; show him a little sympathy. He isn't easy to amuse; but I saw him laugh once or twice at things Nan said.'

Nan sat up in surprise. 'Me? Jinny says I always say the wrong thing.'

'Well, you know, that rather takes in England. They're so tired of the perfectly behaved Americans who are afraid of using even a wrong word.'

Virginia gave a slightly irritated laugh. 'You'd better hold your hand out, Nan, if you want to be Conchita's sister-in-law.'

'Oh, misery! What I like is just chattering with people I'm not afraid of – like that young man we met the other day in London who said he was a friend of yours. He lives somewhere near here, doesn't he?'

'Oh, Guy Thwarte. Rather! He's one of the most fascinating detrimentals in England.'

'What's a detrimental?'

'A young man that all the women are mad about, but who's too poor to marry. The only kind left for the married women, in fact – so hands off, please, my dear. Not that I want Guy for myself,' Conchita added with her lazy laugh. 'Dick's enough of a detrimental for me. What I'm looking for is a friend with a settled income that he doesn't know how to spend.'

'*Conchita!*' Virginia exclaimed, flushed with disapproval.

Lady Richard rose from the sofa. 'So sorry! I forgot you little Puritans weren't broken in yet. Goodnight, dears. Breakfast at nine sharp; and don't forget family prayers.' She stopped on the threshold to add in a half-whisper: 'Don't forget, either, that the day after tomorrow we're going to drive over to call on him – the detrimental,

I mean. And even if you don't care about him, you'll see the loveliest place in all England.'

'Well, it was true enough, what Conchita said about nobody speaking,' Virginia remarked when the two sisters were alone. 'Did you ever know anything as awful as that dinner? I couldn't think of a word to say. My voice just froze in my throat.'

'I didn't mind so much, because it gave me a chance to look,' Nan rejoined.

'At what? All I saw was a big room with cracks in the ceiling, and bits of plaster off the walls. And after dinner, when those great bony girls showed us albums with views of the Rhine, I thought I should scream. I wonder they didn't bring out a magic lantern!'

Nan was silent. She knew that Virginia's survey of the world was limited to people, the clothes they wore, and the carriages they drove in. Her own universe was so crammed to bursting with wonderful sights and sounds that, in spite of her sense of Virginia's superiority – her beauty, her ease, her self-confidence – Nan sometimes felt a shamefaced pity for her. It must be cold and lonely, she thought, in such an empty colourless world as her sister's.

'But the house is terribly grand, don't you think it is? I like to imagine all those people on the walls, in their splendid historical dresses, walking about in the big rooms. Don't you believe they come down at night sometimes?'

'Oh, shut up, Nan. You're too old for baby-talk . . . Be sure you look under the bed before you blow out the candle . . .'

Virginia's head was already on the pillow, her hair overflowing it in ripples of light.

'Do come to bed, Nan. I hate the way the furniture creaks. Isn't it funny there's no gas? I wish we'd told that maid to sit up for us.' She waited a moment, and then went on: 'I'm sorry for Lord Seadown. He looks so scared of his father; but I thought Lord Brightlingsea was very kind, really. Did you see how I made him laugh?'

'I saw they couldn't either of them take their eyes off you.'

'Oh, well – if they have nobody to look at but those daughters I don't wonder,' Virginia murmured complacently, her lids sinking over her drowsy eyes.

Nan was not drowsy. Unfamiliar scenes and faces always palpitated in her long afterward; but the impact of new scenes usually made itself felt before that of new people. Her soul opened slowly and timidly to her kind, but her imagination rushed out to the beauties of the visible world; and the decaying majesty of Allfriars moved her strangely. Splendour neither frightened her, nor made her self-assertive as it did Virginia; she never felt herself matched against things greater than herself, but softly merged in them; and she lay awake, thinking of what Miss Testvalley had told her of the history of the ancient Abbey, which Henry VIII had bestowed on an ancestor of Lord Brightlingsea's, and of the tragic vicissitudes following on its desecration. She lay for a long time listening to the mysterious sounds given forth by old houses at night, the undefinable creakings, rustlings and sighings which would have frightened Virginia had she remained awake, but which sounded to Nan like the long murmur of the past breaking on the shores of a sleeping world.

In a majestic bedroom at the other end of the house the master of Allfriars, in dressing-gown and slippers, appeared from his dressing-room. On his lips was a smile of retrospective satisfaction seldom seen by his wife at that hour.

'Well, those two young women gave us an unexpectedly lively evening – eh, my dear? Remarkably intelligent, that eldest girl; the beauty, I mean. I'm to show her the pictures tomorrow morning. By the way, please send word to the Vicar that I shan't be able to go to the vestry meeting at eleven; he'd better put it off till next week . . . What are you to tell him? Why – er – unexpected business . . . And the little one, who looks such a child, had plenty to say for herself too. She seemed to know the whole history of the place. Now, why can't our girls talk like that?'

'You've never encouraged them to chatter,' replied Lady Brightlingsea, settling a weary head on a longed-for pillow; and her lord responded by a growl. As if talk were necessarily chatter! Yet as such Lord Brightlingsea had always regarded it when it issued from the lips of his own family. How little he had ever been understood by those nearest him, he thought; and as he composed himself to slumber in his half of the vast bed, his last conscious act was to murmur over: 'The Hobbema's the big black one in the red drawing-room, between the lacquer cabinets; and the portrait of Lady Jane Grey that they were asking about must be the one in the octagon room, over the fire-place.' For Lord Brightlingsea was determined to shine as a connoisseur in the eyes of the young lady for whom he had put off the vestry meeting.

The terrace of Honourslove had never looked more beautiful than on the following Sunday afternoon. The party from Allfriars – Lady Richard Marable, her brother-in-law Lord Seadown, and the two young ladies from America – had been taken through the house by Sir Helmsley and his son, and after a stroll along the shady banks of the Love, murmuring in its little glen far below, had returned by way of the gardens to the chapel hooded with ivy at the gates of the park. In the gardens they had seen the lavender-borders, the hundreds of feet of rosy brick hung with peaches and nectarines, the old fig-tree heavy with purple fruit in a sheltered corner; and in the chapel, with its delicately traceried roof and dark oaken stalls, had lingered over kneeling and recumbent Thwartes, Thwartes in cuirass and ruff, in furred robes, in portentous wigs, their stiffly farthingaled ladies at their sides, and baby Thwartes tucked away overhead in little marble cots. And now, turning back to the house, they were looking out from the terrace over the soft reaches of country bathed in afternoon light.

After the shabby vastness of Allfriars everything about Honourslove seemed to Nan St George warm, cared-for, exquisitely intimate. The stones of the house, the bricks of the walls, the very flags of the terrace, were so full of captured sunshine that in the darkest days they must keep an inner brightness. Nan, though too ignorant to single out the details of all this beauty, found herself suddenly at ease with the soft mellow place, as though some secret thread of destiny attached her to it.

Guy Thwarte, somewhat to her surprise, had kept at her side during the walk and the visit to the chapel. He had not said much, but with him also Nan had felt instantly at ease. In his answers to her questions she had detected a latent passion for every tree and stone of the beautiful old place – a sentiment new to her experience, as a dweller in houses without histories, but exquisitely familiar to her imagination. They had walked together to the far end of the terrace before she noticed that the others, guided by Sir Helmsley, were passing through the glass doors into the hall. Nan turned to follow, but her companion laid his hand on her arm. 'Stay,' he said quietly.

Without answering she perched herself on the ledge of the balustrade, and looked up at the long honey-coloured front of the house, with the great carven shield above the door, and the quiet lines of cornice and window-frames.

'I wanted you to see it in this light. It's the magic hour,' he explained.

She turned her glance from the house to his face. 'I see why Conchita says it's the most beautiful place in England.'

He smiled. 'I don't know. I suppose if one were married to a woman one adored, one would soon get beyond her beauty. That's the way I feel about Honourslove. It's in my bones.'

'Oh, then you understand!' she exclaimed.

'Understand –?'

Nan coloured a little; the words had slipped out. 'I mean about the *beyondness* of things. I know there's no such word . . .'

'There's such a feeling. When two people have reached it together it's – well, they *are* "beyond".' He broke off. 'You see now why I wanted you to come to Honourslove,' he said in an odd new voice.

She was still looking at him thoughtfully. 'You knew I'd understand.'

'Oh, everything!'

She sighed for pleasure; but then: 'No. There's one thing I don't understand. How you go away and leave it all for so long.'

He gave a nervous laugh. 'You don't know England. That's part of our sense of beyondness: I'd do more than that for those old stones.'

Nan bent her eyes to the worn flags on the terrace. 'I see; that was stupid of me.'

For no reason at all the quick colour rushed to her temples again, and the young man coloured too. 'It's a beautiful view,' she stammered, suddenly self-conscious.

'It depends who looks at it,' he said.

She dropped to her feet, and turned to gaze away over the shimmering distances. Guy Thwarte said nothing more, and for a long while they stood side by side without speaking, each seeing the other in every line of the landscape.

*

Sir Helmsley, after fulminating in advance against the foreign intruders, had been all smiles on their arrival. Guy was used to
such sudden changes of the paternal mood, and knew that feminine
beauty could be counted on to produce them. His father could never,
at the moment, hold out against deep lashes and brilliant lips, and
no one knew better than Virginia St George how to make use of
such charms.

'That red-haired witch from Brazil has her wits about her,' Sir
Helmsley mumbled that evening over his after-dinner cigar. 'I don't
wonder she stirs them up at Allfriars. Gad, I should think Master
Richard Marable had found his match . . . But your St George girl is
a goddess . . . *patuit dea* – I think I like 'em better like that . . . divinely
dull . . . just the quiet bearers of their own beauty, like the priestesses
in a Panathenaic procession . . .' He leaned back in his armchair,
and looked sharply across the table at his son, who sat with bent
head, drawing vague arabesques on the mahogany. 'Guy, my boy –
that kind are about as expensive to acquire as the Venus of Milo;
and as difficult to fit into domestic life.'

Guy Thwarte looked up with an absent smile. 'I daresay that's
what Seadown's thinking, sir.'

'Seadown?'

'Well, I suppose your classical analogies are meant to apply to the
eldest Miss St George, aren't they?'

Father and son continued to look at each other, the father perplexed, the son privately amused. 'What? Isn't it the eldest –?' Sir
Helmsley broke out.

Guy shook his head, and his father sank back with a groan. 'Good
Lord, my boy! I thought I understood you. Sovran beauty . . . and that
girl has it . . .'

'I suppose so, sir.'

'You *suppose* –?'

Guy held up his head and cleared his throat. 'You see, sir, it
happens to be the younger one –'

'The younger one? I didn't even notice her. I imagined you were
taking her off my hands so that I could have a better chance with the
beauties.'

'Perhaps in a way I was,' said Guy. 'Though I think you might
have enjoyed talking to her almost as much as gazing at the goddess.'

'H'm. What sort of talk?'

'Well, she came to a dead point before the Rossetti in the study, and at once began to quote "The Blessed Damozel".'

'That child? So the Fleshly School has penetrated to the back-woods! Well, I don't know that it's exactly the best food for the family breakfast-table.'

'I imagine she came on it by chance. It appears she has a wonderful governess who's a cousin of the Rossettis.'

'Ah, yes. One of old Testavaglia's descendants, I suppose. What a queer concatenation of circumstances, to doom an Italian patriot to bring up a little Miss Jonathan!'

'I think it was rather a happy accident to give her some one with whom she could talk of poetry.'

'Well – supposing you were to leave that to her governess? Eh? I say, Guy, you don't mean –?'

His son paused before replying. 'I've nothing to add to what I told you the other day, sir. My South American job comes first; and God knows what will have become of her when I get back. She's barely nineteen and I've only seen her twice . . .'

'Well, I'm glad you remember that,' his father interjected. 'I never should have, at your age.'

'Oh, I've given it thought enough, I can assure you,' Guy rejoined, still with his quiet smile.

Sir Helmsley rose from his chair. 'Shall we finish our smoke on the terrace?'

They went out together into the twilight, and strolled up and down, as their habit was, in silence. Guy Thwarte knew that Sir Helmsley's mind was as crowded as his own with urgent passionate thoughts clamouring to be expressed. And there were only three days left in which to utter them! To the young man his father's step and his own sounded as full of mystery as the tread of the coming years. After a while they made one of their wonted pauses, and stood leaning against the balustrade above the darkening landscape.

'Eh, well – what are you thinking of?' Sir Helmsley broke out, with one of his sudden jerks of interrogation.

Guy pondered. 'I was thinking how strange and far-off everything here seems to me already. I seem to see it all as sharply as things in a dream.'

Sir Helmsley gave a nervous laugh. 'H'm. And I was thinking that the strangest thing about it all was to hear common-sense spoken about a young woman under the roof of Honourslove.' He pressed his son's arm, and then turned abruptly away, and they resumed their walk in silence; for in truth there was nothing more to be said.

12

A dark-haired girl who was so handsome that the heads nearest her were all turned her way, stood impatiently at a crowded London street-corner. It was a radiant afternoon of July; and the crowd which had checked her advance had assembled to see the fine ladies in their state carriages on the way to the last Drawing-room of the season.

'I don't see why they won't let us through. It's worse than a village circus,' the beauty grumbled to her companion, a younger girl who would have been pretty save for that dazzling proximity, but who showed her teeth too much when she laughed. She laughed now.

'What's wrong with just staying where we are, Liz? It beats any Barnum show I ever saw, and the people are ever so much more polite. Nobody shoves you. Look at that antique yellow coach coming along now, with the two powdered giants hanging on at the back. Oh, Liz! – and the old mummy inside! I guess she dates way back beyond the carriage. But look at her jewels, will you? My good-ness – and she's got a real live crown on her head!'

'Shut up, Mab – everybody's looking at you,' Lizzy Elmsworth rejoined, still sulkily, though in spite of herself she was beginning to be interested in the scene.

The younger girl laughed again. 'They're looking at *you*, you silly. It rests their eyes, after all the scare-crows in those circus-chariots. Liz, why do you suppose they dress up like queens at the waxworks, just to go to an afternoon party?'

'It's not an ordinary party. It's the Queen's Drawing-room.'

'Well, I'm sorry for the Queen if she has to feast her eyes for long on some of these beauties . . . Oh, good; the carriages are moving!

THE BUCCANEERS

Better luck next time. This next carriage isn't half as grand, but maybe it's pleasanter inside . . . Oh!' Mab Elmsworth suddenly exclaimed, applying a sharp pinch to her sister's arm.

' "Oh" what? I don't see anything so wonderful –'

'Why, look, Lizzy! Reach up on your tip-toes. In the third carriage – if it isn't the St George girls! Look, *look*! When they move again they'll see us.'

'Nonsense. There are dozens of people between us. Besides, I don't believe it is . . . How in the world should they be here?'

'Why, I guess Conchita fixed it up. Or don't they present people through our Legation?'

'You have to have letters to the Minister. Who on earth'd have given them to the St Georges?'

'I don't know; but there they are. Oh, Liz, look at Jinny, will you? She looks like a queen herself – a queen going to her wedding, with that tulle veil and the feathers . . . Oh, mercy, and there's little Nan! Well, the headdress isn't as becoming to her – she hasn't got the *style*, has she? Now, Liz! The carriages are moving . . . I'm not tall enough – you reach up and wave. They're sure to see us if you do.'

Lizzy Elmsworth did not move. 'I can survive not being seen by the St George girls,' she said coldly. 'If only we could get out of this crowd.'

'Oh, just wait till I squeeze through, and make a sign to them! There –. Oh, thank you so much . . . Now they see me! Jinny – Nan – do look! It's Mab . . .'

Lizzy caught her sister by the arm. 'You're making a show of us; come away,' she whispered angrily.

'Why, Liz . . . Just wait a second . . . I'm sure they saw us . . .'

'I'm sure they didn't want to see us. Can't you understand? A girl screaming at the top of her lungs from the side-walk . . . Please come when I tell you to, Mabel.'

At that moment Virginia St George turned her head toward Mab's gesticulating arm. Her face, under its halo of tulle and arching feathers, was so lovely that the eyes in the crowd deserted Lizzy Elmsworth. 'Well, they're not *all* mummies going to Court,' a man said good-naturedly; and the group about him laughed.

'Come away, Mabel,' Miss Elmsworth repeated. She did not know till that moment how much she would dislike seeing the St George girls in the glory of their Court feathers. She dragged her reluctant sister through a gap in the crowd, and they turned back in the direction of the hotel where they were staying.

'Now I hope you understand that they saw us, *and didn't want to see us!*'

'Why, Liz, what's come over you? A minute ago you said they couldn't possibly see us.'

'Now I'm sure they did, and made believe not to. I should have thought you'd have had more pride than to scream at them that way among all those common people.'

The two girls walked on in silence.

Mrs St George had been bitterly disappointed in her attempt to launch her daughters in New York. Scandalized though she was by Virginia's joining in the wretched practical joke played on the Assembly patronesses by Lord Richard Marable and his future brother-in-law, she could not think that such a prank would have lasting consequences. The difficulty, she believed, lay with Colonel St George. He was too free-and-easy, too much disposed to behave as if Fifth Avenue and Wall Street were one. As a social figure no one took him seriously (except certain women she could have named, had it not demeaned her even to think of them), and by taking up with the Clossons, and forcing her to associate publicly with that divorced foreigner, he had deprived her girls of all chance of social recognition. Miss Testvalley had seen it from the first. She too was terribly upset about the ball; but she did not share Mrs St George's view that Virginia and Nan, by acting as bridesmaids to Conchita Closson, had increased the mischief. At the wedding their beauty had been much remarked; and, as Miss Testvalley pointed out, Conchita had married into one of the greatest English families, and if ever the girls wanted to do a London season, knowing the Brightlingseas would certainly be a great help.

'A London season?' Mrs St George gasped, in a tone implying that her burdens and bewilderments were heavy enough already.

Miss Testvalley laughed. 'Why not? It might be much easier than New York; you ought to try,' that intrepid woman declared.

Mrs St George, in her bewilderment, repeated this to her eldest daughter; and Virginia, who was a thoughtful girl, turned the matter over in her mind. The New York experiment, though her mother regarded it as a failure, had not been without its compensations; especially the second winter, when Nan emerged from the school-room. There was no doubt that Nan supplemented her sister use-fully; she could always think of something funny or original to say, whereas there were moments when Virginia had to rely on the length of her eyelashes and the lustre of her lips, and trust to them to plead for her. Certainly the two sisters made an irresistible pair. The Assembly ladies might ignore their existence, but the young men did not; and there were jolly little dinners and gay theatre-parties in plenty to console the exiled beauties. Still, it was bitter to be left out of all the most exclusive entertainments, to have not a single invitation to Newport, to be unbidden to the Opera on the fashion-able nights. With Mrs St George it rankled more than with her daugh-ters. With the approach of the second summer she had thought of hiring a house at Newport; but she simply didn't dare – and it was then that Miss Testvalley made her bold suggestion.

'But I've never been to England. I wouldn't know how to get to know people. And I couldn't face a strange country all alone.'

'You'd soon make friends, you know. It's easier sometimes in foreign countries.'

Virginia here joined in. 'Why shouldn't we try, mother? I'm sure Conchita'd be glad to get us invitations. She's awfully good-natured.'

'Your father would think we'd gone crazy.'

Perhaps Mrs St George hoped he would; it was always an added cause for anxiety when her husband approved of holiday plans in which he was not to share. And that summer she knew he intended to see the Cup Races off Newport, with a vulgar drinking crowd, Elmsworth and Closson among them, who had joined him in charter-ing a steam-yacht for the occasion.

Colonel St George's business association with Mr Closson had turned out to be an exceptionally fruitful one, and he had not failed to remind his wife that its pecuniary results had already justified him in asking her to be kind to Mrs Closson. 'If you hadn't, how would I have paid for this European trip, I'd like to know, and all the finery for the girls' London season?' he had playfully reminded her, as he pressed the steamer-tickets and a letter of credit into her reluctant hand.

Mrs St George knew then that the time for further argument was over. The letter of credit, a vaguely understood instrument which she handled as though it were an explosive, proved that his decision was irrevocable. The pact with Mr Closson had paid for the projected European tour, and would also, Mrs St George bitterly reflected, help to pay for the charter of the steam-yacht, and the champagne orgies on board, with ladies in pink bonnets. All this was final, unchangeable, and she could only exhale her anguish to her daughters and their governess.

'Now your father's rich his first idea is to get rid of us, and have a good time by himself.'

Nan flushed up, longing to find words in defence of the Colonel; and Virginia spoke for her. 'How silly, mother! Father feels it's only fair to give us a chance in London. You know perfectly well that if we get on there we'll be invited everywhere when we get back to New York. That's why father wants us to go.'

'But I simply couldn't go to England all alone with you girls,' Mrs St George despairingly repeated.

'But we won't be alone. Of course Miss Testvalley'll come too!' Nan interrupted.

'Take care, Nan! If I do, it will be to try to get you on with your Italian,' said the governess. But they were all aware that by this time she was less necessary to her pupils than to their mother. And so, they hardly knew how, they had all (with Colonel St George's too-hearty encouragement) drifted, or been whirled, into this wild project; and now, on a hot July afternoon, when Mrs St George would have been so happy sipping her lemonade in friendly company on the Grand Union verandah, she sat in the melancholy exile of a London hotel, and wondered when the girls would get back from that awful performance they called a Drawing-room.

There had been times – she remembered ruefully – when she had not been happy at Saratoga, had felt uncomfortable in the company of the dubious Mrs Closson, and irritated by the vulgar exuberance of Mrs Elmsworth; but such was her present loneliness that she would have welcomed either with open arms. And it was precisely as this thought crossed her mind that the buttons knocked on the door to ask if she would receive Mrs Elmsworth.

'Oh, my dear!' cried poor Mrs St George, falling on her visitor's breast; and two minutes later the ladies were mingling their loneliness, their perplexities, their mistrust of all things foreign and unfamiliar, in an ecstasy of interchanged confidences.

The confidences lasted so long that Mrs Elmsworth did not return to her hotel until after her daughters. She found them alone in the dark shiny sitting-room which so exactly resembled the one inhabited by Mrs St George, and saw at once that they were out of humour with each other if not with the world. Mrs Elmsworth disliked gloomy faces, and on this occasion felt herself entitled to resent them, since it was to please her daughters that she had left her lazy pleasant cure at Bad Ems to give them a glimpse of the London season.

'Well, girls, you look as if you were just home from a funeral,' she remarked, breathing heavily from her ascent of the hotel stairs, and restraining the impulse to undo the upper buttons of her strongly whale-boned Paris dress.

'Well, we are. We've seen all the old corpses in London dressed up for that circus they call a Drawing-room,' said her eldest daughter.

'They weren't all corpses, though,' Mab interrupted. 'What do you think, mother? We saw Jinny and Nan St George, rigged out to kill, feathers and all, in the procession!'

Mrs Elmsworth manifested no surprise. 'Yes, I know. I've just been sitting with Mrs St George, and she told me the girls had gone to the Drawing-room. She said Conchita Marable fixed it up for them. So you see it's not so difficult, after all.'

Lizzy shrugged impatiently. 'If Conchita has done it for them we can't ask her to do it again for us. Besides, it's too late; I saw in the paper it was the last Drawing-room. I told you we ought to have come a month ago.'

'Well, I wouldn't worry about that,' said her mother good-naturedly. 'There was a Miss March came in while I was with Mrs St George – such a sweet little woman. An American; but she's lived for years in London, and knows everybody. Well, she said going to a Drawing-room didn't really amount to anything; it just gave the girls a chance to dress up and see a fine show. She says the thing is to be in the Prince of Wales's set. That's what all the smart women are after. And it seems that Miss March's friend, Lady Churt, is very intimate with the Prince and has introduced Conchita to him, and he's crazy about her Spanish songs. Isn't that funny, girls?'

'It may be very funny. But I don't see how it's going to help us,' Lizzy grumbled.

Mrs Elmsworth gave her easy laugh. 'Well, it won't, if you don't help yourselves. If you think everybody's against you, they will be against you. But that Miss March has invited you and Mabel to take tea at her house next week – it seems everybody in England takes tea at five. In the country-houses the women dress up for it, in things they call "tea-gowns". I wish we'd known that when we were order-ing our clothes in Paris. But Miss March will tell you all about it, and a lot more besides.'

Lizzy Elmsworth was not a good-tempered girl, but she was too intelligent to let her temper interfere with her opportunities. She hated the St George girls for having got ahead of her in their attack on London, but was instantly disposed to profit by the breach they had made. Virginia St George was not clever, and Lizzy would be able to guide her; they could be of the greatest use to each other, if the St Georges could be made to enter into the plan. Exactly what plan, Lizzy herself did not know; but she felt instinctively that, like their native country, they could stand only if they were united.

Mrs St George, in her loneliness, had besought Mrs Elmsworth to return the next afternoon. She didn't dare invite Lizzy and Mab, she explained, because her own girls were being taken to see the Tower of London by some of their new friends (Lizzy's resentment stirred again as she listened); but if Mrs Elmsworth would just drop in and sit with her, Mrs St George thought perhaps Miss March would be coming in too, and then they would talk over plans for the rest of the summer. Lizzy understood at once the use to which Mrs St George's loneliness might be put. Mrs Elmsworth was lonely too; but this did not greatly concern her daughter. In the St George and Elmsworth circles unemployed mothers were the rule; but Lizzy saw that, by pooling their solitudes, the two ladies might become more contented, and therefore more manageable. And having come to lay siege to London Miss Elmsworth was determined, at all costs, not to leave till the citadel had fallen.

'I guess I'll go with you,' she announced, when her mother rose to put on her bonnet for the call.

'Why, the girls won't be there; she told me so. She says they'll be round to see you tomorrow,' said Mrs Elmsworth, surprised.

'I don't care about the girls; I want to see that Miss March.'

'Oh, well,' her mother agreed. Lizzy was always doing things she didn't understand, but Mab usually threw some light on them afterward. And certainly, Mrs Elmsworth reflected, it became her eldest daughter to be in one of her mysterious moods. She had never seen Lizzy look more goddess-like than when they ascended Mrs St George's stairs together.

Miss March was not far from sharing Mrs Elmsworth's opinion. When the Elmsworth ladies were shown in, Miss March was already sitting with Mrs St George. She had returned on the pretext of bringing an invitation for the girls to visit Holland House; but in reality she was impatient to see the rival beauty. Miss Testvalley, the day before, had told her all about Lizzy Elmsworth, whom some people thought, in her different way, as handsome as Virginia, and who was certainly cleverer. And here she was, stalking in ahead of her mother, in what appeared to be the new American style, and carrying her slim height and small regal head with an assurance which might well eclipse Virginia's milder light.

Miss March surveyed her with the practised eye of an old frequenter of the marriage-market.

'Very fair girls usually have a better chance here; but Idina Churt is dark – perhaps, for that reason, this girl might be more likely . . .' Miss March lost herself in almost maternal musings. She often said to herself (and sometimes to her most intimate friends) that Lord Seadown seemed to her like her own son; and now, as she looked on Lizzy Elmsworth's dark splendour, she murmured inwardly: 'Of course we must find out first what Mr Elmsworth would be prepared to do . . .'

To Mrs Elmsworth, whom she greeted with her most persuasive smile, she said engagingly: 'Mrs St George and I have such a delightful plan to suggest to you. Of course you won't want to stay in London much longer. It's so hot and crowded; and before long it will be a dusty desert. Mrs St George tells me that you're both rather wondering where to go next, and I've suggested that you should join her in hiring a lovely little cottage on the Thames belonging to a friend of mine, Lady Churt. It could be had at once, servants and all – the most perfect servants – and I've stayed so often with Lady Churt that I know just how cool and comfortable and lazy one can be there. But I was thinking more especially of your daughters and their friends . . . The river's a Paradise at their age . . . the punting by moonlight, and all the rest . . .'

Long-past memories of the river's magic brought a sigh to Miss March's lips; but she turned it into a smile as she raised her forget-me-not eyes to Lizzy Elmsworth's imperial orbs. Lizzy returned the look, and the two immediately understood each other.

'Why, mother, that sounds perfectly lovely. You'd love it too, Mrs St George, wouldn't you?' Lizzy smiled, stooping gracefully to kiss her mother's friend. She had no idea what punting was, but the fact that it was practised by moonlight suggested the exclusion of rheumatic elders, and a free field – or river, rather – for the exercise of youthful arts. And in those she felt confident of excelling.

13

The lawn before Lady Churt's cottage (or bungalow, as the knowing were beginning to say) spread sweetly to the Thames at Runnymede. With its long deck-like verandah, its awnings stretched from every window, it seemed to Nan St George a fairy galleon making, all sails set, for the river. Swans, as fabulous to Nan as her imaginary galleon, sailed majestically on the silver flood; and boats manned by beautiful bare-armed athletes sped back and forth between the flat grass-banks.

At first Nan was the only one of the party on whom the river was not lost. Virginia's attention travelled barely as far as the circles of calceolarias and lobelias dotting the lawn, and the vases of red geraniums and purple petunias which flanked the door; she liked the well-kept flowers and bright turf, and found it pleasant, on warm afternoons, to sit under an ancient cedar and play at the new-fangled tea-drinking into which they had been initiated by Miss March, with the aid of Lady Churt's accomplished parlour-maid. Lizzy Elmsworth and Mab also liked the tea-drinking, but were hardly aware of the great blue-green boughs under which the rite was celebrated. They had grown up between city streets and watering-place hotels, and were serenely unconscious of the 'beyondness' of which Nan had confided her mysterious sense to Guy Thwarte.

The two mothers, after their first bewildered contact with Lady Churt's servants, had surrendered themselves to these accomplished guides, and lapsed contentedly into their old watering-place habits. To Mrs St George and Mrs Elmsworth the cottage at Runnymede differed from the Grand Union at Saratoga only in its inferior size, and more restricted opportunities for gossip. True, Miss March came down often with racy tit-bits from London, but the distinguished persons concerned were too remote to interest the exiles. Mrs St George missed even the things she had loathed at Saratoga – the familiarity of the black servants, the obnoxious sociability of Mrs Closson, and the spectacle of the race-course, with ladies in pink bonnets lying in wait for the Colonel. Mrs Elmsworth had never wasted her time in loathing anything. She would have been perfectly happy at Saratoga and in New York if her young ladies had been more kindly welcomed there. She privately thought Lizzy hard to please, and wondered what her own life would have been if she had turned up her nose at Mr Elmsworth, who was a clerk in the village grocery-store when they had joined their lot; but the girls had their own ideas, and since Conchita Closson's marriage (an unhappy affair, as it turned out) had roused theirs with social ambition, Mrs Elmsworth was perfectly willing to let them try their luck in England, where beauty such as Lizzy's (because it was rarer, she supposed) had been known to raise a girl almost to the throne. It would certainly be funny, she confided to Mrs St George, to see one of their daughters settled at Windsor Castle (Mrs St George thought it would be exceedingly funny to see one of Mrs Elmsworth's); and Miss March, to whom the confidence was passed on, concluded that Mrs Elmsworth was imperfectly aware of the difference between the ruler of England and her subjects.

'Unfortunately their Royal Highnesses are all married,' she said with her instructive little laugh; and Mrs Elmsworth replied vaguely: 'Oh, but aren't there plenty of other Dukes?' If there were, she could trust Lizzy, her tone implied; and Miss March, whose mind was now set on uniting the dark beauty to Lord Seadown, began to wonder if she might not fail again, this time not as in her own case, but because of the young lady's too-great ambition.

Mrs Elmsworth also missed the friendly bustle of the Grand Union, the gentlemen coming from New York on Saturdays with the Wall Street news, and the flutter caused in the dining-room when it got round that Mr Elmsworth had made another hit on the market; but she soon resigned herself to the routine of *bézique* with Mrs St George. At first she too was chilled by the silent orderliness of the household; but though both ladies found the maid-servants painfully unsociable, and were too much afraid of the cook ever to set foot in the kitchen, they enjoyed the absence of domestic disturbances, and the novel experience of having every wish anticipated.

Meanwhile the bungalow was becoming even more attractive than when its owner inhabited it. Parliament sat exceptionally late that year, and many were the younger members of both Houses, chafing to escape to Scotland, and the private secretaries and minor government officials, still chained to their desks, who found compensations at the cottage on the Thames. Reinforced by the guardsmen quartered at Windsor, they prolonged the river season in a manner unknown to the oldest inhabitants. The weather that year seemed to be in connivance with the American beauties, and punting by moonlight was only one of the midsummer distractions to be found at Runnymede.

To Lady Richard Marable the Thames-side cottage offered a happy escape from her little house in London, where there were always duns to be dealt with, and unpaid servants to be coaxed to stay. She came down often, always bringing the right people with her, and combining parties, and inventing amusements, which made invitations to the cottage as sought-after as cards to the Royal enclosure. There was not an ounce of jealousy in Conchita's easy nature. She was delighted with the success of her friends, and proud of the admiration they excited. 'We've each got our own line,' she said to Lizzy Elmsworth, 'and if we only back each other up we'll beat all the other women hands down. The men are blissfully happy in a house where nobody chaperons them, and they can smoke in every room, and gaze at you and Virginia, and laugh at my jokes, and join in my nigger songs. It's too soon yet to know what Nan St George and Mab will contribute; but they'll probably develop a line of their own, and the show's not a bad one as it is. If we stick to the rules of the game, and don't play any low-down tricks on each other,' ('Oh, Conchita!' Lizzy protested, with a beautiful pained smile) 'we'll have all London in our pocket next year.'

No one followed the Runnymede revels with a keener eye than Miss Testvalley. The invasion of England had been her own invention, and from a thousand little signs she already knew it would end in conquest. But from the outset she had put her charges on their guard against a too-easy triumph. The young men were to be allowed as much innocent enjoyment as they chose; but Miss Testvalley saw to it that they remembered the limits of their liberty. It was amusement enough to be with a group of fearless and talkative girls, who said new things in a new language, who were ignorant of tradition and unimpressed by distinctions of rank; but it was soon clear that their young hostesses must be treated with the same respect, if not with the same ceremony, as English girls of good family.

Miss Testvalley, when she persuaded the St Georges to come to England, had rejoiced at the thought of being once more near her family; but she soon found that her real centre of gravity was in the little house at Runnymede. She performed the weekly pilgrimage to Denmark Hill in the old spirit of filial piety; but the old enthusiasm was lacking. Her venerable relatives (thanks to her earnings in America) were now comfortably provided for; but they had grown too placid, too static, to occupy her. Her natural inclination was for action and conflict, and all her thoughts were engrossed by her young charges. Miss March was an admirable lieutenant, supplying the social experience which Miss Testvalley lacked; and between them they administered the cottage at Runnymede like an outpost in a conquered province.

Miss March, who was without Miss Testvalley's breadth of vision, was slightly alarmed by the audacities of the young ladies, and secretly anxious to improve their social education.

'I don't think they understand *yet* what a Duke is,' she sighed to Miss Testvalley, after a Sunday when Lord Seadown had unexpectedly appeared at the cottage with his cousin, the young Duke of Tintagel.

Miss Testvalley laughed. 'So much the better! I hope they never will. Look at the well brought-up American girls who've got the peerage by heart, and spend their lives trying to be taken for members of the British aristocracy. Don't they always end by marrying curates or army-surgeons – or just not marrying at all?'

A reminiscent pink suffused Miss March's cheek. 'Yes . . . sometimes; perhaps you're right . . . But I don't think I shall ever quite get used to Lady Richard's Spanish dances; or to the peculiar words in some of her songs.'

'Lady Richard's married, and needn't concern us,' said Miss Testvalley. 'What attracts the young men is the girls' naturalness, and their not being afraid to say what they think.' Miss March sighed again, and said she supposed that was the new fashion; certainly it gave the girls a better chance . . .

Lord Seadown's sudden appearance at the cottage seemed in fact to support Miss Testvalley's theory. Miss March remembered Lady Churt's emphatic words when the lease had been concluded. 'I'm ever so much obliged to you, Jacky. You've got me out of an awfully tight place by finding tenants for me, and getting such a good rent out of them. I only hope your American beauties will want to come back next year. But I've forbidden Seadown to set foot in the place while they're there, and if Conchita Marable coaxes him down you must swear you'll let me know, and I'll see it doesn't happen again.'

Miss March had obediently sworn; but she saw now that she must conceal Lord Seadown's visits instead of denouncing them. Poor Idina's exactions were obviously absurd. If she chose to let her house she could not prevent her tenants from receiving any one they pleased; and it was clear that the tenants liked Seadown, and that he returned the sentiment, for after his first visit he came often. Lady Churt, luckily, was in Scotland; and Miss March trusted to her remaining there till the lease of the cottage had expired.

The Duke of Tintagel did not again accompany his friend. He was a young man of non-committal appearance and manner, and it was difficult to say what impression the American beauties made on him; but, to Miss March's distress, he had apparently made little if any on them.

'They don't seem in the least to realize that he's the greatest match in England,' Miss March said with a shade of impatience. 'Not that there would be the least chance . . . I understand the Duchess has already made her choice; and the young Duke is a perfect son. Still, the mere fact of his coming . . .'

'Oh, he came merely out of curiosity. He's always been rather a dull young man, and I daresay all the noise and the nonsense simply bewildered him.'

'Oh, but you know him, of course, don't you? You were at Tintagel before you went to America. Is it true that he always does what his mother tells him?'

'I don't know. But the young men about whom that is said usually break out sooner or later,' replied the governess with a shrug.

About this time she began to wonder if the atmosphere of Runnymede were not a little too stimulating for Nan's tender sensibilities. Since Teddy de Santos-Dios, who had joined his sister in London, had taken to coming down with her for Sundays, the fun had grown fast and furious. Practical jokes were Teddy's chief accomplishment, and their preparation involved rather too much familiarity with the upper ranges of the house, too much popping in and out of bedrooms, and too many screaming midnight pillow-fights. Miss Testvalley saw that Nan, whose feelings always rushed to extremes, was growing restless and excited, and she felt the need of shielding the girl and keeping her apart. That the others were often noisy, and sometimes vulgar, did not disturb Miss Testvalley; they were obviously in pursuit of husbands, and had probably hit on the best way of getting them. Seadown was certainly very much taken by Lizzy Elmsworth; and two or three of the other young men had fallen victims to Virginia's graces. But it was too early for Nan to enter the matrimonial race, and when she did, Miss Testvalley hoped it would be for different reasons, and in a different manner. She did not want her pupil to engage herself after a night of champagne and song on the river; her sense of artistic fitness rejected the idea of Nan's adopting the same methods as her elders.

Mrs St George was slightly bewildered when the governess suggested taking her pupil away from the late hours and the continuous excitements at the cottage. It was not so much the idea of parting from Nan, as of losing the moral support of the governess's presence, that troubled Mrs St George. 'But, Miss Testvalley, why do you want to go away? I never know how to talk to those servants, and I never can remember the titles of the young men that Conchita brings down, or what I ought to call them.'

'I'm sure Miss March will help you with all that. And I do think Nan ought to get away for two or three weeks. Haven't you noticed how thin she's grown? And her eyes are as big as saucers. I know a quiet little place in Cornwall where she could have some bathing, and go to bed every night at nine.'

To every one's surprise, Nan offered no objection. The prospect of seeing new places stirred her imagination, and she seemed to lose all interest in the gay doings at the cottage when Miss Testvalley told her that, on the way, they would stop at Exeter, where there was a very beautiful cathedral.

'And shall we see some beautiful houses too? I love seeing houses that are so ancient and so lovely that the people who live there have them in their bones.'

Miss Testvalley looked at her pupil sharply. 'What an odd expression! Did you find it in a book?' she asked; for the promiscuity of Nan's reading sometimes alarmed her.

'Oh, no. It was what that young Mr Thwarte said to me about Honourslove. It's why he's going away for two years – so that he can make a great deal of money, and come back and spend it on Honourslove.'

'H'm – from what I've heard, Honourslove could easily swallow a good deal more than he's likely to make in two years, or even ten,' said Miss Testvalley. 'The father and son are both said to be very extravagant, and the only way for Mr Guy Thwarte to keep up his ancestral home will be to bring a great heiress back to it.'

Nan looked thoughtful. 'You mean, even if he doesn't love her?'

'Oh, well, I daresay he'll love her – or be grateful to her, at any rate.'

'I shouldn't think gratitude was enough,' said Nan with a sigh. She was silent again for a while, and then added: 'Mr Thwarte has read all your cousin's poetry – Dante Gabriel's, I mean.'

Miss Testvalley gave her a startled glance. 'May I ask how you happened to find that out?'

'Why, because there's a perfectly beautiful picture by your cousin in Sir Helmsley's study, and Mr Thwarte showed it to me. And so we talked of his poetry too. But Mr Thwarte thinks there are other poems even more wonderful than "The Blessed Damozel". Some of the sonnets in *The House of Life*, I mean. Do you think they're more beautiful, Miss Testvalley?'

The governess hesitated; she often found herself hesitating over the answers to Nan's questions. 'You told Mr Thwarte that you'd read some of those poems?'

'Oh, yes; I told him I'd read every one of them.'

'And what did he say?'

'He said . . . he said he'd felt from the first that he and I would be certain to like the same things; and he *loved* my liking Dante Gabriel. I told him he was your cousin, and that you were devoted to him.'

'Ah – well, I'm glad you told him that, for Sir Helmsley Thwarte is an old friend of my cousin's, and one of his best patrons. But you know, Nan, there are people who don't appreciate his poetry – don't see how beautiful it is; and I'd rather you didn't proclaim in public that you've read it all. Some people are so stupid that they wouldn't exactly understand a young girl's caring for that kind of poetry. You see, don't you, dear?'

'Oh, yes. They'd be shocked, I suppose, because it's all about love. But that's why I like it, you know,' said Nan composedly.

Miss Testvalley made no answer, and Nan went on in a thoughtful voice: 'Shall we see some other places as beautiful as Honourslove?'

The governess reflected. She had not contemplated a round of sight-seeing for her pupil, and Cornwall did not seem to have many sights to offer. But at length she said: 'Well, Trevennick is not so far from Tintagel. If the family are away I might take you there, I suppose. You know the old Tintagel was supposed to have been King Arthur's castle.'

Nan's face lit up. 'Where the Knights of the Round Table were? Oh, Miss Testvalley, can we see that too? And the mere where he threw his sword Excalibur? Oh, couldn't we start tomorrow, don't you think?'

Miss Testvalley felt relieved. She had been slightly disturbed by Nan's allusion to Honourslove, and the unexpected glimpse it gave of an exchange of confidences between Guy Thwarte and her pupil; but she saw that in another moment the thought of visiting the scenes celebrated in Tennyson's famous poems had swept away all other fancies. *The Idylls of the King* had been one of Nan's magic casements, and Miss Testvalley smiled to herself at the ease with which the girl's mind flitted from one new vision to another.

'A child still, luckily,' she thought, sighing, she knew not why, at what the future might hold for Nan when childish things should be put away.

14

The Duke of Tintagel was a young man burdened with scruples. This was probably due to the fact that his father, the late Duke, had had none. During all his boyhood and youth the heir had watched the disastrous effects of not considering trifles. It was not that his father had been either irresponsible or negligent. The late Duke had no vices; but his virtues were excessively costly. His conduct had always been governed by a sense of the overwhelming obligations connected with his great position. One of these obligations, he held, consisted in keeping up his rank; the other, in producing an heir. Unfortunately the Duchess had given him six daughters before a son was born, and two more afterward in the attempt to provide the heir with a younger brother; and though daughters constitute a relatively small charge on a great estate, still a Duke's daughters cannot (or so their parent thought) be fed, clothed, educated and married at as low a cost as young women of humbler origin. The Duke's other obligation, that of keeping up his rank, had involved him in even heavier expenditure. Hitherto Longlands, the seat in Somersetshire, had been thought imposing enough even for a Duke; but its owner had always been troubled by the fact that the new castle at Tintagel, built for his great-grandfather in the approved Gothic style of the day, and with the avowed intention of surpassing Inveraray, had never been inhabited. The expense of completing it, and living in it in suitable state, appeared to have discouraged its creator; and for years it stood abandoned on its Cornish cliff, a sadder ruin than the other, until it passed to the young Duke's father. To him it became a torment, a reproach, an obsession; the Duke of Tintagel must live at Tintagel as the Duke of Argyll lived at Inveraray, with a splendour befitting the place; and the carrying out of this resolve had been the late Duke's crowning achievement.

His young heir, who had just succeeded him, had as keen a sense as his father of ducal duties. He meant, if possible, to keep up in suitable state both Tintagel and Longlands, as well as Folyat House, his London residence; but he meant to do so without the continual drain on his fortune which his father had been obliged to incur. The new Duke hoped that, by devoting all his time and most of his faculties to the care of his estates and the personal supervision of his budget, he could reduce his cost of living without altering its style; and the indefatigable Duchess, her numerous daughters notwithstanding, found time to second the attempt. She was not the woman to let her son forget the importance of her aid; and though a perfect understanding had always reigned between them, recent symptoms made it appear that the young Duke was beginning to chafe under her regency.

Soon after his visit to Runnymede he and his mother sat together in the Duchess's boudoir in the London house, a narrow lofty room on whose crowded walls authentic Raphaels were ultimately mingled with water-colours executed by the Duchess's maiden aunts, and photographs of shooting-parties at the various ducal estates. The Duchess invariably arranged to have this hour alone with her son, when breakfast was over, and her daughters (of whom death or marriage had claimed all but three) had gone their different ways. The Duchess had always kept her son to herself, and the Ladies Clara, Ermyntrude and Almina Folyat would never have dreamed of intruding on them.

At present, as it happened, all three were in the country, and Folyat House had put on its summer sackcloth; but the Duchess lingered on, determined not to forsake her son till he was released from his Parliamentary duties.

'I was hoping,' she said, noticing that the Duke had twice glanced at the clock, 'that you'd manage to get away to Scotland for a few days. Isn't it possible? The Hopeleighs particularly wanted you to go to them at Loch Skarig. Lady Hopeleigh wrote yesterday to ask me to remind you . . .'

The Duchess was small of stature, with firm round cheeks, a small mouth and quick dark eyes under an anxiously wrinkled forehead.

She did not often smile, and when, as now, she attempted it, the result was a pucker similar to the wrinkles on her brow. 'You know that some one else will be very grieved if you don't go,' she insinuated archly.

The Duke's look passed from faint *ennui* to marked severity. He glanced at the ceiling, and made no answer.

'My dear Ushant,' said the Duchess, who still called him by the title he had borne before his father's death, 'surely you can't be blind to the fact that poor Jean Hopeleigh's future is in your hands. It is a serious thing to have inspired such a deep sentiment . . .'

The Duke's naturally inexpressive face had become completely expressionless, but his mother continued: 'I only fear it may cause you a lasting remorse . . .'

'I will never marry any one who hunts me down for the sake of my title,' exclaimed the Duke abruptly.

His mother raised her neat dark eyebrows in a reproachful stare. 'For your title? But, my dear Ushant, surely Jean Hopeleigh . . .'

'Jean Hopeleigh is like all the others. I'm sick of being tracked like a wild animal,' cried the Duke, who looked excessively tame.

The Duchess gave a deep sigh. 'Ushant –!'

'Well?'

'You haven't – it's not possible – formed an imprudent attachment? You're not concealing anything from me?' The Duke's smiles were almost as difficult as his mother's; but his muscles made an effort in that direction. 'I shall never form an attachment until I meet a girl who doesn't know what a Duke is!'

'Well, my dear, I can't think where one could find a being so totally ignorant of everything on which England's greatness rests,' said the Duchess impressively.

'Then I shan't marry.'

'Ushant –!'

'I'm sorry, mother –'

She lifted her sharp eyes to his. 'You remember that the roof at Tintagel has still to be paid for?'

'Yes.'

'Dear Jean's settlements would make all that so easy. There's nothing the Hopeleighs wouldn't do . . .'

The Duke interrupted her. 'Why not marry me to a Jewess? Some of those people in the City could buy up the Hopeleighs and not feel it.'

The Duchess drew herself up. Her lips trembled, but no word came. Her son stalked out of the room. From the threshold he turned to say: 'I shall go down to Tintagel on Friday night to go over the books with Blair.' His mother could only bend her head; his obstinacy was beginning to frighten her.

The Duke got into the train on the Friday with a feeling of relief. His high and continuous sense of his rank was combined with a secret desire for anonymity. If he could have had himself replaced in the world of fashion and politics by a mechanical effigy of the Duke of Tintagel, while he himself went obscurely about his private business, he would have been a happier man. He was as firmly convinced as his mother that the greatness of England rested largely on her Dukes. The Dukes of Tintagel had always had a strong sense of public obligation; and the young Duke was determined not to fall below their standard. But his real tastes were for small matters, for the *minutiae* of a retired and leisurely existence. As a little boy his secret longing had been to be a clock-maker; or rather (since their fabrication might have been too delicate a business) a man who sold clocks and sat among them in his little shop, watching them, doctoring them, taking their temperature, feeling their pulse, listening to their chimes, oiling, setting and regulating them. The then Lord Ushant had never avowed this longing to his parents; even in petticoats he had understood that a future Duke can never hope to keep a clock-shop. But often, wandering through the great saloons and interminable galleries of Longlands and Tintagel, he had said to himself with a beating heart: 'Some day I'll wind all these clocks myself, every Sunday morning before breakfast.'

Later he felt that he would have been perfectly happy as a country squire, arbitrating in village disputes, adjusting differences between vicar and school-master, sorting fishing-tackle, mending broken furniture, doctoring the dogs, re-arranging his collection of stamps; instead of which fate had cast him for the centre front of the world's most brilliant social stage.

Undoubtedly his mother had been a great help. She enjoyed equally the hard work and the pompous ceremonial incumbent on conscientious Dukes; and the poor young Duke was incorrigibly conscientious. But his conscience could not compel him to accept a marriage arranged by his mother. That part of his life he intended to arrange for himself. His departure for Tintagel was an oblique reply to the Duchess's challenge. She had told him to go to Scotland, and he was going to Cornwall instead. The mere fact of being seated in a train which was hurrying westward was a declaration of independence. The Duke longed above all to be free, to decide for himself; and though he was ostensibly going to Tintagel on estate business, his real purpose was to think over his future in solitude.

If only he might have remained unmarried! Not that he was without the feelings natural to young men; but the kind of marriage he was expected to make took no account of such feelings. 'I won't be hunted – I won't!' the Duke muttered as the train rushed westward, seeing himself as a panting quarry pursued by an implacable pack of would-be Duchesses. Was there no escape? Yes. He would dedicate his public life entirely to his country, but in private he would do as he chose. Valiant words, and easy to speak when no one was listening; but with his mother's small hard eyes on him, his resolves had a way of melting. Was it true that if he did not offer himself to Jean Hopeleigh the world might accuse him of trifling with her? If so, the sooner he married some one else the better. The chief difficulty was that he had not yet met any one whom he really wanted to marry.

Well, he would give himself at least three days in which to think it all over, out of reach of the Duchess's eyes . . .

A salt mist was drifting to and fro down the coast as the Duke, the next afternoon, walked along the cliffs toward the ruins of the old Tintagel. Since early morning he had been at work with Mr Blair, the agent, going into the laborious question of reducing the bills for the roof of the new castle, and examining the other problems presented by the administration of his great domain. After that, with agent and housekeeper, he had inspected every room in the castle, carefully examining floors and ceilings, and seeing to it that Mr Blair recorded the repairs to be made, but firmly hurrying past the innumerable clocks, large and small, loud and soft, which, from writing-table and mantel-shelf and cabinet-top, cried out to him for attention. 'Have you a good man for the clocks?' he had merely asked, with an affectation of indifference; and when the housekeeper replied: 'Oh, yes, your Grace. Mr Trelly from Wadebridge comes once a week, the same that his late Grace always employed,' he had passed on with a distinct feeling of disappointment; for probably a man of that sort would resent any one else's winding the clocks – a sentiment the Duke could perfectly appreciate.

Finally, wearied by these labours, which were as much out of scale with his real tastes as the immense building itself, he had lunched late and hastily on bread and cheese, to the despair of the housekeeper, who had despatched a groom before daybreak to scour Wadebridge for delicacies.

The Duke's afternoon was his own, and his meagre repast over he set out for a tramp. The troublesome question of his marriage was still foremost in his mind; for after inspecting the castle he felt more than ever the impossibility of escaping from his ducal burdens. Yet how could the simple-hearted girl of whom he was in search be induced to share the weight of these great establishments? It was unlikely that a young woman too ignorant of worldly advantages to covet his title would be attracted by his responsibilities. Why not remain unmarried, as he had threatened, and let the title and the splendours go to the elderly clergyman who was his heir presumptive? But no – that would be a still worse failure in duty. He must marry, have children, play the great part assigned to him.

As he walked along the coast toward the ruined Tintagel he shook off his momentary cowardice. The westerly wind blew great trails of fog in from the sea, and now and then, between them, showed a mass of molten silver, swaying heavily, as though exhausted by a distant gale. The Duke thought of the stuffy heat of London, and the currents of his blood ran less sedately. He would marry, yes; but he would choose his own wife, and choose her away from the world, in some still backwater of rural England. But here another difficulty lurked. He had once, before his father's death, lit on a girl who fitted ideally into his plan: the daughter of a naval officer's widow, brought up in a remote Norfolk village. The Duke had found a friend to introduce him, had called, had talked happily with the widow of parochial matters, had shown her what was wrong with her clock, and had even contrived to be left alone with the young lady. But the young lady could say no more than 'Yes' and 'No', and she placed even these monosyllables with so little relevance that face to face with her he was struck dumb also. He did not return, and the young lady married a curate.

The memory tormented him now. Perhaps, if he had been patient, had given her time – but no, he recalled her blank bewildered face, and thought what a depressing sight it would be every morning behind the tea-urn. Though he sought simplicity he dreaded dulness. Dimly conscious that he was dull himself, he craved the stimulus of a quicker mind; yet he feared a dull wife less than a brilliant one, for with the latter how could he maintain his superiority? He remembered his discomfort among those loud rattling young women whom his cousin Seadown had taken him to see at Runnymede. Very handsome they were, each in her own way; nor was the Duke insensible to beauty. One especially, the fair one, had attracted him. She was less noisy than the others, and would have been an agreeable sight at the breakfast-table; and she carried her head in a way to show off the Tintagel jewels. But marry an American –? The thought was inconceivable. Besides, supposing she should want to surround herself with all those screaming people, and supposing he had to invite the mother – he wasn't sure which of the two elderly ladies with dyed fringes *was* the mother – to Longlands or Tintagel whenever a child was born? From this glimpse into an alien world the Duke's orderly imagination recoiled. What he wanted was an English bride of ancient lineage and Arcadian innocence; and somewhere in the British Isles there must be one awaiting him . . .

15

After their early swim the morning had turned so damp and foggy that Miss Testvalley said to Nan: 'I believe this would be a good day for me to drive over to Polwhelly and call at the vicarage. You can sit in the garden a little while if the sun comes out.'

The vicarage at Polwhelly had been Miss Testvalley's chief refuge during her long lonely months at Tintagel with her Folyat pupils, and Nan knew that she wished to visit her old friends. As for Nan herself, after the swim and the morning walk, she preferred to sit in the inn garden, sheltered by a tall fuchsia hedge, and gazing out over the headlands and the sea. She had not even expressed the wish to take the short walk along the cliffs to the ruins of Tintagel; and she had apparently forgotten Miss Testvalley's offer to show her the modern castle of the same name. She seemed neither listless nor unwell, the governess thought, but lulled by the strong air, and steeped in a lazy beatitude; and this was the very mood Miss Testvalley had sought to create in her.

But an hour or two after Trevennick's only fly had carried off Miss Testvalley, the corner where Nan sat became a balcony above a great sea-drama. A twist of the wind had whirled away the fog, and there of a sudden lay the sea in a metallic glitter, with white clouds storming over it, hiding and then revealing the fiery blue sky between. Sit in the shelter of the fuchsia hedge on such a day? Not Nan! Her feet were already dancing on the sunbeams, and in another minute the gate had swung behind her, and she was away to meet the gale on the downs above the village.

When the Duke of Tintagel reached the famous ruin from which he took his name, another freak of the wind had swept the fog in again. The sea was no more than a hoarse sound on an invisible shore, and he climbed the slopes through a cloud filled with the stormy clash of sea-birds. To some minds the change might have seemed to befit the desolate place; but the Duke, being a good landlord, thought only: 'More rain, I suppose; and that is certain to mean a loss on the crops.'

But the walk had been exhilarating, and when he reached the upper platform of the castle, and looked down through a break in the fog at the savage coast-line, a feeling of pride and satisfaction crept through him. He liked the idea that a place so ancient and renowned belonged to him, was a mere milestone in his race's long descent; and he said to himself: 'I owe everything to England. Perhaps after all I ought to marry as my mother wishes . . .'

He had thought he had the wild place to himself, but as he advanced toward the edge of the platform he perceived that his solitude was shared by a young lady who, as yet unaware of his presence, stood wedged in a coign of the ramparts, absorbed in the struggle between wind and sea.

The Duke gave an embarrassed cough; but between the waves and the gulls the sound did not carry far. The girl remained motionless, her profile turned seaward, and the Duke was near enough to study it in detail.

She had not the kind of beauty to whirl a man off his feet, and his eye was free to note that her complexion, though now warmed by the wind, was naturally pale, that her nose was a trifle too small, and her hair a tawny uncertain mixture of dark and fair. Nothing overpowering in all this; but being overpowered was what the Duke most dreaded. He went in fear of the terrible beauty that is born and bred for the strawberry leaves, and the face he was studying was so grave yet so happy that he felt somehow re-assured and safe. This girl, at any rate, was certainly not thinking of Dukes; and in the eyes she presently turned to him he saw not himself but the sea.

He raised his hat, and she looked at him, surprised but not disturbed. 'I didn't know you were there,' she said simply.

'The grass deadens one's steps . . .' the Duke apologized.

'Yes. And the birds scream so – and the wind.'

'I'm afraid I startled you.'

'Oh, no. I didn't suppose the place belonged to me . . .' She continued to scrutinize him gravely, and he wondered whether a certain fearless gravity were not what he liked best in a woman. Then suddenly she smiled, and he changed his mind.

'But I've seen you before, haven't I?' she exclaimed. 'I'm sure I have. Wasn't it at Runnymede?'

'At Runnymede?' he stammered, his heart sinking. The smile, then, had after all been for the Duke!

'Yes. I'm Nan St George. My mother and Mrs Elmsworth have taken a little cottage there – Lady Churt's cottage. A lot of people come down from London to see my sister Virginia and Liz Elmsworth, and I have an idea you came one day – didn't you? There are so many of them – crowds of young men; and always changing. I'm afraid I can't remember all their names. But didn't Teddy de Santos-Dios bring you down the day we had that awful pillow-fight? I know – you're a Mr Robinson.'

In an instant the Duke's apprehensive mind registered a succession of terrors. First, the dread that he had been recognized and marked down; then the more deadly fear that, though this had actually happened, his quick-witted antagonist was clever enough to affect an impossible ignorance. A Mr Robinson! For a fleeting second the Duke tried to feel what it would be like to be a Mr Robinson . . . a man who might wind his own clocks when he chose. It did not feel as agreeable as the Duke had imagined – and he hastily re-became a Duke.

Yet would it not be safer to accept the proffered alias? He wavered. But no; the idea was absurd. If this girl, though he did not remember ever having seen her, had really been at Runnymede the day he had gone there, it was obvious that, though she might not identify him at the moment (a thought not wholly gratifying to his vanity), she could not long remain in ignorance. His face must have betrayed his embarrassment, for she exclaimed: 'Oh, then, you're not Mr Robinson? I'm so sorry! Virginia (that's my sister; I don't believe you've forgotten *her*) – Virginia says I'm always making stupid mistakes. And I know everybody hates being taken for somebody else; and especially for a Mr Robinson. But won't you tell me your name?'

The Duke's confusion increased. But he was aware that hesitation was ridiculous. There was no help for it; he had to drag himself into the open. 'My name's Tintagel.'

Nan's eyebrows rose in surprise, and her smile enchanted him again. 'Oh, how perfectly splendid! Then of course you know Miss Testvalley?'

The Duke stared. He had never seen exactly that effect produced by the announcement of his name. 'Miss Testvalley?'

'Oh, don't you know her? How funny! But aren't you the brother of those girls whose governess she was? They used to live at Tintagel. I mean Clara and Ermie and Mina . . .'

'Their governess?' It suddenly dawned on the Duke how little he knew about his sisters. The fact of being regarded as a mere append-age to these unimportant females was a still sharper blow to his vanity; yet it gave him the re-assurance that even now the speaker did not know she was addressing a Duke. Incredible as such ignor-ance was, he was constrained to recognize it. 'She knows me only as their brother,' he thought. 'Or else,' he added, 'she knows who I am, and doesn't care.'

At first neither alternative was wholly pleasing; but after a moment's reflection he felt a glow of relief. 'I remember my sisters had a governess they were devoted to,' he said, with a timid affability.

'I should think so! She's perfectly splendid. Did you know she was Dante Gabriel Rossetti's own cousin?' Nan continued, her enthusiasm rising, as it always did when she spoke of Miss Testvalley.

The Duke's perplexity deepened; and it annoyed him to have to grope for his answers in conversing with this prompt young woman. 'I'm afraid I know very few Italians—'

'Oh, well, you wouldn't know *him*; he's very ill, and hardly sees anybody. But don't you love his poetry? Which sonnet do you like best in *The House of Life*? I have a friend whose favourite is the one that begins: "When do I love thee most, belovèd one?"'

'I – the fact is, I've very little time to read poetry,' the Duke faltered.

Nan looked at him incredulously. 'It doesn't take much time if you really care for it. But lots of people don't – Virginia doesn't . . . Are you coming down soon to Runnymede? Miss Testvalley and I are going back next week. They just sent me here for a little while to get a change of air and some bathing, but it was really because they thought Runnymede was too exciting for me.'

'Ah,' exclaimed the Duke, his interest growing, 'you don't care for excitement, then?' (The lovely child!)

Nan pondered the question. 'Well, it all depends . . . Everything's exciting, don't you think so? I mean sunsets and poetry, and swimming out too far in a rough sea . . . But I don't believe I care as much as the others for practical jokes: frightening old ladies by dressing up as burglars with dark lanterns, or putting wooden rattlesnakes in people's beds – *do you*?'

It was the Duke's turn to hesitate. 'I – well, I must own that such experiences are unfamiliar to me; but I can hardly imagine being amused by them.'

His mind revolved uneasily between the alternatives of disguising himself as a burglar or listening to a young lady recite poetry; and to bring the talk back to an easier level he said: 'You're staying in the neighbourhood?'

'Yes. At Trevennick, at the inn. I love it here, don't you? You live somewhere near here, I suppose?'

Yes, the Duke said: his place wasn't above three miles away. He'd just walked over from there . . . He broke off, at a loss how to go on; but his interlocutor came to the rescue.

'I suppose you must know the vicar at Polwhelly? Miss Testvalley's gone to see him this afternoon. That's why I came up here alone. I promised and swore I wouldn't stir out of the inn garden – but how could I help it, when the sun suddenly came out?'

'How indeed?' echoed the Duke, attempting one of his difficult smiles. 'Will your governess be very angry, do you think?'

'Oh, fearfully, at first. But afterward she'll understand. Only I do want to get back before she comes in, or she'll be worried . . .' She turned back to the rampart for a last look at the sea; but the deepening fog had blotted out everything. 'I must really go,' she said, 'or I'll never find my way down.'

The Duke's gaze followed her. Was this a tentative invitation to guide her back to the inn? Should he offer to do so? Or would the governess disapprove of this even more than of her charge's wandering off alone in the fog? 'If you'll allow me – may I see you back to Trevennick?' he suggested.

'Oh, I wish you would. If it's not too far out of your way?'

'It's – it's on my way,' the Duke declared, lying hurriedly; and they started down the steep declivity. The slow descent was effected in silence, for the Duke's lie had exhausted his conversational resources, and his companion seemed to have caught the contagion of his shyness. Inwardly he was thinking: 'Ought I to offer her a hand? Is it steep enough – or will she think I'm presuming?'

He had never before met a young lady alone in a ruined castle, and his mind, nurtured on precedents, had no rule to guide it. But nature cried aloud in him that he must somehow see her again. He was still turning over the best means of effecting another meeting – an invitation to the castle, a suggestion that he should call on Miss Testvalley? – when, after a slippery descent from the ruins, and an arduous climb up the opposite cliff, they reached the fork of the path where it joined the lane to Trevennick.

'Thank you so much; but you needn't come any further. There's the inn just below,' the young lady said, smiling.

'Oh, really? You'd rather –? Mayn't I –?'

She shook her head. 'No; really,' she mimicked him lightly; and with a quick wave of dismissal she started down the lane.

The Duke stood motionless, looking irresolutely after her, and wondering what he ought to have said or done. 'I ought to have contrived a way of going as far as the inn with her,' he said to himself, exasperated by his own lack of initiative. 'It comes of being always hunted, I suppose,' he added, as he watched her slight outline lessen down the hill.

Just where the descent took a turn toward the village, Nan encountered a familiar figure panting upward.

'Annabel – I've been hunting for you everywhere!'

Annabel laughed and embraced her duenna. 'You weren't expected back so soon.'

'You promised me faithfully that you'd stay in the garden. And in this drenching fog –'

'Yes; but the fog blew away after you'd gone, and I thought that let me off my promise. So I scrambled up to the castle – that's all.'

'That's all? Over a mile away, and along those dangerous slippery cliffs?'

'Oh, it was all right. There was a gentleman there who brought me back.'

'A gentleman – in the ruins?'

'Yes. He says he lives somewhere round here.'

'How often have I told you not to let strangers speak to you?'

'He didn't. I spoke to him. But he's not really a stranger, darling; he thinks he knows you.'

'Oh, he does, does he?' Miss Testvalley gave a sniff of incredulity.

'I saw he wanted to ask if he could call,' Nan continued, 'but he was too shy. I never saw anybody so scared. I don't believe he's been around much.'

'I daresay he was shocked by your behaviour.'

'Oh, no. Why should he have been? He just stayed with me while we were getting up the cliff; after that I said he mustn't come any farther. Why, there he is still – at the top of the lane, where I left him. I suppose he's been watching to see that I got home safely. Don't you call that sweet of him?'

Miss Testvalley released herself from her pupil's arm. Her eyes were not only keen but far-sighted. They followed Nan's glance, and rested on the figure of a young man who stood above them on the edge of the cliff. As she looked he turned slowly away.

'Annabel! Are you sure that was the gentleman?'

'Yes . . . He's funny. He says he has no time to read poetry. What do you suppose he does instead?'

'But it's the Duke of Tintagel!' Miss Testvalley suddenly declared.

'The Duke? That young man?' It was Nan's turn to give an incredulous laugh. 'He said his name was Tintagel, and that he was the brother of those girls at the castle; but I thought of course he was a younger son. He never said he was the Duke.'

Miss Testvalley gave an impatient shrug. 'They don't go about shouting out their titles. The family name is Folyat. And he has no younger brother, as it happens.'

'Well, how was I to know all that? Oh, Miss Testvalley,' exclaimed Nan, spinning around on her governess, 'but if he's the Duke he's the one Miss March wants Jinny to marry!'

'Miss March is full of brilliant ideas.'

'I don't call that one particularly brilliant. At least not if I was Jinny, I shouldn't. I think,' said Nan, after a moment's pondering, 'that the Duke's one of the stupidest young men I ever met.'

'Well,' rejoined her governess severely, 'I hope he thinks nothing worse than that of you.'

16

The Mr Robinson for whom Nan St George had mistaken the Duke of Tintagel was a young man much more confident of his gifts, and assured as to his future, than that retiring nobleman. There was nothing within the scope of his understanding which Hector Robinson did not know, and mean at some time to make use of. His grandfather had been first a miner and then a mine-owner in the North; his father, old Sir Downman Robinson, had built up one of the biggest cotton industries in Lancashire, and been rewarded with a knighthood, and Sir Downman's only son meant to turn the knighthood into a baronetcy, and the baronetcy into a peerage. All in good time.

Meanwhile, as a partner in his father's big company, and director in various city enterprises, and as Conservative MP for one of the last rotten boroughs in England, he had his work cut out for him, and could boast that his thirty-five years had not been idle ones.

It was only on the social side that he had hung fire. In coming out against his father as a Conservative, and thus obtaining without difficulty his election to Lord Saltmire's constituency, Mr Robinson had flattered himself that he would secure a footing in society as readily as in the City. Had he made a miscalculation? Was it true that fashion had turned toward Liberalism, and that a young Liberal MP was more likely to find favour in the circles to which Mr Robinson aspired?

Perhaps it was true; but Mr Robinson was a Conservative by instinct, by nature, and in his obstinate self-confidence was determined that he would succeed without sacrificing his political convictions. And at any rate, when it came to a marriage, he felt reasonably sure that his Conservatism would recommend him in the families from which he intended to choose his bride.

Mr Robinson, surveying the world as his oyster, had already (if the figure be allowed) divided it into two halves, each in a different way designed to serve his purpose. The one, which he labelled Mayfair, held out possibilities of immediate success. In that set, which had already caught the Heir to the Throne in its glittering meshes, there were ladies of the highest fashion who, in return for pecuniary favours, were ready and even eager to promote the ascent of gentlemen with short pedigrees and long purses. As a member of Parliament he had a status which did away with most of the awkward preliminaries; and he found it easy enough to pick up, among his masculine acquaintances, an introduction to that privileged group beginning to be known as 'the Marlborough set'.

But it was not in this easy-going world that he meant to marry. Socially as well as politically Mr Robinson was a true Conservative, and it was in the duller half of the London world, the half he called 'Belgravia', that he intended to seek a partner. But into those uniform cream-coloured houses where dowdy dowagers ruled, and flocks of marriageable daughters pined for a suitor approved by the family, Mr Robinson had not yet forced his way. The only interior known to him in that world was Lord Saltmire's, and in this he was received on a strictly Parliamentary basis. He had made the immense mistake of not immediately recognizing the fact, and of imagining, for a mad moment, that the Earl of Saltmire, who had been so ready to endow him with a seat in Parliament, would be no less disposed to welcome him as a brother-in-law. But Lady Audrey de Salis, plain, dowdy, and one of five unmarried sisters, had refused him curtly and all too definitely; and the shock had thrown him back into the arms of Mayfair. Obviously he had aspired too high, or been too impatient; but it was in his nature to be aspiring and impatient, and if he was to succeed it must be on the lines of his own character.

So he had told himself as he looked into his glass on the morning of his first visit to the cottage at Runnymede, whither Teddy de Santos-Dios was to conduct him. Mr Robinson saw in his mirror the energetic reddish features of a young man with a broad short nose, a dense crop of brown hair, and a heavy brown moustache. He had been among the first to recognize that whiskers were going out, and had sacrificed as handsome a pair as the City could show. When Mr Robinson made up his mind that a change was coming, his principle was always to meet it half way; and so the whiskers went. And it did make him look younger to wear only the fashionable moustache. With that, and a flower in the buttonhole of his Poole coat, he could take his chance with most men, though he was aware that the careless unselfconsciousness of the elect was still beyond him. But in time he would achieve that too.

Certainly he could not have gone to a better school than the bungalow at Runnymede. The young guardsmen, the budding MPs and civil servants who frequented it, were all of the favoured caste whose ease of manner Mr Robinson envied; and nowhere were they so easy as in the company of the young women already familiar to fashionable London as 'the Americans'. Mr Robinson returned from that first visit enchanted and slightly bewildered, but with the fixed resolve to go back as often as he was invited. Before the day was over he had lent fifty pounds to Teddy de Santos-Dios, and lost another fifty at poker to the latter's sister, Lady Richard Marable, thus securing a prompt invitation for the following week; and after that he was confident of keeping the foot-hold he had gained.

But if the young ladies enchanted him he saw in the young men his immediate opportunity. Lady Richard's brother-in-law, Lord

Seadown, was, for instance, one of the golden youths to whom Mr Robinson had vainly sought an introduction. Lord Richard Marable, Seadown's younger brother, he did know; but Lord Richard's acquaintance was easy to make, and led nowhere, least of all in the direction of his own family. At Runnymede Lord Richard was seldom visible; but Lord Seadown, who was always there, treated with brotherly cordiality all who shared the freedom of the cottage. There were others too, younger sons of great houses, officers quartered at Windsor or Aldershot, young Parliamentarians and minor Government officials reluctantly detained in town at the season's end, and hailing with joy the novel distractions of Runnymede; there was even – on one memorable day – the young Duke of Tintagel, a shrinking neutral-tinted figure in that highly coloured throng.

'Now if *I* were a Duke –!' Robinson thought, viewing with pity the unhappy nobleman's dull clothes and embarrassed manner; but he contrived an introduction to his Grace, and even a few moments of interesting political talk, in which the Duke took eager refuge from the call to play blindman's-buff with the young ladies. All this was greatly to the good, and Mr Robinson missed no chance to return to Runnymede.

On a breathless August afternoon he had come down from London, as he did on most Saturdays, and joined the party about the tea-table under the big cedar. The group was smaller than usual. Miss March was away visiting friends in the Lake country, Nan St George was still in Cornwall with her governess, Mrs St George and Mrs Elmsworth, exhausted by the heat, had retired to the seclusion of their bedrooms, and only Virginia St George and the two Elmsworth girls, under the doubtful chaperonage of Lady Richard Marable, sat around the table with their usual guests – Lord Seadown, Santos-Dios, Hector Robinson, a couple of young soldiers from Windsor, and a caustic young civil servant, the Honourable Miles Dawnly, who could always be trusted to bring down the latest news from London – or, at that season, from Scotland, Homburg or Marienbad, as the case might be.

Mr Robinson by this time felt quite at home among them. He agreed with the others that it was far too hot to play tennis or even croquet, or to go on the river before sunset, and he lay contentedly on the turf under the cedar, thinking his own thoughts, and making his own observations, while he joined in the languid chatter about the tea-table.

Of observations there were always plenty to be made at Runnymede. Robinson, by this time, had in his hands most of the threads running from one to another of these careless smiling young people. It was obvious, for instance, that Miles Dawnly, who had probably never lost his balance before, was head-over-ears in love with Conchita Marable, and that she was 'playing' him indolently and amusedly, for want of a bigger fish. But the neuralgic point in the group was the growing rivalry between Lizzy Elmsworth and Virginia St George. Those two inseparable friends were gradually becoming estranged; and the reason was not far to seek. It was between them now, in the person of Lord Seadown, who lay at their feet, plucking up tufts of clover, and gazing silently skyward through the dark boughs of the cedar. It had for some time been clear to Robinson that the susceptible young man was torn between Virginia St George's exquisite profile and Lizzy Elmsworth's active wit. He needed the combined stimulus of both to rouse his slow imagination, and Robinson saw that while Virginia had the advantage as yet, it might at any moment slip into Lizzy's quick fingers. And Lizzy saw this too.

Suddenly Mabel Elmsworth, at whose feet no one was lying, jumped up and declared that if she sat still a minute longer she would take root. 'Walk down to the river with me, will you, Mr Robinson? There may be a little more air there than under the trees.'

Robinson had no particular desire to walk to the river, or anywhere else, with Mab Elmsworth. She was jolly and conversable enough, but minor luminaries never interested him when stars of the first magnitude were in view. However, he was still tingling with the resentment aroused by the Lady Audrey de Salis's rejection, and in the mood to compare unfavourably that silent and large-limbed young woman with the swift nymphs of Runnymede. At Runnymede they all seemed to live, metaphorically, from hand to mouth. Everything that happened seemed to be improvised, and this suited his own impetuous pace much better than the sluggish *tempo* of the Saltmire circle. He rose, therefore, at Mabel's summons, wondering what the object of the invitation could be. Was she going to ask him to marry her? A little shiver ran down his spine; for all he knew, that might be the way they did it in the States. But her first words dispelled his fear.

'Mr Robinson, Lord Seadown's a friend of yours, isn't he?'

Robinson hesitated. He was far too intelligent to affect to be more intimate with any one than he really was, and after a moment he answered: 'I haven't known him long; but everybody who comes here appears to be on friendly terms with everybody else.'

His companion frowned slightly. 'I wish they really were! But what I wanted to ask you was – have you ever noticed anything particular between Lord Seadown and my sister?'

Robinson stopped short. The question took him by surprise. He had already noticed, in these free-mannered young women, a singular reticence about their family concerns, a sort of moral modesty that seemed to constrain them to throw a veil over matters freely enough discussed in aristocratic English circles. He repeated: 'Your sister?'

'You probably think it's a peculiar question. Don't imagine I'm trying to pump you. But everybody must have seen that he's tremendously taken with Lizzy, and that Jinny St George is doing her best to come between them.'

Robinson's embarrassment deepened. He did not know where she was trying to lead him. 'I should be sorry to think that of Miss St George, who appears to be so devoted to your sister.'

Mabel Elmsworth laughed impatiently. 'I suppose that's the proper thing to say. But I'm not asking you to take sides – I'm not even blaming Virginia. Only it's been going on now all summer, and what I say is it's time he chose between them, if he's ever going to. It's very hard on Lizzy, and it's not fair that he should make two friends quarrel. After all, we're all alone in a strange country, and I daresay our ways are not like yours, and may lead you to make mistakes about us. All I wanted to ask is, if you couldn't drop a hint to Lord Seadown.'

Hector Robinson looked curiously at this girl, who might have been pretty in less goddess-like company, and who spoke with such precocious wisdom on subjects delicate to touch. 'By Jove, she'd make a good wife for an ambitious man,' he thought. He did not mean himself, but he reflected that the man who married her beautiful sister might be glad enough, at times, to have such a counsellor at his elbow.

'I think you're right about one thing, Miss Elmsworth. Your ways are so friendly, so kind, that a fellow, if he wasn't careful, might find himself drawn two ways at once –'

Mabel laughed. 'Oh, you mean: we flirt. Well, it's in our blood, I suppose. And no one thinks the worse of a girl for it at home. But over here it may seem undignified; and perhaps Lord Seadown thought he had the right to amuse himself without making up his mind. But in America, when a girl has shown that she really cares, it puts a gentleman on his honour, and he understands that the game has gone on long enough.'

'I see.'

'Only, we've nobody here to say this to Lord Seadown' (Mabel seemed tacitly to assume that neither mother could be counted on for the purpose – not at least in such hot weather), 'and so I thought –'

Mr Robinson murmured: 'Yes – yes –' and after a pause went on: 'But Lord Seadown is Lady Richard's brother-in-law. Couldn't she –?'

Mabel shrugged. 'Oh, Conchita's too lazy to be bothered. And if she took sides, it would be with Jinny St George, because they're great friends, and she'd want all the money she can get for Seadown. Colonel St George is a very rich man nowadays.'

'I see,' Mr Robinson again murmured. It was out of the question that he should speak on such a matter to Lord Seadown, and he did not know how to say this to any one as inexperienced as Mabel Elmsworth. 'I'll think it over – I'll see what can be done,' he pursued, directing his steps toward the group under the cedar in his desire to cut the conversation short.

As he approached he thought what a pretty scene it was: the young women in their light starched dresses and spreading hats, the young men in flannel boating suits, stretched at their feet on the turf, and the afternoon sunlight filtering through the dark boughs in dapplings of gold.

Mabel Elmsworth walked beside him in silence, clearly aware that her appeal had failed; but suddenly she exclaimed: 'There's a lady driving in that I've never seen before ... She's stopping the carriage to get out and join Conchita. I suppose it's a friend of hers, don't you?'

Calls from ladies, Mr Robinson had already noticed, were rare and unexpected at the cottage. If a guardsman had leapt from the station fly Mabel, whether she knew him or not, would have remained unperturbed; but the sight of an unknown young woman of elegant appearance filled her with excitement and curiosity. 'Let's go and see,' she exclaimed.

The visitor, who was dark-haired, with an audaciously rouged complexion, and the kind of nose which the Laureate had taught his readers to describe as tip-tilted, was personally unknown to Mr Robinson also; but thanks to the Bond Street photographers and the new society journals her features were as familiar to him as her reputation.

'Why, it's Lady Churt – it's your landlady!' he exclaimed, with a quick glance of enquiry at his companion. The tie between Seadown and Lady Churt had long been notorious in their little world, and Robinson instantly surmised that the appearance of the lady might have a far from favourable bearing on what Mabel Elmsworth had just been telling him. But Mabel hurried forward without responding to his remark, and they joined the party just as Lady Churt was exchanging a cordial hand-clasp with Lady Richard Marable.

'Darling!'

'Darling Idina, what a surprise!'

'Conchita, dearest – I'd no idea I should find you here! Won't you explain me, please, to these young ladies – my tenants, I suppose?' Lady Churt swept the group with her cool amused glance, which paused curiously, and as Robinson thought somewhat anxiously, on Virginia St George's radiant face.

'She looks older than in her photographs – and hunted, somehow,' Robinson reflected, his own gaze resting on Lady Churt.

'I'm Lady Churt – your landlady, you know,' the speaker continued affably, addressing herself to Virginia and Lizzy. 'Please don't let me interrupt this delightful party. Mayn't I join it instead? What a brilliant idea to have tea out here in hot weather! I always used to have it on the terrace. But you Americans are so clever at arranging things.' She looked about her, mustering the group with her fixed metallic smile. With the exception of Hector Robinson the young men were evidently all known to her, and she found an easy word of greeting for each. Lord Seadown was the last that she named.

'Ah, Seadown – so you're here too? Now I see why you forgot that you were lunching with me in town today. I must say you chose the better part!' She dropped into the deep basket-chair which Santos-Dios had pushed forward, and held out her hand for a proffered mint-julep. 'No tea, thanks – not when one of Teddy's demoralizing mixtures is available . . . You see, I know what to expect when I come here . . . A cigarette, Seadown? I hope you've got my special supply with you, even if you've forgotten our engagement?' She smiled again upon the girls. 'He spoils me horribly, you know, by always remembering to carry about my particular brand.'

Seadown, with flushed face and lowering brow, produced the packet, and Lady Churt slipped the contents into her cigarette-case. 'I do hope I'm not interrupting some delightful plan or other? Perhaps you were all going out on the river? If you were, you mustn't let me delay you, for I must be off again in a few minutes.'

Every one protested that it was much too hot to move, and Lady Churt continued: 'Really – you had no plans? Well, it *is* pleasanter here than anywhere else. But perhaps I'm dreadfully in the way. Seadown's looking at me as if I were . . .' She turned her glance laughingly toward Virginia St George. 'The fact is, I'm not at all sure that landladies have a right to intrude on their tenants unannounced. I daresay it's really against the law.'

'Well, if it is, you must pay the penalty by being detained at our pleasure,' said Lady Richard gaily; and after a moment's pause Lizzy Elmsworth came forward. 'Won't you let me call my mother and Mrs St George, Lady Churt? I'm sure they'd be sorry not to see you. It was so hot after luncheon that they went up to their rooms to rest.'

'How very wise of them! I wouldn't disturb them for the world.' Lady Churt set down her empty glass, and bent over the lighting of a cigarette. 'Only you really mustn't let me interfere for a moment with what you were all going to do. You see,' she added, turning about with a smile of challenge, 'you see, though my tenants haven't yet done me the honour of inviting me down, I've heard what amusing things are always going on here, and what wonderful ways you've found of cheering up the poor martyrs to duty who can't get away to the grouse and the deer – and I may as well confess that I'm dread-fully keen to learn your secrets.'

Robinson saw that this challenge had a slightly startling effect on the three girls, who stood grouped together with an air of mutual defensiveness unlike their usual easy attitude. But Lady Richard met the words promptly. 'If your tenants haven't invited you down, Idina dear, I fancy it's only because they were afraid to have you see how rudimentary their arts are compared to their landlady's. So many delightful people had already learnt the way to the cottage that there was nothing to do but to leave the door unlatched. Isn't that your only secret, girls? If there's any other –' she too glanced about her with a smile – 'well, perhaps it's *this*; but this, remember, *is* a secret, even from the stern Mammas who are taking their siesta upstairs.'

As she spoke she turned to her brother. 'Come, Teddy – if every-body's had tea, what about lifting the tray and things on to the grass, and putting this table to its real use?' Two of the young men sprang to her aid, and in a moment tray and tea-cloth had been swept away, and the green baize top of the folding table had declared its original purpose

'Cards? Oh, how jolly!' cried Lady Churt. She drew a seat up to the table, while Teddy de Santos-Dios, who had disappeared into the house, hurried back with a handful of packs. 'But this is glorious! No wonder my poor little cottage has become so popular. What – poker? Oh, by all means. The only game worth playing – I took my first lesson from Seadown last week ... Seadown, I had a little *porte-monnaie* somewhere, didn't I? Or did I leave it in the fly? Not that I've much hope of finding anything in it but some powder and a few pawn-tickets ... Oh, Seadown, will you come to my rescue? Lend me a fiver, there's a darling – I hope I'm not going to lose more than that.'

Lord Seadown who, since her arrival, had maintained a look of gloomy detachment, drew forth his note-case with an embarrassed air. She received it with a laugh. 'What? *Carte blanche?* What munifi-cence! But let me see –.' She took up the note-case, ran her fingers through it, and drew out two or three five-pound notes. 'Heavens, Seadown, what wealth! How am I ever to pay you back if I lose? Or even if I win, when I need so desperately every penny I can scrape together?' She slipped the notes into her purse, which the observant Hector Robinson, alert for the chance of making himself known to the newcomer, had hastened to retrieve from the fly. Lady Churt took the purse with a brief nod for the service rendered, and a long and attentive look at the personable Hector; then she handed back Lord Seadown's note-case. 'Wish me luck, my dear! Perhaps I may manage to fleece one or two of these hardened gamblers.'

The card-players, laughing, settled themselves about the table. Lady Churt and Lady Richard sat on opposite sides, Lord Seadown took a seat next to his sister-in-law, and the other men disposed themselves as they pleased. Robinson, who did not care to play, had casually placed himself behind Lady Churt, and the three girls, resisting a little banter and entreaty, declared that they also preferred to walk about and look on at the players.

The game began in earnest, and Lady Churt opened with the supernaturally brilliant hand which often falls to the lot of the novice. The stakes (the observant Robinson noticed) were higher than usual, the players consequently more intent. It was one of those afternoons when thunder invisibly amasses itself behind the blue, and as the sun drooped slowly westward it seemed as though the card-table under the cedar-boughs were over-hung by the same feverish hush as the sultry lawns and airless river.

Lady Churt's luck did not hold. Too quickly elated, she dashed ahead toward disaster. Robinson was not long in discovering that she was too emotional for a game based on dissimulation, and no match for such seasoned players as Lady Richard and Lady Richard's brother. Even the other young men had more experience, or at any rate more self-control, than she could muster; and though her purse had evidently been better supplied than she pretended, the time at length came when it was nearly empty.

But at that very moment her luck turned again. Robinson could not believe his eyes. The hand she held could hardly be surpassed; she understood enough of the game to seize her opportunity, and fling her last notes into the jack-pot presided over by Teddy de Santos-Dios's glossy smile and supple gestures. There was more money in the jack-pot than Robinson had ever seen on the Runnymede card-table, and a certain breathlessness overhung the scene, as if the weight of the thundery sky were in the lungs of the players.

Lady Churt threw down her hand, and leaned back with a sparkle of triumph in eyes and lips. But Miles Dawnly, with an almost apologetic gesture, had spread his cards upon the table.

'Begorra! A royal flush —' a young Irish lieutenant gasped out. The groups about the table stared at each other. It was one of those moments which make even seasoned poker-players gasp. For a short interval of perplexity Lady Churt was silent; then the exclamations of the other players brought home to her the shock of her disaster.

'It's the sort of game that fellows write about in their memoirs,' murmured Teddy, almost awestruck; and the lucky winner gave an embarrassed laugh. It was almost incredible to him too.

Lady Churt pushed back her chair, nearly colliding with the attentive Robinson. She tried to laugh. 'Well, I've learnt my lesson! Lost Seadown's last copper, as well as my own. Not that he need mind; he's won more than he lent me. But I'm completely ruined – down and out, as I believe you say in the States. I'm afraid you're all too clever for me, and one of the young ladies had better take my place,' she added with a drawn smile.

'Oh, come, Idina, don't lose heart!' exclaimed Lady Richard, deep in the game, and annoyed at the interruption.

'Heart, my dear? I assure you I've never minded parting with that organ. It's losing the shillings and pence that I can't afford.'

Miles Dawnly glanced across the table at Lizzy Elmsworth, who stood beside Hector Robinson, her keen eyes bent on the game. 'Come, Miss Elmsworth, if Lady Churt is really deserting us, won't you replace her?'

'Do, Lizzy,' cried Lady Richard; but Lizzy shook her head, declaring that she and her friends were completely ignorant of the game.

'What, even Virginia?' Conchita laughed. 'There's no excuse for her, at any rate, for her father is a celebrated poker-player. My respected parent always says he'd rather make Colonel St George a handsome present than sit down at poker with him.'

Virginia coloured at the challenge, but Lizzy, always quicker at the uptake, intervened before she could answer.

'You seem to have forgotten, Conchita, that girls don't play cards for money in America.'

Lady Churt turned suddenly toward Virginia St George, who was standing behind her. 'No. I understand the game you young ladies play has fewer risks, and requires only two players,' she said, fixing her vivid eyes on the girl's bewildered face. Robinson, who had drawn back a few steps, was still watching her intently. He said to himself that he had never seen a woman so angry, and that certain small viperine heads darting forked tongues behind their glass cases at the Zoo would in future always remind him of Lady Churt.

For a moment Virginia's bewilderment was shared by the others about the table; but Conchita, startled out of her absorption in the game, hastily assumed the air of one who is vainly struggling to repress a burst of ill-timed mirth. 'How frightfully funny you are, Idina! I do wish you wouldn't make me laugh so terribly in this hot weather!'

Lady Churt's colour rose angrily. 'I'm glad it amuses you to see your friends lose their money,' she said. 'But unluckily I can't afford to make the fun last much longer.'

'Oh, nonsense, darling! Of course your luck will turn. It's been miraculous already. Lend her something to go on with, Seadown, do . . .'

'I'm afraid Seadown can't go on either. I'm sorry to be a spoil-sport, but I must really carry him off. As he forgot to lunch with me today it's only fair that he should come back to town for dinner.'

Lord Seadown, who had relapsed into an unhappy silence, did not break it in response to this; but Lady Richard once more came to his rescue. 'We love your chaff, Idina; and we hope the idea of carrying off Seadown is only a part of it. You say he was engaged to lunch with you today; but isn't there a mistake about dates? Seedy, in his family character as my brother-in-law, brought me down here for the week-end, and I'm afraid he's got to wait and see me home on Monday. You wouldn't suppose my husband would mind my travel-ling alone, would you, considering how much he does it himself – or professes to; but as a matter of fact he and my father-in-law, who disagree on so many subjects, are quite agreed that I'm not to have any adventures if they can help it. And so you see . . . But sit down again, darling, do. Why should you hurry away? If you'll only stop and dine you'll have an army of heroes to see you back to town; and Seadown's society at dinner.'

The effect of this was to make Lady Churt whiten with anger

under her paint. She glanced sharply from Lady Richard to Lord Seadown.

'Yes; do, Idina,' the latter at length found voice to say.

Lady Churt threw back her brilliant head with another laugh. 'Thanks a lot for your invitation, Conchita darling – and for yours too, Seadown. It's really rather amusing to be asked to dine in one's own house . . . But today I'm afraid I can't. I've got to carry you back to London with me, Seadown, whoever may have brought you here. The fact is –' she turned another of her challenging glances on Virginia St George – 'the fact is, it's time your hostesses found out that you don't go with the house; at least not when I'm not living in it. That ought to have been explained to them, perhaps –'

'Idina . . .' Lord Seadown muttered in anguish.

'Oh, I'm not blaming anybody! It's such a natural mistake. Lord Seadown comes down so continually when I'm here,' Lady Churt pursued, her eyes still on Virginia's burning face, 'that I suppose he simply forgot the house was let, and went on coming from the mere force of habit. I do hope, Miss St George, his being here hasn't inconvenienced you? Come along, Seadown, or we'll miss our train; and please excuse yourself to these young ladies, who may think your visits were made on their account – mayn't they?'

A startled silence followed. Even Conchita's ready tongue seemed to fail her. She cast a look of interrogation at her brother-in-law, but his gaze remained obstinately on the ground, and the other young men had discreetly drawn back from the scene of action.

Virginia St George stood a little way from her friends. Her head was high, her cheeks burning, her blue eyes dark with indignation. Mr Robinson, intently following the scene, wondered whether it were possible for a young creature to look more proud and beautiful. But in another moment he found himself reversing his judgment; for Mr Robinson was all for action, and suddenly, swiftly, the other beauty, Virginia's friend and rival, had flung herself into the fray.

'Virginia! What are you waiting for? Don't you see that Lord Seadown has no right to speak till you do? Why don't you tell him at once that he has your permission to announce your engagement?' Lizzy Elmsworth cried with angry fervour.

Mr Robinson hung upon this dialogue with the breathless absorption of an experienced play-goer discovering the gifts of an unknown actress. 'By Jove – by Jove,' he murmured to himself. His talk with Mabel Elmsworth had made clear to him the rivalry he had already suspected between the two beauties, and he could measure the full significance of Lizzy's action.

'By Jove – she knew she hadn't much of a chance with Seadown, and quick as lightning she decided to back up the other girl against the common enemy.' His own admiration, which, like Seadown's, had hitherto wavered between the two beauties, was transferred in a flash, and once for all, to Lizzy. 'Gad, she looks like an avenging goddess – I can almost hear the arrow whizzing past! What a party-leader she'd make,' he thought; and added, with inward satisfaction: 'Well, she won't be thrown away on this poor nonentity, at all events.'

Virginia St George still stood uncertain, her blue entreating eyes turned with a sort of terror on Lady Churt.

'Seadown!' the latter repeated with an angry smile.

The sound of his name seemed to rouse the tardy suitor. He lifted his head, and his gaze met Virginia's, and detected her tears. He flushed to his pale eyebrows.

'This is all a mistake, a complete mistake . . . I mean,' he stammered, turning to Virginia, 'it's just a joke of Lady Churt's – who's such an old friend of mine that I know she'll want to be the first to congratulate me . . . if you'll only tell her that she may.'

He went up to Virginia, and took possession of her trembling hand. Virginia left it in his; but with her other hand she drew Lizzy Elmsworth to her.

'Oh, Lizzy,' she faltered.

Lizzy bestowed on her a kiss of congratulation, and drew back with a little laugh. Mr Robinson, from his secret observatory, guessed exactly what was passing through her mind. 'She's begun to realize that she's thrown away her last hope of Seadown; and very likely she repents her rashness. But the defence of the clan before everything; and I daresay he wasn't the only string to her bow.'

Lady Churt stood staring at the two girls with a hard bright intensity which, as the silence lengthened, made Mr Robinson conscious of a slight shiver down his spine. At length she too broke into a laugh. 'Really –' she said, 'really . . .' She was obviously struggling for the appropriate word. She found it in another moment.

'Engaged? Engaged to Seadown? What a delightful surprise!

Almost as great a one, I suspect, to Seadown as to Miss St George herself. Or is it only another of your American jokes – just a way you've invented of keeping Seadown here over Sunday? Well, for my part you're welcome either way . . .' She paused and her quick ironic glance travelled from face to face. 'But if it's serious, you know – then of course I congratulate you, Seadown. And you too, Miss St George.' She went up to Virginia, and looked her straight in the eyes. 'I congratulate you, my dear, on your cleverness, on your good looks, on your success. But you must excuse me for saying that I know Seadown far too well to congratulate you on having caught him for a husband.'

She held out a gloved hand rattling with bracelets, just touched Virginia's shrinking fingers, and stalked past Lord Seadown without seeming to see him.

'Conchita, darling, how cleverly you've staged the whole business. We must really repeat it the next time there are *tableaux vivants* at Stafford House.' Her eyes took a rapid survey of the young men. 'And now I must be off. Mr Dawnly, will you see me to my fly?'

Mr Robinson turned from the group with a faint smile as Miles Dawnly advanced to accompany Lady Churt. 'What a tit-bit for Dawnly to carry back to town!' he thought. 'Poor woman . . . She'll have another try for Seadown, of course – but the game's up, and she probably knows it. I thought she'd have kept her head better. But what fools the cleverest of them can be . . .' He had the excited sense of having assisted at a self-revelation such as the polite world seldom offers. Every accent of Lady Churt's stinging voice, every lift of her black eyebrows and tremor of her red lips, seemed to bare her before him in her avidity, her disorder, her social arrogance and her spiritual poverty. The sight curiously re-adjusted Mr Robinson's sense of values, and his admiration for Lizzy Elmsworth grew with his pity for her routed opponent.

17

Under the fixed smile of the Folyat Raphael the Duchess of Tintagel sat at breakfast opposite two of her many daughters, the Ladies Almina Folyat and Gwendolen de Lurey.

When the Duke was present he reserved to himself the right to glance through the morning papers between his cup of tea and his devilled kidneys; but in his absence his mother exercised the privilege, and had the *Morning Post* placed before her as one of her jealously guarded rights.

She always went straight to the Court Circular, and thence (guided by her mother's heart) to the Fashionable Marriages; and now, after a brief glance at the latter, she threw down the journal with a sudden exclamation.

'Oh, Mamma, what is it?' both daughters cried in alarm. Lady Almina thought wistfully: 'Probably somebody else she had hopes of for Ermie or me is engaged,' and Lady Gwendolen de Lurey, who had five children, and an invalid husband with a heavily mortgaged estate, reflected, as she always did when she heard of a projected marriage in high life, that when her own engagement had been announced every one took it for granted that Colonel de Lurey would inherit within the year the immense fortune of a paralysed uncle – who after all was still alive. 'So there's no use planning in advance,' Lady Gwendolen concluded wearily, glancing at the clock to make sure it was not yet time to take her second girl to the dentist (the children always had to draw lots for the annual visit to the dentist, as it was too expensive to take more than one a year).

'What is it, Mamma?' the daughters repeated apprehensively.

The Duchess laid down the newspaper, and looked first at one and then at the other. 'It is – it is – that I sometimes wonder what we bring you all up for!'

'Mamma!'

'Yes; the time, and the worry, and the money –'

'But what in the world has happened, Mamma?'

'What has happened? Only that Seadown is going to marry an American! That a – what's the name? – a Miss Virginia St George of New York is going to be premier Marchioness of England!' She pushed the paper aside, and looked up indignantly at the imbecile smile of the Raphael Madonna. 'And nobody cares!' she ended bitterly, as though including that insipid masterpiece in her reproach.

Lady Almina and Lady Gwendolen repeated with astonishment: 'Seadown?'

'Yes; your cousin Seadown – who used to be at Longlands so often at one time that I *had* hoped . . .'

Lady Almina flushed at the hint, which she took as a personal reproach, and her married sister, seeing her distress, intervened: 'Oh, but Mamma, you know perfectly well that for years Seadown has been Idina Churt's property, and nobody has had a chance against her.'

The Duchess gave her dry laugh. 'Nobody? It seems this girl had only to lift a finger –'

'I daresay, Mamma, they use means in the States that a well-bred English girl wouldn't stoop to.'

The Duchess stirred her tea angrily. 'I wish I knew what they are!' she declared, unconsciously echoing the words of an American President when his most successful general was accused of intemperance.

Lady Gwendolen, who had exhausted her ammunition, again glanced at the clock. 'I'm afraid, Mamma, I must ask you to excuse me if I hurry off with Clare to the dentist. It's half past nine – and in this house I'm always sure Ushant keeps the clocks on time . . .'

The Duchess looked at her with unseeing eyes. 'Oh, Ushant –!' she exclaimed. 'If you can either of you tell me where Ushant is – or why he's not in London, when the House has not risen – I shall be much obliged to you!'

Lady Gwendolen had slipped away under cover of this outburst, and the Duchess's unmarried daughter was left alone to weather the storm. She thought: 'I don't much mind, if only Mamma lets me alone about Seadown.'

Lady Almina Folyat's secret desire was to enter an Anglican Sisterhood, and next to the grievance of her not marrying, she knew none would be so intolerable to her mother as her joining one of these High Church masquerades, as the evangelical Duchess would have called it. 'If you want to dress yourself up, why don't you go to a fancy-ball?' the Duchess had parried her daughter's first approach to the subject; and since then Lady Almina had trembled, and bided her time in silence. She had always thought, she could not tell why, that perhaps when Ushant married he might take her side – or at any rate set her the example of throwing off their mother's tyranny.

'Seadown marrying an American! I pity poor Selina Brightlingsea; but she has never known how to manage her children.' The Duchess folded the *Morning Post*, and gathered up her correspondence. Her morning duties lay before her, stretching out in a long monotonous perspective to the moment when all Ushant's clocks should simultaneously strike the luncheon hour. She felt a sudden discouragement when she thought of it – she to whom the duties of her station had for over thirty years been what its pleasures would have been to other women. Well – it was a joy, even now, to do it all for Ushant, neglectful and ungrateful as he had lately been; and she meant to go on with the task unflinchingly till the day when she could put the heavy burden into the hands of his wife. And what a burden it seemed to her that morning!

She reviewed it all, as though it lay outlined before her on some vast chart: the treasures, the possessions, the heirlooms: the pictures, the jewels – Raphaels, Correggios, Ruysdaels, Vandykes and Hobbemas, the Folyat rubies, the tiaras, the legendary Ushant diamond, the plate, the great gold service for royal dinners, the priceless porcelain, the gigantic ranges of hot-houses at Longlands; and then the poor, the charities, the immense distribution of coal and blankets, committee-meetings, bazaar-openings, foundation-layings; and last, but not least onerous, the recurring court duties, inevitable as the turn of the seasons. She had been Mistress of the Robes, and would be so again; and her daughter-in-law, of course, could be no less. The Duchess smiled suddenly at the thought of what Seadown's prospects might have been if he had been a future Duke, and obliged to initiate his American wife into the official duties of her station! 'It will be bad enough for his poor mother as it is – but fancy having to prepare a Miss St George of New York for her duties as Mistress of the Robes. But no – the Queen would never consent. The Prime Minister would have to be warned . . . But what nonsense I'm inventing!' thought the Duchess, pushing back her chair, and ringing to tell the butler that she would see the groom-of-the-chambers that morning before the housekeeper.

'No message from the Duke, I suppose?' she asked, as the butler backed toward the threshold.

'Well, your Grace, I was about to mention to your Grace that his Grace's valet has just received a telegram instructing him to take down a couple of portmanteaux to Tintagel, where his Grace is remaining for the present.'

The door closed, and the Duchess sat looking ahead of her blindly. She had not noticed that her second daughter had also disappeared, but now a sudden sense of being alone – quite alone and unwanted – overwhelmed her, and her little piercing black eyes grew dim.

'I hope,' she murmured to herself, 'this marriage will be a warning to Ushant.' But this hope had no power to dispel her sense of having to carry her immense burden alone.

When the Duke finally joined his mother at Longlands he had surprisingly little to say about his long stay at Tintagel. There had been a good many matters to go into with Blair; and he had thought it better to remain till they were settled. So much he said, and no more; but his mere presence gradually gave the Duchess the comfortable feeling of slipping back with him into the old routine.

The shooting-parties had begun, and as usual, in response to long-established lists of invitations, the guns were beginning to assemble. The Duchess always made out these lists; her son had never expressed any personal preference in the matter. Though he was a moderately good shot he took no interest in the sport, and, as often as he could, excused himself on the ground of business. His cousins Seadown and Dick Marable, both ardent sportsmen and excellent shots, used often to be asked to replace him on such occasions; and he always took it for granted that Seadown would be invited, though Dick Marable no longer figured on the list.

After a few days, therefore, he said to his mother: 'I'm afraid I shall have to go up to town tomorrow morning for a day or two.'

'To town? Are you never going to allow yourself a proper holiday?' she protested.

'I shan't be away long. When is Seadown coming? He can replace me.'

The Duchess's tight lips grew tighter. 'I doubt if Seadown comes. In fact, I've done nothing to remind him. So soon after his engagement, I could hardly suggest it, could I?'

The Duke's passive countenance showed a faint surprise. 'But surely, if you invite the young lady –'

'And her Mamma? And her sister? I understand there's a sister –' the Duchess rejoined ironically.

'Yes,' said the Duke, the slow blood rising to his face, 'there's a sister.'

'Well, you know how long in advance our shooting-parties are made up; even if I felt like adding three unknown ladies to my list, I can't think where I could put them.'

Knowing the vast extent of the house, her son received this in a sceptical silence. At length he said: 'Has Seadown brought Miss St George to see you?'

'No. Selina Brightlingsea simply wrote me a line. I fancy she's not particularly eager to show off the future Marchioness.'

'Miss St George is wonderfully beautiful,' the Duke murmured.

'My dear Ushant, nothing will convince me that our English beauties can be surpassed. – But since you're here will you glance at the seating of tonight's dinner-table. The Hopeleighs, you remember, are arriving . . .'

'I'm afraid I'm no good at dinner-tables. Hadn't you better consult one of the girls?' replied the Duke, ignoring the mention of the expected guests; and as he turned to leave the room his mother thought, with a sinking heart: 'I might better have countermanded the Hopeleighs. He has evidently got wind of their coming, and now he's running away from them.'

The cottage at Runnymede stood dumb and deserted-looking as the Duke drove up to it. The two mothers, he knew, were in London, with the prospective bride and her friends Lizzy and Mab, who were of course to be among her bridesmaids. In view of the preparations for her daughter's approaching marriage, Mrs St George had decided to take a small house in town for the autumn, and, as the Duke also knew, she had chosen Lady Richard Marable's, chiefly because it was near Miss Jacky March's modest dwelling, and because poor Conchita was more than ever in need of ready money.

The Duke of Tintagel was perfectly aware that he should find neither Mrs St George nor her eldest daughter at Runnymede; but he was not in quest of either. If he had not learned, immediately on his return to Longlands, that Jean Hopeleigh and her parents were among the guests expected there, he might never have gone up to London, or taken the afternoon train to Staines. It took the shock of an imminent duty to accelerate his decisions; and to run away from Jean Hopeleigh had become his most urgent duty.

He had not returned to the cottage since the hot summer day when he had avoided playing blindman's-buff with a bevy of noisy girls only by letting himself be drawn into a tiresome political discussion with a pushing young man whose name had escaped him.

Now the whole aspect of the place was changed. The house seemed empty, the bright awnings were gone, and a cold grey mist hung in the cedar-boughs and hid the river. But the Duke found nothing melancholy in the scene. He had a healthy indifference to the worst vagaries of the British climate, and the mist reminded him of the day when, in the fog-swept ruins of Tintagel, he had come on the young lady whom it had been his exquisite privilege to guide back to Trevennick. He had called at the inn the next day, to re-introduce himself to the young lady's governess, and to invite them both to the new Tintagel; and for a fortnight his visits to the inn at Trevennick, and theirs to the ducal seat, had been frequent and protracted. But, though he had spent with them long hours which had flown like minutes, he had never got beyond saying to himself: 'I shan't rest till I've found an English girl exactly like her.' And to be sure of not mistaking the copy he had continued his study of the original.

Miss Testvalley was alone in the little upstairs sitting-room at Runnymede. For some time past she had craved a brief respite from her arduous responsibilities, but now that it had come she was too agitated to profit by it.

It was startling enough to be met, on returning home with Nan, by the announcement of Virginia's engagement; and when she had learned of Lady Churt's dramatic incursion she felt that the news she herself had to impart must be postponed – the more so as, for the moment, it was merely a shadowy affair of hints, apprehensions, divinations.

If Miss Testvalley could have guessed the consequences of her proposal to give the St George girls a season in England, she was not sure she would not have steered Mrs St George back to Saratoga. Not that she had lost her taste for battle and adventure; but she had developed a tenderness for Nan St George, and an odd desire to shelter her from the worldly glories her governess's rash advice had thrust upon the family. Nan was different, and Miss Testvalley could have wished a different future for her; she felt that Belgravia and Mayfair, shooting-parties in great country-houses, and the rest of the fashionable routine to which Virginia and the Elmsworth girls had taken so promptly, would leave Nan bewildered and unsatisfied. What kind of life would satisfy her, Miss Testvalley did not profess to know. The girl, for all her flashes of precocity, was in most ways immature, and the governess had a feeling that she must shape her own fate, and that only unhappiness could come of trying to shape it for her. So it was as well that at present there was no time to deal with Nan.

Virginia's impending marriage had thrown Mrs St George into a state of chaotic despair. It was too much for her to cope with – too complete a revenge on the slights of Mrs Parmore and the cruel rebuff of the Assembly ladies. 'We might better have stayed in New York,' Mrs St George wailed, aghast at the practical consequences of a granted prayer.

Miss Jacky March and Conchita Marable soon laughed her out of this. The trembling awe with which Miss March spoke of Virginia's privilege in entering into one of the greatest families in England woke a secret response in Mrs St George. She, who had suffered because her beautiful daughters could never hope to marry into the proud houses of Eglinton or Parmore, was about to become the mother-in-law of an earl, who would one day (in a manner as unintelligible to Mrs St George as the development of the embryo) turn into the premier Marquess of England. The fact that it was all so unintelligible made it seem more dazzling. 'At last Virginia's beauty will have a worthy setting,' Miss March exulted; and when Mrs St George anxiously murmured: 'But look at poor Conchita. Her husband drinks, and behaves dreadfully with other women, and she never seems to have enough money –' Miss March calmed her with the remark: 'Well, you ask her if she'd rather be living in Fifth Avenue, with more money than she'd know how to spend.'

Conchita herself confirmed this. 'Seadown's always been the good boy of the family. He'll never give Jinny any trouble. After all, that hateful entanglement with Idina Churt shows how quiet and domestic he really is. That was why she held him so long. He likes to sit before the same fire every evening . . . Of course with Dick it's different. The family shipped him off to South America because they couldn't keep him out of scrapes. And if I took a sentimental view of marriage I'd sit up crying half the night . . . But I'll tell you what, Mrs St George; even that's worth while in London. In New York, if a girl's unhappily married there's nothing to take her mind off it; whereas here there's never really time to think about it. And of course Jinny won't have my worries, and she'll have a position that Dick wouldn't have given me even if he'd been a model son and husband.'

Most of this was beyond Mrs St George's grasp; but the gist of it was consoling, and even flattering. After all, if it was the kind of life Jinny wanted, and if even poor Conchita, and that wretched Jacky March, who'd been so cruelly treated, agreed that London was worth the price – well, Mrs St George supposed it must be; and anyhow Mrs Parmore and Mrs Eglinton must be rubbing their eyes at this very minute over the announcement of Virginia's engagement in the New York papers. All that London could give, in rank, in honours, in social glory, was only, to Mrs St George, a knife to stab New York with – and that weapon she clutched with feverish glee. 'If only her father rubs the Brightlingseas into those people he goes with at Newport,' she thought vindictively.

The bell rung by the Duke tinkled languidly and long before a flurried maid appeared; and the Duke, accustomed to seeing double doors fly open on velvet carpets at his approach, thought how pleasant it would be to live in a cottage with too few servants, and have time to notice that the mat was shabby, and the brass knocker needed polishing.

Mrs St George and Mrs Elmsworth were up in town. Yes, he knew that; but might he perhaps see Miss Testvalley? He muttered his name as if it were a term of obloquy, and the dazzled maid curtsied him into the drawing-room and rushed up to tell the governess.

'Did you tell his Grace that Miss Annabel was in London too?' Miss Testvalley asked.

No, the maid replied; but his Grace had not asked for Miss Annabel.

'Ah –' murmured the governess. She knew her man well enough by this time to be aware that this looked serious. 'It was me he asked for?' And the maid, evidently sharing her astonishment, declared that it was.

'Oh, your Grace, there's no fire!' Miss Testvalley exclaimed, as she entered the drawing-room a moment later and found her visitor standing close to the icy grate. 'No, I won't ring. I can light a fire at least as well as any house-maid.'

'Not for me, please,' the Duke protested. 'I dislike over-heated rooms.' He continued to stand near the hearth. 'The – the fact is, I was just noticing, before you came down, that this clock appears to be losing about five minutes a day; that is, supposing it to be wound on Sunday mornings.'

'Oh, your Grace – would you come to our rescue? That clock has bothered Mrs St George and Mrs Elmsworth ever since we came here –'

But the Duke had already opened the glass case, and with his ear to the dial was sounding the clock as though it were a human lung. 'Ah – I thought so!' he exclaimed in a tone of quiet triumph; and for several minutes he continued his delicate manipulations, watched attentively by Miss Testvalley, who thought: 'If ever he nags his wife – and I should think he might be a nagger – she will only have to ask him what's wrong with the drawing-room clock. And how many clocks there must be, at Tintagel and Longlands and Folyat House!'

'There – but I'm afraid it ought to be sent to a professional,' said the Duke modestly, taking the seat designated by Miss Testvalley.

'I'm sure it will be all right. Your Grace is so wonderful with clocks.' The Duke was silent, and Miss Testvalley concluded that doctoring the time-piece had been prompted less by an irrepressible impulse than by the desire to put off weightier matters. 'I'm so sorry,' she said, 'that there's no one here to receive you. I suppose the maid told you that our two ladies have taken a house in town for a few weeks, to prepare for Miss St George's wedding.'

'Yes, I've heard of that,' said the Duke, almost solemnly. He cast an anxious glance about him, as if in search of something; and Miss Testvalley thought proper to add: 'And your young friend Annabel has gone to London with her sister.'

'Ah –' said the Duke laboriously.

He stood up, walked back to the hearth, gazed at the passive face of the clock, and for a moment followed the smooth movement of the hands. Then he turned to Miss Testvalley. 'The wedding is to take place soon?'

'Very soon; in about a month. Colonel St George naturally wants to be present, and business will take him back to New York before December. In fact, it was at first intended that the wedding should take place in New York –'

'Oh –' murmured the Duke, in the politely incredulous tone of one who implies: 'Why attempt such an unheard-of experiment?'

Miss Testvalley caught his meaning and smiled. 'You know Lord and Lady Richard were married in New York. It seems more natural that a girl should be married from her own home.'

The Duke looked doubtful. 'Have they the necessary churches?' he asked.

'Quite adequate,' said Miss Testvalley drily.

There was another and heavier silence before the Duke continued: 'And does Mrs St George intend to remain in London, or will she take a house in the country?'

'Oh, neither. After the wedding Mrs St George will go to her own house in New York. She will sail immediately with the Colonel.'

'Immediately–' echoed the Duke. He hesitated. 'And Miss Annabel –?'

'Naturally goes home with her parents. They wish her to have a season in New York.'

This time the silence closed in so oppressively that it seemed as though it had literally buried her visitor. She felt an impulse to dig him out, but repressed it.

At length the Duke spoke in a hoarse unsteady voice. 'It would be impossible for me – er – to undertake the journey to New York.'

Miss Testvalley gave him an amused glance. 'Oh, it's settled that Lord Seadown's wedding is to be in London.'

'I – I don't mean Seadown's. I mean – my own,' said the Duke. He stood up again, walked the length of the room, and came back to her. 'You must have seen, Miss Testvalley . . . It has been a long struggle, but I've decided . . .'

'Yes?'

'To ask Miss Annabel St George –'

Miss Testvalley stood up also. Her heart was stirred with an odd mixture of curiosity and sympathy. She really liked the Duke – but could Annabel ever be brought to like him?

'And so I came down today, in the hope of consulting with you –'

Miss Testvalley interrupted him. 'Duke, I must remind you that arranging marriages for my pupils is not included in my duties. If you wish to speak to Mrs St George –'

'But I don't!' exclaimed the Duke. He looked so startled that for a moment she thought he was about to turn and take flight. It would have been a relief to her if he had. But he coughed nervously, cleared his throat, and began again.

'I've always understood that in America it was the custom to speak first to the young lady herself. And knowing how fond you are of Miss St George, I merely wished to ask –'

'Yes, I am very fond of her,' Miss Testvalley said gravely.

'Quite so. And I wished to ask if you had any idea whether her . . . her feelings in any degree corresponded with mine,' faltered the anxious suitor.

Miss Testvalley pondered. What should she say? What could she say? What did she really wish to say? She could not, at the moment, have answered any of these questions; she knew only that, as life suddenly pressed closer to her charge, her impulse was to catch her fast and hold her tight.

'I can't reply to that, your Grace. I can only say that I don't know.'

'You don't know?' repeated the Duke in surprise.

'Nan in some ways is still a child. She judges many things as a child would –'

'Yes! That's what I find so interesting . . . so unusual . . .'

'Exactly. But it makes your question unanswerable. How can one answer for a child who can't yet answer for herself?'

The Duke looked crestfallen. 'But it's her childish innocence, her indifference to money and honours and – er – that kind of thing, that I value so immensely . . .'

'Yes. But you can hardly regard her as a rare piece for your collection.'

'I don't know, Miss Testvalley, why you should accuse me of such ideas . . .'

'I don't accuse you, your Grace. I only want you to understand that Nan is one thing now, but may be another, quite different, thing in a year or two. Sensitive natures alter strangely after their first contact with life.'

'Ah, but I should make it my business to shield her from every contact with life!'

'I'm sure you would. But what if Nan turned out to be a woman who didn't want to be shielded?'

The Duke's countenance expressed the most genuine dismay. 'Not want to be shielded? I thought you were a friend of hers,' he stammered.

'I am. A good friend, I hope. That's why I advise you to wait, to give her time to grow up.'

The Duke looked at her with a hunted eye, and she suddenly thought: 'Poor man! I daresay he's trying to marry her against some one else. Running away from the fatted heiress . . . But Nan's worth too much to be used as an alternative.'

'To wait? But you say she's going back to the States immediately.'

'Well, to wait till she returns to England. She probably will, you know.'

'Oh, but I can't wait!' cried the Duke, in the astonished tone of the one who has never before been obliged to.

Miss Testvalley smiled. 'I'm afraid you must say that to Annabel herself, not to me.'

'I thought you were my friend. I hoped you'd advise me . . .'

'You don't want me to advise you, Duke. You want me to agree with you.'

The Duke considered this for some time without speaking; then he said: 'I suppose you've no objection to giving me the London address?' and the governess wrote it down for him with her same disciplined smile.

18

Longlands House, October 25

To Sir Helmsley Thwarte, Bart.
  Honourslove, Lowdon, Glos.

MY DEAR SIR HELMSLEY,

It seems an age since you have given Ushant and me the pleasure of figuring among the guns at Longlands; but I hope next month you will do us that favour.

You are, as you know, always a welcome guest; but I will not deny that this year I feel a special need for your presence. I suppose you have heard that Selina Brightlingsea's eldest boy is marrying an American – so that there will soon be two daughters-in-law of that nationality in the family. I make no comment beyond saying that I fail to see why the virtue and charms of our English girls are not sufficient to satisfy the hearts of our young men. It is useless, I suppose, to argue such matters with the interested parties; one can only hope that when experience has tested the more showy attractions of the young ladies from the States, the enduring qualities of our own daughters will re-assert themselves. Meanwhile I am selfishly glad that it is poor Selina, and not I, on whom such a trial has been imposed.

But to come to the point. You know Ushant's exceptionally high standards, especially in family matters, and will not be surprised to hear that he feels we ought to do our cousinly duty toward the Brightlingseas by inviting Seadown, his fiancée, and the latter's family (a Colonel and Mrs St George, and a younger daughter), to Longlands. He says it would not matter half as much if Seadown were marrying one of our own kind; and though I do not quite follow this argument, I respect it, as I do all my dear son's decisions. You see what is before me, therefore; and though you may not share Ushant's view, I hope your own family feeling will prompt you to come and help me out with all these strange people.

The shooting is especially good this year, and if you could

manage to be with us from the 10th to the 18th of November, Ushant assures me the sport will be worthy of your gun.

Believe me

Yours very sincerely

BLANCHE TINTAGEL

Longlands House, November 15

To Guy Thwarte Esqre
  Care of the British Consulate General
    Rio Janeiro
      (To be forwarded)

MY DEAR BOY,

Look on the above address and marvel! You who know how many years it is since I have allowed myself to be dragged into a Longlands shooting-party will wonder what can have caused me to succumb at last.

Well – queerly enough, a sense of duty! I have, as you know, my (rare) moments of self-examination and remorse. One of these penitential phases coincided with Blanche Tintagel's invitation, and as it was re-inforced by a moving appeal to my tribal loyalty, I thought I ought to respond, and I did. After all, Tintagel is our Duke, and Longlands is our Dukery, and we local people ought all to back each other up in subversive times like these.

The reason of Blanche's cry for help will amuse you. Do you remember, one afternoon just before you left for Brazil, having asked me to invite to Honourslove two American young ladies, friends of Lady Dick Marable's, who were staying at Allfriars? You were so urgent that my apprehensions were aroused; and I imagine rightly. But being soft-hearted I yielded, and Lady Richard appeared with an enchantress, and the enchantress's younger sister, who seemed to me totally eclipsed by her elder, though you apparently thought otherwise. I've no doubt you will recall the incident.

Well – Seadown is to marry the beauty, a Miss St George, of New York. Rumours, of course, are rife about the circumstances of the marriage. Seadown is said to have been trapped by a clever manoeuvre; but as this report probably emanates

448

from Lady Churt – the Ariadne in the case – it need not be taken too seriously. We know that American business men are 'smart', but we also know that their daughters are beautiful; and having seen the young lady who has supplanted Ariadne, I have no difficulty in believing that her 'beaux yeux' sufficed to let Seadown out of prison – for friends and foes agree that the affair with the relentless Idina had become an imprisonment. They also say that Papa St George is very wealthy, and that consideration must be not without weight – its weight in gold – to the Brightlingseas. I hope they will not be disappointed, but as you know I am no great believer in transatlantic fortunes – though I trust, my dear fellow, that the one you are now amassing is beyond suspicion. Otherwise I should find it hard to forgo your company much longer.

It's an odd chance that finds me in an atmosphere so different from that of our shabby old house, on the date fixed for the despatch of my monthly chronicle. But I don't want to miss the South American post, and it may amuse you to have a change from the ordinary small beer of Honourslove. Certainly the contrast is not without interest; and perhaps it strikes me the more because of my disintegrating habit of seeing things through other people's eyes, so that at this moment I am viewing Longlands, not as a familiar and respected monument, but as the unheard-of and incomprehensible phenomenon that a great English country-seat offers to the unprejudiced gaze of the American backwoodsman and his females. I refer to the St George party, who arrived the day before yesterday, and are still in the first flush of their bewilderment.

The Duchess and her daughters are of course no less bewildered. They have no conception of a society not based on aristocratic institutions, with Inveraray, Welbeck, Chatsworth, Longlands and so forth as its main supports; and their guests cannot grasp the meaning of such institutions or understand the hundreds of minute observances forming the texture of an old society. This has caused me, for the first time in my life, to see from the outside at once the absurdity and the impressiveness of our great ducal establishments, the futility of their domestic ceremonial, and their importance as custodians of historical tradition and of high (if narrow) social standards. My poor friend Blanche would faint if she knew that I had actually ventured to imagine what an England without Dukes might be, perhaps may soon be; but she would be restored to her senses if she knew that, after weighing the evidence for and against, I have decided that, having been afflicted with Dukes, we'd better keep 'em. I need hardly add that such problems do not trouble the St Georges, who have not yet reached the stage of investigating social origins.

I can't imagine how the Duchess and the other ladies deal with Mrs St George and her daughters during the daily absence of the guns; but I have noticed that American young ladies cannot be kept quiet for an indefinite time by being shown views of Vesuvius and albums of family water-colours.

Luckily it's all right for the men. The shooting has never been better, and Seadown, who is in his element, has had the surprise of finding that his future father-in-law is not precisely out of his. Colonel St George is a good shot; and it is not the least part of the joke that he is decidedly bored by covert shooting, an institution as new to him as dukedoms, and doesn't understand how a man who respects himself can want to shoot otherwise than over a dog. But he accommodates himself well enough to our effete habits, and is in fact a big good-natured easy-going man, with a kind of florid good looks, too new clothes, and a collection of funny stories, some of which are not new enough.

As to the ladies, what shall I say? The beauty *is* a beauty, as I discovered (you may remember) the moment she appeared at Honourslove. She is precisely what she was then: the obvious, the finished exemplar, of what she professes to be. And, as you know, I have always had a preference for the icily regular. Her composure is unshakeable; and under a surface of American animation I imagine she is as passive as she looks. She giggles with the rest, and says: 'Oh, girls', but on her lips such phrases acquire a classic cadence. I suspect her of having a strong will and knowing all the arts of exaction. She will probably get whatever she wants in life, and will give in return only her beautiful profile. I don't believe her soul has a full face. If I were in Seadown's place I should probably be as much in love with her as he is. As a rule I don't care for interesting women; I mean in the domestic relation. I prefer a fine figure-head embodying a beautiful form, a solid bulk of usage and conformity. But I own that figure-heads lack conversation . . .

Your little friend is not deficient in this respect; and she is also agreeable to look upon. Not beautiful; but there is a subtler form of loveliness, which the unobservant confuse with beauty, and which this young Annabel is on the way to acquire. I say 'on the way' because she is still a bundle of engaging possibilities rather than a finished picture. Of the mother there is nothing to say, for that excellent lady evidently requires familiar surroundings to bring out such small individuality as she possesses. In the unfamiliar she becomes invisible; and Longlands and she will never be visible to each other.

Most amusing of all is to watch our good Blanche, her faithful daughters, and her other guests, struggling with the strange beings suddenly thrust upon them. Your little friend (the only one with whom one can converse, by the way) told me that when Lady Brightlingsea heard of Dick Marable's engagement to the Brazilian beauty she cabled to the St Georges' governess: 'Is she black?' Well, the attitude of Longlands toward its transatlantic guests is not much more enlightened than Selina Brightlingsea's. Their bewilderment is so great that, when one of the girls spoke of archery clubs being fashionable in the States, somebody blurted out: 'I suppose the Indians taught you?'; and I am constantly expecting them to ask Mrs St George how she heats her wigwam in winter.

The only exceptions are Seadown, who contributes little beyond a mute adoration of the beauty, and – our host, young Tintagel. Strange to say, he seems curiously alert and informed about his American visitors; so much so that I'm wondering if his including them in the party is due only to a cousinly regard for Seadown. My short study of the case has almost convinced me that his motives are more interested. His mother, of course, has no suspicion of this – when did our Blanche ever begin to suspect anything until it was emblazoned across the heavens? The first thing she said to me (in explaining the presence of the

St Georges) was that, since so many of our young eligibles were beginning to make these mad American marriages, she thought that Tintagel should see a few specimens at close quarters. *Sancta simplicitas!* If this is her object, I fear the specimens are not well-chosen. I suspect that Tintagel had them invited because he's very nearly, if not quite, in love with the younger girl, and being a sincere believer in the importance of Dukes, wants her family to see what marriage with an English Duke means.

How far the St Georges are aware of all this, I can't say. The only one I suspect of suspecting it is the young Annabel; but these Americans, under their forth-coming manner, their surface-gush, as some might call it, have an odd reticence about what goes on underneath. At any rate the young lady seems to understand something of her environment, which is a sealed book to the others. She has been better educated than her sister, and has a more receptive mind. It seems as though some one had sown in a bare field a sprinkling of history, poetry and pictures, and every seed had shot up in a flowery tangle. I fancy the sower is the little brown governess of whom you spoke (her pupil says she is little and brown). Miss Annabel asks so many questions about English life in town and country, about rules, customs, traditions, and their why and wherefore, that I sometimes wonder if she is not preparing for a leading part on the social stage; then a glimpse of utter simplicity dispels the idea, and I remember that all her country-people are merciless questioners, and conclude that she has the national habit, but exercises it more intelligently than the others. She is intensely interested in the history of this house, and has an emotional sense at least of its beauties; perhaps the little governess – that odd descendant of old Testavaglia's – has had a hand in developing this side also of her pupil's intelligence.

Miss Annabel seems to be devoted to this Miss Testvalley, who is staying on with the family though both girls are out, and one on the brink of marriage, and who is apparently their guide in the world of fashion – odd as such a rôle seems for an Italian revolutionary. But I understood she had learned her way about the great world as governess in the Brightlingsea and Tintagel households. Her pupil, by the way, tells me that Miss Testvalley knows all about the circumstances in which my D. G. Rossetti was painted, and knows also the mysterious replica with variants which is still in D. G.'s possession, and which he has never been willing to show me. The girl, the afternoon she came to Honourslove, apparently looked closely enough at my picture to describe it in detail to her governess, who says that in the replica the embroidered border of the cloak is *peach-coloured* instead of blue . . .

All this has stirred up the old collector in me, and when the St Georges go to Allfriars, where they have been asked to stay before the wedding, Miss Annabel has promised to try to have the governess invited, and to bring her to Honourslove to see the picture. What a pity you won't be there to welcome them! The girl's account of the Testavaglia and her family excites my curiosity almost as much as this report about the border of the cloak.

After the above, which reads, I flatter myself, not unlike a page of Saint Simon, the home chronicle will seem tamer than ever. Mrs Bolt has again upset everything in my study by having it dusted. The chestnut mare has foaled, and we're getting on with the ploughing. We are having too much rain – but when haven't we too much rain in England? The new grocer at Little Ausprey threatens to leave, because he says his wife and the non-conformist minister – but there, you always pretend to hate village scandals, and as I have, for the moment, none of my own to tempt your jaded palate, I will end this confession of an impenitent but blameless parent.

Your aff^{te}

H.T.

P.S. The good Blanche asked anxiously about you – your health, plans and prospects, the probable date of your return; and I told her I would give a good deal to know myself. Do you suppose she has her eye on you for Ermie or Almina? Seadown's defection was a hard blow; and if I'm right about Tintagel, Heaven help her!

BOOK THREE

19

The windows of the Correggio room at Longlands overlooked what was known as the Duchess's private garden, a floral masterpiece designed by the great Sir Joseph Paxton, of Chatsworth and Crystal Palace fame. Beyond an elaborate cast-iron fountain swarmed over by chaste divinities, and surrounded by stars and crescents of bedding plants, an archway in the wall of yew and holly led down a grass avenue to the autumnal distances of the home park. Mist shrouded the slopes dotted with mighty trees, the bare woodlands, the lake pallidly reflecting a low uncertain sky. Deer flitted spectrally from glade to glade, and on remoter hill-sides blurred clusters of sheep and cattle were faintly visible. It had rained heavily in the morning, it would doubtless rain again before night; and in the Correggio room the drip of water sounded intermittently from the long reaches of roof-gutter and from the creepers against the many-windowed house-front.

The Duchess, at the window, stood gazing out over what seemed a measureless perspective of rain-sodden acres. Then, with a sigh, she turned back to the writing-table and took up her pen. A sheet of paper lay before her, carefully inscribed in a small precise hand:

To a Dowager Duchess.
To a Duchess.
To a Marchioness.
To the wife of a Cabinet Minister who has no rank by birth.
To the wife of a Bishop.
To an Ambassador.

The page was inscribed: 'Important', and under each head-line was a brief formula for beginning and ending a letter. The Duchess scrutinized this paper attentively; then she glanced over another paper bearing a list of names, and finally, with a sigh, took from a tall mahogany stand a sheet of note-paper with 'Longlands House' engraved in gold under a ducal coronet, and began to write.

After each note she struck a pencil line through one of the names on the list, and then began another note. Each was short, but she wrote slowly, almost laboriously, like a conscientious child copying out an exercise; and at the bottom of the sheet she inscribed her name, after assuring herself once more that the formula preceding her signature corresponded with the instructions before her. At length she reached the last note, verified the formula, and for the twentieth time wrote out underneath: 'Annabel Tintagel'.

There before her, in orderly sequence, lay the invitations to the first big shooting-party of the season at Longlands, and she threw down her pen with another sigh. For a minute or two she sat with her elbows on the desk, her face in her hands; then she uncovered her eyes, and looked again at the note she had just signed.

'Annabel Tintagel,' she said slowly: 'who *is* Annabel Tintagel?'

The question was one which she had put to herself more than once during the last months, and the answer was always the same: she did not know. Annabel Tintagel was a strange figure with whom she lived, and whose actions she watched with a cold curiosity, but with whom she had never arrived at terms of intimacy, and never would. Of that she was now sure.

There was another perplexing thing about her situation. She was now, to all appearances, Annabel Tintagel, and had been so for over two years; but before that she had been Annabel St George, and the figure of Annabel St George, her face and voice, her likes and dislikes, her memories and moods, all that made up her tremulous little identity, though still at the new Annabel's side, no longer composed the central Annabel, the being with whom this strange new Annabel of the Correggio room at Longlands, and the Duchess's private garden, felt herself really one. There were moments when the vain hunt for her real self became so perplexing and disheartening that she was glad to escape from it into the mechanical duties of her new life. But in the intervals she continued to grope for herself, and to find no one.

To begin with, what had caused Annabel St George to turn into Annabel Tintagel? That was the central problem! Yet how could she solve it, when she could no longer question that elusive Annabel St

George, who was still so near to her, yet as remote and unapproachable as a plaintive ghost?

Yes – a ghost. That was it. Annabel St George was dead, and Annabel Tintagel did not know how to question the dead, and would therefore never be able to find out why and how that mysterious change had come about . . .

'The greatest mistake,' she mused, her chin resting on her clasped hands, her eyes fixed unseeingly on the dim reaches of the park, 'the greatest mistake is to think that we ever know why we do things . . . I suppose the nearest we can ever come to it is by getting what old people call "experience". But by the time we've got that we're no longer the persons who did the things we no longer understand. The trouble is, I suppose, that we change every moment; and the things we did stay.'

Of course she could have found plenty of external reasons; a succession of incidents, leading, as a trail leads across a desert, from one point to another of the original Annabel's career. But what was the use of recapitulating these points, when she was no longer the Annabel whom they had led to this splendid and lonely room set in the endless acres of Longlands?

The curious thing was that her uncertainty and confusion of mind seemed to have communicated themselves to the new world into which she found herself transplanted – and that she was aware of the fact. 'They don't know what to make of me, and why should they, when I don't know what to make of myself?' she had once said, in an unusual burst of confidence, to her sister Virginia, who had never really understood her confidences, and who had absently rejoined, studying herself while she spoke in her sister's monumental cheval glass, and critically pinching her waist between thumb and fore-finger: 'My dear, I've never yet met an Englishman or an Englishwoman who didn't know what to make of a Duchess, if only they had the chance to try. The trouble is you don't give them the chance.'

Yes; Annabel supposed it was that. Fashionable London had assimilated with surprising rapidity the lovely transatlantic invaders. Hostesses who only two years ago would have shuddered at the clink of tall glasses and the rattle of cards, now threw their doors open to poker-parties, and offered intoxicating drinks to those to whom the new-fangled afternoon tea seemed too reminiscent of the school-room. Hands trained to draw from a Broadwood the dulcet cadences of 'La Sonnambula' now thrummed the banjo to 'Juanita' or 'The Swanee River'. Girls, and even young matrons, pinned up their skirts to compete with the young men in the new game of lawn-tennis on lordly lawns, smoking was spreading from the precincts reserved for it to dining-room and library (it was even rumoured that 'the Americans' took sly whiffs in their bedrooms!), Lady Seadown was said to be getting up an amateur nigger-minstrel performance for the Christmas party at Allfriars, and as for the wild games introduced into country-house parties, there was no denying that, even after a hard day's hunting or shooting, they could tear the men from their after-dinner torpor.

A blast of outer air had freshened the stagnant atmosphere of Belgravian drawing-rooms, and while some sections of London society still shuddered (or affected to shudder) at 'the Americans', others, and the uppermost among them, openly applauded and imitated them. But in both groups the young Duchess of Tintagel remained a figure apart. The Dowager Duchess spoke of her as 'my perfect daughter-in-law', but praise from the Dowager Duchess had about as much zest as a Sunday-school diploma. In the circle where the pace was set by Conchita Marable, Virginia Seadown and Lizzy Elmsworth (now married to the brilliant young Conservative member of Parliament, Mr Hector Robinson), the circle to which, by kinship and early associations, Annabel belonged, she was as much a stranger as in the straitest fastnesses of the peerage. 'Annabel has really managed,' Conchita drawled with her slow smile, 'to be considered unfashionable among the unfashionable –' and the phrase clung to the young Duchess, and catalogued her once for all.

One side of her loved, as much as the others did, dancing, dressing up, midnight romps, practical jokes played on the pompous and elderly; but the other side, the side which had dominated her since her arrival in England, was passionately in earnest and beset with vague dreams and ambitions, in which a desire to better the world alternated with a longing for solitude and poetry.

If her husband could have kept her company in either of these regions she might not have given a thought to the rest of mankind.

But in the realm of poetry the Duke had never willingly risked himself since he had handed up his Vale at Eton, and a great English nobleman of his generation could hardly conceive that he had anything to learn regarding the management of his estates from a little American girl whose father appeared to be a cross between a stock-broker and a professional gambler, and whom he had married chiefly because she seemed too young and timid to have any opinions on any subject whatever.

'The great thing is that I shall be able to form her,' he had said to his mother, on the dreadful day when he had broken the news of his engagement to the horrified Duchess; and the Duchess had replied, with a flash of unwonted insight: 'You're very skilful, Ushant; but women are not quite as simple as clocks.'

As simple as clocks. How like a woman to say that! The Duke smiled. 'Some clocks are not at all simple,' he said with an air of superior knowledge.

'Neither are some women,' his mother rejoined; but there both thought it prudent to let the discussion drop.

Annabel stood up and looked about the room. It was large and luxurious, with walls of dark green velvet framed in heavily carved and gilded oak. Everything about its decoration and furnishings – the towering malachite vases, the ponderous writing-table supported on winged geniuses in ormolu, the heavily-foliaged wall lights, the Landseer portrait, above the monumental chimney-piece, of her husband as a baby, playing with an elder sister in a tartan sash – all testified to a sumptuous 're-doing', doubtless dating from the day when the present Dowager had at last presented her lord with an heir. A stupid oppressive room – somebody else's room, not Annabel's . . . But on three of the velvet-panelled walls hung the famous Correggios; in the half-dusk of an English November they were like rents in the clouds, tunnels of radiance reaching to pure sapphire distances. Annabel looked at the golden limbs, the parted lips gleaming with laughter, the abandonment of young bodies under shimmering foliage. On dark days – and there were many – these pictures were her sunlight. She speculated about them, wove stories around them, and hung them with snatches of verse from Miss Testvalley's poet-cousin. How was it they went?

> *Beyond all depth away*
> *The heat lies silent at the brink of day:*
> *Now the hand trails upon the viol-string*
> *That sobs, and the brown faces cease to sing,*
> *Sad with the whole of pleasure.*

Were there such beings anywhere, she wondered, save in the dreams of poets and painters, such landscapes, such sunlight? The Correggio room had always been the reigning Duchess's private boudoir, and at first it had surprised Annabel that her mother-in-law should live surrounded by scenes before which Mrs St George would have veiled her face. But gradually she understood that in a world as solidly buttressed as the Dowager Duchess's by precedents, institutions and traditions, it would have seemed far more subversive to displace the pictures than to hear the children's Sunday-school lessons under the laughter of those happy pagans. The Correggio room had always been the Duchess's boudoir, and the Correggios had always hung there. 'It has always been like that,' was the Dowager's invariable answer to any suggestion of change; and she had conscientiously brought up her son in the same creed.

Though she had been married for over two years it was for her first big party at Longlands that the new Duchess was preparing. The first months after her marriage had been spent at Tintagel, in a solitude deeply disapproved of by the Duke's mother, who for the second time found herself powerless to influence her son. The Duke gave himself up with a sort of dogged abandonment to the long dreamed-of delights of solitude and domestic bliss. The ducal couple (as the Dowager discovered with dismay, on her first visit to them) lived like any middle-class husband and wife, tucked away in a wing of the majestic pile where two butlers and ten footmen should have been drawn up behind the dinner-table, and a groom-of-the-chambers have received the guests in the great hall. Groom-of-the-chambers, butlers and footmen had all been relegated to Longlands, and to his mother's dismay only two or three personal servants supplemented the understudies who had hitherto sufficed for Tintagel's simple needs on his trips to Cornwall.

Even after their return to London and Longlands the young couple continued to disturb the Dowager Duchess's peace of mind.

The most careful and patient initiation into the functions of the servants attending on her had not kept Annabel from committing what seemed to her mother-in-law inexcusable, perhaps deliberate blunders; such as asking the groom-of-the-chambers to fetch her a glass of water, or bidding one of the under house-maids to lace up her dinner-dress when her own maid was accidentally out of hearing.

'It's not that she's *stupid*, you know, my dear,' the Dowager avowed to her old friend Miss Jacky March, 'but she puts one out, asking the reason of things that have nothing to do with reasons – such as why the housekeeper doesn't take her meals with the upper servants, but only comes in for dessert. What would happen next, as I said to her, in a house where the housekeeper *did* take her meals with the upper servants? That sort of possibility never occurs to the poor child; yet I really can't call her stupid. I often find her with a book in her hand. I think she thinks too much about things that oughtn't to be thought about,' wailed the bewildered Duchess. 'And the worst of it is that dear Ushant doesn't seem to know how to help her . . .' her tone implying that, in any case, such a task should not have been laid on him. And Miss Jacky March murmured her sympathy.

20

Those quiet months in Cornwall, which already seemed so much more remote from the actual Annabel than her girlhood at Saratoga, had been of her own choosing. She did not admit to herself that her first sight of the ruins of the ancient Tintagel had played a large part in her wooing; that if the Duke had been only the dullest among the amiable but dull young men who came to the bungalow at Runnymede she would hardly have given him a second thought. But the idea of living in that magic castle by the sad western sea had secretly tinged her vision of the castle's owner; and she had thought that he and she might get to know each other more readily there than anywhere else. And now, in looking back, she asked herself if it were not her own fault that the weeks at Tintagel had not brought the expected understanding. Instead, as she now saw, they had only made husband and wife more unintelligible to each other. To Annabel, the

Cornish castle spoke with that rich low murmur of the past which she had first heard in its mysterious intensity the night when she had lain awake in the tapestried chamber at Allfriars, beside the sleeping Virginia, who had noticed only that the room was cold and shabby. Though the walls of Tintagel were relatively new, they were built on ancient foundations, and crowded with the treasures of the past; and near by was the mere of Excalibur, and from her windows she could see the dark grey sea, and sometimes, at night-fall, the mysterious barge with black sails putting out from the ruined castle to carry the dead King to Avalon.

Of all this, nothing existed for her husband. He saw the new Tintagel only as a costly folly of his father's, which family pride obliged him to keep up with fitting state, in spite of the unfruitful acres that made its maintenance so difficult. In shouldering these cares, however, he did not expect his wife to help him, save by looking her part as a beautiful and angelically pure young Duchess, whose only duties consisted in bestowing her angelic presence on entertainments for the tenantry and agricultural prize-givings. The Duke had grown up under the iron rod of a mother who, during his minority, had managed not only his property, but his very life, and he had no idea of letting her authority pass to his wife. Much as he dreaded the duties belonging to his great rank, deeply as he was oppressed by them, he was determined to perform them himself, were it ever so hesitatingly and painfully, and not to be guided by any one else's suggestions.

To his surprise such suggestions were not slow in coming from Annabel. She had not yet learned that she was expected to remain a lovely and adoring looker-on, and in her daily drives over the estate (in the smart pony-chaise with its burnished trappings and gay pie-bald ponies) she often, out of sheer loneliness, stopped for a chat at toll-gates, farm-houses and cottages, made purchases at the village shops, scattered toys and lollipops among the children, and tried to find out from their mothers what she could do to help them. It had filled her with wonder to learn that for miles around, both at Long-lands and Tintagel, all these people in the quaint damp cottages and the stuffy little shops were her husband's tenants and dependants; that he had the naming of the rectors and vicars of a dozen churches, and that even the old men and women in the mouldy almshouses were there by virtue of his bounty. But when she had grasped the extent of his power it seemed to her that to help and befriend those who depended on him was the best service she could render him. Nothing in her early bringing-up had directed her mind toward any kind of organized beneficence, but she had always been what she called 'sorry for people', and it seemed to her that there was a good deal to be sorry about in the lot of these people who depended solely, in health and sickness, on a rich man's whim.

The discovery that her interest in them was distasteful to the Duke came to her as a great shock, and left a wound that did not heal. Coming in one day, a few months after their marriage, from one of her exploring expeditions, she was told that his Grace wished to speak to her in his study, and she went in eagerly, glad to seize the chance of telling him at once about the evidences of neglect and poverty she had come upon that very afternoon.

'Oh, Ushant, I'm so glad you're in! Could you come with me at once to the Linfrys' cottage, down by St Gildas's; you know, that damp place under the bridge, with the front covered with roses? The eldest boy's down with typhoid, and the drains ought to be seen to at once if all the younger ones are not to get it.' She spoke in haste, too much engrossed in what she had to say to notice the Duke's expression. It was his silence that roused her; and when she looked at him she saw that his face wore what she called its bolted look – the look she most disliked to see on it. He sat silent, twisting an ivory paper-cutter between his fingers.

'May I ask who told you this?' he said at length, in a voice like his mother's when she was rebuking an upper house-maid.

'Why, I found it out myself. I've just come from there.'

The Duke stood up, knocking the paper-cutter to the floor.

'You've been there? Yourself? To a house where you tell me there is typhoid fever? In your state of health? I confess, Annabel – ' His lips twitched nervously under his scanty blond moustache.

'Oh, bother my state of health! I feel all right, really I do. And you know the doctors have ordered me to walk and drive every day.'

'But not go and sit with Mrs Linfry's sick children, in a house reeking with disease.'

'But, Ushant, I just had to! There was no one else to see about them. And if the house reeks with disease, whose fault is it but ours?

They've no sick-nurse, and nobody to help the mother, or tell her what to do; and the doctor comes only every other day.'

'Is it your idea, my dear, that I should provide every cottage on my estates, here and elsewhere, with a hospital nurse?' the Duke asked ironically.

'Well, I wish you would! At least there ought to be a nurse in every village, and two in the bigger ones; and the doctor ought to see his patients every day; and the drains – Ushant, you must come with me *at once* and smell the drains!' cried Nan in a passion of entreaty.

She felt the Duke's inexpressive eyes fixed coldly on her.

'If your intention is to introduce typhoid fever at Tintagel, I can imagine no better way of going about it,' he began. 'But perhaps you don't realize that, though it may not be as contagious as typhus, the doctors are by no means sure . . .'

'Oh, but they *are* sure; only ask them! Typhoid comes from bad drains and infected milk. It can't hurt you in the least to go down and see what's happening at the Linfrys'; and you ought to, because they're your own tenants. Won't you come with me now? The ponies are not a bit tired, and I told William to wait –'

'I wish you would not call Armson by his Christian name; I've already told you that in England head grooms are called by their surnames.'

'Oh, Ushant, what *can* it matter? I call you by your surname, but I never can remember about the others. And the only thing that matters now . . .'

The Duke walked to the hearth, and pulled the embroidered bell-rope beside the chimney. To the footman who appeared he said: 'Please tell Armson that her Grace will not require the pony-chaise any longer this afternoon.'

'But –' Annabel burst out; then she stood silent till the door closed on the servant. The Duke remained silent also.

'Is that your answer?' she asked at length, her breath coming quickly.

He lifted a more friendly face. 'My dear child, don't look so tragic. I'll see Blair; he shall look into the drains. But do try to remember that these small matters concern my agent more than they do me, and that they don't concern you at all. My mother was very much esteemed and respected at Tintagel, but though she managed my affairs so wisely, it never occurred to her to interfere directly with the agent's business, except as regards Christmas festivities, and the annual school-treat. Her holding herself aloof increased the respect that was felt for her; and my wife could not do better than to follow her example.'

Annabel stood staring at her husband without speaking. She was too young to understand the manifold inhibitions, some inherited, some peculiar to his own character, which made it impossible for him to act promptly and spontaneously; but she knew him to be by nature not an unkind man, and this increased her bewilderment.

Suddenly a flood of words burst from her. 'You tell me to be careful about my health in the very same breath that you say you can't be bothered about these poor people, and that their child's dying is a small matter, to be looked after by the agent. It's for the sake of your own child that you forbid me to go to see them – but I tell you I don't want a child if he's to be brought up with such ideas, if he's to be taught, as you have been, that it's right and natural to live in a palace with fifty servants, and not care for the people who are slaving for him on his own land, to make his big income bigger! I'd rather be dead than see a child of mine taught to grow up as – as you have!'

She broke down and dropped into a seat, hiding her face in her hands. Her husband looked at her without speaking. Nothing in his past experience had prepared him for such a scene, and the consciousness that he did not know how to deal with it increased his irritation. Had Annabel gone mad – or was it only what the doctors called her 'condition'? In either case he felt equally incapable of resolute and dignified action. Of course, if he were told that it was necessary, owing to her 'condition', he would send these Linfrys – a shiftless lot – money and food, would ask the doctor to see the boy oftener; though it went hard with him to swallow his own words, and find himself again under a woman's orders. At any rate, he must try to propitiate Annabel, to get her into a more amenable mood; and as soon as possible must take her back to Longlands, where she would be nearer a London physician, accustomed to bringing Dukes into the world.

'Annabel,' he said, going up to her, and laying his hand on her bent head.

She started to her feet. 'Let me alone,' she exclaimed, and brushed past him to the door. He heard her cross the hall and go up the stairs in the direction of her own rooms; then he turned back to his desk. One of the drawing-room clocks stood there before him, disembowelled; and as he began (with hands that still shook a little) to put it cautiously together, he remembered his mother's comment: 'Women are not always as simple as clocks.' Had she been right?

After a while he laid aside the works of the clock and sat staring helplessly before him. Then it occurred to him that Annabel, in her present mood, was quite capable of going contrary to his orders, and sending for a carriage to drive her back to the Linfrys' – or Heaven knew where. He rang again, and asked for his own servant. When the man came the Duke confided to him that her Grace was in a somewhat nervous state, and that the doctors wished her to be kept quiet, and not to drive out again that afternoon. Would Bowman therefore see the head coachman at once, and explain that, even if her Grace should ask for a carriage, some excuse must be found . . . they were not, of course, to say anything to implicate the Duke, but it must be so managed that her Grace should not be able to drive out again that day.

Bowman acquiesced, with the look of respectful compassion which his face often wore when he was charged with his master's involved and embarrassed instructions; and the Duke, left alone, continued to sit idly at his writing-table.

Annabel did not re-appear that afternoon; and when the Duke, on his way up to dress for dinner, knocked at her sitting-room door, she was not there. He went on to his own dressing-room, but on the way met his wife's maid, and asked if her Grace were already dressing.

'Oh, no, your Grace. I thought the Duchess was with your Grace . . .'

A little chill caught him about the heart. It was nearly eight o'clock, for they dined late at Tintagel; and the maid had not yet seen her mistress! The Duke said with affected composure: 'Her Grace was tired this afternoon. She may have fallen asleep in the drawing-room –' though he could imagine nothing less like the alert and restless Annabel.

Oh, no, the maid said again; her Grace had gone out on foot two or three hours ago, and had not yet returned.

'On foot?'

'Yes, your Grace. Her Grace asked for her pony-carriage; but I understood there were orders –'

The Duke interrupted irritably: 'The doctor's orders were that her Grace should not go out at all today.'

The maid lowered her lids as if to hide her incredulous eyes, and he felt that she was probably acquainted with every detail of the day's happenings. The thought sent the blood up to the roots of his pale hair, and he challenged her nervously. 'You must at least know which way her Grace said she was going.'

'The Duchess said nothing to me, your Grace. But I understand she sent to the stables, and finding she could not have a carriage walked away through the park.'

'That will do . . . there's been some unfortunate misunderstanding about her Grace's orders,' stammered the Duke, turning away to his dressing-room.

The day had been raw and cloudy, and with the dusk rain had begun, and was coming down now in a heavy pour that echoed through the narrow twisting passages of the castle and made their sky-lights rattle. And in this icy down-pour his wife, his Duchess, the expectant mother of future Dukes, was wandering somewhere on foot, alone and unprotected. Anger and alarm contended in the Duke. If any one had told him that marrying a simple unworldly girl, hardly out of the school-room, would add fresh complications to a life already overburdened with them, he would have scoffed at the idea. Certainly he had done nothing to deserve such a fate. And he wondered now why he had been so eager to bring it upon himself. Though he had married for love only a few months before, he was now far more concerned with Annabel as the mother of his son than for her own sake. The first weeks with her had been very sweet – but since then her presence in his house had seemed only to increase his daily problems and bothers. The Duke rang and ordered Bowman to send to the stables for the station-brougham, and when it arrived he drove down at break-neck speed to the Linfrys' cottage. But Nan was not there. The Duke stared at Mrs Linfry blankly. He did not know where to go next, and it mortified him to reveal his distress and uncertainty to the coachman. 'Home!' he ordered angrily, getting into the carriage again; and the dark drive began once more. He was half way back when the carriage stopped with a jerk, and the coach-man, scrambling down from the box, called to him in a queer frightened voice.

The Duke jumped out and saw the man lifting a small dripping figure into the brougham. 'By the mercy of God, your Grace . . . I think the Duchess has fainted . . .'

'Drive like the devil . . . stop at the stables to send a groom for the doctor,' stammered the Duke, pressing his wife in his arms. The rest of the way back was as indistinct to him as to the girl who lay so white on his breast. Bowed over her in anguish, he remembered nothing till the carriage drove under the echoing gate-tower at Tintagel, and lights and servants pressed confusedly about them. He lifted Annabel out, and she opened her eyes and took a few steps alone across the hall. 'Oh – am I here again?' she said, with a little laugh; then she swayed forward, and he caught her as she fell . . .

To the Duchess of Tintagel who was signing the last notes of invita-tion for the Longlands shooting-party, the scene at Tintagel and what had followed now seemed as remote and legendary as the tales that clung about the old ruins of Arthur's castle. Annabel had put herself hopelessly in the wrong. She had understood it without being told, she had acknowledged it and wept over it at the time; but the irremediable had been done, and she knew that never, in her hus-band's eyes, would any evidence of repentance atone for that night's disaster.

The miscarriage which had resulted from her mad expedition through the storm had robbed the Duke of a son; of that he was convinced. He, the Duke of Tintagel, wanted a son, he had a right to expect a son, he would have had a son, if this woman's criminal folly had not destroyed his hopes. The physicians summoned in con-sultation spoke of the necessity of many months of repose . . . even they did not seem to understand that a Duke must have an heir, that it is the purpose for which Dukes make the troublesome effort of marrying.

It was now more than a year since that had happened, and after long weeks of illness a new Annabel – a third Annabel – had emerged from the ordeal. Life had somehow, as the months passed, clumsily re-adjusted itself. As far as words went, the Duke had forgiven his wife; they had left the solitude of Tintagel as soon as the physicians thought it possible for the Duchess to be moved; and now, in their crowded London life, and at Longlands, where the Dowager had seen to it that all the old ceremonial was re-established, the ducal pair were too busy, too deeply involved in the incessant distractions and obligations of their station, to have time to remember what was over and could not be mended.

But Annabel gradually learned that it was not only one's self that changed. The ceaseless mysterious flow of days wore down and altered the shape of the people nearest one, so that one seemed fated to be always a stranger among strangers. The mere fact, for instance, of Annabel St George's becoming Annabel Tintagel had turned her mother-in-law, the Duchess of Tintagel, into a Dowager Duchess, over whose diminished head the mighty roof of Longlands had shrunk into the modest shelter of a lovely little rose-clad dower-house at the gates of the park. And every one else, as far as Annabel's world reached, seemed to have changed in the same way.

That, at times, was the most perplexing part of it. When, for instance, the new Annabel tried to think herself back on to the verandah of the Grand Union Hotel, waiting for her father and his stock-broker friends to return from the races, or in the hotel ball-room with the red damask curtains, dancing with her sister, with Conchita Closson and the Elmsworth girls, or with the obscure and infrequent young men who now and then turned up to partner their wasted loveliness – when she thought, for instance, of Roy Gilling, and the handkerchief she had dropped, and he had kissed and hidden in his pocket – it was like looking at the flickering figures of the magic lanterns she used to see at children's parties. What was left, now, of those uncertain apparitions, and what relation, say, did the Conchita Closson who had once seemed so ethereal and elusive, bear to Lady Dick Marable, beautiful still, though she was growing rather too stout, but who had lost her lovely indolence and detachment, and was now perpetually preoccupied about money, and immersed in domestic difficulties and clandestine consolations; or to Virginia, her own sister Virginia, who had seemed to Annabel so secure, so aloof, so disdainful of everything but her own pleasures, but who, as Lady Seadown, was enslaved to that dull half-asleep

Seadown, absorbed in questions of rank and precedence, and in awe – actually in awe – of her father-in-law's stupid arrogance, and of Lady Brightlingsea's bewildered condescensions?

Yes; changed, every one of them, vanished out of recognition, as the lost Annabel of the Grand Union had vanished. As she looked about her, the only figures which seemed to have preserved their former outline were those of her father and his business friends; but that, perhaps, was because she so seldom saw them, because when they appeared, at long intervals, for a hurried look at transatlantic daughters and grandchildren, they brought New York with them, solidly and loudly, remained jovially unconscious of any change of scene and habits greater than that between the east and west shores of the Hudson, and hurried away again, leaving behind them cheques and christening mugs, and unaware to the last that they had been farther from Wall Street than across the ferry.

Ah, yes – and Laura Testvalley, her darling old Val! She too had remained her firm sharp-edged self. But then she too was usually away, she had not suffered the erosion of daily contact. The real break with the vanished Annabel had come, the new Annabel some-times thought, when Miss Testvalley, her task at the St Georges' ended, had vanished into the seclusion of another family which re-quired 'finishing'. Miss Testvalley, since she had kissed the bride after the great Tintagel wedding, nearly three years ago, had re-appeared only at long intervals, and as it were under protest. It was one of her principles – as she had often told Annabel – that a governess should not hang about her former pupils. Later they might require her – there was no knowing, her subtle smile implied; but once the school-room was closed, she should vanish with the tattered lesson-books, the dreary school-room food, the cod-liver oil and the chilblain cures.

Perhaps, Annabel thought, if her beloved Val had remained with her, they might between them have rescued the old Annabel, or at least kept up communications with her ghost – a faint tap now and then against the walls which had built themselves up about the new Duchess. But as it was, there was the new Duchess isolated in her new world, no longer able to reach back to her past, and not having yet learned how to communicate with her present.

She roused herself from these vain musings, and took up her pen.

A final glance at the list had shown her that one invitation had been forgotten – or, if not forgotten, at least postponed.

DEAR MR THWARTE,

The Duke tells me you have lately come back to England, and he hopes so much that you can come to Longlands for our next shooting-party, on the 18th. He asks me to say that he is anxious to have a talk with you about the situation at Lowdon. He hopes you intend to stand if Sir Hercules Loft is obliged to resign, and wishes you to know that you will have his full support.

Yours sincerely
ANNABEL TINTAGEL

Underneath she added: 'P.S. Perhaps you'd remember me if I signed Nan St George.' But what was the sense of that, when there was no longer any one of that name? She tore the note up, and re-wrote it without adding the postscript.

21

Guy Thwarte had not been back at Honourslove long enough to expect a heavy mail beside his breakfast plate. His four years in Brazil had cut him off more completely than he had realized from his former life; and he was still in the somewhat painful stage of picking up the threads.

'Only one letter? Lucky devil, I envy you!' grumbled Sir Helmsley, taking his seat at the other end of the table and impatiently pushing aside a stack of newspapers, circulars and letters.

The young man glanced with a smile at his father's correspondence. He knew so well of what it consisted: innumerable bills, dunning letters, urgent communications from book-makers, tradesmen, the chairmen of political committees or art-exhibitions, scented notes from enamoured ladies, or letters surmounted by mysterious symbols from astrologers, palmists or alchemists – for Sir Helmsley had dabbled in most of the arts, and bent above most of the mysteries. But today, as usual, his son observed, the bills and the dunning letters predominated. Guy would have to put some order into that; and probably into the scented letters too.

'Yes, I'm between two worlds yet – "powerless to be born" kind of feeling,' he said as he took up the solitary note beside his own plate. The writing was unknown to him, and he opened the envelope with indifference.

'Oh, my dear fellow – don't say that; don't say "powerless",' his father rejoined, half-pleadingly, but with a laugh. 'There's such a lot waiting to be done; we all expect you to put your hand to the plough without losing a minute. I was lunching at Longlands the other day and had a long talk with Ushant. With old Sir Hercules Loft in his dotage for the last year, there's likely to be a vacancy at Lowdon at any minute, and the Duke's anxious to have you look over the ground without losing any time, especially as that new millionaire from Glasgow is said to have some chance of getting in.'

'Oh, well –' Guy was glancing over his letter while his father spoke. He knew Sir Helmsley's great desire was to see him in the House of Commons, an ambition hitherto curbed by the father's reduced fortune, but brought into the foreground again since the son's return from exile with a substantial bank account.

Guy looked up from his letter. 'Tintagel's been talking to you about it, I see.'

'You see? Why – has he written to you already?'

'No. But she has. The new American Duchess – the little girl I brought here once, you remember?' He handed the letter to his father, whose face expressed a growing satisfaction as he read.

'Well – that makes it plain sailing. You'll go to Longlands, of course?'

'To Longlands?' Guy hesitated. 'I don't know. I'm not sure I want to.'

'But if Tintagel wants to see you about the seat? You ought to look over the ground. There may not be much time to lose.'

'Not if I'm going to stand – certainly.'

'*If!*' shouted Sir Helmsley, bringing down his fist with a crash that set the Crown Derby cups dancing. 'Is that what you're not sure of? I thought we were agreed before you went away that it was time there was a Thwarte again in the House of Commons.'

'Oh – before I went away,' Guy murmured. His father's challenge, calling him back suddenly to his old life, the traditional life of a Thwarte of Honourslove, had shown him for the first time how far from it all he had travelled in the last years, how remote had become the old sense of inherited obligations which had once seemed the very marrow of his bones.

'Now you've made your pile, as they say out there,' Sir Helmsley continued, attempting a lighter tone, but unable to disguise his pride in the incredible fact of his son's achievement – a Thwarte who had made money! – 'now that you've made your pile, isn't it time to think of a career? In my simplicity, I imagined it was one of your principal reasons for exiling yourself.'

'Yes; I suppose it was,' Guy acquiesced.

After this, for a while, father and son faced one another in silence across the breakfast-table, each, as is the way of the sensitive, over-conscious of the other's thoughts. Guy, knowing so acutely what was expected of him, was vainly struggling to become again the young man who had left England four years earlier; but strive as he would he could not yet fit himself into his place in the old scheme of things. The truth was, he was no longer the Guy Thwarte of four years ago, and would probably never recover that lost self. The break had been too violent, the disrupting influences too powerful. Those dark rich stormy years of exile lay like a raging channel between himself and his old life, and his father's summons only drove him back upon himself.

'You'll have to give me time, sir – I seem to be on both sides of the globe at once,' he muttered at length with bent head.

Sir Helmsley stood up abruptly, and walking around the table laid a hand on his son's shoulder. 'My dear fellow, I'm so sorry. It seems so natural to have you back that I'd forgotten the roots you've struck over there . . . I'd forgotten the grave . . .'

Guy's eyes darkened, and he nodded. 'All right, sir . . .' He stood up also. 'I think I'll take a turn about the stables.' He put the letter from Longlands into his pocket, and walked out alone on to the terrace. As he stood there, looking out over the bare November land-scape, and the soft blue hills fading into a low sky, the sense of kinship between himself and the soil began to creep through him once more. What a power there was in these accumulated associations, all so low-pitched, soft and unobtrusive, yet which were already insinuating themselves through his stormy Brazilian years, and sapping them of their reality! He felt himself becoming again the school-boy who used to go nutting in the hazel-copses of the Red Farm, who fished and bathed in the dark pools of the Love, stole nectarines from the walled gardens, and went cub-hunting in the autumn dawn with his father, glorying in Sir Helmsley's horsemanship, and racked with laughter at his jokes – the school-boy whose heart used to beat to bursting at that bend of the road from the station where you first sighted the fluted chimney-stacks of Honourslove.

He walked across the terrace, and turning the flank of the house passed under the sculptured lintel of the chapel. A smell of autumn rose from the cold paving, where the kneeling Thwartes elbowed each other on the narrow floor, and under the recumbent effigies the pillows almost mingled their stony fringes. How many there were, and how faithfully hand had joined hand in the endless work of enlarging and defending the family acres! Guy's glance travelled slowly down the double line, from the armoured effigy of the old fighting Thwarte who had built the chapel to the Thornycroft image of his own mother, draped in her marble slumber, just as the boy had seen her, lying with drawn lids, on the morning when his father's telegram had called him back from Eton. How many there were – and all these graves belonged to him, all were linked to the same soil and to one another in an old community of land and blood; together for all time, and kept warm by each other's nearness. And that far-off grave which also belonged to him – the one to which his father had alluded – how remote and lonely it was, off there under tropic skies, among other graves that were all strange to him!

He sat down and rested his face against the back of the bench in front of him. The sight of his mother's grave had called up that of his young Brazilian wife, and he wanted to shut out for a moment all those crowding Thwartes, and stand again beside her far-off headstone. What would life at Honourslove have been if he had brought Paquita home with him instead of leaving her among the dazzling white graves at Rio? He sat for a long time, thinking, remembering, trying to strip his mind of conventions and face the hard reality underneath. It was inconceivable to him now that, in the first months of his marriage, he had actually dreamed of severing all ties with home, and beginning life anew as a Brazilian mine-owner. He saw that what he had taken for a slowly matured decision had been no more than a passionate impulse; and its resemblance to his father's headlong experiments startled him as he looked back. His mad marriage had nearly deflected the line of his life – for a little pale face with ebony hair and curving black lashes he would have sold his birth-right. And long before the black lashes had been drawn down over the quiet eyes he had known that he had come to the end of that adventure . . .

All his life, and especially since his mother's death, Guy Thwarte had been fighting against his admiration for his father, and telling himself that it was his duty to be as little like him as possible; yet more than once he had acted exactly as Sir Helmsley would have acted, or snatched himself back just in time. But in Brazil he had not been in time . . .

'One brilliant man's enough in a family,' he said to himself as he stood up and left the chapel.

Forgetting his projected visit to the stables, he turned back to the house, and crossing the hall, opened the door of his father's study. There he found Sir Helmsley seated at his easel, re-touching a delicately drawn water-colour copy of the little Rossetti Madonna above his desk. Sir Helmsley, whose own work was incurably amateurish, excelled in the art of copying, or rather interpreting, the work of others; and his water-colour glowed with the deep brilliance of the original picture.

As his son entered he laid down his palette with an embarrassed laugh. 'Well, what do you think of it – eh?'

'Beautiful. I'm glad you've not given up your painting.'

'Eh –? Oh, well, I don't do much of it nowadays. But I'd promised this little thing to Miss Testvalley,' the baronet stammered, reddening handsomely above his auburn beard.

Guy echoed, bewildered: 'Miss Testvalley?'

Sir Helmsley coughed and cleared his throat. 'That governess, you know – or perhaps you don't. She was with the little new Duchess of Tintagel before her marriage; came here with her one day to see my Rossettis. She's Dante Gabriel's cousin; didn't I tell you? Remarkable woman – one of the few relations the poet is always willing to see.

She persuaded him to sell me a first study of the "Bocca Baciata", and I was doing this as a way of thanking her. She's with Augusta Glenloe's girls; I see her occasionally when I go over there.'

Sir Helmsley imparted this information in a loud, almost challenging voice, as he always did when he had to communicate anything unexpected or difficult to account for. Explaining was a nuisance, and somewhat of a derogation. He resented anything that made it necessary, and always spoke as if his interlocutor ought to have known beforehand the answer to the questions he was putting.

After his bad fall in the hunting-field, the year before Guy's return from Brazil, the county had confidently expected that the lonely widower would make an end by marrying either his hospital nurse or the Gaiety girl who had brightened his solitude during his son's absence. One or the other of these conclusions to a career over-populated by the fair sex appeared inevitable in the case of a brilliant and unsteady widower. Coroneted heads had been frequently shaken over what seemed a foregone conclusion; and Guy had shared these fears. And behold, on his return, he found the nurse gone, the Gaiety girl expensively pensioned off, and the baronet, slightly lame, but with youth renewed by six months of enforced seclusion, apparently absorbed in a little brown governess who wore violet poplin and heavy brooches of Roman mosaic, but who (as Guy was soon to observe) had eyes like torches, and masses of curly-edged dark hair which she was beginning to braid less tightly, and to drag back less severely from her broad forehead.

Guy stood looking curiously at his father. The latter's bluster no longer disturbed him; but he was uncomfortably reminded of certain occasions when Sir Helmsley, on the brink of an imprudent investment or an impossible marriage, had blushed and explained with the same volubility. Could this outbreak be caused by one of the same reasons? But no! A middle-aged governess? It was unthinkable. Sir Helmsley had always abhorred the edifying, especially in petticoats; and with his strong well-knit figure, his handsome auburn head, and a complexion clear enough for blushes, he still seemed, in spite of his accident, built for more alluring prey. His real interest, Guy concluded, was no doubt in the Rossetti kinship, and all that it offered to his insatiable imagination. But it made the son wonder anew what other mischief his inflammable parent had been up to during his own long absence. It would clearly be part of his business to look into his father's sentimental history, and keep a sharp eye on his future. With these thoughts in his mind, Guy stood smiling down paternally on his father.

'Well, sir, it's all right,' he said. 'I've thought it over, and I'll go to Longlands; when the time comes I'll stand for Lowdon.'

His father returned the look with something filial and obedient in his glance. 'My dear fellow, it's all right indeed. That's what I've always expected of you.'

Guy wandered out again, drawn back to the soil of Honourslove as a sailor is drawn to the sea. He would have liked to go over all its acres by himself, yard by yard, inch by inch, filling his eyes with the soft slumbrous beauty, his hands with the feel of wrinkled tree-boles, the roughness of sodden autumnal turf, his nostrils with the wine-like smell of dead leaves. The place was swathed in folds of funereal mist shot with watery sunshine, and he thought of all the quiet women who had paced the stones of the terrace on autumn days, worked over the simple-garden and among the roses, or sat in the oak parlour at their accounts or their needle-work, speaking little, thinking much, dumb and nourishing as the heaps of faded leaves which mulched the soil for coming seasons.

The 'little Duchess's' note had evoked no very clear memory when he first read it; but as he wandered down the glen through the fading heath and bracken he suddenly recalled their walk along the same path in its summer fragrance, and how they had stayed alone on the terrace when the rest of the party followed Sir Helmsley through the house. They had leaned side by side on the balustrade, he remembered, looking out over that dear scene, and speaking scarcely a word; and yet, when she had gone, he knew how near they had been . . . He even remembered thinking, as his steamer put out from the docks at Liverpool, that on the way home, after he had done his job in Brazil, he would stop a few days in New York to see her. And then he had heard – with wonder and incredulity – the rumour of her ducal marriage; a rumour speedily confirmed by letters and news-papers from home.

That girl – and Tintagel! She had given Guy the momentary sense of being the finest instrument he had ever had in his hand; an instrument from which, when the time came, he might draw unearthly music. Not that he had ever seriously considered the possibility of trying his chance with her; but he had wanted to keep her image in his heart, as something once glimpsed, and giving him the measure of his dreams. And now it was poor little Tintagel who was to waken those melodies; if indeed he could! For a few weeks after the news came it had blackened Guy's horizon; but he was far away, he was engrossed in labours and pleasures so remote from his earlier life that the girl's pale image had become etherealized, and then had faded out of existence. He sat down on the balustrade of the terrace, in the corner where they had stood together, and pulling out her little note, re-read it.

'The writing of a school-girl . . . and the language of dictation,' he thought; and the idea vaguely annoyed him. 'How on earth could she have married Tintagel? That girl! . . . One would think from the wording of her note that she'd never seen me before . . . She might at least have reminded me that she'd been here. But perhaps she'd forgotten – as I had!' he ended with a laugh and a shrug. And he turned back slowly to the house, where the estate agent was awaiting him with bills and estimates, and long lists of repairs. Already Sir Helmsley had slipped that burden from his shoulders.

22

When their Graces were in residence at Longlands the Dowager did not often come up from the dower-house by the gate. But she had the awful gift of omnipresence, of exercising her influence from a distance; so that while the old family friends and visitors at Longlands said: 'It's wonderful, how tactful Blanche is – how she keeps out of the young people's way,' every member of the household, from its master to the last boots and scullion and gardener's boy, knew that her Grace's eye was on them all, and the machinery of the tremendous establishment still moving in obedience to the pace and pattern she had set.

But at Christmas the Dowager naturally could not remain aloof. If she had not participated in the Christmas festivities the county would have wondered, the servants gossiped, the tradesmen have thought the end of the world had come.

'I hope you'll do your best to persuade my mother to come next week. You know she thinks you don't like her,' Tintagel had said to his wife, a few days before Christmas.

'Oh, why?' Nan protested, blushing guiltily; and of course she had obediently persuaded, and the Duchess had responded by her usual dry jerk of acquiescence.

For the same reason, the new Duchess's family, and her American friends, had also to be invited; or at least so the Duke thought. The Dowager was not of the same mind; but thirty years of dealings with her son ('from his birth the most obstinate baby in the world') had taught her when to give way; and she did so now.

'It does seem odd, though, Ushant's wanting all those strange people here for Christmas,' she confided to her friend Miss March, who had come up with her from the dower-house, 'for I understand the Americans make nothing of any of our religious festivals – do they?'

Miss March, who could not forget that she was the daughter of a clergyman of the Episcopal Church of America, protested gently, as she so often had before: 'Oh, but, Duchess, that depends, you know; in our church the feasts and observances are exactly the same as in yours . . .' But what, she reflected, have such people as the St Georges to do with the Episcopal Church? They might be Seventh Day Baptists, or even Mormons, for all she knew.

'Well, it's very odd,' murmured the Dowager, who was no longer listening to her.

The two ladies had seated themselves after dinner on a wide Jacobean settee at one end of the 'double-cube' saloon, the great room with the Thornhill ceiling and the Mortlake tapestries. The floor had been cleared of rugs and furniture – another shock this to the Dowager, but also accepted with her small stiff smile – and down the middle of the polished *parquet* spun a long line of young (and some more than middle-aged) dancers, led, of course, by Lady Dick Marable and her odd Brazilian brother, whose name the Dowager could never remember, but who looked so dreadfully like an Italian hairdresser. (A girl who had been a close friend of the Dowager's youth had rent society asunder by breaking her engagement to a young officer in the Blues, and running away with her Italian hair-dresser; and when the Dowager's eyes had first rested on Teddy de Santos-Dios she had thought with a shudder: '*Poor Florrie's man must have looked like that.*')

Close in Lady Dick's wake (and obviously more interested in her than in his partner) came Miles Dawnly, piloting a bewildered Brightlingsea girl. It was the custom to invite Dawnly wherever Conchita was invited; and even strait-laced hostesses, who had to have Lady Dick because she 'amused the men', were so thankful not to be obliged to invite her husband that they were glad enough to let Dawnly replace him. Every one knew that he was Lady Dick's chosen attendant, but every one found it convenient to ignore the fact, especially as Dawnly's own standing, and his fame as a dancer and a shot, had long since made him a welcome guest.

The Dowager had always thought it a pity that a man with such charming manners, and an assured political future, should seem in no hurry to choose a wife; but when she saw that he had taken for his partner a Marable rather than a Folyat, she observed tartly to Miss March that she did not suppose Mr Dawnly would ever marry, and hoped Selina Brightlingsea had no illusions on that point.

At the farther end of the great saloon, the odd little Italian governess who used to be at Longlands with the Duchess's younger daughters, and was now 'finishing' the Glenloe girls, sat at the piano rattling off a noisy reel which she was said to have learnt in the States; and down the floor whirled the dancers, in pursuit of Lady Richard and the Brazilian.

'Virginia reel, you say they call it? It's all so unusual,' repeated the Dowager, lifting her long-handled eye-glass to study the gyrations of the troop.

Yes; it certainly was unusual to see old Lord Brightlingsea pirouetting heavily in the wake of his beautiful daughter-in-law Lady Seadown, and Sir Helmsley Thwarte, incapacitated for pirouetting since his hunting accident, standing near the piano, clapping his hands and stamping his sound foot in time with Lady Dick's Negro chant – they said it was Negro. All so very unusual, especially when associated with Christmas . . . Usually that noisy sort of singing was left to the waits, wasn't it? But under this new rule the Dowager's enquiring eye-glass was really a window opening into an unknown world – a world in whose reality she could not bring herself to believe. 'Ushant might better have left me down at the dower-house,' she murmured with a strained smile to Miss March.

'Oh, Duchess, don't say that! See how they're all enjoying themselves,' replied her friend, wondering, deep down under the old Mechlin which draped her bosom, whether Lord Brightlingsea, when the dance swept him close to her sofa, might not pause before her with his inimitable majesty, lift her to her feet, and carry her off into the reel whose familiar rhythm she felt even now running up from her trim ankles . . . But Lord Brightlingsea pounded past her unseeingly . . . Certainly, as men grew older, mere youth seemed to cast a stronger spell over them; the fact had not escaped Miss March.

Lady Brightlingsea was approaching the Dowager's sofa, bearing down on her obliquely and hesitatingly, like a sailing-vessel trying to make a harbour-mouth on a windless day.

'Do come and sit with us, Selina dear,' the Dowager welcomed her. 'No, no, don't run away, Jacky . . . Jacky,' she explained, 'has been telling me about this odd American dance, which seems to amuse them all so much.'

'Oh, yes, do tell us,' exclaimed Lady Brightlingsea, coming to anchor between the two. 'It's called the Virginia reel, isn't it? I thought it was named after my daughter-in-law – Seadown's wife is called Virginia, you know. But she says no: she used to dance it as a child. It's an odd coincidence, isn't it?'

The Dowager was always irritated by Lady Brightlingsea's vagueness. She said, in her precise tone: 'Oh, no, it's a very old dance. The Wild Indians taught it to the Americans, didn't they, Jacky?'

'Well, I'm sure it's wild enough,' Lady Brightlingsea murmured, remembering the scantily clad savages in the great tapestry at Allfriars, and thankful that the dancers had not so completely unclothed themselves – though the *décolletage* of the young American ladies went some way in that direction.

Miss March roused herself to reply, with a certain impatience. 'But no, Duchess; this dance is not Indian. The early English colonists brought it with them from England to Virginia – Virginia was one of the earliest English colonies (called after the Virgin Queen, you know), and the Virginia reel is just an old English or Scottish dance.'

The Dowager never greatly cared to have her statements corrected; and she particularly disliked its being done before Selina Brightlingsea, whose perpetual misapprehensions were a standing joke with everybody.

'I daresay there are two theories. I was certainly told it was a Wild Indian war-dance.'

'It seems much more likely; such a very odd performance,' Lady Brightlingsea acquiesced; but neither lady cared to hazard herself farther on the unknown ground of American customs.

'It's like their *valse* – that's very odd too,' the Dowager continued, after a silence during which she had tried in vain to think up a new topic.

'The *valse*? Oh, but surely the *valse* is familiar enough. My girls were all taught it as a matter of course – weren't yours? I can't think why it shocked our grandparents, can you?'

The Dowager narrowed her lips. 'Not *our* version, certainly. But this American *valse* – "waltz" I think they call it there –'

'Oh, is it different? I hadn't noticed, except that I don't think the young ladies carry themselves with quite as much dignity as ours.'

'I should say not! How can they, when every two minutes they have to be prepared to be turned upside down by their partners?'

'*Upside down?*' echoed Lady Brightlingsea, in startled italics. 'What in the world, Blanche, do you mean by *upside down?*'

'Well, I mean – not exactly, of course. But turned round. Surely you must have noticed? Suddenly whizzed around and made to dance backward. Jacky, what is it they call it in the States?'

'Reversing,' said Miss March, between dry lips. She felt suddenly weary of hearing her compatriots discussed and criticized and having to explain them; perhaps because she had had to do it too often.

'Ah – "reversing". Such a strange word too. I don't think it's English. But the thing itself is so strange – suddenly pushing your partner backward. I can't help thinking it's a little indelicate.'

The dowager, with reviving interest, rejoined: 'Don't you think these new fashions make all the dances seem – er – rather indelicate? When crinolines were worn the movements were not as – as visible as now. These tight skirts, with the gathers up the middle of the front – of course one can't contend against the fashion. But one can at least not exaggerate it, as they appear to do in America.'

'Yes – I'm afraid they exaggerate everything in America . . . My dear,' Lady Brightlingsea suddenly interrupted herself, 'what in the world can they be going to do next?'

The two long rows facing each other (ladies on one side of the room, gentlemen opposite) had now broken up, and two by two, in dancing pairs, forming a sort of giant caterpillar, were spinning off down the double-cube saloon and all the length of the Waterloo room adjoining it, and the Raphael drawing-room beyond, in the direction of the Classical Sculpture gallery.

'Oh, my dear, where *can* they be going?' Lady Brightlingsea cried.

The three ladies, irresistibly drawn by the unusual sight, rose together and advanced to the middle of the Raphael drawing-room. From there they could see the wild train, headed by Lady Dick's rhythmic chant, sweeping ahead of them down the length of the Sculpture gallery, back again to the domed marble hall which formed the axis of the house, and up the state staircase to the floor above.

'My dear – my dear Jacky,' gasped Lady Brightlingsea.

'They'll be going into the bedrooms next, I suppose,' said the Dowager with a dry laugh.

But Miss March was beyond speech. She had remembered that the fear of being late for dinner, and the agitation she always felt on great occasions, had caused her to leave on her dressing-table the duplicate set of fluffy curls which should have been locked up with her modest cosmetics. And in the course of this mad flight Lord Brightlingsea might penetrate to her bedroom, and one of those impious girls might cry out: 'Oh, look at Jacky March's curls on her dressing-table!' She felt too faint to speak . . .

Down the upper gallery spun the accelerated reel, song and laughter growing louder to the accompaniment of hurrying feet. Teddy de Santos-Dios had started 'John Peel', and one hunting song followed on another in rollicking chorus. Door after door was flung open, whirled through, and passed out of again, as the train pursued its turbulent way. Now and then a couple fell out, panting and laughing, to rejoin the line again when it coiled back upon itself – but the Duchess and Guy Thwarte did not rejoin it.

Annabel had sunk down on a bench at the door of the Correggio room. Guy Thwarte stood at her side, leaning against the wall and looking down at her. He thought how becomingly the dance had flushed her cheeks and tossed her hair. 'Poor little thing! Fun and laughter are all she needs to make her lovely – but how is she ever to get them, at Longlands and Tintagel?' he thought.

The door of the Correggio room stood wide as the dance swept on, and he glanced in, and saw the candlelit walls, and the sunset glow of the pictures. 'By Jove! There are the Correggios!'

Annabel stood up. 'You know them, I suppose?'

'Well, rather – but I'd forgotten they were in here.'

'In my sitting-room. Come and look. They're so mysterious in this faint light.'

He followed her, and stood before the pictures, his blood beating high, as it always did at the sight of beauty.

'It sounds funny,' he murmured, 'to call the Earthly Paradise a sitting-room.'

'I thought so too. But it's always been the Duchess's sitting-room.'

'Ah, yes. And that "always been" –.' He smiled and broke off, turning away from her to move slowly about from picture to picture. In the pale amber candle-glow they seemed full of mystery, as though withdrawn into their own native world of sylvan loves and revels; and for a while he too was absorbed into that world, and almost unconscious of his companion's presence. When at last he turned he saw that her face had lost the glow of the dance, and become small and wistful, as he had seen it on the day of his arrival at Longlands.

'You're right. They're even more magical than by daylight.'

'Yes. I often come here when it's getting dark, and sit among them without making a sound. Perhaps some day, if I'm very patient, I'll tame them, and they'll come down to me . . .'

Guy Thwarte stood looking at her. 'Now what on earth,' he thought, 'does Tintagel do when she says a thing like that to him?'

'They must make up to you for a great deal,' he began impru-dently, heedless of what he was saying.

'For a good deal – yes. But it's rather lonely sometimes, when the only things that seem real are one's dreams.'

The young man flushed up, and made a movement toward her. Then he paused, and looked at the pictures with a vague laugh. She was only a child, he reminded himself – she didn't measure what she was saying.

'Oh, well, you'll go to *them*, some day, in their Italian palaces.'

'I don't think so. Ushant doesn't care for travelling.'

'How does he know? He's never been out of England,' broke from Guy impatiently.

'That doesn't matter. He says all the other places are foreign. And he hates anything foreign. There are lots of things he's never done that he feels quite sure he'd hate.'

Guy was silent. Again he seemed to himself to be eaves-dropping – unintentionally leading her on to say more than she meant; and the idea troubled him.

He turned back to his study of the pictures. 'Has it ever occurred to you,' he began again after a pause, 'that to enjoy them in their real beauty –'

'I ought to persuade Ushant to send them back where they belong?'

'I didn't mean anything so drastic. But did it never occur to you that if you had the courage to sweep away all those . . . those touching little – er . . . family mementoes –' His gesture ranged across the closely covered walls, from illuminated views of Vesuvius in action to landscapes by the Dowager Duchess's great-aunts, funereal monuments worked in hair on faded silk, and photographs in heavy oak frames of ducal relatives, famous race-horses, Bishops in lawn sleeves, and under-graduates grouped about sporting trophies.

Annabel coloured, but with amusement, not annoyance. 'Yes; it did occur to me; and one day I smuggled in a ladder and took them all down – every one.'

'By jove, you did? It must have been glorious.'

'Yes; that was the trouble. The Duchess –'

She broke off, and he interposed, with an ironic lift to the brows: 'But you're the Duchess.'

'Not the real one. You must have seen that already. I don't know my part yet, and I don't believe I ever shall. And my mother-in-law was so shocked that every single picture I'd taken down had to be put back the same day.'

'Ah, that's natural too. We're built like that in this tight little island. We fight like tigers against change, and then one fine day accept it without arguing. You'll see: Ushant will come round, and then his mother will, because he has. It's only a question of time – and luckily you've plenty of that ahead of you.' He looked at her as he spoke, conscious that he was not keeping the admiration out of his eyes, or the pity either, as he had meant to.

Her own eyes darkened, and she glanced away. 'Yes; there's plenty of time. Years and years of it.' Her voice dragged on the word, as if in imagination she were struggling through the long desert reaches of her own future.

'You don't complain of that, do you?'

'I don't know; I can't tell. I'm not as sure as Ushant how I shall feel about things I've never tried. But I've tried this – and I sometimes think I wasn't meant for it . . .' She broke off, and he saw the tears in her eyes.

'My dear child –' he began; and then, half-embarrassed: 'For you *are* a child still, you know. Have you any idea how awfully young you are?'

As soon as he had spoken he reflected that she was too young not to resent any allusion to her inexperience. She laughed. 'Please don't send me back to the nursery! "Little girls shouldn't ask questions. You'll understand better when you're grown up" . . . How much longer am I to be talked to like that?'

'I'm afraid that's the most troublesome question of all. The truth is –' He hesitated. 'I rather think growing up's largely a question of climate – of sunshine . . . Perhaps our moral climate's too chilly for you young creatures from across the globe. After all, New York's in the latitude of Naples.'

She gave him a perplexed look, and then smiled. 'Oh, I know – those burning hot summers . . .'

'You want so much to go back to them?'

'Do I? I can't tell . . . I don't believe so . . . But somehow it seems as if this were wrong – my being here . . . If you knew what I'd give to be able to try again . . . somewhere where I could be myself, you understand, not just an unsuccessful Duchess . . .'

'Yes; I do understand –'

'Annabel!' a voice called from the threshold, and Miss Testvalley stood before them, her small brown face full of discernment and resolution.

'My dear, the Duke's asking for you. Your guests are beginning to leave, and I must be off with Lady Glenloe and my girls.' Miss Testvalley, with a nod and a smile at young Thwarte, had linked her arm through Annabel's. She paused a moment on the threshold. 'Wasn't I right, Mr Thwarte, to insist on your coming up with us to see the Correggios? I told the Duke it was my doing. They're wonderful by candle-light. But I'm afraid we ought not to have carried off our hostess from her duties.'

Laughing and talking, the three descended together to the great hall, where the departing guests were assembled.

23

The house-party at Longlands was not to break up for another week; but the morning after the Christmas festivities such general lassitude prevailed that the long galleries and great drawing-rooms remained deserted till luncheon.

The Dowager Duchess had promised her son not to return to the dower-house until the day after Boxing Day. By that time, it was presumed, the new Duchess would be sufficiently familiar with the part she had to play; but meanwhile a vigilant eye was certainly needed, if only to regulate the disorganized household service.

'These Americans appear to keep such strange hours; and they ask for such odd things to be sent to their rooms – such odd things to eat and drink. Things that Boulamine has never even heard of. It's just as well, I suppose, that I should be here to keep him and Mrs Gillings and Manning from losing their heads,' said the Dowager to her son, who had come to her sitting-room before joining the guns, who were setting out late on the morning after the dance (thereby again painfully dislocating the domestic routine).

The Duke made no direct answer to his mother's comment. 'Of

course you must stay,' he said, in a sullen tone, and without looking at her.

The Duchess pursed up her lips. 'There's nothing I wouldn't do to oblige you, Ushant; but last night I really felt for a moment – well, rather out of place; and so, I think, did Selina Brightlingsea.'

The Duke was gazing steadily at a spot on the wall above his mother's head. 'We must move with the times,' he remarked sententiously.

'Well – we were certainly doing that last night. Moving faster than the times, I should have thought. At least almost all of us. I believe you didn't participate. But Annabel –'

'Annabel is very young,' her son interrupted.

'Don't think that I forget that. It's quite natural that she should join in one of her native dances . . . I understand they're very much given to these peculiar dances in the States.'

'I don't know,' said the Duke coldly.

'Only I should have preferred that, having once joined the dancers, she should have remained with them, instead of obliging people to go hunting all over the house for her and her partner – Guy Thwarte, wasn't it? I admit that hearing her name screamed up and down the passages, and in and out of the bedrooms . . . when she ought naturally to have been at her post in the Raphael room . . . where I have always stood when a party was breaking up . . .'

The Duke twisted his fingers nervously about his watch-chain. 'Perhaps you could tell her,' he suggested.

The Dowager's little eyes narrowed doubtfully. 'Don't you think, Ushant, a word from *you* –?'

He glanced at his watch. 'I must be off to join the guns . . . No, decidedly – I'd rather you explained . . . make her understand . . .'

His hand on the door, he turned back. 'I want, just at present, to say nothing that could . . . could in any way put her off . . .' The door closed, and his mother stood staring blankly after him. That chit – and he was afraid of – what did he call it? 'Putting her off'? Was it possible that he did not know his rights? In the Dowager's day, the obligations of a wife – more especially the wife of a Duke – had been as clear as the Ten Commandments. She must give her husband at least two sons, and if in fulfilment of this duty a dozen daughters came uninvited, must receive them with suitably maternal sentiments, and see that they were properly clothed and educated. The Duchess of Tintagel had considered herself lucky in having only eight daughters, but had grieved over Nature's inexorable resolve to grant her no second son.

'Ushant must have two sons – three, if possible. But his wife doesn't seem to understand her duties. Yet she has only to look into the prayer-book . . . but I've never been able to find out to what denomination her family belong. Not Church people, evidently, or these tiresome explanations would be unnecessary . . .'

After an interval of uneasy cogitation the Dowager rang, and sent to enquire if her daughter-in-law could receive her. The reply was that the Duchess was still asleep (at midday – the Dowager, all her life, had been called at a quarter to seven!), but that as soon as she rang she should be given her Grace's message.

The Dowager, with a sigh, turned back to her desk, which was piled, as usual, with a heavy correspondence. If only Ushant had listened to her, had chosen an English wife in his own class, there would probably have been two babies in the nursery by this time, and a third on the way. And none of the rowdy galloping in and out of people's bedrooms at two in the morning. Ah, if sons ever listened to their mothers . . .

The luncheon hour was approaching when there was a knock on the Dowager's door and Annabel entered. The older woman scrutinized her attentively. No – it was past understanding! If the girl had been a beauty one could, with a great effort of the imagination, have pictured Ushant's infatuation, his subjection; but this pale creature with brown hair and insignificant features, without height, or carriage, or that look of authority given by inherited dignities even to the squat and the round – what right had she to such consideration? Yet it was clear that she was already getting the upper hand of her husband.

'My dear – do come in. Sit here; you'll be more comfortable. I hope,' continued the Dowager with a significant smile, as she pushed forward a deep easy-chair, 'that we shall soon have to be asking you to take care of yourself . . . not to commit any fresh imprudence –'

Annabel, ignoring the suggestion, pulled up a straight-backed chair, and seated herself opposite her mother-in-law. 'I'm not at all tired,' she declared.

'Not consciously, perhaps . . . But all that wild dancing last night – and in fact into the small hours . . . must have been very exhausting . . .'

'Oh, I've had a good sleep since. It's nearly luncheon-time, isn't it?'

'Not quite. And I so seldom have a chance of saying a word to you alone that I . . . I want to tell you how much I hope, and Ushant hopes, that you won't run any more risks. I know it's not always easy to remember; but last night, for instance, from every point of view, it might have been better if you had remained at your post.' The Dowager forced a stiff smile. 'Duchesses, you know, are like soldiers; they must often be under arms while others are amusing themselves. And when your guests were leaving, Ushant was naturally – er – surprised at having to hunt over the house for you . . .'

Annabel looked at her thoughtfully. 'Did he ask you to tell me so?'

'No; but he thinks you don't realize how odd it must have seemed to your guests that, in a middle of a party, you should have taken Mr Thwarte upstairs to your sitting-room –'

'But we didn't go on purpose. We were following the reel, and I dropped out because I was tired; and as Mr Thwarte wanted to see the Correggios I took him in.'

'That's the point, my dear. Guy Thwarte ought to have known better than to take you away from your guests and go up to your sitting-room with you after midnight. His doing so was – er – tact-less, to say the least. I don't know what your customs are in the States, but in England –' the Dowager broke off, as if waiting for an interruption which did not come.

Annabel remained silent, and her mother-in-law continued with gathering firmness: 'In England such behaviour might be rather severely judged.'

Annabel's eyes widened, and she stood up with a slight smile. 'I think I'm tired of trying to be English,' she pronounced.

The Dowager rose also, drawing herself up to her full height. 'Trying to be? But you *are* English. When you became my son's wife you acquired his nationality. Nothing can change that now.'

'Nothing?'

'Nothing. Remember what you promised in the marriage service.

"To love and to obey – till death us do part." Those are words not to be lightly spoken.'

'No; but I think I did speak them lightly. I made a mistake.'

'A mistake, my dear? What mistake?'

Annabel drew a quick breath. 'Marrying Ushant,' she said.

The Dowager received this with a gasp. 'My dear Annabel –'

'I think it might be better if I left him; then he could marry somebody else, and have a lot of children. Wouldn't that be best?' Annabel continued hurriedly.

The Dowager, rigid with dismay, stood erect, her strong plump hands grasping the rim of her writing-table. Words of wrath and indignation, scornful annihilating phrases, rushed to her lips, but were checked by her son's warning. 'I want to do nothing to put her off.' If Ushant said that, he meant it; meant, poor misguided fellow, that he was still in love with this thankless girl, this chit, this barren upstart, and that his mother, though authorized to coax her back into the right path, was on no account to drive her there by threats or reproaches.

But the mother's heart spoke louder than she meant it to. 'If you can talk of your own feelings in that way, even in jest, do you take no account of Ushant's?'

Annabel looked at her musingly. 'I don't think Ushant has very strong feelings – about me, I mean.'

The Dowager rejoined with some bitterness: 'You have hardly encouraged him to, have you?'

'I don't know – I can't explain . . . I've told Ushant that I don't think I want to be a mother of Dukes.'

'You should have thought of that before becoming the wife of one. According to English law you are bound to obey your husband implicitly in . . . er . . . all such matters . . . But, Annabel, we mustn't let our talk end in a dispute. My son would be very grieved if he thought I'd said anything to offend you – and I've not meant to. All I want is your happiness and his. In the first years of marriage things don't always go as smoothly as they might, and the advice of an older woman may be helpful. Marriage may not be all roses – especially at first; but I know Ushant's great wish is to see you happy and contented in the lot he has offered you – a lot, my dear, that most young women would envy,' the Dowager concluded, lifting her head with an air of wounded majesty.

'Oh, I know; that's why I'm so sorry for my mistake.'

'Your mistake? But there's been no mistake. Your taking Guy Thwarte up to your sitting-room was quite as much his fault as yours; and you need only show him, by a slightly more distant manner, that he is not to misinterpret it. I daresay less importance is attached to such things in your country – where there are no Dukes, of course . . .'

'No! That's why I'd better go back there,' burst from Annabel.

The Dowager stared at her in incredulous wrath. Really, it was beyond her powers of self-control to listen smilingly to such impertinence – such blasphemy, she had almost called it. Ushant himself must stamp out this senseless rebellion . . .

At that moment the luncheon-gong sent its pompous call down the corridors, and at the sound the Dowager, hurriedly composing her countenance, passed a shaking hand over her neatly waved *bandeaux*. 'The gong, my dear! You must not keep your guests waiting . . . I'll follow you at once . . .'

Annabel turned obediently to the door, and went down to join the assembled ladies, and the few men who were not out with the guns.

Her heart was beating high after the agitation of her talk with her mother-in-law, but as she descended the wide shallow steps of the great staircase (up and down which it would have been a profanation to gallop, as one used to up and down the steep narrow stairs at home) she reflected that the Dowager, though extremely angry, and even scandalized, had instantly put an end to their discussion when she heard the summons to luncheon. Annabel remembered the endless wordy wrangles between her mother, her sister and herself, and thought how little heed they would have paid to a luncheon-gong in the thick of one of their daily disputes. Here it was different: everything was done by rule, and according to tradition, and for the Duchess of Tintagel to keep her guests waiting for luncheon would have been an offence against the conventions almost as great as that of not being at her post when the company were leaving the night before. A year ago Annabel would have laughed at these rules and observances: now, though they chafed her no less, she was beginning to see the use of having one's whims and one's rages submitted to some kind of control. 'It did no good to anybody to have us come down with red noses to a stone-cold lunch, and go upstairs afterward to sulk in our bedrooms,' she thought, and she recalled how her father, when regaled with the history of these domestic disagreements, used to say with a laugh: 'What a lot of nonsense it would knock out of you women to have to hoe a potato-field, or spend a week in Wall Street.'

Yes; in spite of her anger, in spite of her desperate sense of being trapped, Annabel felt in a confused way that the business of living was perhaps conducted more wisely at Longlands – even though Longlands was the potato-field she was destined to hoe for life.

24

That evening before dinner, as Annabel sat over her dressing-room fire, she heard a low knock. She had half expected to see her husband appear, after a talk with his mother, and had steeled herself to a repetition of the morning's scene. But she had an idea that the Dowager might have taken her to task only because the Duke was reluctant to do so; she had already discovered that one of her mother-in-law's duties was the shouldering of any job her son wished to be rid of.

The knock, moreover, was too light to be a man's, and Annabel was not surprised to have it followed by a soft hesitating turn of the door-handle.

'Nan dear – not dressing yet, I hope?' It was Conchita Marable, her tawny hair loosely tossed back, her plump shoulders draped in a rosy dressing-gown festooned with swansdown. It was a long way from Conchita's quarters to the Duchess's, and Annabel was amused at the thought of the Dowager's dismay had she encountered, in the stately corridors of Longlands, a lady with tumbled auburn curls, red-heeled slippers, and a pink deshabille with a marked tendency to drop off the shoulders. A headless ghost would have been much less out of keeping with the traditions of the place.

Annabel greeted her visitor with a smile. Ever since Conchita's first appearance on the verandah of the Grand Union, Annabel's admiration for her had been based on a secret sympathy. Even then the dreamy indolent girl had been enveloped in a sort of warm haze unlike the cool dry light in which Nan's sister and the Elmsworths moved. And Lady Dick, if she had lost something of that early magic, and no longer seemed to Nan to be made of rarer stuff, had yet ripened into something more richly human than the others. A warm fruity fragrance, as of peaches in golden sawdust, breathed from her soft plumpness, the tawny spirals of her hair, the smile which had a way of flickering between her lashes without descending to her lips.

'Darling – you're all alone? Ushant's not lurking anywhere?' she questioned, peering about the room with an air of mystery.

Annabel shook her head. 'No. He doesn't often come here before dinner.'

'Then he's a very stupid man, my dear,' Lady Dick rejoined, her smile resting approvingly on her hostess. 'Nan, do you know how awfully lovely you're growing? I always used to tell Jinny and the Elmsworths that one of these days you'd beat us all; and I see the day's approaching . . .'

Annabel laughed, and her friend drew back to inspect her critically. 'If you'd only burn that alms-house dressing-gown, with the horrid row of horn buttons down the front, which looks as if your mother-in-law had chosen it – ah, she *did*? To discourage midnight escapades, I suppose? Darling, why don't you strike, and let me order your clothes for you—and especially your underclothes? It would be a lovely excuse for running over to Paris, and with your order in my pocket I could get the dress-makers to pay all my expenses, and could bring you back a French maid who'd do your hair so that it wouldn't look like a bun just out of the baking-pan. Oh, Nan – fancy having all you've got – the hair and the eyes, and the rank, and the power, and the money. . .'

Annabel interrupted her. 'Oh, but, Conchie, I haven't got much money.'

Lady Dick's smiling face clouded, and her clear grey eyes grew dark. 'Now why do you say that? Are you afraid of being asked to help an old friend in a tight place, and do you want to warn me off in advance?'

Annabel looked at her in surprise. 'Oh, Conchita, what a beastly question! It doesn't sound a bit like you . . . Do sit down by the fire. You're shaking all over – why, I believe you're crying!'

Annabel put an arm around her friend's shoulder, and drew her down into an armchair near the hearth, pulling up a low stool for herself, and leaning against Lady Dick's knee with low sounds of sympathy. 'Tell me, Conchie darling – what's wrong?'

'Oh, my child, pretty nearly everything.' Drawing out a scrap of lace and cambric, Lady Dick applied it to her beautiful eyes; but the tears continued to flow, and Annabel had to wait till they had ceased. Then Lady Dick, tossing back her tumbled curls, continued with a rainbow smile: 'But what's the use? They're all things you wouldn't understand. What do you know about being head over ears in debt, and in love with one man while you're tied to another—tied tight in one of these awful English marriages, that strangle you in a noose when you try to pull away from them?'

A little shiver ran over Annabel. What indeed did she know of these things? And how much could she admit to Conchita – or for that matter to any one – that she did know? Something sealed her lips, made it, for the moment, impossible even to murmur the sympathy she longed to speak out. She was benumbed, and could only remain silent, pressing Conchita's hands, and deafened by the reverberation of Conchita's last words: 'These awful English marriages, that strangle you in a noose when you try to pull away from them.' If only Conchita had not put that into words!

'Well, Nan – I suppose now I've horrified you past forgiveness,' Lady Dick continued, breaking into a nervous laugh. 'You never imagined things of that sort could happen to anybody you knew, did you? I suppose Miss Testvalley told you that only wicked Queens in history books had lovers. That's what they taught us at school . . . In real life everything ended at the church door, and you just went on having babies and being happy ever after – eh?'

'Oh, Conchie, Conchie,' Nan murmured, flinging her arms about her friend's neck. She felt suddenly years older than Conchita, and mistress of the bitter lore the latter fancied she was revealing to her. Since the tragic incident of the Linfry child's death, Annabel had never asked her husband for money, and he had never informed himself if her requirements exceeded the modest allowance traditionally allotted to Tintagel Duchesses. It had always sufficed for his mother, and why suggest to his wife that her needs might be greater? The Duke had never departed from the rule inculcated by the

Dowager on his coming of age: 'In dealing with tenants and dependants, always avoid putting ideas into their heads' – which meant, in the Dowager's vocabulary, giving them a chance to state their needs or ventilate their grievances; and he had instinctively adopted the same system with his wife. 'People will always think they want whatever you suggest they might want,' his mother had often reminded him; an axiom which had not only saved him thousands of pounds, but protected him from the personal importunities which he disliked even more than the spending of money. He was always reluctant to be drawn into unforeseen expenditure, but he shrank still more from any emotional outlay, and was not sorry to be known (as he soon was) as a landlord who referred all letters to his agents, and resolutely declined personal interviews.

All this flashed through Annabel, but was swept away by Conchita's next words: 'In love with one man and married to another . . .' Yes; that was a terrible fate indeed . . . and yet, and yet . . . might one perhaps not feel less lonely with such a sin on one's conscience than in the blameless isolation of an uninhabited heart?

'Darling, can you tell me . . . anything more? Of course I want to help you; but I must find out ways. I'm almost as much of a prisoner as you are, I fancy; perhaps more. Because Dick's away a good deal, isn't he?'

'Oh, yes, almost always; but his duns are not. The bills keep pouring in. What little money there is is mine, and of course those people know it . . . But I'm stone-broke at present, and I don't know what I shall do if you can't help me out with a loan.' She drew back, and looked at Nan beseechingly. 'You don't know how I hate talking to you about such sordid things . . . You seem so high above it all, so untouched by anything bad.'

'But, Conchie, it's not being bad to be unhappy –'

'No, darling; and goodness knows I'm unhappy enough. But I suppose it's wrong to try to console myself – in the way I have. You must think so, I know; but I can't live without affection, and Miles is so understanding, so tender . . .'

Miles Dawnly, then – Two or three times Nan had wondered – had noticed things which seemed to bespeak a tender intimacy; but she had never been sure . . . The blood rushed to her forehead. As she listened to Conchita she was secretly transposing her friend's words to her own use. 'Oh, I know, I know, Conchie –'

Lady Dick lifted her head quickly, and looked straight into her friend's eyes. 'You know –?'

'I mean, I can imagine . . . how hard it must be not to . . .'

There was a long silence. Annabel was conscious that Conchita was waiting for some word of solace – material or sentimental, or if possible both; but again a paralysing constraint descended on her. In her girlhood no one had ever spoken to her of events or emotions below the surface of life, and she had not yet acquired words to express them. At last she broke out with sudden passion: 'Conchie – it's all turned out a dreadful mistake, hasn't it?'

'A dreadful mistake – you mean my marriage?'

'I mean all our marriages. I don't believe we're any of us really made for this English life. At least I suppose not, for they seem to take so many things for granted here that shock us and make us miserable; and then they're horrified by things we do quite innocently – like that silly reel last night.'

'Oh – you've been hearing about the reel, have you? I saw the old ladies putting their heads together on the sofa.'

'If it's not that it's something else. I sometimes wonder –' She paused again, struggling for words. 'Conchie, if we just packed up and went home to live, would they really be able to make us come back here, as my mother-in-law says? Perhaps I could cable to father for our passage-money –'

She broke off, perceiving that her suggestion had aroused no response. Conchita threw herself back in her armchair, her eyes wide with an unfeigned astonishment. Suddenly she burst out laughing.

'You little darling! Is that your panacea? Go back to Saratoga and New York – to the Assemblies and the Charity balls? Do you really imagine you'd like that better?'

'I don't know . . . Don't you, sometimes?'

'Never! Not for a single minute!' Lady Dick continued to gaze up laughingly at her friend. She seemed to have forgotten her personal troubles in the vision of this grotesque possibility. 'Why, Nan, have you forgotten those dreary endless summers at the Grand Union, and the Opera boxes sent on off-nights by your father's business friends, and the hanging round, fishing for invitations to the Assemblies and knowing we'd never have a look-in at the Thursday Evening dances? . . . Oh, if we were to go over on a visit, just a few weeks' splash in New York or Newport, then every door would fly open, and the Eglintons and Van der Luydens, and all the other old toadies, would be fighting for us, and fawning at our feet; and I don't say I shouldn't like that – for a while. But to be returned to our families as if we'd been sent to England on "appro", and hadn't suited – no, thank you! And I wouldn't go for good and all on any terms – not for all the Astor diamonds! Why, you dear little goose, I'd rather starve and freeze here than go back to all the warm houses and the hot baths, and the emptiness of everything – people and places. And as for you, an English Duchess, with everything the world can give heaped up at your feet – you may not know it now, you innocent infant, but you'd have enough of Madison Avenue and Seventh Regiment balls inside of a week – and of the best of New York and Newport before your first season was over. – There – does the truth frighten you? If you don't believe me, ask Jacky March, or any of the poor little American old maids, or wives or widows, who've had a nibble at it, and have hung on at any price, because London's London, and London life the most exciting and interesting in the world, and once you've got the soot and the fog in your veins you simply can't live without them; and all the poor hangers-on and left-overs know it as well as we do.'

Annabel received this in silence. Lady Dick's tirade filled her with a momentary scorn, followed by a prolonged searching of the heart. Her values, of course, were not Conchita's values; that she had always known. London society, of which she knew so little, had never had any attraction for her save as a splendid spectacle; and the part she was expected to play in that spectacle was a burden and not a delight. It was not the atmosphere of London but of England which had gradually filled her veins and penetrated to her heart. She thought of the thinness of the mental and moral air in her own home; the noisy quarrels about nothing, the paltry preoccupations, her mother's feverish interest in the fashions and follies of a society which had always ignored her. At least life in England had a background, layers and layers of rich deep background, of history, poetry, old traditional observances, beautiful houses, beautiful landscapes, beautiful ancient buildings, palaces, churches, cathedrals. Would it not be possible, in some mysterious way, to create for one's self a life out of all this richness, a life which should somehow make up for the poverty of one's personal lot? If only she could have talked of it all with a friend . . . Laura Testvalley, for instance, of whom her need was so much greater now than it had ever been in the school-room. Could she not perhaps persuade Ushant to let her old governess come back to her –?

Her thoughts had wandered so far from Lady Dick and her troubles that she was almost startled to hear her friend speak.

'Well, my dear, which do you think worse – having a lover, or owing a few hundred pounds? Between the two I've shocked you hopelessly, haven't I? As much as even your mother-in-law could wish. The Dowager doesn't like me, you know. I'm afraid I'll never be asked to Longlands again.' Lady Dick stood up with a laugh, pushing her curls back into their loosened coil. Her face looked pale and heavy.

'You haven't shocked me – only made me dreadfully sorry, because I don't know what I can do . . .'

'Oh, well; don't lie awake over it, my dear,' Lady Dick retorted with a touch of bitterness. 'But wasn't that the dressing-bell? I must hurry off and be laced into my dinner-gown. They don't like unpunctuality here, do they? And tea-gowns wouldn't be tolerated at dinner.'

'Conchie – wait!' Annabel was trembling with the sense of having failed her friend, and been unable to make her understand why. 'Don't think I don't care – Oh, please don't think that! The way we live makes it look as if there wasn't a whim I couldn't gratify; but Ushant doesn't give me much money, and I don't know how to ask for it.'

Conchita turned back and gave her a long look. 'The skinflint! No, I suppose he wouldn't; and I suppose you haven't learnt yet how to manage him.'

Annabel blushed more deeply: 'I'm not clever at managing, I'm afraid. You must give me time to look about, to find out –' It had suddenly occurred to her, she hardly knew why, that Guy Thwarte was the one person she could take into her confidence in such a matter. Perhaps he would be able to tell her how to raise the money for her friend. She would pluck up her courage, and ask him the next day.

'Conchie, dear, by tomorrow evening I promise you . . .' she began; and found herself instantly gathered to her friend's bosom.

'Two hundred pounds would save my life, you darling – and five hundred make me a free woman . . .'

Conchita loosened her embrace. The velvet glow suffused her face again, and she turned joyfully toward the door. But on the threshold she paused, and coming back laid her hands on Annabel's shoulders.

'Nan,' she said, almost solemnly, 'don't judge me, will you, till you find out for yourself what it's like.'

'What what is like? What do you mean, Conchita?'

'Happiness, darling,' Lady Dick whispered. She pressed a quick kiss on her friend's cheek; then, as the dressing-bell crashed out its final call, she picked up her rosy draperies and fled down the corridor.

25

The next morning Annabel, after a restless night, stood at her window watching the dark return of day. Dawn was trying to force a way through leaden mist; every detail, every connecting link, was muffled in folds of rain-cloud. That was England, she thought; not only the English scene but the English life was perpetually muffled. The links between these people and their actions were mostly hidden from Annabel; their looks, their customs, their language, had implications beyond her understanding.

Sometimes fleeting lights, remote and tender, shot through the fog; then the blanket of incomprehension closed in again. It was like that day in the ruins of Tintagel, the day when she and Ushant had met . . . As she looked back on it, the scene of their meeting seemed symbolical: in a ruin and a fog . . . Lovers ought to meet under limpid skies and branches dripping with sunlight, like the nymphs and heroes of Correggio.

The thought that she had even imagined Ushant as a lover made her smile, and she turned away from the window . . . Those were dreams, and the reality was: what? First that she must manage to get five hundred pounds for Conchita; and after that, must think about

her own future. She was glad she had something active and helpful
to do before reverting once more to that dreary problem.

Through her restless night she had gone over and over every
possible plan for getting the five hundred pounds. The idea of consulting Guy Thwarte had faded before the first hint of daylight. Of
course he would offer to lend her the sum; and how could she borrow
from a friend money she saw no possibility of re-paying? And yet, to
whom else could she apply? The Dowager? Her mind brushed past
the absurd idea ... and past that of her sisters-in-law. How
bewildered, how scandalized the poor things would be! Annabel herself, she knew, was bewilderment enough to them: a wife who bore
no children, a Duchess who did not yet clearly understand the duties
of a groom-of-the-chambers, or know what the Chiltern Hundreds
were! To all his people it was as if Ushant had married a savage ...

There was her own family, of course; her sister, her friends the
Elmsworths. Annabel knew that in the dizzy up-and-down of Wall
Street, which ladies were not expected to understand, Mr Elmsworth
was now 'on top', as they called it. The cornering of a heavy block
of railway shares, though apparently necessary to the development
of another line, had temporarily hampered her father and Mr Closson, and Annabel was aware that Virginia had already addressed
several unavailing appeals to Colonel St George. Certainly, if he had
cut down the girls' allowances it was because the poor Colonel could
not help himself; and it seemed only fair that his first aid, whenever
it came, should go to Virginia, whose husband's income had to be
extracted from the heavily burdened Brightlingsea estate, rather than
to the wife of one of England's wealthiest Dukes.

One of England's wealthiest Dukes! That was what Ushant was;
and it was naturally to him that his wife should turn in any financial
difficulty. But Annabel had never done so since the Linfry incident,
and though she knew the sum she wanted was nothing to a man with
Ushant's income, she was as frightened as though she had been
going to beg for the half of his fortune.

The others, of course – Virginia, the Elmsworths and poor Conchita – had long since become trained borrowers and beggars.
Money – or rather the want of it – loomed before them at every
turn, and they had mastered most of the arts of extracting it from
reluctant husbands or parents. This London life necessitated so

many expenditures unknown to the humdrum existence of Madison Avenue and the Grand Union Hotel: Court functions, Royal Ascot, the Cowes season, the entertaining of royalties, the heavy cost of pheasant-shooting, deer-stalking and hunting, above all (it was whispered) the high play and extravagant luxury prevailing in the inner set to which the lovely newcomers had been so warmly welcomed. You couldn't, Virginia had over and over again explained to Annabel, expect to keep your place in that jealously guarded set if you didn't dress up, live up, play up, to its princely standards. But Annabel had lent an inattentive ear to these hints. She wanted nothing of what her sister and her sister's friends were fighting for; their needs did not stir her imagination, and they soon learned that, beyond occasionally letting them charge a dress, or a few yards of lace, to her account, she could give them little aid.

It was Conchita's appeal which first roused her sympathy. 'You don't know what it is,' Lady Dick had said, 'to be in love with one man and tied to another'; and instantly the barriers of Nan's indifference had broken down. It was wrong – it was no doubt dreadfully wrong – but it was human, it was understandable, it made her frozen heart thaw in soft participation. 'It must be less wicked to love the wrong person than not to love anybody at all,' she thought, considering her own desolate plight . . .

But such thoughts were pure self-indulgence; her immediate business was the finding of the five hundred pounds to lift Conchita's weight of debt.

When there was a big shooting-party at Longlands every hour of the Duke's day was disposed of in advance, and Nan had begun to regard this as a compensation for the boredom associated with such occasions. She was resolved never again to expose herself to the risks of those solitary months at Tintagel, with an Ushant at leisure to dissect his grievances as he did his clocks . . . After much reflection she scribbled a note to him: 'Please let me know after breakfast when I can see you –' and to her surprise, when the party rose from the sumptuous repast which always fortified the guns at Longlands, the Duke followed her into the east drawing-room, where the ladies were accustomed to assemble in the mornings, with their needle-work and correspondence.

'If you'll come to my study for a moment, Annabel.'

'Now –?' she stammered, not expecting so prompt a response.

The Duke consulted his watch. 'I have a quarter of an hour before we start.' She hesitated, and then, reflecting that she might have a better chance of success if there were no time to prolong the discussion, she rose and followed him.

The Duke's study at Longlands had been created by a predecessor imbued with loftier ideas of his station, and the glories befitting it, than the present Duke could muster. In size, and splendour of ornament, it seemed singularly out of scale with the nervous little man pacing its stately floor; but it had always been 'the Duke's study', and must therefore go on being so to the end of time.

Ushant had seated himself behind his monumental desk, as if to borrow from it the authority he did not always know how to assert unaided. His wife stood before him without speaking. He lifted his head, and forced one of the difficult smiles he had inherited from his mother. 'Yes –?'

'Oh, Ushant – I don't know how to begin; and this room always frightens me. It looks as if people came here only when you send for them to be sentenced.'

The Duke met this with a look of genuine bewilderment. Could it be, the look implied, that his wife imagined there was some link between the peerage and the magistracy? 'Well, my dear –?'

'Oh, you wouldn't understand . . . But what I've actually come for is to ask you to let me have five hundred pounds.'

There, it was out – about as lightly as if she had hurled a rock at him through one of the tall windows! He frowned and looked down, picking up an emblazoned paper-cutter to examine it.

'Five hundred pounds?' he repeated slowly.

'Yes.'

'Do I understand that you are asking me for that sum?'

'Yes.'

There was another heavy silence, during which she strained her eyes to detect any change in his guarded face. There was none.

'Five hundred pounds?'

'Oh, please, Ushant – yes!'

'Now – at once?'

'At once,' she faltered, feeling that each syllable of his slow interrogatory was draining away a drop of her courage.

The Duke again attempted a smile. 'It's a large sum – a very large sum. Has your dress-maker led you on rather farther than your means would justify?'

Nan reddened. Her dress-maker! She wondered if Ushant had ever noticed her clothes? But might he not be offering her the very pretext she needed? She hated having to use one, but since she could think of no other way of getting what she wanted, she resolved to surmount her scruples.

'Well, you see, I've never known exactly what my means were . . . but I do want this money . . .'

'Never known what your means were? Surely it's all clearly enough written down in your marriage settlements.'

'Yes; but sometimes one is tempted to spend a trifle more . . .'

'You must have been taught very little about the value of money to call five hundred pounds a trifle.'

Annabel broke into a laugh. 'You're teaching me a lot about it now.'

The Duke's temples grew red under his straw-coloured hair, and she saw that her stroke had gone home.

'It's my duty to do so,' he remarked drily. Then his tone altered, and he added, on a conciliatory note: 'I hope you'll bear the lesson in mind; but of course if you've incurred this debt it must be paid.'

'Oh, Ushant –'

He raised his hand to check her gratitude. 'Naturally . . . If you'll please tell these people to send me their bill.' He rose stiffly, with another glance at his watch. 'I said a quarter of an hour – and I'm afraid it's nearly up.'

Nan stood crestfallen between her husband and the door. 'But you don't understand . . .' (She wondered whether it was not a mistake to say that to him so often?) 'I mean,' she hurriedly corrected herself, 'it's really no use your bothering . . . If you'll just make out the cheque to me I'll –'

The Duke stopped short. 'Ah –' he said slowly. 'Then it's *not* to pay your dress-maker that you want it?'

Nan's quick colour flew to her forehead. 'Well, no – it's not. I – I want it for . . . my private charities . . .'

'Your private charities? Is your allowance not paid regularly? All your private expenditures are supposed to be included in it. My mother was always satisfied with that arrangement.'

'Yes; but did your mother never have unexpected calls –? Sometimes one has to help in an emergency . . .'

The two faced each other in a difficult silence. At length the Duke straightened himself, and said with an attempt at ease: 'I'm willing to admit that emergencies may arise; but if you ask me to advance five hundred pounds at a moment's notice it's only fair that I should be told why you need it.'

Their eyes met, and a flame of resistance leapt into Nan's. 'I've told you it's for a *private* charity.'

'My dear, there should be nothing private between husband and wife.'

She laughed impatiently. 'Are you trying to say you won't give me the money?'

'I'm saying quite the contrary. I'm ready to give it if you'll tell me what you want it for.'

'Ushant – it's a long time since I've asked you a favour, and you can't go on forever ordering me about like a child.'

The Duke took a few steps across the room; then he turned back. His complexion had faded to its usual sandy pallor, and his lips twitched a little. 'Perhaps, my dear, you forget how long it is since *I* have asked for a favour. I'm afraid you must make your choice. If I'm not, as you call it, to order you about like a child, you may force me to order you about as a wife.' The words came out slowly, haltingly, as if they had cost him a struggle. Nan had noticed before now that anger was too big a garment for him: it always hung on him in uneasy folds. 'And now my time is up. I can't keep the guns waiting any longer,' he concluded abruptly, turning toward the door.

Annabel stood silent; she could find nothing else to say. She had failed, as she had foreseen she would, for lack of the arts by which cleverer women gain their ends. 'You can't force me . . . no one can force me . . .' she cried out suddenly, hardly knowing what she said; but her husband had already crossed the threshold, and she wondered whether the closing of the door had not drowned her words.

The big house was full of the rumour of the departing sportsmen. Gradually the sounds died out, and the hush of boredom and inactivity fell from the carved and gilded walls. Annabel stood where the

Duke left her. Now she went out into the long vaulted passage on which the study opened. The passage was empty, and so was the great domed and pillared hall beyond. Under such lowering skies the ladies would remain grouped about the fire in the east drawing-room, trying to cheat the empty hours with gossip and embroidery and letter-writing. It was not a day for them to join the sportsmen, even had their host encouraged this new-fangled habit; but it was well known that the Duke, who had no great taste for sport, and practised it only as one of the duties of his station, did not find the task lightened by feminine companionship.

In the lobby of one of the side entrances Annabel found an old garden hat and cloak. She put them on and went out. It would have been impossible for her, just then, to join the bored but placid group in the east drawing-room. The great house had become like a sepulchre to her; under its ponderous cornices and cupolas she felt herself reduced to a corpse-like immobility. It was only in the open that she became herself again – a stormy self, reckless and rebellious. 'Perhaps,' she thought, 'if Ushant had ever lived in smaller houses he would have understood me better.' Was it because all the great people secretly felt as Ushant did – oppressed, weighed down under a dead burden of pomp and precedent – that they built these gigantic palaces to give themselves the illusion of being giants?

Now, out of doors, under the lowering skies, she could breathe and even begin to think. But for the moment all her straining thoughts were arrested by the same insurmountable barrier: she was the Duchess of Tintagel, and knew no way of becoming any one else . . .

She walked across the gardens opening out from the west wing, and slowly mounted the wooded hill-side beyond. It was beginning to rain, and she must find a refuge somewhere – a solitude in which she could fight out this battle between herself and her fate. The slope she was climbing was somewhat derisively crowned by an octagonal temple of Love, with rain-streaked walls of peeling stucco. On the summit of the dome the neglected god spanned his bow unheeded, and underneath it a door swinging loose on broken hinges gave admittance to a room stored with the remnants of derelict croquet-sets and disabled shuttlecocks and grace-rings. It was evidently many a day since the lords of Longlands had visited the divinity who is supposed to rule the world.

Nan, certain of being undisturbed in this retreat, often came there with a book or writing-materials; but she had not intruded on its mouldy solitude since the beginning of winter.

As she entered, a chill fell on her; but she sat down at the stone table in the centre of the dilapidated mosaic floor, and rested her chin on her hands. 'I must think it all out,' she said aloud, and closing her eyes she tried to lose herself in an inner world of self-examination.

But think out what? Does a life-prisoner behind iron bars take the trouble to think out his future? What a waste of time, what a cruel expenditure of hope ... Once more she felt herself sinking into depths of childish despair – one of those old benumbing despairs without past or future which used to blot out the skies when her father scolded her or Miss Testvalley looked disapproving. Her face dropped into her hands, and she broke into sobs of misery.

The sobs murmured themselves out; but for a long time she continued to sit motionless, her face hidden, with a child's reluctance to look out again on a world which has wounded it. Her back was turned to the door, and she was so sunk in her distress that she was unconscious of not being alone until she felt a touch on her shoulder, and heard a man's voice: 'Duchess – are you ill? What's happened?'

She turned, and saw Guy Thwarte bending over her. 'What is it – what has made you cry?' he continued, in the compassionate tone of a grown person speaking to a frightened child.

Nan jumped up, her wet handkerchief crumpled against her eyes. She felt a sudden anger at this intrusion. 'Where did you come from? Why aren't you out with the guns?' she stammered.

'I was to have been; but a message came from Lowdon to say that Sir Hercules is worse, and Ushant has asked me to prepare some notes in case the election comes on sooner than we expected. So I wandered up the hill to clear my ideas a little.'

Nan stood looking at him with a growing sense of resentment. Hitherto his presence had roused only friendly emotions; his nearness had even seemed a vague protection against the unknown and the inimical. But in her present mood that nearness seemed a deliberate intrusion – as though he had forced himself upon her out of some unworthy curiosity, had seized the chance to come upon her unawares.

'Won't you tell me why you are crying?' he insisted gently.

Her childish anger flamed. 'I'm not crying,' she retorted, hurriedly pushing her handkerchief into her pocket. 'And I don't know why you should follow me here. You must see that I want to be alone.'

The young man drew back, surprised. He too, since the distant day of their first talk at Honourslove, had felt between them the existence of a mysterious understanding which every subsequent meeting had renewed, though in actual words so little had passed between them. He had imagined that Annabel was glad he should feel this, and her sudden rebuff was like a blow. But her distress was so evident that he did not feel obliged to take her words literally.

'I had no idea of following you,' he answered. 'I didn't even know you were here; but since I find you in such distress, how can I help asking if there's nothing I can do?'

'No, no, there's nothing!' she cried, humiliated that this man of all others should surprise her in her childish wretchedness. 'Well, yes – I *am* crying . . . now . . . You can see I am, I suppose?' She groped for the handkerchief. 'But if anybody could do anything for me, do you suppose I'd be sitting here and just bearing it? It's because there's nothing . . . nothing . . . any one can do, that I've come here to get away from people, to get away from everything . . . Can't you understand that?' she ended passionately.

'I can understand your feeling so – yes. I've often thought you must.' She gave him a startled look, and her face crimsoned. 'But can't you see,' he pursued, 'that it's hard on a friend – a man who's ventured to think himself your friend – to be told, when he sees you in trouble, that he's not wanted, that he can be of no use, that even his sympathy's unwelcome?'

Annabel continued to look at him with resentful eyes. But already the mere sound of his voice was lessening the weight of her loneliness, and she answered more gently: 'You're very kind –'

'Oh, *kind*!' he echoed impatiently.

'You've always been kind to me. I wish you hadn't been away for so many years. I used to think sometimes that if only I could have asked you about things . . .'

'But – but if you've really thought that, why do you want to drive me away now that I *am* here?' He went up to her with outstretched hands; but she shook her head.

'Because I'm not the Annabel you used to know. I'm a strange woman, strange even to myself, who goes by my name. I suppose in time I'll get to know her, and learn how to live with her.'

The angry child had been replaced by a sad but self-controlled woman, who appeared to Guy infinitely farther away and more inaccessible than the other. He had wanted to take the child in his arms and comfort her with kisses; but this newcomer seemed to warn him to be circumspect, and after a pause he rejoined, with a smile: 'And can't I be of any use, even to the strange woman?'

Her voice softened. 'Well, yes; you can. You are of use. . . . Thinking of you as a friend does help me . . . it often has . . .' She went up to him and put her hand in his. 'Please believe that. But don't ask me anything more; don't even say anything more now, if you really want to help me.'

He held her hand without attempting to disregard either her look or her words. Through the loud beat of his blood a whisper warned him that the delicate balance of their friendship hung on his obedience.

'I want it above all things, but I'll wait,' he said, and lifted the hand to his lips.

26

As long as the Dowager ruled at Longlands she had found her chief relaxation from ducal drudgery in visiting the immense collection of rare and costly exotic plants in the Duke's famous conservatories. But when she retired to the dower-house, and the sole command of the one small glass-house attached to her new dwelling, she realized the insipidity of inspecting plants in the company of a severe and suspicious head gardener compared with the joys of planting, transplanting, pruning, fertilizing, writing out labels, pressing down the earth about outspread roots, and compelling an obedient underling to do in her own way what she could not manage alone. The

Dowager, to whom life had always presented itself in terms of duty, to whom even the closest human relations had come draped in that pale garb, had found her only liberation in gardening; and since amateur horticulture was beginning to be regarded in the highest circles not only as an elegant distraction but almost as one of a great lady's tasks, she had immersed herself in it with a guilty fervour, still doubting if anything so delightful could be quite blameless.

Her son, aware of this passion, which equalled his own for dismembering clocks, was in the habit of going straight to the conservatory when he visited her; and there he found her on the morning after his strange conversation with his wife.

The Dowager was always gratified by his visits, which were necessarily rare during the shooting-parties; but it would have pleased her better had he not come at the exact moment when, gauntleted and aproned, she was transferring some new gloxinia seedlings from one pan to another.

She laid down her implements, scratched a few words in a notebook at her elbow, and dusted the soil from her big gloves.

'Ah, Ushant –.' She broke off, struck by his unusual pallor, and the state of his hair. 'My dear, you don't look well. Is anything wrong?' she asked, in the tone of one long accustomed to being told every morning of some new wrongness in the course of things.

The Duke stood looking down at the long shelf, the heaps of upturned soil and the scattered labels. It occurred to him that, for ladies, horticulture might prove a safe and agreeable pastime.

'Have you ever tried to interest Annabel in this kind of thing?' he asked abruptly. 'I'm afraid I'm too ignorant to do it myself – but I sometimes think she would be happier if she had some innocent amusement like gardening. Needle-work doesn't seem to appeal to her.'

The Dowager's upper lip lengthened. 'I've not had much chance of discussing her tastes with her; but of course, if you wish me to . . . Do you think, for instance, she might learn to care for grafting?'

It was inconceivable to the Duke that any one should care for grafting; but not wishing to betray his complete ignorance of the subject, he effected a diversion by proposing a change of scene. 'Perhaps we could talk more comfortably in the drawing-room,' he suggested.

His mother laid down her tools. She was used to interruptions, and did not dare to confess how trying it was to be asked to abandon her seedlings at that critical stage. She also weakly regretted having to leave the pleasant temperature of the conservatory for an icy drawing-room in which the fire was never lit till the lamps were brought. Such economies were necessary to a Dowager with several daughters whose meagre allowances were always having to be supplemented; but the Duchess, who was almost as hardened to cold as her son, led the way to the drawing-room without apology.

'I'm sorry,' she said, as she seated herself near the lifeless hearth, 'that you think dear Annabel lacks amusements.'

The Duke stood before the chimney, his hands thrust despondently in his pockets. 'Oh – I don't say that. But I suppose she's been used to other kinds of amusement in the States; skating, you know, and dancing – they seem to do a lot of dancing over there; and even in England I suppose young ladies expect more variety and excitement nowadays than they had in your time.'

The Dowager, who had taken up her alms-house knitting, dropped a sigh into its harsh folds.

'Certainly in my time they didn't expect much – luckily, for they wouldn't have got it.'

The Duke made no reply, but moved uneasily back and forth across the room, as his way was when his mind was troubled.

'Won't you sit down, Ushant?'

'Thanks. No.' He returned to his station on the hearth-rug.

'You're not joining the guns?' his mother asked.

'No. Seadown will replace me. The fact is,' the Duke continued in an embarrassed tone, 'I wanted a few minutes of quiet talk with you.'

He paused again, and his mother sat silent, automatically counting her stitches, though her whole mind was centred on his words. She was sure some pressing difficulty had brought him to her, but she knew that any visible sign of curiosity, or even sympathy, might check his confidence.

'I – I have had a very – er – embarrassing experience with Annabel,' he began; and the Dowager lifted her head quickly, but without interrupting the movement of her needles.

The Duke coughed and cleared his throat. ('At the last minute,' his mother thought, 'he's wondering whether he might not better have held his tongue.' She knitted on.)

'A – a really incomprehensible experience.' He threw himself into the chair opposite hers. 'And completely unexpected. Yesterday morning, just as I was leaving the house, Annabel asked me for a large sum of money – a very large sum. For five hundred pounds.'

'Five hundred pounds?' The needles dropped from the Dowager's petrified fingers.

Her son gave a dry laugh. 'It seems to me a considerable amount.'

The Dowager was thinking hurriedly: 'That chit! *I* shouldn't have dared to ask him for a quarter of that amount – much less his father . . .' Aloud she said: 'But what does she want it for?'

'That's the point. She refuses to tell me.'

'Refuses –?' the Dowager gasped.

'Er – yes. First she hinted it was for her dress-maker; but on being pressed she owned it was not.'

'Ah – and then?'

'Well – then . . . I told her I'd pay the debt if she'd incurred it; but only if she would tell me to whom the money was owing.'

'Of course. Very proper.'

'So I thought; but she said I'd no right to cross-examine her –'

'Ushant! She called it that?'

'Something of the sort. And as the guns were waiting, I said that was my final answer – and there the matter ended.'

The Dowager's face quivered with an excitement she had no means of expressing. This woman – he'd offered her five hundred pounds! And she'd refused it . . .

'It could hardly have ended otherwise,' she approved, thinking of the many occasions when a gift of five hundred pounds from the late Duke would have eased her daily load of maternal anxieties.

Her son made no reply, and as he began to move uneasily about the room, it occurred to her that what he wanted was not her approval but her dissent. Yet how could she appear to encourage such open rebellion? 'You certainly did right,' she repeated.

'Ah, there I'm not sure,' the Duke muttered.

'Not sure –?'

'Nothing's gained, I'm afraid, by taking that tone with Annabel.'

He reddened uncomfortably, and turned his head away from his mother's scrutiny.

'You mean you think you were too lenient?'

'Lord, no – just the contrary. I . . . oh, well, you wouldn't understand. These American girls are brought up differently from our young women. You'd probably say they were spoilt . . .'

'I should,' the Dowager assented drily.

'Well – perhaps. Though in a country where there's no primogeniture I suppose it's natural that daughters should be more indulged. At any rate, I . . . I thought it all over during the day – I thought of nothing else, in fact; and after she'd gone down to dinner yesterday evening I slipped into her room and put an envelope with the money on her dressing-table.'

'Oh, Ushant – how generous, how noble!'

The Duchess's hard little eyes filled with sudden tears. Her mind was torn between wrath at her daughter-in-law's incredible exactions, and the thought of what such generosity on her own husband's part might have meant to her, with those eight girls to provide for. But Annabel had no daughters – and no sons – and the Dowager's heart had hardened again before her eyes were dry. Would there be no limit to Ushant's weakness, she wondered?

'You're the best judge, of course, in any question between your wife and yourself; but I hope Annabel will never forget what she owes you.'

The Duke gave a short laugh. 'She's forgotten it already.'

'Ushant –!'

He crimsoned unhappily and again averted his face from his mother's eyes. He felt a nervous impulse to possess himself of the clock on the mantel-shelf and take it to pieces; but he turned his back on the temptation. 'I'm sorry to bother you with these wretched details . . . but . . . perhaps one woman can understand another where a man would fail . . .'

'Yes –?'

'Well, you see, Annabel has been rather nervous and uncertain lately; I've had to be patient. But I thought – I thought when she found she'd gained her point about the money . . . she . . . er . . . would wish to show her gratitude . . .'

'Naturally.'

'So, when the men left the smoking-room last night, I went up to her room. It was not particularly late, and she had not undressed. I went in, and she did thank me . . . well, very prettily . . . But when I . . . when I proposed to stay, she refused, refused absolutely –'

The Dowager's lips twitched. 'Refused? On what ground?'

'That she hadn't understood I'd been driving a bargain with her. The scene was extremely painful,' the Duke stammered.

'Yes; I understand.' The Dowager paused, and then added abruptly: 'So she handed back the envelope –?'

Her son hung his head. 'No; there was no question of that.'

'Ah – her pride didn't prevent her accepting the bribe, though she refused to stick to the bargain?'

'I can't say there was an actual bargain; but – well, it was something like that . . .'

The Dowager sat silent, her needles motionless in her hands. This, she thought, was one of the strangest hours of her life, and not the least strange part of it was the light reflected back on her own past, and on the weary nights when she had not dared to lock her door . . .

'And then –?'

'Then – well, the end of it was that she said she wanted to go away.'

'Go away?'

'She wants to go off somewhere – she doesn't care where – alone with her old governess. You know; the little Italian woman who's with Augusta Glenloe and came over the other night with the party from Champions. She seems to be the only person Annabel cares for, or who, at any rate, has any influence over her.'

The Dowager meditated. Again the memory of her own past thrust itself between her and her wrath against her daughter-in-law. Ah, if she had ever dared to ask the late Duke to let her off – to let her go away for a few days, she didn't care where! Even now, she trembled inwardly at the thought of what his answer would have been . . .

'Do you think this governess's influence is good?' she asked at length.

'I've always supposed it was. She's very much attached to Annabel. But how can I ask Augusta Glenloe to lend me her girls' governess to go – I don't know where – with my wife?'

'It's out of the question, of course. Besides, a Duchess of Tintagel can hardly wander about the world in that way. But perhaps – if you're sure it's wise to yield to this . . . this fancy of Annabel's . . .'

'Yes, I am,' the Duke interrupted uncomfortably.

'Then why not ask Augusta Glenloe to invite her to Champions for a few weeks? I could easily explain . . . putting it on the ground of Annabel's health. Augusta will be glad to do what she can . . .'

The Duke heaved a deep sigh, at once of depression and relief. It was clear that he wished to put an end to the talk, and escape as quickly as possible from the questions in his mother's eyes.

'It might be a good idea.'

'Very well. Shall I write?'

The Duke agreed that she might – but of course without giving the least hint . . .

Oh, of course; naturally the Dowager understood that. Augusta would accept her explanation without seeing anything unusual in it . . . It wasn't easy to surprise Augusta.

The Duke, with a vague mutter of thanks, turned to the door; and his mother, following him, laid her hand on his arm. 'You've been very long-suffering, Ushant; I hope you'll have your reward.'

He stammered something inaudible, and went out of the room. The Dowager, left alone, sat down by the hearth and bent over her scattered knitting. She had forgotten even her haste to get back to the gloxinias. Her son's halting confidences had stirred in her a storm of unaccustomed emotion, and memories of her own past crowded about her like mocking ghosts. But the Dowager did not believe in ghosts, and her grim realism made short work of the phantoms. 'There's only one way for an English Duchess to behave – and the wretched girl has never learnt it . . .' Smoothing out her knitting, she restored it to the basket reserved for pauper industries; then she stood up, and tied on her gardening apron. There were still a great many seedlings to transplant, and after that the new curate was coming to discuss arrangements for the next Mothers' Meeting . . . and then –

'There's always something to be done next . . . I daresay that's the trouble with Annabel – she's never assumed her responsibilities. Once one does, there's no time left for trifles.' The Dowager, half way across the room, stopped abruptly. 'But what in the world can she want with those five hundred pounds? Certainly not to pay her dress-maker – that was a stupid excuse,' she reflected; for even to her untrained eye it was evident that Annabel, unlike her sister and her American friends, had never dressed with the elegance her rank demanded. Yet for what else could she need this money – unless indeed (the Dowager shuddered at the thought) to help some young man out of a scrape? The idea was horrible; but the Dowager had heard it whispered that such cases had been known, even in their own circle; and suddenly she remembered the unaccountable incident of her daughter-in-law's taking Guy Thwarte upstairs to her sitting-room in the course of that crazy reel . . .

27

At Champions, the Glenloe place in Gloucestershire, a broad-faced amiable brick house with regular windows and a pillared porch replaced the ancestral towers which had been destroyed by fire some thirty years earlier, and now, in ivy-draped ruin, invited the young and romantic to mourn with them by moonlight.

The family did not mourn; least of all Lady Glenloe, to whom airy passages and plain square rooms seemed infinitely preferable to rat-infested moats and turrets, a troublesome over-crowded muniment-room, and the famous family portraits that were continually having to be cleaned and re-backed; and who, in rehearsing the saga of the fire, always concluded with a sigh of satisfaction: 'Luckily they saved the stuffed birds.'

It was doubtful if the other members of the family had ever noticed anything about the house but the temperature of the rooms, and the relative comfort of the armchairs. Certainly Lady Glenloe had done nothing to extend their observations. She herself had accomplished the unusual feat of having only two daughters and four sons: and this achievement, and the fact that Lord Glenloe had lived for years on a ranch in Canada, and came to England but briefly and rarely, had obliged his wife to be a frequent traveller, going from the soldier sons in Canada and India to the gold-miner in South Africa and the Embassy attaché at St Petersburg, and returning home via the Northwest and the marital ranch.

Such travels, infrequent in Lady Glenloe's day, had opened her eyes to matters undreamed-of by most ladies of the aristocracy, and she had brought back from her wanderings a mind tanned and toughened like her complexion by the healthy hardships of the road. Her two daughters, though left at home, and kept in due subordination, had caught a whiff of the gales that whistled through her mental rigging, and the talk at Champions was full of easy allusions to Thibet, Salt Lake City, Tsarskoë or Delhi, as to all of which Lady Glenloe could furnish statistical items, and facts on plant and bird distribution. In this atmosphere Miss Testvalley breathed more freely than in her other educational prisons, and when she appeared on the station platform to welcome the young Duchess, the latter, though absorbed in her own troubles, instantly noticed the change in her governess. At Longlands, during the Christmas revels, there had been no time or opportunity for observation, much less for private talk; but now Miss Testvalley took possession of Annabel as a matter of course.

'My dear, you won't mind there being no one but me to meet you? The girls and their brothers from Petersburg and Ottawa are out with the guns, and Lady Glenloe sent you all sorts of excuses, but she had an important parish meeting – something to do with alms-house sanitation; and she thought you'd probably be tired by the journey, and rather glad to rest quietly till dinner.'

Yes – Annabel was very glad. She suspected that the informal arrival had been planned with Lady Glenloe's connivance, and it made her feel like a girl again to be springing up the stairs on Miss Testvalley's arm, with no groom-of-the-chambers bowing her onward, or housekeeper curtseying in advance. 'Everything's pot-luck at Champions.' Lady Glenloe had a way of saying it that made pot-luck sound far more appetizing than elaborate preparations; and Annabel's spirits rose with every step.

She had left Longlands with a heavy mind. After a scene of tearful gratitude, Lady Dick, her money in her pocket, had fled to London by the first train, ostensibly to deal with her more pressing creditors; and for another week Annabel had continued to fulfil her duties as hostess to the shooting-party. She had wanted to say a word in private to Guy Thwarte, to excuse herself for her childish outbreak when he had surprised her in the temple; but the day after Conchita's departure he too had gone, called to Honourslove on some local business, and leaving with a promise to the Duke that he would return for the Lowdon election.

Without her two friends, Annabel felt herself more than ever alone. She knew that the Duke, according to his lights, had behaved generously to her; and she would have liked to feel properly grateful. But she was conscious only of a bewildered resentment. She was sure she had done right in helping Conchita Marable, and she could not understand why an act of friendship should have to be expiated like a crime, and in a way so painful to her pride. She felt that she and her husband would never be able to reach an understanding, and this being so it did not greatly matter which of the two was at fault. 'I guess it was our parents, really, for making us so different,' was her final summing up to Laura Testvalley, in the course of that first unbosoming.

The astringent quality of Miss Testvalley's sympathy had always acted on Annabel like a tonic. Miss Testvalley was not one to weep with you, but to show you briskly why there was no cause for weeping. Now, however, she remained silent for a long while after listening to her pupil's story; and when she spoke, it was with a new softness. 'My poor Nan, life makes ugly faces at us sometimes, I know.'

Annabel threw herself on the brown cashmere bosom which had so often been her refuge. 'Of course you know, you darling old Val. I think there's nothing in the world you don't know.' And her tears broke out in a releasing shower.

Miss Testvalley let them flow; apparently she had no bracing epigram at hand. But when Nan had dried her eyes, and tossed back her hair, the governess remarked quietly: 'I'd like you to try a change of air first; then we'll talk this all over. There's a good deal of fresh air in this house, and I want you to ventilate your bewildered little head.'

Annabel looked at her with a certain surprise. Though Miss Testvalley was often kind, she was seldom tender; and Nan had a sudden intuition of new forces stirring under the breast-plate of brown cashmere. She looked again, more attentively, and then said:

'Val, your hair's grown ever so much thicker; and you do it in a new way.'

'I – do I?' For the first time since Annabel had known her, Miss Testvalley's brown complexion turned to a rich crimson. The colour darted up, flamed and faded, all in a second or two; but it left the governess's keen little face suffused with a soft inner light like – why, yes, Nan perceived with a start, like that velvety glow on Conchita's delicate cheek. For a moment, neither of the women spoke; but some quick current of understanding seemed to flash between them.

Miss Testvalley laughed. 'Oh, my hair . . . you think? Yes; I have been trying a new hair-lotion – one of those wonderful French things. You didn't know I was such a vain old goose? Well, the truth is, Lady Churt was staying here (you know she's a cousin); and after she left, one of the girls found a bottle of this stuff in her room, and just for fun we – that is, I . . . well, there's my silly secret . . .' She laughed again, and tried to flatten her upstanding ripples with a pedantic hand. But the ripples sprang up defiantly, and so did her colour. Nan kept an intent gaze on her.

'You look ten years younger, you look *young*, I mean, Val dear,' she corrected herself with a smile.

'Well, that's the way I want you to look, my child –. No; don't ring for your maid – not yet! First let me look through your dresses, and tell you what to wear this evening. You know, dear, you've never thought enough about the little things; and one fine day, if one doesn't, they may suddenly grow into tremendously big ones.' She lowered her fine lids. 'That's the reason I'm letting my hair wave a little more. Not *too* much, you think? . . . Tell me, Nan, is your maid clever about hair?'

Nan shook her head, 'I don't believe she is. My mother-in-law found her for me,' she confessed, remembering Conchita's ironic comment on the horn buttons of her dressing-gown.

Presently Lady Glenloe appeared, brisk and brown, in rough tweed and shabby furs. She was as insensible to heat and cold as she was to most of the finer shades of sensation, and her dress always conformed to the calendar, without taking account of such unimportant trifles as latitudes.

'Ah, I'm glad you've got a good fire. They tell me it's very cold this evening. So delighted you've come, my dear; you must need a change and a rest after a series of those big Longlands parties. I've always wondered how your mother-in-law stood the strain . . . Here you'll find only the family; we don't go in for any ceremony at Champions – but I hope you'll like being with my girls . . . By the way, dinner may be a trifle late; you won't mind? The fact is, Sir Helmsley Thwarte sent a note this morning to ask if he might come and dine, and bring his son, who's at Honourslove. You know Sir Helmsley, of course? And Guy – he's been with you at Longlands, hasn't he? We must all drive over to Honourslove . . . Sir Helmsley's a most friendly neigh-bour; we see him here very often, don't we, Miss Testvalley?'

The governess's head was bent to the grate, from which a coal had fallen. 'When Mr Thwarte's there, Sir Helmsley naturally likes to take him about, I suppose,' she murmured to the tongs.

'Ah, just so! – Guy ought to marry,' Lady Glenloe announced. 'I must get some young people to meet him the next time he comes . . . You know there was an unfortunate marriage at Rio – but luckily the young woman died . . . leaving him a fortune, I believe. Ah, I must send word at once to the cook that Sir Helmsley likes his beef rather underdone . . . Sir Helmsley's very particular about his food . . . But now I'll leave you to rest, my dear. And don't make yourself too fine. We're used to pot-luck at Champions.'

Annabel, left alone, stood pondering before her glass. She was to see Guy Thwarte that evening – and Miss Testvalley had reproached her for not thinking enough about the details of her dress and hair. Hair-dressing had always been a much-discussed affair among the St George ladies, but something winged and impatient in Nan resisted the slow torture of adjusting puffs and curls. Regarding herself as the least noticeable in a group where youthful beauty carried its torch so high, and convinced that, wherever they went, the other girls would always be the centre of attention, Nan had never thought it worth while to waste much time on her inconspicuous person. The Duke had not married her for her beauty – how could she imagine it, when he might have chosen Virginia? Indeed, he had mentioned, in the course of his odd wooing, that beautiful women always frightened him, and that the qualities he especially valued in Nan were her gentleness and her inexperience – 'And certainly I was inexperienced enough,' she meditated, as she stood before the mirror; 'but I'm afraid he hasn't found me particularly gentle.'

She continued to study her reflection critically, wondering whether Miss Testvalley was right, and she owed it to herself to dress her hair more becomingly, and wear her jewels as if she hadn't merely hired them for a fancy-ball. (The comparison was Miss Testvalley's.) She could imagine taking an interest in her hair, even studying the effect of a flower or a ribbon skilfully placed; but she knew she could never feel at ease under the weight of the Tintagel heirlooms. Luckily the principal pieces, ponderous coronets and tiaras, massive necklaces and bracelets hung with stones like rocs' eggs, were locked up in a London bank, and would probably not be imposed upon her except at Drawing-rooms or receptions for foreign sovereigns; yet even the less ceremonious ornaments, which Virginia or Conchita would have carried off with such an air, seemed too imposing for her slight presence.

But now, for the first time, she felt a desire to assert herself, to live up to her opportunities. 'After all, I'm Annabel Tintagel, and as I can't help myself I might as well try to make the best of it.' Perhaps Miss Testvalley was right. Already she seemed to breathe more freely, to feel a new air in her lungs. It was her first escape from the long oppression of Tintagel and Longlands, and the solemn London house; and freed from the restrictions they imposed, and under the same roof with her only two friends in the great lonely English world, she felt her spirits rising. 'I know I'm always too glad or too sad – like that girl in the German play that Miss Testvalley read to me,' she said to herself; and wondered whether Guy Thwarte knew Clärchen's song, and would think her conceited if she told him she had always felt that a little bit of herself was Clärchen. 'There are so many people in me,' she thought; but tonight the puzzling idea of her multiplicity cheered instead of bewildering her . . . 'There can't be too many happy Nans,' she thought with a smile, as she drew on her long gloves.

That evening her maid had had to take her hair down twice before each coil and ripple was placed to the best advantage of her small head, and in proper relation to the diamond briar-rose on the shoulder of her coral pink *poult-de-soie*.

When she entered the drawing-room she found it empty; but the next moment Guy Thwarte appeared, and she went up to him impulsively.

'Oh, I'm so glad you're here. I've been wanting to tell you how sorry I am to have behaved so stupidly the day you found me in the temple –' 'of Love,' she had been about to add; but the absurdity of the designation checked her. She reddened and went on: 'I wanted to write and tell you; but I couldn't. I'm not good at letters.'

Guy was looking at her, visibly surprised at the change in her appearance, and the warm animation of her voice. 'This is better than writing,' he rejoined, with a smile. 'I'm glad to see you so changed – looking so . . . so much happier . . .'

('Already?' she reflected guiltily, remembering that she had been away from Longlands only a few hours!)

'Yes; I am happier. Miss Testvalley says I'm always going up and down . . . And I wanted to tell you – do you remember Clärchen's song?' she began in an eager voice, feeling her tongue loosened and her heart at ease with him again.

Lady Glenloe's ringing accents interrupted them. 'My dear Duchess! You've been looking for us? I'm so sorry. I had carried everybody off to my son's study to see this extraordinary new thing – this telephone, as they call it. I brought it back with me the other day from the States. It's a curious toy; but to you, of course, it's no novelty. In America they're already talking from one town to another – yes actually! Mine goes only as far as the lodge, but I'm urging Sir Helmsley Thwarte to put one in at Honourslove, so that we can have a good gossip together over the crops and the weather . . . But he says he's afraid it will unchain all the bores in the county . . . Sir Helmsley, I think you know the Duchess? I'm going to persuade her to put in a telephone at Longlands . . . We English are so backward. They have them in all the principal hotels in New York; and when I was in St Petersburg last winter they were actually talking of having one between the Imperial Palace and Tsarskoë –'

The old butler appeared to announce dinner, and the procession formed itself, headed by Annabel on the arm of the son from the Petersburg Embassy.

'Yes, at Tsarskoë I've seen the Empress talking over it herself. She uses it to communicate with the nurseries,' the diplomatist explained impressively; and Nan wondered why they were all so worked up over an object already regarded as a domestic utensil in America. But it was all a part of the novelty and excitement of being at Champions, and she thought with a smile how much less exhilarating the subjects of conversation at a Longlands dinner would have been.

28

The Champions party chose a mild day of February for the drive to Honourslove. The diplomatic son conducted ·the Duchess, his mother and Miss Testvalley in the wagonette, and the others followed in various vehicles piloted by sons and daughters of the house. For two hours they drove through the tawny winter landscape bounded by hills veiled in blue mist, traversing villages clustered about silver-grey manor-houses, and a little market-town with a High Street bordered by the wool-merchants' stately dwellings, and guarded by a sturdy church-tower. The dark green of rhododendron plantations made autumn linger under the bare woods; on house-fronts sheltered from the wind the naked jasmine was already starred with gold. This merging of the seasons, so unlike the harsh break between summer and winter in America, had often touched Nan's imagination; but she had never felt as now the mild loveliness of certain winter days in England. It all seemed part of the unreality of her sensations, and as the carriage turned in at the gates of Honourslove, she recalled her only other visit there, when she and Guy Thwarte had stood alone on the terrace before the house, and found not a word to say. Poor Nan St George – so tongue-tied and bewildered by the surge of her feelings; why had no one taught her the words for them? As the carriage drew up before the door she seemed to see her own pitiful figure of four years ago flit by like a ghost; but in a moment it vanished in the warm air of the present.

The day was so soft that Lady Glenloe insisted on a turn through the gardens before luncheon; and, as usual when a famous country-house is visited, the guests found themselves following the prescribed itinerary – saying the proper things about the view from the terrace, descending the steep path to the mossy glen of the Love, and returning by the walled gardens and the chapel.

Their host, heading the party with the Duchess and Lady Glenloe, had begun his habitual and slightly ironic summary of the family history. Lady Glenloe lent it an inattentive ear; but Annabel hung on his words, and always quick to discover an appreciative listener, he soon dropped his bantering note to unfold the romantic tale of the old house. Annabel felt that he understood her questions, and sympathized with her curiosity, and as they turned away from the chapel he said, with his quick smile: 'I see Miss Testvalley was right, Duchess – she always is. She told me you were the only foreigner she'd ever known who cared for the real deep-down England, rather than the sham one of the London drawing-rooms.'

Nan flushed with pride; it still made her as happy to be praised by Miss Testvalley as when the little brown governess had sniffed appreciatively at the posy her pupil had brought her on her first evening at Saratoga.

'I'm afraid I shall always feel strange in London drawing-rooms,' Nan answered; 'but that hidden-away life of England, the old houses and their histories, and all the far-back things the old people hand on to their grandchildren – they seem so natural and home-like. And Miss Testvalley, who's a foreigner too, has shown me better than anybody how to appreciate them.'

'Ah – that's it. We English are spoilt; we've ceased to feel the beauty, to listen to the voices. But you and she come to it with fresh eyes and fresh imaginations – you happen to be blessed with both. I wish more of our Englishwomen felt it all as you do. After luncheon you must go through the old house, and let it talk to you . . . My son, who knows it all even better than I do, will show it to you . . .'

'You spoke the other day about Clärchen's song; the evening my father and I drove over to dine at Champions,' Guy Thwarte said suddenly.

He and Annabel, at the day's end, had drifted out again to the wide terrace. They had visited the old house, room by room, lingering long over each picture, each piece of rare old furniture or tapestry, and already the winter afternoon was fading out in crimson distances overhung by twilight. In the hall Lady Glenloe had collected her party for departure.

'Oh, Clärchen? Yes – when my spirits were always jumping up

and down Miss Testvalley used to call me Clärchen, just to tease me.'

'And doesn't she, any longer? I mean, don't your spirits jump up and down any more?'

'Well, I'm afraid they do sometimes. Miss Testvalley says things are never as bad as I think, or as good as I expect – but I'd rather have the bad hours than not believe in the good ones, wouldn't you? What really frightens me is not caring for anything any more. Don't you think that's worse?'

'That's the worst, certainly. But it's never going to happen to you, Duchess.'

Her face lit up. 'Oh, do you think so? I'm not sure. Things seem to last so long – as if in the end they were bound to wear people out. Sometimes life seems like a match between one's self and one's gaolers. The gaolers, of course, are one's mistakes; and the question is, who'll hold out longest? When I think of that, life, instead of being too long, seems as short as a winter day . . . Oh, look, the lights already, over there in the valley . . . this day's over. And suddenly you find you've missed your chance. You've been beaten . . .'

'No, no; for there'll be other days soon. And other chances. Goethe was a very young man when he wrote Clärchen's song. The next time I come to Champions I'll bring *Faust* with me, and show you some of the things life taught him.'

'Oh, are you coming back to Champions? When? Before I leave?' she asked eagerly; and he answered: 'I'll come whenever Lady Glenloe asks me.'

Again he saw her face suffused with one of its Clärchen-like illuminations, and added, rather hastily: 'The fact is, I've got to hang about here on account of the possible bye-election at Lowdon. Ushant may have told you –'

The illumination faded. 'He never tells me anything about politics. He thinks women oughtn't to meddle with such things.'

Guy laughed. 'Well, I rather believe he's right. But meanwhile, here I am, waiting rather aimlessly until I'm called upon to meddle . . . And as soon as Champions wants me I'll come.'

In Sir Helmsley's study he and Miss Testvalley were standing together before Sir Helmsley's copy of the little Rossetti Madonna. The ladies of the party had been carried off to collect their wraps, and their host had seized the opportunity to present his water-colour to Miss Testvalley. 'If you think it's not too bad –'

Miss Testvalley's colour rose becomingly. 'It's perfect, Sir Helmsley. If you'll allow me, I'll show it to Dante Gabriel the next time I go to see the poor fellow.' She bent appreciatively over the sketch. 'And you'll let me take it off now?'

'No. I want to have it framed first. But Guy will bring it to you. I understand he's going to Champions in a day or two for a longish visit.'

Miss Testvalley made no reply, and her host, who was beginning to know her face well, saw that she was keeping back many comments.

'You're not surprised?' he suggested.

'I – I don't know.'

Sir Helmsley laughed. 'Perhaps we shall all know soon. But meanwhile let's be a little indiscreet. Which of the daughters do you put your money on?'

Miss Testvalley carefully replaced the water-colour on its easel. 'The . . . the daughters?'

'Corisande or Kitty . . . Why, you must have noticed. The better pleased Lady Glenloe is, the more off-hand her manner becomes. And just now I heard her suggesting to my son to come back to Champions as soon as he could, if he thought he could stand a boring family party.'

'Ah – yes.' Miss Testvalley remained lost in contemplation of her water-colour. 'And you think Lady Glenloe approves?'

'Intensely, judging from her indifferent manner.' Sir Helmsley stroked his short beard reflectively. 'And I do too. Whichever of the young ladies it is, *cela sera de tout repos*. Cora's eyes are very small; but her nose is straighter than Kitty's. And that's the kind of thing I want for Guy: something safe and unexciting. Now that he's managed to scrape together a little money – the first time a Thwarte has ever done it by the work of his hands or his brain – I dread his falling a victim to some unscrupulous woman.'

'Yes,' Miss Testvalley acquiesced, a faint glint of irony in her fine eyes. 'I can imagine how anxious you must be.'

'Oh, desperately; as anxious as the mother of a flirtatious daughter –'

'I understand that.'

'And you make no comment?'

'I make no comment.'

'Because you think in this particular case I'm mistaken?'

'I don't know.'

Sir Helmsley glanced through the window at the darkening terrace. 'Well, here he is now. And a lady with him. Shall we toss a penny on which it is – Corisande or Kitty? Oh – no! Why, it's the little Duchess, I believe . . .'

Miss Testvalley still remained silent.

'Another of your pupils!' Sir Helmsley continued, with a teasing laugh. He paused, and added tentatively: 'And perhaps the most interesting – eh?'

'Perhaps.'

'Because she's the most intelligent – or the most unhappy?'

Miss Testvalley looked up quickly. 'Why do you suggest that she's unhappy?'

'Oh,' he rejoined, with a slight shrug, 'because you're so incurably philanthropic that I should say your swans would often turn out to be lame ducks.'

'Perhaps they do. At any rate, she's the pupil I was fondest of and should most wish to guard against unhappiness.'

'Ah –' murmured Sir Helmsley, on a half-questioning note.

'But Lady Glenloe must be ready to start; I'd better go and call the Duchess,' Miss Testvalley added, moving toward the door. There was a sound of voices in the hall, and among them Lady Glenloe's, calling out: 'Cora, Kitty – has any one seen the Duchess? Oh, Mr Thwarte, we're looking for the Duchess, and I see you've been giving her a last glimpse of your wonderful view . . .'

'Not the last, I hope,' said Guy smiling, as he came forward with Annabel.

'The last for today, at any rate; we must be off at once on our long drive. Mr Thwarte, I count on you for next Saturday. Sir Helmsley, can't we persuade you to come too?'

The drive back to Champions passed like a dream. To secure herself against disturbance, Nan had slipped her hand into Miss Testvalley's, and let her head droop on the governess's shoulder. She heard one of the Glenloe girls whisper: 'The Duchess is asleep,' and a conniving silence seemed to enfold her. But she had no wish to sleep: her wide-open eyes looked out into the falling night, caught the glint of lights flashing past in the High Street, lost themselves in the long intervals of dusk between the villages, and plunged into deepening night as the low glimmer of the west went out. In her heart was a deep delicious peace such as she had never known before. In this great lonely desert of life stretching out before her she had a friend – a friend who understood not only all she said, but everything she could not say. At the end of the long road on which the regular rap of the horses' feet was beating out the hours, she saw him standing, waiting for her, watching for her through the night.

29

'Do you know, I think Nan's coming to stay next week!'

Mrs Hector Robinson laid down the letter she had been perusing and glanced across the funereal architecture of the British breakfast-table at her husband, who, plunged in *The Times*, sat in the armchair facing her. He looked up with the natural resentment of the male Briton disturbed by an untutored female in his morning encounter with the news. 'Nan –?' he echoed interrogatively.

Lizzy Robinson laughed – and her laugh was a brilliant affair, which lit up the mid-winter darkness of the solemn pseudo-gothic breakfast-room at Belfield.

'Well, Annabel, then; Annabel Duchess –'

'The – not the Duchess of Tintagel?'

Mr Robinson had instantly discarded *The Times*. He sat gazing incredulously at the face of his wife, on which the afterglow of her laugh still enchantingly lingered. Certainly, he thought, he had married one of the most beautiful women in England. And now his father was dead, and Belfield and the big London house, and the Scottish shooting-lodge, and the Lancashire mills which fed them – all for the last year had been his. Everything he had put his hand to had succeeded. But he had never pictured the Duchess of Tintagel at a Belfield house-party, and the vision made him a little dizzy.

The afterglow of his wife's amusement still lingered. 'The – Duchess – of – Tintagel,' she mimicked him. 'Has there never been a Duchess at Belfield before?'

Mr Robinson stiffened slightly. 'Not *this* Duchess. I understood the Tintagels paid no visits.'

'Ushant doesn't, certainly – luckily for us! But I suppose he can't keep his wife actually chained up, can he, with all these new laws, and the police prying in everywhere? At any rate, she's been at Lady Glenloe's for the last month; and now she wants to know if she can come here.'

Mr Robinson's stare had the fixity of a muscular contraction. 'She's written to ask –?'

His wife tossed the letter across the monuments in Sheffield plate. 'There – if you don't believe me.'

He read the short note with a hurriedly assumed air of detachment. 'Dear me – who else is coming? Shall you be able to fit her in, do you think?' The detachment was almost too perfect, and Lizzy felt like exclaiming: 'Oh, come, my dear – don't over-do it!' But she never gave her husband such hints except when it was absolutely necessary.

'Shall I write that she may come?' she asked, with an air of wifely compliance.

Mr Robinson coughed – in order that his response should not be too eager. 'That's for you to decide, my dear. I don't see why not; if she can put up with a rather dull hunting crowd,' he said, suddenly viewing his other guests from a new angle. 'Let me see – there's old Dashleigh – I'm afraid he *is* a bore – and Hubert Clyde, and Colonel Beagles, and of course Sir Blasker Tripp for Lady Dick Marable – eh?' He smiled suggestively. 'And Guy Thwarte; is the Duchess likely to object to Guy Thwarte?'

Lizzy Robinson's smile deepened. 'Oh, no; I gather she won't in the least object to him.'

'Why – what do you mean? You don't –'

In his surprise and agitation Mr Robinson abandoned all further thought of *The Times*.

'Well – it occurs to me that she may conceivably have known he was coming here next week. I know he's been at Champions a good deal during the month she's been spending there. And I – well, I should certainly have risked asking him to meet her, if he hadn't already been on your list.'

Mr Robinson looked at his wife's smile, and slowly responded to it. He had always thought he had a prompt mind, as quick as any at the uptake; but there were times when this American girl left him breathless, and even a little frightened. Her social intuitions were uncannily swift; and in his rare moments of leisure from politics and the mills he sometimes asked himself if, with such gifts of divination, she might not some day be building a new future for herself. But there was a stolid British baby upstairs in the nursery, and Mr Robinson was richer than anybody she was likely to come across, except old Blasker Tripp, who of course belonged to Conchita Marable. And she certainly seemed happy, and absorbed in furthering their joint career . . . But his chief reason for feeling safe was the fact that her standard of values was identical with his own. Strangely enough, this lovely alien who had been swept into his life on a brief gust of passion, proved to have a respect as profound as his for the concrete realities, and his sturdy unawareness of everything which could not be expressed in terms of bank accounts or political and social expediency. It was as if he had married Titania, and she had brought with her a vanload of ponderous mahogany furniture exactly matching what he had grown up with at Belfield. And he knew she had her eye on a peerage . . .

Yes; but meanwhile –. He picked up *The Times*, and began to smooth it out with deliberation, as though seeking a pretext for not carrying on the conversation.

'Well, Hector –?' his wife began impatiently. 'I suppose I shall have to answer this.' She had recovered Annabel's letter.

Her husband still hesitated. 'My dear – I should be only too happy to see the Duchess here . . . But . . .' The more he reflected, the bigger grew the But suddenly looming before him. 'Have you any way of knowing if – er – the Duke approves?'

Lizzy again sounded her gay laugh. 'Approves of Nan's coming here?'

Her husband nodded gravely, and as she watched him her own face grew attentive. She had learned that Hector's ideas were almost always worth considering.

'You mean . . . he may not like her inviting herself here?'

'Her doing so is certainly unconventional.'

'But she's been staying alone at Champions for a month.'

Mr Robinson was still dubious. 'Lady Glenloe's a relative. And besides, her visit to Champions is none of our business. But if you have any reason to think –'

His wife interrupted him. 'What I think is that Nan's dying of boredom, and longing for a change; and if the Duke let her go to Champions, where she was among strangers, I don't see how he can object to her coming here, to an old friend from her own country. I'd like to see him refuse to let her stay with me,' cried Lizzy in what her husband called her 'Hail Columbia voice'.

Mr Robinson's frown relaxed. Lizzy so often found the right note. This was probably another instance of the advantage, for an ambitious man, of marrying some one by nationality and up-bringing entirely detached from his own social problems. He now regarded as a valuable asset the breezy independence of his wife's attitude, which at first had alarmed him. 'It's one of the reasons of their popularity,' he reflected. There was no doubt that London society was getting tired of pretences and compliances, of conformity and uniformity. The free and easy Americanism of this little band of invaders had taken the world of fashion by storm, and Hector Robinson was too alert not to have noted the renovation of the social atmosphere. 'Wherever the men are amused, fashion is bound to follow,' was one of Lizzy's axioms; and certainly, from their future sovereign to his most newly knighted subject, the men *were* amused in Mayfair's American drawing-rooms.

[*The manuscript ends here. Before beginning work on* The Buccaneers *Edith Wharton produced a synopsis (reproduced below) outlining the entire plot of the novel. She followed this outline very closely, so it is likely that the planned ending would have been used if she had completed the novel.*]

This novel deals with the adventures of three American families with beautiful daughters who attempt the London social adventure in the 'seventies – the first time the social invasion had ever been tried in England on such a scale.

The three mothers – Mrs St George, Mrs Elmsworth, and Mrs Closson – have all made an attempt to launch their daughters in New York, where their husbands are in business, but have no social standing (the families, all of very ordinary origin, being from the south-west, or from the northern part of the state of New York). The New York experiment is only partly successful, for though the girls attract attention by their beauty they are viewed distrustfully by the New York hostesses whose verdict counts, their origin being hazy and their appearance what was then called 'loud'. So, though admired at Saratoga, Long Branch and the White Sulphur Springs, they fail at Newport and in New York, and the young men flirt with them but do not offer marriage.

Mrs St George has a governess for her youngest daughter, Nan, who is not yet out. She knows that governesses are fashionable, and is determined that Nan shall have the same advantages as the daughters of the New York aristocracy, for she suspects that her daughter Virginia's lack of success, and the failure of Lizzy and Mabel Elmsworth, may have been due to lack of social training. Mrs St George therefore engages a governess who has been in the best houses in New York and London, and a highly competent middle-aged woman named Laura Testvalley (she is of Italian origin – the name is corrupted from Testavaglia) arrives in the family. Laura Testvalley has been in several aristocratic families in England, but after a run of bad luck has come to the States on account of the great demand for superior 'finishing' governesses, and the higher salaries offered. Miss Testvalley is an adventuress, but a great-souled one. She has been a year with the fashionable Mrs Parmore of New York, who belongs to one of the oldest Knickerbocker families, but she finds the place dull, and is anxious for higher pay and a more lavish household. She recognizes the immense social gifts of the St George girls, and becomes in particular passionately attached to Nan.

She says to Mrs St George: 'Why try Newport again? Go straight to England first, and come back to America with the prestige of a brilliant London season.'

Mrs St George is dazzled, and persuades her husband to let her go. The Closson and Elmsworth girls are friends of the oldest St George girl, and they too persuade their parents to let them try London.

The three families embark together on the adventure, and though furiously jealous of each other, are clever enough to see the advantage of backing each other up; and Miss Testvalley leads them all like a general.

In each particular family the sense of solidarity is of course even stronger than it is between members of the group, and as soon as Virginia St George has made a brilliant English marriage she devotes all her energies to finding a husband for Nan.

But Nan rebels – or at least is not content with the prizes offered. She is, or thinks she is, as ambitious as the others, but it is for more interesting reasons; intellectual, political and artistic. She is the least beautiful but by far the most brilliant and seductive of them all; and to the amazement of the others (and adroitly steered by Miss Testvalley) she suddenly captures the greatest match in England, the young Duke of Tintagel.

But though she is dazzled for the moment her heart is not satisfied. The Duke is kindly but dull and arrogant, and the man she really loves is young Guy Thwarte, a poor officer in the Guards, the son of Sir Helmsley Thwarte, whose old and wonderfully beautiful place in Gloucestershire, Honourslove, is the scene of a part of the story.

Sir Helmsley Thwarte, the widowed father of Guy, a clever, broken-down and bitter old worldling, is captivated by Miss Testvalley, and wants to marry her; but meanwhile the young Duchess of Tintagel has suddenly decided to leave her husband and go off with Guy, and it turns out that Laura Testvalley, moved by the youth and passion of the lovers, and disgusted by the mediocre Duke of Tintagel, has secretly lent a hand in the planning of the elopement, the scandal of which is to ring through England for years.

Sir Helmsley Thwarte discovers what is going on, and is so furious at his only son's being involved in such an adventure that, suspecting Miss Testvalley's complicity, he breaks with her, and the great old adventuress, seeing love, deep and abiding love, triumph for the first time in her career, helps Nan to join her lover, who has been ordered to South Africa, and then goes back alone to old age and poverty.

The Elmsworth and Closson adventures will be interwoven with Nan's, and the setting will be aristocratic London in the season, and life in the great English country-houses as they were sixty years ago.

READ MORE IN PENGUIN

In every corner of the world, on every subject under the sun, Penguin represents quality and variety – the very best in publishing today.

For complete information about books available from Penguin – including Puffins, Penguin Classics and Arkana – and how to order them, write to us at the appropriate address below. Please note that for copyright reasons the selection of books varies from country to country.

In the United Kingdom: Please write to *Dept. EP, Penguin Books Ltd, Bath Road, Harmondsworth, West Drayton, Middlesex UB7 ODA*

In the United States: Please write to *Consumer Sales, Penguin USA, P.O. Box 999, Dept. 17109, Bergenfield, New Jersey 07621-0120*. VISA and MasterCard holders call 1-800-253-6476 to order Penguin titles

In Canada: Please write to *Penguin Books Canada Ltd, 10 Alcorn Avenue, Suite 300, Toronto, Ontario M4V 3B2*

In Australia: Please write to *Penguin Books Australia Ltd, P.O. Box 257, Ringwood, Victoria 3134*

In New Zealand: Please write to *Penguin Books (NZ) Ltd, Private Bag 102902, North Shore Mail Centre, Auckland 10*

In India: Please write to *Penguin Books India Pvt Ltd, 706 Eros Apartments, 56 Nehru Place, New Delhi 110 019*

In the Netherlands: Please write to *Penguin Books Netherlands bv, Postbus 3507, NL-1001 AH Amsterdam*

In Germany: Please write to *Penguin Books Deutschland GmbH, Metzlerstrasse 26, 60594 Frankfurt am Main*

In Spain: Please write to *Penguin Books S. A., Bravo Murillo 19, 1° B, 28015 Madrid*

In Italy: Please write to *Penguin Italia s.r.l., Via Felice Casati 20, I–20124 Milano*

In France: Please write to *Penguin France S. A., 17 rue Lejeune, F–31000 Toulouse*

In Japan: Please write to *Penguin Books Japan, Ishikiribashi Building, 2–5–4, Suido, Bunkyo-ku, Tokyo 112*

In South Africa: Please write to *Longman Penguin Southern Africa (Pty) Ltd, Private Bag X08, Bertsham 2013*

READ MORE IN PENGUIN

Penguin Twentieth-Century Classics offer a selection of the finest works of literature published this century. Spanning the globe from Argentina to America, from France to India, the masters of prose and poetry are represented in by the Penguin.

If you would like a catalogue of the Twentieth-Century Classics library, please write to: ·

Penguin Marketing, 27 Wrights Lane, London W8 5TZ

(Available while stocks last)

READ MORE IN PENGUIN

A CHOICE OF TWENTIETH-CENTURY CLASSICS

Tender is the Night F. Scott Fitzgerald

In *Tender is the Night*, the author distilled much of his and Zelda's life, and the knowledge of the wrecked, fabulous Fitzgeralds adds poignancy and regret to his supple, tender and poetically tantalizing portrait of destructive affluence and spoiled idealism.

Lady Chatterley's Lover D. H. Lawrence

The story of the relationship between Constance Chatterley and Mellors, her crippled husband's gamekeeper, is Lawrence's most controversial novel – and perhaps his most complete and beautiful study of mutual love.

The Sword of Honour Trilogy Evelyn Waugh

A glorious fusion of comedy, satire and farcical despair, *The Sword of Honour Trilogy – Men at Arms, Officers and Gentlemen* and *Unconditional Surrender* – is also Evelyn Waugh's bitter attack on a world where chivalry and nobility were betrayed on every hand.

Cancer Ward Aleksandr Solzhenitsyn

Solzhenitsyn, like Oleg Kostoglotov, the central character of this novel, went in the mid-1950s from concentration camp to cancer ward and later recovered. The British publication of *Cancer Ward* in 1968 confirmed him as Russia's greatest living novelist. 'Solzhenitsyn is a writer of genius, able to illuminate reality through his fictions as no other living novelist can do' – *Sunday Times*

The Amen Corner James Baldwin

Sister Margaret presides over a thriving gospel-singing community in New York's Harlem. Proud and silent, for the last ten years she has successfully turned her heart to the Lord and her back on the past. But then her husband Luke unexpectedly reappears. He is a burnt-out jazz musician, a scandal of a man who none the less is seeking love and redemption.

BY THE SAME AUTHOR

Summer

In its rural settings and its poor, uneducated, protagonists, *Summer* represents a sharp departure from Wharton's familiar depictions of the urban upper class. Charity Royall lives unhappily with her hard-drinking adoptive father in an isolated village, until a visiting architect awakens her sexual passion and the hope for escape. Exploring Charity's relation to her father and her lover, Wharton delves into dark cultural territory: repressed sexuality, small-town prejudice, and, in subtle hints, incest.

The Age of Innocence

Into the world of propriety which composed the rigid code of Old New York society returns the Countess Olenska, separated from her European husband and bearing with her an independence and impulsive awareness of life which stirs the educated sensitivity of Newland Archer, engaged to be married to May Welland, 'that terrifying product of the social system he belonged to and believed in, the young girl who knew nothing and expected everything'.

The Age of Innocence is also available as a Penguin Audiobook, read by Kerry Shale.

Ethan Frome

In an ugly house in the stark New England countryside live Ethan Frome and his wife Zeena. Ethan runs a failing sawmill and a barren farm, but it is his indifferent marriage that distresses him most. When a young girl comes to work for the Fromes, Ethan's fantasies of future happiness turn the fate of all three to obsession and tragedy.

also published:

The Custom of the Country
Three Novels of Old New York
(The Age of Innocence/
The Custom of the Country/
The House of Mirth)

The Muse's Tragedy and Other
  Stories
The Reef
The Buccaneers